X 23

The Life and Adventures of
Trobadora Beatrice
as Chronicled by
Her Minstrel Laura

IRMTRAUD MORGNER Translated by Jeanette Clausen

The Life and Adventures of Trobadora Beatrice as Chronicled by Her Minstrel Laura

A Novel in Thirteen Books and Seven Intermezzos

with an introduction
by Jeanette Clausen and
Silke von der Emde
Consultant: Otto Emersleben

University of Nebraska Press
Lincoln and London

Publication of this volume has been assisted by grants from the National Endowment for the Arts and from Inter Nationes.
First published by Aufbau Verlag, Berlin, in 1974, as *Leben und Abenteuer der Trobadora Beatriz nach Zeugnissen ihrer Spielfrau Laura: Roman in dreizehn Büchern und sieben Intermezzos.*

♾ Library of Congress Cataloging-in-Publication Data
Morgner, Irmtraud. [Leben und Abenteuer der Trobadora Beatriz nach Zeugnissen ihrer Spielfrau Laura. English]
The life and adventures of Trobadora Beatrice as chronicled by her minstrel Laura : a novel in thirteen books and seven intermezzos / Irmtraud Morgner ; translated by Jeanette Clausen ; with an introduction by Jeanette Clausen and Silke von der Emde. p. cm — (European women writers series) Includes bibliographical references.
ISBN 0-8032-3203-9 (cl. : alk. paper) — ISBN 0-8032-8260-5 (pbk.: alk. paper)
I. Clausen, Jeanette 1940– II. Title III. Series.
PT2673.064 L413 2000
833'.914–dc21
99-052824

NATIONAL
ENDOWMENT
FOR THE ARTS

CONTENTS

INTRODUCTION

Irmtraud Morgner, one of the most talented and controversial writers of the former German Democratic Republic (GDR), has also been one of its best-kept secrets. Although her books were widely read in the two Germanies and have been studied by feminist scholars in various countries, none of her works has been translated in its entirety until now.[1] *The Life and Adventures of Trobadora Beatrice as Chronicled by Her Minstrel Laura*, first published in 1974, was an instant success with readers: in the GDR it sold out immediately (forty thousand copies in one year), and in West Germany people flooded to public readings by the author before the novel was even published there in 1976. Today, ten years after the demise of the GDR, *Life and Adventures* still stands out as a unique artistic creation that can be enjoyed on many levels, from a purely entertaining, often hilarious, and fantastic adventure to an incisive feminist critique of political ideology, science, history, and aesthetic theory.

Life and Adventures is the story of Beatrice de Dia, a woman troubadour of twelfth-century Provence whom Morgner recreates with the help of characters and motifs from mythology, literature, fairy tales, medieval tapestries, and fantasy.[2] Unhappy with the misogyny of the Middle Ages, Beatrice makes a pact with Persephone to sleep for 810 years, in order to wait for a time when women's equality will have been realized. Her sister-in-law, the Beautiful Melusine, provides a bridge to the present. Half woman and half dragon, Melusine is Beatrice's informant during her sleep, her ally through space and time, and in her commitment to political action, a foil to Beatrice's picaresque spontaneity and naiveté. After a rude awakening in her Provence château in May 1968, Beatrice eventually makes her way to Paris in the aftermath of the student uprisings. There she leads for a time an outwardly conventional life as a married woman (with clandestine activities on behalf of her pact with 'the Persephonic opposition'), studies Marx, and learns German. A visiting journalist urges her to visit his native land, the GDR, assuring her that it is an ideal country where women are truly free and emancipated.

With the arrival of Trobadora Beatrice in East Berlin in book 4, Morgner sets up a playful confrontation between Beatrice's expectations (nourished by the official GDR party line) and the reality of women's lives in the 'Promised Land.' In Laura Salman, socialist trolley-car driver, writer, and single mother, Beatrice finds her modern-day minstrel and apprentice – or is it Beatrice who is the apprentice? For it is Laura who writes Beatrice's first stories, and it is Laura's theory about how to achieve a mass transformation of consciousness that will save the world from capitalism, wars, hunger, and patriarchy that sends Beatrice on a quest to find a unicorn. When she finally returns to the GDR, she no longer writes erotic love poetry but instead produces three 'Bitterfeld Fruits,' stories that reflect and challenge the cultural policies known as the Bitterfeld Way. The adventures of Beatrice and Laura come to a halt with the trobadora's accidental death the day after the leftist parties win a majority of votes in the French elections of March 1973.

The story of Beatrice and Laura – the allusion to Dante and Petrarch is, of course, intentional – is narrated in thirteen 'books.' The story line is continually interrupted by newscasts, speeches, fairy tales, interviews, poems, theoretical texts, letters, encounters between the author and her characters, parodies of typical GDR genres (for example, the trobadora's self-critique in chapter 14 of book 4 and the satirized 'arrival novel' in chapter 16), and a wonderful array of self-contained stories, each of them linked in some way to one or more of the various threads the author is developing. The thirteen books in turn are interrupted by seven 'intermezzos,' which take place in the GDR during the Cuban missile crisis of 1962. Here we meet several of the novel's characters in their younger days, as well as their parents and other older people whose convictions are rooted in their experiences during the Third Reich and earlier. The intermezzos thus provide a layer of history undergirding the main story, a glimpse of the early years of the GDR that were beginning to fade from memory even for readers of *Life and Adventures* in the mid-1970s. Morgner – or rather, Laura – explains the rationale for the novel's structure in book 8, where Laura tries to persuade an editor that the montage novel is an ideal form for interventions, the novel of the future that can encompass all shifting requirements of day-to-day politics and cultural policy while also conforming to women's life-rhythm with its constant interruptions of childcare and housework. Tongue in cheek? The answer, of course, is yes and no. Like many GDR authors who took their art and their vision of socialism seriously, Morgner had her problems with the censors.

Born in 1933 in Chemnitz (later Karl-Marx-Stadt, now renamed Chemnitz), Irmtraud Morgner belonged to the first generation to be educated in the newly founded socialist state. After receiving her *Abitur*, she studied language and literature with Hans Mayer at the University of Leipzig, graduating with a degree in *Germanistik* in 1956. After a stint as an assistant editor of the literary journal *Neue deutsche Literatur*, she began working as a freelance writer in 1958. She encountered no difficulties in publishing her first three books in the GDR, *Das Signal steht auf Fahrt* (The signal is on 'go,' 1959), *Ein Haus am Rande der Stadt* (A house at the edge of town, 1962), and *Notturno* (1964). But like many GDR writers of her generation who tended to renounce their early work as their thinking changed and matured during the 1970s, she later rejected these texts because of their schematic realism and 'unliterary' character.

In 1965 the GDR publishing house Mitteldeutscher Verlag announced publication of Morgner's novel *Rumba auf einen Herbst* (Rumba for an autumn) for the spring of 1966. But because of a sudden turn in cultural politics following the eleventh plenum of the Central Committee of the Socialist Unity Party, permission to publish *Rumba* was withdrawn and the manuscript never returned to the author. The ever-resourceful Morgner was able to partly reverse this setback by incorporating large sections of *Rumba* into *Life and Adventures* as the seven intermezzos.[3] This experience had profound consequences for her development as a writer: from then on, her most important goal was, in her words, to write *literature*. To ensure that her books would not be misunderstood as political pamphlets, Morgner radically changed her narrative strategies. Far from adhering to the dictates of socialist realism and the Bitterfeld Way, she increasingly found ways to subvert them, especially through her famous humor and through fantasy.

The officially prescribed function of socialist realist literature was, of course, to shape readers' understanding of socialist ideology by representing objective reality in its revolutionary development and progress. To this end, a positive hero/heroine who perseveres against all odds and serves as a role model for readers was de rigueur; 'formalist' elements such as montage, alienation techniques, and other aesthetic experiments were taboo. Proclaimed by Walter Ulbricht in 1959, the Bitterfeld movement elaborated an emphasis on integrating the world of production into the creative arts. Authors were expected to study the lives of average people by working in factories, on farms, or in other state enterprises before writing about them. Workers, in turn, were encouraged to become writers by slogans such as 'Greif zur Feder, Kumpel!' (Take up the pen, Comrade!). These policies are confronted and thematized satirically throughout the novel, beginning in the prologue ('Resolutions'), when Laura tries to persuade the author to buy her manuscript: 'These documents will save you at least ten trips, a hundred hours of production-line research, and a thousand conversations.' Scenes in which Laura or Beatrice read from their works to audiences of women factory workers provide a glimpse of how the policies worked in practice.[4]

Besides using humor and satire as subversive strategies, Morgner challenges the rationalist cultural politics of the Socialist Unity Party by incorporating an abundance of fantastic elements into her novel. The twelfth-century trobadora is helped by the mythological Persephone (whose powers, however, have been sharply curtailed by 'Mr. Lord God'); two lovers escape their workday routine temporarily via a trip to Heaven (which bears an unfortunate resemblance to a prison camp); the dragon Melusine flies between Hades, King Arthur's court, and present-day Europe; a scientist learns how to regenerate human flesh from proteins grown on petroleum fractions; and even Laura's skeptical mother, Olga, eventually turns to Persephone for help. The fictional characters also freely interact with real GDR personalities, such as the poets Sarah Kirsch and Paul Wiens. Thus space and time, reality and fiction, religion and science, past and present merge into a vast mosaic where everything is possible — until a too-harsh insistence on reality upsets the balance, as in the story 'The Tightrope' (bk. 11, ch. 26). Readers will want to discover for themselves the role that losing one's balance plays in the accidental death of the Trobadora Beatrice.

Morgner stated repeatedly that her goal as a writer was to help women enter history, and this theme is evident in most of her books.[5] It is a task that she takes most seriously even as she boldly invents whatever fantastic 'facts' she needs at the moment. As Beatrice tells Laura in book 4, facing realities can only be judged a sign of strength if you have good luck: 'A person who is condemned to life imprisonment and doesn't make plans to escape is not proud but cowardly. . . . I have exited history because I wanted to enter history. To appropriate nature. First of all, my own. Tackle the making of humanity head-on. This end justifies all magical means. Prosit.' Morgner's view of history is evoked most eloquently in chapter 22 of book 8, where Beatrice describes her visit to Diocletian's palace in the Yugoslavian city Split. This city becomes a metaphor for understanding history as a palimpsest. The splendid palace, for example, which has been altered countless times over the course of centuries, bears layer upon layer of historical knowledge and events. Women too have always been part of history, but in order to appropriate it, they must excavate the traces of themselves from under the layers. At the same time, they must begin to actively inscribe history with accounts of their existences as women, a process whose outcome cannot be foretold. As Beatrice muses in concluding the story of her visit to Split: 'How many Lauras does the world structure of today need in order to be marbled with Lauras?'

The idea of writing women into history is, of course, familiar to everyone who has even a nodding acquaintance with feminist literature and scholarship of the last three decades. Morgner, however, writing in the GDR of the late 1960s and early 1970s, did not identify with feminists in West Germany and other Western countries. While acknowledging that the women's movement had been an important stimulus to her thinking, she declared that *Life and Adventures* had been written by a Communist and refused the label 'feminist' for herself for many years. Reading the novel today, we can see that she recognized the limitations of much feminist literature and theory of the time, in particular 'difference' feminism with its emphasis on assumed innate or 'essentialist' differences between women and men.[6] Morgner's own feminist vision is identified already in chapter 7 of book 1, where Beatrice concludes that the goddesses' goal of reinstating the matriarchy is reactionary and decides 'in favor of the third order. Which was to be neither patriarchal nor matriarchal, but human.' It is from this perspective that Morgner critiques the inequities persisting in the GDR despite the official claim that women's equality had been achieved there – and indeed, it was the law of the land – by repeatedly requiring Laura and Beatrice to resort to the Beautiful Melusine's black magic in attempting to accomplish their goals. Another character, Valeska, finally finds the ideal solution by learning how to don 'the uniform of privilege,' that is, to change her gender, more or less at will (bk. 12). Morgner's characters stand the concept of the positive heroine on its head; her detailed descriptions of women's daily lives belie the claims that progressive measures such as free childcare, official nondiscrimination of unmarried mothers, and generous maternity leaves (a single mother like Laura could take up to three years) could close the huge gap between legal equality for women and the reality of their daily lives in the GDR.

Morgner's fearlessness in addressing feminist themes and her exuberant insistence on women's right to sexual pleasure – both taboo subjects in her country at the time – make her unique among GDR women writers of her generation. These qualities also help explain why her books were not published in the Soviet Union, where her erotic scenes were considered pornographic. Her exploration of the themes of *Life and Adventures* and her experimentation with narrative form continued even more radically in the long-awaited *Amanda: Ein Hexenroman* (Amanda: A witch novel, 1983), the second part of a planned trilogy that, sadly, was never finished. At the time of Morgner's death from cancer in 1990, only fragments of the third volume had been completed.[7]

In an interview with Alice Schwarzer, editor of the West German feminist magazine *Emma*, in late 1989, Morgner discussed the importance of laughter as a means of confronting taboos and of coping with the realities of life. She also spoke with regret of being prevented by her illness from participating in the revolutionary events then taking place in Germany, of her horror at the corruption that had been revealed in Honecker's government, and of struggling to come to terms with her own complicity: 'For in spite of everything I too in principle supported this father-land (homeland is something different), because capitalism was and is not an alternative for me, certainly not for women. . . . If this should be my last interview – don't take it as my last word, dear *Emma*-readers: perhaps it is somewhere in my books.'[8]

Readers looking for Morgner's 'last word' in *Life and Adventures* will soon realize that she is having fun at our expense too. Not infrequently, a statement or event that is mentioned almost as if in passing will bring us up short, only to be clarified eventually, sometimes many chapters later. The mix of characters and events from history, fiction, and contemporary life makes us wonder how much significance to attach to particular clues. For example, references to the medieval code of courtly love, which required chivalrous devotion to an unattainable woman, are echoed in journalist Uwe Parnitzke's rueful musings on his marital problems ('Having sex was only possible downwards, love only upwards' [first interm.]). But is it significant that several characters – Gahmuret in the poem 'Water Walk,' the physicist Morolf, and a woman Beatrice meets in Split, Bele H. (Belekane) — bear the names of characters from medieval epic literature? Why does Orlando show up to carry Beatrice's suitcase at the Leipzig train station? Scarcely less unexpected, given the suppression of traditional religions in the GDR, are the numerous Biblical references and quotations that lard the narrative.

Through puzzling or bizarre juxtapositions, Morgner draws her readers into the creative process, so that we too become, along with Laura, Valeska, the Beautiful Melusine, and Beatrice, coauthors of this fantastic text as we read. Not unlike Beatrice, who in her naiveté often misinterprets the motives of other characters and the meanings of events, we may be led astray by our assumptions or by gaps in our knowledge. Some of the theoretical and scientific passages in the novel are easily understandable to the general reader, while others may seem like gibberish to readers unfamiliar with the language of nuclear physics or the chemistry of nutrition science, for example. Some of the literary allusions, such as to *Don Quixote* or *The Thousand and One Nights*, are rather transparent, while other references — among them echoes of Brecht, Thomas Mann, Mikhail Bulgakov, Jean Paul, and Goethe — are anything but. Yet this too is part of the message — as Beatrice and Laura realize in book 4, 'one doesn't have to know everything' — and of the fun of discovery. Who would expect to find a quote (unacknowledged, of course!) from Kahlil Gibran's *The Prophet* in a novel by an East German Communist? But there it is. Readers who happen to know Morse code should take a close look at book 5. These are only a few hints of the surprises in store for readers embarking on the adventure of reading *The Life and Adventures of Trobadora Beatrice as Chronicled by Her Minstrel Laura.*

Notes

1. Excerpts from Morgner's *Life and Adventures* that have been previously published in English translation are: 'Gospel of Valeska, Which Laura Reads as a Revelation on the Day of the Trobadora Beatriz's Burial' (bk. 12), trans. Karen R. Achberger and Friedrich Achberger, *New German Critique* 15 (fall 1978): 121–46; 'Shoes,' (bk. 10, ch. 15) and 'The Rope' (bk. 11, ch. 26, abridged), trans. Karen R. Achberger, *German Feminism: Readings in Politics and Literature*, ed. Edith Hoshino Altbach et al. (Albany: State U of New York P, 1984), 213–14, 215–19; 'Third Fruit of Bitterfeld: The Tightrope' (bk. 11, ch. 26), trans. Nancy Lukens, *Daughters of Eve: Women's Writing from the German Democratic Republic*, ed. Nancy Lukens and Dorothy Rosenberg (Lincoln: U of Nebraska P, 1993), 135–42. These publications were consulted in the course of preparing this translation. Also

published in English translation are two stories from *Hochzeit in Konstantinopel* (Wedding in Constantinople) (Berlin: Aufbau, 1968), 'White Easter' and 'The Duel,' trans. Karen R. Achberger, *German Feminism*, 77–82, 209–12.

2. Virtually nothing is known about the historical Trobairitz de Dia, not even a death date or whether her name was really Beatrice. Preserved are a two-sentence *vida* (life), which Morgner adapts as the opening lines of book 1, and four *cansos* (love songs) attributed to a Comtessa de Dia, as well as a *tenso* (a dispute between two poets) attributed to the troubadour Raimbaut d'Aurenga (d. 1173) that some scholars have seen as evidence of the love relationship between Raimbaut and the Comtessa de Dia. The four *cansos* (two of which Morgner includes in *Life and Adventures*, bk. 1, ch. 9, and bk. 4, ch. 5) and the *vida* can be found in Meg Bogin, *The Women Troubadours* (New York: Paddington Press, 1976), 82–91, 163.

3. The complete text of *Rumba auf einen Herbst* was reconstructed by Rudolf Bussmann, who administers Morgner's literary estate, and finally published by Luchterhand two years after the author's death. A paperback edition was published by dtv in 1995.

4. In fact, the official attempt to establish a movement of writing workers was ultimately deemed a failure. No great or revolutionary art to speak of was produced in GDR workers' writing circles.

5. The most important besides *Life and Adventures* are: *Hochzeit in Konstantinopel* (Wedding in Constantinople, 1968); *Gauklerlegende: Eine Spielfraungeschichte. Mit sechs Fotographien von Lothar Reher* (Juggler's legend: A story of women minstrels, with six photographs by Lothar Reher, 1970); *Die Wundersamen Reisen Gustavs des Weltfahrers: Lügenhafter Roman mit Kommentaren* (The wondrous journeys of Gustav the world traveler: Mendacious novel with commentaries, 1972), and *Amanda: Ein Hexenroman* (Amanda: A witch novel, 1983). For a detailed analysis of this theme, see Silke von der Emde, *Entering History: Feminist Dialogues in Irmtraud Morgner's Prose*, diss., Indiana U, 1994.

6. 'Difference feminism' was popularized in West Germany most prominently by Alice Schwarzer's *Der 'kleine Unterschied' und seine großen Folgen: Frauen über sich. Beginn einer Befreiung* (The 'little difference' and its great consequences: Women on the subject of themselves. Beginning of a liberation) (Frankfurt am Main: S. Fischer, 1975).

7. One story from this work was published by Luchterhand in 1991: 'Der Schöne und das Tier: Eine Liebesgeschichte' (The [male] beauty and the beast: A love story). The work as compiled from the author's literary estate has now been published as Irmtraud Morgner, *Das heroische Testament: Roman in Fragmenten*

(The heroic testament: A novel in fragments), compiled from unpublished papers, edited and with commentary by Rudolf Bussmann (Munich: Luchterhand, 1998).

8. 'Jetzt oder nie! Die Frauen sind die Hälfte des Volkes!' (Now or never! Women are half of the population!) *Emma* 2 (February 1990): 32–39, quote on 32.

TRANSLATOR'S NOTE

In preparing this translation, I have attempted to render Morgner's prose into idiomatic English while retaining characteristic features of her style. Prominent examples are her frequent use of sentence fragments, especially subordinate clauses (beginning with 'because,' 'since,' 'although,' 'which,' etc.) that stand alone; also indirect speech (reported speech that is not introduced by phrases such as 'she said') and long sentences consisting of several short clauses joined by commas. A merging of narrative perspectives or shifts in narrative voice are often eclipsed by such means.

Rather than interrupt the narrative with footnotes, I have chosen to gloss many acronyms and unfamiliar terms in the text itself. Individuals, events, and concepts that are likely to be unfamiliar to readers with little knowledge of the GDR or that have a particular significance in the context are identified in the glossary at the end of the book. In general, names, terms, and concepts from literature, mythology, and history that can be easily located in standard English-language reference works are not identified in the glossary.

For clarification of many details specific to GDR linguistic usage, institutions, or practices, I am greatly indebted to Otto Emersleben, who read the entire translation in draft form and rendered invaluable assistance. Short excerpts from the novel previously published in translation (bk. 10, ch. 15 ['Shoes'] and bk. 12 ['Gospel of Valeska'], trans. Karen Achberger; bk. 11, ch. 26 ['The Tightrope'], trans. Nancy Lukens) influenced my translation of those sections. Petra Seifert read a semifinal draft of the translation and offered helpful suggestions. Any errors that remain are my responsibility.

The Life and Adventures of Trobadora Beatrice as Chronicled by Her Minstrel Laura

In the beginning was the other act. BEATRICE DE DIA

LIST OF THE NOVEL'S MAJOR CHARACTERS

Beatrice de Dia, trobadora
Guilhem de Poitiers, her first husband
Théophile Gerson, storekeeper, her second husband
Raimbaut d'Aurenga, troubadour, her first lover
Alain, student, her second lover
Lutz Pakulat, structural engineer, her third lover
Laura Salman, Germanist, construction worker, trolley-car driver, minstrel
Uwe Parnitzke, journalist, her first husband
Benno Pakulat, carpenter, her second husband
Juliane, Laura's daughter
Wesselin, Laura's son
Johann Salman, engine driver, Laura's father
Olga Salman, Laura's mother
Lutz Pakulat, structural engineer, Laura's sometime lover
Valeska Kantus, nutrition scientist
Uwe Parnitzke, journalist, married to Valeska in his second marriage
Rudolf Uhlenbrook, nutrition scientist, her second husband
Arno, Valeska's son
Franz Kantus, typesetter, Valeska's father
Berta, Valeska's mother
Katschmann, trolley-car driver, Berta's life companion
Oskar Pakulat, carpenter, father of Benno and Lutz
Anna Pakulat, Oskar's wife

Wenzel Morolf, physicist
Gurnemann, physicist

The structural plan of the novel is here recommended to the gentle readers but not imposed upon them, for which reason the table of contents is printed at the end of the book.

RESOLUTIONS

Of course this country is a land of miracles. I realized this when a woman came walking toward me. On my street. One morning in April. The unknown woman asked if I had any money. Since I'm disinclined to conversation when sober, I said good morning. And I was in a hurry, on my way to the nursery school. The woman, who also had a child hanging on her left hand, caught up to me, thrust a package at me with her right hand, and said, 'Five thousand.' We stared at each other. The boys pulled away from us. I was still hearing the amount. As it dawned on me, I tried to let go of the package. But the woman shrank back and buried her hands in the pockets of her coat. Its abundant expanse was filled. The short garment didn't show her knees at all, barely her calves. Although I had every reason to demand an apology from this pushy woman, I apologized. Her brown button-eyes studied my face. I tolerated, who knows why, the unsolicited weight of the package. Only when I felt the circulation in my fingertips being cut off by the packing string did I attempt to set it down on the trunk of a parked car. 'Three thousand,' said the woman. She took a tissue from her coat pocket and rubbed her eyes. Then her nose. Rainwater tickled mine. It dripped down from the part in my hair. The woman's permed curls were already in a state of disarray reminiscent of an unraveled brown sock. Three sobs. At that, I forgot the pain in my fingers. I waited meekly for who knows what. When the wrapping paper was wet through and bulging, I smelled it. 'It's unique,' the woman said through her tears, 'an opportunity, the chance of a lifetime. Seize it.' Her Saxon accent was harmoniously in tune with her round, freckled face. 'Fame,' she continued in this dialect, coming cautiously closer and jabbing at the package with a fat forefinger. 'World renown, guaranteed. You're a writer, aren't you?' Then came a detailed description of a conversation with the local butcher, which is supposedly how she learned of my occupation. She thought the children knew each other from the playground. Now that she was married, she unfortunately couldn't be sure of getting day care. That made prospects for her actual profession uncertain. And she had lost her other one with the death of her friend Beatrice. If I hesitated too long, she wouldn't be able to buy a proper gravestone for this remarkable woman. I gave my condolences. In anticipation. But suddenly the woman stopped talking. I looked indifferently at the sky, which a cloud from the gas works had superfluously darkened. Scraped splinters of glass from the sidewalk with my feet. Doubtful, I ran to the puddle and asked the woman's son to take the package. The boy, who was about three, replied that he was a captain. He told me what his destroyer could do in a sea battle. Richard, my son, described what his destroyer could do. They were using ice cream spoons for warships. Feeling calmer, I ran back and explained that writers don't buy manuscripts, because they can produce their own. The woman started working on a fresh tissue. The deployment of teardrops for blackmail tempered my sympathetic reactions. But instead of cutting the process short by means of the most obvious, simple, true, and in this country not at all dishonorable argument, I concealed my lack of funds, instead casting myself and my profession in a bad light by explaining how the selling of manuscripts interferes with work. And tried to gain time by discussing other business details. Finally I said, 'So you're asking me not only to negotiate for free, but also to pay three thousand marks? Three thousand marks for a gravestone?' — 'Yes, I am,' said the woman, adding that the renowned Beatrice de Dia deserved even greater honors. I said I was sorry that word of her deceased friend's fame hadn't reached me. Since I guessed the fat little woman to be in her mid-thirties and assumed her friends were of the same generation, I thought it would be easy to deflect the impression of being badly educated. To be on the safe side, I reminded her of several geniuses whom an early death had cheated of public recognition during their lifetimes. The woman gave her friend's age as 843. Since the woman seemed to be in perfect mental and physical health, I asked if I had heard correctly. The woman rolled her button-eyes and repeated her appalling statement. At that moment I realized that if the woman wasn't an arch-liar, she was telling a great truth. And I felt the pull. At the same time, noticed dimples in the chubby cheeks across from me. Suddenly the woman brushed the shreds of tissue from her coat, took the package from my hands, and said, 'I was Trobadora Beatrice's minstrel. My name is Laura.' — 'Stop,' I said. Oh, this irresistible pull of curiosity, I'd known all along that I wouldn't escape responsibility. Involuntarily I fumbled with the knotted strings. Laura said, 'After I have the money you can get your claws on it. As much as you please. Everything, for all I care. One thousand, because it's you. These documents will save you at least ten trips, a hundred hours of production-line research, and a thousand conversations. The whole world on five pounds of paper. Seven hundred marks cash and you're a made woman.' I snatched the package from Laura's arms and my son from the puddle and invited her to my apartment. There I handed over my budget for the month in exchange for a receipt. As I cut the strings, I asked Laura why she didn't want to become a made woman. 'I am one,' she replied. 'As soon as I'm able to drive my trolley through the city again, I'll be one. Sedentary occupations don't agree with me. And I wouldn't know how to decide whether people should laugh or cry. No more scribbling for me.' I put my son in dry pants and shoes, dropped him off late, that is, sternly reprimanded, at the nursery school, and was finally able to start reading in the ninth hour of April the third. The documents ideally justified the risk of the purchase. My expectations were absolutely exceeded. I immediately started reordering and editing these sensational testimonies for publication. The book you are reading follows the sources rigorously in describing all essential events. Sections of text are reproduced unchanged in a new sequence that is more accommodating to the reader. – On 7 April I paid my last respects to Beatrice de Dia. Her body had been under refrigeration for three weeks for purposes of scientific research. During the funeral service in the small parlor of the Berlin-Baumschulenweg crematorium I admired the trobadora's face. Everything about it was long and narrow, her forehead, nose, chin; even her lips seemed higher than they were wide, as if pursed in boundless pride. Yet her eyelids were immense bulging hemispheres. Round arch-shaped brows high above them. Black. Her hair, tightly curled at the hairline, hadn't gone gray either. It fell to her upper arms. Even the coffin seemed excessively long to me. A man whom I initially took for a hired funeral orator spoke grandiose, somber words of praise for the beauty of this ageless vision. Laura claimed he was the well-known poet Pomerenke. At the end he promised the deceased that he would forgo poetry, renounce all beautiful sounds, and fight political battles for the trobadora's legacy. Except for Laura, her husband Benno, and me, no witnesses were present.

Berlin, 22 August 1973
Irmtraud Morgner

BOOK ONE

Chapter 1

Which recounts what Laura initially learns from Beatrice de Dia about her strange and wondrous back- and foreground

Beatrice de Dia, a beautiful and noble lady, was the wife of Sir Guilhem de Poitiers. She fell in love with Sir Raimbaut d'Aurenga and composed many fine and beautiful songs for him, a few of which can be found in anthologies of old Provençal troubadour poetry. Next to the distinctive verses of Raimbaut d'Aurenga (French: d'Orange). He loved the game of playing with difficult rhymes and the ambiguity of words. The metric structure of his works reflects great refinement. Convinced of their exclusivity, the chronically indebted count constantly tried to find complicated words ending in -enga to rhyme with Aurenga, and showed disdain for all unaristocratic verse-artists. For this reason Beatrice felt compelled to mention her noble status in her 'Canso of Love Betrayed,' as well as her intellect, beauty, loyalty, and passion. Superfluously. In practice, the gentleman didn't think a bird in the hand was worth two in the bush, as would seem logical. To him, a bird in the hand was worth two in the hand. This experience prompted the contessa to depart the medieval world of men. By unnatural means. Persephone demanded 2,920 hours of work for each year of sleep. The trobadora named the largest number she knew. Her promise was enough for 810 years of sleep. When she had confirmed her promise to Persephone on her word of honor and pricked herself in the finger with a spindle, the magic began to work. Only for her; husband and servants died in the usual way, per the agreement. A hedge of roses grew up around the château. While it was still visible, robber barons tried repeatedly to break through the hedge of thorns. Later people took it for an impassable hill and went around it. In the spring of 1968, an engineer who had been hired to build a highway in the area decided to blast the obstacle out of the way. As he and the explosives specialist approached the red-blossomed mountain of roses to discuss where to place the charge, cursing the fragrance for lowering the construction workers' productivity, the hedge suddenly gave way and opened like a gate. The engineer was dumbstruck. Until he saw the château; then he cursed even louder. For he was anticipating endless negotiations with the Office for Protection of Historic Monuments. The curses awakened Beatrice. After rubbing the sleep from her eyes, she fell instantly in love with the engineer as a consequence of extreme abstinence.

Chapter 2

Wherein the reader finds the words exchanged by the engineer (engr.) and the explosives specialist (ex.sp.) on Monday, 6 May 1968, after Beatrice has fallen in love

EX.SP.: A miracle.

ENGR.: There are no miracles.

EX.SP.: Naturally.

ENGR.: Huh?

EX.SP.: I said, of course. We've often had street battles. But you can see for yourself . . .

ENGR.: A dusty ruin, a dusty female. I'm no American tourist who compensates for his hometown's short history by prostrating himself before every antiquity. I'm a Frenchman. And I'm paying for my son's education. If he wants to build barricades, he'll have to look for another source of income.

EX.SP.: That gives me an idea. We'll sell the miracle.

ENGR.: And?

EX.SP.: We'll be rich.

ENG.: Poor.

EX.SP.: Even poorer?

ENGR.: If the story gets out, we'll lose the job, they'll lock us up . . . Hey, has the ruin gotten you so confused that you're forgetting who the construction site belongs to, along with everything on it?

EX.SP.: The dame is no ruin. And the building is in great shape. Normally our châteaux last through the ages only when they're used as prisons. At our current rate of fifty percent of cases solved, only dilettante jobs are resolved. An educated man like you . . .

ENGR.: I'd guess, eleventh century. Anyway, miracles just don't sell.

EX.SP.: Why not?

ENGR.: Because they don't exist.

EX.SP.: Of course. We'll have to hurry. With miracles, you never know how long they'll last. Only when we have the check in our pocket . . .

ENGR.: You think there's a chance that the miracle is one and it's about to disappear?

EX.SP.: Naturally.

ENGR.: And if it doesn't?

EX.SP.: Demolition contract. It would obligate the buyer to tear down the château by the start date in our highway construction contract. Just recently I read about an American millionaire who paid big money for some old nuisance of a bridge in England. He had it taken down and shipped to California or someplace and put it back up on his ranch. The château is at least twice that old . . .

ENGR.: Which would have to be reflected in the price. Not to mention the money saved on clearing away the rubble . . .

EX.SP.: . . . and the blasting . . .

ENGR.: Our money, all of it.

EX.SP.: Sixty percent for me.

ENGR.: How come?

EX.SP.: My idea.

ENGR.: My project.

EX.SP.: Fifty-fifty.

ENGR.: Sixty percent for me.

(Here followed a long exchange of curses and percentages, according to Laura only vaguely remembered by Beatrice, as well as thumps to the head.)

CLOSING WORDS OF ENGR.: Forty-five percent for you, and the dame.

Chapter 3

WHICH TELLS SECONDARILY OF WEED PULLING AND PRIMARILY OF A REUNION

Beatrice was able to follow the two men's conversation word for word even though it was conducted in southern French dialect. When it was finished, she wrested the engineer from her heart and ejected the gentlemen from the chamber. Clouds of dust rose from her bed, nightgown, and limbs. Beatrice blew into the clouds. Coughed. Sneezed. But didn't call for the servants. Because her sister-in-law had kept her more or less up to date on circumstances in the château and in the world. Hypnopedically. Her stiff joints, her back, and her heart cracked. 'Why in hell did she wake me up prematurely?' Beatrice asked herself in Old Provençal, to exercise her speech organs. For these two men didn't match the trobadora's expectations in the least. Why had her sister-in-law, Marie de Lusignan, suddenly, two years before the deadline, obtained permission to get her up? Close-mouthed female! Busybody! Nonetheless, this reunion was overwhelming. This dance of the dust particles in the sunbeam! It shone through empty leaded window frames; the intact windows were covered with dust. Beatrice ran cautiously to the bench in the window shaft. Her legs, unaccustomed to moving, almost failed her. The bench was as long as the wall was thick: two meters. The remains of the glass shattered as she flung the window open. O Provence! Country leaning to the south with the wind at its back. Mistral-tempered loveliness. Palisade-tempered wilderness. An indescribable pleasure to experience, as if in the shelter of a cave, the raging of the northerly fall wind rushing down the Rhone valley. How it howls. How it hisses. How it resounds in the château. What an instrument! Château Almaciz had always been the most beautiful wind organ in Provence. Beatrice knelt on the stone bench and leaned her head out over the protecting wall. Her hair was promptly seized by the mistral and tousled like the trellised fences of cypresses and poplars on the plain. During short lulls Beatrice listened to the splendid sounds of the midday heat: the sawing chords of the cicadas. And she could already smell the intoxicating fragrances of lavender and rosemary that would soon waft over from the hills. Emotion and inner turmoil brought water to the trobadora's eyes. Their large lids measured out the water as drops that slowly washed her cheeks. Her hair was thoroughly cleansed of dust also. 'High time,' said Beatrice in modern French, which Marie de Lusignan had taught her. Her sister-in-law was generally known by the name 'Beautiful Melusine.' Language lessons she had found time for. Her news reports were short and incomplete. She was always on the go and rarely to be heard; at the moment, not at all. What was keeping her from assigning Beatrice work? 'Wakes me from my sleep, excuses herself for a moment, claims she'll be right back from Paris, and doesn't show up,' grumbled Beatrice in modern French, which felt good on her tongue. Even though it struck her as a bit too elaborately elegant. But it echoed familiarly in the chamber. Beatrice wasn't surprised that Almaciz had survived all the wars. What seemed most astonishing to her was that the windows of her sleeping chamber were still facing in a direction that the position of the sun showed to be south. And the hills at midday were overgrown as ever by the harmlessly lush-appearing, impenetrable thickets of weeds and brambles. And the poplars were still baring their silver in the storm. Of course, there were many more fields than before, many more fruit trees, but still, real Nature far and wide, except for a highway. The monster La Tarasque would prevent a second highway. Two brutes did not a patriarchy make. It wasn't so bad.

Chapter 4

Setting out and entering earth

No sooner had she awakened than Beatrice found herself facing magisterial decisions. Alone. For she knew from experience that a Melusinian moment could take days. If she waited for that moment to pass, Beatrice and humankind would be brought to a halt by two fossils. Besides, the château seemed indispensable to the trobadora for her professional work. Therefore, she allowed herself only fleeting glances at Almaciz. And glanced only fleetingly into the mirror. Timidly at first. But her internal image – defined by an intense physical and mental awareness of strength that appears in the zenith of life – was still consistent with the external one. And her unusual height, once a stigmatizing feature, had also been preserved. Good. The trobadora took a close look around the private chambers of Guilhem de Poitiers to be quite sure. They were deserted. At that, Beatrice heaved a sigh of relief. And concluded that it had apparently been possible to bury her husband and the servants before the hedge of roses grew up around the château. Various comments by the explosives specialist implied that the hedge had plunged steeply down into the moat. Beatrice didn't know exactly when it had happened. In any case, as she looked down from the round tower of the fortress, the only thing she could see on the duckweed-covered moat water was a few rose petals. So without delay, she bathed in the cistern, selected the least tattered dress from her trunk, put it on, and was on her way to Tarascon by late afternoon. The sun had already abated its fury, slanting toward the horizon. The peaks of the palisades were shallower. Beatrice had the mistral at her back. It propelled her southward. Swallows sliced the fragrant, resounding air close above the grasses with their scissor-wings. Aromas of roasting from the earth and plants, weeds and resin. Crickets chirped. Winged by the wind, Beatrice made her way through the swaths in the fields. The grain came only up to her knees; reeds were high above her head. On and on. She thought the south would soon be inside. It felt as if she were entering the earth.

Chapter 5

Laura entertains us with a memory that concerns her private life

Elements: Since Thuringia has no active volcanoes, we decided to plunge into a cave on the last day of our vacation. The journey to communion with boundless Nature, a luxury that for various reasons we didn't want to deny ourselves any longer, was made via railway. Dependents, loss of the illusion that the length of one's life story doesn't limit freedom of decision, half-measures dictated by circumstances, white lies, and related unwelcome trivialities as well as the generous melancholy of September brought us closer to earth. And to the other elements — fire, water, and air — which we knew were driven by the forces of love and hate. The train also carried women en route to the second shift at a cotton mill and mushroom hunters. It arrived at the cave site twenty-seven minutes late. Lutz was carrying a flower-print nylon bag containing maps and an umbrella. The mushroom hunters lugged baskets ostentatiously piled high with birch *boletus* and giant *boletus edulis*. That made me hungry. Lutz didn't think the idea of a full meal beforehand was out of place. To the contrary. The owner of the local tavern welcomed us with a handshake. This greeting, conveyed at the table before taking our order, not sincerely but as if in passing, underscored his distance from the visitors. His wife, broad in the beam and masculine-looking, served a meal she had cooked herself. The host discussed soccer with the regular customers, poured beer, kept track of the tab with pencil marks on beer mats that he dropped one by one from a stack held high in the air, and collected money. When the two of us had consumed three servings of sauerbraten with dumplings, downed two glasses of beer, and paid the bill, we set out for the cave, each with an arm around the other's back. The path was marked by large, brightly colored signs carved on wooden signposts. The above-ground facilities reminded us of the local train station, except that they were conspicuously well maintained; the buildings and benches looked freshly painted. To the left of the reception room were two souvenir stands. On the right, behind a rock garden, were several groups of movable figures in open showcases, mounted on poles two meters tall, similar to wooden Christmas displays but powered by windmills. On the poles were requests for donations and operating instructions. In rhyme. Below them were mailbox-shaped money boxes. Lutz put two groschen in the slot and turned a windmill in the opposite direction to that indicated by the arrows on its blades. The wooden figures, fastened to bands similar to drive belts, moved backwards, fell on their backs in the antipodal phase, and turned up on their backs: miners. The trees were in full leaf. Clouds of dust swirled around our shoes, which were made not of metal but of leather. Heat bore down on the crowns of our heads. At the reception room counter, we bought perforated admission tickets torn from rolls like movie tickets. Next to the cash register were framed photocopies of a ballad about the cave, under glass. The window of the gable side was garnished with greenery tied to tree branches. To the right, in the order listed, were doors labeled 'Ladies,' 'Gentlemen,' 'City Council Administration,' 'Cave Entrance.' When the visitor count reached twenty, the guide called for attention, introduced herself, gave the presumed age of the natural monument as several thousand years, and tore pieces from the tickets at the cave entrance. Then she clicked light switches and urged caution. An iron handrail led downward. Stairs. The cement floor was grooved like in a public urinal and wet too. The lush warmth of autumn quickly evaporated from our clothes. Six degrees Celsius, the guide assured us. Constant temperatures as in healthy bodies. Cold – can one get married cold? Cracks in the vaults had been bridged and sealed with lead filling. The guide gave ambitious names to the wide spaces between the passageways; I heard rooms and halls mentioned. Stalactites and stalagmites, which were distributed sparsely, grew one millimeter every twenty to fifty years owing to calcium-poor water. Lighting compensated for this defect. In the cone of light cast by a spotlight, the visitors admired genuine moss, growing there as a result of frequent tours: proof of popularity. Spotlight presentations on sinter columns, pools of water, and thousand-year-old stalactite curtains. The references to age prompted the male visitors, most well on in years, to compliment the guide. She thanked them with an electric sunrise over the cave lake. At the end of the walk, a photographer led us to a camera on a tripod and lined us up, no obligation, for a group picture, nice keepsake, postcard size, two marks eighty, those interested in purchasing it should report at the photo kiosk after the tour, hold still now. A three-minute shot. The photographer thanked us. I took off my shoes and threw them in the lake. Since we were asked for addresses at the photo kiosk, we decided to forgo the embarrassing document. And because of its incriminating nature.

Chapter 6

In which another man shows up

Beatrice kept going headfirst right through the middle of the earth to the intersection. Where the highway cut through the path. Cut it off. The cars rushing by differed in noisiness, stench, and number from the ones Beatrice had seen during her sleep. Dazed by them and by her sudden awakening, she waited. For the moment when a gap in the line of cars would allow her to cross the road. She waited and waited. After a while she spotted a man in the distance standing beside the road just like she was. He was making rowing motions with his arms. At first Beatrice thought he was waving to her in solidarity because he found himself in the same unfortunate situation, and she returned the greeting. But when he didn't stop rowing, she interpreted the gesture as a traffic signal meant to convey a desire to cross the road. So Beatrice rowed too. And after a short time a car stopped. One car. On the path. A man in his middle years stuck his head out of the open window, looked her over, and asked where she was headed. 'Tarascon,' Beatrice answered in amazement. 'Well then,' said the man. And before Beatrice fully understood or could be surprised, she was seated in a car for the first time in her life. And riding. And had the trunk of a car ahead of her. Constantly. Not always the same one. Strange music came from the walls of the car. Interrupted by strange news reports. For example, a male voice reported, 'On Friday afternoon I was passing through the Rue de la Harpe to the Boulevard Saint-Germain, intending to go up the Boulevard Saint-Michel on personal business. But when I reached the Musée de Cluny, there were armed and helmeted police officers standing with their backs to me, sealing off the entrance. Further up, at the Rue des Ecoles – I'd never seen anything like it – police cars were being more or less prevented from moving by a crowd of people throwing stones; five or six came flying through the air at once. I had to take the Boulevard Saint-Germain toward Saint-Germain-des-Prés and then side streets up to the top. There, on the Rue Soufflot, were several thousand students, including many girls. You got the impression that they couldn't help themselves. Many of them had books and lecture notes under their arms. Many apparently came from Nanterre, where the faculty had shut down, as reported by the noon news. Now I learned that the police were arresting left-leaning students assembled in the courtyard of the Sorbonne to protest the fascist machinations of radical right groups, and the Sorbonne was closed too. They were easy to tell apart: a very few, about thirty, at the level of the Sorbonne, challenging the police in the front line; then all those watching from very close by, ready to interfere at the right moment – some, already nervous, were pulling up traffic signs and wire tree guards, while others advocated that they remain peaceful, refrain from improvisation, and instead prepare a purposeful action against the police provocation on Monday – and finally the great majority, who stood around with their books and notebooks, perhaps at a loss but thoroughly cheerful and also determined not to disperse. As soon as the police attacked, the students flooded back but immediately resumed their position when the police withdrew to their starting point. All traffic was essentially brought to a standstill.' – 'A fine state of affairs,' said the driver. Beatrice delighted him with admiring glances. They were meant not for external assets, since beauty was conspicuously absent, but internal ones. Ethical. No hollow cavalier badge – helpfulness. Self-evident brotherliness. Sisterliness. Beautiful human community. Beatrice admired its representative. 'And I had feared I was too early . . . ' said Beatrice. 'On the contrary,' said the man, pulled off to the left, stopped, lowered the seat backs, and threw himself on the trobadora. She pushed him away. The man said, 'Don't fool around.' She resisted. 'Death is free,' panted the man and asked if she had all her marbles. She resisted with all her might. At that, the man struck her on the mouth so hard it bled, overpowered her with the weight of his fat body, called her vile names, and emptied his pouch. As if relieving himself. After rearranging his clothing, he asked matter-of-factly where he should drop Beatrice off in Tarascon. She got out of the car. 'Silly bitch,' said the man and pulled his car back into the stream of foul-smelling traffic that was surging noisily through the fields.

Chapter 7

A HOLDING CELL WITH TWO DEPOSED GODDESSES DESCENDS FROM ON HIGH

The trobadora raged with wrathful thoughts and uttered the curse 'Holy Mother!' Involuntarily. Not because she held out any hopes. But just as it had eight hundred eight years ago, a holding cell landed suddenly at her feet. It was made of concrete, cube shaped, about eight cubic meters in size. The iron door of the cell was bolted shut on the outside by two poles inserted crosswise through hooks embedded in the cement. Instructions for opening the door were posted on the front. Three surfaces of the cube had air holes with grates over them. A song in two-part harmony rang out through the vents. As she had done so long ago, Beatrice followed the instructions for removing the iron poles from the hooks. The door was pushed open from the inside – the same as before. And the song swelled with that zealous resolve which Beatrice always found offensive. But she masked her aversion with a smile and listened to several programmatic songs. The first part was sung by the divine daughter, the second by the divine mother. Mouths agape, eyes turned inward, Persephone and Demeter were actually singing the same old songs of revenge and prophesying the reinstatement of the matriarchy. On the same straw mattresses? The dungeon had no other furniture. If need be, gods can do without food and drink and thus don't have to depend on sanitary facilities. 'You called us?' asked Persephone when the song was over. 'Yes,' said Beatrice, 'that is, actually, I didn't, or more precisely, not directly, but of course it would be wonderful if you could help me in this unfortunate situation . . . ' – 'Just resurrected and slacking already,' Persephone answered sternly. Then she heaped abuse on Melusine and Co., who still hadn't succeeded in restoring the goddesses to power. Persephone used the words 'slipshod' and 'breach of contract.' For the terms of the pact had required the women mentioned to promise that they would reinstate ancient matriarchal conditions in return for prolonged life. Only those like Beatrice de Dia who seemed unsuited for practical political work were allowed to sleep if they promised to work in support of the cause after awakening. Additionally, the active members of the strategic organization that Persephone had built up over time were required to train the passive, sleeping members hypnopedically and indoctrinate them in the party line. By the time the Beautiful Melusine joined the organization, the opposition had already come together. Relatively unhampered, the confined goddesses could pass resolutions easily but couldn't keep control. The opposition met as a round table between Caerleon on Usk and the future, but a little closer to Caerleon. In 1871 the opposition won the majority. The Beautiful Melusine had belonged to the opposition since 1309. Beatrice was informed hypnopedically by her sister-in-law of the goddesses' reactionary endeavors and quickly decided in favor of the third order. Which was to be neither patriarchal nor matriarchal but human. In their illegal work for this human order, the opposition made use of legal divine miracles. Which were limited. 'There's still a quota on the deeds allocated to us,' Persephone lamented. Her face and hands were blue but darker than her robe. Demeter's basic color was green. Beatrice asked Persephone if she had cut a hole in the wheat field with her holding cell only to complain. 'There's still an arbitrary quota on the deeds allocated to us,' Persephone lamented. 'Sometimes we get three or four entitlement vouchers a year, sometimes only one. But there have also been years when Mr. Lord God didn't grant us a single miracle. He can't kill us because we're immortal; that angers him. But he can keep us idle — that's worse than dead. So please don't waste time cursing, but do something about his absolute dictatorship so we can get out of this dungeon soon. Heaven is for women!' Then Persephone and her mother, Demeter, repeated this last statement twenty-seven times as a canon. Meanwhile, two angels landed in drill formation. They closed the door, replaced the bolts, and fastened four ropes to iron rings jutting out from the concrete walls. Then one angel raised his right arm sharply, and the holding cell floated away.

Chapter 8

Sorrow and Rejoicing

When the apparition from on high had disappeared, it dawned on Beatrice that the Beautiful Melusine had given her very superficial instruction about the world. And she made up her mind to be prepared for surprises of all kinds. Whereupon she scanned the skies. After a while an airplane appeared. But Beatrice waited in vain for the Beautiful Melusine. How intensely she now envied the active members of the organization their powers of black magic. Bereft of support and forced to the edge of the road by the airstreams, Beatrice resumed her journey to Tarascon. Downcast. Plotting revenge. Only her belief in the dragon's appetite for human flesh and the infertile state of her 838-year-old body kept her from despairing. As the sun was setting, Beatrice reached the Abbey of Montmajour. She knocked on various doors, called, whistled. Eventually a door opened. Beatrice asked the sister for a bed for the night. However, it wasn't a sister but the museum director. He said, 'We're not a camp for vagabonds, we're a historical treasure.' — 'I'm a historical treasure too,' countered Beatrice and tried to explain herself. But the man understood nothing. He took her for a student on the run and asked what was left of the Latin Quarter. 'What Latin Quarter?' asked Beatrice. At that the man nodded understandingly, promised not to ask any more questions, and showed Beatrice into his apartment. To a seat in front of a box. It displayed moving pictures. The museum director's wife was knitting in front of the box. Now and then she stopped knitting and burst into speech. Beatrice could make out streets full of people, torn-up streets, and streets blocked off by ramparts. One rampart consisted mainly of an overturned bus. Heads popped up from behind the bus. Also arms throwing stones. Men with helmets, masks, and signs were throwing smoking batons up to and behind the obstacle. Enthusiastic voices were commenting on the moving pictures. The commentaries were frequently interrupted by coughing. Also by songs. 'This outburst of joie de vivre,' said one voice, 'this enthusiastic élan, this brotherly atmosphere. The streets of the Latin Quarter are filled with people. Everyone talks with everyone else, totally uninhibited. Everyone listens to everyone else. A hopeful, festive mood.' When burning cars appeared on the screen, the wife said, 'Where will it all end.' The museum director raised and lowered his shoulders several times and stated a judgment about the historical value of Paris. Then he offered Beatrice a secure haymow. As Beatrice was led past empty sarcophagi carved from stone, she turned down the haymow. She tried out the vacant hollows. They were all too short. Finally Beatrice spent the night under an oleander bush in the monastery courtyard. She lay sleepless as long as the bright full moon hung in the sky. For she was worried about the Beautiful Melusine. Could she have scorched her wings on a burning car? Later clouds gathered, veiling the moon, and lulled Beatrice to sleep after all. It was a deep sleep, full of confused dreams. When she woke up, the sun was already shining in the courtyard. And she discovered the head of La Tarasque decorating the capital of a cloister column. A human leg hung from each corner of his mouth. The sight bolstered Beatrice's confidence. To be sure, the condition of her dress was pitiful, seen in the light. During her tussle with the motorist, the worn fabric had disintegrated in many places. One of the floor-length sleeves was half torn away, the skirt was dragging on the right side, only the embroidery had withstood the assault. Embarrassed, the trobadora hid from the approaching tourists, whose voices were already filling the vaulted rooms. But since she couldn't find a back door, she was eventually forced to mingle with the crowd as she was. She hurried along with lowered eyes. Which is why she first noticed the frayed hems. Pants hems. Skirt hems. The skirts reached the ground too. And they were not just ragged but also dirty. The fashion fad of worn-out pants, some of them trimmed with gaudy patches, was less familiar to Beatrice. Yet she didn't doubt for a moment that these garments belonged to ex-sleepers too. So the trobadora was not an exception! Many had followed her example! Men too! Enraptured by this unexpected revelation that seemed to be grounds for the most favorable prospects, Beatrice hastened to the rag wearers and embraced them all. They didn't seem surprised, had a brief discussion, casually. Few were shorter than Beatrice. Several were taller. Before driving off in their cars, which sparkled with chrome and new paint, they gave Beatrice a small bag. Which she assumed had sugar in it. Beatrice followed them barefoot. She emptied the bag into her mouth as Tarascon with the good King René's castle came into view. Then the earth turned upside down; the fossil bugs fell out of her pockets and were devoured.

Chapter 9

Which brings more lucky coincidences after the LSD dream, as well as an old song by Beatrice de Dia, freely rendered into German by Paul Wiens

Beatrice woke up in a ditch beside the road. Scorched and weighed down by the sun, uplifted by the blue of her visions. Strangely peaceful. Satisfied. Sated by harmony. Only her gnawing hunger got her up and on her way. She eased it temporarily with water from the Rhone. A bus stopped at the bridge that led across the river to Tarascon. Tourists tumbled out of it. The mistral veiled them in clouds of dust. The tour leader screamed out the program: viewing of the castle, the church, lunch. The last part of the program inspired Beatrice. With energetic innocence left over from her dream, the trobadora joined the troop. The dust-cloud camouflage helped her get into the castle of the good King René of Provence free of charge. The castle guide claimed that the last troubadours had sung their songs in the court of this castle. The audience had listened from the loggia and the windows. Beatrice interrupted the castle guide's speech with three apologies and invited the tourists into the loggia. They followed her invitation willingly, no doubt in anticipation of the surprise promised in the tour package. The castle guide and the tour leader, each of whom suspected the other of initiating this development, withdrew into the colonnades with their newspapers. Meanwhile, the trobadora, inspired by hunger, remembered a song she had written 814 years ago. After that momentous incident with the love potion. When she had already reworked Raimbaut d'Orange to make him worthy of poetry. A simple pragmatic measure. Not even limited to female poets. But the Beautiful Melusine had immediately shrieked that this would mislead the public. As if intelligent people would seriously think that a Beatrice de Dia could be so inflamed over a person who not only wore peacock feathers on his hat but also on his poems and even on his soul. If the reality of Raimbaut didn't agree with the image of him that Beatrice had resolutely created — so much the worse for reality. The trobadora's stomach growled. The Americans had been jostling for front seats in the loggia for some time already. Beatrice stood, arms akimbo, and sang:

The one I lost, that cavalier
my song laments for sorrow pure,
For time immemorial shall it be known
how well I loved him evermore.
So grievously for love betrayed
because my love for him I hid,
I suffer in solitude and bereft
at night in bed or when I'm dressed.

The depth of the courtyard lent new dimensions to the trobadora's voice. The tourists crowded between the Gothic columns of the loggia. The castle guide and the tour leader stepped out of their colonnades with open newspapers. Beatrice looked up to the square ceiling that covered the shaft. The ceiling was cerulean blue. But not airtight. Occasionally a gust of wind hissed into the masonry. Beatrice waited until the tourists' murmurs and the storm had abated and sang the second strophe:

How gladly would I him enclose
within my arms at eventide
and offer my fair breast to him
to serve as pillow for his head.
That would yield me greater joy
than Floris had from Blancaflor
To him I give my hair, breath, and heart,
his are my eyes and my life.

The tourists clapped and threw coins down on the flagstones of the courtyard. Beatrice asked for silence for the third strophe and for paper money by introducing herself as guaranteed to be the very last and the very first genuine female troubadour. Then she sang:

Friend, handsome, good, and sensual,
were you but one night in my power
and could I but a single night
lie with you and kiss you softly,
know then how great my hunger were
to have you as my husband dear
were you to promise evermore
to treat me thus as I desire.

Beatrice received the applause haughtily. And refused to bend down to pick up coins. In order to drive up the price. However, she had to collect the paper money with her own hands. At that she felt keenly the absence of minstrels for the first time. At least one female minstrel seemed indispensable. Not just for collecting money or accompanying her on the lute — a respectable trobadora didn't perform in her own voice for a public like this one. Then she was the singer: the minstrel sang. Such an undignified lust for antique artifacts! Women with eyeglasses dangling on chains on their bosoms put their spectacles on hastily and gawked without embarrassment at the trobadora's dress. Two of them reached out to touch it. One offered to buy it. For a hundred dollars. To shake the crowd, Beatrice said, 'A thousand.' — 'Eleven hundred,' a male voice retorted. Then there was a confused babble of voices with various bids. Jostling. Finally the castle guide took pity on

Beatrice and led her into the good King René's garden. Sitting on the good king's stone dais, she counted the bills that had been tossed into her floor-length garment. She counted for a long time. Surrounded by the tall battlements that enclosed the bitter fragrance emitted by the geraniums in the sun. Three cypresses shielded the throne. Beatrice counted 2,750. Then she savored the silence and the royal coincidence. Only the tip-tops of the cypresses moved, swaying and rustling.

Chapter 10

Which is detrimental to the LSD revelation

'Tourism is the Cancer of Our Country' was posted on a gable Beatrice passed on her way to the restaurant. The saying struck her as unjust, because it contradicted the good experience she had just had. She dined on mussel soup, artichokes with sauce vinaigrette, horsemeat steak, Provençal tomatoes, and chilled melon for $10. When she had changed the remaining $2,740 at the current rate at a Bank of France affiliate and stashed the francs between her breasts, the original purpose of her visit to the city came back to her. Because of the monster's well-known keen hearing, Beatrice thought it was appropriate to whisper her inquiries as to La Tarasque's current whereabouts. An old man referred her in a loud voice to the fire department. And even offered to accompany Beatrice to the station house. 'Are you from Paris?' asked the old man unexpectedly. 'No,' Beatrice answered. 'Do you have relatives in Paris?' – 'My sister-in-law must be there. Why?' – The old man was momentarily irritated by the question, but then curiosity got the better of him again. And he inquired whether Beatrice had succeeded in reaching her sister-in-law by telephone, for he still hadn't been able to make connections with his Parisian relatives. 'Maybe they've already set fire to the telegraph office?' – 'Yes,' answered Beatrice mechanically. She had other things on her mind. It wasn't a long way. But siesta time. Empty streets reverberating with heat. Deserted except for a few dogs. Even the mistral had died down. Narrow shadows. Beatrice left the meager shade to her companion. For it was mainly a cold sweat that was streaming from all her pores and soaking the money. Only with great effort was she able to conceal her faintheartedness. Embarrassed by the old man's intrepid demeanor, which she promptly interpreted as a characteristic virtue of his generation. But when Beatrice caught sight of the word 'Tarasque' printed in large letters on a canvas above the fire station door, her conjectures took a turn. Beatrice now guessed that the people of Tarascon or of Provence or of the whole world had gotten ahead of her and were keeping La Tarasque as a house pet. To clean up the city. The country. The world. A useful application of the profane for lofty purposes. Beatrice felt she had been hypnopedically misinformed and her revelation reduced to the level of a discovery made for the second time. Which for practical purposes remained meaningless to the trobadora's immediate plans. Thank God. A red curtain hung at the station entrance. Behind it an old man was sleeping at the desk. Beatrice's companion knocked on the desk and said, 'Alfonse.' The old man awoke with a start and said, 'One franc.' – 'Per person?' asked Beatrice. The man twirled his mustache and replied 'Certainly, Madame.' At that, Beatrice paid three francs, one for the engineer, one for the explosives specialist, and one for the motorist. The old man got up, pocketed the money with thanks, and recited some words of introduction in the southern French dialect. Beatrice was taken aback by the words. Among other things, she learned that La Tarasque was driven through the streets once a year. 'In a cage?' asked Beatrice. 'In the carnival procession,' said the man, again holding the final syllable briefly. Then he nudged Beatrice into the shed. Where the dragon stood. Made of papier mâché painted green, his red spines of foam rubber. His horned head wore a long-haired black wig. On each side of the head with its grotesque human features were two costumed show-window mannequins. Which Beatrice was told to regard as castle guards of the good King René. 'We celebrate the death of the legendary beast every year,' said the old man, slapping the green cardboard. 'No citizen of southern France lets an occasion for drinking pass by. You too must experience the thrilling performance, Madame. Please consider yourself officially invited. Tarascon awaits you with its beautiful sights. More information at the tourist bureau around the corner.'

Chapter 11

Transcript of an interview wherein Irmtraud Morgner (I.M.) tries to investigate obscurities in the testimonies cited thus far by questioning Laura Salman (L.S.) about her identity

I.M.: For the courtly knight, women represented the source of all virtues, the fountain he would draw from for his own endeavors. So the question of whether the man or the woman took the initiative in matters of love was decided a priori in high minnesang. In these circumstances, could a woman brought up as befits her rank possibly see herself as a love poet?

L.S.: Minnesinger. Yet who among us has not, in our younger days or momentarily, stepped out of history, that male sea of egotism. Who has not, while still unbroken by experience, run her head against the wall that separates that sea from the future. For sometimes we seem able to neglect the moment called the Present, in which the two eternities, Past and Future, meet. Inspired by harmonies and Marxism, we overcame the ruins of Chemnitz by flying, every Free German Youth member an athlete. Starting gate at the school observatory. The reactionaries were left behind, teachers who hadn't been exposed yet, who took out their resentment by bullying; schoolboys confused by the class enemy, who snuffled like dogs from one material privation to the next and never found the strength to take a good look at the larger issues. Only people of character started from the school observatory. Organized. To be revolutionary requires, among other things, a certain unconditional quality of character. In a flash, the exploitation of man by man was abolished . . .

I.M.: . . . and the exploitation of woman by man . . .

L.S.: . . . was overlooked in the rush. Things were cleaned up, once and for all, from the bottom up; the burned-out city virtually demanded thorough planning. The steepest flights reach their goal on holidays or election days. Led by the accordion player, singing folk, battle, partisan, and revolutionary songs in Russian, Spanish, Italian, English, and French, we quickly arrived at ideal pastures. Where sensations were aroused as in the eleventh hall of the Musée de Cluny in Paris. This hall is round. It's the only one; the objects on exhibit demand the ideal perfection of a circle. I'm speaking of the famous tapestry series 'The Lady and the Unicorn.' According to the catalog, in five symbolic depictions of the human senses the life of a noble lady is displayed beside the legend of the wild unicorn that, as we know, can only be tamed by a pure virgin. But the meaning of the sixth tapestry is said to be a mystery to scholars even today. The blue and gold tent, held open by the lion and the unicorn so that the medieval lady can be seen, bears the inscription *A mon seul désir*. Which means 'To my only desire.' I don't want to cast doubt on the scholastic subject as deciphered by researchers; Jean Paul was always satisfied with the first subject that came along too. His art unfolded in digressions. But since art is only paid for with life, and countless women's lives are preserved in the tapestries, that is, the lives of the women who knotted them, the allegory couldn't help but pale significantly. In favor of an excessive peacefulness. To which even beasts of prey succumb. Never have I seen a gentler ideal of world harmony; never was the longing for unwarlike conditions so pure and radical: the masculine variant has been suppressed. Thus an image of longing that evolved from despair – extreme conditions produce extreme utopias. Who among us has not refused to obey in moments or years of anger; who, when shipwrecked on the egotistical sea, following her own desire, has not stepped onto this gentle land where plants, animals, and one human species dwell in sisterly . . .

I.M.: Did you perhaps have the urge to disobey when you were a schoolgirl?

L.S.: On the contrary – although my mother had no say at home – quite the contrary. But when I entered the eleventh hall of the Musée de Cluny not long ago, it was like a flight up into long-familiar absolute feelings. The ones that caused the militant longing for peace to grow rampantly in us after World War II, as soon as we spread our bodies out on the hilly Saxon landscape . . .

I.M.: Male bodies?

L.S.: Human bodies. The question about the position contains the ghost of a suspicion that an active relationship to the world is a priori determined by gender. Haven't you ever camped under spruce trees in the Erzgebirge? Or at least picked up a city the size of Meißen and downed it at one gulp?

I.M.: Children always lie down on what they love . . .

L.S.: So you're no poet.

I.M.: Wait a minute . . .

L.S.: Anyone who has had these abilities drilled out of her . . .

I.M.: Female role socialization drills these and other abilities out of you . . .

L.S.: . . . the poetic abilities . . .

I.M.: . . . the creative abilities. Women scientists are just as few and far between.

L.S.: I . . .

I.M.: Nowadays. But I was asking about those days. In a word: Beatrice de Dia is an illusion.

L.S.: A historical phenomenon.

I.M.: A typical case of a legend created for the purpose of correcting history, then. Why shouldn't a woman rewrite her past any way she likes. Nations and peoples have always done it.

L.S.: Beatrice de Dia was a troubadour.

I.M.: A man who wrote poetry in a woman's voice.

L.S.: No.

I.M.: A paradox.

L.S.: Not at all.

I.M.: A medieval love poet of the female sex is a paradox.

L.S.: Yes. As a minnesinger Beatrice definitely went too far.

I.M.: What? Now I've gotten myself into something! Which nobody wants. The impression it makes! 'Have you joined the women's libbers?' my publisher asked me recently. 'Do you need that?' Working with these testimonies is systematically destroying my reputation. People have already started looking for blue stockings under my trousers. Men search my face for ugly traces. And grandiose style doesn't sell anyway. I should have gotten a hardship bonus under these conditions. I must insist on clarity. I demand a logical presentation of evidence or my money back, thank you.

L.S.: You're welcome.

Chapter 12

New outrageous surprises that Beatrice couldn't for the life of her get ready for

After her discovery at the fire station, Beatrice felt relief. Which her mind equated with embarrassing shortsightedness. Who, after all, would be able to step in for La Tarasque and devour both the engineer and the explosives specialist to save Almaciz? Where did the next best monster live? What transportation took you there? Beatrice said goodby to the two old men and bent down to pick up a newspaper. Which was lying on the street. Then she went over to the Rhone wall to fold the paper into a hat. The wall was hot. The newsprint came off on Beatrice's hands. But when the wind came up again, the sun hat didn't stay on the trobadora's head for long. She was forced to take the paper in her hands again and again. Concern for the environment made her reluctant to throw it away, so she finally started reading the thing. Its name was *France Soir*. Beatrice read, for example: 'In the Latin Quarter and the Quartier Saint-Germain-des-Prés, thousands of young people battled with authorities for sixteen hours. End result: 460 demonstrators and 205 police officers wounded and admitted to hospitals. 475 arrests, including 35 foreigners. Damage to seven buses and about twenty automobiles. The skirmishes between the students and police began around 9:00 A.M. and continued throughout the day. Toward 8:00 P.M. they suddenly degenerated into a full-fledged battle. Several hundred policemen with helmets and nightsticks, as well as guard troops carrying carbines, riot police, and special units with haversacks full of grenades, suddenly saw about 10,000 young demonstrators surging toward them following a meeting at the Place Denfert-Rochereau. For the first time in a long while, the street belonged to the demonstrators. The agents of order retreated. The battle ended at around 10:00 P.M. But scattered fights continued here and there until midnight. Wounded persons were picked up everywhere on the Rue de Rennes, from the Saint-Germain-des-Prés church to the Montparnasse station. Specialists from the Prefecture of Police had already begun to clean up the main streets of the Latin Quarter and were loading trucks with all kinds of rubble that was blocking the roadways. The last block of demonstrators, about 200 students strong, who had been joined by a group with black leather jackets, was still occupying the upper end of the Rue de Rennes. About thirty police cars appeared, sirens wailing, from the direction of Boulevard Saint-Germain and approached the demonstrators. Before retreating for the last time, the keepers of the peace threw several teargas grenades at the windows of the apartments from which they had been bombarded all evening by diverse missiles.' Had the Beautiful Melusine vanished because she was taking part in street battles like these? Did such street battles only take place in Paris? Beatrice leaned over the hot wall, stared into the water, and contemplated the swirling patterns. Could street battles even be taking place during a time when Beatrice had been prematurely awakened? After all, the Beautiful Melusine knew that Beatrice had taken on a huge work-debt in order to arrive at humane times. That is, harmonious times, sympathetic to her profession. Were the young people already weary of harmonious conditions? Beatrice felt abandoned by her sister-in-law. Whose name was Marie de Lusignan, because Raimund de Lusignan had married her. The name Melusine came from Raimund's castles Melle and Lusignan, which she had lived in by turns. Because the Beautiful Melusine used to love shutting herself into her chambers to read political books, which at the time required a rare and extremely stubborn taste, people were soon convinced that she practiced secret arts and black magic. And soon they were saying that every eight days she changed at least halfway into a dragon and flew around. Shouldn't that half be able to finish off those fossils? At Almaciz the court society had often heard Melusine lamenting. In the chimney. There the powerless student of politics wept and wailed because she couldn't visit her two children. Beatrice was glad she hadn't had to leave any children behind when, following the Beautiful Melusine's example, she left the medieval world of men. By different means, to be sure. The tyrannical Raimund de Lusignan, however, who had taken their two sons away from his intelligent wife and entrusted their upbringing to an army captain, was knocked out of the saddle during a tournament and broke his neck. Inspired by the memory of this example of justice, Beatrice set out again, because she didn't want to miss the Beautiful Melusine, in any case. Not least in order to call her to account. For she had not informed Beatrice of La Tarasque's decease nor of events that must have preceded certain newspaper reports that were incomprehensible to Beatrice. That vagabond at the hearth of Almaciz would soon have to answer for unforgivable acts of thoughtlessness such as these. Maybe already tonight. So Beatrice stole a scooter and hurried back. When she arrived toward evening, the castle was gone.

Chapter 13

Which presents, in authentic sequence, a list of epithets that fell one by one from Beatrice de Dia's lips at the construction site, formerly Almaciz

Dirty crooks — slime buckets — skunks — sons of bitches — chickenshits — ass-kissers — perverts — morons — worthless bums — pricks — rumble-butts — stink-britches — filthy curs — rotten phonies — fleabags — limp-dicks — snot-noses — vulture meat — horses' asses — booze-hounds — blowhards — good-for-nothings — goons — suck-ups — hose-heads — twits — greedy-guts — scarecrows — loafers — weenies — lamebrains — pond scum — jailbirds — shit-for-brains — con men — cutthroats — bastards — shysters — pimps — men.

Chapter 14

Beatrice turns down a Good Samaritan's offer, with disastrous consequences

When the sun went down behind the weed-overgrown hills, floodlights illuminated the highway construction site. Bulldozers scraped up mounds of earth with their blades; backhoes leveled mounds of earth with their scoops; earth was being loaded onto trucks, conveyor belts, shovels. Algerian, Turkish, Greek, and Spanish construction workers labored under the supervision of French engineers and site foremen. The nationalities were identified for Beatrice by the handyman, who had been watching the distraught trobadora from his trailer. He had never heard of a Château Almaciz. And claimed not to know an engineer or explosives specialist who matched the trobadora's description either. But other than that, he was friendly, invited Beatrice into the construction shack, gave her ham, bread, and olives to eat and wine to drink, and even offered her work. As handyman's consort, for free lodging, meals, and so on. He showed her a camp bed in the trailer that she could use. Beatrice replied that her 808 years of sleep weren't going to be for naught; she wanted to work in her profession. Female troubadours must be urgently needed. Luckily, she was financially independent, and she emphatically preferred sleeping under the open sky to stuffy rooms. The open sky was black like the silhouettes of cypresses and star spangled. The moon hung voluptuously at its zenith. Imaginary lavender fragrance gave spice to the mild air. Beatrice kissed some earth before settling her back down on it. Almaciz was inexplicably gone, Provence was forever! And was an enthusiastic participant in the service of *minne*. It hadn't escaped Beatrice's attention that the trailer's inside walls were papered over with portraits of women. An old newspaper poster heralded in pictures and block letters the latest love story of a Brigitte Bardot. Years ago only noble gentlemen had praised women, and now even non-French highway construction workers had embraced the practice! Beatrice thought that not even eleven Châteaux Almaciz would be sufficient compensation for such progress. And eleven was a sacred number. And Beatrice was euphoric. She drifted happily off to sleep. At the edge of a cornfield. No rustling of leaves, no movements, no footsteps could disturb her deep slumber. When the morning dew awakened her, she had been relieved of her money.

Chapter 15

Wherein Laura delivers the proof demanded by I.M.

1. Societal Basis (Scholarship, following E. Köhler)

a) Subsequent to the acquisition of land through warfare, property was initially allocated according to the principles of an alliance of personal protection and fealty between lord and liegeman, based on mutual obligation. The services, whether they involved war activities or other assistance, were compensated by the lord with gifts, the value and quantity of which were at his discretion. The partitioning of land for use and exploitation was a means of undergirding and further guaranteeing the relationship of allegiance. This allegiance, given out of love for honorable behavior, was known in the tenth and eleventh centuries as *honor.* The vassal's devotion was manifested in this pact by his voluntary service. Its counterpart was the lord's generosity. Later, when estate holdings had become larger, personal ties were reinforced or replaced by the fief contract. However, the hereditary fief required an additional bond between vassal and lord, which was rooted more in the realm of the personal and moral than in legal obligations, for otherwise the service could be terminated at any time. The retinue that the feudal lord assembled at his court ultimately formed the center of power. The courtly ethos, which developed from the special form of love in the court's social life and which was enforced absolutely for the nobility as a whole, was, therefore, ideally suited for binding willing workers to the court and thereby to the lord himself as well as for restraining rebellious workers. The power of newly experienced social intercourse bound the various vassals to the court and engendered a consciousness of creating culture that received its impetus from women, indeed — not by chance — from the lord's wife, the *domna.*

b) With the loss of its military function, the knightly class lost its reason for existence and found a new one in the courtly way of life. Theoretically, people were not ready to give up the glamour of knightly life, but in practice the courtly ethos itself prevailed, whereby mere bravery was perceived as intrusive and demonstrations of military competence unnecessary in day-to-day reality. The knightly class of southern France was the first to reach the stage in which the need arose for a new raison d'être for its existence as a class.

2. The Historical Role of Sir de Poitiers's Wife (Scholarship, following E. Köhler)

Interpreting one's own life as exemplary made a necessity of the desire for its recognition. Since its means of expression was poetry, it follows logically that love, as the source and sphere of its blossoming, was brought out of the private domain into public light. The poetry of *minne* created the chivalric worldview through the class-based idealization of a common human desire. Which even the church fathers had proscribed. Later, Scholasticism rehabilitated it as value free, eligible to be ennobled. The cultural experience of courtly love is based on the ennobling of desire — hence the rationalization of love that is troubling from the perspective of today, this dissection, disputation, systematization. The cultural process takes place in and for society. The elevation of the knight is justified only by public recognition, which determines merit and blame. Thus a feigned love experience will suffice if need be. In any event, there is no place for jealousy in such a concept of love. For jealousy would remove the lady from the public cultural process, from this service to the law of one's own class. So the courtly lady was responsible for enabling the man to fulfill his class obligations at the highest level, whereby the nature of high, that is, courtly love was to be sought in the tension between hope and expectation, the only thing which could guarantee that the lover's efforts would not flag. If base love was not transformed into high love, then each had to be sought in a different place. The meaning of the adoration of the lady, the meaning of courtly love itself, consisted in perfecting and increasing the merit of the male wooer. Thus as long as Beatrice de Dia did not block her source of virtue, that is, did not disturb the tension between hope and expectation in her cansos to Raimbaut d'Aurenga but if possible increased it further, her extraordinary activities were completely accepted. A medieval minnesinger of the female sex is historically conceivable. A medieval love poet of the female sex is not.

3. The Unhistorical Role of Sir de Poitiers' Wife (Supplement to Part 1)

Beatrice de Dia had brought Sir Raimbaut d'Aurenga to the court of Almaciz and inspired him to sing, as custom and husband demanded. The art of this troubadour sounded exceedingly pleasant to the ears of Guilhem de Poitiers, for Raimbaut extolled wealth and virtue as compatible, something his rivals more or less questioned. They made a virtue of their material need while Raimbaut, who was no less poor, would cast a sprat to catch a mackerel. Beatrice thought he was a bad poet. So she pondered how to keep the arrogant troubadour at the court without wounding her pride or denying her good taste. She pondered a long time. Although her imagination had long since erected a complete world into which she disappeared as soon as she had carried out her social obligations. There she experienced the world in harmonies: encircled. Dazzling under the weight of tiredness or weightless cheerfulness: at pure moments. For beyond the maze of court intrigues, news, and one's own or assumed considerations, the distilled essence could be discerned. The residue of the soul. The self-generating drink. Downed at one draught. Everything fell into place right away. First, the sister-in-law Melusine, then her sons, whom Beatrice loved, Almaciz, Provence, stellar vaults, all of it domed. Simply joined to the earth. Right at the bottom. At the rock bottom of the earth. — Now, during a festival Sir de Poitiers asked Raimbaut and a certain Guiraut if they, locked in a tower for a year with a beautiful lady, would prefer to love the lady and be hated by her or to be loved by the beautiful lady, whom they hated. The troubadours disputed the issue in competing poems. Raimbaut in grandiose style as usual, in order to distance himself from his opponent and make his precious truths accessible only to a select few. The obscurities caused the highest listener, Sir de Poitiers, to nod off. When he had stated his decision, which self-evidently fell in favor of Raimbaut, Beatrice came up with her saving inspiration. And the very same day she composed a canso to the arrogant troubadour. In which she fed and praised him with words that disqualified his pretentious art. Sir de Poitiers was surprised by his wife's skills. But not unpleasantly so. The court society, jaded by boredom, received the lady's cansos with applause and were lavish in their praise for the trobadora's beauty, character, and kindness. Since he believed the high nobility was exemplary and, for that reason, chosen and appointed by God to rule, Raimbaut, of course, failed to notice he was disqualified. And he wasn't the only one. Untouched, he continued to adorn his hat and verses with peacock feathers just as before. Until an accident put a sudden end to his poetic and also to his physical life. Heated from singing, he was in the castle garden looking for refreshments for himself and his lady when he inadvertently picked up a pitcher that a stable hand had filled for his beloved. Raimbaut poured drinks for Beatrice and himself. Beatrice downed the cup at one draught. Raimbaut, the connoisseur, took a sip, spat, and poured the rest of the wine into a rosebush. Whereby he was spared the passion that immediately overcame Beatrice. For the wine had not only been thinned with water but also with elixir. The local sorceress, Phesponere, earned her living primarily by preparing love elixirs. For courtiers who wanted to satisfy their base love desires quickly and without resistance with a maid or some such in order to abandon themselves without interference to high love, Phesponere did accurate work. For stable hands, she took a guess. Rest did her old eyes good. The elixir for which the stable hand had traded a peck of oats had been carelessly mixed. A side effect that Beatrice noticed was a confusion of her memory reserves. Raimbaut did too, but in other respects he was unscathed. The confusion resulted from exchanges. But these were not present feelings exchanged for the purpose of erotic connections. No, they were past feelings. Two or three years of childhood. In Beatrice's memory reserves there suddenly appeared views of the sea, celestial charts, and voices of adults saying this was a child who was blessed by God and would bring peace to the land. In Raimbaut's memory reserves there suddenly appeared boudoir intrigues, embroidery frames, and voices of adults saying this was a child who must be married off as early as possible to a Sir Guiges, before he died. At that, Beatrice no longer shrank from the worldview she had secretly created for herself out of necessity. Nor did she doubt or change it just because Raimbaut, to whom she was forcibly chained by passion, didn't fit into the picture. She altered the quarrelsome Raimbaut to match her peaceable image and put it on exhibit in conventional canso frames, shamelessly and conscious of right and wrong. The rounded domes, seven of them in addition to d'Aurenga's, disturbed the court. Outraged it. So much so that Guilhem de Poitiers burned his wife's love songs whenever he found them. But Raimbaut grew silent. Because he suddenly doubted himself, weighed, judged, and compared himself. And he soon died. In his thirty-fifth year of life, around 1173.

Chapter 16

Beatrice takes a job in exchange for a dress and hears exciting news from Paris and Bretagne

Thirsting for revenge, Beatrice rushed back to the construction site. On the way there her red linen dress brushed a wild rosebush, caught, and ripped from the hip down to the ankle-length hem. She held the slit together with her left hand while taking the handyman to task. He was incensed over being suspected of theft. Beatrice threatened to call the police. At that, the handyman laughed heartily and called a few other workers over, who also promptly burst into laughter. The site foreman said, 'If I were you, I'd stay away from the police. Be glad they haven't picked you up yet. Girls like you with no identification papers shouldn't talk so much. You don't have any papers . . . ' – 'Papers! I'm Beatrice de Dia, the owner of Almaciz. I'm going to file a complaint,' said the trobadora. 'Complaint,' said the site foreman in amusement. 'Did you hear that? She's going to file a complaint with our supervisor.' The other men actually snickered. Then they turned their attention to the site foreman, who was reading the following newspaper report: 'Late Tuesday afternoon. The entire Latin Quarter is occupied by police. Five thousand demonstrators, students, and professors have assembled, with permission from the prefecture of police, at the Place Denfert-Rochereau. Their ranks swelling to seven or eight thousand, they try to enter the Latin Quarter. The demonstrators, whose number continually increases, do not advance upon the police barricade but cross the Boulevard Montparnasse in the direction of Boulevard des Invalides. They shout "Free our comrades! We are a small minority." By the time they reach the Pont Alexandre III, there are twenty-five thousand of them. The bridge has been sealed off by a police cordon. The demonstrators must stay on the left bank and follow the Quai d'Orsay to the Chamber of Deputies. Suddenly they cross the Pont de la Concorde in a rhythmical trot. They march across the Place de la Concorde and up the Champs-Elysées. In passing, they throw stones at the police officers guarding the offices of *Le Figaro* and commemorate that newspaper by shouting "Boo!" At 10:00 P.M. they reach the Place de l'Etoile. They sing the "Internationale" at the Tomb of the Unknown Soldier. The red flags they are carrying flank the tomb. Then the floodlights are turned off, so that the Arc de Triomphe is veiled in darkness, and the demonstrators march back down the Champs-Elysées. At the level of the Avenue George V the police have gone into formation. The parade of demonstrators turns across the Avenue George V back to the Left Bank and comes to a halt on the Rue d'Assas. The entire Latin Quarter is still occupied by police units. The demonstrators who have returned from the Place de l'Etoile and others who remained on the Left Bank battle with the police until about 3:00 A.M.' The workers listened to the report with happily excited expressions. And instructed the handyman to listen in on the broadcasts. 'We could hire the girl to listen in,' said the site foreman. 'You need a dress, girlie. You can earn the money for it here. Under the same conditions I offered you yesterday evening — I don't hold a grudge, as you see.' — He was using *tu*! Beatrice was outraged at this disrespectful form of address. She was upset because none of them would believe that her property had been stolen. But no one admitted to having torn down a château. Even the name Almaciz seemed unknown to these people. When they called Beatrice a con artist, she felt somehow trapped for the first time. So she hired herself to the handyman for a dress, lodging, and so on. He sealed the contract with a slap on the trobadora's behind. Then a little case emitting music and voices was placed into her left hand. In her right hand she soon had paper and a pencil. For taking notes. At first the site foreman almost doubted her mental ability. He called her a political virgin and even threw pots at her. At that, Beatrice began to fear the mealtimes. Which the construction workers took in the workers' hut. She would stand in the shade of a walnut tree. Only at noon did the heat-martyred men sit, silent with exhaustion, for a moment at their plates, which Beatrice had to fill for them. Mornings and evenings their questions and discussions started as soon as they sat down. 'What's the news from Bretagne?' they would ask probingly, demanding precise answers. The strikes organized by the General Confederation of Labor, the French Democratic Confederation of Christian Workers, the farmers, and the teachers' unions interested them more than the student riots. Vague answers incensed them. For their patience was also at an end. When the French news agency AFP reported that 22,500 of 28,000 employees from the metal-processing industries in the Loire-Atlantique region were striking, and there were mass firings in nine regions in the west, mealtimes were given over to discussing a strike. At night the handyman lay on top of Beatrice. She put up with it reluctantly. Partly because of his style. The man climbed on from the right, moved like a sewing machine for barely one minute, dropped off to the left, and started snoring. Even her husband, Guilhem de Poitiers, would be an improvement in this respect, as Beatrice remembered him. Had the art of sexual relations declined to such an extent in tradition-rich France? Had progress taken place at the cost of regression? During the night from the tenth to the eleventh of May, Beatrice didn't fulfill her physical obligations but listened to the radio instead. Without being asked. Radio ORTF filled the pauses between reports with music. Beatrice filled them with memories of the real Raimbaut d'Aurenga, who didn't correspond to reality.

Chapter 17

Wherein the reader learns what Beatrice de Dia heard on the radio during the night from the tenth to the eleventh of May

Friday, 5:00 p.m.: Five thousand high school students at the Place des Gobelins.

5:30 p.m.: Place Denfert-Rochereau. Professors, impeccable order. 'Release our comrades.' – 'Fouchet – murderer!' Speakers on the Lion de Belfort. Students and professors are arriving.

7:30 p.m.: Ten thousand demonstrators in the Boulevard Arago, 'Freedom' at the Santé Prison, stones thrown at the riot police.

8:00 p.m.: Rue Monge and Boulevard Saint-Germain. Twenty thousand demonstrators. The students and high schoolers keeping order forestall every clash.

8:20 p.m.: Police barriers at the intersection of Boulevard Saint-Germain and Saint-Michel force the demonstrators to return to the Boulevard Saint-Michel. At the same time riot police, guard troops, and patrol officers block all the bridges in Paris.

8:40 p.m.: Chanting – 'Occupy the Latin Quarter.' On all the streets where police officers are concentrated, the demonstrators get into position.

8:15 p.m.: The first barricade on the Rue Le Goff: cars, billboards, protective fencing from the trees, cobblestones. Barricades around the Panthéon and the Sorbonne, Rue Royer-Collard, Rue Saint-Jacques, Rue des Irlandais, Rue de l'Estrapade, Rue Claude-Bernard, Rue des Fossés-Saint-Jacques.

10:05 p.m.: On the radio stations that have been reporting the events since the beginning, the vice chancellor of the Sorbonne declares himself ready to receive the student representatives. On the same stations the students demand release and amnesty for all jailed comrades before beginning any dialogue. The number of barricades increases; the police bring reinforcements and cordon off the Latin Quarter. Demonstrators retreat, others arrive. By now there are more than sixty barricades, some of them two meters tall.

2:15 A.M.: The police troops are ordered to take down the barricades and disperse the demonstrators. Five hundred riot police, shield in one hand, club in the other, advance onto the Boulevard Saint-Michel, throwing tear-gas grenades. The demonstrators sing the 'Internationale' and the 'Marseillaise' and throw stones.

2:40 A.M.: A first barricade falls on the Boulevard Saint-Michel. The students set fire to their barricades with gasoline to stop the inevitable advance of the police. The police use offense grenades. Barricades, battles, and police barriers prevent removal of the wounded. First-aid stations are set up.

3:00 A.M.: While the students shout 'De Gaulle – murderer!' the police step up their attacks. Many residents pour water out of their windows onto the students to protect them from the effects of the tear gas. The police throw grenades into these residents' apartments. In response to the brutal actions of the police, who continually narrow their circle, Molotov cocktails are hurled from the rooftops, sandblasting equipment is brought over from construction sites, and automobiles are set on fire.

5:30 A.M.: The police clean up the Rue Mouffetard.

6:00 A.M.: The patrols comb the entire area systematically and arrest the demonstrators coming out of the buildings where they had been hiding.

Chapter 18

The gist of Laura's notes on the trobadora's memories of the real Raimbaut d'Aurenga, who doesn't correspond to reality

It doesn't bother me that only five of my cansos have been preserved. They are all from the period after the accident. Probably my esteemed husband burned the false ones by mistake. The ones in which, theoretically, tears flow. The real ones weren't as easy to string together into verse chains. For Raimbaut was beautiful beyond measure. A peaceable being who could summon up patience, laugh at himself, lose, play with children, listen, love – not just men or himself, not just himself in the other, but the other, or even the other in himself. He consistently treated even his own children, nine of them altogether, like little humans, not like property, proofs of potency, or cuddle devices available on call.

He showed them not surges of passion but constant, inexhaustible affection. Once in the knights' hall, he spoke in an aside more or less as follows: 'We men today are surprised sometimes. But we'll be much more surprised later on. And in a very different way, I hope, for there's no end in sight. There'll be no boredom in store for us when the ladies can finally do what they want to instead of what they're supposed to. What will women seen as human beings say about men, compared to women as images men have made of them? What will happen when they express what they feel instead of what we expect them to feel? Recently the wife of a poet said there were no love poems by women. She's right. Very few ladies would want to expose their reputation to intimations of abnormality. Women whose love life is not oppressive are considered sick (nymphomaniac). Men of the same type are considered healthy (sound as a bell). Maybe some fine day we'll stop squandering our nakedness in the stable. Maybe some winter day we won't have to resort to getting the flu to have permission to be weak. Maybe some day we'll allow ourselves to shed a tear without first eating horseradish. Oh, to be courted seriously for once, publicly . . . ' I repeated these words of Raimbaut's out loud so all the courtiers could hear them. Then Guilhem de Poitiers declared me mentally ill, led me out of the hall, and kept me imprisoned in the *kemenate*, the women's chambers, from then on. My class standing protected me from being suspected of witchcraft. But when my sister-in-law had to get out of there to escape being burned at the stake, I wrote an emphatic secret message to the sorceress Phesponere. Who had carelessly plunged me into misery. But Phesponere couldn't be found. In my distress I uttered as many different curses as I could. 'Holy Mother' was heard. I received an offer from Persephone. One. I would have preferred what was offered to Melusine. I had to sleep for 808 years. Melusine was allowed to travel around Europe.

Chapter 19

Beatrice finally heads north

The radio news reports plunged Beatrice into a state of ambivalent feelings. But most of all, worry. She feared for the life of the Beautiful Melusine. Without whose assistance she believed herself lost. The workers' mealtimes were prolonged more and more by discussions of strikes.

Which dealt primarily with wage increases, with money. Politics interested Beatrice more. When she joined in during political debates, she felt coldness from the group. The Muslim handyman thought Beatrice was a *pied noir*, an Algerian repatriate. For she had simply told him, not wanting to befuddle his limited powers of mind, that she had been away from Provence for a long time. His religion didn't include women among human beings. His beliefs defined *pieds noirs* as criminals. In spite of this, he didn't beat Beatrice, didn't expect sexual relations to be performed like a massage, he allowed her to eat at the men's table – so he found her dissatisfaction incomprehensible. Even disruptive. He complained about the trobadora's ungratefulness and asked the site foreman to give her a reprimand. The foreman, who had observed her unworldliness with increasing sympathy, spoke mildly to the trobadora. 'You can't get your dress for free, girlie. Even a married woman has to put out when she wants one.' Then he strongly advised Beatrice to get married. Even a man who wanted or needed to put down roots quickly in a foreign country would find marriage to a native the quickest and best way. Many of his workers could confirm this. Political immigrants could too. 'I reject marriage on principle,' countered Beatrice. 'I reject patriarchal institutions on principle.' The site foreman conceded that he didn't blame teenage girls for expressing such opinions; young people always went along with the latest fashion, and ugly women understandably dragged along behind. But Beatrice, though she wasn't that fresh any more, certainly couldn't be called ugly. The site foreman thought that a pretty woman like Beatrice didn't need emancipation. Comments that were so lacking in charm absolutely didn't become her and were detrimental to her beauty. But if she hurried a little, she'd definitely have opportunities to make a good match. Widowers often made decent husbands; a man with a good retirement pension was not to be scoffed at either. 'If I were you, I'd get busy reading the personal ads,' said the foreman at the end of the discussion. On 12 May the workers decided to follow the call of the union associations CGT, CFDT, Force Ouvrière, FEN, and CGC for a general strike and demonstrations. In the early dawn of 13 May, they gave Beatrice ninety francs for a dress, climbed onto a truck, and headed south. Beatrice turned down the warm invitation from the foreman and the workers to join the demonstration in Marseilles. Slogans painted on the truck were 'Ten years is enough,' 'We congratulate you, General,' 'Down with the police state,' 'Government by the people,' and 'Stop the war in Vietnam.' As the truck disappeared in a cloud of dust, Beatrice headed north. On foot. She bought an Indian midi-dress for eighty-seven francs from a street dealer hawking his wares in front of the papal palace in Avignon. She gave him ninety francs: The dealer had long red hair like Raimbaut d'Aurenga. To bear the strains of walking in the heat more easily, Beatrice kept her goal before her inner eye.

Chapter 20
The dream of Les Baux

Les Baux was the city of her youthful dreams. Beatrice thought there was no place imaginable that could be more revolutionary at the moment, that is, friendlier. During her first life, the court of Les Baux was the renowned meeting place for the Provençal troubadours. Poets vied with each other there in singing contests and courts of love. There were hundreds of them during the heyday of Provençal poetry. Most all of them traveling through would ride up that steep rocky path, receive gifts, and praise the deeds, splendor, generosity, and good taste of the princes of Les Baux. The praises of the princes' wives and daughters were also sung in countless *sirventois* and cansos. Fulco, for example, languished poetically for Lady Adelasia, the wife of his protector, Berald des Baux. Guilhem de Cabestanh loved Berengaria des Baux. In the great rock that formed the city, Beatrice was hoping to meet many women guild members. Who were on strike. Maybe for higher wages. Students, teachers, troubadours, workers — in solidarity. So Beatrice was expecting a gigantic crowd of people, flags, banners, songs. Indeed, song competitions where eligibility to participate was based on ability, not gender. She burned to see the unique city again, hewn from a monolith high in the wild, mountainous landscape, with its ramparts, towers, battlements, dungeons, stairways, balconies, terraces, and all the splendor of the Middle Ages, with no visible transitions between the rock and the elaborate masonry. The way to the loveliest mirage of Provence was long. Beatrice could smell thyme even before the spectacle of nature came into view. These bonelike, weathered, rocky shapes standing upright, naked and colossal in the foliage. The plinths separated from one another by narrow valleys, by chasms. Next to the familiar hollow eyes of the grotto, which Beatrice knew to be animated by saints' legends and fairy tales, were dark squares. Crevices that a stalled motorist described to Beatrice as quarries. Which were closed, to be sure. Years ago the people of Les Baux had exploited them for bauxite, but nowadays they preferred to exploit the tourists because it was less arduous. Other sites were now excavated for bauxite, beyond the Val d'Enfer; the entire area was already undermined. 'And the singers?' asked Beatrice. 'As in all bars,' the motorist replied. 'In Les Baux there are only expensive bars. At the first one on the right, the special of the day costs Fr 140. After a long search I found a pub with an inexpensive dining room where meals cost Fr 18. The wait is at least a half hour; in the expensive dining room you're served at once, of course.' He added that many of the artificially created caves were used as wine cellars. The motorist advised Beatrice to visit the wine cellar of Sarragan. A small glass, free of charge, wouldn't obligate her. Beatrice followed his advice. The abrupt coolness in the passageways and rooms, all of which had square-cornered profiles, brought the trobadora, overheated by sun and longing, back to earth. Whereby the motorist's disconcerting remarks began coming back to her. But not for long, because the barkeeper encouraged her to drink a second glass of rosé. When the trobadora had poured that into her empty stomach too, she could already feel the cool spaces of Les Baux that were half cave, half palace; she could already hear her voice enlarged by the reverberations, by the echoes. The striking masses applauded her speech, which demanded the definitive revolution and the heads of certain fossils; total harmony was proclaimed. Beatrice saw herself celebrated by the women in whose tongues she was singing praises, by the acclaimed men, by all the female and male troubadours assembled in the city: Les Baux on strike rejoiced over her return.

Chapter 21

Wherein Beatrice learns, among other things, about a biocide preparation bearing Raimbaut's name

On her long walk through fields of thyme, vineyards, and almond orchards, Beatrice lost her way several times. Finding a piece of newspaper with the headline 'Orange' under the campsite trash left behind by a group of young people beside the ruins of an aqueduct, she thought she must be very close to her destination. Scraps of sausage were wrapped in the newspaper. The headline with Raimbaut's name filled half the page. Had the d'Orange family (old Provençal: Aurenga) remained loyal to Les Baux? Were Raimbaut's descendants that well known, possibly because of their ancestral profession? Beatrice read the text under the gigantic headline in eager anticipation. It was part of an interview by the GDR weekly *Neue Berliner Illustrierte* (NBI) with a biology professor, Dr. Gerhard Grümmer of Rostock University. The fragment read as follows:

NBI: Professor Grümmer, you're a biologist. What induced you to analyze the American warfare crimes, that is, chemical warfare, so intensively?

PROF. GRÜMMER: I've worked on herbicides, the chemical means of weed control, for many years. The misuse of substances developed by biologists and chemists to support agriculture is directly connected to my research area. I was appalled that findings in my discipline are being used to destroy plants, animals, and human beings.

NBI: You said to destroy human beings . . .

PROF. GRÜMMER: Yes, indisputably. The target of all chemical warfare is always human beings, even though the American warfare substances consisting of herbicides primarily damage vegetation. Destroyed forests and fields disturb the water balance, make agriculture impossible, and cause famines.

NBI: You were the first scientist to visit some of the affected areas in South Vietnam. What did you observe there?

PROF. GRÜMMER: There and in the southern provinces of the Democratic Republic of Vietnam — herbicides were also used to destroy forests in Laos and Cambodia, by the way — I saw the effects. I was in areas, for example, that had last been sprayed three years earlier by the American Air Force. There were no more trees, no bushes, no plants or mosses. In many places the earth had been irretrievably washed away so that the naked rock was exposed.

NBI: How does it happen that these basically useful weed killers can produce such devastation?

PROF. GRÜMMER: The chemicals are applied in greatly concentrated forms and in excessive amounts. In addition to substances that are well known from agriculture, laboratories of the American monopoly have developed warfare agents specialized for military deployment in Southeast Asia. Among these is the desiccant Blue that can destroy rice cultures.

NBI: Have you analyzed this warfare agent yourself?

PROF. GRÜMMER: Yes, in my laboratory in Rostock. The samples reached the GDR via an adventuresome route directly from the United States. In consideration of American friends who helped with this, I can say no more.

NBI: What was the goal of your investigations?

PROF. GRÜMMER: It is possible to neutralize the damage to the plants. If appropriate measures are taken immediately after the spraying of Agent Blue, many nutritional plants can be saved. My investigations were in the interest of developing these countermeasures.

NBI: The active substances of the so-called Agent Orange are considered to be particularly dangerous . . .

PROF. GRÜMMER: Agent Orange contains a dangerous pollutant, tetrachlordibenzodioxin, abbreviated as dioxin. When humans come into contact with it, they are afflicted by serious illnesses.

NBI: What illnesses?

PROF. GRÜMMER: Asthenia, visual impairments, skin diseases, and recurring attacks of unconsciousness. However, individual shipments of the substance are contaminated by dioxin to varying degrees. Orange, which is produced in antiquated installations, in St. Louis, for example, contains the largest amount of toxins.

NBI: Can you explain that in more detail?

PROF. GRÜMMER: The total American production of the substances in Agent Orange would not be enough to meet the needs of agriculture and the U.S. Air Force. Therefore, older factories that had already been shut down — and which had delivered a product very high in toxins — were put back into service.

NBI: Don't these products endanger the Americans themselves?

PROF. GRÜMMER: No. American agriculture has extremely strict regulations concerning pollution. The poisonous charges are intended exclusively for use in Southeast Asia. Many shipments contain fifty times more toxin than is allowed in the United States . . .

NBI: This same dioxin?

PROF. GRÜMMER: This dioxin, contained in Agent Orange, is responsible for the alarming spread of Down's syndrome in Vietnam. This inherited disease, the most severe one known to us, appears five hundred times more often in the areas of Vietnam that were sprayed with chemical warfare agents than in all other countries. It affects children in the womb. These children come into the world, if not dead, then physically and psychically crippled. If these pitiful people live to adulthood, they attain at best the physical development of a ten-year-old and the mental level of a seven-year-old.

NBI: That is genocide.

PROF. GRÜMMER: The entire American war effort in Vietnam was always oriented toward genocide, indeed, toward biocide, ecocide, the destruction of all life, of the environment, pure and simple. We must not overlook the fact that the bombardment of the dikes in the Democratic Republic of Vietnam always served the major goal of producing famines and the deaths of millions of human beings.

NBI: But the struggle of the Vietnamese people themselves and worldwide solidarity have . . .

Chapter 22
The reality of Les Baux

The arduous trek through thyme fields, vineyards, and almond orchards finally led Beatrice into a dead city. Whose ruins could only be viewed after paying an entrance fee. Guided tour, just as though no general strike had been called. Thus Beatrice learned that Les Baux had been razed by order of Richelieu in 1631 after the rebellion of the last Baron des Baux, Antoine de Villeneuve, against Louis XIII. The view of the ruins is now sold as a tourist attraction. The rebuilt businesses are all services: stores, restaurants, hotels, bars. Hunger, thirst, and need for human company forced Beatrice to the front steps of a nightclub, the Queen Joan. Here the trobadora brooded over how to get out of this physical and mental crisis. But the owner of the club, Dr. Adrienne Richard, soon found her. And was about to chase her away, to spare his refined guests the sight of beggars. He had a few rude threats on the tip of his tongue when the trobadora's physical appearance struck him as usable – a bar hostess had just quit. So, Dr. Richard made the famished Beatrice an offer. She protested weakly by naming her profession. 'If you do your work well and the guests don't object, you can sing too as far as I'm concerned,' said Dr. Richard. 'Some of the men like singing.' In the kitchen, where she was served a substantial meal, the unworldly Beatrice would have signed a contract to that effect. If the cosmopolitan Melusine or equivalent hadn't stopped her at the last moment. Indirectly. A secret message suddenly landed on the trobadora's empty plate.

Chapter 23

Which reveals what the Beautiful Melusine's secret message tells Beatrice

Come to Paris as quickly as possible. The cops have nabbed me. I'm in a cell without a chimney, so I can't get out to escort you here. But since I can use my small supply of black magic only for personal aims, the loss is bearable. If you can help out. You must leave at once, hitchhiking; there's no gas in Paris any more. The city is no longer a sea of houses and cars. The streets finally belong to the people. Liberated from fumes and technological overcrowding, Paris is livable again. Suddenly everyone is talking to everyone else. You can easily ask the way to Rue Berthollet 17, fourth floor on the right. But the streets will be congested. Red and black flags everywhere; you'll see the familiar, true, forgotten pictures of the French Revolution. You'll also hear and read a lot of liberated utopian language. However, no joint program of the leftist parties and the trade unions yet exists. Therefore, you must sing for workers and students. Your slogan: More unified action for a government of the people and democratic unity. Report to the strike committee of the Renault plant and to Radio ORTF as soon as you arrive. If you use the poetry of the street, your songs will soon be on everyone's lips. To help you compose in advance while on the road, here's some authentic material of this poetry:

Be realists, demand the impossible.
The barricade blocks the street but opens the way.
Forbidding is forbidden.
All power to the workers' councils.
Don't vacation in Greece, come to the Sorbonne.
Dreams are reality.
Alone we can do nothing.
Talk to each other.
The poetry is on the street.
Being human is not a condition you're born to, it's an honor you must achieve.
On the faculty, 6 percent workers' children; in the reformatories, 90 percent.
Revolution, I love you.

The comrades in the Rue Berthollet will give you appropriate instructions. Don't disgrace me! And don't waste any time trying to liberate me. Help the other prisoners by means of purposeful actions instead. I hope somehow to be able to help myself soon. Let imagination take over!

Destroy the message at once!

M.

Chapter 24
Consciousness lasts until Lyon

Beatrice felt such intense joy over this sign of life from the Beautiful Melusine that she gave no thought to how the secret message had been transmitted. The trobadora cast only a cursory glance into the smoke outlet that the folded paper must have fallen from. Then she set out. Winged by the promise of shelter in her sister-in-law's words, pursued by curses from the bar owner, well fed. Forlorn as she was, Beatrice would have accepted even less comprehensible instructions without protest. Except that she found herself incapable of hitchhiking. Based on experience. Instead, she attempted a quick-march to Paris. In Valence she saw a crowd of about ten thousand strikers. In Tours she swallowed the secret message for reasons of conspiracy and hunger. Just outside of Lyon she lost consciousness.

Chapter 25
Paris, but what's that

Beatrice spent seven weeks in a hospital in Lyon. When she had recovered from sunstroke, a matron helped her get papers and an inconspicuous birth date by providing faked references. And bought her a train ticket. On 13 July at 7:18 A.M., Beatrice finally arrived in Paris. Gare de Lyon. Masses of people were streaming out of other trains too. And moving quickly. Beatrice adjusted to their pace. Was propelled to the exit. Where a gust of gasoline-perfumed air assailed her. The streets didn't belong to the people at all but to the cars. Red or black flags were nowhere to be seen. The crowd of people didn't fall into lines but fled in all directions. No songs. No one spoke to Beatrice. When she asked a hurried passerby the shortest way to Rue Berthollet, he advised her to take a cab or the Metro. He thought walking was a joke or impossible. The trobadora's absolute poverty obliged her to choose the impossible. Rocky canyons of narrow buildings. In front of the door-sized windows were half-grates that reminded Beatrice of lace. Between the sidewalk and the street were unbroken walls of cars. Beatrice could see over them. But felt increasingly smaller the longer she trudged along beside the brightly colored metal. In quick march. But the overwhelming majority of the people were beautiful, carefully dressed in tasteful clothes. Against her will, Beatrice made slow progress, because there were so many striking figures to look at. She would have felt impolite for not admiring their finery, not honoring their efforts. The women looked more alike than the men. Whose bland garments feigned or foreshadowed personality. With the women, the reverse was observable. Some of them looked like devices for transporting clothing. Most of the buildings were transparent below, showing wardrobes behind glass, furniture, books, things to eat, in immoderate variety and selection. Beatrice would have become totally confused if she hadn't forced herself to recall the content of the secret message again and again. In vain Beatrice sought the poetry of the street that the Beautiful Melusine had mentioned. Only flag-bouquets of blue-white-red on churches and similar buildings. Hardly any children. Soon Beatrice also noticed that the people didn't deign to exchange glances. But after an hour she had no strength left for glances either but found it difficult not to be distracted by the onslaught of optical stimuli. Her head ached from the noise and fumes. Maybe the city only seemed so alarming because she was a stranger here? Maybe she had the wrong concept of revolution? In any case, she couldn't let the people whom the Beautiful Melusine called comrades wait any longer. For she didn't want to disgrace her sister-in-law. And she had to start working in her profession as trobadora at long last. Without delay. At Rue Berthollet 17, fourth floor on the right, Beatrice was just in time to meet two students. The others had already gone on vacation. Hospitable reception. Subdued atmosphere. Permission offered to occupy the apartment during the semester break; Comrade Lusignan was still in jail. 'And where am I to sing?' asked Beatrice. The students laughed bitterly. Couldn't understand how a political person could sleep through the reactionaries' election victory. 'Really, was your hospital on the moon?' — 'My hospital was a loony bin,' confessed Beatrice. The students embraced Beatrice and declared that the cops would stoop to any crime. Then the students emptied their wallets into Beatrice's Indian midi-skirt, handed over the apartment keys for safekeeping, and said good-by until the start of the semester. For two weeks Beatrice felt like the guardian of five rooms equipped with little furniture, many brochures, and sixty-seven Melusinian books. Time enough to thoroughly ponder the circumstances that forced the born politician Melusine to idleness and a trobadora to social action.

Chapter 26

Wherein the reader finds an overview of Beatrice de Dia's principle places of residence from 23 July 1968 to 22 October 1969 and the gist of what happens to her

23 July 1968
Beatrice introduces herself in Paris to the publisher Joubert at his Rue Monge office and can't prove her identity, since her papers give her age as thirty-six. Accused of fraud. Banned from the premises.

28 July
Departure for Lyon to persuade the matron to withdraw her statement concerning Beatrice's age. The matron agrees at once and burns the trobadora's papers.

2 August
Arrested during a drug raid in Lyon.

3 August–18 September
In jail in Lyon. Threatened with deportation as a foreigner without a residence permit. Released for lack of evidence.

23 September–2 October
Ice-cream vendor in Aigues-Mortes. Beatrice copies her five surviving songs from a troubadour anthology and on a customer's recommendation, sends them to the newspaper *Paris-Match*.

4 October–18 October
Sells lavender in Cannes. Sends three of her songs to the editor of *Midi-Soir*.

20 October
In Saintes-Maries-de-la-Mer Beatrice saves a child from drowning and receives five hundred francs from its father.

21 October–3 November
Beatrice stays at the Hotel Escorial in Nice for five days, then at the train station.

16 November–20 December

Temporary attendant at the Frédéric Mistral Museum in Saint-Rémy. Sends one of her songs to the local newspaper.

23 December 1968–2 March 1969

Beatrice falls ill with pneumonia and is admitted to the hospital in Aix-en-Provence. The woman doctor on the ward provides fabricated references for a new ID with an inconspicuous birth date.

8 March–1 May

Works as a maid in Marseilles.

3 May

In Arles Beatrice becomes acquainted with the Swedish tourist Johnson, who takes her to a bullfight in the arena. Thereupon, Beatrice flees Provence.

10 May

Return to Paris. The owner of the building at Rue Berthollet 17 has sold all the apartments. The student commune that had rented them was evicted in November. Address unknown.

13 May–16 June

Homeless shelter in Paris.

17 June

Beatrice makes the acquaintance of a Mr. Tailleur, who soon sends her out on the street.

22 October 1969

Beatrice marries Gerson, one of her customers.

Chapter 27

Wherein Laura makes up for the absence of a positive conclusion to the first book by describing certifiably genuine events from her life

Sense of order: My grandmother wrote down the story of her daughter-in-law, Jenny's, hour of death and manner of dying. It was an angry letter. At that, I felt sympathy for my aunt. For the first time. Up to then, I had hated her and her husband. Mainly her husband; her mind was not used to thinking. It groveled to whatever came out of Uncle Kurt's mouth. Grandmother depended on him for support also, because he had gone to high school; his parents had provided for that. They had sent their daughter, my mother, to a cooking school. At the time, my maternal grandfather had worked as a shunter, later as a conductor, then as an engine driver. He and my mother paid little attention to Uncle Kurt; they had no say. If only because they suffered from colds occasionally and couldn't stomach certain foods. My grandmother could respect only healthy people. Uncle Kurt could stomach anything. A narrow, fine-skinned, feminine nose stood out like a deformity on his flat-featured face, which always, even right after shaving, had a bluish sheen from his eyeglasses on down. His broad upper lip barely closed over an incisor with a gold inlay. When my uncle laughed, he would suck saliva from his teeth and stroke his remaining hair with the palm of his hand. His wife had blond hair that was combed through only by the hairdresser. She would skim a comb over her back-combed marcel waves and fasten stray strands with hairpins under the bun at the back of her neck. For their engagement, my uncle supposedly gave her a recording of the ballad 'Tom the Rhymester.' Because of the line 'then he saw a blond woman.' During the war my aunt stored the record in the cellar. During the thirties my uncle sent my aunt to spas for rheumatism several times. My grandmother respected that. She looked forward to those weeks of keeping house for her son. To keep from losing his job as head district accountant, he joined the Nazi party on 30 January 1933 and waited for the Communists. Until 1945 he kept on repeating to his and my parents, since they wouldn't listen, that we had to get the Communists in, then everything would change. After 1945 he kept on repeating that the Communists deserved to be hanged. His and my parents pretended not to hear but carefully closed the windows on such occasions. Glad to have survived and burdened by problems of continuing to survive, they put little stock in words. They granted Uncle Kurt his vituperations because of his ever vituperative soul and because circumstances had removed him from his office and enlisted him as an elevator operator in a cotton mill. My father remarked with satisfaction that the unaccustomed labor had changed his brother-in-law. Who took revenge by paging through notebooks with his chapped hands. Notebooks filled with formulas and stenographic script. Uncle Kurt had also made accurate copies of technical drawings from engineering books about cotton-mill machinery. Soon he was claiming that he had verified the calculations for all the machines in the cotton-mill halls. He described technical discussions with master craftsmen, which seemed to gratify his arrogance to such an extent that he began to consider himself reeducated in engineering. Taking the lead. He accompanied victorious descriptions like these with rasping noises produced by rubbing his curved thumb against the palm of his hand. My grandmother declared that these gestures were the habits of a violinist. Because Uncle Kurt had originally wanted to be a teacher, he had taken violin and piano lessons. My grandfather had even bought a piano, thus acquiring among his relatives a reputation for diminished mental capacity. When my uncle's administrative career made the instrument dispensable, my mother was given custody of it. Although she had never been fond of her brother, she confirmed that he had become a skilled violinist. On Christmas day in 1917, they had played the Bach-Gounod 'Ave Maria' together; at the time, my mother was eight years old and Uncle Kurt seventeen. He practiced every day until his marriage. After that, he took the violin up to the attic and had a house built. Here the childless couple occupied the two tiny second-floor rooms and the kitchen. The ground-floor rooms served as a storage area for candy boxes and other packing material and as a fruit cellar. In the yard surrounding the house, Uncle Kurt had planted so many apple, pear, and plum trees that consuming the harvests from autumn to autumn soon became a primary, barely manageable lifetime occupation. Aunt Jenny took constipating medicines in order to be halfway equal to the task. Uncle Kurt refused cherry trees because he had no use for blackbirds. In 1944 my grandparents had to clear out the ground-floor rooms and move into them to save the house from refugees. Nonetheless, a Silesian couple was quartered there in 1945. My grandfather made friends with them right away and told the old people a lot about Bialystok and Brest, where he had been during the First World War. When he was a young man working as a conductor. He liked to talk about his younger days and about a Russian war prisoner named Sergei. Grandfather transferred his sympathy for this young man to everything from the East. He never let criticism of the Soviet occupation troops pass without a protest. Uncle Kurt suggested that he rent a room in the neighboring barracks. My uncle called the Silesian couple 'Polacks.' They too were shown his notebooks full of excerpts copied with painstaking neatness using needle-sharp red, green, and black pencils. He explained his recalculations using a big slide rule. He bought me a little slide rule and taught me how it worked. I'm indebted to my uncle for my ability to write teacher-pleasing prose. 'Gather material, organize the material, introduction, exposition, conclusion.' He would expound on these and other guidelines, preferably around crowded coffee tables. He would sit far away from me, the better to cut in on the general conversations. He despised human beings for their stupidity, especially women. He seemed not to consider me one until I joined the Free German Youth. I was scrawny, undernourished, had to wait a long time for breasts. As far as organization was concerned, he thought my parents and I were a lost cause; still, he accepted foodstuffs that my father traded textiles for in Poland. For years my father, who belonged to a locomotive brigade, made reparations deliveries to the Soviet Union. He was stationed in Königs Wusterhausen; there and while on the road, he lived in a freight car that was hooked to the tender. Before every trip the brigades took on provisions, so-called *produkti* such as flour, bacon, pearl barley or other grains, and meat. The latter sometimes in the form of lung, heart, entrails. The men would put these innards into sacks and authorize one brigade member to make deliveries to their wives and bring back goods for bartering, for example, textiles, petroleum lamps, sewing-machine needles. Once my father's stoker dropped two jute sacks filled with beef heads and feet at our local railway station. The wives transported them on handcarts to a butcher, who was persuaded with cigarettes to strip off the hides, remove the horns, hooves, and teeth, and divide the rest into portions that would fit into cooking pots. For several days my mother cooked the unwieldy pieces into a sort of headcheese, almost all of which was put up in jars, contrary to my expectations. The apartment and entryway smelled like carpenter's glue. I took a jar to my grandparents. With instructions to say nothing to my uncle and aunt. They were especially envious of the cooking oil my father was able to smuggle in a canister for lubricating oil, until the canister was stolen. Lubricating oil was scarce too. Since the brigade members had no refrigerator, the perishable foods that they lived on during their long trips were smuggled: illegal. For this reason my father would only barter for the family's needs after Uncle Kurt started waiting for war, only for the family's needs. Those needs were great. I could eat four helpings of stew at one meal, also twelve potatoes or potato pancakes. I would faint on an empty stomach. By the time the customs officials knew nearly all the possible hiding places, legal rations had increased to such an extent that my father stopped volunteering for the transit brigade. My grandfather had already died by then. Dropsy. I liked him as well dead as alive. A big yellow handkerchief was wrapped around his chin and cheeks and tied on top of his head, as if his head had the mumps. As grandfather lay on his deathbed, I would take the sheet off his bearded face, stroking it when I knew no one was looking. I couldn't understand why my grandmother couldn't have slept beside the dead man over night. Even in the room next to the chapel where they had laid him out in his frock coat, he seemed the same to me. My grandmother had cut her most beautiful azalea bush and fastened the blossoms to the pillow with stickpins. For the funeral meal she served green-bean soup with marjoram and lovage. No schnapps. Nevertheless, Uncle Kurt started arguing. With me, for lack of Grandfather. The others avoided political discussions. I wore my silver Good Scholar medal on my coat collar and had answers for every question. Uncle Kurt didn't ask questions, because he had answers for everything too. We exchanged declarations of principles in the form of insults. Aunt Jenny confirmed that my father rightly belonged on the list that Uncle Kurt had repeatedly recited, for having made reparations deliveries to the Soviet Union. When Grandmother asked us to be quiet and talk about Grandfather, Uncle Kurt threatened to put her on the list too. Whoever couldn't decide in our favor must be against us. The list would name all who deserved to be hanged. Uncle Kurt and Aunt Jenny were sure that Uncle Kurt and Aunt Jenny didn't deserve to be hanged. To take revenge, I announced that in case of a civil war, I was ready to take up arms against all reactionaries, no matter how close the family relationship. The same for collaborators. On principle, I included my grandmother among them, since she stood by her son and daughter-in-law as well as by me and my parents. I considered my father to be working class and regularly conducted informational discussions to educate him for membership in the Party of the Working Class. At age sixteen I became a candidate for Party membership. During recess the comrade pupils and the comrade teachers would consult on evaluating technical and political aspects of the lessons. I didn't tell the Party that my uncle was waiting for atomic war. When we happened to meet in public, Uncle Kurt would cross the street and look away from me. At home we avoided one another. During the last years before her scandalous death, all I knew about my aunt's life was from hearsay accounts. Grandmother would give them to me unasked when I visited her. Thus I was able to gather that my aunt received one mark household money per day from my uncle, who had meanwhile gotten a job as bookkeeper at the Workers' Consumer Co-op, and that she was only allowed to listen to Western radio stations. No one except Grandmother visited her. Sometimes Grandmother would find my aunt still in bed at noon. Apathetic. After my aunt's death, sacks of dirty laundry were found under beds and on top of wardrobes. My aunt drowned herself in the pond on the military base.

BOOK TWO

Chapter 1
Beatrice de Dia Gerson

Théophile Gerson owned a small greengrocery on the Rue Mouffetard. His shop was just as cramped for space as the neighboring ones, which is why the display tables had to be carried out onto the narrow street every day. Then the produce had to be attractively arranged. The sixty-two-year-old Gerson had always had an artistic bent. His deceased wife had been a roller skater in her younger days; his daughter had taken accordion lessons. On girls to whom he regularly treated himself, he liked full-length black gloves and other elegant attire. Once when he was really in the mood, he asked Beatrice to sing. She sang the first *cobla* that came to mind. Gerson didn't understand the Old Provençal text but was visibly affected. After that, he was convinced he had discovered Beatrice. Their marriage improved his self-esteem. Though Gerson could afford only one shop assistant and never took vacation, he forbade Beatrice to show up in the store. He said the store was drafty, she'd catch cold and ruin her voice. Going for walks in the polluted air of the streets would also be injurious to her vocal mechanism. Indeed, the Paris traffic, the hectic pace, and criminality had made the city totally inhospitable for delicate creatures like women and children. He thought Beatrice should rest up from the stresses of her unprotected female existence, keep house, look elegant on Sundays and holidays, and not go out alone. Of course, Gerson refused on principle to allow his wife to use her voice professionally, just as he forbade her all other employment, citing the law. Until 1965 French marriage law assigned the female marriage partner all household and maternal duties and granted the male partner the right to decide whether his wife could practice a profession. The trobadora followed Gerson's rules strictly, without objection. She seemed to enjoy a roof over her head, meals, and sleep. Gerson was certain he could feel her gratitude daily. Not for a moment did he regret having followed the advice of his friend Hector. Hector, who was married for the fifth time, didn't give a damn about respectable parentage or other measures of reputation; all he needed was gratitude. And in his experience, women who had lost their pride in the struggle for a bare existence were the most grateful ones. He had met all his wives in the red-light district. Beatrice soon made friends with Jacqueline, Hector's fifth wife. Even though Jacqueline believed that marriage was a meaningful institution. In Paris, at any rate. Of course, no one could seriously love her oppressor, but you could come to terms with him. For mutual advantage. She pointed out that small nations and states often turned to their more powerful enemies for protection. In Paris, where she felt trapped, Jacqueline believed marriage was a woman's only hope. For this reason, bald heads, potbellies, and flab drooping down the back didn't bother her. She cooked what her husband asked for, did his laundry, overlooked his quirks, and said what he wanted to hear. Beatrice took pains to emulate her friend's behavior. Before long the two women had gotten their husbands' permission to go shopping together. The purchases they brought home from boutiques seemed to the men relatively insubstantial compared to the money they'd been given. The more so since Jacqueline and Beatrice often spent hours out in the rain looking for bargains, Paris winters are rainy. After these excursions the trobadora was always in a good mood, treating her husband with special attention, indifferent to the just-purchased items of clothing. Sometimes she even forgot to try them on for him. Gerson observed with amazement that his wife was more interested in newspapers than in her purchases. Was she attracted more by the process of shopping than the result? Once when Beatrice entered Gerson's store, drenched and chilled after Christmas shopping, he kissed her affectionately in front of his customers. He even felt that excitement from childhood, a mixture of curiosity and anticipation. And he hastily bought an artificial crocodile-leather bag for Beatrice, to avoid embarrassment. One week before Christmas, a shop for men's formal wear on the Rue François Premier was blown up. The next day the headquarters of the National Guard and the police had to be evacuated because anonymous phone calls announced that a bomb was set to go off at 1:00 P.M. On 22 December the Musée de l'Armée had to be closed following a mine alert. Gerson read with abhorrence the headlines about the wave of terror that was sending Paris into a state of shock and fear and that would seriously interfere with holiday celebrations as well as sales. Beatrice read about it in eleven journalistic variations. On Christmas Eve she put a knit shirt and a bottle of aftershave under the tree. Whereupon the disappointed Gerson decided to save the artificial crocodile-leather bag for his wife's birthday. However, he was abundantly provided with culinary delicacies and erotic attentions. So, on the first day of the holiday season, he indulged his wife's wish that he go for a walk with her. The sidewalks were conspicuously empty, as were the streets. There was so little exhaust in the air that no one got a headache. No empty parking spaces along the streets. Holding hands, M. and Mme. Gerson strolled through the lanes of metal. The Dôme des Invalides was still closed. And the Avenue de Tourville was still barricaded by military vehicles. The mine-clearing operation in the world's largest military museum couldn't be concluded until mid-January, since only twelve mines were found. Flyers distributed by unknown perpetrators at the Hôtel des Invalides had announced thirteen.

Chapter 2

Beatrice's vocal range is uncovered

Even Gerson hung a poster in his show window asking the citizens of Paris to cooperate in finding the perpetrators. From his extensive display of wares, which had to project a tempting, distracting superabundance as well as the soundness of the business, Gerson sold the slightly rotted produce only to tourists who spoke other languages. French customers from outside the neighborhood got produce that was at most one day old, and for his steady customers it was guaranteed fresh. Among his steady customers were a few students. One of them, Alain Lorient, always brought him the newspaper *Humanité dimanche*. Gerson read the paper with interest because he was battling the prevailing conditions, which he perceived as threatening to his business. His interest was transformed into sympathy when the *Humanité* emphatically condemned the terrorist attacks. So Gerson would occasionally buy a daily edition of the paper from the student too. It repeatedly exposed the perpetrators as conscious or unconscious accomplices of right-wing or fascist powers. And all left-radical and anarchist movements were called to battle. Beatrice used the newspaper to keep her soup kettles warm, because she had taken a liking to Alain. A red headband adorned his shoulder-length hair. His lower jaw was so flexible that he could nibble the ends of his mustache. He wore Indian shirts that were so transparent, you could see the sparse whorls of hair on his chest. One day, when a telephoned bomb threat had brought all traffic on the Champs-Elysées and its neighboring streets to a standstill, Beatrice spotted the student in front of the electronics store across the street. Trapped by a mob that was camped around the TV set in the show window. Were the manly men of the powerless forces of order once again pleading for useful clues? Or for respect? Were they again threatening the use of the gigantic police force, which had been sent into one hectic action after another, each more audacious than the last? Were they adding up the cost of these maneuvers? The cost of the bluffs? For the bluffs were possibly even more expensive than bloodless attacks such as the blowing up of the shop for men's formal wear or the inexact mining of the military museum. Was the TV pleading for peace and order? In terms of logic, discipline, and loyalty to Melusine, Beatrice still felt solidarity with the Persephonic opposition. But her sympathies now belonged to the vindictive movement that was planning retaliation. Beatrice had to open the living-room window. Then she could hear Alain's impudent laughter. And Gerson's voice extolling his wares, which mingled with the voices of his competitors. Fog hung over the throng of people and produce. A damp chill crept into the room. Still Beatrice rested her breasts on the windowsill, watching the steep Rue Mouffetard with its displays of flesh and vegetables. The mob dispersed. Alain crossed to the other side of the street. Then occasionally shifted his weight from one leg to the other. He was with a well-dressed man of about forty, who looked conservative compared to Alain. Beatrice noticed that Alain was pointing out to his companion not only Gerson's produce but also his wife. Since the jealous Gerson was occupied at the moment with the weighing of soybean sprouts, Beatrice smiled. Alain touched his outstretched right hand briefly to his temple. But his companion said 'friendship.' At that, Beatrice felt a sudden appetite for smooth, untarnished flesh. Which refused to subside by evening, no matter how she disciplined herself. In her conjugal bed it even got worse. Fortunately, Gerson lay in raucous sleep. Beatrice lay wide awake. Soon she got out of bed, turned on the kitchen light, and found pen and paper. She sat at the counter writing for a long time. Wads of crumpled paper piled up. Finally she realized that she could no longer compose scholastic cansos, those imitations with disguised tenor, baritone, bass. Imperceptibly, perhaps on the brutal paths of humiliation, her own vocal range had been uncovered. Though models for using it did not yet exist. Toward morning she wrote the following poem:

Water Walk

And my ship
was at midlake
rolling
and heeling in the waves,
and the wind chased wispy clouds.

But in the seventh night
Gahmuret came across the lake.
Slowly,
his hair resolute against the wind.
When I saw him
walk across the water,
I gave a start.

He said,
'It is I, don't be afraid.'
I said,
'If it's you,
then call me to come to you
on the water.'

'Come,' he said.

And I climbed out of the ship
and stepped onto the water
and went toward the wispy cloud
that he had just smoked.
He was standing behind the cloud.

As the cloud was swept away
by a squall
and his mouth was naked,
I cried for help
and sank into the waves.

But Gahmuret bent down
at once

and pulled me from the water
of which I had drunk plentifully,
my hair was soaking wet,
and he said,
'You of little faith, why do you doubt?'

And we boarded the ship,
and the wind died down.

Chapter 3

A HOLDING CELL WITH A DEPOSED GODDESS RISES FROM THE UNDERWORLD

While looking for Alain's apartment one morning, Beatrice ended up not far from the Rue de l'Estrapade in a rear courtyard with torn-up asphalt pavement. Beatrice had to climb across drainpipes, piles of dirt and rubble. While trying to dodge a pool of tar, she stepped in a puddle. The muddy water flooded her right shoe. Beatrice cursed. Later she was uncertain whether 'Holy Mother' was one of the curses she had uttered involuntarily. In any case, the already familiar cell suddenly emerged from the construction site's large drainage shaft. A song in one voice came through the grating over the vents. Beatrice lifted the two iron bars that served as bolts to the door. It was pushed open from the inside. Persephone was sitting there alone. She spent three quarters of the year locked up with her mother in the upper world; for the remaining quarter, she had solitary confinement in the underworld. 'But Zeus has long since been overthrown,' said Beatrice, shaking her head. 'Can he still tell you what to do, even though he's in jail?' – 'He's not in jail,' Persephone replied. 'He made a deal with Mr. Lord God. Between men, as it were, the same as Pluto did. Only the deposed goddesses get the dungeon.' – 'I understand,' said Beatrice. 'But were you much better off under Zeus?' – Persephone told her that Pluto had fallen in love with Demeter's daughter one day and asked Zeus for permission to marry Persephone. Zeus was afraid of offending his older brother if he refused, but he also knew that Demeter would never forgive him if her daughter had to descend to Tartarus forever. So Zeus gave a diplomatic answer. And that encouraged Pluto to abduct Persephone. Her mother searched for her tirelessly for nine days and nine nights. Finally she learned from a certain Triptolemos that the earth had suddenly opened up before the eyes of his brothers, a shepherd and a swineherd out on the fields with their animals. The pigs disappeared into the ground. A wagon drawn by black horses appeared. The driver's face was invisible. He had his right arm around a screaming girl — Demeter's daughter. With Triptolemos's eyewitness account, Demeter made her way to Hecate. And then the two of them went to Helios, the all-seeing one, and forced him to admit that Pluto had abducted Persephone — no doubt with the consent of his brother Zeus. Demeter was so outraged at this that she didn't go back to Olympus. She continued wandering over the earth, forbidding the trees to bear fruit and the plants to grow, until the human race was threatened with extinction. Zeus, who feared he would lose his worshippers and thus his divine existence, tried conciliatory gifts. But Demeter swore that the earth would remain infertile until Persephone returned. Then Zeus was forced to send Hermes to Pluto with a message that said: 'If you don't give Persephone back, we're all doomed to die.' Foolishly, however, Persephone had picked a pomegranate in Pluto's garden and eaten seven seeds of the fruit of the dead. When her mother learned of this, she grew even sadder and said, 'I'll never go back to Olympus; never will I lift my curse from the earth.' But after much negotiation a solution was finally found: Persephone would stay with Pluto for three months a year as queen of Tartarus and spend the remaining nine months with Demeter. — Persephone's explanation reinforced Beatrice's secret sympathy for Demeter. The trobadora did not have to hide her feelings as she said, 'For your mother I could blow Paris to bits.' Persephone applauded. Echoes bounced off the courtyard walls. Beatrice was afraid the residents of the building would take them by surprise. Satisfied with her patrol trip, Persephone descended back to the underworld. Beatrice escaped undetected.

Chapter 4

Beatrice loses her way

Beatrice finally learned that Alain must be a member of the notorious Red May commune, which had rented an attic apartment on the Rue de l'Arbalète. So, as soon as Gerson had departed for Versailles in his delivery truck to buy hothouse tomatoes, Beatrice wrapped the poem 'Water Walk' around a bunch of endive and headed for the Rue de l'Arbalète. The endive was to be a pretext: she planned to say that Alain had paid for the endive the last time he shopped at the store and forgotten it. The apartment door was opened by a girl of about five. The mansard rooms were furnished with mattresses and stacks of books. The unpainted walls were plastered with posters bearing figures and words. Beatrice read: 'Go out on the street and punch the first person over thirty you meet in the face. It will always be right.' — 'Fuck the minister of education in the mouth.' — 'Beat up the professors where you find them.' — 'Taking pleasure in destruction is a creative act.' — 'Imperialism and all reactionaries are paper tigers.' The windows were bare. According to the little girl, Alain was asleep. Under the jumble of people covered by a tarpaulin. In the opposite corner two men were smoking and talking. One proclaimed that in hashish, time was the sum total of erotic moments. In mescaline, on the other hand, there was no time. Beginning and end were simultaneous and forever. The world was a state of space and color. You didn't become aware of time again until the effects subsided and the colors faded. But with speed, like Preludin, every action, even passing water, was an event. But listening to Jimi Hendrix was better than pinball. The other one said, 'A revolutionary despises every doctrine and renounces every science in the world. He leaves that up to future generations. He knows only one science, that of destruction. Uncompromising with respect to himself, he must also be uncompromising to others. All feelings of affection, the tender feelings of family affiliation, of friendship, of gratitude must be stifled in him by the single-minded and cold-blooded passion for the work of the revolution. For him there is only one single pleasure, one single consolation, one commendation and satisfaction: the success of the revolution.' — Beatrice listened in fascination. For which reason she noticed too late that the little girl had taken the wrapped-up bunch of endive from her. The girl tossed it into the kitchen and pushed Beatrice in after it. 'The guys put up posters last night,' whispered the girl softly. 'You can wash the dishes while you're waiting. Or cook, if you can find anything. Are your professors assholes too?' — 'No, I'm a housewife,' said Beatrice. — 'And I'm Michèle,' said the girl. 'Housewives have no business in our kitchen.' Beatrice was pushed back out of the kitchen and led to a stack containing Melusinian books among others, with the advice to become emancipated while waiting. Beatrice pulled a brochure with the title *The Sexual Revolution* from the stack. Which promptly fell down and woke up the sleeping men. A young man whose hair covered his face beckoned Beatrice to join him on the mattress. Beatrice followed him. But soon asked to go to the next room. The young man fulfilled this expressed wish and other unexpressed wishes for Beatrice. When the two came back out of the room, Michèle said to Beatrice, 'Are you really that frustrated?' But the young man lifted his hair. Whereupon Beatrice realized that she had fallen for the false Alain. The false one ranked the true one among those who smashed their own feet by piling up stones.

Chapter 5

Mostly indecent writings by the trobadora, inspired by her base love for the false Alain

Roof

Before Gahmuret falls asleep
he puts my hand
on his sex.
I curl my fingers,
the skin releases warmth,
tension,
falls away.
Pressure on hips and knees.
It intensifies
as breaths come less rapidly:
calmness radiates out.
I move carefully.
He follows.
Floods the mattress.
Leaves me stranded on the floor.
The wood leaves its mark on my back.
I watch the swell of his body,
listen.
Collect flotsam:
Snoring, the word 'you.'
My arm falls asleep.
My hand is empty.
Peace.

Chapter 6

Mostly decent writings by the trobadora, apparently inspired by her high love for the true Alain

Space Suit

I am independent,
sitting under the sky
just as under the roof.
Climate doesn't matter,
vegetation,
the tides,
I have space with me.
I'm wearing it.
It fits closely on my skull and hips,
lies lightly on my shoulders,
it falls abundantly
on my waist, belly, and sex,
presses my breasts,
fits my arms and legs
in the width.
But not lengthwise.

It doesn't suit me.
It's uncomfortable.
But star-studded down to my feet.

My space is a body.
I bring it to life,
as it does me.
Serfdom.

Chapter 7

Beatrice studies German and Marx

The true Alain lived in a furnished room on the Rue Claude-Bernard. With his wife. When Beatrice found out that he was properly married, she got drunk on Pernod. Which yielded the most ideal intoxication, for now nothing stood in the way of her high love. She continued to practice base love at the Rue de l'Arbalète, for health reasons. Group sex seemed to her the pinnacle of erotic boredom. A falling out with Jacqueline when Beatrice claimed she couldn't talk her husband out of any more money for shopping. Gerson was glad his wife was devoting herself to sedentary pleasures. To be sure, as a precautionary measure he said 'You'll be sorry if I catch you!' at least once a day, but obligingly accepted the packages that Alain dropped off at the store for Beatrice. The packages contained Marxist books for self-study. They were underlined in red, blue, and green so that Beatrice could easily understand the various degrees of importance. From Lenin's work *'Left-Wing' Communism: An Infantile Disorder,* Beatrice excerpted, in addition to the red-underlined words, most of the blue underlinings and all the marginal notes. Since the true Alain was studying German in order to read Marx and Engels in the original, Beatrice also enrolled in a German course at the Society for Friendship France-GDR. It was an evening course. Gerson drove Beatrice there in his delivery truck and picked her up again. Although no more terrorist attacks had been announced. The police searches were still without results, however. The German teacher said Beatrice was a linguistic genius. After only three sessions, she read without a dictionary a beautiful passage from the German edition of Marx's economic-philosophical writings, which she immediately copied with a felt pen onto the kitchen wall above the stove. The passage read: 'The relationship of male to female is the most natural relation of human to human. Thus it is this relation that shows the extent to which the natural relation of human beings is human or the extent to which human nature has become their nature . . . ' In his letters to Kugelmann, Marx had written the following sentence dear to Beatrice's heart: 'Social progress can be precisely measured by the social position of the fair sex.'

Chapter 8

Kollontai Revelation, read by the 5-year-old Michèle, heard by the 840-year-old Beatrice on a mattress at the Red May commune

Probably what amazes you the most is that I can give myself to men just because I like them, without waiting to fall in love with them? You see, one needs time for falling in love; I have read many novels and know how much time being in love requires. But I have no time. We have so much work in our region; there are so many important problems to solve. When did we have time in all these years of the revolution raging about us? Always haste and hurry, one's thoughts always filled with a thousand burning issues. Of course, there are calmer periods too . . . So, then you realize that you like this or that person; but understand me please: there's no time for falling in love. And besides – you barely get to know a man and there you are; he's ordered to the front or transferred to another city. Or you have so much to do yourself that you forget him . . . But that's precisely why you learn to treasure the hours when you meet someone by chance and feel happy together . . . Tell Mother to calm down . . . Certainly I'll do something stupid for love at some point. Not for nothing am I her daughter and Grandmother's granddaughter . . . And there are people whom I love – and how I love them . . . not just Mother . . . others too, Lenin, for example . . . Don't smile. I'm very serious. I love him much more than all the men that I liked and hooked up with. When I know I'm going to hear and see him, I'm transported for days . . . For him I could even give my life. Then there's Comrade Gerassim. Do you know him? The party secretary in our region. There's a human being . . . You see, I love him. Really and truly. I will always defer to him, even when he's not right, because I know that his intentions are always good and right . . . When that scandalous intrigue against him began last year – maybe you remember – I couldn't sleep a single night . . . And how we fought for him then. I got the whole region moving. Yes, I really love him!

Chapter 9

A man named Uwe Parnitzke

At an evening of public discussion of the Friendship Society, which was campaigning for diplomatic recognition of the GDR, the true Alain showed up again in the company of a striking man already known to Beatrice. The well-dressed gentleman spoke up several times. Alain, the discussion leader, had introduced him as his friend Uwe Parnitzke, who would accompany the Leipzig Opera Ensemble on its tour of France as their reporter. Parnitzke orated in barbaric French, did nothing to conceal his insecurity, threw away all opportunities for effects. Beatrice heard comprehensive descriptions of ideal conditions. She listened with rapt attention. When a representative of the press tried to make fun of Parnitzke, Beatrice cut the microphone cord. Whereupon the event had to be cut short because of technical difficulties. And Beatrice took the opportunity to invite Parnitzke and Alain to a bar. There Parnitzke admitted that this was his first visit to France. Soon he was giving an enthusiastic description of the demonstrations of 13 May and 29 May 1968 in Paris, which he evaluated as follows: 'May 1968 in France was not a lost or betrayed revolution. It was the experiment of a revolution in its successive phases. First, the sudden revolt of an influential minority; then the beginning of a common struggle. Then during a work stoppage by the proletariat but still before the overthrow of power, the play of oppositions between the classes and strata who could have joined forces for the revolution. Finally, precisely because these oppositions could be neither overcome nor eliminated: the decision by the still-intact power apparatus.' Parnitzke adjusted the knot of his necktie. And lifted his chin to free the skin pinched by his stiff white shirt collar. The true Alain curled his shoulder-length hair into ringlets with his forefinger and gave three cheers for women. Beatrice gave three cheers for Parnitzke. Pleased and embarrassed, he made a dismissive gesture. Spoke about his contributions to the discussion, which he thought were unsuccessful. 'The only thing missing was a certain sparkle that comes from presumptuous behavior,' said Beatrice, adding that she appreciated such shortcomings. Parnitzke replied that he needed history, not pity. No one who wanted to tackle a larger problem could do without the support of history. Beatrice embraced him on the spot. 'Science requires that one call to account all forces, all groups, parties, classes, and masses at work in the affected country,' Parnitzke quoted distractedly, 'so that one doesn't determine politics based only on the desires and views, on the degree of class consciousness and battle-readiness of a single group or party. Only when the underclasses no longer want the old ways and the upper classes can't continue in the old ways, only then can the revolution triumph.' Beatrice applauded the logical clarity of the quotation. Alain's red headband had to be used for catching teardrops. The young man melancholically said May 1968 was the most beautiful month of his life, explaining, 'All of a sudden I became aware that all social structures are made by human beings and that human beings can change them. A hopeful, festive mood. Lenin also said, "the revolution is the festival of the oppressed and exploited." In my department we debated day after day with professors and teaching assistants. Political subjects as well as philosophy, but most of all a program of demands and measures opposing the old-fashioned patriarchal university operations. A radical reorientation of teaching methods; full voting rights for students on all issues and at all levels; new partnership relations between teachers and learners. This collective search for truth, this serious and passionate desire to understand each other, this thirst for collaborative governance – wonderful.' Beatrice regretted sorrowfully that she had been kept away by sunstroke. Then she cursed the cops who were still holding her sister-in-law in jail and eyed Alain's Indian shirt with pleasure. It was not only transparent but also unbuttoned. Uwe Parnitzke kept a cardigan on under his gray jacket in the overheated bar. He swallowed various tablets as a precautionary measure, apparently mistrusting his physical strength. Beatrice admired his gentle, bright-colored eyes. With which he ventured shy glances. Without lowering them. Even the true Alain looked at women only with eyes averted. But interrupted the conversation at regular intervals with random cheers for the female sex in general. Which Parnitzke seemed to take seriously. 'Would my assistance be agreeable to you?' asked Beatrice. – 'In what way?' asked Parnitzke. – 'I'm 840 years old. Could you tackle a more serious problem with me behind you?' – Unrestrained laughter from Alain, who was satisfied that his wine was having an effect. Parnitzke said, 'We need legends.' And he explained this in all seriousness. Members of noble families, for example, whose family trees reached back to the Middle Ages, had an advantage over other people who knew nothing of their past. Even if the other people now belonged to the ruling class. For these other people, the simple ones whose ancestors didn't seem noteworthy for history books, were lacking a certain instinctive success factor. Which confers an unearned decisiveness, calmness, pride. The West German journalist Marion, countess of Dönhoff, had claimed in an interview never to have had problems asserting herself as a woman. Parnitzke, who felt he belonged to the ruling class not only politically but also by reason of gender, had been encouraged by the countess's confession to proceed along similar lines as Beatrice. 'For the expropriated and the women, who were formerly not considered worthy of being recorded in written history, are not therefore automatically without history,' said Parnitzke menacingly. 'Reality cannot be created or abolished with words, though it can be silenced. We must break this silence. We must create a legendary historical consciousness.' Parnitzke shook Beatrice's right hand, kissed the trobadora on the left and right cheek and then the left again, and invited her to the German Democratic Republic. Besides giving her his Leipzig address, he also wrote the Berlin address of his first ex-wife, Laura, on a matchbook cover. And advised Beatrice warmly not to overlook the impressive material gains of May 1968, despite the election victory of the reactionaries. He reminded her of the 35 percent minimum wage increase, guaranteed by law in all professions, and in agriculture a full 56 percent, which benefited close to four million workers. For another fifteen million, the wage increase they had fought for amounted to at least 10 percent, often 15, and in some cases 20 percent and more. Also, expanded rights for social activity within the companies, in many places shorter working hours and the government's acceptance of a return to the forty-hour workweek as a short-term goal, general increases in retirement pensions, and for many young people an additional — fifth — week of paid vacation. As was well known, Waldeck-Rochet had said that no comparable progress had been achieved since the liberation in 1944 . . . The true Alain praised Parnitzke's erudition, adding that most of the wage increases had already been eaten up by price increases, and ordered generous helpings of escargots.

Chapter 10

The trobadora's last two Parisian poems

I

And branches grew round about,
arteries and veins:
a hedge.
When it had grown up over my head
I thought I was blind.
Gradually the eye grew accustomed to the twilight.
The sky is red now,
but near.
Star-spangled with innards,
clouded over with muscles.
So far no rain.
I listen to rumbling juices,
my eyes follow
the meandering coils of the small intestine,

the skin registers resonances of the heart.
Restless.

II

Before I fell in love with him
I made an image
of him.
I took it in
as a sublet.
When I felt desire
I brought out the image.
When I was satisfied
I put it away.
One day it came unbidden,
and didn't leave
when I wanted it to.
And came and went from then on
as it pleased.
And wouldn't leave.
Ate the furniture, walls, streets, the city.
Last of all, me.
It is I.

Chapter 11

Wherein the reader learns what Parnitzke tells the trobadora in the Jardin des Tuileries about the country to which he has warmly invited her

In our country the working class, under the leadership of its Marxist-Leninist party and in alliance with the farmers and other working people, controls the power of the state for the good and welfare of all the people. The class of capitalists and big landowners has been disempowered. Socialist society structures its entire life on the basis of the highest form of democracy: socialist democracy. Working people participate actively in state government and in solving the problems of economic and cultural growth through the organs of the state, the trade unions, and other mass organizations. In socialism there is true political freedom. Socialism puts an end, for all time, to control by private ownership over the means of production, the cause of the splitting of society into classes engaged in relentless struggle against each other. It is based on the firm economic foundation of socialist ownership of the means of production, which exists in two forms: ownership by society as a whole, by the state; and cooperative ownership through voluntary collectivization by the small producers of goods in agriculture and the trades. Socialism does away forever with the anarchy of production, economic crises, and other social upheavals. The socialist state plans the socialist economy, which is developed based on the most advanced achievements in science and technology. The productive forces have unlimited leeway for their development. The attainment of a higher level of productivity than in capitalism is the primary task, in order to ensure the superiority of socialism over all other systems. Socialism solves the greatest social problem: it eliminates the causes of man's exploitation by man and thus exploitation itself and the exploiter class. In socialism there are only two allied classes, the working class and the farmers, but they have changed too. The working class has become the leading force in society. The farmers have taken the path of the socialist economy. The voluntary collectivization of the farming community is an outstanding event in the socioeconomic history of humankind. The common interests of the two forms of socialist ownership bring the working class and the collective farming class closer together, consolidating their alliance and making their friendship unshakable. A new form of intelligence that is faithfully devoted to socialism issues forth from the people. The conflict between city and country, between intellectual work and physical work that is typical of exploitative societies is gradually eliminated in socialism. The unshakable social, political, and ideological unity of the people is developed on the basis of the fundamental interests that the workers, farmers, and intellectuals have in common. In socialism the principle 'From each according to his abilities, to each according to his achievements' has been realized. It ensures that the members of society are materially interested in the results of their work, offers the opportunity of optimally linking personal interests with those of society, and creates a powerful incentive for improving work productivity, the economy, and the people's well-being. The working people's awareness that they are working not for exploiters but for themselves and their own society produces enthusiasm for work, innovation, creative initiatives, and social competition by the masses. The goal of socialism is to satisfy the people's increasing material and cultural needs more and more completely through uninterrupted development and perfection of social production. For millennia the masses of people suffered under the elementary effect of social laws; now they control these laws, and their activity on behalf of building a socialist society and defending peace against imperialist warmongers is steadily growing. In socialism there are equal opportunities for all. Everyone has the opportunity to develop his abilities, gain an education, and cultivate a well-rounded personality. The right to work, to recreation, to education, to medical care, to care during old age and illness or with loss of the ability to work is guaranteed. There is equality of citizens of all races and nationalities, equality of women and men in all spheres of political, economic, and cultural life. Socialist society guarantees true freedom of personality. The highest expression of this freedom is the liberation of the people from exploitation. Therein, above all, rests true social justice. Socialist law incorporates this justice and ensures true legal security. Socialism is also the result of a great revolution in ideology. It creates the most favorable conditions for the flourishing of science. Millions of people benefit from the achievements of culture and science. A socialist culture is developing. Marxism-Leninism is the ideology of socialist society as a whole. The misanthropy produced by private ownership is a thing of the past. The collective bases of life and work for people in socialism will prevail. Relations among people are characterized by comradely cooperation and mutual help.

Chapter 12

Parnitzke finds the optimal woman in his life; Beatrice buys a train ticket to the Promised Land

A short time after Parnitzke's description of the Promised Land, those two or three magically acquired childhood years suddenly reappeared in Beatrice's head. With a view of the sea, celestial charts, and voices of adults saying this was a child blessed by God who would bring peace to the land. Having thus recovered her composure, Beatrice strolled through the evening streets of the Latin Quarter with Uwe before his journey home. Beatrice left the last traces of her sympathy for Persephone's legal party supporters, who wanted to replace existing injustices with other ones, on the Rue Ortolan. There a violinist and two guitar players were playing virtuoso musical pieces in medieval style. The guitar players sat on the sidewalk. Hunched over, in order to read the music lying before them in the dim light. The violinist's music lay on the roof of a car. People quickly gathered around the musicians. Coins were thrown down. Cars honked their horns and crowded the listeners. Applause after every piece. The violinist thanked them by bowing deeply several times and pointing to the guitar players with his outstretched arm. Uwe put a bill into an envelope, stuck it under the violin music, and turned away in embarrassment. On the Rue Saint-Médard Beatrice called Uwe her ally and told him her real profession. At that, he confessed he had suspected something of the sort. And fell in love with her on the spot. Before midnight he told Beatrice she was the optimal woman of his life. After this remarkable evening, Beatrice kept her visits to the false Alain to a bare minimum. And stopped composing poems in honor of the true Alain. What Beatrice found even more convincing than the ideal picture Uwe had painted and his fondness for legends were his divorces. What a country it must be, thought Beatrice, in which a man like this is rejected twice. When she found out that Hector had discovered hand grenades under Jacqueline's bed, she bought a ticket to Berlin at the Gare de l'Est.

FIRST INTERMEZZO

WHEREIN THE READER LEARNS WHAT THE BEAUTIFUL MELUSINE COPIED FROM IRMTRAUD MORGNER'S NOVEL *RUMBA FOR AN AUTUMN* INTO HER 7TH MELUSINIAN BOOK IN 1964

The article had to reach the editorial office before midnight. One hundred and fifty lines. The first ten were no problem. Topical tag line, autumn, the sea, the peninsula with the institute's buildings, former chocolate factory and so forth, a drunk could write the beginning. But the series was titled The Productive Force of Science; at some point you had to get to the issue.

'Eventually we have to get to the issue,' this Armenian had said between the soup and the main course, in excellent German, almost without an accent; maybe he was after a Nobel Prize. Presumably most of these people were. You only had to look at them, only had to watch what they ate. The Armenian ate zwieback. 'It's time for us to get to the issue,' he'd said, 'what you don't accomplish between thirty and forty, you'll never accomplish.'

Dull thuds, in rapid succession: the slamming of the automatic doors. Uwe Parnitzke was thrown against the seat back. The horn sounded. All that Uwe could see in the window was his own reflection. He should have listened to his wife and refused the assignment.

He paged hastily through his steno pad. He'd written twenty pages and more today, but none of it was usable. Not only the foreign scientists but also those from the institute who were participating in this conference admitted without hesitation – and with a certain degree of pride, for they hadn't a clue about the immediate needs of the press – that solutions to the problems they were working on would perhaps have practical significance eighty years from now, and that their research was outrageously expensive, becoming more expensive all the time, and so forth. Even the connection to the topical tag line, which was really obligatory for a report on the work of an institute for nuclear physics – Uwe had the idea as soon as he found out about the assignment, although the political situation was not yet acute – even that simple connection had to be forced. A sign that the entire venture was a failure. Uwe should have gone on vacation with Valeska. Either write something about the issue or go on vacation, yessir. 'At age thirty you have to get to the issue,' the Armenian had said. His name was Paremusian or Taresmusian or Karemusian or something like that. Uwe ate a second helping and this Igor Dideldumian nibbled zwieback, presumably because ambition had destroyed his stomach. He polished off two big packages of the stuff and talked incessantly, his coal black eyes glittering with fanaticism. Uwe was also thirty. He would rather have talked with the Englishman at his right, the Englishman sat at his right and Prince Igor on the left, but the Englishman was listening to the Armenian too. Uwe was thirty. His stomach was in perfect shape.

The lights of the city reflected on the windshield.

'I haven't seen the sea yet,' said Prince Igor, 'but it belongs to me. Virtually. If I sail the sea in my mind, it belongs to us. Whatever you really want, you will accomplish.' He used the masculine article *der* for *das Meer,* the sea; probably the masculine was the only way he could imagine such an imposing force as the sea. Uwe had been twenty the first time he saw the sea. At twenty, the sea was endless. At thirty, it had shores. The other conference participants talked about the food, the female lab techs who were serving the meal, and, of course, politics. War, yes or no, and the like. Nobody except Igor and a certain Dr. Wenzel Morolf talked about the sea. The others were all normal. What they were doing seemed supremely normal: analyzing film, taking measurements; most of them were probably perfectly normal number-crunchers, guys you could talk to. If you could. But Igor didn't let anyone else have the floor. Uwe, at any rate, heard nothing but Igor's metallic voice, his rhythmical monster-sentences. He was also thirty, but his stomach was all right. Except that he had a hard time falling asleep at night, because I feel that I'm running out of time, said Igor. At twenty you don't understand what that is, time. It's a category that doesn't exist until you're thirty. At thirty it turns up for the first time. When you've become a human being and you're not just physically there but also intellectually really there, at that moment, on top of the mountain, you see the end for the first time. And you understand what it is: time. Up to then you've only talked about not having enough time. But suddenly you feel the monster that will never leave you from then on, that pursues you, especially at night. That chases you; I take it to bed with me and get up with it, and it won't be any different for you, Professor Gurnemann, even if you don't eat zwieback. Do you like riddles? A dog has a pan tied to its tail. When the dog runs, the pan bangs on the pavement. Question: At what speed must the dog run before the banging of the pan becomes inaudible? They all think about it, the institute director Gurnemann, his colleagues, the Englishmen, the West Germans; everyone ponders. The Englishman chews while brooding; I nibble my zwieback, after a while I have pity on them and give the ridiculously obvious answer: zero.

The train stations they were passing now had better lighting. The thudding of the joints in the rails was slower. Vacation-house communities. Villas. New housing developments. Suburbs. Uwe had to start writing now, at once. He was out of time.

For he lived in this city. Not since childhood. But in the summer of 1945, he had ended up here. And since then he'd lived in the city. First, in one of the three western sectors, then in the eastern sector, then in the west again, and from 1949 until now in the east without interruption. Twelve years in a neighborhood with two or three tenement buildings behind every apartment building. The apartments in the tenement buildings were now officially designated as difficult to rent out. Uwe lived in a front-facing building. It was so conveniently located that he could have jumped from the kitchen window onto the roof of a passing S-Bahn train. The trains used to cross the border; here and there they still did. Uwe knew the city only with this border. He was used to this state of affairs. For these days every city had a border, a visible or an invisible one.

I should have stayed with science, he thought, I'll chuck my job and do science again. Or I'll become a foreign correspondent. Or we'll have children, a son who will become a scientist when he grows up.

He wrote all night. Toward morning when the first train went by, roaring, grinding, rhythmically pounding, louder and louder, really loud, the house shaking from the pounding, even the lamp resonated, toward morning the desk was covered with pages of writing. And the typewriter keys were sticky. And the lamp was still holding back the darkness behind the windows. And fatigue came. And sleep was a long way off. Uwe couldn't catch up with it. In half-sleep, a few dreams. Which were haunted by Valeska. All his dreams were haunted by Valeska. A tall Valeska. He was always shorter than she. Although she didn't wear high-heeled shoes. In reality she was shorter than he, even with high heels. This bothered him in his half-sleep. When fully awake he would never have admitted – not even to himself – that he could only love superior women. Oh, this ill-fated longing – Valeska was the same type as Laura. Did he have to make the same mistake again? Why in the world was he attracted to such admirable creatures when he knew they would make him impotent in the long run. Having sex was only possible downwards, love only upwards. His sensitive nature also got in his way sexually. He couldn't help envying egotistical men who could concentrate exclusively on themselves during physical love. He'd probably never get there. Even if he lived forever in this conveniently located house, which, remarkably enough, had not yet collapsed from the shuddering of the passing S-Bahn trains. Roaring, grinding, rhythmical pounding, louder and louder, really loud, the windows rattled, the lamp resonated: the second train was heading into town. But Uwe didn't really hear that one. And the ones after that, not at all. He only heard his voice trying to summon sleep. He talked to his room. I'm a man who has no father, that SA-brownshirt isn't my father, and my mother wasn't worth anything either. Days she worked in the spinning mill, and evenings she looked for a man to marry. And when this brownshirt promised marriage, she let him take her. But then he was promoted and a black-haired woman was out of the question. And she took hot baths and swallowed quinine. But I was born anyway. I was sent to my grandmother's, and I stayed with her, even after a man to marry had turned up. But Grandmother had no use for me either. Nobody had any use for me. And I had no use for anyone. I struggled along on my own. In the rear courtyard where we played. At school. When I lost my grandmother because she stopped going to the cellar when the alarm sounded. And at the university nobody helped me either, when I got in trouble and was sent to production for two years and Juliane died and Laura left me. And Valeska has her own problems. Everyone has their own problems. What do you have when you have a wife? Nothing. You can't have anyone. You only have yourself. Even when I love, I can't cross that line. Love is my creation too. I can't borrow a life. One doesn't live on in one's children. One only lives oneself. Everyone has to come to terms with his life on his own. People who are afraid to be alone are afraid of themselves. They're terrified of their inner emptiness. You can only experience things actively. The greater the consumption of experience, the smaller the person. Everyone must try alone to fill this monstrous hole that was created when we buried God. Killing him was difficult. But summoning up the strength to put oneself in his place is incomparably more difficult. If you're not strong enough to patch the leak, your boat will sink. I'm strong enough. I'm getting to the issue. I'm a man who doesn't need a father, said Uwe.

And the room understood him. It looked pretty run-down, but it wasn't bare. It could get along without Valeska. It had a do-it-yourself paint job: yellow walls, blue ceiling.

Uwe hoisted the typewriter back onto the desk. While bending over to pick it up, he said, 'It must go back where it belongs,' and it went back where it belonged. He said, 'I have to pick the paper up too,' and he gathered the pages scattered on the carpet. The activity of making coffee was also accompanied by the appropriate words. Then he told the editor that he wasn't about to concoct a story out of nothing and went on his way.

A bright dome of morning hung overhead. Uwe didn't feel fatigue, even though he hadn't slept. The streets had been sprayed with water. He traveled through a tidied-up city. The traffic moved around him. Concentrically. Uwe ate his way easily through the buildings. Then he got on the S-Bahn and digested the walls. All the way to the physicists' peninsula.

From the opposite shore the peninsula, occupied by a tall tree, the tower of an idled accelerator, and various buildings, looked romantic. So Uwe didn't take the ferry over. He went by land. That way, you didn't notice that it was a peninsula. That way, it was part of the rather simple village, whose residents preferred to get around on bicycles, staring curiously at the out-of-towners. The physicists counted as locals. Even though quite a few of them lived in the city. The institute was located inconspicuously at a corner of the village. When the accelerator, now out of date and only fit for demolition, was being built, the institute was the talk of the village. But ever since the local women working there as lab techs had reported that the physicists worked with scissors and studied pieces of film, the institute was no longer interesting. Physicists who didn't build atomic bombs were uninteresting. Because they weren't real physicists.

Uwe presented his journalist pass; the doorman nodded. When someone with a doctorate arrived, the doorman opened the window and said, 'Good Morning, Herr Doktor.' Uwe had no title. Those with no title had to be thankful if they were nodded to. Uwe nodded back. He walked past the tall tree and the ugly little brick building where, not too long ago, chocolate candies had been produced and the director now resided. The refectory, a barracks, had been added on to Monsignor's chocolate-Gothic administration building. Professional and lay workers didn't have separate refectories, there was just the one barracks where they all took their meals, physicists, mathematicians, engineers, skilled workers, secretaries, lab techs, cleaning ladies. The physicists wore the habit of the order. The fashionably orthodox wore their white lab coats long, the others wore short ones with slits up the side. Many lay brothers and almost all lay sisters had white lab coats too.

The brothers who were participating in the conference shed their habits before entering the parlatorium, the conference room. Uwe didn't shed his insecurity. He dragged it through the corridors of the institute, which smelled like well-roasted capacitors. He dragged it through the first floor, where the lab, the workshop, the library, and the computer were housed. He carried it up to the second floor, where the experimental physicists had their cells. Every cell had a blackboard with a tray for chalk and erasers, a desk with scissors and other tools, a chair, a bookshelf, a coat hook, a window with milk glass in the lower half, blue tile floor, two meters by four meters seventy six, and a door painted a different color than all the others, each one unique like the entrances to beehives. On the third floor, where the theoreticians' offices and the parlatorium were located and the walls were covered with pictures of saints — Copernicus, Galileo, Giordano Bruno, Newton, Cavendish, Coulomb, Ampère, Galois, Gauß, Minkowski, Maxwell, Planck, Einstein — he felt a little sick. But he pulled himself together.

And entered the parlatorium. A long, narrow room, on the front wall a triptych blackboard that reached the ceiling. Its wings were covered with numbers, letters, graphs, and a drawing that looked like a headless stick figure or a grasshopper. On the altarpiece were nonsense words.

The men were seated around a large rectangular table, men exclusively. Dr. Wenzel Morolf had told Uwe that physics was a vital science for vital men. So it was a masculine science. We men, thought Uwe to himself, and discreetly pulled a chair away from the table and sat down in a corner.

On the table were thick files of skyscraper-like drawings that were composed of little St. Andrew's crosses. Mostly the crosses were piled up on the horizontal axis of the first quadrant in a Cartesian coordinate system. Or they were clustered between the coordinates without touching them. The men called these computer-generated drawings 'plots,' and talked about them officially in English or Russian, and unofficially in English, Russian, Swabian, Saxon, Rhinelandish, Bavarian, and Plattdeutsch. Uwe didn't understand in any language. All he could do was listen to the voices, often many of them at once, for there was no discussion leader. Whoever had anything interesting to say was listened to. Whoever wasn't interested in a particular problem left the room and strolled in the corridor. Uwe could only watch the men and guess. He loved this game. Wherever he was, he watched people and thought about what kind of life might match them. He tried different lives on people, like trying on clothes. Sometimes he did this for a long time; sometimes he couldn't think of anything suitable. But sometimes it fit right away. With this Armenian, for example, it seemed to fit right away.

For the British professor next to him, on the other hand, Uwe had a hard time finding something suitable. Horse face, kiss-curls, diamonds set in gold on his pinky finger, turtleneck sweater, pipe. A man smokes cigarettes. A manly man smokes a pipe. Uwe guessed him to be in his early forties. He's the oldest of the conferees by far. He cleans his pipe while the Armenian explains his theory of time. He speaks very little. Does it bother him that he's over forty? Does he feel superior or inferior to the younger men? Is he modest, or does he just act that way? What kind of life would fit a closed book like this? There are people that don't appeal to one. This man doesn't appeal to Uwe. The Armenian does, but the Englishman doesn't.

The skinny Indian doesn't either, the one they say is world-renowned. Among the living physicists, only one was world-renowned for Uwe: Oppenheimer. They wrote that he had intellectual sex appeal. Could you write something like that about one of these men? Maybe Monsignor. Uwe thought of the institute director as Monsignor. Monsignor was a good-looking man. Uwe didn't like to admit these things, but he was forced to admit that this guy, who at age thirty-five had been a professor for who knows how long, was damned good-looking. Large, wide-set eyes, behind glasses to be sure, but that didn't matter, light blond hair, cut short, parted in the middle, unwrinkled skin, unwrinkled suit made of silk or something like it, athletic build, small hands, wedding ring. The day before yesterday, when the debate had lasted until 2:00 A.M., with cognac at the end to toast the Soviet missiles in Cuba, Monsignor was the only one who didn't drink anything. And he had left at midnight. He looked at his watch several times, and he disappeared at twelve on the dot. Taking small, precise steps. Precise.

Disciplined. Matter-of-fact. We men, thought Uwe. Valeska would deny that, of course. But Valeska wasn't a regular woman either. Monsignor barely raised his voice when he spoke. He didn't wave his hands about like this Dr. Wenzel Morolf. He was economical. Brilliantly economical, without a doubt. But intellectual sex appeal? This Dr. Wenzel Morolf, who had been totally drunk the other night, might have some. Maybe. But none of the others. None except the Armenian.

A heterogeneous face: fanatically hard eyes, feminine mouth. Igor always took part in the discussion. It was hard for him to sit still. Sometimes he got up and paced back and forth in the parlatorium. Lurking. When someone spoke too long, he would say something clever to call attention back to himself. Only Dr. Wenzel Morolf didn't react. He drew abstract patterns on paper when the Armenian was speaking. He seemed not to like him. Uwe liked him. He had attracted his attention right away. Attention at any price. He found him rather insufferable but couldn't help watching him. So, what kind of a life would suit this little man, whose voice was almost always to be heard, Russian, English, German? Probably his parents were intellectuals, perhaps he was always the best in school. He suffers from being so short, he takes on a tremendous amount, he enrolls in the university. Among equals, now he's one among equals, it takes a long time for him to come to terms with that. He still hasn't come to terms with it, as the condition of his stomach proves. Maybe he has taken on too much. But he can't go back; he pursues the goal he set himself as a boy. He can't really rejoice over partial successes. Rejoicing is a release of tension; for him there is no alternation between tension and release. For him there is only tension, ambition eats him up, traffic moves around him in concentric circles. And the city. And the sea. The city belongs to him, the sea belongs to him. I, the city, I: the sea. But he feels sick at the parlatorium door. Actually, on the way there, as he passes the expensive instruments for processing material produced at monstrously high expense. The institute employs over a hundred people, nine institutes are collaborating on one part of a problem, thousands are represented by the men around this rectangular table. One person alone can't accomplish anything. Not even a genius. Not even if he imagines that he can eat up cities. But he doesn't allow himself a vacation, he sleeps on his desk, he can't watch calmly as a day passes, ambition is eating me up.

Dr. Wenzel Morolf went to the blackboard and talked to the blue numbers and letters and graphs and the drawing that looked like a headless stick figure or a grasshopper. The stick-grasshopper was called Graph or Feinmann Graph or something like that. The Swabian sitting in front of Uwe turned around occasionally and tried to explain something to him. But Uwe didn't understand him, not even acoustically. He'd never in his life spoken with a Swabian before.

But he scarcely understood Monsignor and Dr. Morolf and the others either when they tried to explain something to him. Their voices sounded remarkably distorted, as if they were reaching him through a telephone line with a lot of interference. Only the Armenian was easy to understand. But since the physicists could easily make themselves understood to one another as well as to Uwe, he asked himself where these people were living. Not in this city, at any rate. And not on this earth, either. For wars were going on here. Cold ones and other ones. At the moment, maybe even new ones. In the Caribbean Sea maybe new ones at this very hour. And the physicists were talking about research projects that might yield practical significance in eighty years! Where were these people living?

At that, Uwe looked them over, one after the other. He tried different dimensions on them. There were some with aristocratic noses, whom the fifth dimension might fit, but most of them Uwe could definitely imagine with pork knuckles and beer. What you really want you will achieve, thought Uwe. I'm a man who doesn't need a father.

BOOK THREE

Beatrice finds a message in a bottle — Laura calls the find 'Bottle-Post Legend'

But at the Gare de Lyon, Beatrice de Dia got in the wrong car. The nonstop train traveled through the night. The trobadora slept well and woke up the next morning not in Berlin but in Hamburg. She took advantage of the detour only for a sightseeing tour of the harbor. During which she fished a bottle out of its oily waters. Laura later dubbed the message that the trobadora claimed was sealed in the bottle the 'Bottle-Post Legend.' The strange document reads as follows:

1

There are events in the world that I can't understand. My current residence is dark. I'm writing blind. The paper is damp from gastric juice. After writing everything down, I'll put the document in a whiskey bottle. It was swallowed yesterday and will leave the fish the natural way.

2

The inexplicable part began with a droning noise that slowly swelled up, memory drove me out of bed. During the night of 23 October. Since no sirens sounded, I opened the window. I was dazzled. By strings of flares that lit up the city and the sky. The sky glistened. Angels and cherubs covered it like shingles on a roof. Their garments were stiff with silver. They flew in squadrons. The speed of the wing beats made their wings appear segment shaped. The first squadron of angels was scattering rose leaves, the second one leaflets, the third was swinging censers. There followed two squadrons of angels bearing books and five bearing lassos. Then seven squadrons of cherubim. The pommels and handles of the swords brandished by the cherubim were embossed with sparkling jewels. All movements were executed in drill formation. Between the ninth and tenth squadron of angels flew the Lord. Without wings. His gold brocade garment was decorated with peacock feathers and sable fur. From each epaulette there loomed four engraved shafts hung with sky blue and scarlet standards. The train was so long that it clattered across the gasometer roofs. His head was encircled by curly angel hair, finer and whiter than that used to decorate Christmas trees. His equally fine and white beard was a yard long. The Lord wore a halo as well, which was fastened to his long curly wig with golden wires, and an aureole. Singing angels were holding it. The Lord was directing their song with a paper scroll. I woke Jonah up.

3

I shared his bed. Since April. During the day he worked at St. George's cemetery, I worked at the plant nursery across the street. I could watch him unloading wreaths. The cemetery compost heap was visible from the barracks window where my worktable stood.

4

When the word of the Lord had come down, we fetched the atlas. There we found Nineveh on the Tigris. Jonah said, 'I don't know the Lord.' Relieved, I got into my clothes. We left the house and the city with a suitcase. At Sappho we gave a captain eight hundred thousand liras in ferry money for a place in the 'tween deck. During the crossing to Tarshish, our ship approached a lighthouse. It stood on a paved island. The skeleton of a great fish was bleaching on the shore.

5

But a wind came up, and a storm came down upon the sea and battered the ship. The mariners cried out, each one to his god, and threw gear into the sea to lighten the ship. It drifted out of control in the storm, gigantic waves overran it, water burst through. All the passengers helped, although they were seasick, all except Jonah. Some mariners looked for him. I found him asleep in a hold of the lower deck. He was lying on a full sack between crates and barrels. The sack was leaking; something white was seeping out. I tasted it. Sugar. A barrel rolled past my feet toward the bulkhead. I braced myself on an upright beam. My petroleum lamp, which I had hung on the beam, rocked to and fro in arcs of 120 degrees. An ear-splitting tumult of noises from which you could clearly make out the crashing of breakers, irregular engine rhythms, the clanking of chains, Jonah's snoring. He lay on his back, his chin jutting up, right hand in the sugar, left hand on his heart; his green shirt was unbuttoned. I watched indulgently, left the room, and threw up over the railing.

6

The hurricane raged for three hours. Then I slept too. For a good fourteen hours. A rat awakened me. I bathed quickly, rubbed ointment on my elbows where the skin was raw from bouts of lovemaking, and took the best dress from the suitcase. When I was satisfied with my reflection, I made my way to the lower deck. Jonah's green shirt lay on his berth. I went through the passageways, climbed an iron ladder, looked into holds, visited the mess hall. When I had thoroughly searched the ship's belly, I went to the upper deck. Clear sky, white crescent moon on a blue gray background, dry flanks, breeze. Gulls were circling the lifeboat, perching on the lowering mechanism, shitting on it. An officer touched two fingers to the brim of his cap, passengers promenaded. A dog was sleeping beside the stairs to the commander's bridge. Gentle swells under my feet. They did not take me to the one I desired. Cursing, I leaned over the railing, lumpy with drops of old oil paint. Blue green water to a depth of about ten meters, bow and stern spattered with foam, a shark's fin. I pointed it out to a sailor. He laughed. When I asked where Jonah was, the sailor spat over the railing. After a while he said that's where Jonah was. Since I didn't believe the man, he told me about the monstrousness of the storm, cloudbursts and swelling waves, damage to the rigging, and filth that the seasick passengers had bestowed upon the ship. He also reminded me that Jonah had slept through the storm. Significantly, when they finally found him, the ship owner went to him and said, 'Why are you sleeping? Get up, call out to your God, that we may not perish.' At that, Jonah had scratched his chest with his left hand, licked sugar from his right hand. The engineer had said, 'Come, let us cast lots, that we may know for whose sake we are faring so badly.' — 'And when the lots were cast, it fell upon Jonah,' said the sailor. 'All the same, we asked, Why do you fare so badly? What is your work, and where are you from? Jonah answered, I am a graveyard worker and fear the Lord. For I am fleeing from him. Then even the most courageous ones were seized by fear, they all cried out, Why have you done this? — Because I was supposed to preach against the great city of Nineveh, Jonah answered. We deliberated what we could do to quiet the elements. But Jonah said, Take me and throw me into the water, then the sea will grow calm. For I know that the great storm has come over you on my account. — We struggled in vain to reach the shore for a while longer. Then we called out to the Lord, saying, O Lord, let us not perish for the sake of this man's soul, and do not put upon us innocent blood, for you, Lord, are doing what pleases you. And we took Jonah and threw him into the sea. And the sea stood still from its raging.'

7

When I had heard the course of events, I was plunged into sadness and threw the narrator over the railing.

8

During the failed attempt to rescue him, two mariners drowned. I wept and fasted for three days and three nights. Then I put on the green shirt that Jonah had left behind and went on land at Tarshish. In a harbor tavern I ordered a funeral meal and wine for all the guests. The meal was served in earthenware vessels. In one bowl a reddish soup bubbled with drops of grease and chunks of white fish. Cream shaped like a rose and lemon slices on the side. Tomatoes, cucumbers, and herbs were arranged on small plates, roasted slices of eggplant and calabash, sweet and hot peppers, bacon. It glistened like satin. Also served were smoked mackerel, escargots, crabs, sea urchins that smelled like love. Beside carafes of vinegar, oil, and wine were bowls of spices. The bread was warm and cottony soft. I picked it apart with my fingers. My pleasure-weakened palate was cleansed by its taste. The largest platter was heaped with roasted and boiled mutton and beef. Garlic, mushrooms, and fried onions surrounded it; butter melted on still-bloody slices garnished with grapefruit slices, olives, grated horseradish. Stalks of fennel were served with it. I emptied the platters, for I was filled with sorrow. And I quenched my thirst with wine, and the guests drank to my health. Then I told them of my misfortune. And there was no one who failed to shed tears for Jonah's sake. After I had prayed to him, I threw my glass into the sea and danced until morning.

9

A ship took me back to the shores of my city. Its towers were wreathed by clouds. Paper-dragon kites tossed between cranes and chimneys. The roofs glistened wetly. The fence along the shore was coated with creosote. I climbed over it, unobserved. The walkways wobbled under my feet. Well-worn granite flagstones, broken in some places, pebbled sidewalk, patterned asphalt with wartlike bulges where weeds were growing through, cement. A cold wind blew through the street canyons and Jonah's shirt. The velvet cuff on the right sleeve was worn off. The breast pockets were full of tobacco crumbs, pens, and papers. That changed my appearance. Men hurrying by looked at me. Dogs pissed on the walls of buildings. Colorful leaves sailed from the trees lining the streets. Boys walked past me carrying cases emitting music. The nursery was working on its autumn program. My absence was recorded as vacation. Until the Sunday before Advent, I made ten to twelve wreaths every day, not counting bouquets. The twig bindery was set up in front of the store. Only a narrow strip in the middle of the sidewalk was open for pedestrians.

10

The winter was hard, the price of flowers high. On the side streets the snow was several meters high in places, the newspapers reported battles, I froze the fingers of my right hand. They were red and swollen and hurt when I made wreaths. Jonah's papers, which I had hung on the walls of my room with thumbtacks, blistered. Ice sprouted from the carpet. Birds fell from trees, frozen solid. On clear nights the stars froze fast in the sky, keeping welders busy with their tools until noon. They wore hooded coats lined with bear hides and asbestos masks. The fire-engine ladders they stood on to work swayed in the wind. On Sundays and holidays I slept with the welder named Kurt.

11

Toward noon on 21 March, a great fish was sighted near the coast. He broke open the ice with his back. It gleamed like chrome. He spouted columns of water from his forehead toward the clouds. Then they burst. The rain melted the ice barricade that the fish had jammed up against the shore. The sea overflowed and submerged the streets of the city. The mayor went aboard an assault boat and collected seventy thousand volunteers. They positioned 130 howitzers, mortars, and close-range artillery. On sandbags that secured the steep coastline. The house I lived in was near the coast. From the kitchen window of my third-floor apartment, I could follow the battle maneuvers. Twenty-one thousand three hundred and eight shots were fired at the fish. All the glass in unopened windows shattered. Toward evening the fish spewed a human body over the city wall and disappeared.

12

I stretched clothing over the empty window frames. Water streamed out of the stove. I slept more restlessly than usual. Toward morning Jonah tumbled into my apartment, on top of me. I was silent under his hands. Drained by hopeless waiting, out of the habit, and incapable of lying, I lay motionless beside the one I desired. Then Jonah lost his desire too. Now suspicious, now jealous, struck down by abrupt good fortune, we quarreled, O reunion, a complete and total failure.

13

Wisdom returned. First of all, to Jonah's hands. Upon waking, I asked if he'd been resurrected. At that, he fell back and lay as if lifeless. I poured water on his face. It was pale. His hair was sopping wet. It reached to his shoulders. Algae and fish bones were stuck in his beard. I kissed Jonah's lips. After a while I felt the edges of his teeth, the roof of his mouth, papillae, tasted tobacco, my mouth was filled. When I felt certain that life had returned to Jonah, I got up and went to the kitchen. Jonah was sitting on the bed when I returned with bread and wine. His thighs were spread apart, his knees bent, his left foot under the right calf, the instep of his right foot tucked into the crook of his left knee. In the hollow between heel and calf, his open hands lay crossed. The bread scattered over the floor. I spilled wine and stood still and looked. His skin was transparent, his body opened up under my eyes: dense branches. Birds lived there, martens, monkeys. Some leaves were nibbled by caterpillars. The leaves glistened greasily. Spider webs were stretched between leaf stems. Blue fruits hung in abundance. I listened to the chirping of the cicadas, plucked a fruit, ate.

14

After Jonah had bathed, shaved, and trimmed his hair, I asked how he had been saved. 'By a miracle,' he replied. His bath water was algae green. 'And why did you flee from the Lord?' I asked then. 'Because he believed in me,' he answered. Then I gave Jonah his green shirt back. He smelled it, put it on, patted the empty breast pockets, and began his description of the miracle. It lasted three days and three nights. When he was finished, I fell into a deathlike sleep, whereby many remarkable details were forgotten. However, I can still clearly remember the beginning and the end of the miracle. When Jonah's strength had ebbed from hours of swimming in the stormy sea, so that he could no longer keep himself above water, he was caught in a subterranean current. He was rapidly swept away in the water. It was light green. Enclosed air bubbles floated past him, algae, fish, octopuses, hundreds of sky-high obelisk-like shapes, lined up like trees along a boulevard, the spaces in between were crowded with animals, the swarms around Jonah grew thicker and thicker, he gulped air bubbles to keep from suffocating, the darkness deepened, suddenly he was lifted upward, at the same time he felt pressure on all sides, the water receded, shortly afterward he lost consciousness. When he awoke again, he was in darkness. His hands grasped fish bones, mud and slime clung to his skin and clothes, and he cried for help. After a time the Lord put a light on his head, like the kind miners wear, and spoke. Jonah didn't dare defend himself but did ask for leniency. He pointed out that a laborer who dug graves every day would understandably have other things on his mind after work. Besides, sermons about cities doomed to destruction could be interpreted as business advertising. The Lord was unrelenting. 'In many months I swam around the world three times,' said Jonah. 'Strange blind sea creatures brought me news of the continents whose shores the great fish was passing, I heard thousands upon thousands of creatures die beside me, I walked on their corpses, which were dissolved by the fish's gastric acid, I slept on their bones and skeletons, I was immune to the acid through the miracle, I dreamt of you day and night, and my longing made me gaunt. When the fish had half digested my clothes and love-hunger had made me ill, I promised obedience. Then the Lord spoke to the fish. The fish obeyed the command unwillingly, having just swallowed a ray. I flew across the wall on a ballistic path, the ray leading the way!'

15

With Jonah the season came back. He soon took a job. Not at the St. George cemetery across from the nursery but at the municipal graveyard next door, to be on the safe side. Some days he brought wreaths that were still in good condition for me to refurbish. In the evenings we strolled through the streets. Quicksilver lamps illuminated the foliage of the trees. Young women walked with their beaux from one island of shade to the next. Old women walked their dogs. Dust had been wiped away to form letters on the chassis of parked cars. The moon hung in the web of overhead wires that latticed the streets. Trains scraped sparks from the wires. Circles of light alternating red, green, and yellow, newspaper vendors. We always bought the evening paper.

16

On June ninth the Lord appeared above the city with drumrolls and songs. On the tenth with barrel organs and songs. The throats of thousands of angels retched them out. Thousands upon thousands of angels turned the cranks of thousands upon thousands of barrel organs. The singing intensified to an ear-splitting roar. The organs were painted with hellish scenes of torture and slaughter, they were full of hidden pipe and flute registers that warbled sweetly. When the din of oaths, curses, and heavenly melodies had swelled to thunderous levels,

Jonah signaled me that he was ready to jump out the window to save me. I refused his offer and went into the water.

17

The water was cold and turbulent. The sky was low. It gave the sea a grayish color. When clouds burst, I floated on my back and licked raindrops. I queried haddocks, flounders, and swarms of herring, dived down to the starfish, asked octopuses for advice. All the creatures willingly gave me information. The ships' crews were silent. My eyes scanned the shores of many countries. After six days of fruitless searching, I approached a shark. He swam around me in concentric circles. His asymmetrical tail, the upper half extended in the shape of a crescent, made fanning motions. The lower dagger-jaw of his mouth gleamed white. When my breath was getting short and the ungainly mouth was gaping, I asked if the great fish who had sheltered Jonah in his belly for seven months had been seen. The shark turned abruptly away from me and swam three circles. Then he gave me to understand that nothing like this had ever happened to him, and he had lost his appetite; at present the great fish was staying near the Faeroe Islands. The shark called the fish his friend and asked me to tell him to enjoy his meal. I surfaced hastily, getting water in my lungs. Bouts of coughing slowed my progress. My hands grew stiff. My hair froze. My salt wounds burned. The sea frothed. Icebergs were floating in it. In desperation I called out my friend's name and slapped my arms in the black water. Then throngs of dolphins appeared, surrounded me curiously, supported my exhausted body, and asked how Jonah was doing. I described the danger he was in. The dolphins called him brother. Taking turns on their backs, I rode to the Faeroese coast. On the seventh day of my expedition, I sighted on the lee side a chrome-gleaming mountain range with sparse vegetation. It was swarming with creatures. Rolls of thunder at regular intervals. Light quivering of the sea. The dolphins swam toward the mountain range. Then I recognized it as the great fish's back. People were building a wooden granary on it. The upper half of his dorsal fin disappeared in the clouds. Walruses and black-spotted cattle rested between his meter-thick scales. Dwarf pines were planted around the spout hole on his forehead. Hundreds of monstrous teeth jutted out of the great fish's mouth. He was asleep, snoring, in the calm water of a cove. My courage flagged at the sight of his impenetrable body. The dolphins brought me back, carried me to the fish's left eye, and threw jellyfish against its armored lid. As it opened, they ordered me to smile.

My hair turned white under its red gaze. Smiling, I asked it to give Jonah shelter again. Outraged, the great fish spewed columns of water toward the sun. The water evaporated with a hissing noise. The vapor clouded the stars. I told the fish of love that would enable me to separate from Jonah for his sake. The fish said he was weary and planning to retire. He had already rented out his back. He would only rent to people who didn't have to shun the light of day and were dependable in delivering fodder. He wanted peace and quiet. The great fish gnashed his huge teeth. A roar like an avalanche of rocks descending. His eyelid drooped halfway over the blood-red pupil. 'But you are a great fish,' I said to the great fish. 'You need not fear the Lord. Do you even report to him?' — 'God forbid,' said the great fish. He assured me that he'd never been subject to any Lord. I congratulated him and asked what would then prevent him from following his fishy heart. 'Nothing,' the great fish answered, 'but the Lord is the Lord.' To keep the great fish from falling asleep, I started dancing. Slowly I snapped my right middle finger rhythmically against my palm, stamped vigorously on the dolphin's back, whirled around, pointed, smiled. The eyelid opened; the red pupil began to glitter. I swayed my shoulders and hips, placed my palms under my breasts, speeded up the rhythm. When the great fish opened his maw lecherously, I leaped onto his tongue. I caressed it with my fingertips, stroked his palate, tickled his throat. Because of the vast distance, I could only cast a fleeting glance into the belly. Soon the great fish declared that he was ready to give Jonah shelter if I accompanied him, otherwise not. The unexpected prospect of never having to be separated from Jonah again made me sing. The great fish shook the tenants and vegetation from his back and set out to sea with me. I stretched out on his tongue.

18

On 26 June we reached the shore of my city. The great fish spat me from the roadstead over the city wall. I found Jonah smoking in the basement. His hair had grayed, like mine. That same night the great fish swallowed us. We've been living in his belly for three months. Are the sunflowers already blooming? Answer us!

BOOK FOUR

Chapter 1

The trobadora's arrival in the Promised Land

At the Hamburg-Altona train station Beatrice met a sailor from the GDR city of Greifswald. He lent the trobadora the fare to Berlin and found her the right train. Beatrice shared a compartment with people of retirement age. Finding their conversations reactionary, she withdrew into her dreams of the future. At the Friedrichstraße station Beatrice crossed the border. She got into the line of those waiting for clearance. To help them pass the time, she sang the beautiful Provençal song *Ad un fin aman von datz*. Translated into English, the first stanza would go something like this:

To a lover, well-disposed,
did the lady's offered favors
show the time and place of joy.
The prize beckoned him to the ev'ning.
With heavy heart he paced all day,
and anxious spake and sighed:
Day, how do you last so long!
O woe!
Night, your delay is my death!

The waiting passengers eyed Beatrice in embarrassment. The border police, who apparently thought the song referred to their work tempo, called for silence and patience. Later Beatrice followed the example of some long-maned young men by tucking the right hank of her hair behind her right ear. Then she reached through the slot at the passport counter, grasped the police officer's hand behind the glass pane as it was about to pick up her papers, shook the hand and congratulated its owner on his liberation. The startled officer thanked her while pointing out that the day of liberation is celebrated on 8 May. He found nothing to object to, however, whereupon he asked Beatrice the reason for her journey. 'To settle in paradise,' said Beatrice. The answer aroused his suspicions again. He admonished Beatrice to give precise answers, in keeping with the seriousness of the situation, adding that the German Democratic Republic wasn't a paradise but a socialist state. 'Thank God,' said Beatrice and raised her right fist in greeting, 'now I'll finally find work.' The police officer returned the greeting by raising the right index finger of his outstretched hand to the brim of his cap. Smiling, he assured her that the right to work was guaranteed by law to all citizens of his country and that there was a great shortage of workers. Every working person who wanted to help solve important problems would be welcome. Beatrice thanked the police officer and praised the gleam of his even white teeth, which set off his brownish skin tone beautifully. The smile disappeared. Throat-clearing. Embarrassed coughing. Return of the passport through the slot with a wish for a speedy recovery. The baggage control registered no objections.

Chapter 2

FURTHER EXALTED AND CONFUSING MOMENTS AFTER ARRIVAL

Shortly after the gate had been opened for Beatrice, the trobadora saw a short fat woman who seemed nicer and more trustworthy than all other women she had seen so far. The woman wore a blue uniform. Beatrice had a suitcase. When she set it at the woman's feet to ask her the location of the nearest employer for troubadours, the woman stood silent for a moment, her eyes wide with astonishment. Then she turned around abruptly. Ran away. And threw up at the entrance of the hall for westbound travelers. Beatrice took a while to recover from this strange encounter. Then she went to the entrance of the hall too and watched the gulls eating the vomit. Beatrice perceived the traffic noise as silence. The air as country air. She crossed the Schiffbauerdamm in a solemn mood. Reached the riverside. Spat into the Spree. A flock of ducks quacked across the water. Swans came swimming over, gulls flew toward her. A swarm of children also moved slowly toward Beatrice. The children were holding each other's hands. Five rows of garlands. Behind them were a young woman and a young man. Beatrice addressed the young man, 'Excuse me, Mr. Nursery-School Teacher, could you tell me where troubadours . . . ' – 'Nursery-school teacher!? You must be new here,' huffed the young man, tapping his forehead with his index finger. 'Yes,' said Beatrice. With an offended expression, the young man kissed the young woman and left. Two trolleys were slowly crossing the hump that the Weidendamm Bridge made in connecting to the street. Squeaking and scraping noises. Beatrice attributed the silence to the local men's efforts on behalf of their looks, concluding that they competed with each other not with snappy cars but with snappy bodies. At that, it seemed unimportant to Beatrice that she had lost the addresses of Parnitzke and his first ex-wife. Besides, the sky was even higher here than in Provence. So high that its color wasn't recognizable. Wonderful homecoming! Endlessly longed for! Beatrice was convinced that the possibility of finally entering history more than made up for the loss of her mother tongue. Moved, she sat down on her suitcase and enjoyed her increased value. Beatrice looked for further signs on the faces of those walking or driving by. And watched the neon letters on the railroad bridge with interest. Of course, the hall for westbound travelers interested her less than the rest of the station. So she began walking, mingling with the people standing around. With suitcases. Without. She looked at the people curiously. Young people. Women. Men. Two of the men Beatrice was scrutinizing addressed her, asking a figure that the trobadora took to be a train number. She replied that she didn't want to leave but was overjoyed to have just arrived. The men didn't seem inclined to share the trobadora's joy conversation-wise. Working escalators from and to the municipal train station displayed to Beatrice several kilometers worth of rolling images of native inhabitants. The two rolling images were going in opposite directions. Beatrice took an hour to let the moving sights confirm her preconceived views. Then a casual reach into her jacket pocket reminded her of reality. The money that the Greifswald sailor had lent her to finance the trip was running out. Determined to support herself now and henceforth by honest work, Beatrice asked several people for the address of the employment office for female troubadours. Blank looks, shrugging of shoulders, winks. Has she lost her marbles. Indignant lip-smacking, abusive language, slaps on the rear, laughter, lectures on the political, moral, and medical significance of the laws against prostitution. Beatrice accounted for the disconcerting answers by the presumably incomprehensible form of her questions. Was the German language so askew on her tongue despite her fanatical efforts to learn it? Was her French accent preventing her from making herself understood at home? Was the trobadora's hope that she would immediately be able to sing in German perhaps an illusion?

A long-haired youth carrying a portable radio in the crook of his arm helped Beatrice temporarily out of her confusion with a few brusque words. He recommended that she apply at the Administrative Office of Concerts and Guest Performances.

Chapter 3

Wherein description of wanderings in the Promised Land begins

Since Beatrice could understand nothing of the directions the young man gave her, he loaded her onto the rear seat of his motorcycle. And drove through many streets and plazas. The streets were mostly bare. The plazas weren't exactly garages either. Beatrice, who was already accustomed to traveling surrounded by metal, suddenly perceived herself as large beyond measure, as if she had grown. Even though her size was unremarkable, compared to the average height of the people on the streets. The unpretentious views awakened supremely good feelings in her. The young man drove Beatrice to the Administrative Office of Concerts and Guest Performances. And carried her suitcase, which had separated her breast from his back during the ride, up to the personnel department. There Beatrice thanked him with a kiss of the hand, turned around, and requested a position as trobadora from the indignant secretary. When the young man had disappeared and the secretary had cast enough contemptuous glances, she referred Beatrice to the dance music department. The director asked to see her professional membership card. Beatrice replied that no membership cards had been issued in the twelfth century and told him the highlights of her life story. While she was speaking, the director left his seat behind the desk. He approached Beatrice cautiously. When she had finished and was about to start singing the 'Canso of Love Betrayed' as a sample of her art, he spread out his arms. Beatrice thought he was going to embrace her so she could feel his welcoming joy. But abruptly found herself deposited politely outside the door. For a moment Beatrice stood there stunned. But upon hearing a female voice in the distance giggle that they had their share of crazies, the trobadora became suspicious and offered resistance. The little man, whose physical strength was no match for the trobadora's, babbled in his desperation that publishing houses have many female employees. If Beatrice could type, her prospects for employment would be favorable. She would then have daily contact with art, for which she obviously had a great liking, and a living to boot. 'Saboteur,' said Beatrice and pressed the man harder against the elevator door with the weight of her whole body. 'Help,' the little man whispered. But since no help was in sight in the spacious hallway, the director, worried about his authority, surrendered the address of the largest publisher of belles lettres in the GDR. Beatrice, convinced she had caught up with a saboteur, saw herself forced by lack of money to let go of him for the time being. But took note of his name. This displeased the man so much that his trouble-fearing brain began working feverishly. The trobadora's scandalous behavior triggered his worst fears. He suddenly realized that he could be prosecuted for criminal mischief. Referrals were a confidential matter, after all. What would happen if the director of the Aufbau-Verlag had no sense of humor? The little man strained to think of a business that stood as far as possible from ideology. His dilemma gave him the idea of ardently extolling the VEB Circus as a better suggestion. Its director had long been asking for a powerful woman with a good imagination. But up to now it had been impossible to fulfill the request, so the position was still vacant. Beatrice would have an excellent chance. Surprisingly, the trobadora was relatively pleased with this white lie. So that Beatrice wouldn't have time to change her mind, the relieved man placed his company car at her disposal.

Chapter 4

Recounting in the trobadora's words and perception what the chauffeur of the company car told her of his friend's story

World concept: One evening after work, Ferdinand Frank, insurance agent, spotted in the newspaper of the man next to him on the subway an announcement that shook him. Deeply, especially since his occasional symptoms had recently been diagnosed by a rheumatologist as signs of age. At that, he had become acutely aware that he had only left Berlin as an army private. Since then he had felt the press of time and an irresistible anxious urge to develop a concept of the world before it was too late. He contemplated motorcycles, cars, speedboats, and even dreamed of a helicopter that could lift him out of the depths of the streets, sky high. This dream was surpassed by the possibilities offered by the ad, inasmuch as they were outside of Frank's way of thinking. To Frank they seemed daring. Only in daring undertakings could he see a solution. Only rigorous life changes seemed appropriate at his age. In addition, the amount called for by the advertisement was less than the lowest price of a drivable car. Since Frank feared, for unclear reasons, that the newspaper might be sold out, he negotiated with his seat mate, who sold him the *Berliner Abendzeitung* after he finished reading it. As the subway train emerged from underground and swept up onto the trestle that crossed the Schönhauser Allee like a centipede, Frank's mind was made up. He got out at the Dimitroffstraße station, squeezed through the barrier and the masses of people pushing down the stairs, and hired a taxi. It took him to the remains of a garden-plot colony on Greifswalderstraße that the advertiser had listed as the viewing site. Women exhibitors running around in house slippers over the surviving strawberry plants helped lay cables between carousels and swings, gave information, and assured Frank that he was not too late. The trailers all looked alike. Light brown wood, metal side strips painted red, the coiled chains hanging on the tailgate were red also; everything was like new. The seller sat on a bulldozer hitched to the advertised object. Right away, he demonstrated the trailer's maneuverability, then showed Frank its fabric and interior furnishings as well. Although the seller was obviously a showman, Frank didn't hesitate. Years of relevant professional experience enabled him to draft a proper sale contract in short order. When it was signed, Frank asked the seller, who claimed to be scaling down his business for reasons of age, to haul the trailer to Schönhauser Allee, where Frank's apartment was. On the way there, they stopped at the savings bank, where Frank withdrew the sum specified by the contract and handed it over. Oddly, the landlady started talking about gypsies. The neighbors declared the purchase to be a consequence of Frank's sudden loss of his wife, which had presumably been harmful to his mental health, and spoke in gently regretful tones. Nevertheless, Frank gave notice at the insurance company and moved furniture from his apartment in the rear building into the trailer, which was parked in the courtyard. Children helped him. He hired a hauling contractor for his first trip. It took him out of the walls of the Prenzlauer Berg district, where he was born and had grown old, over Pankow, Karow, and Buch to Bernau. The bulldozer operator complained that they were using too much gas. Frank paid reluctantly, even though an unexpected inheritance had made him relatively independent. Between birches and pines, he looked for new concepts. Since, to his amazement, he found none, he had himself towed further. This time to the south. The tractor-trailer rig recruit declared the chassis to be unusable, having broken down twice already. Frank felt cheated by the showman. And thus confirmed in his view of that profession. Happy. When he was looking in the direction of the traffic. After stops in Fürstenwalde and Beeskow, both times parking the trailer at the edge of town and again waiting in vain for the longed-for feeling of foreignness, he hired two tractors to tow him to Doberlug-Kirchhain. As fast as possible, for he hoped to escape what was following him by speeding. Several times during the drive, the wagon jerked and shook as though something were being ripped away, so that Frank gave a happy start and hurried to the back window. To no avail; the city tagged along behind. A gigantic train. He dragged it after him over highways and country roads, brick roofs for the most part, older buildings with identical trim, war-scarred with iron balcony railings or worn balconies with rusting cross sections of sawed-off iron girders, new high-rises, Lenin von Tomski, playground climbing bars, double-decker busses, the solar eclipselike light of the Dimitroffstraße gas works, garden plots, border security posts, Mont Klamott, the insurance building, Zillen, the Treptow memorial, the electronic appliance factory, the Warsaw Bridge, Ostkreuz, the trestle of the elevated railway over the Schönhauser Allee, the rear courtyard with its garbage cans and two mountain ash trees that all windows of the apartment looked out onto. Frank yelled orders to the tractor operator, urging him on, out beyond Doberlug-Kirchhain. In vain. No matter where he headed, he never arrived. He was always hitched to his city, cut through the middle by a border. He was at home everywhere and compared his concept of the world to the foreign one and found it beautiful and sought to change the others according to his image.

Chapter 5

Wherein the Reader Is Told, among Other Things, Why a VEB Director Grabs the Beautiful Melusine's Bosom

The director of the VEB Circus received Beatrice cordially. Couldn't for the life of him remember having made a call to the Office of Concerts and Guest Performances. He had no position for a powerful woman with a good imagination. But listened willingly to all the stanzas of the

'Canso of Love Betrayed,' which Beatrice had composed in 1158 for the unreal Raimbaut d'Aurenga. The first stanza, translated into German by Mr. Franz Wellner, would go like this in English:

I'm forced to sing, no matter what I do.
Such agony for him whom I desire,
for whom I am consumed as by naught else.
Not how in charming grace I favored him,
not rank nor mind nor beauty regards he.
Leaves me behind, abandoned and betrayed
as I'd deserve if I had been a monster . . .

The performance amused the circus director. He applauded, took two glasses and a bottle of schnapps from his desk drawer, and poured drinks for himself and Beatrice. The trobadora saw this procedure as promising. After the toasts were exchanged, she expected to be hired. But the director, after downing his schnapps with a grimace, regretted that he couldn't offer Beatrice employment in her field. All current programs of the individual circus operations under his supervision were already supplied with musical clown performances. Fully staffed in other respects as well. All he needed was a highly qualified animal trainer. Because of an accident. In the Circus Eos, two lions had bitten a trainer so severely that she had to be hospitalized. The director spoke of the risks to the artists in this profession and other disadvantages of the roving life. Beatrice spoke of the advantages of the roving life. At that, the trap door of the air shaft sprang open. The director was startled. Strange plaintive cries were heard. Then the statement: 'People believe great truths more readily in unlikely clothing.' Beatrice didn't believe her ears. But felt the strange excitement that always preceded her poetic inspirations, sudden decisions, and related productive states. Finally she pulled herself together and cried out, 'Is it you, is it you at last, free? I must be crazy.' —'Who are you talking to?' asked the director, more than baffled. 'My sister-in-law Marie de Lusignan, who was jailed in France for nearly two years. Awaiting trial? I'm telling you, nearly two years in detention, awaiting trial. Just imagine those conditions. Appearing in human form was always risky for her. And I wait and wait until I'm blue in the face. Literally. Can you imagine a trobadora as a greengrocer's wife? In spite of her inconspicuous disguise, the cops must have found out somehow that my sister-in-law can do magic and feared that she might falsify the election results. The police don't realize how powerless Persephone is. If my sister-in-law could do political magic, France would have long since become a socialist country. Have you never heard of the Beautiful Melusine?' — The director had ample experience with con artists. Therefore, he reverted to a businesslike tone, curtly and gruffly demanding a qualifying certificate. Since the trobadora possessed nothing in writing, she asked permission to present a practical one and called out, 'Are you ready?' — 'Always ready,' replied the voice from the air shaft. 'I don't need any ventriloquists,' said the director, who was now losing patience. 'I need an animal trainer, madame, an animal trainer, if you understand what I mean. However, I have no beasts of prey in my office!' — 'But I do,' said Beatrice, and whistled, putting her thumb and index finger into her mouth. Then there was a blast of wind, a howling and hissing. The trap door clattered, flew wide open, clouds of dust rose up: through the air shaft of the VEB Circus administration building the Beautiful Melusine appeared in the flesh. In the shape of a Sphinx: half dragon, half woman. Beatrice celebrated her reunion with her sister-in-law by ardently embracing and kissing the upper, female half. The director struggled to regain his composure quickly, since the female half, like the other half, was naked. So he left his desk, stepped across the armored back toward Beatrice, confessed to having worked twenty-one years as a magician, congratulated her with collegial admiration on the trick, and placed his left hand under the Beautiful Melusine's left breast. To check the material. Surprised for a second time, he admitted defeat as a magician and promptly hired the trobadora under a seasonal contract.

Chapter 6

Wherein Irmtraud Morgner tries by means of a solemn oath to persuade certain male readers to keep on reading

Gentlemen!

Hereby I do solemnly swear based on my own observation that the physical Beatrice de Dia was a woman who matched today's ideal of beauty completely. I guarantee that she looked absolutely youthful. Even on her deathbed, her figure could be described as flawless. The poet

Guntram Pomerenke cited 92-61-90 centimeters as her typical measurements. Had Beatrice not met the prevailing standards of beauty and age at the time she bore witness, you, gentlemen, would of course cast doubt upon Beatrice's general truths, dismiss her particular women's-rights ideas straight away as defective and toss this book into the fire. For in contrast to men, whom you understand as differentiated beings with differentiated needs, you think of women as monolithic. For which reason you trace all their cares, problems, and suffering back to one single defect. And this single optimal defect is of course yourselves. Gentlemen, bluntly stated: your middle part. — In the hope that my pragmatic explanation makes you, gentlemen, inclined to grant the right of existence not only to the works of the hunchbacked Herr Kant (Immanuel) and similar eminent authorities, I remain,

with socialist greetings
Irmtraud Morgner

Chapter 7
Instructive crossing to Leipzig

The Circus Eos was still in its winter quarters in Leipzig. The trobadora took the train to her first job. In the dining car she ate a tough schnitzel with red cabbage and fried potatoes. Beatrice quelled her rising irritation at having to chew so hard by striking up a conversation with her neighbor. The neighbor was a soldier serving a fixed term. A private whose professional goal was commissioned officer. Using simple sentences suitable for note-taking, he explained various maneuvers that Beatrice could view from the train window. What impressed her most were the caterpillar tractors that had left wavy tread marks on the roadways along the railroad track. Deep wavy grooves were filled with water. The design of the caterpillars was different from the ones the Beautiful Melusine had shown the trobadora hypnopedically during her sleep through World War II. Beatrice was reasonably well informed about military subjects, also economic ones, but her sister-in-law had grossly neglected the moral side. The soldier told the trobadora that the People's National Army was supported in these maneuvers by the staffs and units of their brother armies, the Bulgarians, Hungarians, Poles, Soviets, and Czechs; the members of the air force and air defense troops were always ready and in a position to reliably protect the socialist camp's airspace. 'Do dragons show up on radar screens too?' asked Beatrice. The soldier gave her to understand that he found discussion of children's toys inappropriate in military conversations. Beatrice worried about Melusine, who would be choosing air travel, as always. Distractedly, the trobadora proved to the soldier that she was well versed in the theoretical foundations of Marxism-Leninism also. Then the soldier showed Beatrice in confidence an ad that he had placed in the newspaper *Wochenpost*. The ad, which he had cut out and saved in his passbook, ran as follows: 'Who wants to take a chance? Soldier, 19 yr., 1 m. 72, lt. brn. hair; int. mus., photog., winter sp., seeks attr. dk-haired slim f. (18–25) w/ progr. worldview as penp. Cottbus-Frankf. area prefd. Marriage not imposs. Letter w/ photo (w. be returned) to 523 DEWAG 95 Zwickau.' — At first, it was the abbreviated words that impeded Beatrice's understanding of the ad, then her preconceived ideas. After the soldier had explained his action in terms of lack of opportunity and provided a translation, Beatrice waxed enthusiastic. For she was convinced that he was the first man she had met who would tell his wife the tales of the thousand and one nights. She ordered a bottle of red wine, since there was no more champagne. The waiter requested immediate payment because the shift was changing. Beatrice paid her bill and her neighbor's from the advance on her wages. She attributed the soldier's loss of composure to the mundane character of the drink. To raise the soldier's spirits, Beatrice said that she'd like to hear one of his stories sometime. 'Have you ever met a woman whose husband tells her the tales of the thousand and one nights?' the soldier asked. — 'Not yet, but you have,' answered Beatrice. — 'Me,' the soldier said indignantly. 'What do you think I am?' Adding that he would only consider full-blooded women. Besides, he had never led a dissolute life or put girls off with idle talk. There ensued a short lecture on healthy, clean sexuality. Beatrice couldn't follow the lecture. She blamed this inability on a headache: after the Bitterfeld stop, overpowering odors had penetrated the train. The soldier didn't neglect to mention that maneuvers and armaments would be superfluous once the exploitation of man by man was eliminated in all countries. 'And the exploitation of woman by man?' asked Beatrice. — 'What?' said the soldier. Beatrice attributed his lack of understanding to the ideal conditions in his country. After the train had already reached Möckern, Beatrice hastily told the soldier a dark fairy tale, appropriately revised and updated, that would cast the ideal conditions in the proper light and prevent the young man from mistaking achievements for self-evident facts.

Chapter 8

Verbatim text of the fairy tale Beatrice tells a soldier to encourage his gratitude

Once upon a time, there was a girl named Obilot. She lived in a dreadful country. The king was so rich that he could give his portrait to all his female subjects for their baptism. It was painted by the best artists; the arts flourished in this country. The only thing the king demanded in return for his gift was love. The king looked like a wild boar. All the women admired him and deceived their husbands by displaying his image behind their closed eyelids during marital relations. Girls pictured their chosen ones as wild boars before falling in love. All the girls except Obilot. She loved a man. He was beautiful of head and stature, a baker by profession. Every morning he threw a hot breakfast roll against her window. Every evening she opened her bedroom door to him. By tradition of the country, the king's picture hung there; the girl's parents were respectable people, and she was living under their roof. To ward off the portrait's superior strength, Obilot dubbed the baker an emperor. With the truth of her love she took off first her clothes, then her hair, skin, fat, and finally all her flesh. Her skeleton found its resting place next to the baking trough where the baker kneaded his dough in the early morning hours.

Chapter 9

Wherein the reader is finally told of a Pyrrhic victory

At the central train station in Leipzig, Beatrice was greeted by the antipodean artist Orlando. He brought her three chrysanthemums and greetings from Madame Eos, the circus director. Since the trobadora's suitcase was too heavy for Orlando's arms, he hired a porter with a baggage cart. Orlando lay down on his back on the cart and raised his legs. When his shoe soles were vertically exposed to the sooty glass roof of the station, the artist told Beatrice to throw the suitcase toward his shoes when he gave the order. Beatrice did as she was told. Orlando caught the suitcase with the tip of his right foot, upended it, shifted it to the left foot and back again, and continued in this way to the exit. While the porter and Beatrice transported the cart across the stairs of the east hall, Orlando made the suitcase spin like a top. Performed balancing acts with his eyes blindfolded and other tricks until they reached the circus director's apartment across from the winter quarters. Madame Eos greeted Beatrice warmly and led her through a pair of bead curtains. Over animal hides. The trobadora was offered a seat on a pillow-laden sofa. She could barely find room. The pillowcases were embroidered with horses and proverbial sayings. On a baroque desk stood autographed photos in gold frames. On the walls hung shelves holding files, circus literature, the stuffed head of a polar bear, porcelain animals, wineglasses, and other crystal. A round table stood under a Japanese lamp. Tablecloth of crocheted lace. Its fringes brushed the padded seats of four gold-painted chairs. Madame Eos sat down in a red wing chair that set off her white curls beautifully. 'The accident suffered by your colleague during training has delayed our departure,' said Madame Eos in measured north-Saxon tones. Beatrice was quickly getting used to this intonation. Its decided pleasantness was so confidence inspiring that the trobadora refrained from fabricating a previous circus career. Through her demeanor, Madame Eos reinforced Beatrice's regained conviction that century-long sleeps were not a rarity. The fact that the men she had met so far knew no ladies from other time periods proved nothing except how insufferable those men were. Or how uninhabitable France was for women who weren't willing to trace their origin back to a man's rib. Beatrice told her life story in detail, because Madame Eos kept saying 'interesting,' 'indeed,' and 'charming'; meanwhile, she made a telephone call. While hearing the description of the singing contest between Raimbaut d'Aurenga and Beatrice held in 1152 in the palace of Count Valentinois, Madame Eos got the idea for a directorship. At once she had Beatrice put on the nightgown she had slept in for 808 years. 'Marvelously anti-fashion,' said Madame Eos. 'Little one, we'll create a medieval Orpheus number for you, the first musical Sphinx-trainer act in the world. Your maxi-skirt will have to be slit up both sides, of course.' Madame Eos immediately fetched a pair of scissors. Beatrice found the expression 'little one' inappropriate coming from the lips of someone at least 775 years younger than she. An hour later Beatrice was already standing in the circus arena. Giving the scene builder directions for constructing an imitation chimney that would cut through the four-pole tent. Without a chimney the Beautiful Melusine wouldn't be able to land. Without the Beautiful Melusine the trobadora wouldn't be allowed to sing. When the scene was finished the next morning and the Sphinx was sprawling in the sand shortly after the whistle signal, Madame Eos was touched to realize that the director of the VEB Circus had written the literal truth in his telegram. Madame Eos had never before met a circus artist with powers such as these. She threw out her idea of a directorship and released Beatrice from singing. Because it would detract from the show effect. 'Scandal!' screamed Beatrice. Unaware that contradicting them is the least effective form of interaction with retired women animal trainers. Besides, Beatrice's behavior was so stunningly inexplicable to Madame Director that she could only see it as harebrained and unfathomable. So she made a big scene. Beatrice wasn't slow either. Reinforced by three years of Raimbaut's childhood, her character, after overcoming certain physical crises, had recovered to the extent of refusing compromises. In the end, Beatrice threw the contract down at Madame Director's feet and turned away. Toward the curtained exit. Red plush, the folds billowing in the drafty air. The musicians were practicing above the plush. The bandmaster held his funneled hands to his mouth and asked through the funnel whether the musical accompaniment was being dropped. 'All of it,' said Beatrice. And tripped over the Beautiful Melusine. At that the Sphinx lashed the sand with her armor-plated tail so that the dust flew, rose into the harsh-smelling air of the arena, flew three rounds about the trapeze, and spoke: 'Moralists are squeamish. But politicians are smart. The end justifies the means. If they read you in the newspaper first, you will also be allowed to sing.' Then Melusine landed, fished the contract out of the sand, handed it to the director, and promised Beatrice on her honor that her interests would still be guaranteed. So the trobadora was pacified. Madame Eos promptly had the already printed posters of predators shredded and new ones printed. Writing the text was difficult because she didn't know how to surpass the old title, 'Trained Animal Acts: World Sensation.' Finally she settled on 'The Most Sensational Animal Trainer of All Time.' On 21 March 1970 Circus Eos went on tour. Their first engagement was in Karl-Marx-Stadt. In Halle they had to extend their stay from four days to eleven because of the huge demand for tickets; in Weimar they stayed two entire weeks giving two performances a day in a sold-out tent. The VEB Circus director sent Beatrice a congratulatory telegram. In it, he asked the trobadora for a report on her successful visit to Weimar for the monthly magazine *Artistry Today*.

Chapter 10

The most sensational enchanted animal trainer of all time reports on her arrival in Weimar

Goethe Park: the wind blows warm in my ears. Wafts into the wood, rocking the branches covered with tender green webs. The earth yields softly under my feet. The high muddy water of the Ilm sloshes as it meanders through the valley. Visitors on benches read brochures; I buy one too. In the garden house, as I look at the view from the windows of Goethe's study, poetry seems to be a successor institution. The walls of the stone-floored room next to the kitchen are overwhelmed with views of Rome. Watercress along the riverbank. I envy the real herd of sheep, envy the German shepherd dog rolling in the grass even more, and the sparrows bathing in dust. At least take a walk, with arms raised, palms outstretched as when listening to music — not at all. I pick a violet for Melusine. I press it in the 1840 edition of a book on the symbolism of dreams, just purchased in the antiquarian bookstore. Young Pioneers from the children's home ride by. Two slight-statured music students from Ceylon are leaning on the bridge railing in the tribhanga pose. And I admire the adventuresome beards and hairstyles of the architecture students and their girls, whose faces are adorned with intense colors. Uncertainly, I pass them wearing my conservative attire. Metal brooms, wielded by overall-clad men, scrape dry leaves from the paths. Insistently visible on all sides is the intent to preserve this once-and-for-all order against the burgeoning powers of the imminent summer. Trees creak. Bird songs and droppings fall from the treetops. The words *Francisco Dessaviae Principi* inscribed on a boulder have been chalked over with rhombuses.

Chapter 11

Verbatim text of a secret pact of mutual assistance between the would-be politician Melusine and the would-be trobadora Beatrice

Bound by a specific pact system that the undersigned parties, in dire straits and powerless, were forced to transact with the disempowered powers of the underworld and the upper world, the said parties have agreed, for their part, to draw up a pact of mutual assistance. Herein the trobadora Beatrice promises to provide agitprop art to the born politician Melusine in support of her ideological work. Melusine promises to supply inspiration, resp. peace and quiet for meditation, to her sister-in-law by means of black magic. The agitprop art is to be produced for capitalist relations, the overthrow of which is the focus of Melusine's illegal activity. Battle cry of the requisite protest songs: A woman today who can afford to have character must be a socialist. In keeping with her abilities, Beatrice shall concentrate her activity, to be kept secret from the disempowered powers, on socialist relations, carrying out work that changes and shapes morality. The contractual partners expect greater effectiveness through specialization and protection from ivory-tower idiocy through collaboration.

signed Melusine
signed Beatrice de Dia

Chapter 12

Which reproduces word for word a letter to the editor of the Karl-Marx-Stadt *Free Press*, titled 'Desecration of Our Cultural Heritage'

As a woman who passionately admires the circus arts, I always look forward with great interest to the guest performances of our national circus. Since health considerations required me to reside in Karl-Marx-Stadt temporarily, I naturally attended a performance of the Circus Eos, which I hold in high esteem. The poster for the program 'Most Sensational Animal Trainer of All Time' listed a name that seemed familiar. But, of course, I did not think it possible that a state-owned enterprise would allow this sort of tastelessness, which is tantamount to desecration of a famous name, that is, of our cultural heritage, and is an insult to all women. For in fact, Beatrice de Dia was the name of a female troubadour from Provence in the twelfth century. I protest the disparaging misuse of a progressive woman's name. I condemn the mendacious announcement, calculated to catch fools, of a cheap magic act that is actually a striptease. In the name of the Venceremos brigade, I demand the withdrawal of this slapstick performance, in which a Sphinx costume is misused to revive the reactionary theories of Max Funk and his gang on females as half-humans and the missing link between anthropoid and *Homo sapiens.* Have the ideological winds of the Circus Eos died down?

Laura Salman, Trolley-Car Driver
1055 Berlin, Osterstraße 37

Chapter 13
FLIGHT ON A DRAGON'S BACK

At the request of Madame Director Eos, the newspaper clipping service VEB Progress provided Beatrice with all printed materials that mentioned her name. The postal worker brought Laura Salman's letter to Erfurt, along with a collection of flattering reviews. In the morning Beatrice threw the reviews into the stove in her trailer, in the evening she threw the letter at the Beautiful Melusine's head. Then she climbed on her back, thrust her heels into the armor-plated flanks, and put her sister-in-law to flight in the direction of 1055 Berlin. For the trobadora had immediately recognized the address at the end of the letter as the one she had misplaced, that of Parnitzke's first ex-wife. The Beautiful Melusine pounded the muggy night air furiously with her wings. Whereby a rattling noise was generated, comparable to that produced by striking plastic dishes together. Beatrice could even feel the leathery hide brush her ears at times, so powerfully did the wings reach out. The Beautiful Melusine also made sharp turns and steep fluctuations in altitude in order to punish Beatrice's behavior. Which the Sphinx could not help but perceive as insulting. Was ingratitude her reward for helping by word and deed? Did this out-of-touch contessa believe she would always get special favors? Did she perhaps imagine that it was already possible for women to live without pragmatism? 'Your advice has amputated my honor,' said Beatrice. — 'Indeed,' said Melusine. — 'The circus act has made me look ridiculous as a trobadora,' said Beatrice. — 'Not even a great male poet can become famous all at once without a scandal,' Melusine replied. 'Better tainted than dead.' The beautiful half of her body gleamed in the moonlight. Her figure was as well preserved as her sister-in-law's. And like hers, felt a bit coarse to the touch. Beatrice had to hold tight to her neck to avoid being thrown off by the wind and the abrupt turns. Melusine's breasts were covered by a kind of chemise. In her anger at her sister-in-law, Beatrice couldn't refrain from asking if the garment was meant as the sign of a corrective change in her forward movement. 'I'm cold,' answered the Beautiful Melusine. 'I'm not one of those women who quote theories of frustration to cover up their conformity. I've adapted and put on clothes, for you. I wanted to spare you the dirty work, my love; a female troubadour's potential public has well-entrenched habits that must be taken into consideration before you can try to improve upon them. Life is not pure. And only those who don't work make no mistakes.' Melusine's style of speech reminded Beatrice of certain debates among the members of the Paris commune. Also, the armor-plated back was so sharp that Beatrice was soon suffering from seating discomfort, for which reason she couldn't properly enjoy the beauties of a nocturnal flight on a dragon's back. Since the air was clear, the sky seemed to Beatrice to be everywhere. Above her it was star-studded all over, below her in heaps. The lights of the populated areas, which she took for clusters of stars, intensified her fanatical mood. Above Wittenberg the trobadora burst into speech accordingly.

Chapter 14

Trobadora Beatrice's self-criticism above the Luther city, Wittenberg

Instead of progressive powers, I have depended on ghosts of the past. Instead of love, I have sown hate. I have yielded opportunistically to the pressure of unclear elements. I have shortsightedly followed a direction that would sacrifice the goal for the journey. This direction counts on ambition, addiction to praise, and unprincipled behaviors, which put an end to solidarity. Down with the slogan 'the end justifies the means,' for reprehensible means defile the noblest ends. Giving in to evil ways means preserving or even promoting evil ways. The trolley driver Laura Salman has opened my eyes with her letter. I thank her for her helpful criticism and promise to learn from it.

Chapter 15

A farewell with serious consequences

Toward morning the Beautiful Melusine landed on a smokestack of the Dimitroffstraße gas works in Berlin instead of on Laura Salman's chimney. For she'd had enough of the trobadora's accusations and self-reproaches. 'Sentimental claptrap,' said the Beautiful Melusine, 'dumb people with initiative are the worst imaginable human type for politics or the military. See how well you get along by yourself.' Thereupon, Beatrice canceled their allegiance and declared the mutual assistance pact null and void, to punish Melusine for her insulting words. Her sister-in-law accepted the termination. Laughed so hard, in fact, that her armor-plated belly bumped the smokestack. But she soon began coughing. Because thick brown smoke was billowing out of the opening of the smokestack. It obscured the thicket of buildings in Prenzlauer Berg that had just emerged from the night. The rows of gas-works furnaces disappeared, also the cooling towers, steaming fire engines, mounds of coke, crane installations, railway sidings, the trolley station. And the two women could only hear each other. The last cough-interrupted words that Beatrice heard from the Beautiful Melusine were: 'Impatient people must depend on miracles. You're punishing yourself.' As a gust of wind dispersed the smoke, the Sphinx was already aloft in the polluted air. She circled the steel scaffolding of the dome three times. Then she headed south and quickly vanished from Beatrice's sight.

Chapter 16

The trobadora finds Laura and herself

Beatrice relished the heroic taste of her decision made in dire straits. The smokestack was 136 meters high. Since the trobadora intended to forego miracles from now on, without recanting, the first serious test of her own strength was getting down. Beatrice fought off her fear by counting the iron rungs. She was at 273 when she touched the ground. Covered with soot. The coating camouflaged her. And thus she succeeded in leaving the factory grounds without a pass; the porter even said good morning to her. However, taxi drivers emphatically refused to transport Beatrice unwashed. The men and women at the trolley stops glared Beatrice away from them. So the trobadora was forced to ask the way to Osterstraße 37 on foot. The smell of the gas works was still very noticeable in front of the desired building. The style of the façade reminded Beatrice of simulated woodworm infestations in imitation period furniture. Entrance via courtyard. Apartment on the fourth floor, right. Cardboard name plate. Working doorbell. The two women recognized each other at once. Although Beatrice tumbled into Laura Salman's house with the above-mentioned self-criticism. In need of a bath. Although Laura had gained considerable weight since their first meeting at the Friedrichstraße train station. By now she could hardly see her feet. Next to her, Beatrice's reflection in the wardrobe mirror seemed excessively tall and gaunt. She kept her composure while Laura laughed until tears came to her eyes over the self-criticism and disappeared into the bath. Where she had to start the water heater. Beatrice stepped uncertainly into the heated water. Which improved the acoustics of the bathroom. Beatrice felt her voice sounding refined, as in the cave concert halls of Les Baux, as she tried to describe her Paris meeting with Parnitzke. 'In him, for the first time in my life I found a man who is bigger inside than outside,' said Beatrice. 'He even understands that there's a connection between historical consciousness and self-consciousness. Which is why it isn't enough simply to give the expropriated their material possessions back. Are you feeling better now?' — 'Much better,' said Laura. 'Was Uwe unable to take his eyes off you? On the one hand, you're his ideal type.' — 'And on the other hand? At any rate, he's an endearing person,' said Beatrice. 'When I heard that two women here had left him, I thought to myself: That's the place to go! Can you really be so choosy?' — Unmoved, Laura soaped the soot from Beatrice's back. Conceding, however, that she believed Uwe to be not only an honorable human being but also a typical phenomenon. Not until after her bath did the trobadora find out that the letter to the editor had been authored by a student at the College of Communication and Transportation, a woman who was completing her practicum in Laura's brigade. So Laura hadn't even seen Beatrice's circus act, only heard about it in the student's critical description. And at the latter's request, allowed the use of her name, because the student believed a proletarian voice would carry more weight. Incidentally, Laura had stopped driving trolleys through Berlin months before publication of the letter. Instead, she was working light duty that had been assigned to her until her maternity leave began. 'The changes I was feeling for the first time when you met me were treated as an upset stomach for seven weeks until the doctors thought of the obvious,' said Laura cheerfully. 'Of course, this country is a land of miracles. But I didn't realize it until I began making a human being and met one. Who was already old, ancient. Does one feel superior when one is ancient?' — 'On the contrary,' said Beatrice, 'only someone who knows everything or nothing can feel superior. Do I look ancient?' — Laura smacked her lips indignantly. — 'Of course, I must look it, otherwise you wouldn't know . . . ' — 'But you said yourself . . . ' — 'I didn't say a word, not one word about my past, not even to Uwe. After all, I . . . ' — 'Beatrice de Dia, wife of Herr Guilhem de Poitiers and Herr Théophile Gerson. Parnitzke, of course, introduced you as Comrade Gerson . . . ' Only then did the two women realize that they were using *du* with each other. And they admitted defeat and embraced. United in the conviction that one doesn't have to know everything. Indeed, that sometimes there is nothing to know and that only confusion would arise if one tried to find out.

Chapter 17

WHEREIN IS DESCRIBED WHAT BEATRICE DE DIA FOUND OUT, LITTLE BY LITTLE, ABOUT LAURA'S PAST LIFE

Laura was the only daughter of the engine driver Johann Salman and his wife, Olga. In the twelfth grade of the school Laura attended, the comrade boys chose the People's Army and the comrade girls the humanities. Laura enrolled at Humboldt University. In her first semester, she fell in love with the economics major Axel. Who was good looking and fit Laura's body perfectly. So he soon got her with child. In fear of her parents' disapproval, Laura swallowed quinine. To no avail. Then fear of possible damage to the fetus turned Laura's anxiety into panic. She appealed to physicians, who, not wanting to commit a crime, offered her no help but did humiliate her. A gynecologist with two degrees asked, 'Did you think fun was free of charge?' One who had only a Ph.D. demanded fun for himself and a thousand marks. A woman whom Laura told about the quinine said feebleminded children were a punishment from God. Finally Laura resorted to a knitting needle. And inflicted a dangerous injury. But was discharged from the hospital. When Axel picked her up there, she said good-by to him forever. In her second semester she fell in love with the philosophy professor K. and sat in the first row whenever possible to hear his lectures. In her third semester she married the graduate assistant Uwe Parnitzke. Who was quiet and hard-working and didn't fit Laura's body. Sometimes she sang fight songs to lute music for him; as a member of the university choir, she had access to a large repertoire of this genre. Sometimes they went together to performances by the folk-art ensemble. Since Uwe was an even-tempered, disciplined, and unselfish person, Laura could live in near-freedom from monthly anxiety, and in contrast to many other female students, was able to take her state teacher's exam without having interrupted her studies. Research assistantship. Laura's fear of having suffered damage from her abortion proved to be unfounded. In the first year of her assistantship, she gave birth to a baby girl. Who was given the name Juliane. The director of the institute arranged for a day-care space for Juliane. The happy mother dropped her daughter off at childcare in the morning, picked her up in the evening, washed diapers and all the other family laundry, cooked, shopped, cleaned the apartment, took the baby to the doctor, took care of her when she was sick. Uwe, a journalist, was often away on business trips at the time. Laura fell behind with the commentary she was writing for an edition her professor was working on. He pronounced her research reports on the poet Frank Wedekind to be increasingly unsatisfactory. Sometimes she conducted seminars unprepared. Sometimes even dropped her daughter off at childcare with a slight fever in order to keep up with her teaching responsibilities. In 1958, eleven days before her first birthday, Juliane died of pneumonia. Soon thereafter Laura charged herself with lacking ideological clarity and asked to be transferred to production. During the following years, she worked for the State Enterprise Construction in Heidenau and on renowned construction sites in the republic. In 1959, after five years of marriage, Laura divorced Uwe, who characterized her behavior as proletarian-worship, gold-digger romanticism, and a detriment to family life. Since 1965 she had been a trolley driver in Berlin.

Chapter 18

An offer is made to Laura

The truthful report moved Beatrice to qualify Laura as her minstrel. 'We have sought and found each other,' said the trobadora enthusiastically. Laura, who couldn't imagine exactly what a minstrel was, assumed she would be applying for a service job along the lines of domestic worker or baby-sitter. Whereby her exuberance was severely dampened. Therefore, she felt the following fundamental declaration was called for: 'In the first place, every human being, no matter what gender, should clean up their own dirt. And in the second place, driving a trolley is not my occupation but my profession.' — 'Wonderful,' Beatrice replied, 'sedentary people aren't suited to be minstrels.' She tried to convince Laura that the job she was offering would be easy, since writing poetry wasn't required. As is well known, in the old days minstrels had composed many texts themselves — songs, fairy tales, whole epics. But she would definitely write all the songs herself; all she would need was lute playing, some interpretations, and a certain amount of organizational assistance. This information diffused Laura's suspicions and put her into a conciliatory mood but didn't change her mind. The only explanation Beatrice could find for the current unpopularity of this profession was a lack of qualified workers. Because she knew from reading the newspaper that local poets traveled across the country no less often than the Provençal troubadours had done. Were all GDR poets able to present their works to good advantage? Loudly enough? Compared to factory lecture halls, the Provençal castles were intimate chambers. Did all the poets of this country have voluminous voices? When the audience was small or disinterested, the Provençal troubadours would often simply sit and watch, letting the minstrel carry the entire program. Beatrice had also had male minstrels. But female minstrels were useful in a greater variety of ways: taking care of uninteresting or unreasonable rendezvous that the trobadora couldn't afford to turn down for reasons of etiquette would have been part of the female minstrel's usual work. Beatrice hastened to assure Laura that she wouldn't have to deal with these situations if she took the job. Laura reminded her indignantly that she'd taken the position at the Greifswalderstraße station to sell trolley tickets and do a respectable job of producing her child. In a word, she requested a different topic of conversation and made coffee. Beatrice couldn't help praising the coffee. Laura couldn't help disapproving of the letter to the editor and the self-criticism. For being too true. 'You lack pragmatism,' said Laura. 'Thank goodness,' said Beatrice, 'and you lack character.' 'Thank goodness,' said Laura and told an all-too-true story.

Chapter 19

Which recounts the story that Laura characterized as too true

Café au contraire: Our women's brigade was drinking cappuccino at the Alexanderplatz Espresso recently when a man who was a feast for the eyes entered the establishment. So I whistled the scale up and down and looked the gentleman over, up and down. As he passed our table, I said, 'Damn!' Then our brigade discussed his feet, which were sockless; we estimated his waist measurement at seventy centimeters, his age as thirty-two. His fashion shirt clung to his shoulder blades, indicating a lean build. Narrow head with protruding ears, blunt-cut hair that some backwoods barber had shaved up the neck so the hairline didn't reach his shirt collar, which is my specialty. I recommended that he take up rowing to correct the bad posture of his beautiful shoulders. Since the gentleman was seated at a corner table, we had to talk very loudly. I ordered a double vodka for him and me and drank to his health while he tried to convince the server there had been a mistake. Later I went to his table, said excuse me, but didn't we know each other from somewhere, and sat down on the chair next to him. I insisted that the gentleman look over the wine list and asked his preference. Since he had none, I pressed my knee against his, ordered three rounds of slivovitz, and threatened revenge for the insult it would be if he didn't drink up. Although the gentleman was neither appreciative nor amusing but speechless, I paid the bill and escorted him out of the bar. In the doorway I slipped my hand as if by accident across one cheek of his behind, to check the tissue structure. Since I could find no shortcoming, I invited him to the Cinema International. An inner struggle that was becoming increasingly visible on his pretty face now distorted it into a grimace but finally overcame his consternation and loosened his tongue, so that the gentleman burst out, 'Look here, you have outrageous manners!' — 'No, ordinary ones,' I replied. 'You're just not used to being treated like a lady.'

Chapter 20

Wherein Laura's inventive spirit finally wins a narrow victory

Laura's story plunged Beatrice into despair. So much so that she locked herself in the bathroom. Sitting on the edge of the tub, she could hear the promises of her friend, who was rattling the doorknob: veal cutlets, Cinzano, Mozart. Beatrice found the promises tasteless, indeed, insultingly inappropriate. At that, her teardrops fell onto her skirt faster than the water into the tub. And the rattling noise in the water pipes awakened associations of machine guns. All her hopes mowed down, everything wiped out with one salvo. 'I'm a corpse,' said Beatrice as she came out of the bathroom after a while. 'A wandering corpse. Only too true. Like history. Which is an oath of manifestation. Ach, Laura, goddamn me.' — 'Ach, Beatrice, goddamn me,' replied Laura with a guilty conscience and escorted her friend onto the balcony. There the heat of the sun reflected back from the plaster walls. Small stones and other debris that the last rain had washed out of the plaster crunched under their feet. Fine ashes fell from the smoggy sky. A grayish brown gasworks cloud hid the sun temporarily. There was barely enough room for the two women on the roofless balcony. Beatrice sat leaning forward on her chair. Laura sat spraddle-legged and leaning back, her hands clasped over the lower half of her rounded belly. Which is why the statement 'It's not all that bad' came easily from her lips. 'What?' shrieked Beatrice, as if a nerve had been struck by the dentist's drill, 'I've slept 808 years for nothing. All of a sudden, I understand that I'll still have to deny my vocation: deny myself. No wonder I can't find proper employment. Customs don't allow it. One can't find what doesn't exist. A passive troubadour, an object that sings of a subject, is logically unthinkable. A paradox.' — 'It's a joke,' acknowledged Laura. 'In this country eroticism is the last domain that belongs to men. In all other areas the laws of our land grant women equal rights. Must you take issue professionally with this last domain of all things, which can scarcely be captured in legal terms and which understandably the men stubbornly defend? Couldn't you find something else . . . ' — 'No,' said Beatrice brusquely. 'Now it no longer distresses me that I still haven't met any female professional colleagues either. If female troubadours are, in principle, felt to be just as impermissible today as eight hundred years ago, then nothing more exists now than then. Could you perhaps tell me how to persuade Persephone to give me eight hundred more years of sleep?' — 'No,' said Laura. Also brusquely. She condemned conclusions like these as weak. Actually, she shared her father's view of people who don't face the realties of life. Accepting the realties wouldn't have to mean wholesale affirmation, she continued. In any case, the process of life demanded pride, realpolitik, a talent for improvisation. And consisted of the ability to struggle through. Miracles, okay, but no private ones for slackers. And anyway, there were no stories that are too true. There were only true and untrue stories. And since Laura could easily prove that she had lied . . . ' — 'Frivolous tricks,' said Beatrice. Hastily, Laura asserted that private miracles were frivolous tricks. Beatrice called Laura squeamish. Facing realties could only be judged a sign of strength if you had good luck. 'A person who is condemned to life imprisonment and doesn't make plans to escape is not proud but cowardly. Didn't you also bewail the lack of solidarity among women? That's natural among those who have been humiliated for millennia. Their hope of escaping from a hopeless situation could only be based on miracles, that is, on individual actions. I have exited history because I wanted to enter history. To appropriate nature. First of all, my own. Tackle the making of humanity head-on. This end justifies all magical means. Prosit.' – 'Prosit,' said Laura but had a soft drink instead of wine. Then she scraped one fingernail for a while in the dirt of the unplanted flower box, which wasn't going to win any balcony contest. When the third June bug had bumped against her forehead, her inventive spirit finally started working. Soon Laura said, 'In the first place, history isn't true; in the second place, I know a young man who wants to be a nursery-school teacher; in the third place, my mother always feels better when she visits the new districts in Karl-Marx-Stadt, where you can see young men washing windows and hanging up laundry. Know what? You give the circus your resignation and get a job as a contributor to *Magazine for Women;* the editors will arrange for you to move to Berlin, I'll find an apartment for you in the neighborhood, and now let's have fruit salad with whipped cream.' – '*Magazine for Women?*' asked Beatrice. 'Is there actually . . . it's surely impossible that . . . ' – 'In this country nothing is impossible,' Laura answered from the kitchen, inserted the beaters into the mixer and turned it on.

Chapter 21

Wherein a temporary end to the wanderings in the GDR and a pragmatic invention of the trobadora's are described

Beatrice bought the latest issue of the women's magazine recommended by Laura as well as two back issues, in order to prepare her application. By analogy to another local magazine that published photographs of female nudes, Beatrice expected male nudes in the women's magazine. Her expectations were not confirmed. Nevertheless, she resigned from the circus without giving notice, paid off the breach of contract from her salary savings, and spent the rest on a poetry generator. The PGH Progress in Glauchau built the unit based on the trobadora's cryptic instructions. Beatrice had the apparatus installed on the Sonnenberg in Karl-Marx-Stadt. In a courtyard framed by a front-facing building with side wings and a tenement building. The electronically controlled apparatus was the size of a kiosk, and from the outside looked something like an orchestrion, owing to the slightly delayed reaction of the striking mechanism and the jerky movements of the plaster figures, which daily received a fresh coat of paint applied by automatic brushes. The three-dimensional details of the figures were gradually smoothed over by the oil paint and replaced by new ones, a change that can be observed in similar fashion on ships' hulls. Beatrice took lessons for three weeks from the PGH electricians to become acquainted with the control panel and gauges that filled the inside of the poetry generator. A variable price list was mounted on the outside of the machine, which was equipped with numerous red, green, and white signal lights. The price per syllable was between seven and thirty-two cents, depending on the thematic category; the surcharge for end rhyme was generally twelve cents apiece and twice that amount for internal rhyme. The cheapest of the nine categories was usually chemistry or automation and during unfavorable weather, agriculture; the most expensive was love. The customers stated their wishes with respect to category, meter, and length into a microphone. Their voices were recorded on tape, translated by a complex mechanism into the latest computer language, and transferred to punch cards. At the start Beatrice had to process between thirty and forty punch cards per day. Decoding them took up more than half the production time and had comprised ten of the eleven weeks of the training period as well. Love with end rhyme was most in demand. When Beatrice had become accustomed to her four square meters of machine-crowded work space and gotten some practice, she would fasten each punch card onto the coffeepot handle with a clothespin as the card operator tossed it onto her table and compose directly into the typewriter. The printing of the poem, price calculation, and collection of payment were done automatically. Since Beatrice was skilled in the most popular and most expensive category, the demand increased; at times, long lines of people formed in front of the apparatus. Soon the trobadora, who had to deduct only 20 percent income tax and 20 percent social security from her earnings, could give up her furnished room in the tenement building and rent one in the front building. Nor did she lack for lovers, for she subjected her activities in the poetry generator to a pledge of confidentiality.

SECOND INTERMEZZO

Wherein the Reader Learns What the Beautiful Melusine Copied from Irmtraud Morgner's Novel *Rumba for an Autumn* into Her 14th Melusinian Book in 1964

Uwe didn't even have a real father-in-law. Katschmann called himself 'life companion.' He'd been living with Berta for three years. Uwe had her invite him for a meal once in a while. When Valeska was out of town.

Uwe arrived just in time for supper. Sweet-smelling steam drifted across the table. Katschmann wanted a hot meal in the evening. But not too hot: he waited for Berta to taste his soup.

Uwe flooded his palate with cocoa soup. When he sucked it through his teeth, it lay foaming on his tongue. Sweet. Sickeningly sweet. A local specialty. Uwe was used to other ones. Where he came from, they ate rice pudding with cinnamon sugar and bratwurst.

'Don't you like it, Uwe?'

'I like it.'

'Would you like another helping?'

'No.'

'Why not?' Berta stood up and poured her soup into his bowl. She usually stood while eating. Because from above, it was easier to watch the plates being emptied. Her eyebrows were raised high on her creased forehead. She watched the table as if it were a running slot machine. And she always won. But she wanted to win high. She spread bread for Katschmann the way he liked it, pushed plates back and forth, and described what was on them.

Katschmann clinked his spoon on his cup. Berta brought sugar. Berta praised Uwe. The more they ate, the more she felt her affection returned.

'And you? When are you going to eat?'

'Does anyone want pickled mushrooms? Or herring in oil?' She started describing what was on the table again: nice butter, nice bread, nice cold cuts, nice cheese, nice eggs . . .

'I'm not blind,' said Katschmann.

'But you could go to church once a year. Yes, I know, I know what you're going to say, but I must remind you that Frau Wieseke's husband used to have good eyes too, and all of a sudden . . . You wouldn't be able to drive any more if you . . . Edgar, once a year won't kill you.'

'I'm against religion,' said Katschmann.

'Me too,' said Berta and sat on the edge of her chair. 'I am too, and so is Uwe, and Valeska too, right, Uwe? Would you like schlackwurst or cheese on your bread, Edgar.'

'Schlackwurst,' said Katschmann.

'We're of one mind,' said Berta. 'A family that's not of one mind on all questions isn't a family. We're a family. We say there's no God. But if there is one after all . . . You see, it would really be best if you went to church at least once a year, just in case.'

Katschmann's head loomed over the table like a spherical red buoy. Berta attempted to maneuver a helping onto his plate with the salad server, without success. Katschmann pushed his plate away with his right arm and stopped chewing. And lost time. And that was presumably what aggravated him the most. Eating seemed to be part of an immense workload that he took on every day. He dealt with it methodically and so thoroughly that it had given him blood-pressure problems. The illness gave him a bright complexion; he looked healthy and strong and hard to figure out. Only when he was very angry did he get alarmingly red. Since Valeska was away and Uwe took his meals with his mother-in-law when she had first shift, he was often alarmingly red. And always for the same reason. For several days Berta had been pursuing him not just with goodness but also with God. He had talked her out of this God before moving in with her. Suddenly this God was back again. Katschmann was convinced that Berta had been influenced by something, some kind of trend. He had a sixth sense for them. He said, 'We reject God.'

'Yes,' said Berta, bowing her head. Her thinning gray hair was permed and fastened with numerous clips and combs.

Katschmann slid his plate back toward him again. Berta stood up again and circled the table. It reached her waist. Which she no longer had but still marked with belts.

'We don't need a God,' said Katschmann.

'Yes, I know,' said Berta. She couldn't say no. Goodness was her downfall. That's how she had ended up with this man. She had met him on the S-Bahn, as she explained afterwards, when it was already too late. Katschmann was coming from work and Berta from her shift, and blind chance seated them across from one another. Uwe had met Valeska entirely by chance as well. Because he had been sent to production on probation, where he met Valeska's father. Life was decided by chance meetings like these. Terrible, it was best not to think about it. Berta had it better. For her nothing was by chance. Until three years ago, certainly not. And now all of a sudden, pretty certainly not. A God made chance happenings into laws. A God brought order into any chaos. A God was practical. Had Berta dredged him up again because he was so practical? Maybe you needed a God when you were forced to make the same hand movements thousands of times a day. Maybe she couldn't sit at an assembly line without him anymore? Or she couldn't come to terms with the blind chance that had seated Katschmann across from her in an S-Bahn train. Katschmann must have told her all the details of his bad luck on that occasion: wife deceased, two boys at home, the boys with nothing to eat, no one to take care of the apartment. Help. Berta volunteered to help. She cooked for the boys, got Katschmann's apartment in order, did his laundry, and came once a week to do the housework, gratis. Valeska was outraged. Valeska said, You'll wear yourself out. Berta promised to tell Katschmann to hire a housekeeper. Uwe didn't doubt that she had firmly resolved to talk with Katschmann about this. She surely resolved again and again. But she couldn't bring herself to do it. Then Valeska and Uwe got an apartment and moved out, Katschmann's older son joined the army, and the younger one was looking forward to his *Abitur* and the joys of fatherhood. Berta was told to take in a lodger. Katschmann was available. Berta didn't want to. But once again she couldn't say no. Katschmann gave his apartment to the younger son, who had married in all haste, and moved in with Berta. He'd been living with her ever since. On questionnaires he listed her as 'life companion.' Did Berta need a God because she'd been unfaithful to Franz?

The droning of motors poured through the closed windows. Berta hunched her head down on her shoulders. The city evoked memories of itself. With the noises of its daily existence, which could be defined as U.S. Air Force or Royal Air Force or Armée de l'air.

'If we have to go through that again . . .'

Katschmann, who had just bent his bald head over his plate and set his lower jaw into regular horizontal motions, turned red again. 'If . . .'

Berta smiled apologetically on Katschmann's behalf and nodded for Uwe. Her cross-eyed gaze turned to both of them. Katschmann gripped his fork handle between his thumb and index finger and beat time on the tablecloth with the prongs. 'If . . . what's that supposed to mean, if . . . '

Uwe turned away, but he heard the beats. Steadily thudding beats. Soft. Table beats. Beating the bushes. Heartbeats. He wanted to take the fork from Katschmann's hand and say something to Berta, but he couldn't help thinking, Can you talk about it that way. Can you lose yourself in the situation that way. If. Wasn't insecurity expressed in that 'if'? Had Berta been influenced by something after all, some kind of tendency that one should challenge? Katschmann didn't let himself go like Uwe and Berta. Katschmann sat up straight, as if he were presiding at a meeting. And now he sat even straighter, and his weary eyes, which lay slantwise on his face, pressed down by the drooping of his eyelids, had a hard expression as he posed the question in their midst. A question of conscience? A trick question? He said, 'Excuse me, but who is making history today?'

'I know,' said Berta, 'but sometimes I get scared anyway.'

'A Communist is never scared.'

'I know,' said Berta, 'but just like now . . . '

'Fear makes you weak,' said Katschmann. 'And weakness is dangerous.' He started eating again. He said, 'We're invincible.'

'Yes,' said Berta, 'but you could go once a year, just in case.'

Uwe understood Berta. Uwe understood Katschmann. But he was glad anyway when Katschmann left the apartment. Katschmann was usually on the go. Either driving the S-Bahn or on a volunteer assignment. But he was no traveler. He always stood at the same spot. Even while driving. Uwe envied him.

But he liked the apartment better when Katschmann wasn't there. It was larger without him. You could move about in the rooms without being afraid of bumping into the furniture. The living-room furniture belonged to Berta: sideboard, sofa, china cupboard, table, four chairs. All the pieces except the chairs were covered with crocheted doilies. Berta worked on them while Katschmann read underlined passages to her from his books. Berta was always inventing new patterns.

When Uwe was visiting her, she didn't crochet. Because then she always made mistakes, so she said. When Valeska was visiting, she wasn't allowed to crochet. Valeska rejected doilies. Uwe liked them. Not because they were pretty, but because Berta had made them. Everywhere on the ugly, old furniture that Berta had bought cheap or received as gifts in the course of her hard life lay her dreams woven of artificial silk yarn.

'Will you crochet me something for my desk?'

'For your desk?'

'Yes.'

'But Valeska . . . '

'For my desk, not hers.'

'Yours?'

'Yes.'

'Really?'

'Yes.'

'Your nice desk?'

'Yes.'

'And what shall I crochet?'

'Anything,' said Uwe.

'Maybe a flame pattern?'

'Doesn't matter,' said Uwe.

'I'll give some thought to a new flame pattern,' said Berta and closed her protruding eyes. Then she stretched out both arms, raised her hands high, lifted her first two fingers, pursed her lips, summoned up her deep fairy-tale voice, and said, her eyes still closed and beating time with her hands: 'I'llgive – some – thoughtto – anew – flamepat-tern.'

Uwe had no father. But he finally had a mother. Berta was his mother. He loved her so much that he was embarrassed to tell her. He even thought he looked like her. Valeska was quite different. Valeska could live without parents. Valeska didn't need a God. Not even tonight. Even now, a human being was enough for her. Berta needed a God when she had to live alone. For twenty-seven years.

Thirty-two years ago Berta wanted to marry the unemployed type-setter Franz Kantus. Supposedly the banns had already been posted when Hitler proclaimed the Third Reich. Franz had to emigrate. The brownshirts were after him. Berta had to decide from one day to the next, and she couldn't do that. She was expecting a child. She listened to Franz, she listened to her parents, she didn't want to hurt anyone, and then it was too late. Franz had told Uwe that only a lucky chance had enabled him to escape across the border. Until 1937 Berta would occasionally get a sign of life from him via comrades. Then nothing.

She raised her daughter alone. She worked on the assembly line. Then. Now. Was she still working just for the money? Was there any other reason to keep working on an assembly line nowadays? Maybe this God wasn't really a God but a sort of dream figure. A human being can't live without dreams. One like Berta, who had worked like a machine for over thirty years and was still a human being. Maybe she had to create a dream figure for herself because she didn't have a human being she could dream about. Maybe Franz was a person one could dream about. When he stopped writing to her, she surely must have suspected that he had found someone else, maybe a Russian woman. A young man can't live alone indefinitely, every human being has strengths and weaknesses, and so on. But she didn't let that destroy his image. Maybe she even made a religion out of this love? Every great love is a kind of religion. Maybe she was still in love with him now?

'Shall I use yarn or silk?'

'For what?'

'For the doily for your desk.'

'Silk,' said Uwe.

'White or yellow?'

'Doesn't matter.'

'And what if you don't like it?'

'I like all the things you make.'

'Really?'

'Really.'

'But if you don't like it, you don't have to take it.'

'I'll surely like it,' said Uwe.

'I'llgive – some – thoughtto – anew – flamepat-tern,' said Berta softly, her eyes closed, her arms stretched out, her hands curved up, first two fingers extended, and tapped gently around on the table, always tracing the new pattern.

If she was able to make a religion out of this love, she loves him still, thought Uwe. I'd love him too, if I were a woman. Everybody at the printer's likes him. Without him I couldn't have swallowed the Twentieth Party Congress. Why didn't they live together? Why did she live with this Katschmann? Did she perhaps love them both? Did her wide-angled gaze fall on both of them? Or had Franz become a stranger to her when he returned, rehabilitated, in 1955? Can a person one has loved so much become a stranger? How could Uwe know she had loved him so much? He knew. He knew it because she was so much like him, ach, Berta, if I didn't know that you exist and that I can come to you when I'm in a bad way, who knows if I could have lasted in this stressful business. Naturally, you have no idea what a newspaper is, you read it, but you have no idea of the newspaper mechanism you must adapt to or fall flat. But you can listen, you have the wonderful ability to listen even when you don't understand: you're always there for me, all the time. Even when I don't see you, I feel the shelter of your love over me. I've looked for this shelter with all the women I've loved. I didn't find it. Not even with Valeska. I need you. I understand you. I understand that you need that kind of shelter too, and you've gotten it back now. You need it now. I need it now. Katschmann is a person who means well. I took him in because there was too much space under my roof. Most of it was reserved for a grandchild. But I probably won't have one. So I have to rent out space.

Katschmann came back. He tossed a bundle of brochures onto the table among the skeins and doilies that Berta had spread out and said, 'You'd have to read them ten times to exhaust their meanings.'

Uwe paid no attention to him. He watched Berta taking apart doilies and winding the silk onto empty yarn rolls, her lips pursed, her eyes half closed. He thought, I'm a person who had no mother. I got in my grandmother's way too, I got in everybody's way, I had to make my own way, I was always cold, even at school. Whenever I had a friend, I hung on him so much that pretty soon he wanted nothing more to do with me. I was jealous of all my friends. I longed for somebody who'd be there just for me. I wanted the girls I loved to be there just for me too. I wanted to have somebody the way someone has their mother. I wanted to forget my cold childhood. But you can't forget a thing like that. You drag it around with you until the end. At the university I was so cold that I went through a lot of girls. Every time I plunged in all the way to the borders of existence. Every time I made a religion out of it. Laura and Valeska brought me to my senses. But one person alone can't fill the immense hole that was created when we buried God. One person alone isn't strong enough to patch the hole to keep the boat from sinking. I'm not strong enough alone. I can't get to the issue alone. I'm a person who needs a mother.

'You haven't told us what happened to you today,' said Berta. 'Was it nice, Uwe, did you learn a lot?'

'To be sure,' said Katschmann, 'the question of science, right now, when the powers-that-be, you know, the string-pullers, my personal opinion is, we can't lose any time, we must work feverishly like these scientists.'

'Which ones?' asked Berta.

'The ones Uwe is reporting about.'

'Where?' asked Berta.

'In the newspaper,' said Katschmann. 'You have to study the newspaper every day, I tell you, and you can contradict me, you have to work through it twice these days to halfway exhaust its meaning. And then you have to go to work the way these scientists go to work: The battle is waged in the sphere of material production.'

'It's a conference,' said Uwe.

'I'm not against conferences,' said Katschmann. 'I'm going to say something now, and you can correct me, if there is a productive force, and science is one, there'll be a report about it, if someone is a productive force, he has the right to hold a conference. Naturally, you can disagree about the right time. This situation wasn't a vacation for Uwe. But in principle he has the right, and I tell you, and maybe you'll agree, I say, in this situation we need more reports like that.'

'What kind of reports?' asked Uwe.

'Like the one about the conference of the Soviet scientists.'

'It's an international conference, Edgar.'

'The main thing is for the report to be good.'

'I haven't written it yet.'

'Then get started now. I tell you, and this is my personal opinion, the Americans want to take over Cuba. We have no time to lose. Let the scientists be an example to you.'

'Edgar, they're working on problems that can perhaps be exploited for practical purposes in eighty years.'

'What?'

'Yes.'

'The Soviet scientists too?'

'The Soviets too.'

'All of them?'

'Not all, but the two who are at the conference, yes.'

'In this situation we need everyone,' said Katschmann.

Berta raised her hand like a schoolchild who wants to ask a question. 'Uwe, have you heard . . . '

'Naturally,' said Katschmann, 'if you work for the newspaper . . . '

'But it's not in the newspaper.'

'Then it's not true,' said Katschmann.

Berta nodded at Katschmann and smiled apologetically at Uwe. Then she said, 'Supposedly the Russians have missiles in Cuba . . . '

'I heard that too,' said Uwe.

'Who from?'

'From the scientists,' said Uwe.

'Where do these scientists come from?' asked Katschmann.

'Different places,' said Uwe. 'Besides our scientists and the West Germans . . . '

'So.'

'Yes,' said Uwe, 'and ours can travel all over too. I can't get a visa, but they . . . '

'They ought to bring that out in the open,' said Katschmann. 'I'm going to say something now, and maybe you'll agree, I tell you: They have to bring the scandal to the public in a report.'

BOOK FIVE

Which presents in their basic form a small selection of the works that Beatrice de Dia authored with the poetry generator

Calling Formula of a Lover's Poem

— ———
◡— ◡—◡◡ ◡—◡◡
— ———
◡— ◡—◡◡ ◡—◡◡
— ———
◡— ◡—◡◡ ◡—◡◡

Voices of the Steelworkers

—◡◡◡ ◡—◡ ◡◡ —◡ ——◡
——— —◡
— ◡◡◡◡ ◡
—◡◡◡ ◡ ◡ ◡—◡
—◡◡◡ ◡—◡ ◡◡ —◡ ——◡
——— —◡
— ◡◡◡◡ ◡
—◡◡◡ ◡ ◡ ◡—◡

Provocation for B. D.

◡◡
◡◡◡◡ ◡— ◡◡◡— ◡
—◡ ———
◡——◡ ◡— — ◡◡ ◡ —◡ —◡—◡ ◡
◡—— ◡◡ — ◡◡◡◡
—◡—— ——— ◡◡— ◡—◡
—◡◡ ◡ ◡◡◡ ◡◡ ◡—◡ ◡

Conversation with the Moon over Leuna II

— ◡ — ◡   ◡ — ◡ ◡   ◡   ◡ — — ◡
◡ —   ◡ ◡   ◡ — ◡
— ◡ — ◡   ◡ — ◡ ◡   ◡   ◡ — — ◡
◡ —   ◡ ◡   ◡ — ◡
— ◡ — ◡   ◡ — ◡ ◡   ◡   ◡ — — ◡
◡ —   ◡ ◡   ◡ — ◡

BOOK SIX

LOVE LEGEND BY LAURA SALMAN, WHICH BEATRICE DE DIA PASSES OFF AS HER OWN WORK TO THIRTEEN MALE AND SEVEN FEMALE EMPLOYEES OF THE BERLIN S-BAHN

Ever since being on maternity leave, Laura had worried about Beatrice. She schlepped her swollen belly restlessly from wall to wall, gazed out the windows toward the gasometer dome that towered over the roofs, when there was a southerly wind, she also opened the window. Since Osterstraße was only moderately traveled, she could hear the hissing noise of the trolleys from time to time. Then she would involuntarily picture the poetry generator, which Beatrice had described as a nine-cubic-meter booth. At that, the very pregnant Laura felt claustrophobic. Melancholy letters from Beatrice reinforced Laura's belief that the trobadora was deteriorating in the poetry generator, where she sang of anonymous subjects at piecework rates. Laura's inventive spirit was preoccupied. Even at night when the baby was trampling her diaphragm, she looked for a solution. The saving inspiration was obvious. But required great organizational efforts. Laura didn't shy away from them. After several telephone calls and discussions in person with her station manager, the Party secretary, the director of the cultural center, and the second secretary of the Writers' Union, a connection between the employees and Beatrice de Dia was established. First of all, contractually. Laura was responsible enough to understand that sometimes you had to lead a horse to water, even such an obstinate one as Beatrice. So Laura got ready for resistance or protest against high-handed dealings, braced herself for a rage-inspired lightning-quick visit from the trobadora, and assembled ample persuasive arguments. All for naught. To Laura's great astonishment, Beatrice sent the contract for a reading at the Railway Workers' Cultural Center back to the S-Bahn administration by return mail and wrote to Laura asking her to send the story mentioned in the contract. Laura wrote back that the employees wanted to hear a recent story of Beatrice's own production. Beatrice replied that she could provide only poems of her own production, since she had never written any stories. 'Never! Goddammit!' Laura yelled, pounding her fist on the letter that contained the message. 'Here I'm chasing around with a big belly, overcoming prejudices, convincing Pontius and Pilate of the need to rescue a poetic talent – and then it's all going to fall through because of ten pages!' Laura had calculated that if need be, Beatrice would have fifteen days to produce a new story, a day and a half per page. – 'Always bellyaching,' she grumbled, among other relevant bons mots; she loathed impractical people. But disappointment gnawed at her most of all. For her views of poetry agreed, more or less, with Goethe's statement, recorded as follows by Eckermann: 'To write prose, one must have something to say; but he who has nothing to say can still make verses and rhymes, where one word inspires the next, and in the end something comes forth that is really nothing but still looks as if it were something.' – Laura had sung Beatrice's praises as a great poet. Would the station manager suspect her of false claims? Could she risk making a fool of herself with the people she hoped to be working with again soon? Could she expose her friend to a depressing false start as an employed person? Laura pondered various possibilities for eliminating the risks. Finally she decided on the least expensive variation, recalled her experiences at the state-owned construction company in the Heidenau district during the Cuba crisis of 1961, and poured out her inventive spirit in a love legend. In a half-reclining position; sitting was already very difficult for her, as was standing. The love legend ended up eleven verses long and was written in Beatrice's voice as well as in her name. Laura sent the piece off three weeks before giving birth. Beatrice recognized her hand in the legend and wrote back enthusiastically, 'You're my better half!' The event was salvaged and took place in a friendly atmosphere. The union leadership served coffee and sweet rolls to go with the legend. There was unanimous praise for the legend's political import and the woman character's choice of profession, while the moral quality of certain passages was seen as deficient. For example, the fact that male authors describe naked women shouldn't lead a female author to describe naked men. Belles lettres meant 'good literature,' after all. The love legend that Beatrice de Dia passed off as her own work to thirteen male and seven female workers of the Berlin S-Bahn reads as follows:

1

The news reached me during dinner. I didn't understand it right away, the meat was tough, the innkeeper turned away from the bar toward the radio. He pulled it out from the shelf a little, adjusting the volume so that the announcer's voice drowned out the noises of conversation and dishes, but keeping his ear close to the fabric covering of the speakers. The noises subsided, increased again; then there was silence. The wall behind the shelves was mirror glass. It doubled the schnapps bottles, the cigarette packets, the room. The men looked for their reflections between the displayed items. Except for me, there were only men in the tavern. Their faces were tanned up to their eyebrows, their foreheads were pale, with no traces of mortar. Anton reached for the rucksack lying between his boots under the table, I remember that perfectly. Even though years have passed since then. With more news reports of this kind. I knew the men by name. I had recently started working with them. Our construction site was on the other side of the river. No one whistled as the stranger entered. He sat down at my table. His hair was conspicuous, like that of people who wear wigs, lifeless but thicker and not as well combed; at first glance it looked black.

2

Two bricklayers had missed their buses. After eight glasses of beer, they invited the stranger to join their card game. I ate another helping. When raising my arm to lift the fork to my mouth, I could feel my shoulder. After my second day of work, my arm had trembled when not supported. We were still checking each other out, the workers and I, but no longer furtively. After work I sat in the tavern with them. They waited for their buses, I waited for evening. The stranger wasn't one of us. He wrote the card-game scores in tiny numerals on the margin of a newspaper. He held the pencil with almost outstretched fingers that were shorter than the back of his hand; pale, unblemished skin covered with hair that was thicker toward the sides. Each time he wrote down the scores, he looked up at the clock, which had ornate wood carvings stacked around it. The top of the shelf, stained brown from smoke, reached the ceiling. After paying for my meal, I joined the card players and ordered beer, a bottle. The stranger drank from a glass, I envied him. The radio announcer repeated the report of the blockade. The stranger lost two games. When the other tables were empty, I asked to play too. The stranger paid the bricklayers their winnings and drew a new score chart on the newspaper margin. When I had lost my third game, one of the bricklayers put his hand on my shoulder. His name was Edwin. Our brigade called him 'pig champion' because when he was plastering, he supposedly got more mortar on the floor than on the wall. Meanwhile, plastering was fully mechanized. Ash particles drifted across the tabletop, which vibrated from the card playing. The innkeeper washed glasses. Edwin took his hand from my shoulder and laid it on my knee. The stranger narrowed his eyes. They lay at a slant, rising up to his temples. The tabletop was split; Edwin had stuck his cards into the crack. Sometimes he deliberated until all the flies had settled on the smooth-scoured wood. The announcer reported the general mobilization on the island once again. The window fan shook the tin ventilation flaps and the diagonally hung curtains. Edwin breathed into my ear. The stranger coughed. Above the bridge of his nose, a V-shaped artery stood out on his brow. Black-framed iris, ocher spots on a green background, I placed my hand on Edwin's. In the right corner of his mouth hung a cigarette with a long, intact ash, his lips and right cheek were nicotine stained, I looked at his cheek. Edwin was insisting that we leave. I got up, gave the stranger my hand, and left on his arm.

3

We reached the train station quickly. It was built on an embankment that bore two pairs of tracks. We looked toward them. He said, 'You could just as well give me a kiss.' His hair burned in my hand. He closed his eyes like a woman. I did as I was told. Then we went to the tunnel that led to the platforms. Lamps with grilles over them at the top of the domed ceiling. The grooved, black-painted supporting walls reminded you of a urinal. We looked at the train schedule pasted onto the whitewashed arch. 'What would you like,' he asked. 'I'd like you,' I said.

4

'My place or yours,' he asked. 'Mine,' I said. After my divorce I had no apartment. During the week I slept in an attic room at the cultural center, on Sundays in my bedroom at my parents' home. When I was hired, I'd been promised a furnished room in the neighborhood; very few of the construction company's workers lived in the little town. My parents lived in Karl-Marx-Stadt. The cultural center belonged to the construction company. Supposedly it was an inn that had seen better days. The moneys from the cultural fund had been used to remodel the ground floor with the work of volunteers. The upstairs had been repainted. Only the neon sign was lit, closed today, I had keys, the janitor was a Red mountain climber, we went up the wooden stairs in our stocking feet. The room had been carved out of the storage loft and like it, smelled of dust and clutter. A forty-watt bulb hung on a cord from the ceiling, on the latch of the skylight my bricklayer's gear. Blue-and-white-checked bedding. We rammed our teeth against each other's lips and rasped our tongues until spit ran from the corners of our mouths, yanked at each other's clothes, got out of them, our hands played on our bodies as if on instruments. Boards creaked. Louder as we came together. I tossed my head, probably I also clawed down his back, the battle raged rhythmically fast and inexorably toward the climax. It was reached as I heard a yell, and my mouth overflowed. I bore the weight of his damp body for a long time. When he lifted himself from me, I moved to the right. He lay down on my left side. I gazed with pleasure at his sweaty, glistening face. Later I sat up. His skin spanned his body tightly. Moderately padded with fat, it concealed the branching of blood vessels. Freckles on the upper sides of his arms and down his back to the belt line, strikingly developed muscles on shoulders and rib cage, then indistinct sparse hair from the hollow of his throat downwards. Narrow hips, deep, flat waist, short legs with knobby knees, a pretty, middle-sized organ. I kissed it.

5

After midnight we thanked each other, exchanged names, and parted. When the janitor kicked his climbing boots against the door in the morning as usual, I missed a feeling of emptiness. I was surprised, said 'yes' to let him know I was awake, looked at the wavy pattern on the slanting wall above me. I looked at it every morning, I'd already made out a horse and a boot or Italy. To the left of the horse, a toe print. I got up, collected my clothes from the floor, calculated. Eighteenth day. The stained brown deal boards were marked by outlines of heels and shoe soles, cigarette ashes in the washbowl, no water in the pitcher. The janitor brought water from the kitchen for the waiter who had the next room. I had to make do on the second floor. Ladies' restroom. I put on my overalls without washing. They were stiff with mortar on the chest and thighs. The construction site was nearby. In the first weeks I didn't change clothes in the construction workers' shack. I missed the apprentices' construction site. There'd been three of us there. One woman had married and moved to Leuna, one had had a baby, now I was the only woman in the company who worked on the scaffold. The brigade had accepted me reluctantly, the workers' protection act doesn't allow women to cart bricks, for example; the site director had guaranteed it. Since the introduction of the *Objektlohn*, the policy of paying by the job, the men were worried about money again. During the forenoon Anton and I raised the left pediment; at the time, we still used the old method of one brick, one slab of mortar. But keeping pace with your partner, that's what they called the method invented by our company leader and publicized by the newspapers. Our brigade only built third floors. At breakfast, conversations about the new policy and the blockade. The girl Friday brought milk. Drinking beer during work hours was forbidden by voluntary commitment. No one seemed afraid. My skin exuded the smell of Bruno's body. Before evening I knew that I loved him.

6

For three days I had no appetite. I hardly slept. On the fourth day Bruno showed up at the construction site. I didn't see him right away. We were pouring cement, I was running the lift, when you're doing that, you can scarcely take your eyes from the hoist. Anton yelled, 'Company.' He was my mentor and had committed himself to my political education; then he was going to retire. Bruno said, 'Come.' I said, 'How.' I had remembered him as younger. We ran across a stubble field to the river. On the riverbank we fell over each other. On my back I lay with my eyes closed. The other way around, I watched Bruno. In front of his ears, where his hair was gray, his skin was wrinkled. He raised his shoulders to his chin, wrapped his arms around his head, his palms were arched, his fingers outstretched, his mouth tight-lipped as if in agony, his eyes moved behind their tightly shut lids, I exerted myself, his face burst open like a wound, his hands closed part way, Bruno turned his head, grass got under his fingernails, earth. Toward evening we lay quietly, Bruno calm, I euphoric: peace.

7

It lasted until seven. Then we were so cold we had to leave the riverbank. Reluctantly we approached the town, avoided the tavern, the clubhouse, the truck trailer in which the codriver was waiting for Bruno. The chestnut trees on the railway embankment had lost most of their leaves. We looked at the two pairs of train tracks. I said, 'In heaven we'd have peace and quiet.' 'How do you know that?' asked Bruno. 'From my grandmother,' I said. 'Let's go,' he said. We tried to bribe the young woman at the counter with 50 marks. She demanded 100, since the place didn't exist as far as she was concerned. The tickets cost 573.20 marks. Transportation was by trolley.

8

When the tracks began to curve upwards, the angel let go of the handle and started the engine. Bruno moved to the other seat as instructed. Both seats were facing the direction of the tracks, the seat backs over the wheels. When the incline of ascent exceeded 160 degrees, we had to put on our seat belts. The tracks gleamed in the darkness. Our breath froze into snow. When I looked down, it was like being with Bruno, only longer. The angel flapped his wings in our faces.

9

Heaven was densely populated. The registration office was in a high-rise in the city. Selection took place in the courtyard. Our written request was granted on the basis of false statements. We were given garments with slits in them and a letter of referral. A camp had been set up in a quiet area for the love department, 728 barracks, barbed-wire barricades, trenches. Heaven dogs of various breeds ran around in them. A bed was assigned to us in barrack number 361. In contrast to our fellow residents, we used it regularly. At first. Use was permitted only with clothes on and under a doctor's supervision. Every third inmate was a member of the heavenly health service. Included in the surveillance was, among other things, the administering of electrocardiograms. Nevertheless, we were blissful. At first. The occupants changed frequently. The married couples all complied with the heavenly regulations, sooner or later. By right the camp was open only to married couples. Its official designation was transition camp. Sometimes residents gave up after the first day. Then their slit garments were burned on the roll-call square, with musical accompaniment. In the case of later conversions, closed clothing was handed over in the dressing room. We paid little attention to camp life, mostly lying next to each other, looking at each other. Bruno's beauty had a tinge of ugliness. That made it unique, kept me occupied. I admired it effortlessly. At first. When we weren't otherwise engaged, we exchanged conjectures about the Cuba crisis, I described reinforcements we used, door gauges, lintels, Bruno talked about different kinds of fuel and accidents. After four months we had our first quarrel. We blamed the preventive health measures. That night we knocked out the guard, ran to the ends of heaven, and leaned over the balustrade. The earth was still blue.

10

Our deed was found out. We hid in a bunker for three days. When a 'wanted' description of us was issued, we fled across the border. After interrogations about the morale and military objects in the enemy camp, we were welcomed into hell. A commander with red wings decorated us with the Order of Defectors. It entitled us to use of all the machines. We decided for the composite, three by three meters, air-conditioning, waiter service, we negotiated over stationary mirrors, electronically controlled mirrors, love detectors, gimbals, gimbals programmed for ninety-two variations, pipe organ, striking mechanism, garrote, and vexation machine, a detector-driven device that changed the partner's appearance, gender, and desire. We used the latter to suppress the hatred that developed. To no avail; even the couples who used the most modern units turned into poor devils. Within a short time, nothing distinguished them from the mob that loafed about the streets, grumbling, cursing, fighting. After I had broken Bruno's right ring finger, we decided to go home.

11

We got back to the little town on earth via the airlift. It was spring. The town was still standing, in fact, it had twelve new houses. The first person we ran into was a coal carrier. We questioned him. He looked us up and down, finally remembering that the Americans had halted the blockade at the time, he couldn't remember the exact details. We said good-by to him and departed, each to our own place. Because of a shortage of workers, I was hired back immediately. Anton had retired. Bruno visited me once a week. Later, less often. Now he lives in Dresden.

BOOK SEVEN

Chapter 1

WHEREIN LAURA GIVES BIRTH TWICE

Laura gave birth to a baby boy on 22 August 1970 at 3:40 P.M. in the large delivery room of the Charité Hospital. He weighed 6 pounds 350 grams. She named him Wesselin. When Wesselin weighed 9 pounds, Laura had not yet received literary confirmation that the trobadora's meeting with the railway workers had come to a fruitful conclusion. Wesselin started crying whenever Laura took off his diapers. He seemed to be sensitive to cold. He could tolerate a bare bottom more easily when his head was covered; in water, he was quiet. Laura had taught herself the bath hold, for which the left hand goes under the baby's left armpit with the lower arm supporting the head, by reading infant-care literature. When Wesselin weighed 10 pounds and his mother was still waiting for confirmation of her friend's literary recovery, her displeasure and feelings of responsibility became acute. And Laura's inventive spirit began once more to search for ways to influence Beatrice de Dia's life process in a positive way. Finally Laura narrowed to three the measures that could be a catalyst for poetry and decided in favor of the simplest one. Such that she wrote a letter offering her friend Lutz, in case Beatrice had still not found a suitable lover. Lutz seemed to Laura an improvement compared to the poetry generator and relatively suitable, since he was married and tormented by conscience. She thought a relationship with an 840-year-old woman might unburden his conscience and was willing to do without him for her own and Beatrice's sake. To her letter of solidarity, she appended a memoir in which she took pains to present Lutz to good advantage.

Chapter 2

LAURA'S MEMOIR OF LUTZ PAKULAT

Stones: On the way to Heiligendamm, we encountered four hikers and a rotting bird. It lay on its back in the sand, its wing feathers spread, its belly open. Along the shore the sea was still congested, the cracking ice stretching far out over the breakwaters, then an open strip, white horizon. Since the sky was the same blue gray color as the open strip, the sea seemed to have been raised to form a dome over the swarms of gulls. They flew around us, screeching. When they landed on the snow-covered ice floes, they disappeared in the brightness, which blinded us. When they flew up, their white bodies plunged into the anti-sea and drifted there like chunks of ice. I alternated walking on my shoe soles and my hair. Gentle splashing and gurgling. Breakers drenched the beach ice white underneath. When the water ebbed, the ice became glassy. Lutz pointed out buoys, three ships, and a lighthouse tower in the distance. Gentle breeze. Scraping noises in various pitches. The surf had washed heaps of stones to one side of the breakwaters. I pointed out vapor trails to Lutz, clouds, and especially the sun. It floated in solemn pallor. I also declared that I didn't want to be dragged away. From the steep coast, water flowed as in a gorge. It washed under the thawed-bare sandy beach, emptied into rivulets, filled puddles, ponds; the water barriers made you look down anyway. Shells, lotion bottles, the remains of a stone-reinforced fortress. Lutz leaned down first. The stones were hard under our feet; they gave way, rolled. We felt our way forward slowly from one pile to the next. Lightened by the weight that we loaded into our pockets, without eyes for each other, surrendering to the toil of choosing. We balanced on overflowing abundance, wallowed with eyes and hands, gathered up the bounty with relish, white, gray, black, red, veined with many colors, patterned. When we walked, our treasures slapped against our thighs. Lutz looked for meaningful shapes, I looked for ones that felt good in my hand. Gentle ovals, polished; I never expected to find that which is indestructible in the air, only under me. I, who am sometimes its eversion, can finally sink back, uplifted. The rotting bird was probably a crow. When we got to Heiligendamm, we ate bratwurst and coffeecake.

Chapter 3

Wherein everything goes according to plan

Beatrice answered the letter by a surprise visit that interrupted Laura's breast-feeding. The trobadora emphatically refused to tolerate any intrusion into her personal affairs. Laura told her about the day Wesselin had smiled for the first time. Was able to induce a smile as well and mimed the difference from Wesselin's earlier convulsive expressions, the kind described in parenting manuals as typical infant behavior. Laura covered the bald spot on the back of her son's head with her hand. Beatrice wasted many words on the quality of the legend that Laura had authored but none on the rounded shape of the back of Wesselin's head. This was distressing to Laura, an underestimation of physical creations as compared to intellectual ones. Lutz Pakulat arrived late for supper. 'Stop stamping your feet, Wesselin is asleep,' said Laura. 'Will do,' said Lutz. A man at the age that is euphemistically called the 'best years.' Tall, lean; what was lacking on top of his head he grew under his nose. He made hasty excuses for his late arrival on account of business. Even when he was seated in the armchair, his haste clung to him. He seemed to do his relaxing in a hurry too, his eating for sure. 'Do you even know what you're eating?' asked Beatrice. — 'Know? Laura is someone I trust; it's enough for me if she knows,' said Lutz, chewing. 'A phenomenon of the times,' said Laura apologetically. 'For us, eating is normally thought of not as an enjoyable part of life but as a necessary one. Eating is an act of consciousness. The higher the consciousness, the lower the gastronomic culture. The director of the regional building company where I worked for a while bolted his food during meetings, or he ate it cold, whenever he had time. When he didn't have time, he lived on bockwurst. He took a certain pride in that, by the way. His nickname was Caesar. Pleasurable eating during serious meetings would probably have struck him as somewhat suspicious. He was committed to this style. A question of habit. For Lutz, eating is similar to filling the gas tank of a car.' — 'I'll have another fifty liters,' said Lutz, chewing. Beatrice furrowed her brow. So Laura hastened to explain that not only could Lutz build and repair houses but also radios, stoves, antennas, shoes, furniture, hallways, vacuum cleaners, whatever; he could do everything. 'Except eat. It must be because of rhythm. You two probably have a different rhythm in this respect. Revolutions are always a bit puritanical. Because they go after the whole thing, work first and then pleasure. Although they know that the whole thing is a finite value, the end itself, after which there is nothing else, complete idealism as it were, they still want the whole thing somehow. At any rate, they chase after it as if possessed . . . ' — 'You're really espousing your principles today,' said Beatrice. — 'I always try to adapt to my guests,' said Laura. — 'And how do you accomplish all that,' asked Beatrice reverently. — 'I have a concept,' said Lutz. 'If you want to make something of your life, you have to have a concept.' He admitted that he wrote for the company newsletter occasionally, structural engineer by day, writer by night, so to speak, and that he'd been most pleasantly surprised. By Laura's announcement, which had led him to expect a strange phenomenon instead of a nice young woman. 'There's definitely a demonic aspect to poetry,' Beatrice replied, 'and especially in the unconscious, where all common sense and all rational thought come off badly and which therefore is so incredibly effective. Likewise, its highest degree is reached in music, which is so high that no rational thought can grasp it, and an effect dominating everything radiates from it that no one is able to account for. That's why religious cults can't do without it. It is one of the first means of miraculously affecting people.' Lutz laughed heartily. Assured Beatrice once more that she was a pretty young woman. Beatrice assured Lutz that he was a pretty young man. He gave an affected laugh. But quickly overcame his insecurity by giving detailed descriptions of his construction sites. Beatrice got a general impression of colossal spaces and force fields. During his recital of dialogues between site foremen and the site leader, the phrase 'will do' caught her attention. She could only half listen, because her undivided attention was concentrated on Lutz's appearance. That same evening the trobadora returned to Karl-Marx-Stadt and burned down the poetry generator. The next day she rented a furnished room in Oranienburg, because she couldn't count on getting authorization to move to Berlin. She visited Laura rarely. Strikingly pale. Lutz gave Laura the excuse of a suddenly announced conference outside of the city. Between feedings, which lasted a long time because Laura had to supplement them with the bottle and her son took forever to burp, she sometimes thought briefly with surprise at how easily the love project she was promoting seemed to be proceeding. When Beatrice sent the first story she'd written in her life, Laura felt like a patron.

Chapter 4

Which presents the trobadora's first story

Prunus spinosa: On his way home one night, Ludwig of Oranienburg fell and was pierced in the breast by a blackthorn twig. He was a young man at the time, tired from wine and from dancing, and he clutched at his shirt — the star of love rises and shines only during dawn and dusk. The next morning, when Ludwig had slept it off, he discovered the splinter over his seventh left rib while bathing. He tried several times to pull it out, to no avail. The thorns resisted. He was in a hurry anyway, a tile layer by trade. At work, where he was mostly on his knees, he didn't feel hampered or disturbed, he escaped infection, so he didn't worry about it and before long, scarcely noticed it. He would have forgotten the thorn altogether if it hadn't started growing in the spring, branching out over his skin. So that most of the girls to whom Ludwig applied himself complained about it. He cut back the black-crusted thicket. During the year it grew back. He had to prune the rose plant every spring. Soon he married and fathered three children. One day, when the children were already grown, his daughter saw him furtively sharpening the shears and putting them to use. She asked him what had caused the growth. He spoke at length, for he didn't know what to say. Asked why he was acting that way, he retreated into anger. When he ran out of curses, he was surprised and put the scissors back into his wife's sewing basket. The blackthorn grew half an ell every year. Ludwig took an outdoor job. In the summer to keep the foliage green as long as possible, in the winter to give the bare branches a rest. He laid flagstones on two new esplanades in his hometown and several kilometers of sidewalk. Because he was always surrounded by nature, he no longer spent his vacations traveling but on the balcony. His wife had designated it his special place and moved one half of the conjugal bed out there. Since he spurned medical help, his sons and most people avoided him. Only his daughter visited him occasionally. Usually in February, to cut shoots. When placed in water in a warm room, they quickly produced white blossoms, which appeared before the leaves did. Many of the men with whom Ludwig worked appreciated him because of the leafy roof, which was soon large enough to protect several people from rain showers. On fine autumn days, when their mouths were dry from heat and dust and no beer was to be had, they chewed the tart blue fruits and spit the stones in the sand they were laying the flagstones on. When Ludwig was sixty, the rosebush had made him thin. His feet hurt from the weight of the bush, which twisted around him up to his brow and blocked his view, so that he moved uncertainly on the streets. Because of his girth, he had long since been unable to use public transportation. So he gave up his job and settled beside the highway between the villages of Kiekebusch and Königs Wusterhausen. The following night, when drivers had their lights on high beam because of the rain, roots burst through his back. They gradually rooted his body into the ground. The blackthorn stands on the right side of the road to Königs Wusterhausen. Young people occasionally answer the call of nature behind it, children and older couples the call of love.

Chapter 5

Another offer is made to Laura

To Laura, her friend's first story seemed unmarketable but nevertheless an impressive proof of the fact, widely circulated and sometimes doubted in her country, that art can be organized. Serious art — the production of poetry was probably unpredictable. The successful event was clouded by her discovery of a lump on Wesselin's left groin. He screamed. And her neighbor, Frau Kajunke, wasn't home. So Laura loaded her son into the baby stroller and hurried to the outpatient clinic. For about an hour she stood, perspiring with fear, at a diaper box in the waiting room, trying in vain to calm Wesselin. When she was called into the treatment room, Wesselin had fallen asleep. When she undressed him, the lump had disappeared. The doctor diagnosed a hernia that would need surgery before he started school. Return home in light rain. Beatrice was waiting for Laura at the apartment door. With the urgent plea that she start working for her as minstrel. She, Beatrice, had already written another story and in the near future had to perform for the workers of the Pump Storage Works in Hohenwarte, for a border troop of the People's National Army, for the Women Lightbulb Workers and so forth; it would be impossible to cope alone with the wealth of obligations. Of course, Laura refused the offer again, since she already had a profession. After the leave to which she was legally entitled, she obviously wanted to drive trolleys again. She would be assured of getting day care. She couldn't understand how a woman like Beatrice could have such bizarre expectations. Three hours of manipulative sorrow, such as Laura had previously experienced only with men. Flattering talk about how Beatrice felt that Laura was her sister in spirit: irreplaceable. 'I'm no domestic servant,' said Laura. 'I'm looking forward to the week after next.' After washing Wesselin's diapers, she explained that she had become accustomed to standing while driving. Left hand on the control button, right hand on the brake valve, ahead of her the ribbon of track that the train ate up, at sixty, at eighty kilometers per hour, bridges, steep railway embankments, brown from the rust of the brake dust, train stations, also rusty, houses, signal lights green, yellow, red, quays, silos; you felt the thump of the rails under your feet and the speed of the train and how full it was. The overfilled commuter trains rode heavily and gobbled a lot of electricity. You could really feel a train only if you stood. Beatrice claimed to be cured of her wanderlust. She didn't need to know the world; she would create it. Had perhaps Lutz recently become a man who listened to the tales of a thousand and one nights?

Chapter 6

The Trobadora's Second, Not Invented, Story, as Presented to the Kurt Huhn Border Troop of the People's National Army

Marie de Montpellier was married at age eleven to the Viscount of Marseilles, Barral. And thus forced to cede her rights to Montpellier to the children of her stepmother, Agnes. At age fifteen Marie returned to her paternal home as a widow with a substantial inheritance. They took away her riches and married her off a second time, to the Count of Comminges, who was still married to two other women at the time, which didn't faze people in those days nor was it condemned by the church if one was allied, like the Count of Comminges, with the persecutors of the Albigenses. Marie bore him two daughters but was treated cruelly by him, so she returned home. But there her sufferings were so great that she forgot those in the house of the Count of Comminges and went back to him. However, horribly tormented once again, she was forced to flee a second time. Luckily her father, Wilhelm, died just at this time. And since his marriage to Agnes wasn't recognized by the Pope, because his first wife was still alive, Marie de Montpellier gained her inheritance rights. For which reason Peter the Second, King of Aragon, married her. The marriage was celebrated at Montpellier. When night fell, the King refused to consummate the marriage. Great embarrassment on the part of the guests, deep pain on the part of the bride. No one could explain the refusal of the good, young, poetry-writing, and always gallant king, for the bride was not ugly. But the coquettish young Countess Mireval, a guest at the wedding, was more beautiful. She smiles; she seems to know the reason for the refusal. And since the king surrounds her with all the charm of a troubadour, the entire court is soon in on the secret. And so they recruit the beautiful countess and convince her to sacrifice herself on behalf of consummating the marriage. She doubles her coquettishness. The king, a Spaniard, glows. He throws himself at her feet. He finally attains his goal. The countess will receive him secretly tonight in her château at Mireval. The beautiful night approaches. The good king mounts his horse without breastplate or greaves, and rides and rides – the nightingale sings sweetly in Languedoc nights – and rides to Mireval. A certain chambermaid or a certain page receives him at a certain rear gate and leads him by the hand through gardens, dark passageways, and rooms into the chamber. It is dark. The countess's chastity permits no lamp. The good king is happy. When he is very happy, all the doors open suddenly and the entire court mob of Montpellier and Aragon swarms in, at the lead the beautiful, laughing Countess of Mireval. The king is filled with consternation and sees what he has done. Aragon and Montpellier are united by the law of nations, and the power base increases. However, now King Peter is still more irritated with the queen. He turns away from her even more decisively and leaves her to a lonely life in Château Mireval. The lands of Aragon and Montpellier bemoan the lack of legitimate heirs. So it happened one day that the king was leaving the stud farms of Lattes very cheerful and excited. A nobleman from his retinue named Guilhelm d'Arcale had the good idea of speaking thus to the king: 'Milord, instead of going hunting now, we could visit the queen, our lady, at Château Mireval. Your Majesty could spend a second night with her, and we would, if it please Your Majesty, stand watch with candles in our hands. And God in his mercy would bless you with a son.' The king, moved by these words, did as the nobleman advised. And the next morning he cheerfully took the queen behind him on his horse and rode to Montpellier with her. The citizens of the town were so delighted at their princess's happiness that they held great feasts and invented for the occasion a dance called *le chevalet,* the wooden horse, which perhaps is still known today in Montpellier. However, that night gave life to the king known in history books by the name Jacob the Conqueror. Nevertheless, the good King Peter could not entirely conquer his aversion to Marie de Montpellier and divorced her. In order to marry another Marie, the niece of Amalric, King of Jerusalem. Marie de Montpellier went to Rome to make a complaint to the Pope and block the divorce. She died there. By poison.

Chapter 7

Scandalous verses and sleeves for Lutz

Laura wrote cheerful letters to her parents in Karl-Marx-Stadt and to Beatrice in Oranienburg. The letters contained news along these lines: 'While having his diapers changed, Wesselin discovered that he has legs. Grabs for them the moment I lift the blanket. When he gets hold of a leg, he laughs, sometimes he bleats, beside himself with joy. When the leg disappears, he's amazed. Starts looking for it. When he finds it, joy as before and so forth. Made it through the combined tetanus, diphtheria, and whooping cough vaccinations without a fever. Drank his tummy full after the shot and fell asleep. Eating is supreme pleasure, hunger is supreme pain. For the last two weeks no disposable diapers to be found.' Upon her first visit to Beatrice's apartment in Oranienburg, Laura happened to find on the trobadora's cluttered desk a piece of paper with a scandalous verse. She threw the original at Beatrice's head, then into the stove. On the paper was:

Beautiful
defiled by time and women
are you
most beautiful resting
on your back
when the column of air presses your skin
onto innards and bones
and your flesh is intensely
revealed.
Hard on thighs and breast
gentle around the hollow of the navel
a pull
that I follow
under the words of my tongue
under its strokes
suddenly
just now you age
first among the kings
the last

whose tyranny I sanction
I exist in the prison of your body
world is made of your flesh.
From this sex
no prettier one seen
may it make
its teardrops: pre-secretions of desire.
My mouth awaits the burning of semen
baptismal cry
and I kiss the telltale hands.

Beatrice took Laura's overly sensitive reaction for an effect of abstinence and offered to give Lutz back. Not even passionate relations could ever have moved her to quarrel with a woman over a man. Laura said no thanks. Reconciliation over Hungarian beef soup from a can. A great need to communicate on the trobadora's part. She informed Laura that she could observe strange things about Lutz when he was giving definitions, which was his specialty. 'As soon as he heads toward a definition, all that is accidental falls away from him,' said Beatrice. 'The dark blue eyes, the mustache, the thinning hair. His face falls away like a plaster mask; only the scaffold remains standing, an open construction whose parts are fastened together with rivets. During definitions I see the reinforcements under his face and the buttresses and supporting beams of his shoulders, for his sweater is missing too. And the ample ready-to-wear pants are missing too. When he gives definitions, I can look through him. Did you observe the same kinds of things?' — 'I could have,' said Laura. 'I don't doubt that I could have. If I'd wanted to.' — 'I don't understand,' said Beatrice. 'You will,' said Laura. 'After all, pity isn't the right feeling that one wants to have toward a lover in the long run.' — It was incomprehensible to Beatrice that Laura could feel sorry for a man who had a wife at home with children and a mistress with equal rights. In the old days mistresses cost the men a lot of money, but mistresses with equal rights cost nothing, were independent, sensible, and without danger of scandal. There was nothing more convenient, so why these inappropriate feelings? — 'A person who constantly demands success and superiority of himself is pitiful,' said Laura. Beatrice vehemently denied that men in the GDR were forced to constantly demand success and superiority of themselves. — 'Customs are worse than people,' said Laura, 'and they live longer. For example, Lutz says his brother Benno is a failure, his life messed up. Benno is a carpenter with an *Abitur*. Lutz claims that their father got furiously angry at the kid. I think he gripes about Benno so much because he secretly envies him.' – 'Does he also secretly envy female trolley-car drivers with college degrees?' asked Beatrice. – 'Lutz doesn't envy women on principle,' Laura answered and dragged out an art history book to show her friend the descriptive text that went with the photographs of an early Greek bronze statuette. Nevertheless, Beatrice did a reading for the Olga Benario Women's Brigade of the Signal and Insulation Technology Plant, wearing a red coat with jacket sleeves from Lutz. And didn't present her own works, as had been announced, but some verses by Raimbaut d'Aurenga that she happened to remember. Understandably, the women didn't accept Beatrice's excuse that she couldn't do any better without the help of a minstrel. Because they had to get along without household help. And because you couldn't earn an *Ökulei* with this Raimbaut d'Aurenga. Apparently the word *Ökulei* appealed to Beatrice right away, giving marvelous wings to her imagination. Its translation, *ökonomisch-kultureller Leistungsvergleich,* cultural-economic productivity competition, meant nothing to her. When asked about her experiences in factories and other reality research for her literary work, Beatrice had nothing to report. That made an impression. Consequently, her reception was cool and the honorarium modest. Beatrice was offended. Laura couldn't feel sorry for her. Instead, she too criticized the performance and the program. Beatrice tried to justify the patched-together piece with writer's block and the showy sleeves that were fashionable in her time. Since women used to wear their arms uncovered, but custom required sleeves now and then, especially at religious ceremonies and solemn occasions, sleeves had become an independent item of clothing. This had led easily to the custom of lovers' exchanging sleeves with each other. Beatrice grumbled about the poverty of symbolism in objects today. In her time feelings could be expressed symbolically in a number of different ways. At the very least, by the color of one's clothing. Green meant the beginning of love, white meant hope, red was passionate love, yellow was fulfillment, blue was fidelity. Various nuances could be expressed by putting colors together, which is why jackets were often sewn together from patches. Today not even belts were given a meaning. Laura rejected such meaning prescriptions as Scholasticism.

Chapter 8

Which reproduces the text describing a bronze statuette, shown meaning-prescriptively by Laura to her friend Beatrice while talking about Lutz Pakulat

The bronze statuette of a seated man from the Alpheus Valley was created between the ninth and eighth centuries B.C.. Its limbs are as fine as wire, symmetrical when seen from the front; viewed from the side, they are constructively united in geometric angles into an abstract figure. Yet it is impossible to view it as an ornamental figure, like a piece of jewelry. Rather, all the elements of a Greek sculpture organically emphasizing the pose find clear and pure expression in this wire figure: the nakedness, which reveals the limbs; the relaxed attitude of each limb, and – despite the symmetry – in the frontal view a powerfully reaching, contrasting movement of above and below that firmly anchors the person. As a particular and most sublime effect of this geometrical abstraction, there emerges an equivalence and thus a relationship of all the limbs to one another, which, owing to the absence of facial features, is undisturbed by questions of the person's who-when-where and simply manifests the dynamism of the figure very purely and powerfully. It is a scaffolding style that foreshadows the façade of an architectonic scaffold in the figure, constituted by the arms and lower thighs.

The geometric style gets its name from the simple ornamental designs found on vases from this period. Its characteristic features are the straight lines and right angles of which the patterns are composed. Figurative representation is initially unknown in this style, appearing very sparingly and spreading further only by stages. Owing to the seeming meagerness and underdevelopment of geometric art, geometric style is generally granted only a modest chapter within the history of Greek art, more that of a prelude that elucidates its rapid rise from the lowest depths to glory as an independent and significant achievement. But in fact, this art of the geometric style is not only a beginning of Greek art but also a genuinely Greek beginning, a most significant and unique achievement by which Greek art is actually inaugurated and founded.

Seen from the lofty standpoint of human history, it is remarkable that geometric style, using the most unplastic means imaginable – geometrically unexciting, linear, demanding surface and signifying surface – still succeeded in expressing plastic, bodied forces that point the way to Greek sculpture of the classical period; thus, the people who represent this style are inaugurating a stage of humanity that goes beyond the Archaic elements of the Egyptians and Assyrians and bears the seeds of Greek art within it. But in a language that goes back to the beginnings of art, including the Egyptian and Assyrian, and could be called childlike. It is as if a boy who has not yet mastered the language of his fathers and can only stammer, nonetheless represents and gives expression to a way of life that will transcend that of his fathers and ancestors, signifying the beginning of a new life-form. Cultures such as the Egyptian and Near Eastern blossom and develop in their own sphere, but this development is enlargement, refinement, complication; it becomes wiser and more mature, but it is also an aging process that is denied the step to the truly new, the completely different. For that, a new youth, a new childlike state is required. This youth and childlike state are expressed in the primitiveness of geometric style – no deficiency, no lack of ability, but the advantage of freshness and generative power, readiness for the new, to which the earlier, antiquated cultures were denied access. To be sure, it is equally remarkable that what is fulfilled on a grand scale as human destiny also befalls geometric style on the smaller scale. It also develops within itself, reproduces, and refines itself; it grows old too. In order to arrive at a new stage – the tangibly concrete, nonlinear, unsilhouetted, natural human figure filled with flesh and blood – it too requires an impetus from the outside and new impulses.

Chapter 9

Exchange of Experience through the Telephone Line

Because of overload, the trobadora only rarely left her furnished room. For which reason Beatrice and Laura had to conduct their friendly relations primarily by telephone. Beatrice's landlady complained that the conversations were too long. So the trobadora found herself forced to pay Frau Buche a twenty-mark phone user's fee in addition to the official charges. The following affords a partial insight into one of these telephone dialogues, written down from memory by Laura:

L.: Are you still alive?

B.: And how. Lutz really isn't made of wood.

L.: But not of steel either. There's no such thing as all those company functions that he calls home about these days.

B.: There are too. He's a genius. He believed you right away when you said that I'm 840 years old. Let's see a ground-floor member of his profession match that.

L.: He has raised the art of definition to a magic discipline. He calls you a 'nonlinear system,' the atom bomb a 'doomsday machine'; what you understand you can also control, he says. With his explanations he tidies up his head just like his desk, where he won't tolerate any unfinished tasks. He doesn't marvel at anything any more.

B.: You're belittling him.

L.: He belittles himself. Systematically. He has systematically trained himself not to marvel at anything, in order to do more work.

B.: But he knows how to love.

L.: Of course. Those who make a virtue of achievement are universal.

B.: Why don't you talk about something you know more about.

L.: Sure.

B.: Well then.

Chapter 10

Wherein the Reader Finds the Third and, for Now, the Last Story by the Trobadora

Night walking: When I can't sleep, I go for a walk. On rooftops; older ones are covered with sheet metal. My heels tap on sheet zinc, bricks, slate, tar paper, wood; two or three alternating steps on sooty duck boards, they're only that long; you need hours for a single dance. In the meantime, the moon is someplace else or has disappeared. I leap over cross streets from one gable top to another. I prefer gabled roofs, balancing with outstretched arms, spitting into gutters; on the other side of the deep street canyons and courtyards is water; the sky is open to me too. Berlin lights it up day and night. The sky is gray when I can't sleep. If I run into cats coupling on the duck boards, I interrupt my dance and greet the moon: Olisbos. Streets and courtyards are deserted; I see plaster, granite slabs, asphalt, garbage-can lids, treetops, cars. I don't lift up their lids. I lift up the lids of saddle roofs, hipped roofs, miniature hipped roofs, pyramid roofs, conical roofs, mansard roofs, lean-to roofs, terrace roofs, flat roofs, serrated roofs, and cupolas. I see working men and women in factories and beds; I see sleeping men, women, children, dogs, parakeets, two rats on the pews of the Marienkirche. I see Lutz lying down, feet at the back of his neck, his wife tosses her head, moans, doesn't scream. But I don't like to go for walks when I can't sleep.

Chapter 11
Surrender and rebellion

Beatrice was lying down on the job. Failed to deliver literary-historical lectures about herself to the Society for Dissemination of Scientific Knowledge as contractually promised. Was absent from a literary ball for which posters at the S-Bahn stations had listed her name in bold letters next to the names Sarah Kirsch and Volker Braun. Forgot a reading at the Berlin Lightbulb Works. Stopped writing. – Laura obtained a day-care space and started driving S-Bahn trains through the streets of Berlin again. Four days after she started work, Wesselin came down with bronchitis. Laura took sixteen days leave to care for him. Eight working days later, the pediatrician diagnosed German measles. At short intervals there followed angina, diarrhea, and bronchitis again. Laura was absent more than two out of three months of work during a severe personnel shortage and got a lecture on how it's damn impossible to make a work schedule with women. She kept her predicament from her parents, in order to spare herself their disapproval. Even so, Laura's father wrote distressing letters in which Juliane's name was mentioned. In these papers, only the handwriting seemed familiar. But who does know his father? Laura thought he was a very beautiful man. When he was forty, she had created an image of him. Since that time she had never kissed him. Her mother wrote letters, dredging up her fundamental objections to Laura's change of profession. Laura didn't answer the letters. But in the face of her overpoweringly mounting fear, she could no longer defend the triumphant optimism with which she had countered the foreseeable difficulties of raising a child alone. After the pediatrician diagnosed an abnormal weakness of Wesselin's immune system, declared day care to be counterindicated, and recommended care in a private home, Laura burst in on her friend's Oranienburg idyll. Without further ado, baby Wesselin was wheeled into Beatrice's living room. Accompanied by jars of baby food, powdered milk, and a list of instructions. Lutz took cover in bed. Laura bade them farewell to take care of urgent business.

Chapter 12

THE TROBADORA'S CRY FOR HELP REACHES THE EARS OF THE BEAUTIFUL MELUSINE

Don't make me guilty of this innocent child's death, don't let Laura lose her second child, fly Wesselin to the nearest outpatient clinic at once, before he chokes, I'll take back my termination of our mutual assistance pact and anything else you want. Forgive me . . .

Chapter 13

THE BEAUTIFUL MELUSINE'S DIAGNOSIS, PROCLAIMED THROUGH THE PIPES OF THE TILED STOVE, REACHES THE EARS OF THE TROBADORA

The baby is vomiting because he's been overfed with mush, he's screaming because his diapers are full, he's coughing because Herr Pakulat never stops smoking. Change Wesselin's diapers, give him a stuffed toy, and open the window. Without a miracle you can't even help a baby, let alone the world . . .

Chapter 14

DECISIONS AND LAURA'S FIRST PERFORMANCE

Laura got a year's leave from the personnel department of the Berlin S-Bahn. Upon her return to Oranienburg, she found Beatrice out in front of the house. The trobadora was pushing the stroller with both hands. Back and forth. Wesselin was asleep. Lutz had fled. Because screaming children can't be controlled by definitions. So Beatrice had given him his walking papers. Sobered. Probably also satiated. One who has long gone the way of flesh is suddenly inclined to intellect and great deeds. 'I think that's the last image I'm going to make of a man,' said Beatrice. 'Down with gilding the lily. Up with dynamite!' —Laura's savings were respectable but not enough to live on for a year. So she came back to the trobadora's offer and was hired as her minstrel, starting immediately. For wages, with the condition that she would be able to take proper care of Wesselin. Instead of an aptitude test, Beatrice asked for a story to compensate the Berlin Lightbulb Works for her canceled program.

Laura wrote a story titled 'Gabriel' in Beatrice's style and presented it as the trobadora's intellectual property to the Yuri Gagarin Women's Brigade. Attributing the author's absence to illness. In truth, Beatrice was taking care of Wesselin. For Laura's first performance, which took place in a corner of the dining hall, the union leadership served the women tarts. The younger women lightbulb workers found fault with the story's entertainment value in a hurry, because the nursery schools and day-care centers closed at 6:00 P.M. The older women were more leisurely with their questions, asking about the author's workplace and showing theirs. A conveyor belt. The sight of it encouraged Laura to confess that she had written the story at the diaper table. Between her son, Wesselin's, feedings. She would be more careful when composing reports about her son's growth and development for parents and friends. The confession earned her two hugs as she said good-by.

Chapter 15

Wherein the reader finds the story that Laura presented at her first performance as minstrel at the Berlin Lightbulb Works

Gabriel: The tavern had been recommended to me. I asked the way there early Sunday morning. I had left my cash register on Saturday afternoon. The town was crossed by a highway that dropped steeply down to it. A neo-Gothic town hall had been built along the road: this was no village. The church door stood open, a male alto voice rang out and across the market square, large as a courtyard. The tavern was behind the church. An enameled metal nameplate, picturing a monk with an overflowing beer stein, hung next to the door of the one-story building, no sign above the door, Ave Maria. I went up five steps that were worn to a slant. The door to the bar was stuck. I lowered my head involuntarily. An old man sat at the window. His trunk and legs formed an axis that met the polished floor under the table and the back of the chair at acute angles, his heels on the edges of his slippers, his hands around a steaming enamel pot. I said hello. The old man bent over the pot, tipped it, took a sip, and said hello too. Then he rubbed the back of his hand against his face where it was shaven and asked what I wanted. I asked for beer. He replied, as had been predicted, that he wasn't going to get up for a beer. I was satisfied and ordered two beers. An old woman scurried out of the darkness. She wiped a quarter-square-meter linoleum-covered tabletop with a rag, also the seat and back of the nearest chair. The table was oval. Three men were sitting there. All the other tables, except the one on which the owner's arms rested, were empty. I had to sit down. 'How long are you going to stick around?' asked the owner. 'He doesn't mean it that way,' whispered one of the men at the table, the older one; the younger ones giggled. 'A long time,' I said and gave them to understand that this was my only reason for making the detour. According to the map, the town had no tourist attractions. I spread the map out on the green linoleum of the table. The paper was frayed at the folds. I had drawn circles in ink around the places I had visited, thirty-eight circles in seven weeks. I pointed out the circles and asked them to consider that only two days per week counted; I spent the other days sitting behind a cash register. 'Sorry,' said the owner. 'I'm closed on December 31.' He scraped his slippers on the floor. A fly bumped against the low ceiling at irregular intervals. I deciphered the rhymed inscription on a bone hanging from the ceiling on a thread. It urged the guests at the regulars' table to tell lies. I called the owner to the regulars' table. 'If I catch the guy who bad-mouthed me, I'll punch his lights out,' he said. Then he stood up, placed his palms on the sides of his bulging vest front, and shuffled to the bar. The back of his vest bulged too. I hastened to assure him that I'd had most favorable recommendations. The owner brought two glasses of beer. The next half-hour was spent in conjectures concerning the person responsible for sending an outsider to the Ochsenschenke tavern. I described the person as male. The men racked their brains. I drank. Waited for them to tell lies. Looked at the vest back, which bulged over the shoulder blades. Yawned. Mice had kept me awake. Mice or rats running around under the floorboards of the barracks, barns are hard to come by. There are plenty of construction sites everywhere that are empty on the weekend. I always had an assortment of keys and picklocks with me. This time I didn't need them, the construction site for the new dam had a watchman. With difficulty I came to an understanding with the watchman. His dog wagged its tail. I was cold. I didn't know where my life was going. Saturdays I took my sleeping bag along to work. The sales area was as wide as a soccer field; it was high too, neon lights on the ceiling. After sitting under that roof for five days, I wanted sky. No matter what it looked like, whether sun was falling from it or rain. The main thing was sky, this roof. The women at the cash registers next to me thought I went hiking for my health or because the small town bored me or because my apartment was infested with dry rot. I had left a new apartment in a large city voluntarily. That kind of luxury I could do without. Not the kind that was found on the street. Playing with defective hiking maps. I longed for precise maps. For dense networks of roads. For the possibility of walking or climbing over everything: the absolute hiking experience. My understanding that these foolish longings could never be fulfilled depressed me. As did the prospect of having to run a cash register all my life. Plagued by restlessness, I hastened along without really enjoying the views bestowed on me along the way. New customers came clomping through the door. The owner cursed; they rapped their knuckles on the top of the regulars' table before sitting down. The young men received them by singing an army song. It told of love and the start of the fall harvest. The farmers asked the owner if I was his successor. He said I was normal, mentioned the state-owned Ratskeller and the fact that he and his wife hadn't had a day off or a vacation for fifty years. I explained that most of the taverns shown on the map were closed altogether or for their day of rest. The owner turned around. Two humps were emphasized by the satin of the vest. Near the shoulder blades, they stood steeply from his back, then gradually fell to the belt line. A strikingly upright posture. His hands turned the beer tap as if they wanted to break it off. A tower-shaped bar display was covered with names of old cigarette brands. It was smoke brown like all the other merchandise and the walls where they weren't covered by pictures, announcements of songfests, and documents of the NAW, the National Reconstruction Works, or fanned skat cards under glass. I was still waiting. The owner brought a round of schnapps, courtesy of a local soldier on leave. 'Two hundred and eleven more days,' said the soldier. The owner didn't drink. And refused cigarettes on the grounds that passive smoking was healthier and cheaper. The explanation disappointed me. The soldier on leave offered to run home and bring back a legend. I too felt like getting up, thought about the hedge roses heavy with rose hips that lined the highways in this area; sometimes straw hung on them. I longed for the crickets' shrill chirping, recalling a white poplar with its leaves ringing in the wind like a flock of birds taking off. The legend was handwritten, thirteen pages long. The soldier swayed as he handed it over to me. Although the tavern's small windows, stuck into openings in the thick walls as in shafts, were shaded by leafy plants, making reading difficult, I was able to figure out that the manuscript began with a report about a villa. One located on the seashore, surrounded by walls, cypresses, and fast cars and presided over by a countess. The pornography that followed was no more explicit than the descriptions of golden objects and materials. The soldier watched me and slapped the owner on the back. It sounded like the rattling of a harlequin's wand. The owner fended off the blows with his bare elbow. Curly white hair stood out from his open shirt collar. His bare skull and face loomed above his neck. Two lines ran from the bridge of his nose to his lower jaw, forming an equilateral triangle with his chin. The lines formed furrows on both sides of his mouth; in profile the hanging cheek pouches hid his mouth. Tufts of gray bristles roofed over his eyes. His eyebrows were constantly in motion, usually not as a pair. Camouflage colored pupils. Sparks in his eyes. The vacationer said, 'If she isn't married, there's no point.' The man next to him snatched the pages from the table and stuffed them in his left inside jacket pocket. The farmers asked me if I wanted to get my start on the duck farm or as an economist. There were other jobs open too, nursery school, good pay, fresh air. 'Save your breath,' said the owner, 'she's starting at the bank on January 1. After five years of taking correspondence courses, she'll meet Sorembig's son Frieder and write programs for the computer in Greiz.' The owner described the city of Greiz and the company that he claimed would acquire the computer in May 1976 for 2.3 million English pounds. I laughed. In satisfaction at finally glimpsing the resources of the goal that had been recommended to me. The owner took off his food-spattered vest. The guests looked at the ceiling. Serious, flushed faces. As the owner described the phenomenon of love that would instantaneously and irresistibly ally me with Sorembig, the teacher, during our first meeting at the Elsterberg train station, I heard strange noises. They were similar to those made by flies bumping into things in flight, only louder. I confessed to a preference for mendacious stories. The owner's voice grew harsh, then changed to speech-song. So I learned that Frieder would father two children with me, after marrying me. Automobile. My mother-in-law would raise the children. After they reached school age, the family would travel to a foreign country every summer. Margitte, the older child, would be bitten by a viper northeast of Dubrovnik at age eleven. I cried out. The old man's voice verged on a coloratura; the intensity of tone changed constantly, as well as the direction. Smoke that had collected under the ceiling moved in scattered clouds, as if a shifting wind were blowing in. The viper bite is not life threatening. Margitte takes training as an electrical fitter and becomes a heat technician, the son becomes a lieutenant in the navy. Frieder receives a good pension and dies at age seventy-six in our weekend cabin, I survive him by four years. The owner put his vest back on. The men lowered their heads. The humps on his back shrank down to their original size. I paid and left the bar. I wanted to be alone with the pleasant prospects that had come to me so unexpectedly, exceeding all expectations. Sunny highway. Haste left me, this foolish longing, all uncertainty; I walked onward with a light step. Leisurely at first. Then slowly. Toward evening I reached the dam, threw myself from the dam wall, and drowned.

THIRD INTERMEZZO

Wherein the reader learns what the Beautiful Melusine copied from Irmtraud Morgner's novel *Rumba for an Autumn* into her 21st Melusinian book in 1964

'Now, baby.' The voice came from above, from a height. 'Now, baby, that's enough of those silly memories.'

'I'm not a baby, and I insist that you at least let me keep my memories.'

'No way,' said Lutz. 'Look, Karla, don't get me wrong, but there's no point.'

Did everything have to have a point?

'Baby, I think you've gone nuts.'

Nuts. Her mother thought so, Lutz thought so, who else, if you please, who else?

'You're so touchy today. Is anything wrong?'

'Listen, Lutz, you remember when our group was writing a five-act play because all the plays we could find were bourgeois garbage? There was nothing we thought we couldn't handle. We cleared away the old town hall with pickaxes and shovels, all the rubble of the town hall, remember? And everyone wanted to study. They all said you could learn everything. Ach, Lutz, what a wonderful time it was, in those days. Nothing to eat, but we were happy. Everything was simpler somehow, you know, easier to keep track of. Things were still happening in the youth association. A fighting spirit. Enthusiasm, when I think about how we celebrated the seventh of October . . . The early days were the happiest time of my life.'

'But you can't be sorry that knowledge has replaced faith.'

'Why not?'

'Is faith more than knowledge? Is the primitive worth striving for? Only laypeople find it easier to grasp, baby. By the way, we're not as complicated as you think. The mythology of the nonswimmers, you know.'

So I'm a nonswimmer. Seven years of housework and helping out a little in the co-op, and suddenly you're a nonswimmer. One who would sink hopelessly when they threw you in the water.

'Ach, Karla, baby, no, you really are a baby.'

Ever since they were married he'd called her 'baby.' And he also thought 'baby.' And she thought 'boy.' And they lived with these stereotypes. More precisely, under the cover of these stereotypes. Even if they could be new every day – prescriptions for maintaining a happy marriage advised being new every day as a sure method – even if they succeeded in doing the impossible, it wouldn't be any use. Because they wouldn't notice it. Karla was sure they wouldn't notice it. When you have an object right before your eyes, you don't see it any more. All that remains is the illusion that you once produced of it while it was still far away. A stereotype.

'You're romanticizing your memories,' said Lutz.

'Ach, you and your cool common sense. Let me have my little corner of romanticism.'

But in this Lutz was merciless. He said cool common sense was a reactionary cliché, reactionary through and through, yessiree, handed down through generations, and it showed. It dated from a time when common sense was a problem for those in power and so forth, a relic, as I said, that must be resisted. Lutz resisted it for a while. And concluded by asserting that common sense was the best thing about human beings – what really made them human. You couldn't praise common sense enough. Lutz was on his favorite topic; he rollicked about at an altitude where it never smelled like diapers and a thousand trivial things.

'Finished?'

'If we agree, sure.'

Did you always have to agree? Agreement, what did that mean anyway, in this marriage where one participant is a nonswimmer?

'No,' said Karla.

No? The self-confident voice leaned down toward her. No? 'But, baby, when your parents talk about the good old days, you get upset. Yet you do the very same thing. And so you shouldn't be surprised when you don't hit it off with my brother.'

'Ach, Benno – give me a break. When we were his age, we were different people. Remember, every week we did our *subbotnik*, our volunteer project . . . '

'I know, I know, but you can't live from the past forever; you have to . . . '

'What?'

'At some point, you have to . . . '

Of course. The same old song, the one he always sang to his father. But Oskar Pakulat didn't listen, and he was right not to. In this respect Karla understood her father-in-law better than her husband. Actually, it was the irrepressible old Pakulat who had gotten her out of the worst of it, back then. Her parents had said, We've been deceived once, we don't believe in anything anymore. All her parents did was complain. But you could talk to Pakulat. It used to be that you could talk to Lutz. But now he just talked alone. Now Karla only felt like a listener. And she said, 'I'm not giving up the romanticism of the early days.'

'Hopeless,' said Lutz, 'hopelessly senile like my father. For him socialism has to be hard work, otherwise he gets suspicious. No feeling for a romanticism that can be measured in money. Karla, you're getting old.'

'So are you,' said Karla.

'Of course, I'm living.'

'What does that mean anyway, living?'

'It's quite simple; for me it means: build houses, invent things, throw things away, fight your way along, take your lumps . . . '

Quite simple. His desk was always neat. Probably love played a much greater role in a woman's life than in a man's. Probably men were built to be much more practical anyway. Karla knew some men who could fall in and out of love at will.

'You're so serious. What's the matter with you? Is anything wrong?' When Karla was serious, Lutz always pestered her with questions until she gave up. She was the family clown who chased Lutz's cares away, the life of the party who cheered him up when he came home tired. Why else did you have a wife? Karla had time enough to be serious when he wasn't there. And when the children were asleep. Was Karla ever really serious? At twenty she'd mostly been cheerful, so she was cheerful, it's that simple. Probably people knew each other worse and worse, the better they knew each other.

'You've been overdoing it, baby. It's that simple.'

For him, everything was always that simple. Even when they first met, he was like that. They'd known each other for a while when they met. They had worked together in the Free German Youth group writing the five-act play; more than twenty people who called each other 'youth pal' had written pieces of it. Then they had decided, along with these same twenty people, to enroll in the ABF, the Workers' and Farmers' Faculty. And they were both in the same class, the math-science curriculum.

Lutz sat in front of Karla. She had his furry head right before her eyes six to seven hours a day; whenever she wasn't distracted by the teacher or the blackboard, she had to stare at his light brown mop, whether she wanted to or not. It was so thick that from behind, you couldn't see his ears, and close to the crown, right in the middle, where many guys get a bald spot, there were some light-colored strands. At the nape of his neck too. The back of his head was flat, and the light strands of hair poked his shirt collar. From behind, Lutz looked as if he had no neck. When he was called on and didn't know the answer, he would grip some nape hair between his second and third fingers and stroke it with his index finger. This gesture was a sure sign that Karla had to tell him the answer. While doing so, she would lean way across the desktop. When he dropped down again – he sat down by plopping abruptly down on the folding seat – his light brown thatch was sometimes so close to her eyes that for a few moments she couldn't see. So that she was aware only of its bitter smell. And of the desire to touch it. She felt this desire for the first time during a chemistry class.

Two months later one of the usual dance evenings was held in the ABF dining room. Lutz wasn't dancing. He only danced when he had a goal. If there was no goal, he didn't dance. He looked the girls over: to bed or not to bed. He didn't like any of them. So, don't bed. So, don't dance. So, schnapps.

Of course, that evening Karla didn't yet know why he wasn't dancing. She thought: shy. In between dances she glanced over at him occasionally. Otherwise, she was busy. She had two dance partners who kept her busy. Two clinch technicians. 'Clinch technician' was what Karla called the men who put both hands on their dance partner's back, pressed the side of their head against her hair, and shifted from one leg to the other in time to the music without moving from the spot. Operators, in other words. Guys you had to battle with. Karla enjoyed battling. With words. With looks. In a sporting manner. Dance-sport. More sport than dance. But not bad, not dangerous. Because you were on guard. It was logical to be on your guard during battle. Tango, slow fox-trot, English waltz. Karla stepped to and fro in a corner with her partners. Occasionally she watched Lutz from this corner. He was leaning his crossed arms on the bare tabletop – they got tablecloths only on state holidays. He sat there staring like he did at school when he didn't know the answer. At school he stared at the inkwell. Here he stared into his schnapps glass. Once in a while, he looked up. But he never blinked an eye. He remained stone-faced, and his eyes, which were quite large and actually pretty, were rolled way back; it looked as if he had pulled his brows across his eyes like a curtain, so nobody could look inside. English waltz, slow fox-trot, tango. Karla's dance partners were pushing for a decision. Karla stood rhythmically in the corner with the one and then the other, watching Lutz get drunk over the shoulder of the one and then the other. And toward eleven she sensed that she was feeling sorry for him. When she sensed that, she was lost. But, of course, she didn't realize it yet. She didn't realize it until two days later, and then it was too late. But at eleven she still felt safe. Now her dance partners were starting to press their lips against her neck from time to time and that sort of thing. Karla was very busy. Karla thought: indifferent. Indifference spurred her to call attention to herself: Dammit all, don't you see me. Lutz didn't see her. Lutz guzzled schnapps. Karla thought: shy. Shyness prompted her to let down her guard. She shook off her dance partners and sat down next to Lutz. Just like that. Unarmed. So as not to intimidate him even more. Lutz laughed into his schnapps glass, that was all.

'Aren't you dancing?'

'No,' he said.

'Why not?'

'Because.'

'Not even with me?'

'Not even with you.'

'And if I ask you to?' She asked him. She, the girl two dance partners had competed for all evening, asked this guy looking at her stone-faced if he would deign to be so kind. He didn't deign. He simply turned down the invitation. Nobody had ever turned down an invitation to dance from Karla. Because she'd never had to ask anyone before. Not until this evening, around eleven. Around eleven she said, 'May I have the next dance?'

'No,' he said.

At that moment, at the latest, she should have had her guard up. But she did nothing. She didn't even think about it. All she thought was: Dance, he has to dance with me. It was a question of prestige for her to force him to it.

'I'm not a dancer,' he said.

'Liar. I've seen you hopping around before.'

'So?'

'Yes.'

'When?'

'Two months ago, no, just a minute, it was May 17, yes, May 17.'

'Who with?'

'With that sex bomb from 2a. I thought she was going to inhale you.'

At that moment, at the latest, Karla ought to have realized that a nondancer who danced the last dance with the sex bomb from 2a wasn't so shy that she needed to feel sorry for him. But she realized nothing. She talked and talked. And since he kept on sitting there stone-faced, hardly looking at her, she thought: He's afraid of me. And tried to get across to him that he didn't have to be afraid. And finally she said, 'All right then, if you don't want to, I don't either.' And with that, she was done in. With that, she had done herself in. She had played right into his hands. Without a struggle. Without realizing it.

And he realized it, of course. Although he was quite drunk. And he played it smart: he said good-by politely and left. Friday evening. Just before midnight. On Saturday there were no classes. Beautiful summer weather. Karla went swimming. Karla went to the movies. Good mood. A little boisterous. By Saturday afternoon Karla realized that she had fallen in love. That evening she called him up. He came. So, to bed.

So, wake up. Karla immediately looked strenuously at the keys of the blue piano. She took off the upper and lower boards of the housing and looked at the piano's insides: pin block, hammers, the iron frame with the strings stretched over it. She felt light-headed from the harsh aroma that the mechanism exuded, from this adventuresome, daring, daydream-inducing aroma.

And the memories continued, smooth as silk. A bare room, white-washed, strips of paper with writing on them nailed on the bare walls, the strips half a meter wide, the letters almost as wide, red letters, red cloth on the table and a bowl of fried potatoes. Twelve forks are spearing the browned potato chunks. Lutz says, mankind only asks itself questions it can answer. Wenzel Morolf sticks his fork into his upper left jacket pocket. Eleven forks spear the bowl empty. Wenzel pushes his chair back with two fingers, Wenzel sits leaning back, his legs crossed, one foot jiggling, his hands are twisting an empty cigarette pack, his eyes are narrow, black narrowed eyes watching the bowl get emptied. But his fork stays in his pocket. Even if he had to starve, the fork stays in his pocket. 'So mankind only asks itself questions it can answer. Aha.' An inflammatory 'aha.' Several of them. Steeply rising forehead, high-ridged Roman nose, ascetic mouth, almost without lips, pointed chin, black narrowed child's eyes, doubt. Wenzel doubts everything Lutz says. So, mankind. Aha. 'Who is that, mankind? I don't know him, he's never introduced himself to me. You know him. It's enough if a trusted individual such as yourself knows him. It's quite enough if you know that he asks himself questions. Questions, then. Aha. What is that, a question? Something to eat? A jewel for the nose? Pornography? Ladies, I must disappoint you, I have a liking for good pornography, but unfortunately I must disappoint you: it's an answer. A question you can answer is an answer. So mankind asks itself answers. And that's a pile of crap. To my taste, masturbation is a pile of crap, ladies.' The ladies are wearing blue work shirts. The ladies won't stand for being addressed as 'ladies.' They reject that bourgeois nonsense, they eat from the serving bowl, they're not afraid to go after the old town hall with a pickax, away with the old garbage, let's have the new state, we are the state. And there are eleven of us, twelve counting Wenzel. But Wenzel is on the wrong track politically. Lutz personally took him under his wing, to straighten him out. Since then he's even farther off the track. Lutz constantly has to unmask him. When he's finished eating, he throws his fork on the red tablecloth and unmasks him. 'You doubt everything,' he says. All Wenzel sees is the red cloth. Wenzel says, 'Where doubt stops, stupidity starts.'

'Defeatist.'

'Montesquieu,' says Wenzel.

Lutz slowly gains momentum. Wenzel jiggles his foot, his eyes are even narrower, he has a matchstick between his lips, leaning back, all the way back: I, Wenzel Morolf, no god, but who's better? We were. There were eleven of us. Seven guys and four girls, whom Wenzel calls 'ladies.' He talks only to the 'ladies,' the others are as good as absent as far as he's concerned. Even when he's arguing with Lutz, he faces the 'ladies.' I had brought Wenzel into the group because he played well. Lutz had been against it. But the dormitory evenings were too quiet for me, and so I simply brought him along. And he promptly threw out our entire program. He played all evening, the piano, the guitar, the banjo, he called attention to himself immediately, singing and playing all evening. To begin with, cultural heritage. Lutz was all for cultural heritage too, heritage was approved, then French chansons, none of us understood French anyway, and then jazz, 'nobody knows you when you're down and out' and so forth, then nothing but jazz. And after we had danced like lunatics for a while, Lutz said jazz was cosmopolitanism, and cosmopolitanism was decadent, we rejected decadence. We didn't reject it right away, Lutz had to present the proof several times. The chain of proof was flawless. Flawless chains of proof were his strong suit. We rejected unanimously. Wenzel poured beer in the piano. But he came back. He reeked of arrogance, but he came back. Although Lutz was constantly proving to him how far off the track he was. Although you absolutely couldn't depend on him otherwise, he came back and intruded.

'You're intruding,' says Lutz.

'Aha,' says Wenzel several times, inflammatory. Did he only come so he could intrude?

'He only comes to class so he can intrude,' said the physics teacher. Wenzel read detective novels under the desk during physics class, refused to answer simple questions, tried to lead the teacher onto slippery ground. The physics teacher could find no errors in his written work. Physics interested Wenzel. History didn't. Every other possible subject that had nothing to do with him, but not history, of all things. History was the main focus. He was barely getting a four in main focus. If you got a five in main focus, you failed the *Abitur*.

'We've formed study collectives,' says Lutz. 'If you don't make an effort, you'll flunk history next year. We've decided that no one in our class is allowed to flunk. Karla leads the study collective for history.'

'I like Karla,' says Wenzel.

'I'm not interested in whether you like my fiancée; I'm interested in when you intend to start doing something in history.'

'Never,' says Wenzel, 'but I'll come to Karla's group.'

Usually Lutz weighed every one of Wenzel's words. He weighed them, and then he worked them into chains of proof. But now, of all times, he doesn't. Now he's not even interested in whether this Wenzel likes his fiancée. He seems to be very sure of his ground. Sometimes he acts shy, but he's sure. Others make love into a circus with jealousy and other foolishness. Lutz asks if things have a point, jealousy has none, so there, it's that simple. For Lutz, everything is simple. Karla had called him up, and he'd come over, and they'd slept together, it was that simple. And tomorrow maybe Wenzel would come to her group, because that was settled, also quite simple. Wenzel had made up his mind to hang onto his laziness. He sat in the state library every day, but maybe he'd come anyway. Why? Where's the point in that?

'The meaning of life is work,' says Lutz. 'Lazy people aren't living.'

'If that's true, then the dumb ones who have to work hardest in order to achieve anything at all would be living the most intensively. Do you live intensively in math?'

Lutz has a two in math. He has only twos, while Wenzel has all ones and a four and, of course, a crummy assessment of society. Lutz says, 'Talent isn't something you earn.' He speaks softly as always, his index finger at his mouth to curb the words and mute their decibel level. Not soft speech as such: soft speech on principle. 'Talent isn't something you earn.'

'Aha.' Several times. 'Aha. Recently you defined talent as work. Which tailor does your brain alterations, anyway?'

'Talent carries an obligation,' says Lutz. He tickles his nose with his index finger. Then he places it vertically on his lips again. He knows that the subjects he's talking about speak for themselves and require no noise. Whoever doesn't take on the effort of listening is out of luck. Whoever is bothered by the constant nose tickling and touching of the face is not interested in the subjects but in effects. Wenzel needs effects. Irony, swear words, bons mots; he even admits that he uses these expressions less for their meaning than for the effect. He claims that truth is rarely brilliant because it has to be repeated too often. Lutz rejects effects on principle. Lutz says softly, 'Talent carries an obligation.'

'For doing volunteer construction work, I know. Every brick a coffin nail in the sword of imperialism. But recently you said that talent is mysticism; a human being can learn everything.'

'If he has a talent for learning, yes.'

'Wise.'

Lutz smiles. He's done it. He's gotten this arrogant individualist, who, of course, has petit bourgeois origins, once again. Lutz gets them all. He's feared by the ABF teachers and students. He's proud that he is feared. At meetings sometimes even Karla is a little afraid of him. Usually he's almost shy, or at least he acts that way. But behind a speaker's podium, he grows taller. When Wenzel speaks up in the full assembly of students and teachers, there's laughter. When Lutz speaks up, nobody laughs. With Wenzel you never know what to expect, with Lutz you're sure. You can depend on Lutz. Always. Consistent scholastic performance, helpful, punctual, loyal. Lutz is faithful to his wife. Lutz is husband material.

It smells of fried potatoes. It smells of brawling. Karla can no longer clearly see the other ten who are still sitting at the table. Maybe mix a little bit more and kissy-face, blurry, very blurry. Only Lutz and Wenzel are there, very clearly, in all details, Lutz's canvas jacket and Wenzel's black eyes and his hair that sits on his head like a wig, and the fried potato smell, very clearly, yes.

'And if you have a talent for laziness?'

'You don't need talent for being lazy,' says Lutz.

'You bet you do,' says Wenzel, jiggling his foot, 'and how, talent alone is not sufficient for being lazy. Laziness also requires character, a lot of character, ladies. Little characters have to be diligent, because they always need an alibi to justify their existence, to themselves, to other people: I did thus and so today, I didn't live my life in vain, and forgive us our trespasses, amen. When there's no alibi, they can't sleep. Because they're afraid, the little people. They're afraid of death, the dear little people, that's why they have to do something for their immortality every day. The sweet little people have to create immortal works every day. And what does the author of an immortal work have from his immortal work when he has rotted away? Fanfare! Strong characters don't need an alibi. They don't have a need to justify themselves to anyone. They lie in the sun. They can afford to care less about recognition, they rest in themselves. We crap on posterity, ladies; we live. Kisses.' Wenzel had gotten to his feet. He crosses the meeting room, taking big strides. He walks pigeon-toed and stamps his heels on the floor so that the table wobbles. Lutz is furious. But the others find Wenzel's new theory quite interesting. Quite interesting is, of course, not enough for Wenzel. So he won't rest until Lutz unmasks him as reactionary and the others accept the theory. Then he'll drop the theory, as always, and put forth another one, as always. In this case, the new one goes: 'The little people philosophize about life, the great ones make something out of it. Dante lost Beatrice; she died when he was twenty-five but not for him. He made something out of this love. He made it immortal.'

'And what does he have from this immortality when he has rotted away?' asks Lutz. 'What does this Dante have?'

'The greatest satisfaction imaginable,' says Wenzel.

'But you just said . . . '

'A man of character says the same thing all his life. Whoever has none keeps learning and changes his mind. I allow myself the luxury of having no character.'

'We have no use for people without character,' says Lutz.

'Aha.' Several times. 'Aha. I get it.'

'So why don't you leave, if you get it?'

'Because I like it here.'

'What do you like?'

'The experiment. Physicists are curious. Physicists have a soft spot for experiments.'

'Socialism isn't an experiment,' says Karla.

'If it weren't an experiment, it wouldn't interest me,' says Wenzel, 'finished products don't interest me. You interest me.'

Karla looks at Lutz. Lutz looks at Wenzel. Lutz says, 'You have absolutely no conception of politics, you smart-ass.'

'Yes, I do,' says Wenzel, 'the world must be ruled by experts: by royalty. Physics is the queen of science. So the world must be ruled by physicists. Ladies and gentlemen, elect me and the world will have peace.'

A pose. Grandfather's pose, when he played the role of selfless pirate.

Lutz says, 'First, let's see if you're even accepted to the degree program.'

'Why wouldn't I be?'

'With a four in history?'

'I'm not going to study history.'

'With a three average?'

Wenzel holds his hands to the stove. Lutz clears the table. Lutz is right, Wenzel can't be saved, a Saint-Simonian can't be saved. Besides physicists, Saint-Simon at least accepted mathematicians, chemists, physiologists, writers, painters, and musicians for his intellectual world order. Wenzel only accepts physicists. This stinkingly vain, ambitious, unpredictable nut-case only accepts himself, only himself. Lutz is right; Wenzel can't be saved. A state that depended on such Wenzels would be desolate. Lutz is right, Wenzel is talented but undependable, you can't accept him into the degree program. A state needs dependable people.

'If I'm not admitted to the program I'll topple the government,' says Wenzel. 'Anyway, the question of the meaning of life is a bogus question. Life is neither meaningful nor meaningless. Of course, you can give it a meaning, for the sake of simplicity, Lutz does it constantly, with both hands full, embellishment is in style again. But does such a great, indestructible thing need embellishment? Life is – enough. The meaning of life is living.' Said he and leaves the room. In two long strides.

BOOK EIGHT

Chapter 1

WHICH BRINGS UP THE SUBJECT OF AN EARTHLY SECRET SOCIETY

When Laura had reported her appointment as minstrel to the Magistrate of Greater Berlin, Department of Finance, Center for Taxation, where her work was recognized as tax-deferred freelance employment, Beatrice released her friend from this function. Unofficially. And appointed her secretary general of the Sibylic Secret Society of the World Order. She said women needed neither Persephonic opposition nor art to become liberated but rather a genius. 'Oh Lord, genius,' said Laura with a sense of impending doom, doubled her vigilance, and pondered the best tactical alternative. Then she hailed her friend's decision to renounce the profession of trobadora as a sensible and logical step. People who were hell-bent on going headfirst through a wall were ultimately no more effective than those who went rump-first. To take the erotic domain away from men, the last one officially granted them here, would be tactically unwise at this time. Because in this way, men could express the authoritarian needs drilled into them by thousands of years of tradition with the least serious consequences. Anyhow, many women held to tradition in this arena only as a kind of grammar rule. And you could at best feel sorry for a man who seriously believed the feigned dependence and weakness of his professionally and financially independent wife, who was doing the statistical average of 80 percent of the housework and childcare at the same time. In any case, he was nothing to write songs about. Laura said she thought the profession of trobadora was premature not because there were no women who thought of themselves as subjects, but because the necessary subjects to sing about didn't yet exist as social phenomena or were hidden by customary practices. The possibility of leading a horse to water was power dependent. And up to the present day, that meant male dependent. 'Exactly,' said Beatrice. 'Here is where our society must position the lever.' — 'How many members does our society have?' asked Laura. — 'Two, counting you,' Beatrice answered. 'I'm the president. The smaller a society, the less deadwood.' — 'And what lever are you going to use?' asked Laura. — 'Ask me no questions and I'll tell you no lies,' replied Beatrice, adding that not everything could be democratically discussed in secret societies, for reasons of security. Laura thought the secret society was a poet's absurdity. So she tried to treat Beatrice indulgently, like a child. This was difficult for Laura, she was still inexperienced in dealing with poets. But cunning in a practical way. Mindful of a certain chess champion's wise words about the fanaticism-inhibiting effect of diaper pails, Laura constantly found pretexts for getting Beatrice to at least push Wesselin's stroller. And despite having been relieved of her responsibilities, Laura continued to pursue her minstrel activities. Which for the moment were limited to the defensive writing of business letters. Because all kinds of editors and publishers were sending reminders to deliver poems, reportages, stories, and the like. When Beatrice declared her intent to renounce the profession of trobadora and artistic endeavor altogether, Laura decided to offer the Aufbau-Verlag a montage novel.

Chapter 2

Interview by the Beautiful Melusine (B.M.) with the Soviet chess grand champion Dr. Soloviov (Dr. S.), which she incorporated into her 4th Melusinian book as the 19th chapter

B.M.: There are some relatively good women chess players, but no absolutely good ones. How do you explain that?

DR. S.: Not only historically.

B.M.: In science and art, women must measure up to the male competition, which is seen as the standard. Why are chess competitions held separately by gender?

DR. S.: Because a woman is absolutely incapable of fanaticism. Take Bobby Fischer, for example. He knows nothing except chess, not even romance novels. And yet he is definitely accepted as a male human being — a female human being of his type would be seen as a bogeywoman. Although this female human would hardly be more distant from normal life than Herr Fischer . . .

B.M.: What does the normal life of a woman consist of, in your opinion?

DR. S.: Not her sociologically determined burdens. But children. Their presence, demands, requirements, poesy are barriers to fanaticizing the intellect. A child's existence puts intellectual objects in perspective to reality, relativizes them, sometimes also drastically ironizes them. If I were to take over half the care of my sons from my wife, that is, if not only she had equal rights, but I did too, then I could only qualify for the regional division.

B.M.: According to that, the price of women's emancipation would be the decline of the art of chess.

DR. S.: The decline of professional chess in the style that is played at world championships today, at any rate. But perhaps another reason why the royal game doesn't appeal much to women is that it's warlike. Chess players have to work up anger at their opponent in order to get in shape for the match. A mere victory doesn't satisfy the monomaniacal Fischer. He thirsts for the psychic destruction of his opponent. He usually accompanies his attacks with loud comic-strip exclamations: 'Crunch!' 'Smash!' 'Crash!' — 'After the sixth game I could feel Petrosian's ego crumbling,' he confessed with satisfaction in a TV interview.

B.M.: Doesn't sport per se have a warlike component?

DR. S.: One combats this officially by propagating the unifying spirit of sport, to the tune of march music. Some weight lifters curse their weights, the better to lift them to full height.

B.M.: I don't believe that women can or should enhance their self-confidence with the belief that they have wrestled another person to the ground. Perhaps they intrinsically lack the impetus to prove themselves in this way. Women are self-sufficient systems. Relatively unsportsmanlike . . .

DR. S.: If one takes the male concept of sports as the norm.

B.M.: Dr. Soloviov, your second occupation is physics. Do you believe that women are also relatively unscientific?

DR. S.: If one takes the male style of scientific thought, which inclines to intellectual fanaticism, as the norm and relativizes against this norm: yes. Scientific findings have an appearance of neutrality. The way to these findings reflects the personal hand of the scientist: his thought patterns. The way the questions are formulated, the choice of research subjects also betray this hand. If women, freed from their sociologically determined burdens, were to obstruct and foil the work of research, a new way of thinking could accrue to science. Intellectual fanaticism has produced outstanding scientific and artistic results. Intellectual realism could produce results that would be no less outstanding. Of a different kind. It is a virtue for which we lack the vision, for the time being. The vision determined by material interests. Morality can trigger secondary changes, but not fundamental ones.

B.M.: That is absolutely selflessly sensible. Am I correct in my assumption that you preach wine in public and secretly drink water?

DR. S.: You are correct.

B.M.: And what does your wife say about that?

DR. S.: When I make concessions to her in interviews, she comes down a notch.

B.M.: Thank you.

Chapter 3

Alarming confession and a redemptive animal

When Beatrice actually gave Wesselin a bath, Laura believed her friend had recovered. Then she discovered a strange text among the papers that Beatrice had given the boy to play with. Wesselin loved to rip up paper. After tearing it, he always threw the larger piece away. The text read as follows: 'A jumbo is made by using a five-liter bottle; these can be found near restaurants, warehouses, or grocery stores. Such a bottle usually has a screw top and a ring for carrying it with one finger. Fill the bottle three-quarters full with gasoline, and one-quarter with extra heavy lubricating oil mixed with axle grease. Seal the neck of the bottle with a gasoline-soaked cotton ball fastened securely with wire. When it is time to throw the jumbo, the cotton (or rag) is ignited. The bottle will burst upon impact. The gasoline, oil, and grease will ignite and burn with a napalmlike effect.' Called on the carpet, Beatrice admitted collecting this and similar recipes. On behalf of the Sibylic Secret Society. Personally, she definitely preferred the theoretical deployment of jumbos; as is well known, small military secret societies use the lever of blackmail with good success. Why should a really small secret society do without it? 'By diverting one airplane, for example, we two powerless women could force a government to abolish the antiabortion statute. How about it?' – Laura said sorry, she'd have to call the police. 'No,' shrieked Beatrice and declared she had the best intentions. Laura countered, 'If you have the best intentions, you have nothing to fear from the People's Police.' – 'Yes, I do,' shrieked

Beatrice, 'they'll hand me over.' Since Laura understood nothing but was determined to protect her workers' and farmers' state from terrorists and her friend from foreign agents, Beatrice was finally forced to make a confession. It dealt with the two young men, on the 'wanted' list in Paris and in all of France for terrorist attacks, who were actually women. Named Jacqueline and Beatrice. 'Crimes like these must be avenged with the severest punishment,' said Laura and pondered. Beatrice expressed regret for her acts and cited revolutionary impatience as a mitigating circumstance. 'She who wants to change the world must have patience,' countered Laura sternly. 'It's hard for the likes of us to keep our goals modest. But success depends on just that. Much is always welcome. A little is good.' Laura read from Lenin's book *'Left-Wing' Communism: An Infantile Disorder*: 'The surest means to discredit and damage a new political (and not only political) idea consists in championing it and taking it to absurd lengths. For every truth can become an absurdity if one makes it "exorbitant" (as old Dietzgen used to say), if one exaggerates it, if one extends it beyond the limits of applicability; indeed, under these conditions it will inevitably become an absurdity.' Laura searched for a solution that would be good for her country as well as for Beatrice. She searched a long time. Then she remembered the white stag in the first verses of the romance *Erec* by Chrétien de Troyes. The creature, personified legal custom (Old French: *costume*) used by King Arthur as a kind of theory of busywork, finally gave Laura the saving inspiration of the unicorn.

Chapter 4

Wherein Laura recommends the unicorn and a quest to the trobadora

Of course, this country is a land of miracles. The war-torn cities have been rebuilt, the forests have been restocked, their game population is impressive. But one species is still absent up to the present day. Here and elsewhere. It's believed to be extinct. And so far, scientists have found no evidence that could shake this belief. And the politicians were glad it was unshaken. For different reasons. The capitalists see it as a threat to their existence, the socialists to their reputation. Medicinal mass influence is generally considered an atrocity. Could it be that for this reason the species was systematically exterminated in areas where it didn't die out? Nobody looks for the unicorn anywhere except in fables these days, at any rate. I'm that Nobody. Admittedly, I haven't found it yet. Those who travel abroad in tour groups will be supplied. Not with atrocities. But your identification papers are grounds for the best hopes. If you proceed conspiratorially. If a state should learn that you are pursuing the unicorn, however, you're lost. And the unicorn too. For it's now well known that its spiral horn is relatively worthless. The pulverized horn is an aphrodisiac. But the dried essence of a single unicorn brain could shape the convictions of six to twenty million people. Not unlike the fluoridation of the drinking water, which achieved a reduction of tooth decay in the Karl-Marx-Stadt district, an elevated ideological level could be achieved by monocerosization of the drinking water. Bypassing the time- and energy-draining long way around via brains, without these money-gobbling mass media and other orthodox methods of propaganda. Which are relatively ineffective. Six to twenty million people with a low to reactionary ideological developmental level could be transformed, via a one-time infusion of one unicorn energy-unit (the smallest unit, corresponding to the average amount of dried essence of one unicorn brain) into the drinking water, into intelligent, kindly, peaceful world citizens of Communist persuasion. For our country one-fifth of a unicorn energy-unit (ueu) would be ample. The amount required per unenlightened brain may seem small. But it is large when one considers that the earth is inhabited by 3.6 billion people. Thousands upon thousands of unicorns would have to lose their lives to liberate the earth quickly and without bloodshed from capitalism, wars, hunger, and patriarchy. The need could only be met by breeding the animals – a method that cannot be reconciled with illegality. So we are left with the scientific method. Which requires the death of one single animal. Track it down! Kill it! Even if you abhor hunting on principle. And don't feed your bounty to the first available crowd of people who despise female troubadours. Deliver it conspiratorially to researchers; it will be easy to interest a few scientists in the project. For what scientist of character doesn't long to see the world controlled by reason. The dried essence will therefore be quickly analyzed. Then will come laboratory experiments for synthetic or biosynthetic production, technological calculations for mass production, within a few months the rationalization of producing convictions should be theoretically concluded. Enterprises with antiauthoritarian leadership strike me as predestined for illegal production of unicorn energy. Do not shrink from the bloody deed, that you may prevent bloody deeds, once and for all. The means to power are always available to us, but it's up to us to choose how we use them. The intelligent, kindly creature's hair is short, like a horse's, white in color, its physical build and gait are also horselike but softer. Luxuriant mane, tail reaching to its hooves. A gun is not required for the quest. Unicorns are brought down by swear words.

Chapter 5

Beatrice sets out on her quest

Beatrice declared that she had a large supply of swear words at her disposal and was not afraid of Interpol. Conducting research in France would be too risky for her. But she would gladly and thoroughly search through all other countries. Discreetly, of course. She said the quest instigated by Laura matched ideally the conceptions of the Society of the New World Order. Conspiracy was a matter of honor for the president of a sibylic organization. Beatrice did not mention that she had to keep her venture strictly secret from her sister-in-law, Melusine, so as not to be exposed for dilettantism; the Persephonic opposition punished the formation of factions by removal from life. Beatrice told her sister-in-law that she was taking a trip to generate protest songs that would support Melusine's mass projects. At that, the born politician jubilantly remembered the mutual assistance pact and readily conjured up the necessary currency. Laura wept a few tears because she couldn't go with the trobadora, for childcare reasons. Beatrice consoled her by promising to deliver abundant travel reports. Laura suggested 'Anaximander' as a code word for the unicorn. On 1 January 1971 Beatrice crossed the state border of the GDR at Hohenwarte.

Chapter 6

Negotiations between the editor in chief of the Aufbau-Verlag publishing house (AV) and Laura (L.) over the offer of a montage novel

AV: Why doesn't Beatrice de Dia come in person?
L.: I'm her authorized collaborator.
AV: So, the author comes from a bourgeois background . . .

L.: How so?

AV: Or something similar. Worldviews can be cast aside much more easily than habits. As the example of the famous poet B. proves. In contrast to most of his colleagues, he acquired not domesticated women but brilliant ones. Whom he put to work for him. Producing ideas and plans is a pleasure; carrying plans out is hard work. Thus the oeuvre of the famous poet, who surely did not have more ideas or plans than other great poets, turned out to be astonishingly extensive. He also had female collaborators who provided material for the production of ideas. And incidentally, he stole like a genius. How many 'ghostwriters' does Beatrice de Dia have?

L.: She's traveling alone. As her minstrel, I have, in principle, about the same status as a professor's assistant. I wasn't able to admire my professor. I admire Beatrice. I'm working to line my own pockets, so to speak. Are you trying to warn me of myself?

AV: The novel you offer is no novel but a collection of stories. Are you aware that anthologies of stories don't sell well?

L.: The orthodox novel form requires sustaining a concept over several years. In view of violent political movements throughout the world and an appalling information explosion, that is possible nowadays only for lethargic or stubborn characters. What I'm offering is the novel form of the future. Which is part of the operative genre. All right?

AV: Oh.

L.: In a contract for such a work, I would agree, in cooperation with an editor, to obtain suitable material from the trobadora and prepare it for publication. All the publisher's requirements in terms of figures, deletions, and additions could be taken into account; all priorities and shadings of day-to-day politics could be incorporated without serious harm to the work. The operative montage novel is an indestructible genre.

AV: Ah.

L.: An absolutely ideal genre for interventions.

AV: You don't say. But why in the world does Beatrice de Dia write short prose?

L.: Short prose is in keeping with her temperament and her lifestyle. Writing is a daily, life-essential activity for her; it also deals with everyday things: that which confronts her every day. These events are difficult, in the long term impossible to predict. They constantly shift her views of the world. To write a novel in the usual sense, that is, to sustain a concept for several years, for example, one must adopt a kind of writing that disregards the experiences and encounters of the epic 'I.' For Beatrice, writing is an experimental process. Short prose is compressed air, in concentrated and very intense form. Apart from temperament, short prose is in keeping with a normal woman's life rhythm, which is socially and not biologically conditioned and constantly diverted by the interruptions of household responsibilities. Lack of time and unforeseeable interruptions force her to quick drafts without leisurely fine-tuning. I can either go full speed ahead or not at all.

AV: You can only go full speed ahead or not at all? You? I thought Frau de Dia was writing the novel?

L.: Oh, right, beg pardon, yes, of course. It's not from modesty that I prefer an ensemble novel of short prose to the orthodox novel form. To deal precisely with something small achieves more than skimming everything. An ensemble of short prose brings the life movement of the epic 'I' clearly into the book with no need to frame it with respect to content. Truth about life in books cannot exist without the author's belief in himself. A mosaic is more than the sum of its stones. In the composition they have a strange effect with and against each other under the eye of the viewer. Reading should be creative work: pleasure.

AV: What capacity to address reality do you ascribe to short prose?

L.: Our society has a tendency to totalize; all revolutions have such a predilection. You can only write short stories with the consent of the readers. They have the job of completing the total. The genre is based on the reader's productivity. Short prose gives an extract, the detail. Precisely. Precision of detail carries more weight than the heaviness of wishy-washy epic literature. And it has to be wishy-washy, because epic literature can't be forced. It must develop gradually. In art nothing can be forced. It is a living thing. I ascribe to short prose a greater capacity to address reality than long prose, because in this case less is more.

AV: So, we'll send you the contract as soon as you've provided an outline.

L.: And the advance?

AV: When Beatrice de Dia has returned the signed contract to us.

Chapter 7
Laura waits and waits for news

Beatrice de Dia was not heard from for two months. Laura waited in vain for reports, which she wanted to turn into money. Obtaining funds for her minstrel's wage was now her chief occupation. When Aufbau-Verlag insinuated in well-chosen words that the trobadora might be traveling in order to shirk her responsibilities, Laura sent an outline for the montage novel. But before long Laura too believed her friend had vanished, never to be seen again. And she reproached herself. For her rigorous therapy. Which had been intended to dampen Beatrice's emancipatory fanaticism. Relativize it. And Laura pushed her baby stroller sadly through the capital city of Berlin. Every day between noon and 3:00 P.M. except when it was raining. She favored a certain side street whose continuation under a different name ended at the S-Bahn grounds. The section she covered was named Roelckestraße. It led from the gas works and heavy auto traffic to cemeteries, hospital barracks surrounded by lawn, garden plots and day-care centers. The stroller could be taken apart to be made larger as the child grew, a so-called combination model. Laura doubted that it would reach the sports-car stage. It was also lopsided, something she had overlooked in the haste of buying it. Buying a stroller before the birth, when you have plenty of time, is forbidden by superstitious tradition. Laura weighted down the stroller a little more heavily on the right side to compensate for the flaw. Her father, Johann Salman, had installed a brake on the left front wheel. Because of the height of the chassis and its static characteristics, Laura could park the stroller in front of stores with its brake locked, as long as Wesselin couldn't sit up. The springs didn't stand up well to being wheeled up and down over curbs. The iron frame of the seat was covered with grayish oilcloth, the canopy with black. To keep Wesselin's tummy from sticking up over the edge of the stroller, Laura replaced the mattress with a flat foam-rubber pad. And early on, fastened her son to straps that could be buckled to the chassis. Wesselin chewed the bright blue color from the felt-lined front breast strap of the harness, which was shaped like suspenders for lederhosen. Red-colored objects tasted best to him. And keys, if they had filed bits. Laura kept her apartment keys away from Wesselin for reasons of hygiene and thought she could please her son with metal slugs she had bought specially for him and sterilized by boiling. Wesselin refused the substitute. He waved his arms when Laura pushed him under trees with sparrows perched in their branches. The moving branches had been sawed off the lime trees on the part of the street where houses stood. These excursions took place between Wesselin's second and third meals. When Wesselin had fallen asleep, Laura fled from portable radios, nail-hammering garden-plot owners, ash-spewing cars, and vacuum cleaners howling through open windows. Wesselin couldn't bear buzz saws or church bells, even when he was awake. The noise most excruciating to his ears was a sewing machine that the neighbor woman used rarely and then so quietly that only Wesselin's desperate bawling made Laura aware of it. Every day she carried the stroller up and down three flights of stairs.

Chapter 8

Appendix to the Novel Outline That Laura Provided to the Aufbau-Verlag

Dear Colleagues,

Since literary work, according to the results of my inquiries, is still measured by the principle of ideological quantity, permit me to make a suggestion for improvement. It could transform the royalty guidelines into a qualified material lever.

1. Theoretical Bases of the Suggested Improvement (Thesis).
   Outlines of novels are unnecessary, for writers who stick to them are not writers. Because they beat outlines to death to achieve length, which requires not creative effort but staying power. Writing, however, means thinking something through to the end. Word by word. Therefore, at the commencement of a project the word order is, in principle, no less uncertain than the inner logic of the story. Unforeseeable turns of events are based on this inner logic. They are climaxes of the adventurous undertaking. Which is an experiment, not a pretense. The scientist experiences such turning points in a similar way when his theory suddenly can no longer be reconciled with a fact he has bumped into. The experience is incidentally depressing and predominantly auspicious. It ignites the fuse for a new theory. A scientist awaits it with suspense. A writer does too. As long as he doesn't allow steamroller-outline publishers to turn him into a manual laborer.

2. Practical Bases of the Suggested Improvement (Antithesis).
   Outlines of novels are necessary, for publishers who do not demand them are not publishers (any longer).
3. Conclusion (Synthesis).
   The dialectical publisher makes a virtue of necessity and measures royalties by the degree of deviation (DD). The degree of deviation describes the difference between outline and finished manuscript. The higher the degree of deviation, the higher the royalties. The DD can be used simultaneously as an indirect measure of the amount of gray matter (GM) used during the writing (1 DD = XGM).

signed Laura Salman, Germanist
Trolley Driver, at present, Minstrel

Chapter 9
Everyday life with a mysterious ray of hope

Laura's mother showed up regularly, with freshly coifed hair, for unannounced rush visits to admire her grandson. Her father could observe his grandson's growth process only four times a year, because he wasn't willing to throw more money down the throat of the railroad, where he had worked for fifty-one years — on principle, Johann Salman used trains only when he had a free ticket. Grandmotherhood had made his wife, Olga, unprincipled, which aggravated her husband. So much so that he didn't speak to her before or after the grandson-visits. He could be silent for days when he was seriously aggravated. That is, about spending money. The purchase of his last new suit, which Olga had pushed through after months of preparation, cost her four silent days. So Olga Salman had been through a period of conversational fasting when she arrived at her daughter's and, consequently, had a lot to make up for. Her favorite topics of conversation were Laura's research-assistant days at the university and baby-stroller models. She rejected as too dangerous the high-chassis type of stroller with a shallow seat that you had to buckle the child into. Laura had selected that one because nothing else was available. Olga Salman complained that she had dreams of seeing the child Wesselin tip over along with the foolish buggy, which ought to be illegal. She demonstrated in the living room various possibilities of tipping over. Up to now Laura had been successful in concealing her minstrel activity from her parents by claiming that she worked at home, addressing envelopes. Olga Salman approved of her daughter's temporary occupation, she approved of everything that was done for her grandson's welfare. She could still get all worked up over Laura's professional career path. She thought it was a downward movement and an appalling underachievement for a woman with a college degree. Falling back on some respectable office work or other such as executive secretary, that Olga Salman could still have understood. But engine driver? Can a philologist whose university education was paid for by the state, whose Party group had approved her for six months in production, really traipse around in rubber boots on construction sites for six years? And on top of that, for nothing, because instead of coming back to scholarly work with a strengthened class-consciousness, Laura went to work for the S-Bahn. Which her mother found even more incomprehensible in light of the father's irregular hours that were so disruptive to family life. Frau Salman found this odious, and unfeminine to boot. And besides, this damned railroad paid badly too; only idiots would work for that money nowadays, but daughters probably took after their fathers, unfortunately. 'Sometimes occupations do run in families,' countered Laura, 'if they are families.' Then she asked her mother to consider that eventually the need to go back and forth several times a day between the acts of stooping over that are indigenous to housework and those heights where ideas are to be found had become too energy-draining for her. Because it was depressing. Anyone who constantly had to battle disqualifying startup conditions in competitive ventures, the way it is in scholarly work, and who also had character, had a right to opportunism. Juliane's death, which not only Olga Salman assumed to have occasioned Laura's abrupt decisions, was not mentioned. Nobody suspected that Laura had, above all, wanted to save her marriage by changing her profession. Because Uwe felt that Laura was superior. And consequently, that he was inferior: this depressed him. Embarrassed silence. At that, Olga Salman felt it was time to tell about the anniversary celebration of her husband's fiftieth year of service. The wives had been invited too, apparently because word had meanwhile gotten around about how lousy the lives of railroaders' wives were. Along with a speech of appreciation by the station manager, they had received a bouquet of flowers, a gift basket with salami, vodka and confectionery, a silver locomotive relief on a marble stand with an engraved plaque and five hundred marks, ten marks for every year of service. So, for the sixtieth anniversary there would be six hundred marks, for the seventieth seven hundred, for the hundredth one thousand, and so forth; loyal railroad workers could get rich. Said she and started washing windows. Took down the curtains from all the windows while she was at it and washed them in the bathtub with the newest laundry detergent. In her younger days she had done the dirty work from necessity; with increasing age her selective resistance decreased. Now she took note of what she had within reach to keep herself busy. Constantly. She even left the table several times during the noon meal. Because she usually placed the potato kettles and vegetable bowls at a distance. Absurdly, Laura had long thought. Only gradually did she figure out the meaning of this careful breathlessness. —While this was going on, Laura was surprised by mail from Odessa; the sender was none other than Beatrice de Dia. At that, Laura felt ashamed of her suspicions and faintheartedness, fought down her wanderlust, and gave her curiosity free rein. But who can describe her disappointment when, instead of descriptions of exotic regions, she took from the wrapping paper a literary portrayal of her great aunt. Anaximander was not mentioned. Was this her return on a therapeutic quest that was supposed to enlarge Beatrice's knowledge of the world? Had Beatrice traveled to the Black Sea to write half-truths about Laura's great aunt without interference? Laura was at a loss to explain how Beatrice had gotten knowledge of certain intimate family details, which she shamelessly dragged into the light of language. Laura was outraged that the trobadora presumed to write as if she were Laura. Laura was pleased that events in her family were considered worth writing about. She was glad that Beatrice, whom she had successfully kept from her parents so far, was thinking so seriously about her. In short, she revised the piece a little and gave it to the most impatient creditor. Who actually published the revised revision after a lengthy period in storage. But the letter accompanying the package from Odessa was so mysterious to Laura that she filed it away without trying to decipher it.

Chapter 10

Wherein Beatrice describes Laura's great aunt as 'Berta of the Blossoming Bed'

Berta of the Blossoming Bed: 'The fun of getting old is disorder,' she said on her ninety-third birthday. By then she could no longer see the bouquet that her great-grandchildren brought. Manfred and Anne were not her flesh-and-blood great-grandchildren; my Great Aunt Berta hadn't had children. From childhood on, her life expectancy had been believed to be short. Now she had outlived all her brothers and sisters. Even my grandmother, who had never been able to watch her older sister having half a roll for breakfast. The great-grandchildren described the bouquet of chrysanthemums to her and asked which vase it should go into. 'I want it cut up,' said Berta, 'chopped fine with the bread knife, what I don't eat today will be dried in the oven. Now that I can no longer use the magnifying glass, I finally know what flowers taste like.' She giggled. Her foster daughter, Lotte, whom Berta had lived with since her fall, laughed the loudest and exchanged glances with her husband. To be on the safe side, he remarked that as far as he was concerned, nothing was too good for Berta, and brought the conversation back to the topic of my grandmother. Although she was also a character, she was held in higher esteem by the family because of her more easily analyzed behavior. For example, my grandmother used to eat three or four rolls for breakfast, as soon as financial crises and war conditions no longer prevented her from doing so. She spoke with contempt of people who didn't eat properly, except for reasons like these. She could respect only people who were completely hale and hearty. Visibly hale and hearty, that is, well-nourished people, who proved in flesh and blood that they were successful. But never could her colossal appetite have driven her to such unnatural desires as those just mentioned, which possibly even hinted of stinginess in Lotte's family. Berta told the story of her fall while washing windows as a joke. The woman could find something favorable even in the gloomiest events. On this day her pious toughness gave me the creeps. For which reason I, like Berta, hardly touched the cake. She sipped barley-malt coffee and stretched her arms and legs out of the bed to show her bruises. She'd never had much more than bones to show. During normal times my grandmother had weighed twice as much as her sister, which is why she couldn't actually acknowledge Berta as a woman. Especially since Berta occasionally read books after her husband, Emil's, death. An activity that my grandmother granted only to people with nothing to do. A proper housewife always had to have things to do. Since Berta could no longer read with the magnifying glass, she listened to the radio. Systematically, she still knew the German-language radio programs by heart. To go with the cake, she demanded 'Europa Cup Soccer Atvidaberg FF versus BFC Dynamo' from Manfred's portable radio. Hand over her mouth, Lotte complained unintelligibly against the reporter's voice. The great-grandchildren raised their arms high to the loudly swelling roar of the crowd. Anne rose to her feet to celebrate Dynamo's second goal. Berta listened, smiling with sightless eyes. Manfred envied her full head of hair. It framed the tiny skull-like face. In contrast to my grandmother, Berta had not only grown ugly with age. The late years of her life, like the hour of truth in love, had instead clearly revealed this woman's essential importance. It surpassed the physical significantly. During halftime Berta raised her head from her pillows and said, 'I took some tow out of the mattress and stuffed tea in, all the supplies my sister had left me as my inheritance. One sleeps like on a newly mown meadow.' She giggled again. So that Lotte and her husband had to laugh again too and exchange glances. Although they were prepared for all kinds of things. Whoever lived with Berta always had to be prepared for all kinds of things. Dire things. When she spoke, she preferred to bring up subjects that the family had, by general agreement, urged her to keep silent about. When talking about places to sleep, she would embarrass them by bringing up the conjugal bed, whose frame she had planted in the earth of her garden plot after Emil's burial. She used it, covered with plastic wrap, as a cold frame for raising lettuce and chrysanthemums, until her fall from the chair had put an end to that scandal. The nickname 'Bed Berta' stuck, however. The fact that this half-blind woman had washed windows every week seemed strange even to me, by the way. Frequent window washing was the only clearly defined household task that she continued after Emil's death. Unexpected outcome of the soccer game. Manfred boasted about his six hundred marks at the State Enterprise Construction, financial advisor Anne boasted about getting a day-care space, Berta about Emil's fear of the sun. He would never have sat in the yard without a shirt on, a shirt was a blotter, he used to say; you have to wear a shirt. They probably found the hoarse giggling inappropriate because it was directed not outward but inward, where it rumbled and shook Berta's rib cage. Seriously. The foster daughter's fears were even exceeded, however, by Berta's asking at suppertime about her great-grandchildren's marriage plans. Thereupon, Gerda's illegitimate child and that dimwit Emil, at least, were dragged into a family festivity where conversations about successful lives were called for. Desperate efforts to elevate the spoiled atmosphere by talking about my unspoiled grandmother failed. Berta's interest in long-winded conversations about marriages had long been a mystery to the family, since she'd wasted no words about her own and didn't even regret it. She had married the first man who came along, an event that by the conventions of her day was every girl's life goal, and she had done so casually, as if there were, in effect, no great differences in these matters. She had stood out as disagreeably clever in the village school and at her job. The farmers' sons wanted women who were capable of hard work, as a single woman Berta would have been considered an incomplete person, the dimwit Emil wanted a wife too, so why spend time looking? The news that it was not Anne but Manfred who still believed married life was highly desirable brought Berta to tears. Giggle-tears, which she wiped away with a paper napkin. The flower prints left red spots of color on her cheeks. 'You probably have to be blind to see this beautiful disorder clearly,' she said after a while and asked for two chrysanthemum leaves in her barley-malt coffee.

Chapter 11

Strange and wondrous letter accompanying the package from Odessa

Dear Laura,

On the shores of the Black Sea, I had the opportunity to consider the pros and cons of your life and times and hope that I can soon return the favor. My accomplished and influential sister-in-law's consent has already been received. As soon as she has time, she'll obtain authorization to get a celestial vehicle on its way. Because those who don't love live one life less, as the deposed goddess Demeter always says. And if you don't yet feel the lack at this moment, because your attention is so beautifully absorbed by Wesselin, in the long run the natural course of things would nevertheless insist on its rights. After all, the old goddess only separated the human species, which originally contained both sexes, into two genders in order to heighten the intensity of their life. My sister-in-law, Melusine, recommended the generating of twenty-year-olds, whom she described as the optimal variant under the prevailing conditions, and suggested Lutz's son from his first marriage. However, since I know your bias concerning the appropriate age of men, I negotiated a moderate solution. So keep a good beer ready for the next little while.

Warmest greetings from
your Beatrice.

Chapter 12
Reprimands and warnings

Laura sent Beatrice the publisher's contract poste restante to Odessa for signature. With a note that was supposed to calm Beatrice. In the note Laura had written that Beatrice didn't need to worry about the concept or other technical problems, a serious book was not planned, Beatrice would have the prospect of little work and a tidy sum of money. Beatrice sent the contract back unsigned and answered with an enraged letter. She called Laura's intentions for producing the book disgraceful. With such plans you could write neither a good book nor a bad one but no book at all. As long as Laura remained incapable of believing she could produce the world's greatest minstrel poetry, she shouldn't even think of trying such a thing. Raimbaut d'Aurenga had composed even his silliest occasional verses convinced that they were a revelation; nothing could come of nothing. Woman's worst flaw was her lack of delusions of grandeur. In order to do a great deed, you first of all needed courage to want something great. Laura was lacking in this, as were most women. Beatrice said novelists were people who hid their ideas in the heads of other people, from cowardice. And Beatrice warned her friend absolutely to avoid a great work. She wrote: 'That's exactly what our best people suffer from, precisely those in whom the most talent and the most tireless striving resides. Goethe suffered from this too and knew that it harmed him. For the present day wants its rights; the thoughts and feelings that come unbidden to the poet every day, these will and must be expressed. But if one has a greater work in mind, nothing can compete with it, all other thoughts are turned away, and one is lost meanwhile even for the comforts of life. What effort and expenditure of intellectual energy are required to organize even one great whole in oneself, and what energies and what a quiet, undisturbed situation of life to then express it well and truly in one flow. If one has hit the wrong note in the whole, every effort is wasted. Furthermore, if one is not fully the master of his material with such an expansive subject, then the whole will be deficient in some places and one will be chastised; and from it all comes nothing but discontent and paralysis of the poet's powers instead of rewards and joy for so much trouble and sacrifice. If, on the other hand, the poet takes up the subject each day and if he always brings a fresh outlook to that which is offered him, he will always create something good, and if he is unsuccessful once in a while, nothing is lost.'

Chapter 13

Which begins with a forged document and ends with a tantrum

By his presence, which exuded earthy cheeriness and discipline, Wesselin saw to it that his mother took Beatrice's principled letter in stride. So she forged her friend's signature, whereby her financial problems were soon alleviated. Laura washed diapers and bedding after Wesselin's first meal, which was at 6:00 A.M. Laura needed no clock to organize her time, since nature had given one to her son. Child breeding demands a strictly regimented schedule that normally runs counter to the nature of adults. Together with forced sedentariness, this schedule mechanism is one of the punishments for motherhood. For they deny that which is so conducive to creative work and impossible for women in everyday life: improvisation. Beatrice believed that said punishments were assigned to women by culture, not by nature. Laura had forbidden herself to meditate on these traditional conditions for reasons of behavioral economy. Even while doing laundry and similar tasks. Since she knew that housework lasted that much longer the less one concentrated on it. Laura's former husband, much like Lutz, would commence to palaver about world politics when he entered a kitchen; in this way Uwe had been able to spend hours washing dishes. Laura suspected that Beatrice had similar bad habits. For this reason their separation seemed to her a fortuitous act of providence of a kind that inhibits violence. Laura boiled the diapers in a two-handled kettle that her mother had used for making marmalade for the winter. When paper diaper liners and Spee could be bought, the diapers came out spotless; Spee is a laundry detergent with whiteners. At the child-welfare clinic, there were women who placed ironed diapers on the baby scale. Laura was sorry that these women couldn't iron away the bacilli before they touched their children; still, she felt compelled to wear a white smock, for reasons of hygiene. She boiled undershirts and baby smocks in a goose-roasting pan that her grandmother had bequeathed to her. The balcony was useless for drying laundry, because its massive façade extension almost eclipsed its interior and couldn't support a roof. So

Laura treasured a spin dryer, whose howling sounds Wesselin listened to with rapture, as her most important new acquisition. Even so, the clotheslines hanging in the bathroom were never empty. In contrast to the designs now customary even in luxury apartments, the bathroom had a window. Laura gratefully overlooked lopsided doors and the balcony drain that was placed too high, so that it filled with water whenever it rained and in the case of cloudbursts could flood Laura's living room and the one below it. When Laura, after much running around and other time-wasting activities, was told by the insurance company that people with this insurance policy had to bear the financial consequences of such natural disasters on their own, she began to get annoyed over Beatrice's principled letter. Finally she actually threw a book against the wall and shrieked, 'Impatience and delusions of grandeur will be your downfall!'

Chapter 14

Nocturnal appearance of the Beautiful Melusine with soot and theory

At the midnight hour, three hours after her shriek, Laura's tiled stove exploded. With a low-volume roar. Laura had been disturbed from light sleep before; mothers of small children sleep only lightly, listening like animals on open hunting grounds. Weeping and wailing had startled Laura. She was lying on a cot about four meters from the disaster area. Her blanket was weighted down with shards. Soot made her throat dry. Coughing, she worked her way out of the rubble and was about to hurry into the next room where Wesselin was sleeping. Then a light began to glow in the darkness. A white light. It grew larger as the soot and dust subsided. When the circle of light had expanded to a diameter of one meter, it could be identified as the aura of a Sphinx. Its dark winged-dragon's body squatted on the heap of shards; the fair skin of its female human head and breasts seemed to be the light source. Laura attributed the apparition to the lentils. After eating legumes in the evening, she occasionally suffered from nightmares. 'Damn lentils,' said Laura. The Sphinx cleared her throat, spat contemptuously into the room, and spoke. 'You have made a serious mistake. Recant! Cease your wicked meddling! For impatience is Beatrice de Dia's unique talent, delusions of grandeur are her extraordinary virtue. Whoever breaks her of talent and impatience, as was done to her sisters for millennia, will be guilty before God, who cannot be male. Nor female either. Thus, must be both; deficiency contradicts the divine principle of perfection. Understood?' — 'Yes,' answered Laura obediently, for the Sphinx's voice had an extortionary undertone. Nevertheless, Laura summoned the courage to excuse herself for a moment to check on her son in the next room. She shined her flashlight cautiously toward the crib. Wesselin lay quietly on his back; his head was turned to one side and wreathed by his arms and fists, making sweet snuffling sounds. After Laura had superfluously tweaked the blanket, she returned to the living room, reassured. There the Sphinx was still squatting on the heap of shards, whereupon Laura concluded that the disturbance could not have been caused by the lentil soup alone. But since her son was unhurt and healthy, all was well with the world. Even with supernatural night visitors. The Sphinx snorted fire from an enviably beautiful nose. Laura involuntarily touched her own, which was no source of light but simply allowed perception through its round nostrils. To be sure, the existence of supernatural night visitors was incompatible with Laura's worldview, but ever since Beatrice de Dia had entered her life, Laura found that consistency was not absolutely necessary for a worldview. In fact, she now found inconsistencies agreeable because they transported one into previously unknown animated states. When her former coworker Grete unceremoniously denied Beatrice's existence because it contradicted logic, Laura answered as follows: 'If Beatrice is big enough to bring us in person the unwritten history that was not made by men, we should at least be big enough to believe in her.' At that, Grete had accused Laura of speaking in riddles, which must be considered an out-of-date form of testimony. Laura had contradicted her. However, the sharp-eyed Laura doubted whether the GDR could be home to supernatural Sphinxes. Therefore she asked the human-headed dragon: 'Do you have a residence permit?' — 'Cybernetics teaches us that the highest form of interaction by a cybernetic system with its environment consists in the system's construction of an inner model of the environment,' answered the Sphinx in a transformed, matter-of-fact voice. 'Games in and with this model lead ultimately to the construction of other possible models, of possible environmental situations, lead to models that are in reality models of fantasy worlds. That applies not only to mathematics. In principle it is also possible to develop physical theories based on accepted natural laws that we more or less know do not exist in reality. The fundamental facts of cosmogony known today, for example, can be represented by a multitude of cosmogonical models. And these models have actually been constructed. It is certain that at most one, perhaps not even one, of these models can be correct but not several of them. We can also imagine a model of future communist society; indeed, we can construct several models. A real equivalent of these models does not exist.' Laura protested by interrupting: 'Beatrice is a human being.' The Sphinx giggled and flapped her dragon wings so that clouds of soot rose up, choking Laura. But when Laura had recovered from her coughing fit, she continued protesting. As follows: 'Beatrice is a human being like me, which is more than can be said of you. So kindly prove your identity, if you're going to force your way into other people's apartments at midnight, trespassing carries a jail sentence, hey, who are you?' The sphinx brushed her blond hair from her left eye with her left dragon leg and spoke: 'I am Beatrice's sister-in-law, my name is Marie de Lusignan. They call me Beautiful Melusine. A societal model constructed in the course of the activity of *Homo ludens* need not function only to achieve better understanding of prevailing conditions; of much greater historical importance are those models that nothing real corresponds to in the present or future and that something real will correspond to in the future only because society applies its energies to turning this model into reality. Marx, for example, developed such a model. Luther's ninety-five theses also represented a model. The effect of this theological model at the time was enormous, although it never became a social reality. The same is true for many a social utopia. On this theme, a text with which the writer Hermann Hesse introduced his *Glass Bead Game* has this to say: "Though in certain respects and for frivolous people, nonexisting things may be more easily and irresponsibly represented in words than existing things, for the god-fearing and conscientious historian it is just the other way around: nothing resists representation in words more strongly and nothing needs more urgently to be brought to the attention of human beings than certain things whose existence is neither provable nor probable, but which are brought one step nearer to being and to the possibility of being born by the very fact that god-fearing and conscientious people treat them to some extent as existing things." I'm flying to the Mediterranean. Good night.' —'Good night,' replied Laura, fascinated. The Sphinx had already squeezed herself far into the chimney. Only her dragon's tail still hung from the stovepipe. It was armor plated and reinforced with spikes. As she disappeared, the spikes clanked against the metal of the pipe.

Chapter 15

Wherein, among other things, the reader can peruse a document that verifies Laura's people-creating art

Laura's living room was uninhabitable for three weeks, to say nothing of the dirty work of cleaning up and the damage to furniture, carpet, and wallpaper. Then an elderly stove fitter took pity on her for money, kind words, and big eyes. He accused Laura of heating floor polish or closing the doors of the stove too fast. At first, Laura vehemently denied having taken the trouble of lighting the stove when the temperature was so springlike. But since she didn't dare to offer this authoritarian specialist the Beautiful Melusine as an alibi, she eventually took the blame herself. For consolation, her neighbor Herta Kajunke gave her a brass trolley-car ignition key. Collector's item. Without Herta, Laura would have continued to think of the S-Bahn as one means of transportation among others. Laura stored the ignition key in the glass cabinet. Johann Salman, who had always left the transmission of news to his wife, suddenly surprised his daughter with a letter. Wherein he announced that his grandson urgently needed a father. Children who had to grow up without a father would come to a bad end. Besides, Wesselin should be given a teaspoonful of honey every day. Laura couldn't have been more amazed. For Johann Salman never spoke about women's business. And was always distant in other respects as well; his wife was probably that way. Laura couldn't imagine that he'd ever been unfaithful in their long years of marriage. However, neither could she imagine that he hadn't been unfaithful. Beatrice's silence about Anaximander calmed and reassured Laura. She figured the silence was a tacit understanding. A woman who had read all the romances of Chrétien de Troyes ought to know who Anaximander was. The medieval chivalric romances were *Bildungsromane*, novels of development. Which were supposed to teach the courtly virtues of *mâze* and *treue*, moderation and fidelity. To this end the knight Erec, for example, first had to abandon himself immoderately to marital love and make love to excess. Knight Ivain, however, had to go on quests immoderately and pursue knighthood to excess. Neither matched the image of a courtly person. Then the knights thoroughly learned moderation in an exemplary way: Erec had to go on a quest, and Ivain went home. Sometimes it seemed to Laura that, in principle, Chrétien's people-creating endeavors had been cut out of a picture book. Which did Laura's not altogether clear conscience good. At the beginning of May she received a color postcard with the words: 'Here more than half the territory is streets, every fortieth person dies in a traffic accident, Anaximander nil. Your unhappy Beatrice, Los Angeles.' Two weeks later Laura received a card that said: 'Here people are literally starving on the street. Still no trace of Anaximander. Your depressed Beatrice, Calcutta.' On 12 July the postman brought a piece of mail with the return address 'Beatrice de Dia, Zagreb, poste restante.' It contained the following report titled 'Conclusion': 'When Professor S. yielded to his family's wish for a new house and was occupied with planning it, he decided in favor of fundamental amenities. The children's playrooms were housed in nuclear-blast-proof bunkers that cost several times more than the house. After moving in, the American professor preferred to spend what little free time he had with the children, even moving his desk, where he usually worked through the night, into the playroom. S. was a physicist and a member of the Atomic Energy Commission of the United States. Later he began to have doubts as to the functionality of the windowless rooms and sought better alternatives. Again fundamentally; he wanted to invent a blast-proof play-bunker for children. This plan required theoretical groundwork: the usual scientific approach by way of books and statistics. By chance, Professor S. came across statistical material on child mortality. He transferred it to graph paper. The curves depicting the data for the countries in which nuclear fallout was deposited owing to the earth's rotation and the prevailing winds after test bomb explosions were similar to one another. They showed that during the sixties one of every hundred children died. Professor S. concluded that the radioactivity produced by a local nuclear war would be many thousands of times higher and would distribute fallout over the earth to an extent that would effect the self-destruction of humankind: The children would die before they were capable of reproducing. So the professor had windows cut in the play-bunker and went on lecture tours with the statistical material.' Laura was moved by reading the report. And gladdened: it seemed to her a sign of recovery, a fruit of her human resource management that functioned by not quite honest means, a document of people-creating art. In a thank-you letter to Zagreb, Laura sent an urgent reminder for detailed news of the great, wide world. Travel substitute. Housewife compensation. Consolation for stationary activity. Nor did she forget to mention that Beatrice's sister-in-law, Marie de Lusignan, had flown to the Mediterranean.

Chapter 16

Celestial vehicle with identified contents

Laura's habit of sleeping with the balcony door open in the summer was a vestige of her childhood. For fresh air was hardly to be expected at Osterstraße 37. When the winds were westerly, stenches were delivered by the gas works, with northerly winds by the State Enterprise Isokond, and otherwise by normal automobile exhaust. Laura accepted these annoyances primarily to feast on the sound of birds chirping. It began at dawn and created in the stone and cement surroundings an illusion of forest. Which found expression in Laura's dreams. Her summertime dreams were green. Suddenly one of them was out of bounds. Blue. For Laura was hearing squeaking noises that her subconscious attributed to coots. Images of water followed: seascapes. They beached Laura into wakefulness. Nighttime. After a while a bluish light shone through the balcony door. But no sign of sunrise. Had some state-owned enterprise used up its entire advertising budget to drive Laura's sleep away with neon lights? She sprang furiously from her bed to find out for sure. At that, the celestial vehicle came to a halt. Right above the balcony. It hung from ropes, had cardboard clouds, and resembled in other ways as well the baroque swings sometimes lowered by ropes in operas. Filled with angels. In the celestial vehicle, which rocked gently above Laura's balcony, there sat a man. Stiff, as if bone injured, legs and body in a straight line with the beginning and end of his back barely touching the blue bench: actually, he was lying down. Sleeping. Arms spread out on the backrest of the bench like wings. His weathered jeans showed his kneecaps to full advantage. His face was covered by a cap. At the sides of the cap pale shoulder-length hair. On a piece of cardboard hanging around his neck on a cord, like an identification tag for a child ready to be sent out the door, the following particulars were listed:

First and last name: Benno Pakulat
Date of birth: 17 August 1944
Place of birth: Leipzig

Marital status: Single
Education: Expanded Upper School, *Abitur*
Occupation: Carpenter
Address: 110 Berlin-Pankow, Florastraße 14
Place of employment: State Enterprise Construction Berlin

Social assessment by the union local: Our colleague Pakulat is known to us as a dependable worker. His brigade elected him their union representative. He is actively involved in the rhythm section of our singing club and shows class awareness in discussions. The children's vacation camp has in him an enthusiastic helper. Last year his brigade was honored as Collective of the Year. Colleague Pakulat is also a member of the Society for German-Soviet Friendship.

Attention! The cap can only be lifted in a clockwise direction.

Laura followed the directions and found Benno Pakulat's face pale, even featured, and less youthful than she had expected from Lutz's descriptions. As the cap fell from her hand, the theatrical apparition disappeared along with the headgear.

Chapter 17
Confessions of Faith

A tax assessment notice disclosed Laura's minstrel work to her parents. So that she couldn't keep Beatrice de Dia's existence from them any longer either. Laura gave a brief biographical and philosophical sketch of the person and concluded with a definition. Because Beatrice had occasionally described a minstrel as a kind of supportive base. Her work was especially useful as a stationary point; even men were more willing to go on quests when they knew they had shelter in the form of marriage or similar security behind them. 'Don't be dumb enough to let another guy convince you that a woman needs a man,' said Olga Salman unexpectedly, 'men should clean up after themselves.' The news of Beatrice had enraged Johann Salman. 'Don't tell us any fairy tales,' he said, adding that he hadn't left the church to be talked into other lies. Then he sipped chicory coffee reproachfully and declared in a voice loud enough to be heard by stokers on moving locomotives, 'I don't believe in miracles!' – 'But in . . . ' said Laura and was hard pressed to keep silent about the Sphinxlike ghost, Melusine. 'But in reality,' he said. And not a word about the quality of the cake they were all devouring. Olga had baked it herself and lugged it to Berlin from Karl-Marx-Stadt. His inattentiveness, of course, annoyed Olga and insulted her; her ordinary state of mind was regained. Brief parental discourse with assigned roles on the topic of real coffee, whereby her father attacked the stupidity and weak character of the addicted, as usual. Her mother despised people who could fall asleep after drinking coffee. When Laura found a propitious moment to follow her into the kitchen to protest that Beatrice had worked in a poetry generator on the Sonnenberg in Karl-Marx-Stadt, Olga raised her chin to look at her daughter through the reading lenses of her bifocals. Of course, there followed comments about the poor state of Laura's health as a consequence of her unforgivable choice of profession. A girl in their neighborhood had gotten a well-paid position in television after completing her state examinations. 'Beatrice's hands feel like stale breakfast rolls,' countered Laura. 'Her facial expression is a little stiff, as if her skin were too tight, like after a face lift, but I don't believe it, the girl is really perfectly preserved, even rather beautiful. When she gave me a kiss good-by, it was like a plastic bubble flying against my cheek.' Laura fetched from the drawer the remains of the medieval smock that Beatrice had wanted to throw in the ragbag. Her mother tested the quality of the faded material by stretching it between her hands, then smoothing it out, and checking for wrinkles. Held it up to the light too, smelled it, inspected the back side of the embroidery and the insides of the seams. Meanwhile, she griped about the terrible state of affairs at the railroad. Father still had vacation time coming from last year, unlawful conditions. Every worker in this country got himself a vacation spot in the summer, only the railroad workers couldn't plan on anything. Not all of them, not everyone put up with such treatment. A certain Kurt Schuster, for example, had reserved two vacation spots for himself and his wife through the travel bureau last February and had taken off in August for two weeks in Prerow. Although that guy in the personnel department at work really shouldn't have let him take the requested vacation because of an engine-driver shortage. But Kurt Schuster had simply taken his vacation, and that was it. Father would have to take his in November or April, they hadn't been out of their four walls for seven years, railroad – some life! 'We'd like to sleep for eight hundred years too!' Johann Salman, who had been watching the two women for a while unobserved and openly from the doorway, ignored these complaints. Because he heard them constantly.

But not the wish. That got him started. For he despised people who wanted to be old in their youth and young in their old age, incapable of abandoning themselves to life or surrendering to it, weaklings. He made this plain in closing words. In thirty-four years of marriage, Olga Salman had learned to swallow her arguments. Down to the gall, where they were collected and processed into undefined bitterness. Which was then abruptly unloaded at almost regular intervals onto the next best object that got in her way. If none did, she could always fall back on a former sergeant who lived nearby in Karl-Marx-Stadt. Although in Laura's case marital-freedom training had been unsuccessful, for which reason she had been spared damage to her health of the aforementioned kind and was unbroken, though tactically proficient from experience, she also chose to remain silent. And the fact that she was forced to live primarily on her savings despite her job was concealed. By serving expensive meals. Upon leaving, Olga Salman repeated several times, 'Nice family. You wait for months until everyone is together, bake a cake, sweat over your hairdo, and no sooner are you in the door, they start quarreling. And on top of it, over foolishness.' – 'There are no miracles,' Johann Salman replied. 'Unfortunately,' said his wife.

Chapter 18

Wherein the Reader Finds an Astonishing Letter to Laura from the Staff Leadership of the Berlin S-Bahn

To Colleague Laura Salman
1055 Berlin
Osterstraße 37
RE: Staff Discussion

Dear Colleague,

In reference to the letter from your friend Beatrice de Dia of 14 July of this year, we inform you that the forging of personal information is a punishable offense, according to Article 11, Paragraph 2. Travel delegations are determined not by noble ladies but by the union leadership. Since no complaints concerning your performance of official duties have come to our attention and there are no technical reservations about your request for reinstatement after three years of child-care leave, we request in your own interest that you appear for an interview at 10:30 A.M. on 21 July in room 19.

With socialist greetings
(signature)
Müller

ENC.: Copy of the above-mentioned letter

Chapter 19

Which reproduces the copy of the letter that Beatrice de Dia supposedly wrote to the staff leadership of the Berlin S-Bahn

Beatrice de Dia
present address Split
Plinarska 17, c/o Sarič

Dear Colleagues,

I hereby request a free train ticket Berlin-Prague-Budapest-Zagreb-Split for the trolley-car driver Laura Salman, who is temporarily on leave from employment with your company. Concurrently, I request that arrangements be made for her passport and the provision of foreign currencies necessary for travel. My friend Laura Salman, a responsible GDR citizen, must depart immediately owing to urgent family circumstances. Split is the city of her birth. Information to the contrary is not true. Thank you in advance for your trouble.

Respectfully,
(signed) Beatrice de Dia

Chapter 20

All kinds of trouble and a telegram

'She's crazy,' cried Laura after reading the mail, startling Wesselin. 'She must be crazy; I've driven her crazy.' Wesselin started crying. Laura bustled desperately about her home base. Which could be characterized as an offshoot of Classical Cultural Heritage style. Ground-floor façade decorated with square stucco blocks, narrow balconies, decorative walls protecting chimneys that had to be lengthened and thus exposed after the building was finished because the furnaces smoked, wood-framed pasteboard doors. Over the colossal stone balustrade of the balcony, Laura had a view of the half-length portrait of a pretentious new yellow housing development that openly professed its roof and furnace heating. Between the TV antennas there were even lavatory ventilation batteries. Out from this flat tar roof stood, from left to right, a siren, three smokestacks, a piece of the Hotel Berlin, a lot of TV tower, and the scaffold of a gasometer dome. In addition, here and there between the sirens and the smokestacks there rose from the horizon white or gray mushroom clouds of smoke; their shape kept Laura informed of the wind conditions. This constant view onto the world could give no information about the seasons, except when it snowed. After her worst fears, which were based on Laura's invention of Anaximander, practical concerns also presented themselves. Maybe Split was simply too boring for Beatrice? Maybe she was longing for a travel companion? Without regard for the upcoming staff discussion in which Laura would have to apologize for her friend's wicked, jesting letters, longing suddenly welled up. Hope ran wild. What Laura had thus far consistently kept under lock and key forced its way into the open. 'Damned wanderlust,' said Laura, and wiped Wesselin's nose. Then she telegraphed to Split, Plinarska 17: 'Forget Anaximander stop come home stop please send arrival time stop Laura.'

Chapter 21

Which reproduces a Melusinian letter to Laura

Dear Laura Salman,

With reference to the celestial vehicle that I sent recently with a young man on board for your consideration, I wish to inform you that the apparition can be repeated at any time. You need only inform me by telephone (22 88 020) of your wishes in a timely fashion, so that I can apply for magic vouchers and disburse them. If you don't drop his cap, you may view Herr Pakulat as long as you like and spray him with beer. He will also willingly give you information when you take off his left shoe and sock and grasp his big toe. The showings are provided without obligation. The amount of time to think it over I leave entirely to your discretion. For information other than that indicated here, however, I cannot make Herr Pakulat available, since the danger of explosion is still acute.

With black magic greetings,
(signed) Melusine
present address Caerleon on Usk

Chapter 22

WHEREIN A DOCUMENT IS PUBLISHED THAT BEATRICE HAS DELIVERED TO HER FRIEND LAURA INSTEAD OF AN ARRIVAL DATE BY A YOUNG WOMAN WHO INTRODUCES HERSELF AS TAMARA BUNKE

Split is an organism that is related to Laura. You can't get enough of it. I lived there for 45 dinars per day. In a private room of category one. A thoroughly rouged and powdered lady at the travel bureau had requested payment in advance of 220 dinars for it. Since the city was still unknown to me at the time, my interest in having a chimney was still active. Which is why I wanted to see the room before paying. In a pleasant Austrian dialect, the lady expressed indignation at my lack of trust in her solid business, described her offer as the last accommodation but one, snatched the rental agreement, and took my last hope of finding anything inhabitable ten minutes later. My experiences in Istria, where signs reading 'Sobe,' 'Rooms,' 'Camera' were displayed everywhere, should have reassured me. Especially since the threatened loss was located outside of the walls of Diocletian's palace. I wanted to live inside those walls. For financial reasons I had resolved to bypass the intervention of travel bureaus henceforth. Actually, I had only entered the travel bureau to ask for a city map. Was I unable to bear the lady's offended expression? Was I provoked by the unspoken dishonoring suspicion of insolvency? I paid and entered the palace through the south gate. Which is avoided by photographers of postcards and art books. Because it is the least profitable, museum-wise. The entire south face of Diocletian's palace is the least profitable, museum-wise. The palm trees in front of the south face are perhaps supposed to soften the impression of irreverence, but in fact they intensify it. These trees, withered by heat and street dust, are useless for idylls. Even in the mist. Which casts light blue and pink hues on the water and silver on the land. It rises at the west of the bay. Cypresses pierce the scorching sky. Perhaps the timeless romanticism of the sea surges beyond the palm palisade of the south face, the heavily trafficked street along the shore notwithstanding. History is located behind the palisade. In a natural, almost human manifestation. The south gate leads first of all to darkness, windless space, and stairs. Upward. Over smooth-trodden square stone blocks requiring long strides, I reached the antechamber in a throng and palaver of tourists: the vestibule. A hazy sky hung over the open cupola of the round building. The uncoated brick structure radiated noonday heat. In its niches, which according to the guidebook were once filled with sculptures, were crumpled papers and American wives posing for photos. The husbands balanced their cameras on their stomachs. From the back, I would have taken their subjects, long-maned blondes squeezed into white jersey pants, for daughters. From the front they were a depressing sight. The efforts of sixty-year-olds to look forty can have attractive results. Trying to look twenty at retirement age creates impressions far beyond the ridiculous. Tragic. These female bundles of energy, whose physical appearance revealed the effort expended on cosmetics, fitness training, and starvation diets, lounged in plastic chairs in the peristyle. I was soon able to occupy a red chair. In order to enjoy the crowds in the market behind the east colonnade, the Romanesque bell tower, and the cathedral. The chair belonged to the left café built into the west colonnade. This pleasure cost me an expensive soft drink; the waiter was there in no time. Which is why I avoided chairs from then on. And ate my meals on the stairs after that. The peristyle, a kind of open-air theatre, is surrounded by stairs. Similar to a water basin; a paddling pool is an unsuitable comparison, since the deified emperor's splendid ceremonies were once conducted there. Today the peristyle is the square in the middle of the city. Other ancient palace structures were also preserved because they were given a new purpose. In the Middle Ages the imperial mausoleum was turned into a cathedral, and the Jupiter temple became a baptismal chapel. But the infiltration of the tyrant's fortress had begun already in the seventh century. All during my stay in Split, making jumbos and waiting for the Beautiful Melusine seemed to me a waste of time. Impatience melted away. And this urge for cleanliness. Physical and mental. I bathed only when swimming in the sea. I didn't rinse the salt from my hair and head. Soon I felt myself permeated through and through by crystals that were growing. Seven days. Diocletian had had the palace built in ten years and moved into it in 305 A.D., after he supposedly had voluntarily renounced the Roman throne. His retirement seat was originally a combination of luxurious villa, Roman army camp, and Hellenistic fortress. In 615 A.D., when Avars and Slavs destroyed the once mighty Salona during their advance to the sea from the North, the homeless Salonites sought refuge within the solid walls of Diocletian's palace. At first, the palace's spacious cellar rooms served as the Salonites' dwelling place. Later they continued on through the institutions of the edifice by transforming the representative imperial premises into apartments. In the style of the respective historical period. New buildings were erected too, wherever there was space. In the course of centuries, honeycomb was joined to honeycomb. The palace's protective walls served to defend the city and have therefore been completely preserved. Is Laura's pragmatic, inventive spirit based on views like these? When Frau Sarič led me to the room of category one, which I had rented without seeing it, I didn't lose my composure. The palace organism had prepared me. To me, the most beautiful expression of its essence was the end wall. Which is said to have originally reflected its entire length (215 meters) into the sea and is praised as one of the most beautiful open façades of ancient architecture. Buildings tower over its walls. The windows, which were set randomly into the walled-up ancient openings, damaged the arcades, the half-columns, and the façade ring. The roofed promenade, now walled up, which once offered the weary emperor protection from bad weather and the heat of the sun and afforded a wonderful view of the sea and outlying islands, is decorated by the present-day inhabitants with well-laden clotheslines, birdcages, tin cans with geraniums growing in them. Infected by the magic of this irreverent picture, which suggests trust in physical creative energy and unshakable composure, I gazed calmly at the rags. With which Frau Sarič had completely covered the parquet floor of the bedroom. The rags were clean, Frau Sarič rearranged the ones that had gotten out of place under my feet, offered me in Italian café *naturale*, schnapps *naturale*; in the collection of rags, I saw a historical organism composed of the corpulent woman's clothes. Already the next day she kissed me on the forehead and told of having to raise three children alone because her husband lived in Brazil for twenty-two years. Now he sat bare chested in the kitchen in the evenings. Car tires lay in the corridor. My suspicion that I was sleeping in the marital bed of a former Ustaše member did not disturb my sleep. A strange historical optimism that is foreign to Laura had come over me. Even calmness comes readily to me. Karl-Marx-Stadt fanaticizes one. That's why I was immediately attracted to this hasty house-gathering valley basin. I can visualize it more clearly than Almaciz. The Christian church combated heathen customs most successfully where it unscrupulously co-opted them. Berlin never developed such a good appetite. It has always crossed out whatever didn't fit on the fashionable menu. This reworking of history for ease of use may illustrate conditions of the day. In force and thoroughness. Vision, wisdom does not profane organisms. I am rooted in the twelfth century. By virtue of art. Laura is rooted in the legendary. By her nature. Does she know this? A certain Bele H., whom I met in the cellar rooms of Diocletian's palace, told me that history had appeared to her in the shape of her deceased grandfather on 17 June 1953 in lecture hall number 40 of the old Leipzig University. Owing to circumstances, in legendary form. 'For only the history of the powerful is written down in books,' said Bele. I would have thought this woman was my mouthpiece if she hadn't been night-blind. But she not only clung to me as we passed through nearly fifty dark cellar rooms, she also stepped on my feet. She said her present occupation was research engineer. Her place of residence, Zwickau. Her voice came toward me in a large basilica-like cellar room. Bele was surrounded by West German tourists, whom she could not distinguish optically. Acoustically she did well, the arrogant intonation of the Saxon dialect aroused my sympathy right away. When a man from Kiel tried to put a five-mark piece in the rear pocket of her pants, I led her away into a tiny adjoining room. And through many passageways and arches back into the light. There she took the floor again, to discuss in a tendentious manner Brecht's poem about the reading worker. 'Here the poet raises questions about creativity that are not found in books. About the slaves who built cities, for example, who left nameless but visible traces of their abilities: about men. I'm waiting for the poet who could let a female worker who reads raise questions,' said Bele H. 'The slaves of the slaves, who could leave no visible traces of their abilities.' — 'You'll probably wait in vain for a male poet,' I said. 'The female poet is close at hand . . . ' — 'Eh,' Bele H. replied. Since she had hoarded the per diem money allotted to her as a member of a trade delegation, she was able to extend her officially allotted stay by two vacation-like days. We spent them in the medieval streets of the old city. Which was swarming with children. We avoided the market place in the evenings. Between 7:00 and 10:00 P.M., it is a marriage market. The young people stood shoulder to shoulder, all of them beautifully formed, strikingly well dressed. Their chatter blended together into a uniform mass of sound. Caught in a square-cornered, lighted façade space. Bele and I observed its roof from the safety of a side street. It was black. Clear and star-studded. After Bele H. had noticed the first shooting star, she spoke: 'Nobody who strives for greater things can do without the assistance of history. This certainty of being rooted. Self-consciousness that creates awareness of tradition. Pride. A nobleman who can lean on his family tree, for example, has an advantage over workers and women who believe they are standing alone.' – 'Do you know Uwe Parnitzke?' I asked, because her opinions reminded me of his. She didn't answer. In Split I acquired a certain understanding for the ragged garb of young visitors and the Americans' lust for antiques. The palace attracted the yearning ones, the starving. For seven days my feet strolled on the historically grown façade remains of Frau Sarič. And I didn't miss the absent chimney for a moment. For in Split I didn't feel dependent on miracles – if I disregarded the American female tourists. Ignoring them was impossible. In this jumble of peoples, which brings money to the tourist attraction day after day, one recognizes the American women right away, not only in groups but also individually. These victims of the terror of success, whose idol is youth, fit into the organism of the old town of Split like ball gowns on the nude beaches of Crveni Otok Island. When I made a stop in Rovinj, the hotel was plagued one night by excessive noise. It came from a group of Italians and lasted long past midnight. I guessed there were about a hundred people. The next morning it turned out that the noise had been produced by a men's society that numbered eighteen. Aroused by their approaching experience of the Red Island, which one can cross over to from Rovinj by boat. On the ship, which lay tilted in the water because the excited men spurned seats, they asked me and other passengers over and over again the exact way to the nude beach, which was the goal of their journey. Although they were assured that they couldn't miss it, they remained mistrustful. The way one mistrusts a very great good fortune, so as not to jeopardize it. Upon arriving, they hung around bashfully behind bushes with cameras ready. Until about noon they at least kept their socks on. They attached importance not necessarily to youth but to proximity. Oh joy, being allowed to look for hours at a naked woman's skin! In Split I comprehend a woman's skin. In contrast to her brothers, who sit in university chairs thinking about the world, she tastes of it. That is why Laura is crossed by streets and tracks and rivers which deposit objects in the fabric of her body, animate objects and inanimate ones. The disorder increases with increasing age, the sense for order decreases, as does the fear of abundance. Wherein woman knows she is suspended. In Split I understand in terms of an organism the regal gait of many Dalmatian women, whose husbands enjoy their weekend forenoons boating on the sea or lounging in the baths and their evenings in restaurants. Also the sovereign acceptance of age, externally letting themselves go, seeming slovenliness. The American women were a glaring contrast to the dignity of the old Dalmatian women. Can looking out the kitchen window every day onto an infiltrated slave-holding fortress make one so indestructible? The view from Laura's kitchen offers cement. Our sandwiches tasted best next to the mausoleum sphinx. Bele H. drank red wine with hers, I drank milk from the carton. During the siesta we laid our heads in the shadow of a currency-exchange chart. I was grateful to the travel-bureau lady for her offended expression. Which had led me to water and made me drink. Seven days of recovery from my Self. How many Lauras does the world structure of today need in order to be marbled with Lauras?

Chapter 23

Legendary dream yarn

When the young woman who had introduced herself as Tamara Bunke had left, Laura remembered having once seen the name in the newspaper. In capital letters. In a death announcement. She also remembered the following sentence from Che Guevara's diary: 'The country that I drench with my blood is the only piece of earth that belongs to me.' At night her great-grandfather spoke to Laura in her sleep more or less as follows: I am seventy-four now and forever. Eight children survive me. Nothing is left. In our village I was known as a man who could do everything. Everything, that meant: read, repair watches, build furniture and stables, cure illnesses, make rain. Meta knew what I could really do. When a cow had trouble calving or lightning struck the hay barn, people sought my advice. Most of them were poor; the rest were tightfisted. Nothing remains of what I could really do. My father spoke German as a foreign language. My mother cursed in Sorbian. People said she had the evil eye. She showed me how to make rain. Whatever didn't grow in the field inherited from my father had to be earned by doing odd jobs, knotting tulle, working as a railroad-crossing attendant or a night watchman. In winter there were shoes to repair. In summer mowers were needed. Year in and year out, my wife brought work home in a pannier from the tulle factory in Plauen. Meta worked at the neighboring cotton mill. Twelve hours a day. Rough skin pulled threads from the tulle. It tolerated children's hands the best. The five- and six-year-olds liked knotting. When I worked as a night watchman, my wife tended the crossing gate. My wife was quiet. Her frequent pregnancies had exhausted her body. I liked it. She didn't look like her sister Meta. The gate attendant's hut we lived in was located on the Annaberg line. I knew all the train personnel who drove this stretch of track. When I went through the village on my job at night, I journeyed through heaven with Meta. Weekdays she ran a Feinflyer. Sundays she visited us. The children called her Potschappel Auntie because a distant relative who used to live in Potschappel had left earrings to her in her will. Blue stones the size of pupils set in gold hanging on wire rings. The weight stretched out the holes in her earlobes. She saw with four eyes. In the war of 1870–71, I carried the earrings in the lining of my jacket. At Dijon I ran my bayonet through the neck of a Prussian sergeant instead of a Frenchman and was wounded myself. That's probably what saved me. And when I was back home, working odd jobs at my visible lifework, I thought about how the world could be organized, and I was restless and found three models. The only one that succeeded is a kind of religion. And there's nothing left of it. Meta said I would have been a miserable lover if I had been the Kaiser. Her braided hair reached down to her behind. As I lay dying I remembered her jealously.

Chapter 24

Which presents the Minstrel Laura's first wanderlust story

Descent: The apartment was located in the rear building, above the office of Grün's wine business. In the courtyard, which all windows faced, there were empty bottles standing around or stacked in crates, also demijohns, buckets, cartons, trash cans, and big iron baskets, usually filled with water and peeled potatoes. Cats strolled on the flat roof of the one-story building across the way. The hallway smelled of dead flowers. Its wide walls were covered at eye level with printed papers. All the walls of the apartment bore these yellowed papers, which Anke had cut from newspapers, magazines, and advertising pillars. Anke is my divorced girlfriend. I hung my clothes in the wardrobe next to the ones she had left there, and waited half a day for Lutz, and a night and half of another day. During this time I got the dust off the furniture, floor, and carpets, built fires in the stoves, washed moldy bits of food from dishes, bought flowers and a lot of food, and listened to old Italian cansos from a record player and three loudspeakers. A man sang alto. Unearthly sounds, you couldn't imagine angels singing better. Anke had a child too. Her former husband traveled abroad looking for girlfriends. There was schnapps in the refrigerator. I waited as we had agreed. Lutz is used to housewives. Three rooms and a kitchen, cemeteries are a good place to make love. My apartment isn't covered with paper. I'm ashamed. Thirteen naked days. I looked at seascapes, skyscrapers, pine trees, Notre Dame of Paris, schnapps bottles with foreign names on their labels, female and male nudes and nude scenes. In the lavatory even the door was covered with them. All the photos were in color. Some of the postcards had canceled postage. The theater posters in the kitchen bulged from the steam. Transfer images of the world. That is our share. Mine. That much is certain when I say 'I.' When I say 'I am a woman.'

Chapter 25

Which relates a surprising trobadorean sign of life from Beatrice, interpreted by Laura as evidence of general recovery

Dear Laura,

Of course nobody can expect respectable poetry from an 841-year-old trobadora. Usually one writes poetry up to age eighteen, in unusual cases until thirty, in extraordinary cases until seventy. Prose is in keeping with my age; for Professor Wenzel Morolf it is out of place. He works at the Institute for Nuclear Physics in the Siberian Department of the USSR Academy of Sciences. I met him here in Genoa. So please commission a canso immediately from a suitable woman poet who knows Russian. Money is no object. Of course, you can't tell her that. To give her an idea of this man's beauty, I'm sending the partial transcription of a speech attuned to my intellectual capacity that Morolf, when asked about his research subject, delivered to me in a hotel hall. To be sure, the gentleman's intellectual elegance has been flattened by the interpreter's rough translation. Sarah Kirsch, for example, would seem well suited. Has Wesselin started walking?

Best greetings,
Beatrice

P.S. Lauretta, dear Lauretta mine,
When will we meet again so fine . . .

Chapter 26

Enclosure from the Trobadora's Letter, Containing Excerpts of Suggestive Arch-Poetic Views That Open Up the Field of Research on Inanimate Matter

Theory and experiments have proven that every elementary particle has a double – a particle with the same qualities except, let us say, the electrical charge and spin. Particles and antiparticles are often compared to a pair of gloves. The 'antiworld' is a mirror image of the world that actually exists.

The first to observe a particle of antimatter in cosmic rays was a member of the Academy of Science, Skobeltsyn. The particle behaved in a most unusual way. Only some years later did it become clear that it was an antielectron, subsequently named 'positron.' Later, at the big American accelerator in Berkeley the antiproton and the antineutron were discovered, and at the accelerator in Geneva they discovered the nucleus of a heavy hydrogen isotope, the antideuteron. Recently scientists in Serpukhov isolated the nucleus of the light helium isotope, antihelium.

Through this series of experiments the possible existence of antimatter was demonstrated theoretically.

The first concentration of antimatter, long hovering in space, was extracted in Novosibirsk in the form of an intensive positron bundle. One can even have one's photograph taken in the bright ray of antimatter, as French President Georges Pompidou did during a visit to our institute.

We assume that we will soon obtain not only light particles but also antiprotons – the primeval substance of antimatter. Then we will be able to conduct a rather exotic experiment. Parallel to an antiproton bundle, we will run a positron bundle with the same velocity. The bundles will form antiplasma in which atoms of antihydrogen arise. Those will be the first antiatoms on earth and perhaps in the entire universe, assuming that antistars and antigalaxies do not exist. From antiatoms one could theoretically form chemical compounds and constructions of any degree of difficulty, including living antiorganisms.

But we'll leave that to the authors of futuristic novels for now.

For scientists, however, it is now time to think seriously about annihilation fuel. Particles and antiparticles do not tolerate each other and disintegrate on contact. Thus the matter and antimatter, organized as particles, atoms, and molecules, are transformed into electromagnetic oscillations – gamma rays and light quanta. In this way the greatest possible amount of energy per unit of fuel mass is released – thousands of times the energy released by a nuclear or thermonuclear reaction and billions of times the energy of the best and most modern rocket fuel. This enables us to speak of the scientific basis for flight to distant stars.

Soon we will possess a greater quantity of antihydrogen than we had of plutonium, the primary nuclear fuel in the 1940s when we were just beginning work on the problem of the atom. Scientists needed five years from the discovery of nuclear fission to the exploitation of atomic energy. Even if we are less fortunate with antimatter and need ten times more time for exploitation, fifty years are a minuscule amount of time to open humankind's way to the stars.

Chapter 27

Laura's letter of reply to Beatrice de Dia, Genoa, poste restante

Dear AntiLaura,

I can't tell you how happy I am. And there is much that I don't understand; one doesn't have to understand everything. Of course I resumed my regular occupation immediately, visited Sarah Kirsch, and presented your request. She couldn't accept the commission, since she has fallen behind with her poetry translation commitments because of a two-year-old son. While we were talking, Wesselin nearly swallowed a little red horse belonging to her son. She advised me, as a last resort, to engage a male poet to write the canso for Professor Wenzel Morolf and was kind enough to make a few phone calls in this regard. To determine their aptitude for the task, she began the phone calls with a test question: What would you do if you woke up as a woman one day? Ten of the eleven men asked reacted with embarrassed silence, revulsion, shock; one of them was actually revolted by the idea, as if it were comparable to Gregor Samsa's transformation into an insect.

I have an appointment with the eleventh poet, who found the idea attractive, on 7 October. Wesselin has tonsillitis.

Best greetings,
Laura

P.S. I had to express my delight at receiving your letter by writing a story. It deals, as you may guess, with our grammar rule, Anaximander. I'm enclosing the piece for the fun of it.

Chapter 28

Laura introduces Anaximander for the fun of it

Monoceros: They say it was so wild that it couldn't be caught by anyone, only by virgins. It ran up to me when I was ten years old, that's no miracle. The gang was playing cops and robbers. I was hiding in a blooming elderberry bush, rubbing ants from my arms and legs, wetting the welts from ant stings with spit, and listening through the sweet fragrance of the umbels. It resounded in my head. Now and then I thought I heard falling rocks, waited for it in fact, despite my desire to be undiscovered. But not forgotten. As I crouched in an uncomfortable position that made my limbs fall asleep, my delight in the inaccessibility of my hiding place at the bottom of a porphyry quarry began to yield to worry that this game might long since have ended and another one begun that I was excluded from. The unicorn freed me from the conflict between curiosity and ambition. All of a sudden, it was standing at the bush, spearing leaves on its spiral horn like warehouse packers spearing cash register receipts. When I gave a start, it made itself invisible. It was so shy, even with itself, that it preferred to remain invisible. This preference suited me fine. After it had eaten three umbels, I was allowed to get on its back. Its hair was short like a horse's, white in color. Its body and gait were also horselike but softer; the jolting of its hoofbeats was transmitted relatively painlessly to the rider's head. It climbed the steep porphyry wall effortlessly. I held onto its mane. I was the first to reach the meeting point but with a greater effect than the last robber. Because the unicorn had remained invisible, it looked as if I was floating. The two cops keeping watch thought I was flying. They stood paralyzed by fear, unable to catch me. I enjoyed my triumph, dismounted, and got out of there. In fear of spoiling the moment or losing the unicorn to the leader if it suddenly became visible. The leader always took everything he liked. I didn't dare tell about it at home either. My mother didn't allow house pets. The unicorn could be kept secret because it was undemanding and dependable. It ate only words and kept its promise not to show itself until my deflowering. When it wasn't going places with me, it lay under my bed in my room at home. The secret gave me feelings of superiority and the strength to be inconspicuous, the better to observe things. I gave in to temptation only once and used the unicorn to win the high jump competition at a BdJM athletics event. Whereupon our teacher, Herr Adler, actually raised my grade in English by one point, since a sound mind had to dwell in a sound body. Adler wore his SA uniform even when demonstrating gymnastic routines on the apparatus. The air-raid shelter seemed safe to me with the unicorn there. In mid-May 1945, I lay with the unicorn on a bleaching tarpaulin spattered with shot splinters and saw that the air space was a sky. When foraging for supplies, it carried more than a handcart load, escaping with the hard-won booty when patrols appeared, and also helped harvest potatoes. It scraped away earth with its front hooves and speared the tubers. My mother was surprised that my basket got full so quickly, mostly with damaged goods. Its horn also purloined sofa cushions, damaging the birds of paradise and tropical plants embroidered by my mother. I wasn't sorry. The cushions were useful under Anaximander's head but bothersome when karate- chopped into place on the sofa; only visitors dared to lean against them. Since starting secondary school, I called the unicorn Anaximander. Inspired by a philosophical remark of my history teacher's. The naming occasioned a grammatical sex change. I was in favor of it. Since the way to school was long and the streetcars overfilled, I used Anaximander as my means of transportation. Every morning I floated across ruins. The air route saved ten minutes. My mother didn't like to get up early either. I think she felt humiliated all her life. That's why she withdrew early into her pride. There she thought about the trials and tribulations of the world, calculated debits and credits, and established justice: women are coolies, but men are swine. That's how she pulled through. And she was glad she had a daughter, and she wanted to pull me through too. At age fifteen I had my first period, and she thought it was time to introduce me to bookkeeping. She observed uneasily that I was becoming more like my father. He had thirteen brothers and sisters. She must have thought her father-in-law was a monster. She thought affectionate gestures such as kisses — she spoke the word in dialect — were pretexts. Men all wanted the same thing. At the time, I was exchanging caresses with boys of the same age whom I didn't think capable of doing it. But I checked out adults in that regard, my parents first of all. And next, chiefly teachers, opera singers, pastors and my grandfather on my mother's side, whom I had believed to be the most proper human being imaginable. I pictured all of them in raunchy acts. The world had become sinister. Exciting. The airborne means of locomotion absolutely matched my moods and opinions at the time: since the air-raid alarms had stopped, the year seemed to consist only of holidays. The ruined city notwithstanding. Because of it. When I went with Anaximander to clean bricks, he had a banner tied to his flanks. When I spoke to families during our campaigns for political reeducation, I made use of Anaximander's supernatural abilities to accelerate the persuasive process. To this end, I hung posters on his invisible body. He made them move like living images in the hallways where the meetings took place. Successfully. Only once did an old woman suffer a religious relapse when the images moved. Since cheating when doing school assignments was generally considered an act unworthy of a progressive pupil, I rarely used the highly qualified Anaximander for this purpose. I only required him to steal lab materials from the desk of the chemistry teacher, whom I believed to be reactionary, and to deliver letters. I wrote them to various boys. Not simultaneously. Nevertheless, Anaximander was disobedient at times. The letters I wrote to my friend Jochen were delivered by Anaximander with his lip curled. My mother's bookkeeping was concerned with values. Before I left for Leipzig, where I was enrolled in the university, my mother swore that the stakes were out of proportion to the event. A married woman had obligations. But I should enjoy life as long as I was still single. I looked forward to defloration with curiosity and fear and hesitated almost a year. My first sexual intercourse was an act of pity. I remember the laborious, painful penetration that I endured for the sake of the man who had seemed friendly and above all trustworthy beforehand. And afterwards too; that's why I was able to overlook the unfortunate incident. Considering that it lasted only a short time, two or three minutes with the lights out. I believe that I even begged him to be careful, although there had been a rustling of paper, which raised hopes of a condom. Besides a mixture of self-surrender and subjection, which reading had prepared me for, I remember only great fear and a few spots of blood on the sheet. The event made a sentimental impression on me. Because of its sinful character. In any case, it made you grown up: ambivalent. So Anaximander left me that same night and never returned.

FOURTH INTERMEZZO

Wherein the Reader Learns What the Beautiful Melusine Copied from Irmtraud Morgner's Novel *Rumba for an Autumn* into Her 28th Melusinian Book in 1964

As Uwe was riding into the city today, it received him with warmth that hung trapped between the buildings. The light, pale sky above the city seemed to be contemplating a storm. As Uwe crossed the median strip, he felt familiar cellar fumes rising through ventilation grids: cool, stale air from the underground traffic. Uwe turned around and continued walking on the median, across the ventilation grids, on the cement that occasionally trembled from the underground traffic. Barely noticeable. But Uwe felt tingling on the soles of his feet. A voluptuous feeling of relief washed over him. The light, pale city sky above him was a Gothic vault: nave, aisle, transept. Uwe walked slowly with firm steps, he had time. He thought: I'm a man who looked for a new father. My real father, whom I hated even as a child because he withheld his name from me, all the children had their father's name except me, my real father was someone I learned to hate for sure, after the war, for certain sure. And then I stripped him away from my life and grew up alone, independent. And I looked for a new father, one you could look up to, one you could pledge yourself to, one you could believe in. His face was present everywhere, on pictures and monuments, in every city, here too; you could sing and read about him, and some people I respected, because they had been true to their convictions under the gallows during those twelve years, called him Daddy. The first book that introduced me to the ideas of the great revolution was his *Brief Biography.* I excerpted almost all of it and passed the test for the Good Scholar's medal a short time later. Bronze. I gave lectures about the great life that was briefly described in 250 pages. His name was never mentioned without the embellishment of an attributive adjective or an appositive. And at age eighteen, on my second father's birthday, I entered the ranks of those led by HIM. For HE was said to have inspired all the heroic deeds and victories that had been won: *sa Stalina, sa rodinu* – for Stalin, for the homeland. Then came 5 March 1953. I sat in my student room and listened again and again to the news that was broadcast at short intervals starting in the early morning hours of 6 March, surrounded by the endless train of funeral music. The endless train resounded for four days, and on his burial day, at the hour when the coffin was lowered into its resting place, sirens howled. I stood honor guard at the feet of a statue that had been hastily brought in. Tubs of flowers were crowded around me; it was as if the earth had opened its summer treasure troves early, for everything was coming apart at the seams anyway. I'm a man who has lost a father.

The median was split by two lines of track that emerged from the deep and rose up to a roof that was borne by pylons. They called it *Magistratsschirm*, City Council umbrella. You could walk under its shelter.

The storm came up and hurled itself under the roof. It was now drawing crowds from both sides of the street; Uwe walked in company. Gusts of wind from the side streets assaulted the shelter-seekers. Scraps of paper were swirled through the air. But up above, the traffic rolled on in a steady rhythm. Uwe remained unscathed and kept to his resolve.

The first raindrops splattered onto the pavement. Umbrellas were placed in position. Then the rain descended upon the city. The storm blew sheets of water under the roof.

Uwe fled into the nearest train station and bought a ticket that spooled out of an ancient appliance. The yellow train was there in no time. Uwe boarded it and rode dry through the rain for a few minutes along the buildings at the third-floor level. Then the train plunged into the deep whence it had come, where it belonged, and there was no longer any weather. Timeless cellar air, violet light, increasing and decreasing decibel level according to the speed of the train, a forest of poles to hold on to. Several meters of safety from storms.

Then Uwe transferred into a yellow train that had never seen a storm, nor the sun either, of course. He entrusted himself to it.

The train passed under the avenue that had once borne HIS name. It no longer bore HIS statue either.

Uwe didn't have to think about anything for the time being. He didn't have to watch where he was going. He let himself be transported.

He reached the editorial office around noon. The boss was out. Uwe told Plischka they should send someone else to the conference, he wasn't the right man for this kind of thing.

'We don't have anyone else,' said Plischka.

'I'm not going there again, at any rate,' said Uwe.

'You have to; it's your assignment.'

'But I don't know anything about it.'

'Then you'll just have to get into it,' said Plischka. 'Or you'll have to change jobs.'

Change jobs. He said that to all the incompetent journalists. They were all incompetent except him.

Uwe left the office and took off along side streets. In an empty lot, some children were struggling with a kite.

But Valeska still hadn't written. Maybe he really was incompetent.

Uwe flagged down the first taxi that came his way and asked to be taken to where the city was green. No other city that he knew was this wild about camping. For a while he wandered through the sun-scorched pine forest, getting stones in his shoes, pine cone splinters, sand. But then he felt drawn toward the water, irresistibly.

The Spree strutted in the pale sun, lapped against the shore, rippled in the reeds. It let boats race over its back, wind-driven boats, motor-driven, hand-driven; it decked itself out with gulls and sails and with polished mahogany. It had fetched down the summer blue of the sky and was rocking it to sleep.

A city just made for dreaming.

But Valeska hadn't written one single time.

A barge was moving slowly across the lake that was connected to its neighbor. Was it moving on its own power? Was it floating with the current? Uwe lay down on his back. His dreams sank into the water, laden with thoughts, with memories, a barge loaded down with brooding, and a wind came up from the port side . . .

—when I was a barge, a young one with very little draft, I didn't need a motor, for I had the current and the current belonged to the river and the river belonged to HIM: I belonged to HIM with my small freight; and I traveled a world that was organized, systematized, comprehensible, full of horizons, a finite world, and, of course, I was stable when I was a barge —

The wind brought cool air, dampness, and Uwe's suit was getting clammy and surely wrinkled and probably stained—but that didn't matter, after this defeat nothing mattered. Uwe was absolutely without talent for technical things; he always had been and always would be. And probably even his daughter, Juliane, would make fun of him, if he still had her, and it had to turn out this way when a blind man tried to write about colors. Could a woman like Valeska love a blind man, a half-blind man who groped his way around uncertainly and was delicate, frail. Maybe he was frail by nature; you couldn't choose your character. There were some people who were born for the barricades. Kantus might be one of them, and then there were others. Uwe was one of the others. One of the dreamers. One of the quiet ones. The loud dreamers had chances these days, but the quiet ones? He was wrong somehow, he felt it even as a child; as a child he had wanted to be altogether different. At that time he always wanted to lead a gang but only succeeded twice. Twice he prevailed against himself, and he thought that was the beginning of a new stage in his life. Many other new stages followed. Almost every year he proclaimed a new stage for himself. For example, when he was accepted to secondary school, when he joined the youth organization, when he stripped that unfathomable Christ and his own natural father from his life and looked for a new father. One you could look up to, one you could pledge yourself to, one you could believe in. Easily. Because he could be seen. And his voice could be heard. And his army had freed Uwe from the nightmare of his natural father. And those who had taken Uwe in when he had no bed of his own and no grandmother said, *We will be victorious because the great Stalin is our leader.* And then the insecurity that had always haunted him gradually disappeared. And in the curriculum vitae that he sent with his application papers to register at the university, he called this the beginning of the decisive stage. And then came 5 March.

—but I kept on going, as always I entrusted myself to the current that HE had guided and that now had to guide itself in his name, and the stability was gratifying, when I was a barge, until the day the current shifted —

That was the hardest blow of his life, the one he probably still hadn't recovered from.

Shortly before it, he had been chosen as an assistant for the *Grundlagenstudium*, the foundation course in Marxism-Leninism. He immediately convened a meeting; he was grateful to the instructor, Jasak, for his willingness to assume leadership of the meeting. Uwe had known him for over four years and knew what he could expect from him.

Jasak, the son of a professor who had lectured on race theory and now held a university chair in the western part of the city, had broken with his parents. Nonetheless, he felt burdened by his family background and was at pains — perhaps without even being aware of it — to compensate for this defect by special diligence. He was known for his thoroughness and adherence to principles, 'take it easy,' he would say, 'when the line is clear . . . '

Uwe pulled himself together and prepared a speech: support for Jasak.

But then it turned out that Uwe stabbed him in the back by doing this.

Jasak spoke about the Party Congress, numbered twentieth in the chronology, with the same highly concentrated acuity, with the same stone-faced expression as he had the last time. He spoke about the disclosures as if they went without saying, as if they had already gone without saying. And with the same self-assurance and severity that had always made him stand out, he denounced those who still refused to see the light. Only the conclusion of his speech diverged a nuance from the usual: Jasak said, Long live the great Lenin.

For Uwe, Jasak's change of direction was so appalling that he needed time to take it in. But then he struck out in all directions with words and gestures, and nothing mattered to him. *Sa Stalina, sa rodinu.*

He defended the image of the *giant* whom he had chosen for his second father and without whom, so it seemed to him at the time, he wouldn't have become a self-aware person. He would have liked to punch Jasak in his stone face that looked as if his change of direction hadn't cost him an inner struggle. He thought: treason. And later he worked himself farther and farther into an opposition that Jasak recorded carefully in a book with numbered pages. And one day he added it up and filed the petition to delegate Uwe to production on probation.

Uwe worked for a year as an unskilled laborer in a print shop. The same one in which Franz Kantus sat at the typesetting machine. The same one that printed the newspaper that Uwe now wrote for. Franz had encouraged him to write. Actually, Uwe stayed with the newspaper because Franz was there. Later he lived with Franz. Uwe owed him everything.

Evening descended upon the lake, early and unsummery, absorbing the last warmth of the October day. The water turned black; in this neighborhood the night seemed to collect itself before rising: line up in puddles according to size, ready, halt, count off . . .

– it was a nice time, when I was a barge, the world was finite, and one man understood it for everyone, and the weak found protection under the shelter of his greatness, when I was a barge, but now I'd rather live under a roof that I have helped to build, although that's more difficult, especially for the weak, it's simpler to hang your heart on one person than on millions, it's easier to read in one face than in a science, but I'd rather live in a world that is infinite and incomprehensibly full of work and questions and hungry for talents, although it takes more strength to get a boat afloat yourself than to drift: I never want to be a barge again —

The lake lay naked in the twilight, stripped of its block-and-tackle adornments. No boat caressed its back. Then the shores on the other side disappeared. And the night ironed away the wrinkles from its skin.

Sleep. Finally. Waiting for the moment that one never experiences, which is surely just as uncertain as gliding into death. Letting oneself drop into nothingness where the unchecked dreams dwell; the entry to the moment is blue. Uwe is already in the entryway. A reddish spot rotates through the trees, changes color, red violet, blue violet, black, soon black will arrive, soon the light will go out, the moment is incredibly black, the moment, the moment. But it doesn't arrive. Again. For three days it hasn't come.

Uwe could no longer write the way he used to; he said to himself: I am a man who has a hard time getting to the issue, maybe I'll write drafts all my life, up to now I've only done drafts, à la Störtebeker, à la Stalin, à la Laura, à la Valeska, à la Franz, I'd like to be like Franz, if he finds out about it there'll be trouble, he always says don't cling to people, stick to the subject, but for me, every subject has a face, the big one has Franz's face, the little one has the Armenian's face, his black eyes have haunted me for three days, I can't watch the days go by, and my nights are sleepless. I can't work because I'm thirty-one years old and I still haven't gotten to the issue, I'm the issue, but I don't know who I am, I still haven't found myself, I'm a production of stages, my life up to now is a collection of variants on other people's lives, I'm a man who has lost a father.

When he woke up, something was hitting him in the face. He reached for it with his hand, but the blows didn't stop; he couldn't see anything either. At first he thought someone had struck him blind. His hands were stiff, when he tried to move, he felt resistance, cold, wet, wetness fell into his face, collecting and running in rivulets down over his forehead and temples, itching. Cold lay upon him and under him, and he still couldn't see. He just comprehended that it was raining; he thought: I slept, finally, and then he saw the tree overhead.

And got up.

And went to Berta's.

She didn't actually say hello. She said, 'I thought it was Katschmann.'

'Are you disappointed?'

'I'm waiting for him,' said Berta.

'Does he have to work?'

'Until six, now it's nearly eleven, maybe something has happened?'

'He'll come,' said Uwe. Actually he hoped for the opposite. Although he didn't hate him. Sometimes he even admired him. But he always pictured an insect when he thought about him. And if he then didn't look in a mirror right away, he would feel an external skeleton on himself too. He was afraid of Katschmann, the way you can be afraid of something you know intimately.

'I haven't finished the doily yet,' said Berta. 'I have several things to finish, I have to sew a dress for myself . . . '

'But there's no hurry . . . '

'Yes, there is,' said Berta. 'There's a hurry for the dress.'

Women were remarkable creatures. Some of them ran around in the same getup for years, Berta did for decades, and all of a sudden they got something into their head, and it didn't suit them any more, and they had to have a new one right away. Valeska's taste was unpredictable in the same way.

Katschmann certainly hadn't been born with an external skeleton either. He had acquired it through the years. Perhaps the first one's name was 'obedience.' A soldier who had served time, land-registry official, Eastern Front: obedience. Probably the great collapse took place for him then, but apparently he had soon found something else to hold on to. He was a Soviet prisoner of war, maybe he had even come across someone from the National Committee, in any case, he must have constructed a new skeleton without delay; presumably, he forced the transformation quickly and rigorously and subjected his life henceforth absolutely and selflessly to the new principle. Perhaps it remained alien to his nature for a long time, however hard he tried; he underwent retraining, he became an electrical fitter and then worked his way up to engine driver. His energy and his will were admirable, he meant well, he always drove the same route, dependable, there are coachmen, drivers, and leaders, my trains are always full, my trains drive hard and use a lot of electricity, left hand on the control button, right hand on the driver's brake valve, ahead of me the ribbon of track that the train eats up, at sixty, at eighty kilometers per hour, bridges; steep railway embankments, brown from the rust of the brake dust, train stations, also rusty, houses, signal lights, green, yellow, red, quays, silos, a museum built of white marble, a palace of marble and gold with hundreds of paintings, the pictures praised Gori's great son in hundreds of situations, in a style: heroic; it seemed as if an artist had painted them, next to the palace stood the house he'd been born in, a tiny farmer's cottage, beautiful in its modesty, surrounded and almost crushed by templelike walls, he had been in Georgia for only one day on a reporting assignment many years ago, he felt the impact of the rails under his feet, you can only feel the train when you stand, I always stand, regulation no. 2: *Fahrt frei – Halt erwarten*, all clear ahead – be prepared to stop. I pull the lever of the driver's brake valve slowly toward me, the power of the train rears up under my feet, I pull into the station to respectful applause . . .

'He's drunk,' said Berta.

'Who?'

'I was just in the kitchen. I thought I heard something fall, but it was Katschmann, he was staggering around the kitchen.'

'The main thing is, he's here.'

'But he never drinks. I can't even put beer on the table.'

'I really only wanted to ask you if Valeska has written to you.'

'No,' said Berta, 'I don't like to write letters either. Maybe somebody got him drunk.'

'I'm going now,' said Uwe. But he couldn't leave. Katschmann staggered up to him and pressed him against the wall with his spongy body. His round head swayed right before his face, a big red schnapps-reeking buoy. Uwe braced his hands against Katschmann's shoulders; it was like taking hold of dough.

Suddenly Katschmann turned around and said, 'So my wife-to-be has company.'

'I had no way of knowing . . . '

'But I did,' said Katschmann, 'maybe I'm not good enough for you any more?' He reached for Berta's arm.

Berta pulled her arm away.

'Have you forgotten that he walked out on you once?'

Berta stood up straight, her eyelids half shut over her protruding eyeballs.

Katschmann stepped falteringly toward Uwe again but missed him, fell against the door. He pounded on the door with his fists and yelled, 'She belongs to me, Franz, she belongs to me.'

Uwe had a hard time pulling him away from the door and onto a chair. Only when he was seated and Uwe's arm was holding him to the chair back did Katschmann recognize him. His gray eyes, which lay slantwise on his face, pressed down sideways by the drooping of his eyelids, cleared at once. He stopped trying to strike out, he pulled his shoulders back and straightened his back, at once he was all there, as soon as he recognized Uwe. And he apologized.

And the next minute he asked about the article.

'It isn't finished yet,' said Uwe.

'Why?'

'Because it isn't finished yet.'

'That's no answer.'

'Yes, it is.'

'I could be mistaken, you can contradict me, but I tell you: In this situation that's no answer.'

'I contradict you.'

'With what right?'

'Aha.'

'In this situation I demand . . . '

'By the way, the Soviet Union is withdrawing her missiles from Cuba, according to TASS, Uncle Edgar, according to TASS.' Uwe watched with satisfaction as Katschmann's prominent ears lost color. Even the best radar ears were at the moment apparently incapable of receiving an official argument. Katschmann seemed to be dependent on his brain. His shoulders fell forward, his back bent, he said, 'I know, I don't understand it, nobody understands it because it's a mistake, I tell you, and you'll agree with me, it's a mistake, but for tactical reasons, you understand, a discussion of mistakes now would only make everything worse.' He dragged a bottle from his jacket pocket and took a sip. And it made him drunk again. He babbled something about retreating and that it wouldn't have happened if HE were still alive. And then he said with a tongue heavy from schnapps, 'We've been betrayed. The Russians have betrayed us.' And his head fell forward. Uwe braced himself against Katschmann's shoulders and sat him up straight again, he grabbed onto the doughy flesh. But Katschmann wouldn't let them put him to bed. He puked his guts out in the bathroom. When he came back out, with a damp head, he said, 'It's all shit. But I won't let anyone take Berta from me. We're getting married.'

BOOK NINE

A WOMAN NAMED PENTHESILEA BRINGS LAURA A ZINC BOX FROM VALESKA KANTUS, CONTAINING HADEAN STORIES AND WONDROUS PROSPECTS FOR NEW RESEARCH IN THE FIELD OF ANIMATE MATTER

While Wesselin's spirits were being darkened by misery occasioned by the growth of two incisors in his upper jaw, his mother received a zinc box. The woman who delivered the box, fifty-five centimeters long, thirty-two centimeters wide, and seventeen centimeters deep, refused the chair that Laura offered her. 'I must avoid the extreme bending that is required for sitting,' the woman said, chewing gum. The box was soldered together. The flesh of the woman's hands seemed even harder to Laura than that of the trobadora. Who was named as the sender of the box. The woman called herself Penthesilea. Laura recalled having read the name in books. 'Didn't a certain Achilles once fall in love with you?' asked Laura facetiously. 'After he had chopped me up in a duel,' answered Penthesilea, also facetiously, putting her right thumb and index finger to her teeth and pulling a string of chewing gum to arm's length. 'After all, Achilles wasn't so strong that he could fall in love with a woman like me. Only in death did I seem desirable to him. Even heroes need a downhill slope in order to function.' Penthesilea tipped back her curly Afro, threaded the string of gum back into her mouth, and laughed so immoderately that Wesselin started whimpering. Penthesilea held one of her shirt cuffs into his playpen. Wesselin stuffed the fabric between his jaws and chewed assiduously. Laura doubted that the shirt could meet minimal hygienic standards. Its material was reminiscent of a sheet from a lover's bed. Laura suspected that Penthesilea couldn't sit down because her jeans were too tight. Or too worn-out. 'You can lie down on the sofa,' said Laura. 'I'd rather have a schnapps,' said Penthesilea. 'How's Beatrice?' asked Laura. 'The way young people are, marvelous,' answered Penthesilea. 'Did you meet Beatrice in Genoa?' asked Laura, after bringing the schnapps. Penthesilea fished out her gum, stuck it under the tabletop, downed the schnapps, and replied, 'In Hades. I'm in a hurry. Passing through. I have to be back in Caerleon on Usk the day after tomorrow. I happened to meet your friend Beatrice on the 3,721st Elysian Field. She was searching. To no avail, like me. With so many new arrivals, it's no wonder that the organization leaves something to be desired. During the three months that Pluto has Persephone with him as his wife, the situation is even more chaotic. Because the deposed queen of the underworld cripples the service workers' discipline with her songs of revenge, which decry wars as the worst perversion of the patriarchy. About half the work force is devils. The other half was taken over by Pluto. To be sure, he has been stripped of power too, but he's made a deal with the devil, which is why he isn't sitting in a holding cell like Persephone but can move about, under guard. Eighty thousand dead from starvation every day, nothing but skin and bones, children with swollen bellies. Among the arrivals from Vietnam are creatures who have partly or totally lost their human appearance. I'll mention only the charred lumps of flesh of the napalm victims, the deformities caused by contact poisons, the bodies torn apart by bombs, the ones dismembered by torture. One former prisoner had been torn in two. "The Americans tied my arms and legs to two different helicopters, took off, and tore me apart," he told us. I've seen a lot in life. My former profession made me callous. That's why I was chosen for this courier job. But it wears me out. Over 90 percent of the Vietnamese arrivals are civilians. Some of the U.S. pilots who were shot down over Vietnam still carry a scrap of material around with them with the American flag printed on it and under it an appeal in fourteen languages. In the most important European languages, in classical and modern Chinese, in Vietnamese, and in the languages of its neighboring countries. The appeal says, "I am an American citizen. I don't speak your language. An unfortunate accident has forced me to ask you for food, shelter, and protection. Please take me to someone who can guarantee my safety and arrange to have me sent back to my people. My government will make it worth your while." Those who died a natural death take the cripples and fragments for walks on the Elysian Fields. I'm glad that I have business in Hades only rarely. When I met Beatrice, I had come down to bring the director of the 3,721st field her summons to Caerleon. The director, Conzetta is her name, was born in Palermo. She was a worker in a fish factory. She's waiting out in front of the building now. I don't want to keep this bashful soul waiting too long. Best greetings, as I said, from Beatrice, and in the box she sends you miscellaneous writings by a certain Valeska, who was just checked in as clinically dead at age forty. Traffic accident. Whether the resuscitation efforts that doctors from earth announced over loudspeakers have been successful, I cannot say. I had to go back. By way of Aornon. I always use the Aornon exit. Good-by.' Penthesilea loosened the wad of gum from under the tabletop, stuffed it into her mouth, and disappeared, chewing. Was this another woman who had rescued herself across the ages with sleeping draughts? Was she a con artist? Or a trickster? Laura remembered that not long ago the *Berliner Zeitung* had published warnings about a female trickster. A check of Laura's wallet yielded no cause for concern. In the zinc box, which Laura had opened by a plumber, there were, in fact, miscellaneous writings by a certain Valeska. Laura sold the miscellaneous writings to the literary magazine *Sinn und Form* for publication under the title 'Hadean stories and wondrous prospects for new research in the field of animate matter.' Under the rubric 'Remarks,' she noted: 'Valeska Kantus, b. 1931, d. 1971, Biologist. The printed text is based on a posthumously discovered manuscript. It contains the stories written on the backs of the pages of a popular science monograph. Since the Rudolf Uhlenbrook listed as the author of the monograph is probably an invention of Valeska's, the reader will find the papers reproduced true to the original, for technical reasons printed seriatim. The beginning of the reversed text is always indicated by the parenthetical notation R.U. = Rudolf Uhlenbrook, the beginning of the stories by V.ff. = Valeska continues. The translation from the Hadean was done by Beatrice de Dia.'

Valeska Kantus: Hadean stories and wondrous prospects for new research in the field of animate matter

(V.) Divorce in a Melancholy Key

1

Uwe was more beautiful than all other men I've known and know now. Kinder. More just. If we had met each other a mere hundred years later, we might have been able to enjoy each other for a long time. As it was, we were both soon plotting escape. Which was a conflict for both of us.

2

A natural event finally distanced me from Uwe. On the third of June I left the outpatient clinic, self-sufficient. As a closed system. The authorized court was housed in a distant building. I picked up the marriage certificate from the apartment and arrived at the fortresslike building early in the forenoon. I presented my request to the doorman. He asked if I had the necessary papers and money with me and showed me inside the labyrinthine walls after I had presented my identification papers. There I couldn't achieve my goal by sticking to the whole truth. Which was cheerful in spite of everything. Cheerful grounds for divorce are no grounds. I struggled to recite the ominous reasons that I had laboriously gathered.

3

A vestibule rampant with space, extravagantly high ceilings, yet economical, in the hallways miserly. Art Nouveau. So, the way he threw money out the window was ominous. He threw it out for clothes or for books he had misplaced, for medications; he was always taking some kind of pills or drops, perhaps prophylactically. He had no confidence in his body. Which was organically healthy, as the doctors assured him; in any case he was harmoniously built, slim, a gentle face with a severe Roman nose, a hesitant look behind a curtain of eyelashes, an abundance of brown hair, everything according to my taste. But not Uwe's. He admired muscle men and could not seriously believe that they turned me off. Maybe that's why he was always buying deodorants, because he thought his body stank, so to speak. Yes, he was always out of money; that was ominous. But he also earned less than I. And that depressed him. Against his convictions, it depressed him. His convictions, of course, required him to be glad about it. And he always kept to what was required: he was proud of me.

4

Where the hallways intersected, the walls bore inscriptions pointing the way; their numbers commanded respect. Barricades with beams hanging on iron-footed poles. Signs on similar poles requesting caution on the waxed floors. His way of seeing the darkest side of every private event was ominous too. Uwe had acquired this habit during the three years of our marriage; I'd never noticed it before. If he couldn't find the manuscript of a reportage he'd written for his newspaper, his first thought was that he'd left it in the S-Bahn. If he asked for vacation time, it was with the expectation of being turned down. If the two of us were invited somewhere, he was convinced that the hosts were actually interested in me, not him. Then he'd sit around with a long-suffering expression. For a long time I thought he was bored, so I'd try to talk about something amusing. But after such efforts, he would clam up entirely, which I took as an indication of inferior quality on my part. Wrongly, as it turned out. By chance. If his French friend, Alain, hadn't gotten him drunk during a visit, I would still believe the things Uwe made himself do. After his schnapps-induced confession, I said, 'But isn't it more honorable to be loved by a human being than by a creature, dammit all.' — 'Theoretically, yes,' he said. — 'I'm good at this and you're good at something else. Do you think I love you because you represent something?' I shrieked. 'I love you because you are something, that's a lot more, dammit all. That's not significant for your colleagues and who knows, whoever else makes snide remarks around there. It's only significant for me because I love you, isn't it enough for you that I love you?' — 'Yes,' he said. From conviction. He was an empathic person, a rarity among men. Capable of falling ill from sympathy. If I told him that my back hurt, I could be sure he would soon feel pain in his. Uwe was attentive by nature, considerate, not the least bit authoritarian. All qualities that he unofficially perceived as weaknesses. And probably struggled against. I perceived them as strengths, which wasn't much comfort to him. His casual gait with toes pointing sharply outwards, which his colleagues at the newspaper called Chaplinesque, overplayed his insecurity. Was it a wound? Did he always end up with women he thought were superior because he had missed having a mother all his life?

5

The waiting room of the municipal district court was located on the fourth floor in the ninth cross-corridor on the left. Under number 379. The number was painted on a metal plate hanging from an elbow mount. Similar signs hung above all the doors. All the chairs and benches in the waiting room were occupied. By women. How many of them were in the enviable position of having to suppress the whole truth in order to achieve their goal? At any rate, his sloppiness was another ominous sign. This ability to mess up a room in no time with books, newspapers, articles of clothing, manuscripts, dirty cups. Oh, his external sloppiness was really a pain in the neck. If you overlooked his internal love of order. He was absolutely incapable of lying. A few of Uwe's colleagues wrote articles about equal rights for women, as he did, and accepted in other respects the agenda of the day. Which was guided by traditional customs. Uwe believed in what he wrote. So much so, that he was depressed when he didn't act accordingly. He made fun of his colleagues and friends who dubbed him 'Prince Consort' after my promotion. 'You guys act like we're still in the postwar years pulling handcarts,' he would say loudly, adding that marriage wasn't a hierarchical institution any more. Yet he only perked up when I was sick in bed and dependent on his help.

6

On the right wall, a news-sheet board covered with cotton bunting, with photos of Lenin tacked onto it. On the left, framed pictures of Walter Ulbricht and Willi Stoph under glass. Across from them official notices and price lists on a bulletin board between curtains. An advance payment of ninety marks was indicated for my husband's and my combined monthly income. The most ominous part of the half-truths I collected, which predictably the court later judged to be serious, almost escaped me. Because it was self-evident. Was there even one woman waiting there who didn't cite it? So for the sake of completeness: insufficient help with the housework. Yet I don't want to suppress the fact that Uwe really did have two left hands. Not only by reason of culture but also by nature. This hampered his efforts to combat laziness and moral inertia. Actually, I suffered less from my double burden than he did. It only made me tired. It gave him a guilty conscience. Which was eventually expressed by hostility. Apparently toward my habit of writing on the backs of nutrition science manuscript pages. Fairy tales and the like, that's how I refreshed myself. I facetiously called these fantastic creations 'Paralipomena for a Man.' Who, of course, was Uwe. He refused to be this man. He said, 'Fantasy is an escape, a sign of capitulation.' I said, 'On the contrary, it's a sign of sovereignty. Indeed, of sovereign treatment of the stuff of reality, as children do when they draw pictures, for example.' – 'But it indicates a conflict,' Uwe replied. And I agreed with him. 'A conflict between expectations and reality,' said Uwe sharply. And I confused him completely by admitting he was right about that too. And then he lost no time in becoming suspicious of me. Of being duplicitous, so to speak, for I had described socialism as the best there was and myself as a utopian. He said the contradiction was obvious and antagonistic. Uwe offered as proof the definition 'A state of consciousness is utopian when it is not congruent with the surrounding "state."' He called my fairy tales 'counterimages.' It was a bitter quarrel. The loudest one I ever had with Uwe. And yet it was a sham battle. Although Uwe rejected all my answers on principle. I told him, for example, that my fairy tales were actions, not models. 'Substitutes for actions,' he yelled, interrupting. 'No,' I yelled back. 'They are proofs of love,' I yelled, 'for you, because I want to be fair to you and your kind, one needs strength for that, one needs a lot of strength for patience and historical justice, my dear, your sloppiness and naive laziness cost me a second shift every day; that would embitter me as a scientist, if I couldn't keep myself in a certain utopian state of suspense. Maybe it's even a type of therapy but an active one, not comparable to religion or the substitute religion you used to practice, maybe you still do, my father thinks so anyway. If I want to be historically just, I can't blame you personally for your traditional habits; they're the generally prevailing ones. But I can't blame our country for them either; that would block my vision of the great advances it has brought about by law in only twenty-five years, that is, in principle I have to accept my situation as it is. And I do, no one can step out of history, I'm coming to terms with it. But not passively. That would be the end of me. Without the suspense that I create on the backs of manuscript pages to refresh my body and soul, I'd be a dead loss as a scientist. My optimism, my cheerfulness live on this suspense between the poles of reality and Communism; without this suspense I would lose the ability to love men.'

7

The curtains had brown roses printed on them. I found out who was ahead of me, a woman whose beauty made her easy to remember, and I waited, standing, for the time being. I found it difficult. I couldn't bear to wear belts any more either, although the waistbands of my skirts still fit. I looked in vain for grieving expressions. Fatigue was much in evidence, but not those faces ravaged by emptiness that fill streetcars and buses in the mornings. Toward noon the first man appeared. In his late forties, he was the oldest person there up to the time I was called into the office. A young woman was waiting for me at the typewriter. The woman waved in a friendly way toward the smooth-worn chair, inserting forms with carbon paper into the typewriter. On these she entered detailed personal information and, to my amazement, the terms plaintiff and defendant. A weak attempt on my part to contest the terms because that which has grown, history, is not prosecutable. The woman's friendliness diminished. She informed me that petitions and suggestions for improvement were processed in another office and asked me the grounds. I listed the ones I had collected. This female legal expert asked when our last marital intercourse had been. I named the date of my surprise attack. Because of overload, she requested a document drawn up in triplicate, in which I was to cite the grounds for my application. The woman wrote the following on the form and read it back: 'The plaintiff is seeking a divorce because the marriage has lost its meaning for the parties.' I was given a carbon copy after paying ninety marks. At the next stop a woman sitting behind a large cash register requested neither justification nor grounds for payment but the desired amount. Confused, I handed it over and accepted a narrow paper receipt.

8

The document about the history of our marriage, which I had promised on my word of honor to deliver, occupied me for three days. As a historical text, for it proved that my new situation had, in fact, separated me from Uwe. I had feared the opposite. I didn't feel the fatigue anymore either. Ever since he felt inferior, Uwe radiated fatigue suggestively whenever he entered a room. The way other people radiate activity, an entrepreneurial spirit. On the second day I found a bouquet of daisies on my desk. On the third day Uwe thanked me for my initiative. With melancholy. Which enhanced his beauty even more. For it was not only a feature of his character, it was a social phenomenon. Which enhances; an elegiac person who has enough insight to let others alone can be beautiful more easily than an intense person who makes demands. I expressly wrote that we had married for love and that my husband was an honorable person. And repeated it before the judge at the first oral hearing. Uwe explained his consent to the divorce by accusing me of superiority. The lay judges, two elderly men, nodded. The judge raised her eyebrows. Too steeply, it seemed to me. Although I could only convey half the truth, out of consideration for Uwe, I had expected more respect. For Uwe. Tragic characters command respect. He was a victim of improvements. I had to separate from him because he had taken on too much. After the judge had thoroughly ascertained the details of the division of household goods, the absence of children expedited the process. To such an extent that the second hearing was finished in fifteen minutes.

9

After the verdict was pronounced, Uwe invited me to the nearest bar for a schnapps. I accepted the invitation and refused the schnapps. When Uwe asked why uncomprehendingly, I cut him off by declaring alcohol to be unhealthy for fetuses.

(R.U.) 'Since the agricultural production of our foodstuffs basically differs very little from conditions of earlier times, outstanding chemists have repeatedly studied the problem of synthetic food production. In principle it is no longer difficult to synthesize any organic materials whatsoever. In the last forty years, fats and oils have been produced synthetically, the synthesis of sugar and carbohydrates is being studied, and the artificial production of products containing nitrogen is not too far in the future. Thus one can generate the necessary organic substances not only through agriculture but also industrially, through chemical synthesis or microbiological processes. But is this industrial production of foodstuffs possible in the near future?

'Let us first examine the nutritional needs of human beings. If we disregard water, there are five essential elements: protein, carbohydrates, fats, vitamins, and minerals. The energy content of the nutrients must include 2,500 to 4,000 calories daily. The need for vitamins and minerals is modest but indispensable. This requirement presents no difficulties because these minerals can be produced cheaply and vitamins are already produced industrially.

'There is a fundamental difference between the carbohydrates and fats as compared to the proteins. The carbohydrates and fats are the energy suppliers that can replace each other in the organism. They are burned in the body and thereby lose their chemical individuality. The organism's fats have a structural and physiochemical task in addition to their energetic one, for they build the lipoid systems and dissolve vitamins. In addition, 3 to 6 grams of unsaturated fatty acids are essential for the organism.

'The proteins are the organism's only suppliers of nitrogen. They are constructed of amino acids (peptide chains) and break down into amino acids in the intestine, forming the building blocks for the structure of the protein occurring naturally in the body. Of the 20 amino acids necessary for the organism, 8 must absolutely be contained in the nutrients in a specific proportion, which is why they are called essential amino acids. For children, a ninth one, arginine, must be present. The remaining amino acids can be produced by the organism itself if it has a source of nitrogen, for example in the form of one of the amino acids or ammonium salts. Surplus amino acids are burned by the body; surplus nitrogen is excreted in the urine. Compared to the fats and carbohydrates, the proteins are the most expensive part of the dietary requirements.

'Lack of protein in human beings is essentially a lack of essential amino acids, for the protein content alone does not determine the quality of the diet. Some vegetable products (peas, soybeans, yeast) are characterized by a high protein content, but their amino acid makeup is not ideal. Breast milk has the most favorable amino acid makeup of all foods. But since human beings receive mother's milk only at an age that the readers have already outgrown, it can be considered here only as a standard. In so doing, it becomes apparent that cow's milk comes close, that wheat flour contains only a third of the optimal amount of lysine, and that there is very little tryptophan and methionine in peas and very little leucine in soybeans. Therefore, the first task of the chemist is to establish a diet to balance the amounts of the essential amino acids. Usually, there is a deficiency — especially in vegetarian diets — of lysine and methionine, sometimes also of leucine and tryptophan. If one adds these supplements to the vegetable proteins, they become equivalent to the animal proteins.'

(V. ff.) Evangelization: Since Valeska was working on a nutrition science project that could not be published or talked about, for reasons of espionage, Clemens took an interest in her profession. Especially because word had gotten around that the academic institute was engaged in synthetic meat production. Clemens asked for confidential confirmation or samples. To counter the tiresome questions without violating her pledge of secrecy or casting doubt on her scientific reputation, Valeska resorted to the archaic method she had hitherto avoided for reasons of respectability. Because doing magic is classified among the successful but industrially not exploitable laboratory experiments. With fairylike abilities you can at best perform in the circus nowadays. Valeska wanted a scientific career. In an institute that employed 157 scientists, among them 11 women. Clemens read with colored pens and a ruler. Valeska devoured. He preferred books that put the world in order. She preferred books that described how to make a world. In view of the hypothesis that all activities which took place in the course of development were programmed into a human cell — that a human being therefore carries all possible living beings recorded in hidden programs of his cells, has the living universe within him, is the universe himself — she had decided to specialize in protein. Naturally, because she wanted to collaborate in studying experimentally and theoretically this wonderful phenomenon, obvious in the euphoria of love but not yet explained scientifically. Since the technical requirements for such research can neither be acquired nor used by individual scientists, they cannot choose a research subject independently of conditions. Professionally, conditions had brought Valeska to nutrition science. Privately, she concentrated on various domesticated animal species. Wistar rats, which she needed for experiments, seemed promising to her at times. Eventually, she decided on partial restorations. In order to combine the useful with the pleasurable, for that which is human. Specifically, during the course of love play, Valeska had often felt a desire to taste of Clemens's flesh. Only because of the earthly impossibility of replacing the desired morsels had she held back. Not least from tactical considerations. A female scientist who is unmasked as a fairy would logically, in view of the often cited fact that women's brains on average weigh less than men's, cast suspicions of mysticism on her female professional colleagues also. In order to keep widespread mental feelings nebulous, Valeska had to approach her task deliberately. She made Clemens promise secrecy on his word of honor. In addition, Clemens swore several oaths. His occasional wish to be consumed by a woman had seemed only metaphorically achievable up to now. The unexpected prospects spurred him on, and he spoke, 'Verily, verily I say unto you, unless you eat of the flesh of the son of man and drink his blood, you will not have life within you.' And 'Whosoever eats my flesh and drinks my blood will have everlasting life.' Pressed for time, Valeska first took a choice morsel located below the left collarbone. Given its age, she thought a buttermilk marinade appropriate, after the hair was singed off. She treated the flesh like game during cooking as well. When done, the meat was still firm, tough to the bite, sweeter than horsemeat, beyond measure and indescribably delectable like love itself. Clemens was very satisfied too. He regretted that Valeska had replaced the excised piece immediately, for which reason the pain lasted only a short time. Valeska would have given in to his wishes if she had been working in a self-contained apartment, out of danger of being accused of cannibalism. Under more favorable conditions, she fulfilled his wishes. And permitted him to taste of her as well; doing magic for her own needs was even easier. Clemens and Valeska grew accustomed to the feasts. Soon they believed for moments that their bones bore each other's flesh. Valeska's talents, which were actually intended to show Clemens, in a way that wasn't prohibited, that the world's 15-million-ton protein deficit could be covered, reinforced Clemens's tendency to mythologize women. That is, the division of labor between man and nature. Valeska sensed a pedestal. This humiliation soon spoiled her appetite and her desire to use magic for producing partial restorations from nutritional yeast raised on petroleum fractions.

(R.U.) 'When we consider the synthetic, but not the biosynthetic, industrial production of food, it must be emphasized that synthesizing the protein part of the diet is not connected to the complex problem of protein synthesis. This point can be explained by the fact that nutritional proteins are completely hydrolyzed in the alimentary canal, broken down by fermentation, and enter the blood only in this form. So it is a matter of microbiological or chemical production of amino acids. The mixture of amino acids would have to be supplied to the organism in a form such that each one of them is processed in the alimentary canal at the pace of a slow digestive process.

'In the field of medicine, synthetic forms of diet already exist. They are aqueous solutions consisting of a mixture of amino acids (representing the protein complex), glucose (representing the carbohydrate group), the ethyl ester of linoleic acid or some other representative fatty acid derivative, and the necessary vitamins and minerals. Apart from its medicinal significance, this fact proved that nourishment via synthetic substances is possible. At present, a series of amino acids can only be produced from costly raw materials. But with production on a larger scale and new production processes, these costs can also be lowered. Such was the case with methionine, for example. When it found widespread application in cattle breeding and was synthesized from propylene, the prices fell considerably. The case of lysine and glutamic acid is similar. If microbiological processes are employed, synthetic protein foods can be produced even more cheaply. It is known that all microorganisms have protein-containing cytoplasm, and many of them can be used as nutrients. Nutritional yeast, for example, which is raised on agricultural sugar wastes or on monosaccharides, is well known. In addition, there are species that develop on hydrocarbon and carbohydrates if they are supplied with the necessary minerals (ammonium salts and phosphorus salts). There are microbes that live on methane, paraffin, and a range of other substances.

'Based on these facts, the French scientist Chamagnar proposed the cultivation of nutritional yeast on petroleum fractions and the use of proteins thus produced for animal feed. At the present time a plant near Marseilles produces about one ton of protein-yeast concentrates per day by this method. From one ton of paraffin-hydrocarbons one can obtain

800 to 1,000 kg of yeast with a protein content of 40 to 45%. Its only deficiency consists in its low methionine content. The manufacturing cost of one ton is said to be between 300 and 400 marks.

'To be sure, the use of this product as fodder or food requires that it either be enriched with methionine or supplemented with substances rich in this amino acid. The world's 15-million-ton protein deficit could be covered if only 1% of the world's yield of paraffin-petroleum were processed by this method. That process is very tempting, particularly since bacteria have been discovered that develop on petroleum hydrocarbons and could provide a rich yield of methionine.'

(V. ff.) *Taraxacum officinale:* I'd like to be on the bleaching plain, for example, near the brick-paved island where the carpet frame is set up. The carpet beater hangs on it. The dust that is beaten from carpets and bedside rugs is blown to the east by the west wind, which is why I prefer the right half of the plain. Clay soil. Putting down deep roots wouldn't be necessary there. In view of the fact that all the households bleach their laundry and there is abundant rainfall on the north side of the low mountain range, my basal rosette never has to touch ground. Still, the tip of the root is seventeen centimeters deep. The earth is a red brown color, closely packed and saturated with fecal matter; the cesspit in the yard is emptied twice a year, in the spring through a chain of vacuum tubes into a city-owned tank wagon, in late fall onto the plain. The pit is covered by two cast-iron plates. When the children cross it on foot, scooters, or tricycles, the plates clatter; when they clatter a lot, the wife of the building supervisor scolds from the pantry window. The supervisor's wife has a goiter. She bleaches at night. Only on short grass, not on newly mown. Before she lays out the laundry, sorted according to type, to form narrow passages crossing each other at right angles like rows between flower beds, she drags a rake across the plain. Then she combs the plain for the likes of us. She jabs the wind-ruffled marsh dandelions from the earth with a kitchen knife and tosses them onto the compost heap in her backyard. Kitchen knives are too short for me. A piece of root always remains in the earth. I feel the cut but not pain. But not joy either or desire: I am. The supervisor's wife sprays the bedding and towels with a garden hose every two hours. Plentifully when there is no moon. Her thumb and index finger narrow the opening of the nozzle, the wetness streams out, regulated by water- and finger-pressure. Puddles collect on the fabric. I drink my fill. In two or three weeks, the rosette of coarse-toothed leaves is back again. The young leaves, rich in vitamins A and C and bitter substances, are harvested by the retired Herr Nussek as a wild vegetable. After that they pass through a basket, bowls, mouths, stomachs, and intestines. The retiree drinks infusions of my leaves and roots when he's lost his appetite, has indigestion or liver disorders; whosoever eats my flesh and drinks my blood will abide in me and I in him. The retiree lives on the third floor on the right. His wife, addicted to white laundry, mourns a tablecloth. Her granddaughter's dress is also stained by the milky juice that flows in the hollow stem of the blossom and in the ribs of the leaves. The juice comes out when I've been injured. Her lover weighed heavily. He rode her and the lawn down. In spring the stem bears a yellow basket of flowers. The flowers contain both kinds. I wait for nothing. Am sedentary by nature. Nary a thought of traveling or other fantasies. Longing is as unknown to me as satiation. Bees crawl on my pistil, looking for honey. When I have faded, the wind or children blow my seeds into the air. Hundreds of seeds with hair parachutes. They rise, fly, land softly somewhere or other. Some may fall on infertile areas but not all; I am indestructible: immortal. Even if the supervisor's wife takes a bread knife to the weeds some washday and I wither on the compost heap. Painlessly. Sometimes I'd like to be a plant, for example, a dandelion, or lesbian.

(R.U.) 'Now to the fats and carbohydrates. Synthesis of the saturated fats is easy. During the Second World War, a synthesis was developed in Germany by which several tons of synthetic butter were produced, which, however, contained small amounts of harmful additives. That does not rule out the possibility of synthesizing fats of the highest nutritional quality.

'The synthesis of carbohydrates is somewhat more difficult. The major problem involves not so much the fact that the targeted synthesis of complex carbohydrates has not been solved but rather that the carbohydrates in our diet – sugars, starches – are very cheap. In contrast to the proteins, where there is a great shortage, carbohydrates are abundantly available. But this does not mean that by perfecting the chemical method – at some still unknown time – the advantage of synthesis may not surpass agricultural means of producing carbohydrates.

'One could ask why we do not pursue the production of synthetic fodder, to ensure that human nutritional needs are met through cattle breeding. There is a very simple reason: Only 7 to 20% of the fodder is utilized by the animal, since the greatest part serves the animal's own requirements. If, for example, 6 million tons of protein are required to meet the needs of 250 million people annually, meeting this need with products of cattle breeding requires 100 million tons.

'Now, what about the concern that in the future we will get our nourishment from pills? There is a reassuring answer to this question, for the daily requirement of water-free protein, between 80 and 100 g amino acids, 450 g carbohydrates, and 100 g fat will not be compressed into pills. One can transform these substances into foods that are tasty and varied and can be consumed with relish.

'Almost all natural proteins of our foodstuffs are tasteless and odorless. This can be verified, for example, by raw meat that has been washed out until it is colorless or by the casein of washed-out quark, a cheese-protein. It cannot be otherwise, for the proteins are high-molecular-weight substances and therefore nonvolatile, odorless. The same is true of the high-molecular-weight carbohydrates (starches, fats). They acquire odor and flavor only through natural admixtures or supplements and in particular from substances that originate during cooking, roasting, or baking of the nutritional raw material through the interaction of the amino acids with the sugars and fats.

'Every taste consists of four components: sweet, salty, sour, and bitter. Only these four can be distinguished by the receptors of the tongue. If we try to test-taste while holding the nose – shutting off the sense of smell – then every possible taste variation can be mixed from only four solutions of sugar, salt, acid, and bitter caffeine. The sense of smell, which is connected to taste, is much more difficult. The combination produces what is called "flavor" in English and is achieved in normal foods by heating and by the addition of spices. The appetizing aroma of the mixture of substances originates through cooking, roasting, and baking. This process is also easy to replicate by heating various amino acids with various forms of sugar.

'At the Institute for Simple Organic Compounds of the USSR Academy of Sciences, the following was established: If one of the fatty acids is added to a heated mixture of amino acids and the corresponding sugar, the aroma changes; in so doing, one can produce synthetically the appetizing aroma of roast chicken or beef pot roast. If traces of trimethylamine oxide are added, the aroma of saltwater fish is produced. Thus it will not be very difficult to give synthetic foods their specific aromatic note.'

(V. ff.) Petrifaction: On the way back from a nutrition science conference, we passed through a little town in Thuringia. The building façades on the market square were being restored for the twentieth anniversary of the founding of the state. As is my wont, I stopped to ask the way to the local antiquarian bookseller. I approached three women of indeterminate age. They stood deep in conversation. Loaded shopping bags hung from their hands. These and their skirts marked their gender, beyond fashion or the need for validation, a self-evident neutrality that evidenced not resignation but plantlike stubbornness, consistency. Such phenomena, conspicuously noticeable especially in small towns, command respect with me, I spoke softly. The women consulted each other and also asked passersby, whom they addressed by name. Nothing definite was brought to light about an antiquarian bookseller but much about a secondhand store, also art dealers and life stories. When I had told mine, the women enumerated tourist attractions, last of all and in confidence a sort of natural monument. It was said to be located on the third floor of an apartment building. They said the apartment belonged to the daughter; I was to identify myself as a foreigner and mention the name Madrasch, the surname of one of the dialect-proficient women. The chauffeur of the academy-owned car cursed the dictates of the one-way streets. We found the house with difficulty, because I was looking for a façade of a characteristic style or at least an old-fashioned one. The reality was a nondescript prewar building. Polished stairs with enameled signs urging caution. Greenery on window ledges and at the curves of the banister. Jute doormat. The chauffeur introduced me as an English delegation to a climacteric woman hesitantly opening the door. My lack of freely convertible currency seemed to reinforce her distrust. The demand for hard currency heightened our curiosity so much that I handed over twenty marks for fear of being turned away. The woman gave her name and the number of persons in her family. The small square apartment hallway smelled of snake-oil liniment and fried bacon. Xylolith floor. Crocheted covers on the brass door handles. Frau Brak's right hand pointed toward a white-painted door with curtains stretched over its window insert. Before it could be opened, the chauffeur and I had to push aside a low shoe rack. The attraction was a petrified human being. It stood in the middle of the room, surrounded by objects. Or held up by them. Light entered the room through two large drape-covered windows opposite the door, presumably direct sunlight; the light in our eyes made the objects that darkly filled the room look like an irregular grid. The room could be entered only through an aisle leading to the object; according to information from Frau Brak, it had been put in place later. Frau Brak spoke in high quavering tones that she seemed to press from her belly with both hands. She said her three-member family was entitled to a two-room apartment. We had to enter the aisle sideways, the narrow side of the body pointing toward the petrifaction. Frau Brak introduced it as her late mother. The towering walls, reaching to the ceiling, consisted of furniture, dishes, bedding, keepsakes, art objects, cardboard packaging, and flowers made of wax, paper, or chenille. Dust and twilight nestled in the cracks. A smell of moldy second-crop hay. Frau Brak showed us a broken place on her mother's hand: the middle finger had been broken off and stolen by a French visitor. Initials and dates had been carved in the lower arms and calves. The wrinkled face was undamaged. At first glance, sandstone. Gray, dust-blunt strands of hair hanging down, black hairpins holding a nest-shaped braid at the back of the head. Tied tight over the short-sleeved green dress was a brightly patterned apron that did not emphasize any physical protrusions but had a wadded handkerchief in the right apron pocket. The bare feet were clad in felt slippers. The stone felt like solidified sediment. However, the greenish color of the hands was reminiscent of diabase. What we learned about the life and strange end of the war-widow Kaden has remained indelible in my memory. When Luise Kaden left her parents' apartment after a quarrel and rented the one her daughter lived in now, the building was new. The walls and windows were bare. The plaster was still damp. It smelled bright. First, Luise Kaden hung marquisette at the windows. Then she bought a bed, table, chair, and armoire and covered the nakedness of the walls. One year after moving in, she had it wallpapered. Now the rooms looked respectably livable to parents and relatives. Although the wallpaper didn't reach the ceiling. But the ceiling paint feigned brocade. The stone floor was gradually covered with carpets. The stone disappeared rapidly. Entirely, when the only daughter moved out to get married. Now the war-widow Kaden spent her small pension primarily on objects, for after the experience of inflation she had given up on saving and found no pleasure in meals consumed in isolation. After her forty-fifth year, she began devoting herself to bargain purchases of matching and mismatched durable objects and their care; later on she collected and assembled systematically. Well into old age, to maintain the feeling of fullness of life. Thus the objects came closer and closer to her; the rooms grew smaller, encroached on her. The bedroom filled up first. Then the kitchen, bath, corridor; Luise Kaden must have spent her last days and nights standing in the living room. Propped up by walls all around. According to the police report, when the apartment was forcibly opened in February 1945 by request of the landlord, Luise Kaden's right upper arm had been pierced by the pendulum point of a wall clock wedged between two leather armchairs stacked on top of each other. The death certificate recorded the cause of death as suicide. Frau Brak, who had lived in Cologne since her marriage and maintained contact with her mother only by letter after the war started, was not successful in officially challenging the findings, which she believed to be incorrect. Although she traveled to Thuringia under great adversity immediately upon receiving news of the death. The doctor who had issued the death certificate had meanwhile been inducted into the *Volkssturm*, the Nazi territorial army, and it was impossible to find a competent replacement in the confused last months of the war. Frau Brak resisted burying her mother under the stigma of suicide, especially since she had discovered that the deceased's unusual condition made haste unnecessary. Frau Brak believed then and now that the cause of death was a type of silicosis. Since she had lost her apartment and belongings in a bombing in October 1944, she decided to take over her mother's apartment and life mission and wait for the war to end. She emigrated with her two small children; her husband had fallen at Smolensk. When she moved in, the other tenants inspected her with curiosity mixed with horror. Sometimes people stopped on the street or inched away from her in shopping queues. The landlord and other witnesses who were present when the apartment was broken open had started the gossip. The landlord regretted it later and also that at first he had wanted to force the apartment to be vacated for refugees from East Prussia. Then artillery fire and the passing invasion of American troops demanded people's attention. But Frau Brak complained that she was still avoided by some people and suffered from loneliness. Although she officially claimed that her mother had been cremated. Only the landlord was in on the secret. She said he had also advised her to go to the train station now and then on a Sunday afternoon with flowers and a watering can. Claiming that her mother's grave was in the local cemetery would quickly be proven to be a lie in a small town where everyone saw everything. Frau Brak confessed that she envied her colleague at work who had put up a bench at her parents' grave site, a pleasant place to sit in the shade of tall chestnut trees in the summer. To my surprise, the woman's initial distrust abruptly turned into trust as soon as I said, when asked my occupation, that I was a biochemist. Although my German, which I speak with a Saxon accent even when trying not to, must have at least cast doubt on my English guise. At any rate, I learned all the details of how Frau Brak transferred the overflowing contents of the bedroom, bath, and corridor by night into a shed in the yard. Obtaining food demanded so much of Frau Brak during the first year after the war that she could hardly find time for her affair of honor. The responsible authorities also seemed disinterested and overburdened with other things. In June 1947 Frau Brak took a job at the post office, but until then she and her son and daughter lived from the contents of the shed. Frau Brak sold the things on the black market or swapped with farmers for provisions. From the urge to live and a kind of fatigue that sets in after many futile trips to offices, from resignation, laziness, possibly also because of the excessive demands of having to learn a profession and bear the entire responsibility for two children, the matter of honor concerning the cause of death was postponed and postponed again and finally dropped. Feelings of gratitude for her inheritance and respect for the dead induced Frau Brak to live in restricted space and leave the living room to the deceased. With all the objects just as they had surrounded her in her last hours, to compensate for funeral, coffin, burial plot, and graveside plants. Frau Brak pointed out that the cost of these things was much less than the rental value of the room. Not to mention the isolating effect of the memorial; even today the building was called 'House of Mystery.' She had come to terms with it. Since her daughter was at the university and her son had signed up for a term with the People's National Army, she didn't miss the living room as much as before. To be sure, the children, in contrast to Dr. Wurche, continued to deny the possibility of petrifaction of human beings but no longer picked a fight over this topic at every visit. One had to excuse them for speaking hatefully of their grandmother, because they had only known her dead. The benefits brought about by the exchange value of the inheritance in times of famine had been forgotten as quickly as the times themselves. But nicknames clung to one. Even her fiancé still called the daughter Witch Brak when he was irritated or wanted to irritate her. Frau Brak protested that her daughter would be proud of this name some day. Incidentally,

Dr. Wurche, a friend of the landlord's, was the first to confirm the petrifaction. By chance. He'd been looking for a sublet; like me, he also had a doctorate or Doctor Eng. or Doctor Phil. or some such, a nice old gentleman. The landlord believed he was a brilliant astronomer and was convinced he would achieve fame eventually. He had also brought in the first visitors, all foreigners; he demanded 40 percent of the receipts. If his wife couldn't shop at the Intershop occasionally, she threatened divorce. He was a trained hairdresser. He had built the aisle. Incidentally, a young American had offered twenty thousand dollars for the petrifaction, but exporting antiquities from the GDR was against the law. Anyway, Frau Brak couldn't ask her mother to be on exhibit in a private museum owned by capitalists, next to pop culture and other perversions. Aside from certain financial interests on the part of the landlord, whose good will she depended on to a certain extent after all, she had nothing against local visitors. Especially since she too was unshaken in her conviction that the petrifaction would attain world renown some day. Her distrust was directed solely toward employees of the housing authority and sanitary inspection. Now that Dr. Wurche had died and she knew no other scientist with appropriate expertise, Frau Brak asked me, after my tour, to prepare a scientific report. She said she could write the letter to the local branch of the travel bureau herself. Frau Brak initially offered a 2 percent share, later on 3, 5, and finally 10 percent of the profits for the report, fervently describing the favorable location and the anticipated financial interest of the responsible state authorities in exploiting the natural monument as a museum. When I still hesitated, she reminded me of civic obligations. The landlord had hopes of selling the building to the city, when the opportunity presented itself, for an exorbitantly high price and under the condition that he be granted the position of museum director. Since he was from a bourgeois background, with reactionary attitudes, and had threatened Luise Kaden with action for eviction several times while she was alive, it was necessary to take him by surprise. Especially since his claim to fame lacked any legal basis; after all, he was not related to Luise Kaden by either blood or marriage. A Belgian visitor had believed not only the mother but also the daughter to be saints and behaved accordingly. In any case, Frau Brak didn't see why she, who had somehow sensed even in childhood that she was different, should end her days as a post-office employee. The shortage of workers at this institution was catastrophic; overtime was the order of the day. At Christmas they had to recruit schoolboys in order to even come close to handling the onslaught of work. She really deserved a quiet position such as museum director. If the city fathers were efficient and combined the tourist attraction with an Interhotel, the income in freely convertible currencies could be substantial. The attraction would undoubtedly become world famous in a very short time, most definitely if the immortal woman's daughter took over the leadership. Because everything was hereditary. To expedite the process, she had removed the rugs from the xylolith floor. Frau Brak asked me not to omit this from the report. It would surely yield the basis for a sensational research project that could help me gain world recognition. I replied that facts always formed the Archimedean point from which even the most important theory could be turned upside down. In this respect nothing was more interesting to a true theoretician than a fact that directly contradicted a hitherto generally recognized theory, because that is where his real work would begin. Then I refused with thanks, on the grounds that I was employed by a scientific institute whose research object was subject to secrecy. Our parting took place in a businesslike atmosphere.

(R.U.) 'Another important problem is the consistency of food. A mixture of water-insoluble synthetic powders or yeast that contains "compensatory" taste additives can be processed just like flour. Thus, for example, it is already possible to produce an excellent protein biscuit from petroleum yeasts. With substances that form gels and are easily digestible (agar-agar, starches, purely synthetic polyvinyl alcohol, and others), one can use these nutritional powders to make doughs, puddings, aspics, and jellies.

'Grains of caviar, meat fibers, and many other things can be produced from such colloids or directly from the yeast protein mass. As an example I can cite the fact that in such a manner the Institute for Simple Organic Compounds produced black caviar that could not be distinguished from true caviar in appearance or taste. With the necessary protein compounds, synthetic foodstuffs (meat, doughs, jellies, puddings, caviar) can be given any desired flavor. Of course, the consistency, taste, and smell of foods of animal origin can be produced not only in mixtures of amino acids but also in yeast protein. This synthesis is also possible with vegetable proteins, for example, legumes. Semi-synthetic meat of this type is already produced industrially in the United States.

'Obviously, this diet will find its way into our life only gradually. First, natural foods can be refined by means of the amino acid and protein complexes, and the lack of essential amino acids can be remedied. But soon they will achieve independent significance. Let us leap forward in time and imagine that an economically acceptable synthesis of dietary needs has replaced the traditional production processes. A few giant factories now produce all the population's foods. Agriculture is a thing of the past, except perhaps for the cultivation of fruit and flowers. The industries that hitherto supplied agriculture with machinery, fuels, fertilizers, and pesticides are also obsolete. Many occupations will change. I dare to say that these are not idle dreams, although relatively little has been achieved up to now. This prospect raises a problem of tremendous significance that will require the mutual cooperation of chemists, biologists, physicians, and economists.'

(V. ff.) Conjectural biographical report of a thirty-eight-year-old woman: At the age of thirty-nine Valeska started a family. With Gerda and Marie. Gerda had two daughters, Marie had a son, suddenly the three women had two daughters and two sons. Riches that they previously had to deny themselves. Their boyfriends didn't live in the building. It was on the Prenzlauer Berg. High-ceilinged old rooms; the women had exchanged their apartments for a whole floor of five rooms, formerly a physician's practice. Each woman had a study; the kitchen, nursery, and family room were accessible to all. After the stresses of moving had been overcome, one woman took responsibility each week for grocery shopping, cleaning, or childcare. Since all the adult family members were equally accustomed to housework, they gained free time every day. The children were all preschool age, the mothers were not on shift work. Two of them could have gone to the theater or the cinema every evening; there couldn't be that many good plays or films. But there were also meetings and books and scientific work. O wondrous freedom, exotic, almost uncomfortable at first. It was even hard for Valeska not to rush to work or to stroll leisurely past shops when going home in the evening. The way home, which used to be a tunnel that she hurried through with her head lowered, gradually acquired streets, façades, clouds. That the form of affection expressed by serving someone meals can be not only practiced but also experienced by women was amazing to her. Especially when the table was set for her in the evening. Seven diners sat around it. Valeska had always wanted a large family. The only children were especially glad of their unexpectedly acquired brothers and sisters, bragged about them. And about their three mothers and three fathers; they quickly got over the loss of privileges. Upbringing made easier. Brotherly life: that is, sisterly. Gerda had her degree in electrical engineering, Maria in finance economics; Valeska was finishing her postdoctoral thesis ahead of the deadline. Accustomed to having her energies fragmented, forced to think and act simultaneously, Valeska at first sat restlessly at her desk in her room. Laboriously she learned to give up the frenetic activity that had been drilled into her as a life rhythm. Then she realized that saving time had degenerated to miserliness. She had lost the ability to relax and read the newspaper, a book, or scientific literature to such an extent that it required effort. Of course, a mother can never forget her child to the point that concern about its well-being would vanish from her mind and make the storage areas in the brain available for other things. Obviously, a woman must be more talented than a man if she wants to achieve the same things. In professions that require the person to exhaust herself, in science, for example, that becomes clear; in others it doesn't. The women just wear out sooner from the double burden, which is strictly contrary to the ideal of beauty. Valeska's father visited the family of women regularly. The children called him Grandpa Franz. He told them fairy tales in which Marx and Siberia appeared in person. The children called Valeska's mother Grandma Berta. She knitted for the family. Rudolf showed up irregularly. Distance maintained the attachment for years. Without overexertion or excessive demands. Valeska waited for Rudolf differently now than she used to. More calmly, the days without him were not wasted time; passion no longer diminished that which was given or distorted that which was desired. Love lost its dogmatic system with the character of a natural event that overpowers the world with grand gestures. Events and objects approached their own value, by comparison. In friendly company there was variety, beautiful human community.

FIFTH INTERMEZZO

Wherein the Reader Learns What the Beautiful Melusine Copied from Irmtraud Morgner's Novel *Rumba for an Autumn* into Her 35th Melusinian Book in 1964

Shawm Twist I

> But he said to him: My son, you are always
> with me, and all that is mine is yours. LUKE 15:31

The house floated slowly out into the night. Pakulat checked the ark over to be sure it was floating well and safely. He shuffled through the cellarway, which was shored up by wooden beams, making sure that no lights were on behind the lath doors. Then he locked the outside doors of the house and yard and checked to see that all the hallway windows were bolted. He dragged himself from floor to floor, past the apartment doors, some of which had rough plywood surfaces instead of carved wooden frames and glass panels. Finally Pakulat climbed the stairs to the attic. He shined a flashlight through the compartments, which still had gray fireproof paint on them, shut the skylights in the roof of the drying room, and lifted the ladder from the exit hatch where the chimney sweep had left it. Then he returned to his apartment, secure in the knowledge that the ark was invulnerable to water and fire and thus ready for the night.

The apartment was empty. Pakulat realized immediately upon unlocking the door that it was still empty. He had to turn the key twice, and he didn't bother to switch on the light in the corridor. He didn't want to see the emptiness.

'Good-for-nothing,' he said and took refuge in the kitchen. He put the soup back into the oven and looked over at the table. 'He'd just better come,' said Pakulat. Without the table, the kitchen would have been empty too. The table was the only thing he could hold on to. The table and the locks hanging next to each other in a row on the wall, eight padlocks. And the keys to the locks hung beside them on a ring.

Pakulat took the ring from the nail and counted the keys. He counted seven. For weeks he'd counted seven. For weeks one had been missing.

'He'd better come,' said Pakulat and shuffled back and forth, from the door to the window, from the window to the door, four steps to, four steps back. Actually, it should have been impossible for him to get past the table. Because it was wider than the kitchen. Actually, his wife shouldn't have succeeded in putting this gigantic table in this tiny kitchen. But she had succeeded.

'Ten o'clock and not home yet, our father would have thrown us out if we'd ever tried to get away with that,' Pakulat said to the table, 'even once – and I've put up with it for weeks, the kid has it too good, young people have it too good . . . ' He leaned on the square tabletop, which stood on thick lathe-turned legs. He saw the flowered pattern on the oilcloth cover. He saw the large, bright surface that the table carved out of the darkness. He thought: all clear. And he said, 'He'd better come . . . '

The kitchen, to Pakulat, was the large, bright surface of the table that had made space for itself with its broad sides between the walls. And behind them, hard for Pakulat to tell how far behind, for he had lost one dimension, somewhere behind them the city began, also a surface. 'He's probably hanging out with those hoodlums again,' said Pakulat. He dragged his slippers through the kitchen once more before going into his son's room to see if his suspicion could be confirmed by evidence.

The trumpet was missing from the top of the armoire. Pakulat groaned with rage. But he also felt a certain satisfaction in having guessed correctly. And he didn't look around the room any further. He knew the trumpet was missing, he knew that nude photographs from the monthly *Magazine* were tacked up on the wall above the bed: he knew what was going on.

And he shuffled back into the kitchen and said, accompanying each word with a blow of his fist on the table, 'He needs his pants kicked.' Then he pushed a chair up to the table, took his wallet out of his hip pocket, threw it onto the oilcloth-covered tabletop, and sat down. He shook out the big wallet, crumpled from sitting, as he had always done on payday, when his wife waited for him to come home from the tavern. He never came late; he drank four beers and four shots, and then he came. But he still felt the need to throw the coins and bills onto the table, as if in passing. And that moment was really the best part of payday. Of course, he didn't look at Anna while doing it. He didn't look at anyone. But he was sure that she was watching him, like after a touch-fall, for example. Today he had also drunk four beers and four shots, and today he also felt the need to throw down his pay, as if in passing. But no one was there to watch him. Anna had died six years ago, and Benno was hanging out with bad company.

Pakulat took the bundle of keys from the wall, took out a key with notched edges, stuck it into one of the seven padlocks, and opened it.

His neighbor was sitting at the window, as always. He sat in a wing chair, his legs and half his upper body wrapped in a blanket. His yellowed hands lay on the armrests. His head hung forward slightly. Large, dull eyes stared from the withered face.

'How's it going?' said Pakulat.

'Good Lord,' said the old man. His dark eyes that lay in their sockets like cold campfires stared fixedly at the window. Every time Pakulat unlocked the door, they were staring at the window.

'It's too dark to see anything.'

'The street,' said the old man.

'You can only see the street when it's light out.'

'My street,' said the old man.

'Do you know what's lying on the table over there?'

'I see the street.'

'My last wages are lying there. One more week and that's the end of it.'

'I see my street.'

'One more week and not a day longer. I don't need the money. What I need is peace and quiet. I've earned it, right?'

'I want to see my street.'

'Tomorrow, Grandpa, tomorrow when it's light out, you can see it again. Now let's get to bed.'

'I'm not tired,' said the old man.

'My pension and the little bit of rent money won't go far, of course. Doesn't matter; I have a son who earns good money, my older boy, you know, engineering degree, not bad, Lutz was always capable. But the younger one. Ten-thirty and not home yet. What do you say about that? I say: disgraceful.'

'I have to see my street.'

'A fellow slaves away on construction year in and year out, but do you suppose that good-for-nothing thinks it's necessary to wonder where the money comes from? I would've had what it takes to get educated too; otherwise I wouldn't have two brainy sons. My father couldn't buy me any books, but I knew where I belonged, I was a different kid when I was Benno's age. If the war hadn't gotten in the way, I could have been the conductor of a shawm band at age seventeen. I was talented all right, no doubt about it. We played at demonstrations and rallies, *when we're marching side by side,* the good songs, yessiree, and my son? What's my son doing with the talent he inherited from me?'

Pakulat stroked the side of his hand across the table, pushing the bills and coins toward him. He slowly gathered the money together, weighed it in his hands, and looked at it, turning his head a little to the right. He held his hard, crooked palms close to his left eye. It was big, so big that the eyelids could hardly hold it. And it was blue and very mobile. It forced a look of curious anticipation from the tired face. Actually, only from the left side of the face. The piercing gaze of a glass eye festering in the socket had caused the right side to grow stiff.

'I'm going to bed,' said Pakulat. 'It's time for bed now.' He sat down on the window seat and folded his tattooed arms across his belly. His short neck sank into his shoulders.

'The street,' said the old man. Maybe Pakulat only imagined that he said it. For what was sitting there in the armchair, had sat there for years and years, was a shell. Life had trickled out of it little by little and seeped away in the stonework of the street. And now the shell was empty. Pakulat noticed for the first time that the shell was empty. And he reached for the lock and turned the key to the right. And he would have liked nothing better than to throw the key away.

Pakulat hung the lock back on its hook. It was small and rusty, and looked shabby next to the shiny steel coat of the lock belonging to Marquardt, partner in the firm Marquardt and Marquardt, Metalsmiths. Marquardt and his wife had moved into Pakulat's father's apartment, not as it was but after painters, masons, and carpenters had worked on it for two months. Every Saturday afternoon Marquardt took two cases of beer from the trunk of his car. Then in the evening he stood on the balcony singing *Star of Rio, you could be my destiny . . .*'

When Pakulat had locked away his neighbor, he was alone again with the two canaries, which were sleeping in a covered cage. The cage hung at the height of the ceiling lamp next to the window.

Pakulat leaned against the tulle-covered windowpane. He felt the cold of the glass through his shirt, he felt the dark surface of the city on his back. A surface brought to life. A gigantic surface teeming with bodies and surging around the house. Day and night. Even when the students were asleep, they didn't let go of this city.

Pakulat slid off the window seat and pulled down the blind. Although he knew it was pointless. Although he knew that everything was futile. Since yesterday everything was futile.

Pakulat toyed again with the idea of selling the house. He had inherited it three years ago from his father. Actually, Pakulat had wanted to bequeath it to his oldest son right away. But Lutz, who was living in a sublet at the time, couldn't even be persuaded to move into his deceased grandfather's apartment. And Benno didn't want the house either. Nobody wanted the house that Pakulat's father had built years ago with his wife's surprise inheritance, in part by his own hand because he was a carpenter too, and he had believed it would maintain his heirs. Now it was just barely maintaining itself, crudely stated. For in contrast to the expenses, the rental income hadn't changed since 1912. That was why Pakulat couldn't find a buyer for the house. Nobody could find buyers for these kinds of rental properties any longer. Houses like these could only be given away. And Pakulat had been unsuccessful in that too. With his sons, in any case. To be sure, the plaster of the façade was riddled here and there with holes from grenade splinters, but giving it away to some government office or other was out of the question. Because it was impossible. Because you couldn't throw a house out of one of its windows.

Pakulat sat back down at the table. 'For all I care, he can come whenever he wants to,' he said to the table. The table was the only thing left to him in the house. Because the son he was waiting for was lost. He had lost him yesterday.

Pakulat remembered waking up early yesterday, earlier than usual. With an image of coffee under his nose. Whenever he felt as if he could carry houses away, he smelled coffee. He had gotten up quietly so as not to wake Benno, eaten two eggs and half a pound cake, packed a white shirt and a necktie in his bag, wedged his saw under his arm, and gone whistling off to work. He hadn't accomplished much that day because he constantly had the smell of coffee under his nose and had to whistle a lot, always thinking of the *Program with Musical Accompaniment* that Benno had presented to him the evening before – not given: presented. The program announced the last number as 'Orchestra of the 17th Expanded Secondary School, conducted by Benno Pakulat, *When We're*

Marching Side by Side.' Pakulat clinked his hammer, sloshed mortar over the reinforcement, swung the lift in so hard that the scaffold trembled. 'Will do,' he said. And slowly a decision took shape in his mind. At lunch time he passed around a case of beer, told his men he had to leave an hour earlier today, and put the most senior team member in charge for that hour. And at a quarter to three, Pakulat shed his carpenter's gear, put on his white shirt, tied his necktie, and took the bus to the business district.

The streets were crowded at this hour. The factories and government offices were spilling out what was left of the people after the workday. A heterogeneous stream squeezed its way through the narrowly walled channel, fatigue and haste jolted together, yielding a mean of tenacious movement that filled the inner-city delta of streets in the late afternoon. The roofs of cars floated on the sluggish stream like scum on sewage. Whirlpools formed in front of the lighted show windows. Pakulat was caught in these whirlpools several times. He went into all the music stores on the square. Finally he made a purchase, reasonably priced and of good quality.

Naturally, the streets were still full of people. Naturally, as soon as he stepped out of the store with his purchase, Pakulat was adrift again in the sluggish stream of bodies that pushed him, pressed, shoved, slowed him down, and assailed him with their odors. Naturally, Pakulat thought once more: all clear. But he navigated, just so. In reality, Pakulat had always navigated. He knew his way around in the streets. He was at home in this city, which was old and relatively well preserved. And which had a lot of relatively well-preserved inhabitants of Pakulat's age, as he found out that evening. Naturally, he also saw students, but they were not the majority. Pakulat lifted the case tied with string the way one lifts a forefinger, attention, and drifted safely to the school. It was a red-brick building whose sixty-year-old façade, menacing, stingy, was garnished with iron hooks. Some of them were hung with captioned bunting stretched across frames made of wooden slats.

Pakulat didn't stop bashfully at the entrance like the others. The parents' assembly with *Musical Accompaniment* would take place in the gym, so Pakulat took the shortest route to the gym. Unfit for military service, thought Pakulat, walking through worn-down corridors. Through a hall portal flanked by teachers and laurel trees. Through all the rows of benches. He took a seat in the first row. 'So,' he said. All he could get out was that little windy word. The one he always resorted to when he needed order. Support. Discipline. But the little windy word was powerless against the disorder that the excitement had created in his head.

And he had to wait a long time. First, for the beginning of the program and then for the end. Couldn't Benno also have opened the program? The best numbers were always either at the beginning or the end. Pakulat sat with legs apart on the low exercise bench, the gift on his lap. The principal gave a speech, a resolution, voted on by raised hands, protesting the sea blockade of the Republic of Cuba by the United States as well as the instigation of world wars, the school choir sang, poems were recited, endless. Pakulat clapped to encourage the pupils to speed up. He drummed his fingertips on the boxed instrument tied with string. After all, anybody could read poetry out loud, anybody could read. But playing an instrument, leading an orchestra, that took talent . . .

Pakulat's instrument lay buried in rubble, tempered by heat, warped – who knows. He'd had to save a long time for it, because he was often out of work. When he couldn't find work as a carpenter, he worked as a hod carrier. And schlepped until his legs were bowed. But he didn't bow down to anyone.

He hadn't bought himself another shawm after the war. At first there weren't any, and then he didn't have time. But wasn't it a shame about his talent?

– to conduct again, to lead a band again, tum-tatum-ta lalala *and sing the old songs,* garden party, sports festival, agitprop, brawl, Pakulat will be there, Pakulat to the rescue, a wrestler with an empty belly, touch-fall. Anna, I won't marry a man who goes to nudist camps, Anna knew at least five hundred songs, when she started singing, she didn't stop, the school choir is sight-reading, foolishness they know by heart and folk songs they sight-read, two weeks in a country house with the choir and I've got the young people to the point where they're singing folk songs by heart and sight-reading foolishness, will do, orientation, guide, lead, to head up a demonstration again with the armored might of the marching band behind you, metallic shawm chords, the bell sounds of the Turkish crescent, the beating of drums and timpani and cymbals, to use your baton to get them marching in step once more, left, two, three, four, *the new age follows us,* and along the street stand veiled ladies, monocled faces, bourgeois types, those were really demonstrations, not the feeble slouches you have nowadays, it took courage to march behind a red flag, *when we're marching side by side* –

Pakulat drummed his fingertips on the packaged shawm. He was sure he could bring that choir around. As he had brought his son around. All of a sudden. But legally. There was nothing that didn't go off legally. Sooner or later. This one was going off rather late. Thick-headed kid. Done. Otherwise he wouldn't be playing my favorite song, thought Pakulat, probably that's the breakthrough, probably he'll lead a shawm band someday too, I've achieved a breakthrough . . .

'And now by special request . . . ' His son's sonorous voice startled Pakulat out of his daydreams. He wiped his hand across his face and scratched the smile from the corners of his mouth. The first two fingers of his right hand rested on his thumb. Pakulat looked toward the stage in anticipation. The young man, wrinkle-resistant suit, ready-to-wear, 230 marks, new shoes, 52 marks, nylon shirt, 75 marks, Pakulat couldn't remember what he had paid for the Lincoln tie, the young man, Benno, moved aside the microphone he had just spoken into, exchanged a few more words with his musicians, who were sitting behind cardboard signs, took the trumpet from the piano, and turned his back to the audience. What did he want with the trumpet, conducting with a trumpet? I'll have to buy him a baton, thought Pakulat.

The parents stopped murmuring. The father lifted his right hand slightly, the first two fingers resting on the thumb. His son stamped his foot four times.

Sports festival, agitprop, brawl, demonstration, the armored might of the marching band, left, two, three, four, Pakulat marched in his wrinkle-resistant suit, legs straight, pulse excellent, breathing no problem, just the way an immortal marches.

He marched for quite a while, because he could only hear with his left ear. Then he stopped short. Since he knew that the dress rehearsal had taken place in the director's presence, he thought: public conversion. He used to belong to the Freethinkers, and he knew that public conversions were very effective. He thought: first, the negative example, to symbolize the hoodlums' past, and then it'll come. He concentrated on what was to come in order to endure the musicians' noise and their remarkable contortions more easily. The piano player tapped his foot on the floor instead of the pedal. The kettledrum player squandered his energies on various pot-sized drums and in general acted like a pot vendor at an open-air market. The bass player didn't have a bow. The brass section played with hollow backs, the higher the sound, the hollower their backs, they played with their eyes closed, paying no attention to the conductor. No wonder that Benno lost interest and blared away too, each of them played something different. The instruments had no sheet-music holders. The kids played with flushed faces, legs wide apart, bellies thrust forward indecently, they squeezed and squeezed, and what came out of these instruments? One note. A shawm would produce four times that much.

While Pakulat was thinking about the senseless waste of energy and talent, rocking the gift on his knees, he was suddenly struck by something familiar. Like a blow with brass knuckles. If you don't sing, I'll knock your eyes out. Take him away. He recognized his favorite song, hammered to pieces, syncopated, twisted. Benno called this twisted. The son of Pakulat the carpenter had made an old workers' song into a twist?

Pakulat reached for his money. And stuffed it back into the wallet. And stared fixedly at the oilcloth-covered tabletop, his head inclined a little to the left. And saw that the flower pattern wasn't there any more. Just a little bit ago he had seen it, it had been like new, and now it was almost gone. Only traces of color were still visible. And narrow dark lines where knives had sliced in all directions. And printer's ink in the shape of reversed letters. And a big brown burn hole that Anna had made when the bunker lamp had fallen out of her hand. And circles left by hot kettles and plates. And a few soup stains that were still fresh. Pakulat smeared them away with his hand. He knew that wasn't the right thing to do. But he was too tired to get a rag. He was afraid to get up and look around. He said, 'The house is like new.'

Nobody answered. Since yesterday he was alone. Abandoned. Mortal.

He took the soup kettle out of the oven, wrapped it in newspaper and then in a cloth, and set it on the table. He looked only at the kettle and the paper and the cloth. But even so, he noticed cracks in the stove tiles. And it seemed that plaster had crumbled from the door casing. He thought: shock wave. Although he knew that was baloney. But he couldn't choose his thoughts. Seven parties lived in his house. He wouldn't have rented to any of them, if it were up to him. Nobody could choose their thoughts.

Pakulat sat down again, reached behind him, fingering until he felt coolness, metal, half-circle, and the hasp. He took it and the key ring from the hook, inserted a flat key into the curved slot, turned the key to the left until he felt resistance, and pressed the bolt back. The hasp snapped open.

'Where is your landlady?'

'In bed.'

'And why aren't you in bed?'

'Because I still have work to do, as you see.'

'All I see is that you're reading.'

'Absolutely right.'

'Reading isn't work.'

The young man, whose face, upper chest, sharply angled arms, backs of hands, and open book were carved out of the darkness by the light of the table lamp, put his hand to his mouth, pulled a whitish string out between his teeth, making it longer and longer, thinner and thinner, then stuffed it back into his mouth, and kept on chewing.

'You've got a light on late into the night and your landlady can hardly afford a cup of coffee.'

'I pay for the light.'

'Oh.'

'The light and the whole apartment. The two-room apartment costs thirty-seven marks, and I pay fifty for one room.'

'What with?'

'With my scholarship grant.'

'In other words, my money. I insist that you not throw my money out the window.'

The young man pressed the radio button and raised the antenna. Yelling. Strange words.

'Inconsiderate behavior!'

'The old lady doesn't sleep anyway.'

'Your landlady isn't old.'

'You don't call sixty old?'

'When you make that kind of noise, she certainly can't sleep.'

'She can't sleep because she thinks I might be in bed with my girlfriend.'

Pakulat locked the student away. He knew what was going on. He had keys for all the parties. Only not for Benno.

Pakulat hung the lock back on the empty hook, to the right of the lock belonging to the family of Senior Inspector ret., which consisted of Herr Senior Inspector ret., Frau Senior Inspector ret. and Fräulein Daughter. It – the pronoun 'she' wouldn't have matched her looks – it played the piano on Sundays and holidays, and Herr Senior Inspector ret. claimed that this fully made up for his grand piano. The block leader himself had taken the grand piano belonging to the songstress Herzfeld.

The house floated on the waters of the night. The ark was invulnerable to water and fire. For it was made for the man and for his wife and his three sons. The man who was seen to be righteous for this time. Who had taken to himself every kind of clean and unclean beast, male and female. In the same manner of the birds under the heaven. And every sort of food also. *And the waters increased and lifted up the ark and bore it high above the earth.* And the man who sat in the ark, alone, for his wife had died and Max had been killed in action, and Lutz was married, and Benno was hanging out with bad company, the man who had a key for all who were with him – although he didn't believe most of them worthy to sit in the rooms – for all of them, only not for Benno, this man asked himself why he didn't kick open the windows and doors and lift the roof off the ark.

'Good-for-nothing,' said Pakulat.

The kitchen shrank. Wrinkled walls around him. Nails stood out from the worn floorboards like warts. The water paint was coming loose in bubbles from the ceiling. All of a sudden. The house had aged all of a sudden. The day before yesterday it had still been as it was in 1912, and at one blow it had aged. By decades, by centuries, so it seemed to Pakulat. He would have felt six hundred years old, if he hadn't once belonged to the Freethinkers.

Only the table had stayed the same. Just as big. Just as bright. Just as young. The oilcloth cover was worn out and the flowered pattern was gone, but the table was indestructible. The dead were indestructible.

Anna had put the table in the kitchen when she was pregnant with Benno. People had said the table was much too big for the tiny kitchen and wouldn't fit even if everything were cleared out. But Anna had bought it. 1944. When the sirens howled almost every night and no one in the building was dumb enough to acquire furniture or children. Anna had scraped money together for an unsuitable table. And made room for it. Hard to tell how she had done it. Pakulat was in a punishment battalion. The senior inspector stopped saying hello to Anna. The sergeant's wife stopped letting her children play with Lutz. Max was missing in action. Her father-in-law badgered her because she hadn't talked her husband out of his dangerous undertakings. Her mother kicked the bucket on the trail of refugees. In the last weeks her legs swelled so much that she could only wear slippers. She stood in the park restaurant in her slippers, washing dishes. And she bought the table in her slippers.

She gave birth in the air-raid shelter, and she was badly off afterwards. Benno was so puny that the doctors offered hardly any hope. But Anna pulled him through. She diapered him on the big table. Later, she went hungry so her child wouldn't have to go hungry. But Benno was still puny, even after his father, back from the war, went foraging for food to get him fed. Benno suffered through all the childhood diseases. At age five his tonsils were taken out, and a year later he broke his calf bone while sledding. When he started school, he was the littlest one in his class. His grade in sport was a four. His son's sufferings oppressed Pakulat as if they were his own. He loved him differently than he did Lutz, who was fifteen years older and won all his fights and was giving political speeches at age fourteen, in public; maybe he loved him a little like a grandfather loves his grandson.

Benno was sickly until his sixteenth year. Then he shook off his illnesses and grew and became strong. Pakulat was overjoyed that little Benno had suddenly turned into a young man more than a head taller than he. And he regretted it. And he didn't permit it. Sometimes. Yesterday evening, for example. The person who conducted the orchestra yesterday evening, that was little Benno for whom Father had brought a present. But he had behaved as little Benno had never done: ill-mannered, ungrateful, vulgar.

'He spit at me,' he said to the table. 'It was as if he had spit at me. And at you too, Anna, and all those who kicked the bucket so he could live and all those who slave away so he can study: my son. I'm stuck with a son like this.'

Pakulat had run home, half sick from disappointment and shame and rage, and waited for Benno, as he was waiting for him now. He had shuffled through the kitchen, four steps to the window, four steps to the door, past the icebox on which the wrapped box with the shawm lay, and waited for his lost son. Who was not yet completely lost yesterday. Who could still be saved via the bridge of remorse.

'Salud,' his son had said when he came home yesterday. And stopped in the doorway. Grinning. And that wasn't remorse. There was no bridge. Indignation struck his father dumb.

Benno seemed to observe this with satisfaction. In any case, he braced one elbow in the doorway and dangled his free leg. And sniffed snot loudly up his nose. And chewed gum.

'So, did you like the shawm twist?'

'Stop chewing,' Pakulat yelled.

'Why?'

'Stop chewing, I tell you.'

'I see that our side is enthused.'

Pakulat yanked his tie down.

Benno flinched. He held his right arm up to his face for a second. Then he braced his elbow in the doorway again and dangled his free leg. And sniffed snot loudly up his nose.

'Don't you have a handkerchief?'

'Yes.'

'Can't you stand still?'

'I won't let you break me to harness.'

'And I won't have you spitting on me, understood?'

'No,' said Benno. He reached for the door handle, stopped in midturn, hesitated a moment but seemed unable to resist, and mumbled that he was hoping to achieve a breakthrough.

And at that, Pakulat lost it. His memory even suspected him of throwing a fit. 'I have a bad memory,' he said to the table. But he admitted having dished out curses and blows.

Benno stood and took it, seemingly unmoved. He had let go of the door handle again and stood in the door, legs apart, his slightly spread arms dangling. This made his shoulders seem wider than usual and his head disproportionately small. Maybe it was also because his pale hair was cropped short. His face was so small that there was only room for eyes and a mustache. His lashless eyelids were straining wide open.

'Dandified whippersnapper, seventeen and a mustache, anything to stand out, making your father look foolish . . . '

'Nobody needs to make you look foolish, you make yourself . . . '

'And you aren't ashamed.'

'You aren't ashamed either.'

'Get your ass out of here,' Pakulat had yelled.

'I was just leaving,' Benno had said. 'Salud.'

Then he had disappeared behind the white painted door and hadn't shown up again. Until now. Now it was eleven thirty. Pakulat stared at the door. He saw that the paint was worn off to the left of the handle.

'Brat,' said Pakulat. He said it several times. Until his rage returned. And he held onto it for a while, making self-exonerating reproaches. He announced the most important ones to the table. He said, 'I should have been stricter with him. Persuading is well and good, but you can't persuade an ox, the only thing that works is a pole between the horns, some of them you have to force . . . '

He wandered around in the kitchen again. He held forth into the stillness that became denser and denser. 'Don't let it bother you, Pakulat,' he said. 'You can kiss my ass, you can all kiss my ass, all of you . . . ' But he let it bother him anyway. He couldn't make any headway against the emptiness that was suddenly gobbling up everything that seemed safe. Nothing was safe from it. He himself least of all. All the houses he had built had gone down in the darkness that he was floating on in his ark, the whole city had drowned, and he felt like opening the ark's windows and doors. Because he was mortal. And so it was all the same whether he died in the ark or drowned. Since yesterday he was as good as dead anyhow.

What was he waiting for? For somebody to still need him after all? Lutz didn't need him. The company didn't need him anymore either. Today they had paid him his second-to-last wage, as usual, the way they paid everyone their wages, next please. And in a week, when he got the last one, they'd probably also say next please. Nobody had asked him if he wanted to keep on working. Naturally, he would've had to say no if someone had asked him. Probably they all knew he couldn't do it any more. But at least they could have asked him. Once. No. They had written him off. Probably they'd already forgotten him. He'd get an invitation to the company party every year, out of pity, for old people they felt pity at best, and that would be the end of it. He was no longer Pakulat, carpenter, wrestler, conductor, unemployed worker, prisoner, detained soldier, company leader, instructor, brigade leader. He was some 'old man.' Probably they'd been calling him 'old man' for a long time, he just hadn't heard them. Because he could only hear in one ear any more. The other one was deaf from beatings during interrogation.

Pakulat reached for the lock again. But then he let it hang after all. It belonged to the family that lived above him and had no time for sleep. The father, mother, and daughter trampled across the floorboards until after midnight and again at four-thirty in the morning. The father banged away on the linoleum with the vacuum cleaner every day, the mother polished the aluminum windowsills every day, the daughter beat the bedside rugs every day. The family was vegetarian by religion and worked at the VEB slaughterhouse. Pakulat had had a key to this family's apartment for twenty-nine years. All that time, every window of their apartment had a flag whenever there was an occasion for it.

At night the flags were brought in and, if necessary, dried on the floor. As soon as day dawned, they were hanging out again, freshly ironed. Pakulat didn't need to open the lock. He had the key. That was enough.

He put on another briquette and wiped his coal-grimy hand over his left eye. 'Crap, damned crap,' he yelled. 'Shit and crap.' Then he peeled the cloth and paper from the kettle and ate the soup he had cooked for Benno. He ladled it mechanically into his mouth, his head turned a little to the right. When the soup was gone, he scraped the bottom of the kettle two or three times before he noticed. 'Ungrateful riffraff,' mumbled Pakulat. Fatigue burned under his eyelids. His artificial eye felt too tight. But he didn't take the glass eye out of its inflamed socket. He didn't want to be one-eyed when Benno came. And he would come, he could come any moment, it was twelve-thirty already.

For a second or two, he even thought that Benno had already come. Probably when he had nodded off. In any case, he saw Benno standing in the door and dangling his free leg. The door was like new, and Benno was combing through his pale hedgehog hair with his curved fingers. And sniffing snot up his nose and twirling his mustache, which was blond and skimpy and all the rest. But then he heard Benno's voice too, and the door was shabby again. Benno had a brown, sonorous voice that didn't suit his pale complexion at all. And what he said didn't suit him for sure. His name was Pakulat, everyone knew he was the son of Pakulat the Communist, and he said, 'You can take that invalid horn and shove it.' 'Invalid horn,' he had said. He called a shawm 'invalid horn.' The sergeant had called it 'cripple horn.' Before he was a sergeant, he'd said that once. And since then Pakulat had the key to the ornate lock that hung next to the vegetarians'. The sergeant, who, of course, was long since no longer a sergeant but a bookkeeper, collected anything that was decorated with scrolls: old watches, porcelain, door handles. He had wanted to buy the door handle from the door of Pakulat's summer house. But Pakulat hadn't taken him up on it. He couldn't remember why any more, at any rate, one word had led to another and finally the sergeant, who wasn't yet a sergeant at the time but already had the tone of voice, said, 'You'll be this small, you, depend on it, this small, I tell you, this small with your cripple horn.' He had stared in fascination at the tiny crack he had made between his thumb and index finger. And then he had pinched his finger and thumb together. But it couldn't be proven that he was the one who had put the police on the trail. One of the group had been executed. If Pakulat's suspicion was right, there was a murderer living downstairs. But it could also be that someone else had squealed on him. Someone else in this house . . .

'Good-for-nothing,' Pakulat mumbled drowsily. But he couldn't make up his mind to go to bed. He yawned and clung to the table. His arms, with their sleeves rolled up to the elbows, lay stretched out on the tabletop as far as they could go. His fingers curled around the edges, fingertips touching the plinth.

Then the table started shrinking, slowly, it could no longer hold its own against the walls, it had no strength left. The walls moved closer together, tighter and tighter, jail, prison, solitary confinement. Four tiny steps to the window, four tiny steps to the door, for thirteen months. And behind the window high up on the wall, invisible, somewhere, behind bars: the airspace. In the door a hole to spy through. The walls covered with scratches, carvings, letters, numbers, rhombuses with a line through lengthwise.

— and the bucket in the corner, and the bowl, the bowl is empty, the trustee brought the bowl empty, number 7311 to interrogation, light, brass knuckles, water, *star of Rio,* if you don't sing, I'll knock your other eye out too, light, *you could be my destiny,* if you're queer, you get more from the clink, brass knuckles, we make soap out of deaf-mutes, water —

'Benno,' mumbled Pakulat. He felt pressure on his forehead. And couldn't see. And smelled a strong chemical odor. And a dull whirling getting stronger and stronger.

It took a while before he realized that he was lying with his face on the tabletop. The skin of his forehead stuck to the oilcloth. His heartbeats pounded into him. He was sweating. But he forbade himself to notice this. And he didn't want to remember that Anna had died in a similar position. Six years ago. But Anna didn't let you forbid her anything. She came and went as she pleased. And she was fifty-one. Six years ago and today and forever. Only Pakulat had gotten older and older, without realizing it. And suddenly he was so old that he had his second-to-last wage in his wallet. And in seven days he would get the last one, and then it was closing time. Then he would sit at the window and stare down at the street like his neighbor.

Where disorder reigned. The garbage cans often stood at the curb for days before they were emptied. Children played rich man-poor man-beggar man-thief. Dogs crapped in the front yards. The sides of the streets were blocked by cars. Portable radios blared late into the night. In the early morning hours women dragged small, sleepy children behind them. The advertising pillars were plastered with fashion posters. Here and there, dustmops were shaken out of windows. The political slogan was missing from the display window of the produce shop. Every evening drunks staggered across the cobblestones as if it were always payday. Teenagers smooched in the recessed doorways. Disorder, everywhere disorder. No different than at the company Pakulat would leave in a week. He'd been the director once, for more than a year; that was seventeen years ago, the owner had taken off and somebody had to take charge, some dependable person had to get up the courage. Pakulat was dependable and got the job. 'Will do,' he said and thought, it's not even a construction company any more, it's a demolition company, anyone can tear down a few ruins, anyone can do that, anyone, anyone. But what with, he asked himself when he had taken over the company. No tools, no money, no construction workers. Nazis who had been kicked out of other places were sent to him as workers. He, the delegate who had never allowed anyone whose papers weren't in order on the construction site, was supposed to hire Nazis once he had become company director. That was more than he could stand. After a year he was replaced and was finally able to do what he'd been planning for twelve years: restore order to the site; see to it that every construction worker had the proper papers. For nine years he worked as a union instructor here and there, usually away from the family. When his wife died, Benno was eleven years old. Pakulat couldn't leave him on his own. He had also grown tired of the everlasting moving around. And he was sick of wearing himself out with bosses who gobbled work and you had nothing to show for it. Or hardly anything. Or at any rate not much. Not enough. To hell with those pig-headed so-and-sos. Pakulat wanted to do something you could get hold of again for a change. Something that would last. That would outlive him. He wanted to work the way he had worked in his youth. High up on the scaffold.

A week from now he had to come down from the scaffold. And what would happen the minute he turned his back? Someone else would join the brigade, someone he wouldn't have allowed on the site before. And the someone had presented himself yesterday. Pakulat had demanded to see his papers, and the kid had said he wasn't in the union. Without batting an eye, as if he was talking about the weather. At the end of his working days, Pakulat had to face the fact that his successor was a phony. Of course, the kid wouldn't become brigade leader right away. Benno had to study too, before he could be a geologist. But it wasn't impossible that before long this guy with no papers could be in charge of a construction site and do as he pleased. It was possible that Benno would soon be deciding what happened to the earth. Could Pakulat step down with a clear conscience if this was his replacement?

The walls moved closer together again, the ceiling pressed down, the sky, which was an airspace . . .

Pakulat yanked a lock from the hook and opened it with a hollow key.

'You're sitting in the dark.'

'Yes,' said the little old lady.

'Did you work the late shift?'

'Yes.'

'Why don't you turn the light on?'

'Don't need a light.'

'But you can't see what you're eating.'

'I don't want to see any more,' said the little old lady, turning on the lamp. It hung from the ceiling on a rod wrapped around with cord, a silk-covered shade with a gathered blind and five lights. Only one of them was on, however, maybe fifteen watts. And the shade was completely dark. You couldn't see the walls. Only pictures surrounded the little old lady, furniture and pictures.

'Do you always have to work the late shift?'

'Yes.'

'Why?'

'Because I couldn't care less.'

'I don't understand.'

'I couldn't care less.'

'At your age you have to think of your health.'

'Nobody else thinks about it, why should I, of all people, think about it.'

'You're at least as old as me.'

'Yes,' said the little old lady.

'And why are you still working?'

'Because I can't look at the pictures all day long.'

The pictures, in black frames of different sizes, filled the spaces between the ornate pieces of furniture. Infants, children, and young men smiled behind glass. The photos of infants hung higher up. If you looked closely you could distinguish two faces that appeared again and again. The one was photographed in brown and white, the other in black and white. Most of the brown-and-white photos hung above the sofa and showed the little old lady's fiancé in various poses, sprawling on a polar bear hide, seated wearing a dress, standing beside a small palm table in a sailor suit with a school satchel and a bag of candy. Half-length portraits showed him wearing a schoolboy's cap, later a bowler hat, and last of all a spiked helmet. Her son's pictures hung on the other side of the room around the sideboard. He too was pictured, among other poses, sprawling, with a bag of candy, and with various kinds of headgear. In the last picture he had on a steel helmet. Like the last picture of his father, it had straw flowers and a crepe veil on the lower right corner.

'You don't get enough sleep.'

'I know,' said the little old lady,

'Sleep keeps you well.'

'I'm not going through that again.'

'You should take better care of yourself.'

'The next time nobody will survive anyway.'

'You've worked enough in your lifetime.'

'Maybe it's already started. I didn't listen to the radio today.'

'You should go to bed.'

'Maybe it's the second flood that Biblical scholars have prophesied. Cuba is supposed to be such a paradise.'

Pakulat locked the little old lady away at once. But the tides of the night had already seized him. They tossed him to and fro, and the waves washed over him. Because the ark was only invulnerable to water and fire. It was made for the man and his wife and his three sons. But it did the man no good to believe that he was seen as righteous for this time. He had taken to himself every kind of clean and unclean beast, male and female. And in like manner of the birds under the heaven. And every kind of food also. But when the waters rose, they did not lift up the ark and bear it away over the earth. When it came, that which one called 'flood' for the sake of simplicity, there were no miracles. When the great flood came, it swallowed the righteous and the unrighteous. And the makers of the flood.

And the earth would again be without form and void. And it would be dark down in the depths . . .

'Benno,' Pakulat cried out. He was startled by his own voice. The light from the kitchen lamp cut into his eyes. The earth, he thought. He knew, of course, that the earth was a sphere. Everyone knew that nowadays.

And Pakulat believed that he also saw it that way. But in reality he only saw a surface. And everything that stood and grew upon it he also saw only in two dimensions, the city for example, and the house and his neighbor and the vegetarian and the Senior Inspector ret. and the student and Benno, he saw them all only in two dimensions. For one had been taken from him. And life had seemed to him only a function of societal quantities ever since. And now that it was in danger, it seemed so to him also. And he would have felt afraid, although he felt somehow safe in his ark, hard to say why, perhaps because he had the big table with him, but he would have felt afraid if the lost son had returned home. But it was nearly one, and Benno was still not back. Benno was in danger. The earth was in danger. The earth was unimaginably large. Benno was unimaginably small. And blood of his blood. And flesh of his flesh. Pakulat feared for Benno.

'Just yesterday they ran into somebody again,' Pakulat said to the table, 'seriously injured. I always say, don't walk around half asleep out there, look where you're going, but young people don't listen, maybe he's come back by now and I didn't notice . . . ' Pakulat pulled himself up on the table, pushed open the scarred door, groped his way through the dark corridor, felt for the door handle, and opened it. Pakulat turned on the light. The bed was empty.

He sat down on the edge of the bed. The cool air of the unheated room closed in on him. Ach, Benno, you good-for-nothing . . .

Pakulat noticed a dog-eared book lying on the night table. 'That looks like hell,' he mumbled, reaching for it. He read, '*Spanish Conversational Grammar.*'

Pakulat got to his feet again, four steps to, four steps back. Spanish! His son didn't even think it was necessary to tell his father what he was studying. Didn't a father have a right to know what his son was doing? What did you have children for, if you couldn't be part of their lives? Spanish. What did you have heirs for if they couldn't be saved from the mistakes the father had made long ago. At Benno's age Pakulat had also gotten involved in all kinds of things, fishing, metalsmithing, shoemaking, cabinetmaking, and all kinds of livestock. But then his father had said that's enough of that, and he had listened to his father and concentrated on one thing and become a carpenter. If you wanted to turn out decent, you had to concentrate on one thing. But Benno didn't listen to his father. Benno did a little of this and a little of that and now Spanish, of all things. He had a four in Russian, but he had time for this foolishness. Spanish! Pakulat had a good memory, he could still remember exactly how he had felt at age seventeen, yessiree. He had experience. Which he had to pass on. Which he passed on every day, at the construction site, on the streetcar, in the store, every time there was an opportunity. Only Benno got nothing from him. Probably his son was a pig-headed so-and-so. There were always pig-headed so-and-sos.

As Pakulat turned around again to take four steps toward the window, a strange spot on the wall caught his left eye. Pakulat hesitated before looking more closely. He knew that nude photos hung above the bed.

He knew what was going on.

But then he looked anyway. And discovered among the nude photos the picture of a young man with curly black chin hair and a beret. Pakulat squinted, put an eyeglass to his eye, squinted again . . .

He couldn't reorient himself right away after this discovery, which made the room different. Had he overlooked the bearded man up to now?

Could you overlook something like that?

His sleepiness melted away. Pakulat turned on the electric heater and puffed up the pillow. 'I must find him,' he said, although the kitchen table was far away, put on his overcoat, and left the room.

He groped his way down the stairs, which were still very well preserved, it seemed to him, like new, he thought. Just a little while ago, the wood had seemed worn, but now it was quite smoothly polished again. He passed four apartment doors, two of which had rough plywood surfaces instead of carved wooden frames and glass panels, squeezed through the porch door, and unlocked the outside door.

And climbed out of the ark, which suddenly seemed invulnerable again to water and fire. And let it float alone out into the night.

BOOK TEN

Chapter 1

TEXT OF A SENSATIONAL TELEGRAM FROM RAPALLO

AM ON ANAXIMANDER'S TRAIL STOP BEATRICE

Chapter 2

LAURA TALKS ON THE TELEPHONE WITH THE BEAUTIFUL MELUSINE

Laura was so taken aback by the telegram that sleep eluded her. After walking around in the apartment for seven nights, she came back to a certain offer by dialing the telephone number 22 88 020. The heat in the phone booth was worse than during dog days. The coin-operated phone was a bottomless pit. But after the tenth groschen it did produce a connection, accompanied by rattling noises, to a voice with a dynamic speech pattern that reminded Laura of her mother, Olga. And made her want to hurry. So Laura kept it short and requested, with some embarrassment, the exhibit Benno Pakulat for an informational interview without obligation. The voice confirmed delivery for the coming evening. Laura did not wait in vain.

Chapter 3

INFORMATIONAL EXCHANGE BETWEEN LAURA SALMAN AND BENNO PAKULAT, SCENE ONE

Scene: *Room with open balcony door.*

Time: *Night in late summer.*

Laura in her nightgown, knitting at the balcony door. Squeaking noises. Blue light. Then a celestial vehicle from on high. In the celestial vehicle, Benno Pakulat. His face is covered by a cap. Laura lifts the cap without waking the sleeping man and sprinkles his face with beer. Then she timidly removes the shoe and sock from his left foot and grasps his big toe, which she does not let go of during the entire scene.

LAURA (*whispering*): Do you love children?

BENNO (*in a monotone, without opening his eyes, low volume*): Yes, now that I know what children are. Before that I only sounded off about it, if you know what I mean.

LAURA (*also low volume*): No.

BENNO: Man, can't you picture that kind of dude, a totally average guy, as the saying goes. You hung out with my brother long enough. To Lutz, children don't really exist until he can have a conversation with them. Before that he doesn't know what to do with them, and to him, children aren't equal human beings you have to take seriously anyway; he's just like our father that way. Which is why old man Pakulat gave me such a hard time, for example, over the milestone problem, if that means anything to you. In politics old man Pakulat found any number of milestones, but for me, lady, where was the milestone on me that told you: until such-and-such a day I'm a lump of clay you can make anything out of, and after such-and-such a day I'm an individual you have to respect. One who now needs clay of his own.

LAURA: Hey, that smells suspiciously like antiauthoritarian education, which was not grown on GDR soil. Haven't you heard of affirmative action plans for juveniles and for women or extracurricular activities for young nature lovers . . .

BENNO: I'm not talking about our state affairs or laws, which are super, I'm talking about morals, family affairs. He who oppresses other people cannot be free himself, the saying goes, but my high-proof Communist father didn't put up with back talk, okay, little sister?

LAURA: How do you mean that?

BENNO: Little brother then, for all I care — all these language problems, sisterly is a made-up word too, or have you ever heard of the state council sending sisterly greetings anywhere?

LAURA: You're brazenly trying to butter me up.

BENNO: Me — never! I've had it up to here with women.

LAURA: With women too?

BENNO: For sure.

LAURA: You're a misanthrope.

BENNO: A philanthrope, lady, or do you think a woman who denies a father visitation rights to his daughter is human?

LAURA: Oh, you have a daughter?

BENNO: Two. When my first daughter was three years old, it hit me during afternoon tea like a ton of bricks, so to speak, that I had no clue what this is, a daughter, a child. My paternal ass took itself colossally seriously at birthday parties, but in actual fact I was a deadbeat. It's the truth; I'd been asleep, slept through it all for three years, and now I was turning myself inside out talking stupid baby talk, crawling around like an idiot on the rug and under the table with stuffed animals, I whinnied like a horse, I even sang 'All My Little Duckies' and stuff like that, if you've been at women's hen parties you know all about it. But of course you don't know old man Pakulat, my esteemed role model, who only made mistakes in order to learn from them; you aren't asking the right question, comrade. Me, on the other hand, that same evening, razor-sharp and persuasive to the max, my wife at the time actually wanted only one child, but when I'm in top form my charm can melt a heart of stone, hydrochloric acid, it's the truth.

LAURA: Why do you act younger than you are?

BENNO: Huh?

LAURA: I don't understand why you still talk and dress and use whatever other tricks to resist becoming an adult, which, in fact, you already are. Late twenties, if my information is correct. Why don't you want to be an adult?

BENNO: Because adult males make me puke.

LAURA: And adult females?

BENNO: I was always into older women. Young chicks who giggle day and night could never get me up, my ex-wife was fifteen years older than me, but it's not what you're thinking, comrade. I didn't dump her for being too old, she dumped me.

LAURA: Divorced?

BENNO: Wasn't necessary, we weren't married, on principle. I don't know if you're familiar with that MO; what young dude wants to be seen as an old married wimp? But of course we lived together, fifth floor tenement house, I converted two efficiencies into one apartment, out of sight, any amount of sunlight up there under the roof, now I'm up to my butt in the basement, and Mr. Biology Degree is nesting in my masterpiece.

LAURA: Your ex-wife's present partner . . .

BENNO: Her husband.

LAURA: So she apparently was a woman who wanted to get married . . .

BENNO: What do you mean apparently, she only had to open her mouth; one word and I would have gotten hold of Mr. Justice of the Peace, with the ring, with a bouquet and ring and the whole ball of wax, am I a monster? But she's one. Forbids a father to see his children, and do you know what the Juvenile Authority says?

LAURA: You have visitation rights.

BENNO: Exactly. I have visitation rights, and their mother has custody. But visitation rights are a discretionary provision, lady, not law. Of course, the custodial parent officially gets a good and serious talking-to, their immoral selfishness is brought to their attention, with reminders that children aren't property and all that. I don't even claim that I brought up my first daughter. But I was a father to my second daughter, a real one, not some dude with visitor status. I got my little girl dressed in the morning and took her to day care, I picked her up in the evening, gave her a bath, fed her, changed her diapers too, of course. When she was sick, I didn't pass the buck to my wife, I sweated it out myself at diaper tables and in doctors' waiting rooms, I tossed and turned all night and bawled my eyes out for fear sometimes. I don't have to tell you that this kind of thing creates bonds, lady. It's the only thing that does; watching doesn't generate serious experiences, only contact, understanding, touching do. When my second daughter started talking, she called me and my wife Mama. When in hell is our state going to pass laws to protect the interests of our working fathers?

Startled, Laura lets go of toe and cap. The apparition disappears squeaking into the air.

Chapter 4

Wherein the reader learns what the Beautiful Melusine copied from a magazine into her 73d Melusinian book

Forty years ago F. S. Hammet studied the consequences of surgical removal of the internal secretory parathyroid glands in rats. If they are removed, the secretion they release into the bloodstream is absent, which has most serious consequences for metabolizing calcium. The calcium concentration in the blood drops rapidly; usually death follows within two days. In Hammet's experiments, however, certain rats proved to be more resistant and survived the operation somewhat longer. This group of more resistant rats differed from those that died sooner in only one respect: they had been regularly handled by the laboratory staff, while the less resistant rats had been raised without being handled at all. Hammet's studies were overlooked for a long time. But some years ago their significance was recognized. Since then, the research has been continued. The rats used have been bred to be virtually identical in terms of their genetic material. In the experiment the genetically identical animals are divided into two groups. One group remains untouched by humans and other animals; the second group is petted at specific intervals according to a strictly normed procedure. Now when both groups are exposed to severe distress – the Canadian researcher H. Selve, originally from Austria-Hungary, introduced the English word 'stress' for this – it is tolerated better by the rats that were petted than by the ones that were not. The stress can take the form of withholding food and water, restricting freedom of movement, infections, injuries, and overexertion. With this kind of stress, the hormonal secretions of the adrenal glands increase. These hormones, which influence the metabolism, increase resistance to stress. When the distress is increased, the two adrenal glands increase their hormonal secretions, and with continued distress, the adrenals enlarge. This enlargement is not seen in rats that have been petted, despite the distress. They also gain more weight and are more easygoing than rats that were not petted. Even the ability to learn is surpassed in rats that were petted as compared to those that were not. They learn to find their way to the food in mazes better; they make fewer mistakes and avoid blind alleys. The state of their nerves also seems to be healthier.

Chapter 5

LAURA'S EXPRESS LETTER TO BEATRICE DE DIA IN RAPALLO, POSTE RESTANTE

Dear Beatrice,

Please come back at once. You have been elected to the PEN Club. The speech in your honor was delivered by the poet Dieter Meicke. I asked for a copy of the script, so you can take a look at it. The summer is much healthier here too. Wesselin can already say your name. See you soon!

Laura

ENCLOSURE

Chapter 6
Enclosure for the Express Letter to Rapallo, Poste Restante

State Railway Pool: You get the best views of the sea in the washbowl. Standing, toes curled upward by the basin, mirror-waves playing about the ankles. The lack of a relatively abundant water supply, which the state railway pool had in common with other public swimming pools, was more than offset by soot, flying ash, and the sights and sounds of the adjoining railway depot. To me, this institution is optimal. I visited it regularly as a child, in the height of summer daily. The walk there took more than half an hour. It started at the top of Hilbersdorf hill, where the pavement of Dresdener Straße was laid under giant maples. Shaded. At the curve I usually stopped and looked down, away from all adverse events. The croissant-shaped roofs of the two boiler houses were fitted into the valley basin, as were the administration building and switch tower, signal bridges, water cranes, coal bunkers, coal depots, swimming pool, diving boards. When the air current released the smoke rising from the boiler house and locomotive smokestacks from the valley, I could recognize the pattern of tracks crossed by trains, departing freight cars, and shunting locomotives. The tracks quivered gently in the shimmering heat. The path downhill through the stunted, soot-laden forest stretched out in a pleasantly agonizing way, for the smells of smoke and swamp were already unmistakable. When the wind was northwest, I could understand the pool attendant's shunting orders and swearing before I reached the clearing. Some years the oak-roller-moth excrement, which fell from the trees they had eaten bare, rustled in the dried-up foliage like rain. Heat and the chirping of crickets above the clearing seemed like a mountain of sunstroke. That's what I had to plow my way through in the end by foot and sweat. Dazed, I bought a ticket from the pool attendant's knitting wife and went to the chassisless passenger car, the changing cabin for the swim club members and their equally privileged family members. I was family, so I didn't need to worry about my dress or lunch when I stirred up the water. Finally. It had a delicately stagnant smell and a harsh taste. When I let myself fall perpendicularly from the three-meter board into the water, it looked dark brown, then greenish brown, and before I surfaced, green and foaming with air bubbles. It burned the eyes and cleared the nose as if with a bottle brush. By June it already took on a viscous appearance. Although the pool attendant defended the purity of the water with harsh, scolding speeches, delivered through a megaphone.

During the cold season he was on the road, working as a plate-layer; during swimming season he was sedentary. On a tall white-painted chair frame that stood in the mud. Beside the swimming pool, at the level of the dividing rope. The rope required the pool visitors to decide whether they belonged to the first or second category of human beings. Naturally, I decided for the first. Before I knew how to swim, I would hold onto the rail and slither my feet up and down the algae-slippery pool walls. After I had acquired that ability, it interested me very little, which is why I only used it for getting out of the water and onto one of the diving boards as fast as possible. The diving boards stood in the mud too. It squished gently between your toes. Near the pool, parallel to it and of the same shape, was a sand basin. The sand was grayish brown, mixed with ash that the wind blew over from the depot. A wire-mesh fence separated the pool from the cinder heap where the adjoining engine graveyard stretched out. The grass was gray and so were the birch leaves; all colors quickly went gray, on fabric too. And on bodies. A short stay on the horizontal bars and monkey bars, which were located on the drifting sand mishmash, and you needed a swim. My parents' scolding at the sight of my blue lips and protruding ribs, held up to me as the harmful consequences of addiction to swimming, could be countered by natural arguments in the state railway pool. Nowhere was the pleasure of swimming more saturated by trouble and aggravation than in this German institution. Officially, the attendant demanded through the megaphone that the eager swimmers cleanse themselves in the washroom beforehand, seriously he was interested in his chickens. They strutted between the bodies sunning themselves on blankets on the lawn. He took pains to see that the darkness of his complexion surpassed that of his guests. Oh joy, to stand on the coconut mat of the three-meter board with ash raining down on my skin and the roar of through trains and whistling of locomotives, when the board started shaking under the pressure of my feet and lifted me out into the undefined luxury of anticipation. The trip ended headfirst. Sometimes I felt the muddy bottom on the top of my head. I had flown through the sea.

Chapter 7

Everyday life with Oranienburg mystery

Laura worried about Beatrice. Who was wandering around, bewildered, in foreign countries. Alone. Actually: left alone. Laura had sent her friend away. The minstrel's natural cheerfulness faded under self-reproaches. For she had often read enviously of male friendships that, without being homosexual, had a beautiful intensity: a mutual undertaking reinforced them. At best, an idea. Elaborating and defending created bonds. That sort of activity between men and women on the other hand was mostly short-lived, because it was threatened by sex storms. But Laura had found friendships among women even more rarely than solidarity. In part because friendships need time. Of necessity, most women's hobby was the second or third shift: housework, children. Young women would be most likely to have energy left over for the daily journey from the diverse acts of stooping over that are indigenous to housework to those heights where ideas are to be found. The 841-year-old Beatrice de Dia, who had come to Laura in a miraculous way, had to be seen as an ideal case, despite all vexations. Unique. And Laura absolutely wanted to hold onto the hopes she had pinned on Beatrice. At some point, her friend would have to sow her wild oats; at some time, she would have to become rational. Because she was wise. Going to endless trouble to bring women history in person was wise. Too wise? Laura's worries increased to such an extent that she occasionally found Wesselin's crying annoying. He started bawling every time she left the room. He chose the left corner of the playpen next to the sofa for crying. The playpen was tied to the sofa so that Wesselin couldn't walk the playpen around. He wept the wailing corner wet in just a few minutes. But kept on playing meanwhile, so as not to lose any time. When Laura entered the room, Wesselin switched abruptly from extortionary screams to laughter. Without interrupting his playing. His favorite toys were wheels. His grandfather had screwed several onto the playpen. Also onto Grandmother's kitchen table and the broom closet, ignoring Olga Salman's protests. He had listened uncomprehendingly to Laura's protests against the rearrangement and remodeling of her apartment from the standpoint of playing. Johann Salman could seriously ask his grandson, who had just started to say his first words, 'What shall we play now?' And he wasn't just acting pleased when Wesselin spun the wheels. Wesselin called wheels 'deez.' To be sure, Johann Salman only indulged in play when children were available as a pretext. He apparently understood adulthood as a condition that called for a certain corseting of movement. Laura had never seen tears in her father's eyes. She doubted that the efforts made by Johann Salman and men like him to satisfy the masculine ideal were honored with conviction by Olga Salman and women like her. Voluntarily. Uwe had been the right partner for Johann Salman in political debates. Of course, Johann valued interminable conversations with homegrown extravagances. And Karl-Marx-Stadt. He believed it was the most proletarian city in the GDR. Recently he had written to Laura, advising her to place an ad for a marriage partner and prescribing two tablespoons of wheat granules daily for Laura and Wesselin. He distrusted everything that was artificial, including art. He rejected nylon socks, also heat-pressed oil, and inorganic fertilizers. He thought that synthetic foodstuffs, which were being developed in the Soviet Union, in the United States, and presumably also in Laura's country, were toxic imitations, which he refused to have anything to do with in times of peace. He and his wife nourished themselves whenever possible with uncooked or gently cooked vegetables, natural honey, and foods you could buy in health-food stores. When Laura paid the rent for Beatrice's Oranienburg apartment and picked up the mail, the landlady called the junk that the room was furnished with 'antiques.' She called her husband a wreck, in his presence. 'Look at that wreck,' she said cheerfully. He sat silently in an armchair, his artificial leg beside him. Landlady Buche dusted the artificial leg and mentioned in passing her deprivations since the First World War and said only dummies would marry cripples. 'Fifty-two years of fishing, one vacation after another – would you be such a dummy?' Laura sorted letters fiercely. Like the residents in the house and Beatrice, the husband called his wife Ma Buche. Among reminders of business matters and invitations, Laura found a peculiar letter of reply from a certain Christoph Arnold. He indicated that he had done all the requested research and finally learned the following: 'After reciting certain prayers and observing fast days, they make the figure of a man from clay or lime, and when they speak the SHEM HAMEPHORASH over it, the figure comes to life. And although it cannot speak, it understands what they say and command; it also does all kinds of housework for the Polish Jews but is not allowed out of the house. On the figure's forehead they write EMETH; that means "truth." But such a figure grows every day, and although it is very small at first, it eventually gets taller than all members of the household. To take away its strength, which finally all in the household must fear, they swiftly erase the first letter, aleph, from the word EMETH on its forehead, so that only the word METH – that means "death" – is left. When this happens, the golem falls down in a heap and dissolves into clay or lime as before . . . They say that such a Baal Shem in Poland, named Rabbi

Elias, made a golem that grew to such a size that the rabbi could no longer reach its forehead to erase the letter *E*. Then he got the idea that as his servant, the golem should take off his boots; he thought he could erase the letter on its forehead when the golem knelt down, and so it happened. But as the golem turned into lime again, the whole weight fell on the rabbi sitting on the bench and crushed him.'

Chapter 8

Speech for an apparatus, delivered by Laura Salman, addressed to the ceiling

I sit out my evenings in front of the cabinet. Of necessity. Voluntarily. And gladly. Usually busy with needles that devour bands. The needles beat high tapping sounds from the wicker chair. When I rest my elbows on its arms, the wicker presses deep patterns into my skin. If I change the pressure, it creaks an answer. One lives well with furniture that can talk. Plugged in to an electric socket, the apparatus emits bands from its window, which is enclosed in wood and foil. The band is certainly made close by and at an uncertain distance behind the window. In a manner that is unclear to me. My father can't explain what electricity is, but he can repair electrical appliances. The mechanic who came by recently in a service vehicle threw his toolbox on the table when he saw my apparatus. He claimed to have completed 1,826 service calls this year, but none for a model like this. And he replaced a defective tube with a new one. With success; at that, a word of defense and justification seemed called for. I spoke from joy as well. Especially about the respectable band quality. The mechanic didn't dispute it and said such old models weren't worth repairing. I was sure that he couldn't explain what electricity is either and found this reassuring and in order, because I thought that people had always lived in harmony with objects that were difficult to explain: on intimate terms through habituation; possibly the organism of a tree by comparison would be even more difficult to explain. I accepted the warranty card for the new tube and paid without adding a tip. For I don't have to represent anything: the apparatus is a use object. In the evenings it emits band, sometimes so much of it that I can't move the needles fast enough. Then it piles up in the room in baroque folds or hangs there. It is made of images and sounds. And while thus occupied, I have cries from Wesselin as a fixed noise in my ears. He sleeps in the next room while Rostock and Moscow and Detroit and the Mekong pass through my fingers. Today I process beautiful belts of land, great feats of production, race riots, state actions, and a Vietnamese corpse, plain purl stitch. All the items of clothing I have made in this way for myself and Wesselin favor this pattern. Everyday clothes. When they're worn out, you throw them away and put on new ones.

Chapter 9

TEXT OF AN OUTRAGEOUS TELEGRAM FROM ROME

ANAXIMANDER FOUND STOP BEATRICE

Chapter 10

LAURA'S EXPRESS LETTER TO BEATRICE DE DIA, ROME, POSTE RESTANTE

Dear Beatrice,

Please come back at once. You have been elected to the City Council Assembly of Berlin. Also a letter of reply that seems suspicious to me has arrived from a certain Christoph Arnold. The late summer is ideal this year. Wesselin is walking. If no one takes his hand, he holds on tight to his left ear. See you soon!

Laura

ENCLOSURE

Chapter 11

ENCLOSURE FOR THE EXPRESS LETTER TO ROME, POSTE RESTANTE

Summary report of the present state of negotiations between the poet Paul Wiens, on the one hand, and Trobadora Beatrice's minstrel, on the other hand, concerning the composition of a canso for Professor Dr. Wenzel Morolf: The meeting arranged by Sarah Kirsch between the minstrel Laura and the poet Paul Wiens began at 5:10 P.M. local time on 1 May 1971, in the foyer of the Berlin Conference Center. As the book bazaar visitors were being urged by the marshals to leave because of closing time, the gentleman slowly came into view. Before that, he was besieged. From time to time, individual people holding papers in their hands had burst through the mob surrounding him. Some of the sheets had patterns drawn on them, some had words, some had patterns and words. I asked for information and learned that the papers with words written on them were sold at fixed prices. The monies were to be deposited in a collection box for the Vietnam Solidarity Committee. When the marshals had freed the table behind which the poet Wiens sat smoking, I was able to look at his display. Various stacks of books and a scant square meter of cardboard. Pasted on it were printed and typewritten pieces of paper where you could read every which way in different unsystematic arrangements:

V erses L yrics for
T o A ll
O rder L ife situations

Are you having trouble in your collective?
Are you on the wrong track?
A PURE RHYME WILL ALWAYS HELP
Even to cure lovesickness . . .

Systematic schooling of emotions:
Adults two lines for 1 mark
Rhymed for double price, i.e., 2 marks
Magic spells 1 mark surcharge
Guaranteed results!
Upon request the composition will be treated confidentially.
Children and professional poets pay half of half price.

Presenting my social security card, which shows my profession authenticated by the tax authorities, I placed a confidential order for a canso of three stanzas, rhymed and fortified with magic spells, for half of half price, in Russian. For the additional request to translate the canso into German, the poet asked forty marks per line plus 30 percent express surcharge. The contract was signed verbally by both parties around 11:00 P.M. the same day in the Ganymede restaurant. Negotiations took place in a comradely atmosphere. Since then I've been sending the poet a written reminder every month.

signed Laura Salman
Minstrel

Chapter 12

INFORMATIONAL EXCHANGE BETWEEN LAURA SALMAN AND BENNO PAKULAT, SCENE TWO

Scene: *Room with open balcony door.*

Time: *Night in early fall.*

Laura in her bathrobe, knitting at the balcony door. Squeaking noises. Blue light. Then a celestial vehicle from on high. In the celestial vehicle, Benno Pakulat. His face is covered by a cap. Laura lifts the cap without waking the sleeping man and sprinkles his face with beer. Then she confidently removes the shoe and sock from his left foot and grasps his big toe, which she does not let go of during the entire scene.

LAURA (*matter-of-factly*): Why did your wife really leave you?

BENNO (*with eyes closed*): Well.

LAURA: Aha.

BENNO: No way aha, or do you maybe also crave guys to whom you can say, you're so beautifully brutal?

LAURA: On the contrary.

BENNO: Oh.

LAURA: So if you don't mind . . .

BENNO: A woman who was hung up on my brother for years isn't used to being treated well. Or did Mr. Engineering Degree get over himself with you?

LAURA: Lutz always came in a festive mood.

BENNO: Cool. His second incarnation must've been mega-optimal. Compared to the first incarnation; that was his marriage to this scientifically talented Karla, if you know what I mean. You couldn't invent a worse loser than Lutz's first incarnation. Because Karla's obligatory housewife role truly burdened my brother. With a guilty conscience. Which was served warmed-over every day by Father State's propaganda; that gets to you. For a while my brother-boy tried to get rid of his guilty conscience by taking the bull by the horns: he dried the dishes and did the stuff they crank out whole TV series about. He helped out, the poor guy—when I hear the word 'help,' I cock my revolver. Or did your one-time husband happen to thank you every time you lifted a finger at home? But naturally, this way out soon seemed too much like work for Mr. Engineering Degree. Because it interfered with storming the fortress of science. It's true. Advancing to the rear was the only other choice: the second incarnation, as the name says. Marriage to a 786-percent devout housewife who relieved Lutz of his guilty conscience. Promotion to breadwinner. Sweetie, do you want this, sweetie, do you want that. And prompt service isn't even all, the woman shows gratitude too. That's luxury. Magnificent professional upswing. Titles on the wall, medals on the chest, automobile, happiness. Which, however, is soon clouded by certain tendencies that the first marriage-variation had insinuated into Mr. Engineering Degree: my brother had tasted blood. So an emancipated girlfriend became indispensable. You, lady, generously sacrificed yourself in this role for a while . . .

LAURA: I didn't sacrifice myself; in my generation I emphatically prefer this role to being a housewife.

BENNO: Bingo. But what did you feel toward Lutz's second wife? Guilt? Jealousy?

LAURA: Solidarity.

BENNO: And solidarity for my ex too?

LAURA: No.

BENNO: Lucky for you. I was starting to think you'd lost the will to live. Support-check father doesn't do it for me, no freaking way. I'd like to see what you'd do if they ever downgraded you to support-check mother.

LAURA: You mean if they took my Wesselin away from me? Murder. I wouldn't survive it. Losing a lover is hard sometimes. But losing a child is like having your arms chopped off, or your legs, or both together . . .

BENNO: What did I say, she made a cripple of me. And not even for revenge or like that; we didn't separate as arch-enemies. She chopped me off for convenience, it's a fact, for the sake of simplicity, so the children don't give the new father problems. Because when children have two fathers to compare, naturally a sort of competitive situation crops up between the two fathers. And she wanted to spare the successor to my throne that strain. And herself too. No doubt. Friction, where the mother instinctively sides with the children, undermines love. Maybe they even arouse jealousy in Mr. Biology Degree; there are guys who are actually jealous of their own children. Adults who ship off children like piece goods should be thrown in the slammer. *(with a changed voice)* Because our children are not our possessions. They are sons and daughters of life's longing for itself. They come through us, not from us. We can give them our love but not our ideas.

We can give their bodies a home but not their souls. For their souls live in the house of tomorrow, which we cannot visit, not even in our dreams. If we wish, we can try to be like them. But we cannot make them be like us. Because life does not go backwards and does not stop at yesterday.

LAURA (*reverently*): Are you speaking in tongues?

BENNO: In quotations.

LAURA: Judging by what you're saying, you must be a man from a picture book. And where's the catch?

BENNO: What catch?

LAURA: You know, the one your wife threw you out for. Too much alcohol?

BENNO: Too little ambition.

LAURA: Lazy.

BENNO: So are you also one of those dames who calls every worker with brains lazy if he doesn't go full speed ahead to qualify himself out of the working class? My wife was constantly after me with some self-study recommendations or other, it's true. Have you got that kind of drive for higher things too? And for these synthetic duds from the Exquisite Boutique – why not just plaster your belly with paper money? And if there's no car in the household, the outlook is all gloom and doom. Shit status symbols. Can I eat a three-piece furniture suite? Why should I imitate the acquisition mode, just because it comes from the West? Okay, the anticonsumer mode comes from there too; over there every nonconformist trend is marketed conformistically in no time, but that can't keep me from having my own ideas about luxury living. Which is not to be confused with luxury consumption.

LAURA: Was your ex a consumer?

BENNO: For sure. Buying stuff got her high. Save and buy, what a pain; this upward mobility is a pestilence. It kills me.

LAURA: Did your wife have a profession?

BENNO: Skilled textile worker; by now she's probably made master craftswoman, Mr. Biology Degree has enough of a head start. For sure, she needs a man to look up to. Can a master craftsman look up to a carpenter? The whole time we were together, the poor dear had to put her qualification on hold, to maintain the traditional difference – a low blow.

Laura laughs.

BENNO: Why aren't you crying?

Startled, Laura lets go of the toe and cap. The apparition disappears squeaking into the air.

Chapter 13

WHEREIN THE READER LEARNS WHAT THE BEAUTIFUL MELUSINE COPIED FROM KRUPSKAYA'S MEMOIRS INTO HER 94TH MELUSINIAN BOOK

When Ilyich and I moved to the Smolny Institute, we were given the room of a former teacher. Behind a screen stood a bed. To enter the room, you had to go through the washroom. You could get to Ilyich's study on the elevator. One delegation came after another. A particularly large number of delegations came from the front. When they came to Ilyich, they usually met him in the reception room. The soldiers stood there crowded together, listening motionless to the words of Ilyich, who stood at the window enlightening them about something or other. Here, in this endlessly overcrowded Smolny, Lenin lived and worked. Everyone was drawn to the Smolny. A regiment of machine gunners guarded the Smolny. This regiment stood on the Wiborg side in summer 1917 and found themselves completely under the influence of the workers in that part of the city. On 3 July this regiment was the first one to revolt, ready to plunge into battle. Kerensky had decided to make an example of this regiment. The soldiers were disarmed, led to a square, and branded as traitors. The machine gunners were now seized by an even stronger hatred of the provisional government. In October they had fought for the Soviet power, and then they took over the protection of the Smolny. One of the machine gunners was assigned to Lenin; it was Comrade Sheltishov, a peasant from the governing district of Ufa. He was boundlessly naive. There was nothing that did not amaze him; he was astonished by the alcohol-burning stove, especially the fact that it burned . . . I worked from morning to night, at first in the Wiborg district and later in the People's Commissariat for Education. There was nobody to really look after Ilyich; Sheltishov brought him the noon meal and bread – Ilyich got the same ration as everyone else. Sometimes Maria Ilyichna brought something to eat, but since I wasn't home, there was nobody to see to it that Ilyich took his meals regularly. Not long ago a young man named Korotkov, who was twelve years old at the time and living with his mother, a cleaning woman in the kitchen of the Smolny, told me that she had once heard footsteps in the kitchen, and looking in, she saw Ilyich eating a piece of black bread with herring. When he saw the cleaning woman, he was a little embarrassed and said smiling, 'I got hungry . . . ' In the end, Schotman's mother, a Finnish woman, adopted us. She was very attached to her son and very proud that he had participated as a delegate in the Second Party Congress and helped Lenin to hide himself in those July days. Now cleanliness and order reigned in our house, the way Lenin liked it. Now she gave instructions to Sheltishov, the cleaning woman, and the serving girls in the dining room. Now I could leave the house with peace of mind, for I knew that Lenin's physical needs were taken care of.

Chapter 14

LAURA CONSULTS THE ABV

When Laura went to pick up mail again, Landlady Buche handed her the letters with the remark that she preferred male renters; you could understand why. Women were always washing or cooking something. And if they got pregnant, you couldn't throw them out, just like that, either, you were always afraid. 'Do you have children too, by any chance? Oh Lord, I always said to my husband, children are capital that isn't working for you. The Möbius woman, ground floor on the right, nursed her baby drunk, and now it has yellow jaundice, yesterday a gentleman was here who offered 120 marks for the room.' Laura put 10 marks in Landlady Buche's apron pocket and entrusted herself to the competent neighborhood authority, the ABV, with a letter of reply from a certain Eberhard David Hauber. Laura suspected that the grotesque letter was in code and that Beatrice was in the clutches of a secret service. Had some scoundrel used Beatrice's mental confusion for his sordid purposes? Had she been blackmailed? The ABV noted Laura's conjectures and promised to have the case investigated. The letter from the certain Eberhard David Hauber, return address Strasbourg, read as follows: 'Heinrich Müller, mint-master of St. Gallen, has invented an automaton weighing fifteen quintals and does presently shew the same to the towns-people for a fee in the house of Councilor Hommel. Next to the machine sits a wooden man, clothed from head to toe, and this he calls Hartmann Holzhalb. The latter holds in his right hand a notched stick, and with his wooden shoulder, elbow, and hand does brandish it about as well as a living man. With his left hand he puts a mouth-piece to his lips, and by moving his lower jaw-bone whilst speaking, he causes full clearly a human voice to be heard. The answer he gives to questions posed to him is never without rhyme. If one looks upon him from the front, he turns his eyes straight ahead of himself. If one observes him from the side, he turns his eyes thence. He regards with his naked eye, and also through eye-glasses, the money that is offered him, pages of printed paper, and the spectators, whose clothing and posture he can also name. He willingly lets himself be touched all over. But when one tries to lift his leg, he sighs for pain from gout. Yet when his legs are let go of again, he laughs as if to split his sides.'

Chapter 15

Second wanderlust story of the minstrel Laura

Shoes: There was a woman, Walli was her name, who preferred small-statured men. Love seemed more enjoyable with them: exchanging roles was easier. She married a man named Sigmund. He could wear her sweaters, she his shirts. On their honeymoon they indulged their longing to be the other or have him near by exchanging articles of clothing. The symbolic act and the smell of the desired body that lingered in the material comforted, calmed, and excited them. Later the woman recognized the added advantage that even their shoe size was the same. She made the most of it after the birth of her first son, when the great, joyous emotion of this event was displaced by the demands of her chosen occupation of secretary. She had abandoned her goal of spending years studying medicine for family reasons. Sigmund, who completed his *Abitur* at the Workers' and Farmers' Faculty the same year as Walli, with a grade average one point lower than hers, was studying engineering. In Dresden. He visited his family in Leipzig almost every weekend. Walli could get along without his help, she was a strong woman. She had carefully completed the exam for her *Abitur* despite labor pains, which began during the Russian test. Anyway, she was used to work by birth, she came from a farm family. To bear the separation more easily, Walli bought a pair of brown lace-up shoes and gave them to Sigmund with the request that he wear them occasionally in Dresden. As soon as he had completed his state examinations, she wanted to apply to the Humanities Department of Karl-Marx-University to pursue Slavic studies. After work, when her son had been picked up from day care, fed, put to bed, and the housework was done, she energetically read Russian-language books. When her son was almost three years old, she gave birth to a daughter. Sigmund passed the state examination with a grade of two and found a position as engineer in Karl-Marx-Stadt. There and on business trips, he wore Walli's shoes, whenever he felt he wasn't being observed. When he had worn holes in the soles and run down the heels, Walli had the shoemaker repair them and saw to it that good material was used, leather if at all possible. She put the Slavic studies out of her mind and set herself the goal of a degree in elementary education as soon as her daughter, who for health reasons couldn't spend the whole day at the child-care center, was old enough for nursery school. After the birth of her second son, Walli looked forward to ending nearly four years as a housewife and returning to her job as a secretary. Especially since the family had been assigned an apartment in Karl-Marx-Stadt. At small evening parties at home, when Sigmund and his colleagues from work partake liberally of wine and swap business-trip stories and their wives help themselves to dessert and knitting, Walli usually puts on the shoes and folds her arms across her chest. Otherwise she keeps the shoes, when her husband isn't wearing them, in the living-room cabinet next to the crystal and china.

Chapter 16

Text of an absurd telegram from Venice

ANAXIMANDER FOUND STOP EXPECT HUNTING REPORT SOONEST STOP BEATRICE

Chapter 17

Informational exchange between Laura Salman and Benno Pakulat, scene three

Scene: *Room with open balcony door.*

Time: *Autumn night.*

Laura in her bathrobe, knitting at the balcony door, her legs wrapped in a blanket. Stops knitting now and then to blow on her hands. Squeaking noises. Blue light. Then celestial vehicle from above. In the celestial vehicle, Benno Pakulat. His face is covered by a cap. Laura lifts the cap without waking the sleeping man and sprinkles his face with beer. Then she takes off his left shoe and sock with a practiced hand and takes hold of his big toe, which she does not let go of during the entire scene.

LAURA (*vigorously*): So you're mad at your brother.

BENNO: I'd be glad if I had one.

LAURA: What?

BENNO: For me, brother isn't a kinship relationship but a social one or whatever. But he who oppresses others is asocial, and a representative of the working class whose brigade is constantly striving for some kind of title has no dealings with asocial elements. As you make your bed, so you must lie in it, let's say. You could easily be my brother, lady, it's the truth.

LAURA: You probably have no idea how a person lives when they never have an eight-hour day. Nor a real weekend either. Even on vacation, Lutz constantly dragged work along. Reference books, documents that piled up because in the daily grind he had no time for serious reading – in science and technology only those who know everything that's going on or nothing at all can have a voice. There are surely some people who effortlessly manage a workload like that plus responsibility. But Lutz is neither physically nor intellectually a strong person. Nothing comes easily to him, he has to work hard. And without a head start. Your family had, as far as I know, hardly any books. At a time when many of his future fellow students were reading for fun, stockpiling literary cushions to support their backs, Lutz was digging out fox's dens or whatever. And then he suddenly found himself faced by virtue of his family tree with the fact of representing the ruling class, a representative, a person to be respected, who wasn't allowed mistakes, weak performances, or uncertainties. Pull off that kind of strongman act on the spot without violence. Just try it – but you didn't try it. You took the easiest way out.

BENNO: And you?

LAURA: Yes – but I tried.

BENNO: And now you have a guilty conscience? Man, don't let this dumb performance mindset cloud your common sense, lady. This one guy in our company, whose brigade has the highest percentages and the most far-out competitive initiatives, his kids ran away at age sixteen, seventeen, one after the other; he's got four. All four got married still wet behind the ears, because nobody had time for them at home. Three of them have children and are already divorced. Obviously, escaping into marriage didn't solve their problems but raised them to a higher level, so to speak. Intensified. With responsibility and obligations, where is a young person supposed to find love for children and patience and understanding when he's carrying around a deficit in that respect. Try sticking your hand in a naked man's pocket. What good are the brigade mate's high economic percentages to Father State if psychologists and doctors have to take care of his children. Crutches, which of course cost money — but I don't even want to talk about money; socialism is made for human beings after all, and the economy is for human beings too and not the other way around.

LAURA: You're really making your brother worse than he is.

BENNO: He could be 207 percent better. It's the truth. Of course, as long as he's uncomfortable dealing responsibly with his children, he can't. I really believe that responsibly dealing with children makes a man better: more patient, more empathic, gentler, wiser. Sometime I'd like to have a supervisor who's a real father. You've failed, comrade lady. According to your conscience. You should have enlightened your comrade lover to the fact that he doesn't stand only to lose convenience but also to gain a world. A watchful citizen can't just pass along a dead-loss conscience like that.

LAURA: I recommended Lutz to someone else because I didn't love him anymore. Love needs mystery.

BENNO: And you'd seen through him.

LAURA: Beatrice de Dia seemed more suitable for him too. And healthier. Such a great woman writer . . .

BENNO: Doesn't exist.

LAURA: What?

BENNO: There aren't any great women writers. Can't be. Greek culture was based on slaveholding, modern culture on holding women as slaves — a carpenter with an *Abitur* isn't as dumb as you think.

LAURA: You're too modest.

BENNO: Oh, you'd like to systematically weaken the ruling class by qualifying work teams until only dummies are still workers . . .

LAURA: Demagogue.

BENNO: Class enemy.

LAURA: Peace.

BENNO: But not the kind you have between states. Not just a world-peace movement on a grand scale. But one on the small scale too. So this shit war between the sexes will finally be over. I'd love to be for something like marriage.

LAURA: Ach.

BENNO: It's the truth. And you? Didn't you tell my brother that marriage would undermine love or something like that?

LAURA: Yes.

BENNO: And now, what do you say now?

LAURA: Every human being knows that he must die some day. He says so too, admits everything. But does that mean he seriously believes it? I believe you can only live in mortal conviction of being an exception. Who will make it through somehow.

BENNO (*dreamy-voiced*): We men today are surprised sometimes. But we'll be much more surprised later on. And in a very different way, I hope, for there's no end in sight. There'll be no boredom in store for us when the ladies can finally do what they want to instead of what they're supposed to. What will women seen as human beings say about men, compared to women as images men have made of them? What will happen when they express what they feel instead of what we expect them to feel? Recently the wife of a poet said there were no love poems by women. She's right. Very few ladies would want to expose their reputation to intimations of abnormality. Women whose love life is not oppressive are considered sick (nymphomaniac). Men of the same type are considered healthy (sound as a bell). Maybe some summer day we'll stop squandering our nakedness on the construction site, maybe someday we'll allow ourselves to shed a tear even when we're not slicing onions. Ach, to be courted seriously for once, publicly. When women's emancipation leads to that, I'm their man.

Moved, Laura lets go of the toe and cap. The apparition disappears, squeaking, into the air.

Chapter 18

Wherein the Reader Learns What the Beautiful Melusine Copied from Laura's Notebook into Her 189th Melusinian Book

Faust in the Deutsches Theater on Schumannstraße. The production was four years old. Worn out. Which made the style stand out very prominently. The fit is more clearly evident on worn-out clothes than on new ones. The aged Faust was very good. He spoke his verses without operatic intonation. Simply. Which revealed their beauty in its nakedness. And their malice and their relevance, and their power. As long as Faust was old, his words were brand-new. Virtually modern. As soon as Faust was young, he had to speak like an old man. Which somehow rubbed the excellent actor Düren the wrong way. He helped himself out of the jam by haranguing. And he harangued until the end; the verses were barked out at top speed. Mephisto kept the lead. Two or three words per line were all he put in his mouth. Whoever couldn't fill in the text from memory from these fragments must be intellectually impaired for technical reasons. Now, verse texts are not made more contemporary by beating them to death. The Gretchen role was also staged historically. Gretchen's limitations were easy to recognize. Faust's limitations as a lover, which are equally time bound, were not presented. Maybe because the directors, Heinz and Dresen, didn't see their behavior in such situations as time bound. Naturally, I am far from insinuating that Herr Dresen, for example, would burst into ecstatic speech upon sight of a foolishly disciplined teenage girl. Herr Düren, who played the aged Faust as an ultimately clever man and who was unable to suddenly play dumb when rejuvenated, mumbled his enthusiasm so it wouldn't be understood as a sexual cry of desperation. Of course, whole generations of male intellects were inflamed, like Goethe, by a 'little flower' they found while walking along in the woods; that's not defamatory. What can you do? Human beings get used to everything. And when they've talked themselves into a statement long enough, they finally believe it. That's the way customs arise. Conventions. And naturally, they must be performed as conventions in the theater. The young Faust's enthusiasm is — apart from the sex steam — just as conventional as Gretchen's downcast eyes, for Gretchen is by no means a wild 'little flower' in the sense of a piece of nature but rather a cultivated plant. After her pregnancy Faust makes his appearances in this production only as a prompter. For the prison scene the directors locked Gretchen into a one-cubic-meter-sized holding cell that was bolted shut with a crowbar. The cell stood alone on the huge, empty stage. In this way the directors brought the production to a grand close.

Chapter 19

Hunting report from Trobadora Beatrice, delivered to Laura by a woman who introduces herself as Aspasia

1

When I saw the cars that were locked out before the city walls, I was as good as certain of my goal. Although I had lost the trail in Mestre. Not far from the Ponte della Libertà, which connects the industrial area with the lagoon. Such a sensitive creature as the unicorn can't survive one day here, for the exhaust fumes from the petrochemical plant would kill even stones. Besides, a person who has been pounded by the traffic must inevitably succumb to the architectonic splendor of Venice when he sees the stockpiled heap of metal. Which reminds you of a gigantic auto graveyard. So I concluded logically that Anaximander would have had no other choice. And I regretted having to refrain from betting, for reasons of conspiracy.

2

'The city will hit you like a blow,' a travel acquaintance from the second class had prophesied. In Italy I had learned from experience to travel only second-class. Because anyone in that country who can and must spend that much money for a first-class ticket, because there's not enough for a chauffeur, belongs to a social class that cares about dignity. That's a job. It takes so much attention that natural inclinations must be sacrificed. On the Turin-Milan route, for example, I encountered in first class members of this voluble and communicative people who could sit for hours next to or opposite one another without exchanging a word. Barely even a glance. To say nothing of any sort of pleasantries or helpful gestures. Maybe the men needed all their strength to endure suit jackets, shirt collars, and neckties in temperatures over forty degrees Celsius. Those insignias of social standing, without which dignity-creating distance is even more arduously acquired. In any case, these people were unsuited for research. The train pulled slowly into the trap. A terminus station. Overfilled, as is normal for all train stations afflicted by mass tourism during the season. The customary sense that human beings are weighed by the ton. Even when liveried servants greet them subserviently. Even when they camp out or sleep on the floor in garish noble rags. A plethora of porters instead of the usual self-service carts for suitcases. Not until I left the train station did the prophecy turn out to be true.

3

The first blow was struck not by the masonry but the silence. For I was coming from Rome. And other garages. Where your ears become so hardened that they cease to be sensitive to human noise. A city just for people? For technical reasons – but the truth was too priceless for me to believe it unequivocally right away. Whoever fights his way through lanes of cars for months at a time, up to his neck in auto bodies, will soon feel that his head is his height. On the bare Piazzale Roma, I grew abruptly. Gained authority. And surpassed myself. Oh joy, to walk literally on footpaths toward waters. Exclaves. Ideals. All city streets should be flooded! – 'Gondola?' The question interrupted my futurological inspirations but seemed appropriate to them. Dazed by pastels, I smiled, ignoring all painfully won principles of behavior. And the gondolier, a gray-haired beauty with a twirled mustache, grasped my suitcase. And escorted me, the red ribbons of his straw hat fluttering in the morning breeze. I walked along, no umbrella, dazzled, marvelously released as if by requited love. The light hung hazily over the water of the Grand Canal and upon it in pale blue and pink patches. Which were bumped up and down against each other by the waves and mixed together. Such water on level, limestone-covered earth! Even when I observed intense negotiations between gondoliers and customers on the mooring, it didn't affect my high spirits. On the contrary, I was even moved to exclaim at the refined elegance of the boats. The boats rocked between poles. Which were unworked, crooked. That intensified their Mannerist artistic effect. Their black paint reminded you of coffins or pianos. Blue green tarpaulins, red seat cushions, brass fittings: the color combination equaled the aesthetic perfection of the shape of the boat in every respect. I took my new guidebook out of my pocket. To look up the exact names of the pensions that I had put on the short list according to finance theory while on the train. Then I happened to glance at the table listing the gondola charges. I was familiar with the table, of course; I never approached capitalist cities uninformed. 'From the Piazzale Roma train station to a downtown hotel 1,500 lire for one to two persons and four pieces of luggage.' Seeing this reassured me. But gave me back a trace of that watchful tension I had drilled into myself as normal travel behavior. The trace sufficed for the question 'How much?' My suitcase was already in the gondola. 'Ten thousand,' said the gondolier. The price averted the insidious danger of high spirits. Belatedly. Whereby I saw myself forced into a defensive position in the haggling that followed. Still, the gondolier quickly dropped four thousand. Then he followed the pattern that Parisian boutique salesladies have down to perfection. First phase: praise for the customer and his taste, which implies prosperity. Second phase: defamatory speeches about the customer, which imply a lack of money. Whoever survives the first phase unscathed is a strong character. Whoever survives the second phase – which must be initiated abruptly in order to have its full effect — is an athletic character. Eye to eye with the pastel shades of the Grand Canal and its reflections of Byzantine-Gothic façades, I had to demonstrate athletic prowess of character. And forego individual treatment and proximity; in the theater the box seats and those closest to the stage are also considered the most desirable. So I fell into line. And was pushed. Onto the mass transport vehicle, vaporetto. There I was as far from the water as a bus driver from the street.

4

Squeezed in by sweating bodies, I remembered judgments of other travel acquaintances who had tried to take the bread from the prophet's mouth. For example: 'Venice has an unhealthy climate.' — 'The glory of Venice was built on crime.' — 'Venice is nothing but a museum, pure highway robbery.' — 'Venice is a sinking ruin, eaten away by dry rot.' I used the changing spaces that formed between the heads surrounding me as windows. Which carved out views for me. From the allocation of rounded arches, pointed arches, tracery, columns, balconies, mosaics, and statues, I obtained an image of enchanting dignity and arrogance. Which favored stone from the second story on up. Downwards, leprous plaster or exposed brick walls; in the windows of the palaces grime-covered glass, boards, darkness from which laden clotheslines shone forth. The bow wave of the vaporetto washed the lower fourth of the gates. They were rusty, eaten away by rust, starting to rot. The stairs to the gates, which were exposed for a moment by the furrow behind the bow wave, were decorated with mussels and algae. At some of the gates were skiffs tethered like animals to the walls of buildings or to planks. Some planks were painted with blue-and-white or red-and-white stripes resembling cords. I was convinced that I was only days away from Anaximander. Or hours. Maybe I had been quite close to him once, or several times, without realizing it? I had discovered and followed his trail on the sandy forecourt of the St. Ambrose pilgrimage church in Rapallo. And I'd been able to pursue it through Carrara, Livorno, Sienna, Tarquinia, Rome, Perugia, Arezzo, Rimini, Ravenna, Ferrara, Padua, all the way to Mestre, as I said before. Probably Anaximander had leaped into the sea and swum to Venice in order to obliterate his trail. Did he suspect that he was being pursued? Whenever the vaporetto docked, which happened fourteen times before the St. Mark's stop, the bodies surrounding me changed. And different hair blew into my face. I experienced the melancholy fairy tale backdrop of the Grand Canal with concentrating knees. Which were clasping my suitcase.

5

A cardboard suitcase. Actually, I should have transported my travel equipment in sacks strapped to a pack frame. Because I was dependent on contacts, owing to the hunt. Rich people could wear prosperity or convictions while so occupied, I was left with only one fashionable alternative: anticonsumer style. Which the Pension Atlantico not far from the Bridge of Sighs seemed well suited to. In its basement it housed the sales agent of an international student travel agency; it was mainly their customers who crowded the cheap little hotel. After hoisting my suitcase over two sleeping bodies in front of the reception desk, I felt like a travel wimp. And I quickly hid my uncertainty behind an expression that I tried hard to copy from the receptionists' bored faces. A mirror beside the key rack made these efforts easier. A few days later it turned out that the two girls were the owners of the hotel. They usually served breakfast carelessly and without hurrying. The shuffling sounds of their slippers were accompanied by the gondoliers' cries of 'oi' — the canal intersection in front of the hotel required acoustic signals. The breakfast room was never lighter than semidarkness, which is probably why its walls, crumbling with dry rot, had been only superficially hung with raffia mats and fishing nets. Nevertheless, here too I was not spared the typical burden of lone women travelers who do match the fashionable norm in age and size. The burden is created by the certainty or the feeling of being looked up and down. Nowhere was I able to escape this burden. And it increased. Since my departure from Berlin, it had at least doubled. And there would be no end in sight before I found Anaximander. That's why I had gotten used to bolting my food as fast as possible while staring at something. Some neutral thing, of course, for example, the patch of sunlight lying like a doormat at the hotel entrance. Thus a couple caught my eye one morning. They squeezed themselves into underground style not only by means of leather luggage but also by new, clean articles of clothing. Influenced by wide-ranging travel activity, I immediately felt, besides pity, a certain aversion to the new arrivals because of their nonconformist, that is, tasteless behavior. The aversion may have been caused primarily by envy. Because for weeks I had squeezed myself into greasy jeans that I didn't dare ruin by washing. And I longed for an accessory that would identify me externally as a complete person. But only Christoph Arnold and Eberhard David Hauber had answered my letters. Unsatisfactorily. The leather-luggage woman's accessory was relatively old. I took him to be one of those intellectuals who squire a woman at least twenty years younger around with them as a status symbol, to display their bountiful success. When the man took the baseball cap from his bald head, the woman seemed at least thirty years younger. The couple looked around the pantry-sized foyer in all seriousness for chairs. After waiting for ten minutes, the man yelled distorted Italian words. That intensified my aversion. For I hated these potato-eaters, who plagued the country every summer with arrogance and metal. Strangely, the man did not escalate his linguistic efforts but soon fell silent. Without showing signs of resignation. The two sat down on their leather suitcases. The young woman became engrossed in a newspaper whose layout seemed somehow familiar to me. The man paged through a book and read sentences from it now and then. For example: 'Bourgeois futurologists claim that in the future robots will take power away from human beings, rob them of all meaningful activity, level out their needs, and thereby totally degrade them morally in the end. But what will really happen?' Or: 'This undifferentiated and global restriction of possible future robots is questionable, not least because we recognize, from the Marxist-Leninist standpoint, the fundamental limitlessness of human knowledge and therefore also the human ability to simulate creative processes.' The young woman answered without looking up in monosyllables or in wordlike sounds. The logodramatic scene interested me more and more. The syllable combination *Ökulei* changed my mood. So that I left the breakfast I had ordered with an empty stomach and hastened to the sound source. My ears rang laurettially, that is, like home. All of a sudden, I felt homesick. For a country I was not born in. How about that! In any case, we greeted each other like members of a labor party delegation.

6

During the subsequent exchange of experiences, I found out that the Olga Benario Women's Brigade of the Berlin Signal and Insulation Technology Plant had not won the cultural-economic productivity competition, despite my reading. Probably because of my reading. 'You really made a mess of things that time,' said the young woman, who introduced the man not as her husband but as her father. I didn't remember the name Karin Janda. But of course, I had heard of the philosophy professor Leopold Janda. And his daughter's devastating criticism aggravated me to this day. Although I had long known that verses by Raimbaut d'Aurenga won't win you a flowerpot, much less an *Ökulei* – then and now I found the complete expression, *ökonomisch-kultureller Leistungsver-*

gleich, cultural-economic productivity competition, unpoetic. 'Wouldn't you like to patch things up soon?' said Karin, who still worked as a librarian at the plant. 'We don't hold grudges; only those who don't work make no mistakes: Lenin.' Nudge in the ribs, slap on the left shoulder. 'Our women need political literature that will blow their minds.' The professor kissed my hand in embarrassment. I assured him that I hadn't expected him to answer my letter anyway. He said his negligence was unforgivable and offered as an excuse his preparation for the international conference on problem-oriented logic in Rome, which had just ended. Also, he called me 'dear Frau Magpyloni' and promised to help me. Indirectly. He said he was engaged in pure research that would not immediately yield results that were exploitable for practical purposes. But he had friends whose assistance he could facilitate. Roberto Venterulli, for example, resided in Rome, a world-class robot builder. 'He has brought the mechanical robot to highest perfection and lends them out as well. At popular prices. He has established lending stations in all the larger cities of Italy; the one here is somewhere in the ghetto. During the tourist season the demand for male dolls is said to be especially high. If you are interested in creativity robots, however, you'll have to be patient for a few more decades.' I said a disgruntled no, thanks, obtained a very reasonably priced room for father and daughter, and offered my services as guide.

7

For I felt superior and responsible. As one would toward children. Because I had a four-day head start in Venice, and outside Venice a gigantic one. Leopold Janda had traveled widely but never in this city. His daughter had left her socialist country's camp for the first time in her life. Three weeks ago. You could still smell the local air of Frankfurter Allee on her, so to speak. And the guileless behaviors of the people there. Which suddenly, shaken by longing, I felt to be a luxury. A life luxury, which overshadows every consumer luxury. Full of familial emotions, I accompanied Karin and Leopold Janda through streets where only stores and restaurants lodged in the ground floor. 'The golem was an artificial man that was made from lime by Rabbi Löw of Prague,' said the professor. 'According to the old legend, which, like numerous other masterpieces of world literature, expressed man's hitherto unfulfilled dream of making artificial creatures or machines that possess specific human creative abilities, which he can make use of. With the development of the computer and of new logical systems that explore the logical regularities of creative thought, for the first time in history human beings have scientific grounds for asking: Is the time ripe for creating robots who can carry out not only physical and routine intellectual work but also creative work? Is it possible to develop robots who can solve problems that are unsolvable for human beings, who will launch ideas that hitherto could not be thought by human beings?' The merchandise drew closer to the potential buyers in front of the display windows. Fashion merchandise, gold, souvenirs, ingredients for extolled Lucullan specialties in ornamental arrangements. Leopold Janda couldn't pass the thousands upon thousands of colorful glass-bead necklaces without touching one every now and then. Other than that, he attacked certain scientists who dodged answering the above-mentioned question. By trying to set absolute limits to the further development of robots. 'Some people claim, for example, that the robot can only do routine intellectual work but never creative work,' the little man proclaimed, looking up. 'Yes,' I said, filled with foreboding. Looking down. But the professor was unstoppable. 'This fear of the robot and the opinion that it could ever be more than an aid is the expression of a decadent society that is incapable of solving the problems of the scientific-technical revolution for the good of mankind,' he ranted. Karin sauntered. Looked calmly at buildings and merchandise. Did not ask for money. 'Youth exaggerates everything,' the father mumbled with resignation. At the market square I wanted to get away. Because yesterday on the Campo St. Polo I had already discovered my third horse apple. The first two I had found in the vicinity of the Pesaro Palace. Since it must be assumed that keeping horses in a city with water streets is impossible, I judged the finds to be unmistakable evidence. Could a sight as attractive as a unicorn go for a walk in Venice at any time of the day or night without being exploited by the tourist industry? Was Anaximander using a magic cape? Or was he perhaps invisible by nature? At the market square Janda hastily bought his daughter a bag of corn, sprinkled her with it, photographed her covered with pigeons, and pushed on. Where the devil was he going? Is there anywhere to be found a formation more refined than this open surface surrounded by a shortage of space? Is there any building on earth that can surpass the beauty of the Doges' Palace? Its boundless dignity is overpowering. It had struck me at first sight as the only possible place of refuge for Anaximander. I had rushed through the halls laden with paintings in a feverish condition. *Grandezza*, wherever the eye could see. Until I got to the weapon collection. There the walls are adorned with implements of slaughter. All over, the murder tools are arranged in patterns, rosettes of swords and spears, friezes of diverse kinds of axelike blades, shooting-iron arabesques, meandering ammunition, suits of armor in various adult and children's sizes. I had left the palace sobered. In absolute certainty that unicorns would flee its pink-and-white marble walls. So if I had now made my way to St. Mark's Square, then only to provide the two Jandas with profitable art experiences — I was losing time. An inestimable loss for hunters. 'I could stand it here for a week,' said Karin. 'From early to late, no normal human being to be seen, only tourists and service businesses and art; that gets on your nerves. But this place is still relatively the best. For me. But I'd really like to know what the German Writers' Union was thinking when they delegated you to come here. Are you maybe supposed to be studying capitalism?' — 'What? The Writers' Union didn't delegate me,' I said, baffled. 'Who else would it be?' said Karin. The professor asked me to excuse her left-radical tendencies. Shortly before their departure he'd had the worst hassles with her for leanings in the opposite direction, disciplinary action in the singing club and so forth; little children, little sorrows, big children, big sorrows. Why was Leopold Janda pressing toward the ghetto quarter? Did he have an interest in my hiring a robot companion? Not until the Bridge of Christ or the Tempter did I come up with a pretext for saying good-by.

8

Toward 10:00 P.M. the professor, accompanied by his daughter, sought me out in my room and informed me that he had found the location of the lending station in the ghetto. Leopold Janda praised the robots as solid craftsmanship. Karin contemptuously recommended ready-to-wear. She mentioned a few amazing items she had seen with her own eyes in the Beate Uhse shops; capitalism exploited even the most eccentric tastes. Annoyed, I made my room available for sightseeing. Its two windowsills, barely two meters above the canal, were ideal theater seats. The regular evening performances with music and song took place before well-lit, guaranteed expensive backdrops. I mentioned the Bridge of Sighs as the most expensive backdrop. Which no gondolier fails to show his guests. Consequently, the windows I had rented provided a representative overview of the pleasure outings. In Venice gondolas are only used for pleasure outings these days. Freight is transported in motorboats. Which sometimes spoil the romantic style of the performances. Rarely in darkness. Leopold and Karin Janda sat down on the windowsills as if on TV armchairs. 'It is patently obvious that the development of a new generation of problem-solving or creatively active robots, so-called creativity robots, would produce such wide-ranging radical changes in human ways of being that science today is unable to fully recognize their dimensions,' said the professor. 'But is a perspective of that kind even real? More than this, is it actually desirable? Let us begin with the question of how to realize such a perspective. Many scientists doubt it. Their reservations are based scientifically on the following: robots can process only programs or algorithms that are entered into them. The heart of creative thought is the solving of problems, that is, the posing and answering of questions that cannot be solved by any known algorithm. That is why no programs can be written with which the robot can solve problems or carry out creative work. Only human beings are in a position to solve problems. Although at first glance this argument seems tempting, I would like to question it.' Karin questioned too. Mainly the value of the Dolle-Minna movement. 'Or is there a fundamental difference if I'm exploited by my husband or by an industrialist? Women who want to accomplish something here must get into politics and make enormous social changes; anything else is masturbation.' The professor cleared his throat in embarrassment. I felt both speeches to be meddling. In my personal affairs. Not until the hour of midnight, which the campanile sounded, did they leave.

9

Toward noon on my sixth day in Venice, I discovered three posters on building number 23 in the Via Garibaldi. One announced a folk festival with a Communist wedding. One recalled the seven martyrs who had been shot to death by the Fascists in the presence of the townspeople on 3 August 1944. On the third was written by hand: *A mon seul désir.* Was Anaximander perhaps in hiding in the traditional Castello quarter? Was there even an uninhabited spot in the narrow, laundry-hung streets where children swarmed? Was the individualistic slogan a code? Drunk with the success of the hunt, I stumbled to the quay where three freight ships lay moored. The sea rocked them gently in St. Mark's basin. St. Giorgio Maggiore floated in the mist. In front of it, the black silhouette of a gondola. I knew that the gondolier was standing on the stern. I saw that he stood on the water. Balanced. Ballet. Enraptured, I tumbled into the nearest restaurant. Without reading the posted menus carefully. I only read the large print – for financial reasons, I could never select la carte meals. Tourist special 1,200 lire, I read. And ordered and ate and drank. The bill punished me for my unforgivable frivolity. Every time I had let myself be carried away by hunger, thirst, or mood in capitalist countries, I'd had to pay dearly for it. This time the waiter demanded 1,900 lire. Because the place setting, wine, and service were not included in the advertised 1,200 lire price. Tormented by homesickness, I searched until darkness fell. Doggedly. I wanted to force the luck of the hunt.

10

When I returned to the Pension Atlantico, tired and unsuccessful, the professor offered me some lire. For the doll rental. 'It shouldn't fail because of money,' he said. 'If I didn't have it, I wouldn't lend it to you; my publisher in Munich paid quite well. On behalf of our copyright office, of course, everything on the level, Frau Magpyloni, no crooked deals, you can pay me back in marks when you have the chance. Let us now pose the question of how a human being solves problems. Will he find the unknown problem-solving algorithm (PSA), that is, the rules and procedures with which he can answer the questions posed in the problem without any prior assumptions or, more precisely, without a specific problem-solving program (PSP)? Even the most primitive method of problem solving, the so-called trial and error method, represents a PSP, although in a very elementary form. In other words, even a human being cannot solve a single problem without a specific program. But this PSP is still primarily used spontaneously by human beings today because they are almost completely ignorant of the rules, in particular the logical rules of problem solving. This often misleads bourgeois scientists to locate the origin of the idea in the subconscious, as a function of intuition, and to interpret it as a process that is not rule governed.' I could only hold onto myself with an effort. But I believe that I succeeded in refusing the offer of money with a poker face and neutral words of thanks. 'I've struggled along as an incomplete person for months, I can stick it out the last days without an escort too,' I said. Certain that Janda wanted to corrupt me shortly before I reached my goal. With a personal solution. In order to prevent the social one.

11

At that, I not only closed the blinds to keep the rats out, following the house rules, but also turned the key twice in the lock. Then I spent a longish time in front of the big blind mirror that hung between the windows. The mirror was genuinely blind. Glass manufacturers in Murano displayed newly produced blind mirrors. Which were more expensive than the same models of usable design. A guide to exhibits had informed me that American customers are partial to imitations of antiques. I'd had to pay 30 percent more for my perfectly faded, weathered jacket than for the same model made with new material. Karin Janda called this antifashionable fashion 'conformist nonconformism.' Did she create her decisive sayings herself? Was Janda trying to throw me off course from personal motives? Had he been put on my trail by the Persephonic opposition? The bed sloped toward the canal as well as toward the floor. The pleasure-outing traffic had died down. I lay there brooding. Listening to the stillness. Which was broken now and then by drunken voices. And by the splashing sounds of sewage water pouring out of the houses.

12

At dawn the garbage scow startled me out of my brooding thoughts, which had still not found a way out. Should I let Leopold Janda know that I saw through his plans? Should I tell him and his daughter to their faces that the trick of worming their way into my confidence with a veneer of Marxism and GDR passports wouldn't cut any ice with me? Karin laid it on too thick. Should I go underground? I opened the right venetian blind a crack. The garbage scow employees were hanging empty black plastic sacks on the door handles and collecting full ones. The motor produced putt-putting noises that reminded you of farts. A rat drew a gentle V-shaped bow wave through the water. How did articles by a man like this get into the GDR weekly newspaper *Sonntag*? I combed the newspaper clipping, with a signed dedication from Janda, for fishy statements. I read: 'The possibility of producing problem-solving robots depends on putting the logical process carried out more or less spontaneously by human beings into the form of a program that can then be used by the robot for solving problems. More precisely: A PSP must be created that allows the robot to find the relevant PSA with which it can answer the questions posed by the problem, answers for which no algorithm is known. Hitherto, it has been assumed that construction of creativity robots is impossible primarily because of the inadequate level of technology. However, it has been shown that it was not the state of computer technology but primarily the limitations of logic, which has so far made the production of creativity robots impossible. For thousands of years of history, under the influence of Aristotle, logic has been concerned almost exclusively with the logical laws of concepts and statements. So far, it has largely ignored other forms of thinking that play a particularly important role in creative thought, as, for example, questions, problems, or ideas. Therefore, it was impossible for logic to investigate the logical laws of creative thought. With the development of problem-oriented logic, that is, logic that is concerned with the logical laws of the problem, the theoretical foundations can be created to permit formulation of a PSP that consciously makes use of this regularity.' The explanation seemed conclusive. At the canal intersection, a shouting match had broken out between two gondoliers. They were blaming each other for having almost caused a collision between the boats. Perhaps Janda wanted to drive Anaximander away from me? On behalf of the Persephonic opposition? Or for private reasons; his daughter had mentioned once that he had been married for twenty-one years. Maybe he was only interested in Anaximander's horn? To pulverize it for use as an aphrodisiac. Deserted by sleep, I paced the stone floor. Which was no less bumpy than the one in St. Mark's church. By lifting my heels up sharply, I could bump the bare ceiling beams with my head. Gondolas were jostling each other on the canal again. Had Laura revealed to Melusine the plan of changing the world via medicinal mass influence? Would I shortly be exposed for dilettantism? Or for forming factions, then I could expect to lose my life. I waited in hiding until Janda and his daughter had left the hotel and crossed the bridge.

13

I paid the hotel bill during the siesta. And got away unnoticed despite my luggage. In the noonday heat only Germans and dogs were on the street. Later I heard ringing and rattling sounds. Then choruses of voices. Under the colonnades of the Procuratie, where the most expensive shops and cafés of Venice are lodged, I was delayed by a demonstration parade. The rhythmically speaking choruses demanded profit sharing and a sales associates' strike for Saturday. I joined the parade briefly. To shake off a woman who I thought was following me. I stopped at four pensions, to no avail: weekend crowds. The *diretissimo* drove away right under my nose. The suspicious woman suddenly came toward me on the Campo Morosini. And said hello. At that, I pushed open the gate of the first palace I came to and ran through six rooms.

14

The door of the seventh room was closed by a drape. With a tentlike decoration. Cerulean blue silk, with gold ornaments worked into it. The ornaments reminded you of drills or corkscrews. Close under the tent roof, that ended in a church-tower-like point, a fringed diagonal curtain. Embroidered with the slogan: *A mon seul désir.* At the golden peak of the roof hung a pennant. A noise distracted me from my fascination. I looked around involuntarily. But couldn't see anything suspicious. As I turned back to the tent again, it had opened. And the unicorn stepped out. Saddled. Its hair was short like horsehair, white in color; its body and gait were also horselike but softer. I strapped my cardboard suitcase to the saddle, mounted the animal, rode out, and left Venice heading north.

SIXTH INTERMEZZO

WHEREIN THE READER LEARNS WHAT ELSE THE BEAUTIFUL MELUSINE COPIED FROM IRMTRAUD MORGNER'S NOVEL *RUMBA FOR AN AUTUMN* INTO HER 35TH MELUSINIAN BOOK IN 1964

Shawm Twist II

> But you should rejoice and be of
> good cheer, because this your brother
> was dead and came to life again, he
> was lost and now is found. LUKE 15:32

The city bore fog. It had rolled its amorphous hulk across the roofs, which supported it on their ridges and pointed gables. It sagged in the streets. Down to the rows of windows on the second floor, sometimes even to the first floor. Pakulat passed only stubs of façades. But he knew the way. Savings bank. Crystal. Porcelain. Plants. Buy and Sell. Colonnades.

The fog had not yet penetrated to the cross vaults. The ribs and transverse arches stood out clearly in the light of the show windows. The crowns remained in semi-darkness. Where they belonged, for they had water spots. Pakulat didn't need to turn his head to the right to see that they had water spots. They'd had them forever, since the first time Pakulat had set foot in the colonnades. He was still a child at the time. And the antiquarian bookstore had been a toy store. And instead of old books there'd been tin figures in the window, hundreds of them, thousands, ach, surely many thousands, depicting the Battle of Fehrbellin. And Pakulat had stamped his feet and screamed, 'I want the Battle of Fehrbellin I want the Battle of Fehrbellin I want . . . ' And his father had yelled, 'You'll get a slap upside the head . . . ' And his mother had said, 'What are people going to think, that little uhlan over on the right can't cost much.' And Pakulat had gotten the little uhlan over on the right, and now he experienced that moment of holding the tin figure in his hands. And he felt the coolness of the metal on his palm.

But the colonnades lasted only a moment, and then the fog was back again. It had nearly buried the city. It tasted of soot. Pakulat held a folded handkerchief to his mouth. But it wasn't moistened, and it had no rubber loops like soldiers' goggles. But the smoke was cold too and not at all comparable. And the fog only looked like smoke. Maybe it didn't even look like it. Maybe it was just ordinary thick autumn fog. Pakulat only had one eye, after all. And its keenness vacillated. Sometimes he saw extra clearly. Sometimes he could see the outlines perfectly. Probably he was seeing extra clearly at the moment. The island was far away after all. And so far it had always worked out somehow. It wouldn't have occurred to Pakulat to doubt that it would work out this time too if he hadn't discovered that bearded man over Benno's bed. Naturally, he had nothing against this man, who looked like an athlete. He'd always had a liking for sportsmen, and maybe basketball was a serious sport. But this fellow, two meters tall, who gave four-hour speeches without notes, gesturing wildly with his arms the whole time, didn't seem especially confidence inspiring either. Such a fiery temperament was perhaps all right for a lover. But Pakulat pictured a statesman differently. At any rate, the man was too young. And that's probably why he hung over Benno's bed. And in spite of everything, it was good that he was hanging there. It had given Pakulat new hope. Maybe his son wasn't lost after all. Pakulat had to find him.

He took his hands out of his pockets in order to make faster headway. It was as if the street were moving toward him under his feet like a conveyor belt, unending, and he was actually walking in place. A drunk appeared for a few moments out of the swathes of fog surrounding him, belched, and bumped into him. The silhouette of a car floated by.

Pakulat hurried through the cottony nothingness that had soaked up the city, his city. Something was urging him on, without consideration for pulse or bronchia, something was driving him forward. But gradually it became clear to him that it was foolish to run aimlessly around on the streets. He turned around and headed toward the school. Systematic, he thought, I have to search systematically. He rang the caretaker's bell. A light appeared in a first-floor window; after a while it was opened, and a woman's tousled head peered out.

'Have you seen my son?'

'A drunk,' said the woman. The window slammed shut, the light went out.

Pakulat stood alone in a city with hundreds of thousands of inhabitants. That he knew his way around in. That he had helped build. Where he had been born and wanted to be buried. Of course, as a dead man it was nothing to him if he rotted away in this city and not someplace else. Of course, it was altogether foolish to think about death. The mean life expectancy gave Pakulat thirteen more years. But that number was only an average. In comparison, Pakulat did not have an average life behind him. So it was easily possible that he'd get even older. Strange that he now thought continually about getting older. It had been going around in his head for some time. Precisely, since the site foreman had said to him, 'Well, old man, one more month and that's the end of it.' However, it was possible that he hadn't said 'old man' at all but something quite different, and Pakulat had only read that into it later. But the site foreman had said 'the end of it'; Pakulat could remember that very clearly. The end of it, then. A week from now was the end of it, and Pakulat was running through the fog that was about to swallow the city. Its gigantic, amorphous hulk, which sagged so far down in the streets that it almost touched the asphalt here and there, didn't spare a single building. It ate its way deeper and deeper into the city that Pakulat had spent decades building. One decade most certainly for nothing, and Pakulat could count himself lucky that the city had been left relatively unscathed in comparison to other cities. But this time luck couldn't be counted on. This time his whole lifework was at stake, so to speak. Pakulat considered 'lifework' to be a highfalutin expression of the intellectuals, toward whom he felt an elemental distrust and antipathy. 'Lifework' was totally out of the question for him. But it was at stake, so to speak. The stakes were in a totally different place, of course, on an island where they grew pineapples and grapefruits that were sold in produce shops for high prices at Christmas time. More precisely, not on the island either but at the highest authority. Pakulat knew his way around in this area. He saw clearly. He only saw with his left eye. He could no longer see anything but this area. Up to the moment when his son seemed lost. Also in this area. Then it shrank. Then it seemed to shrivel up into a spot with a diameter no greater than the length of a boy's shoe. The gigantic, amorphous hulk threatened to devour the city and all the houses Pakulat had built and all the residents whom Pakulat didn't know but for whom he had a sort of fraternal feeling whenever he recognized them by their familiar dialect somewhere to the north or the south, where people spoke differently. He loved his city and its inhabitants. But he could only think about one, one among hundreds of thousands who probably didn't deserve it, who was alone in the world with his father; the world: that was the city. He had run away from his father, and now his father was searching for him. And he would find him, for the world-city was finite.

The father, who had been lost for a while and feared for the city and its inhabitants and even for his lifework, so to speak, felt fear again, exclusively for his son. His supply of love, which he had given away all his life, generously and mostly without expecting anything in return, was almost exhausted. What was left he needed for Benno. Pakulat noticed that he was carrying the ark that he had climbed out of a while ago on his back.

The school's foundation walls and parts of the second story stood directly before him. He could even make out seams in the wall. Because lantern moons hung abundantly in the tufts of fog. And he also smelled the city, whose fumes the amorphous hulk had pressed into the streets. But all Pakulat could feel was what he carried on his shoulders: the ark and the uncertain fate of his son.

But of course his mind, which was alert and kept getting more alert the colder it got, told him that he was by no means alone in this city and that it would make sense to get help. From whom? Lutz was out of town. His daughter-in-law mustn't find out about all this because she couldn't stand Benno. If Pakulat went to an old friend, he could expect reproaches. And the friend couldn't put him on the trail either. Benno didn't socialize in those circles. Besides, it was possible that the matter would then somehow become official and be brought before the Party. And if Pakulat went to the police, the matter would also become official. Going to the police was premature. Police were the last resort. Pakulat couldn't take the last step before the first. The school had been the first. But only the first one that came along. No wonder the caretaker's wife took him for a drunk. Anyone who thought there would still be pupils at school two hours past midnight must be drunk. Or desperate. But Pakulat wasn't desperate. He had never permitted himself any such thing, and he never would. Drunk, thought Pakulat. He had a strong will. It was so strong that it could get Pakulat drunk without schnapps. For a moment. Then Pakulat felt sober again and thought it would make sense to go first to Benno's friend Nero who, as his name suggested, played the drums in the orchestra. Pakulat knew that Nero's name was actually Matzke, Danny or Manny or Stanny Matzke, and that he was a barkeeper's son. And, of course, that he was dumb; probably he'd been born dumb, for children conceived in a drunken stupor were either idiotic or dumb. And barkeepers were always sozzled. They guzzled their bellies full at the construction workers' expense, and if things went well, they drove a Wartburg. Old Matzke's bar surely did well. Bars at the end of the streetcar line always did well. So he drove a Wartburg too. At the construction workers' expense. Or would he try to convince Pakulat that he worked harder than a carpenter, for example? But a carpenter couldn't buy a Wartburg on his wages. Pakulat hated barkeepers, who took money out of his pockets on payday then and now. Thirty years ago one of them had sued him for trespassing, and since then he had hated them.

Pakulat walked through the smoke brown dive, which was no bigger than an ordinary room; he bumped his feet against chair legs and the foot of a tiny table. He sat down on a wobbly chair and ordered a lager, as always. He didn't always order it here. For some time they had been holding their meetings in the back room of a different bar. This one didn't have a back room.

The barkeeper set down the glass and said, 'You've driven my customers away.'

'How so?' asked Pakulat.

'Don't play dumb; you know exactly what I mean.'

'Nope, I'm sorry,' said Pakulat.

'Me too,' said the barkeeper and tried to take the glass away again. But Pakulat didn't let him. Both of them held onto the glass. The beer sloshed back and forth. Pakulat felt wetness on his face. And in a flash a brawl was underway. Pakulat wasn't slow, but suddenly he had several uniformed men to fight against, brownshirts, as he realized to his amazement.

In court the barkeeper, whom Pakulat had believed to be trustworthy, claimed that Pakulat had thrown beer in his face and the SA men had come along by chance. Pakulat, on the other hand, had clearly seen at least one of them come out of the kitchen. But Pakulat had no witnesses. He was found guilty of trespassing concomitantly with damage to property and had to pay a fine, six hundred marks. That was a lot of money for a young carpenter who had been unemployed for two years with a wife and child and an empty apartment. He had to fling six hundred marks down the barkeeper's schnapps-stinking gullet. And the barkeeper, who as Pakulat realized during the hearing had staged the whole show in order to buddy up to the SA, because he had a nose for politics, maybe also because this way he got rid of his old junk and picked up new chairs cheaply, this miserable barkeeper renovated and established a storm troopers' bar at Pakulat's expense.

And ever since, whenever he went to a tavern, Pakulat first had to pass through that storm troopers' bar. And one of the four beers was always wasted. He needed one to wash away that memory. But now he had no beer available. Now there was nothing for him to do except run. And the hour in which he was sentenced to finance a storm troopers' bar stretched out. At least one kilometer.

When he had run all the way through the hour and, out of breath, reached the block where the son of the barkeeper Matzke must live, he looked for the name on several doorbell plates by the flame of his lighter.

– Seifert,

Hannemann,

Merkel, he had called a member of the parents' council a nosey parker, leather coat, motorcycle,

Mutschler,

Neukirch, finger in every pie, no manners, a four in civics class, dyed hair,

Fischer, keeps to himself,

Thieme, show-off,

Kuddelka, the apple doesn't fall far from the pear tree,

Matzke –

Pakulat pushed the little white button down below the level of the plate. Then he took two big steps away from the door, stamped his feet, knocked his feet against each other, and said, 'Filthy weather.' And tipped his head back onto his neck. After a while, probably as long as you had to wait in Matzke's bar until your beer came, a 'hello' came out.

'Herr Matzke, is your son at home?'

'My husband is out of town.'

Aha, the boy was married already too, barely of age and already married. Probably had a kid.

'Listen up, girl, I have to talk to your husband for a minute, it's urgent.'

'Hey, do you mind, what are you thinking of, who are you anyway?'

When Pakulat had yelled a few details of his identity and the matter at hand up into the mist, he was told, 'My son is asleep.'

So it was the old lady. Pakulat had been running around the city for over an hour, and the old lady didn't even want to wake up her son.

'Criminal investigation department,' said Pakulat.

'Be right there,' came the prompt response. And the light went on right away in the stairwell. And Nero, one meter ninety, opened the door. 'Evening. How goes it? Long time no see . . . '

'Do you know where my son is?'

'My son?' Nero yawned. His masculine face had creases like a baby's.

'Hey, young man, I'm talking to you.'

'Yeah, yeah, of course, sure thing, I mean, just a minute. Your papers, please.'

'Papers?'

'*Propusk*, your pass, get it?'

'Impertinence.'

'Vigilance. Otherwise anyone could come and say they were the police . . . '

'Oh that, no, that was just a joke, my name is Pakulat, and I thought you could tell me . . . '

'Well, that's some joke. Man, you gave me a scare.'

'So.'

'Well sure. Man, I was shaking in my boots when I unlocked the door.'

'That's not what it seemed like.'

'If you let the criminal investigators know you're scared, you're gone.'

'Gone? If you have a clear conscience, you don't have to be afraid.'

'Right,' said Nero, yawning, and looked at his wrinkled pajama pants hanging out of his bathrobe. 'Yeh, *du hast recht*, you're right.'

'What do you mean, *du*?'

'Aren't you a comrade?'

'Of course, but you could still address me as *Sie*.'

'I say *du* to all the comrades, know why? Because then they think I'm one, and they skip the propaganda. Don't you want to come upstairs?'

Pakulat refused the invitation and presented his request once more. But Nero couldn't tell him where Benno was either. He said Benno had gone home directly after class. He'd been in a hurry.

'Maybe he's with the wife,' said Nero.

'With the wife? My wife is dead.'

'I mean, with his, not yours . . . '

Pakulat braced his hands on his coat-padded hips. 'What do you mean? What are you . . . '

'Oh, you know how it is. Between men: a hot woman.' Nero was sorry, but unfortunately he didn't know the hot woman's address, and Pakulat said good-by.

Nero looked down at him in a friendly way, patted him on the shoulder, and said, 'Don't worry, Grandpop, he'll come back. If he's with Kitty, he's well taken care of.'

The door banged shut, the key rattled. Pakulat was alone in the city again. He was carrying the ark on his back again. The house was on Martinstraße, and yet he somehow had it on his back. On Martinstraße it was a house and an ark. When he carried it on his back, it was actually only an ark. Strange. The ark weighed heavily, for it had two stories after all, and in 1912 they didn't build with hollow bricks. But Pakulat couldn't set it down. He had miraculously grown together with it, like a snail grown together with its shell. Sometimes it was possible not to think about it, but even when he was tired he couldn't get rid of the load; at best he could crawl into it.

So he crossed over to the trolley stop at the end of the line, of course, it wasn't running at this hour, sat down on the bench in the shelter, and crept into his ark.

And naturally, they were all right there: his neighbor, the student, the Senior Inspector ret. with the songstress Herzfeld's piano, the Battle of Fehrbellin, Marquardt the metalsmith, partner in the firm Marquardt and Marquardt, the Star of Rio, the storm troopers' bar, the two canaries in their cages, the vegetarian family, the little old lady with the pictures, his mother-in-law, who had kicked the bucket on the trail of refugees and lay buried wrapped in a blanket somewhere along the road, and the sergeant.

And Anna.

Anna lay in a zinc bathtub, dressed, wrapped in blankets, sleeping. She had a pair of motorcycle goggles on her forehead. The others sat near the exit, with bags hanging on their shoulders, some of them with gas masks. Pakulat and Lutz sat near the breach in the wall. But Anna slept whenever the antiaircraft gun wasn't firing. She could sleep like a baby. When he thought about her, Pakulat almost always saw her sleeping that way in the zinc bathtub.

— that was a woman, solid, beautiful without artifice, a miracle that she took me, short and feisty as I was, women used to look for the essentials, modest, thrifty, decent, can't find a decent woman any more, my third personal ad and nothing, bleached hair, cigarettes, no papers, so, old people's home, if I don't find another wife I'll have to move into the old people's home, franchise for the great hereafter, where one tries to outdo the next one with how many illnesses they have and what kind and healthy people are spoken of with contempt, I don't want to be buried alive, I want to live, live, but the women are ruthless, they do it with schoolboys, morality is a matter of character, no Kitty could get her claws into me, I was interested in other things at seventeen, but Benno, that good-for-nothing, you think you have a decent son, the women will take everything you've got —

Pakulat crept up under the roof. The wind blew through the skylights. The slate roof clattered. Stick together, thought Pakulat. An elemental feeling of solidarity washed over him. Rough seas. Stiff breeze from the northeast. Waves over the side. The men had to stick together. Of course, Benno wasn't a man yet, otherwise he wouldn't have let some Kitty get her claws into him, he was still green and naive, period. But he wasn't dumb. Sure, he had stuck his father's personal ads on the frame of Lenin's picture that hung in the parlor and got the slaps in the face he deserved, but wasn't his distrust of his father's marriage plans altogether justified? At first, Pakulat had thought: childish jealousy. But now Benno's disapproval struck him as almost justified. Yessiree, men had to stick together. Pakulat was even ready to admit Nero into their circle. Because Nero was quite different. Tonight absolutely everything was quite different. The house was old and full of cracks and the kitchen door had scratches and the pattern on the oilcloth cover on the table was almost gone, you couldn't see the city, but otherwise everything looked quite different. Even this Nero. Up to now he'd only had dyed hair and no manners and a big mouth and a four in civics. And today he said that Pakulat was right and used the progressive *du* with a reactionary accent. Pakulat steered his ark through the night at forty knots, certain that after a two-week stay in a country house, he'd have Nero to the point of singing folk songs by heart and sight-reading foolishness. Something could be made of Nero, in any case. And since Pakulat had found out that a bearded man hung over Benno's bed, he hoped that something could still be made of his son. Only he had to find his son first. Ach, Benno, you good-for-nothing . . . The ark was barely rocking. Pakulat lay becalmed. And lay. And lay.

When he woke up, it was light already. And the fog had lifted. And, of course, the city promptly looked different than usual. For the moment, Pakulat only saw a few houses, but they were enough for him. When he was still a child, the houses at the end of the streetcar line had constantly changed. Every time he came by here, he discovered something new on the houses, a strangely shaped balcony for example or a window that wasn't a window but had been walled shut. Then he grew up and stopped being amazed. Because a grown-up isn't amazed. A grown-up knows what's going on. And since then the houses had stood timelessly stiff and stolid. Even the new ones, which had replaced the bombed-out buildings, changed nothing in the nature of the image that Pakulat had carried around for nearly fifty years. Up to the moment that he woke up. And forgot the ark for a moment. Because he was thinking about the bearded man over Benno's bed and maybe also about what the highfalutin intellectuals called 'lifework' and so forth. But as he said, he had to be economical with his love; when Benno was found, he could be generous again, but for now the world would have to wait. And then as he said, he had grown together with the ark like a snail with its shell. When he woke up, he crept out. But, of course, he had the ark on his back again. And when the foundation walls had pressed deeply enough into the flesh of his back again and his shoulder blades started to hurt, the image of the end of the streetcar line was there again, the one Pakulat had carried around with him nearly fifty years. And he stood up, stepped out of the shelter, and set out for home.

When he got to Martinstraße, where the ark was a real house standing there even though he was carrying it on his back, Pakulat saw that the curtains behind Benno's bedroom window were drawn. Pakulat hastened up the steps. He came back, he's here. Benno, that good-for-nothing . . .

The apartment was empty. The electric heater was still humming in Benno's room. Dry, warm air attacked Pakulat. He didn't defend himself.

He dragged it with him into the kitchen, dragged it back and forth, four steps to the window, four steps to the door, past the kitchen cupboard where the wrapped case with the shawm lay. 'Invalid horn' Benno had called it, ach, Benno, you good-for-nothing. Pakulat made himself a cup of coffee, sat down at the big table, but in this case that didn't help, of course, ate breakfast, buttered bread, put his handsaw in his satchel, and put on his cap. But then he took it off again, because it occurred to him that it would be good to leave a note, something like: Come to the construction site right away, your father. Or: Call my site foreman right away 57 68 3, Father. Pakulat went into Benno's room again, because he wanted to leave the message there. Besides, he needed paper and a pencil to write it with. When he wanted to unlock the desk, he noticed that the key was missing. Benno had something to hide! Maybe letters from this Kitty?

Curiosity forced Pakulat to open the lock with the skeleton key. The desk had been rummaged through. Notebooks, stationery, newspapers, pencils lay on top of each other. Order, merciful daughter of heaven.

While straightening up, Pakulat found a blue book. Its cloth-protected covers were locked together. So, secrets behind lock and key; Pakulat respected them and put the book back in the desk. But then he thought about the fact that children really shouldn't keep secrets from their parents. Secret things were bad things. Pakulat put the book in his satchel and went to work.

On the way there he was tempted several times to reach into his satchel. But he controlled himself. Even on the streetcar, where he had a seat. He placed both hands on the cracked, mortar-splattered leather and looked out the window. The glass pane trembled and clattered and had flaws and modeled the people behind it like a distorting mirror. Lots of people were up and about at this hour. Pakulat saw mostly young people. Strange. The university lectures started at 8:15 A.M., at the earliest. But Pakulat saw students. Maybe they were having a production day. But the students couldn't all have production day at the same time. In any case, Pakulat saw nothing but distorted images of students. Short-cropped hair, bangs on boyish foreheads, high-peaked caps, meter-length scarves, dark circles around eyes, skintight pants, high-heeled shoes, towering hairdos. So now they dominated the streets already at 6:00 A.M. Now they were usurping the city at this early hour. His city. That he had helped to build. His lifework, so to speak. What would they do with it?

Pakulat looked through the warped windowpane by turning his head a little to the right. His blue eye, so big that his eyelids could hardly hold it, moved back and forth very rapidly, nystagmus-like. The left side of his face had wrinkles. The right side was smooth and rigid as always. The piercing gaze of the glass eye got lost behind the crowded bodies of the passengers. Pakulat reached into his satchel and broke open the lock of the blue book. It resembled the lock in the kitchen, the one with the missing key. He hadn't dared to break open the one in the kitchen. Now he had to dare everything. It was a question of his lifework, so to speak, and his son. At this moment the two seemed almost identical in nature.

He was seized by a curious excitement as he opened the oilcloth-protected book covers. No motto. No quotation. The first page was empty. Pakulat started turning pages. Angular letters, connected slantwise and straight, made patterns on the paper in wavy chains of sentences. Pakulat raised and lowered his shaggy eyebrows. Normally, he would have refused to decipher anything written so untidily. Laboriously he began to read.

Hölderlin swears by schnapps. Get 'em drunk and have at it. Kat drinks only pop. Kat says schnapps makes you impotent. Kat has a real person's eyes. I'm going to blow that tall guy away if he calls her Kat again.

Chopped up the teacher's desk today. Far out. Humongous hassle. Teachers' conference, student assembly, parents' council, and other fun stuff to look forward to. First interrogation after the crime: Why did you chop it up, Who was behind it, What Western literature was the tool. Pause. Principal yells; everyone is expelled. Principal yells to beat hell. It gets serious. Why? If we knew, we wouldn't have to sit our butts flat on school benches; instead we could put them on exhibit for money. In other words: we'd made it through seven class periods and were ready to physkultur sanimatsen, play handball. But the schoolyard wasn't up to date, and the old bat folk-dancers were rehearsing in the gym. Back we go to the classroom with the ball and like that. Of course it's forbidden just the same as arriving late, cheating, playing skat in music class, giving your buddy answers, skipping demonstrations, saying 'du' to teachers, sawing off chair legs, being bored in civics class, flirting with female teachers, falsifying grades, twisting FDJ *songs, and that sort of bull. But the masses are invincible. So we, thirty-two masses strong, into the classroom and heave the ball. All of a sudden, somebody shoots Schiller off the wall. Far out. We've shot down about sixteen pictures already. But this time it felt up-to-date weird. Even to me. Just like I feel sometimes with Kitty. But totally different. Commandante throws Schiller into the wastebasket. Armstrong pulls the nail out of the wall. Kat nails the wastebasket shut with it. Kat pounds nails like a real person. The next minute the desk has had it. It's that simple. But the director asks questions.*

The train rumbled through a curve. Pakulat lost his place. The neon light flickered. At the next stop more students got on.

Old Pop is a vending machine for babble. Groschen in, speech out. Five-pfennig piece does it too. Five got you war and all that today. Boring. He has cool scars. Grenade fragment, he says. In the shoulder, out the back. A regular hole. Far out. But only a fragment. I thought it was a bullet and all that.

Movies with Kitty. Got physical afterwards. It doesn't hurt her. It would surely hurt Kat. I'd never do anything like that with Kat. I like the little fat ones. Kat isn't fat at all. Maybe you can't exactly tell. She always wears such thick sweaters.

Maybe she's just starting to fill out. Kitty is filled out. Excellent feeling. She always doesn't want to. She says, I could be your mother. I wish. But I talk her into it. Far out. Because I'm going to marry her. Then I won't have to be careful. If the studs in my class didn't know how to take precautions and all that bull, we could open a nursery school. They're all crazy about Kitty. There's nothing going on with the teenage girls. All they do is giggle. They're all stupid except Kat. Kat isn't a teenager anyway. Kat plays soccer. I'm the goalie. She's the wing up to date on the right. Save. Split knee. Kat plays like a real person. That tall guy plays like a maniac. If he ever fouls Kat, I'll beat him to a pulp.

Pakulat wiped the sweat from his forehead. The students in the car jostled each other.

Castro on TV. Our babes think he's sexy. He talks like a real person. But too fast. It's all Greek to me. The extracurricular dude says our Spanish will be in shape by the time we get our Abi. They say Fidel yakked for four hours. In front of about ten million people. Stamina. Cigar. He answers hecklers. The crowds talk with him. When he's sweating, he rolls up his sleeves. When he gets hoarse, the crowds yell take a break and go wild. You can march and dance to the Cuban revolutionary march. You can do all kinds of things with it. Me and my Barbudo Stompers are going to make a rumba out of it. We'll perform it at the club, when my beard is ready. Old Pop orders me to shave it off. That beard will come off when the Cuban revolution is victorious. Kat says I look ten years older with a beard. Kat talks like a real person. The revolutionary march is catchy.

Old Pop in the newspaper. Picture and story. He wants to make something out of young people. To him, young people are a lump of clay to be kneaded. The tall guy says, Convict. I knock him out.

Ampère is a cool dude. Uses a moving coach for a blackboard and in an attack of mathematical ecstasy, chalks elegant calculations on it. Far out. Always steamed up. Electrodynamics. Electromagnetism. Verses for his wife. A type of Esperanto and all that. Ampère gets enthused like a real person. I'd like to be like Ampère. 5:00 P.M. *rugby practice.*

Production day. The master tells me that the engineers are counted as administration and the cleaning women as productive workers. Caviar for old Pop. He likes a bad worker better than a good high school student. Every day the same song about the workers' hard-earned dough and that I'm misusing the musical talent I got from him and that young people have it too good and get everything handed to us and all that — man, keep that garbage to yourself. And we don't get anything handed to us. But old Pop doesn't understand that because he only thinks in terms of campaigns. Last year when I still wanted to study math, he said, Numerical formalism. Since the campaign has gotten going and I don't want to anymore; it's the science of the future. If that's what the future looks like, I say crap on it; I'll make my own, up to date. Where math is math and black is black and white is white, not one thing today and another thing tomorrow and the day after tomorrow something else again, depending. I have a brain to think with, not some machine that operates by punch cards. All the same brain-calculators, cards punched the same for all of them, that would suit old Pop. That would be simple. That would be a life. But not for me. Muchas gracias. Slap in the face. Old Pop knows what's happening. He always knows what's happening. But he puts on his pants one leg at a time too: preaches about the future and measures it with the same standards as in postwar days pulling handcarts. I say, Everyone gets all excited because our company's production has fallen 1.7 percent compared to the month before. Old Pop says, But compared to 1936, it's risen 320 percent. Far out. I say it out loud. Old Pop carries his past around on his belly in a street vendor's tray. I say that and more of the same. Humongous hassle. I'm ungrateful and politically in the toilet. Studying was his dream and all that. Mother told me a different story. Because old Pop doesn't remember that he was weak in mental arithmetic. Learning is a privilege for him, not work, and a student is a guy who's supported at other people's expense and should constantly mumble prayers of thanks to his benefactors. If I dump the whole mess and start working in a factory, I'll be something: a worker. I can compete with old Pop, who was already a carpenter at my age and all that. If I finish my Abi and attend the university for five years, I'll sink to the level of egghead. Kitty understands everything.

The streetcar went faster and faster. The streets were black with students.

Blockade. Paredón para los terroristas. Council of the Barbudo Stompers. If the missiles aren't effective, we'll have to attack. Everyone is for interbrigades. When it gets to that point, we'll join voluntarily. I'll take my horn along. Venceremos.

Pakulat stood up, pushed through the overfilled car to the exit, and jumped off. Then he ran back a ways to a taxi stop. No taxi in sight. Only would-be riders. Pakulat joined them. Beside him stood a man. Leaning on a lamppost. About three meters away. A young man. The same height. Tied to a post. Blindfolded. Ten men step forward. Ten rifle muzzles. Fire. Three meters from Pakulat, a young man's back explodes. Pakulat's uniform is spattered all over with blood. He takes a few steps away from the young man. That would have cost him his life back then. Today he could get away with it. Nowadays he saw a back explode only once in a while, when someone was standing about three meters away from him. Twenty years ago he had seen it many times. But only once from three meters away. His buddy was executed and Pakulat had to watch, because they suspected that he had connections to Greek partisans too. He had to watch countless times. He lived through this minute countless times.

'Tedious business,' said Pakulat to the young man. 'Usually these cars stand around in droves, but when you happen to need one . . . '

Pakulat ran to the other side of the street and waved at every taxi that came along. When he had flagged one down, he suddenly knew what was going on. And was irritated for not thinking of it sooner. It was obvious: Benno was staying in the cottage. Probably because he didn't want to apologize to Pakulat. He was bullheaded like his father. And quite a stud, as it turned out. Maybe he was staying in the cottage with that Kitty. Pakulat urged the driver on. The numbers on the taximeter changed so fast that Pakulat involuntarily reached for his hip pocket, where his wallet and wages were. Of course, money was no object in this case. But you didn't have to throw it down the throats of these starving taxi drivers either. You could've walked. If you'd thought of it earlier. Earlier was half an hour ago. Long ago. An eternity. Earlier, Pakulat didn't have a key for his son. But now, good Lord above, he had a whole bunch of them. And none fit exactly. He'd never in his life seen such a complicated lock. No idea how this tricky mechanism worked. These young guys were unpredictable. And totally different. Pakulat never would have believed that a human being could be so different. Somehow he had hoped that Benno would be like him. That is, better. Because he was his son after all.

The building façades receded. The airstream wafted a sharp smell of chemical waste into the car. Stones struck the chassis. The car bounced across a little bridge, whitecaps on the river to the right and left, then wooden fences, wire fences, junk fences, and finally the skeleton of a privet hedge. Pakulat had reached his goal. He passed the garden gate, the slippery path, the cottage door – 'Benno.'

No Benno answered, no Kitty. And the flame of his lighter didn't produce the wanted persons from the cottage darkness behind the window shutters either. Besides, it smelled as amazingly stale as ever. If Benno had been staying here with a Kitty, it would definitely smell different. Like perfume or other stinky stuff. A woman who was capable of seducing a minor would also wear perfume.

Before Pakulat left, he shined the light into his toolshed. He couldn't pass by without making sure his treasures were there. Assembled here was everything that directly and indirectly belonged to a set of carpenter's tools: angle iron, mallet, pickax, cross ax, carpenter's ax, broadax, claw hammer, various bucksaws, handsaw, groove saw, backsaw, various chisels and drills, tongs, crowbar.

Pakulat had wanted to leave his tools to his eldest son. But he lay buried somewhere in the Pripet marshes. When Lutz started his apprenticeship, a carpenter needed only a hammer, a saw, and an ax. And Benno didn't even need that for his so-called apprenticeship. All he needed was a place to sit and paper and pencil and books. Carpentry was a profession. But geology? Benno wanted to scratch the earth with paper and pencil. Maybe also with some kind of drills and hooks. But he had no use for the tools Pakulat had inherited from his father and painstakingly saved through the war. He didn't even look at them. He had no eye at all for such things. Of course, nowadays the carpentry profession was almost outdated. Montage construction required crane operators, welders, mixers, fillers, jointers, sealers. Pakulat worked as a filler. But that didn't stop him from finding beautiful things beautiful. And the tool set was beautiful; it was a state, a state.

'Useless to stand around here,' said Pakulat. His son had stayed away a whole night, and he was frittering away time with the museum. Instead of proceeding systematically. For example, against the teacher. Parental home and school. But what a school! Where desks were chopped up and workers' songs were twisted. And boys had nothing on their minds except women. And how they had them on their minds. Pakulat couldn't remember ever having had women on his mind that way. And if he had, he would have been ashamed to write it down. These kids talked about sacraments, so to speak, as if they were breakfast rolls. But not in German. What was in that diary was a scandal, but it wasn't German. And 'old Pop' was simply impertinence. Pakulat wasn't old. Sure, in a week he would get his last wages, but he wasn't going to be pushed out. Least of all by his son. For whom a flag was probably just a piece of red fabric. Who had wild ideas in his head. Getting married was a wild idea. And interbrigades were too. Not bad ideas really. But not especially good ones either. Was wanderlust a good idea? In a political sense? Pakulat looked at everything in the political sense. Because they'd put out one of his eyes. What was Benno looking for in that country whose temperament gave Pakulat cause for alarm? And a statesman with that kind of temperament? And a population that even danced to the 'Internationale'? Revolutionary romanticism, thought Pakulat. Could a glutton for pathos yearn for revolutionary romanticism, could a hard-boiled kid like Benno yearn for anything? Could you even take seriously a seventeen-year-old boy who wanted to marry some Kitty? Questions upon questions. Still: someone who wrote *Venceremos* couldn't be lost. Pakulat locked the yard gate, got back in the taxi, and gave the address of Benno's teacher. A teacher knew everything. By virtue of his profession. A teacher was almost as infallible as a father. A teacher from this school too? Had the principal been present at the dress rehearsal of the cultural program? If so, then the song had been twisted with the principal's knowledge. If so, the teacher wasn't worth anything either. Like master, like man. Besides, the teacher was much too young for a confidential matter. Could Pakulat be expected to take a dressing-down from a thirty-year-old? As the taxi stopped in front of the building where the teacher lived, Pakulat got a better idea: Katerbaum.

Off to see Gustav Katerbaum! Pakulat had known him since his youth. They had been together in detention, awaiting trial, and after 1945 they'd worked together for a short time on the Antifascist Committee. For the last twelve years, Katerbaum had been the director of the company where Benno was fitting out his fitter's certificate while getting his *Abitur*. Fitting out! Other boys from his class worked on construction, as bricklayers to be sure, but at least they worked, Benno fitted out! Maybe he was fitting out a special shift in honor of something or other?

Katerbaum lived in a little house at the edge of the city. The driver cursed the bad condition of the street. Pakulat didn't listen. Pakulat thought: Budjonny could take care of everything.

When the car stopped, Pakulat squirmed out the door, pressed the doorbell with his thumb, rang, and rattled the gate until a window was unbolted. Pakulat explained his concern. Loudly. As loudly as he could. Frau Katerbaum held her hand behind her ear and said, 'What, how was that again?' Then she vanished. Her hand behind her ear.

A few minutes later boots came stamping across the gravel. The warrior Katerbaum in uniform emerged from the thicket of ornamental shrubs.

'Red Front,' said Pakulat, startled.

'What's wrong? Test run or serious?'

'My son is gone.'

Katerbaum lowered his head as if he wanted to spear Pakulat on the point of his Van Dyke beard. 'And you're sounding the alarm for that?'

Budjonny, thought Pakulat. Happily. Redeemed, almost. The familiar feeling of order and discipline was back again, the one with which he had survived what was difficult in his life, and the table, the gigantic Spartan table that Anna had forced into the tiny kitchen back then. The individual was powerless. Discipline added the individuals up into a force. Benno had no discipline. Benno chopped up desks and wanted geology when math was needed and called his father 'old Pop' and sniffed snot up his nose and admired some crazy loner like this Ampère. Everything looked different on this day, but Budjonny had stayed the way he was. Budjonny and Pakulat. Made of iron.

After Pakulat had explained himself and cleared away the distrust, Katerbaum took him upstairs to his study. But he didn't know where Benno was either.

He fetched a schnapps bottle and glasses from the bookcase and said, 'He'll come back.'

Pakulat listened to the words, the familiar voice. His agitation subsided. He no longer felt alone. He thought: One million six hundred thousand . . . 'Long time no see,' he said.

'Lately my older son has been coming in late too.'

'Night shift?'

Katerbaum twirled his mustache. 'Night shift – so to speak . . . '

'I always told my father when I had something going on, training for example, do you remember how we trained together, unemployment compensation, nothing to eat, and we trained . . . '

'Yeah, yeah, I know. Your boy is coming along all right, the apprentice trainer told me . . . '

'So.' Pakulat cleared his throat. 'No wonder. If we'd had nothing but studying to think about when we were young, Gustav . . . ' Pakulat raised his arm and slapped Katerbaum on the back. Asked him did he ever think about how they used to play music together? Did he still remember the general strike? Or 1925: The rightists had thrown Pakulat out of the union, and the construction workers elected him 123 to 17 as the delegate of the General Assembly. Or 1927: Katerbaum took his seat in the city parliament of M. as the only Communist and acquired the nickname Budjonny when he discovered a case of corruption. 'Those were battles; those were victories!'

'Yes,' said Katerbaum and put schnapps and glasses on the desk.

'Do you remember . . . '

'Yes, I remember. Maybe he got drunk and can't find his way home?'

'I always found my way,' said Pakulat. 'But if you want to make your staff car available for a good cause, your job doesn't start until eight . . . '

'I don't have a staff car anymore.'

Pakulat leaped to his feet. 'Are they trying to . . . '

'I've been replaced,' said Katerbaum, unbuttoning his uniform jacket. 'Changing of the guard, goddamn me.'

'So.' Pakulat clung to the windy syllable. So. The old guys pulled the wreck out of the dirt and the young ones . . . Pakulat circled the armchair that Katerbaum was sitting in. He didn't know what to make of his old friend's words. Changing of the guard? Was he putting on a show to hide his sorrow? Did he have to put on an act in front of someone who would get his last wages next week and that would be the end of it? Goddamn me, was getting old that difficult? Goddamn me, yes; Katerbaum had said that too. 'Changing of the guard' and 'Goddamn me.' Pakulat felt his bullheadedness swelling up bigger and bigger. When it had swelled to the size of a pumpkin, he said, 'I have no intention of retiring.'

'Me either,' said Katerbaum. 'I'm going to keep on as director of planning for a while yet.'

Pakulat stopped short. What was this, Katerbaum was giving up, Budjonny admitting defeat . . . 'Just a minute! Are you trying to say that it's fair to . . . '

'Fair! That's hogwash, what a load of bull, a crock of shit. You think you're dealing with a reasonable person, and all of sudden he comes at you with a crock. Fair! Of course, it's not fair. Even my grandson who still shits his diapers knows it isn't fair. It's right, so *basta.* Every generation has its task, anything else is poppycock. Yessir. Poppycock, I say, poppycock. Of course, I'm an engineer. I busted my rear end to get that diploma while working full time in those days, it's no picnic when you're pushing fifty. But I don't know any foreign languages, for example. At fifty you can't get another language into your skull. My replacement can read Russian and English without coffee. Guys like us can't even formulate a sensible idea without coffee, but he . . . '

'And experience,' said Pakulat, digging his hands into his pants pockets.

'Bernd was my assistant for a year. A highly qualified skilled worker. Goddamn me, the companies should be scrambling to get guys like him, but no . . . Experience! You can gain experience. Anyone with big plans needs bold young people, fireballs . . . '

Katerbaum gripped the stem of a schnapps glass between his first two fingers and pushed it across the table to Pakulat. Then he poured. Pakulat picked up the glass, said something, but didn't drink. He held it in his hand for a while, then set it back down on the scratched tabletop. He let his hand lie on the table. And looked at it, his head tilted a little to the right. He lowered his head until his left eye, which was so large that the eyelids could hardly hold it, was right over his chapped hand. The piercing gaze of his glass eye was directed toward the bookcase. Then Pakulat raised his head slightly again. And turned his big blue eye toward Katerbaum. Who sat across from him. Behind the desk. Leaning back. His arms propped on the armrests. Flat. Pakulat sat on a chair, and Katerbaum sat in the armchair. Herr Katerbaum. All that was left of Budjonny was the mustache. And it wasn't worth much anymore.

'Man alive,' said Pakulat softly to the stranger. 'Man alive, you can't saw off the branch you're sitting on. We old people have to stick together.'

'Against who?' Katerbaum raised his bushy eyebrows like an awning, picked up the phone, and dialed.

'What're you doing? Calling the police?'

'Police! I'm calling the Wonder-Shopper.'

'Wonder-Shopper, damn foolishness.'

'Of course, it's foolishness. But at that age we did all kinds of foolishness too. Hello. Katerbaum. Good morning. Sorry to bother you. What? So I almost didn't catch you . . . Actually, Herr Pakulat just . . . No, his father. Is by any chance the son . . . look, you can feel free to . . . He really isn't? Any idea where he might possibly . . . Aha, thanks a lot. Good morning then, sorry to bother you.'

'Who are you talking to anyway?'

'With your son's lady friend, don't look as if you were going to eat me.'

'With my son's lady friend . . . You mean with this Kitty . . . '

'Kitty is good, Kitty suits her. I call her the Wonder-Shopper. The director of our sales office, you see, a cute kid, maybe thirty-five at the most . . . '

'So,' said Pakulat, 'so.' All he had was that little windy word. He gasped it out a few more times. Then he wrote down the address of the sales office director and left.

And went back into the city. Feeling cold. Bleary-eyed. It still wasn't really light out. As long as the fog didn't disperse, it couldn't get really light. But the fog had risen; it had pushed away from the ridges of the roofs and pointed gables and was hanging over the city like a gigantic cloud. No weather for flying, thought Pakulat. Whenever he looked at the sky he thought: flying weather — or, no weather for flying. He only had one eye. And when he went swimming, everyone could see the scar on his back. But nobody could see that his sky was shattered, shot to pieces, mutilated, that only an airspace still remained above him. And nobody had ever noticed that he had to go down to the cellar, near the breach in the wall, when he wanted to remember his wife. And that he could never really see her forehead because it was covered by safety goggles.

No weather for flying, thought Pakulat, walking faster. And groaning, because the ark weighed down on him. Because he was trembling under its weight. But he couldn't get rid of it. He would have to carry it around with him all his life. He hated it. Because he hated the Battle of Fehrbellin. Because he always needed one of the four beers he drank on payday to get through the storm troopers' bar. Because whenever someone was standing about three meters away from him, he involuntarily waited for his back to explode the next minute. Oh, he hated this damn ark. And he loved it. There were sixty-five years in it. What was a recommendation for improvement compared to a brawl. What was a successful partisan attack compared to a 1 percent increase in productivity. Who didn't love his life. And who wouldn't want to get eight hundred years old. That's why the ark was not invulnerable, as long as his son was lost. Pakulat wanted to live on in his son, he had to live on in him, he had to find him so that the ark could withstand the virtual flood that had washed over the earth for years. In a week Pakulat would get his last wages and that would be the end of it, but his son could fortify the ark so that the flood would remain virtual and the inventors of the flood would stop putting their invention to the test. When the son boarded the ark, his father could say, *That is the sign of the covenant that I have made between me and you and all living souls with you forever after: / My rainbow have I placed in the clouds, it shall be the sign of the covenant between me and the earth. And when it happens that I bring clouds over the earth, then shall they see my rainbow in the clouds. / And then I will remember the covenant between me and you and all living souls among all flesh, that there may not come another deluge to cause all flesh to perish.* This is how the father would speak if he had the power of biblical language and made up the value of millions upon millions of fathers and if he had found his son, who would have to yield the value of millions and millions of sons. But Pakulat didn't even know if Benno was worth anything at all. As long as he still hadn't found him, he couldn't say anything. And he could only hope.

And walk a little faster. And read the piece of paper with the sales office director's address. Motteler Str., it said. Motteler Straße was far away. It must be somewhere north. Pakulat had to pass through the city from south to north. He had to call the construction site and say he was coming in late today or not at all and then he had to pass through the city. Which he had helped to build and the students had now taken over. Every year there were more students. And soon Benno would be one of them. Were the students lost sons too? Pakulat went to a phone booth and called the construction site and told the foreman a white lie. Then he walked on. Now through streets that had aged during the night. Now through streets that corresponded to his imagination, because they were his imagination. He went through an aged or a timeless city, depending on whether he was doubting or hoping. When he hoped, he didn't need to raise his head to see that the coping of the cross vault had water spots. They had been there forever. Ever since Pakulat first set foot in the colonnades and saw the Battle of Fehrbellin in the show window; ever since he'd held the little tin uhlan figure in his hands. When he doubted, he could even feel the shabbiness of the ark he was carrying on his back. And he could sense why his sons didn't want it. Nobody who was young wanted something that was finished. A finished world was for people who had their lives ahead of them, a reason to take one's life. But Pakulat almost had his life behind him. Pakulat needed a finished world. At the end of his life he was touching something that was finished. His life goal. Finally. He was touching on it. He had such great respect for it, because he was only touching on it. Benno had no respect. He walked around in the ark without looking where he was going, slammed the doors, scratched up the floor with his shoes. He slept soundly through the nights in it, as if that were something to take for granted. And as soon as he woke up, he practiced wild sounds on his trumpet. When Pakulat doubted, he sensed that Benno would totally remodel the ark, not tear it down, but remodel it. As if it weren't finished. As if it were only raw material for his imagination. Raw material, thought Pakulat. Sadly. And began to hope. When he was really so sad he could puke, he began to hope. Ach, Benno, you good-for-nothing . . .

Pakulat got on a streetcar that could take him to Motteler Straße. To this Kitty. To this thirty-five-year-old woman who was doing it with a minor. Because no decent man had taken her. Or because she hadn't gotten one of the few who'd been spared by the war. Or because she was perverse. A thirty-five-year-old woman who did it with a minor must be perverse. Pakulat knew what was going on. Why was he going to see her, if he knew what was going on? Maybe to let himself be fooled into thinking she was different too? She was that way and not different. And it was totally out of the question for Pakulat to allow his son to marry a woman like that. He would talk to him, that's how it is, and be done with it. He didn't need to talk with this female but with his son. And for that reason he had to find him. But where?

Pakulat got off the streetcar and sat down on one of the benches on the open square in front of the university. On the only one that was empty. The others were occupied by students eating breakfast. Pakulat saw a large surface brought to life: short-cropped hair, bangs on boyish foreheads, high-peaked caps, meter-length scarves, dark circles around eyes, skintight pants, high-heeled shoes, towering hairdos. And a wad of sandwich paper that had been thrown on the lawn. 'So,' said Pakulat. He said only that little windy word. Usually he would have said more, usually he would have said all kinds of things to the girl who threw paper on city property. But today he only said 'so.' And reached for the oilcloth-covered book that was still in his coat pocket. He felt a little ashamed when he saw the broken lock. But there was nothing else he could have done. And actually his son was to blame. A son didn't lock things away from his father. A decent son didn't do that kind of thing. Everything in that book was stuff a decent son didn't do. Almost everything. *Venceremos* was good. Interbrigades were understandable, but the rest of it . . . Where did he get the rest of it? Pakulat had tried to shield his son from the bitter experiences he himself had had. Benno was supposed to avoid repeating the mistakes his father recognized. Under those circumstances, wouldn't he have become an ideal Pakulat? From what was in that book you could conclude that Benno was no Pakulat at all, let alone an ideal one. He was making his own mistakes. He was totally different. He had fantastic ideas about grenades. He was occupied with nothing but unimportant things. He just lived and lived and lived, instead of concentrating on the essential. The essential was *Venceremos*. But in German. Why didn't Benno write it in German? Why did he chop up desks? Would he maybe chop up the ark too? Pakulat turned pages and read. Foreign, thought Pakulat, it's all foreign. Ampère. Spanish. Jazz. Rugby. Maybe he was dying with it. Maybe everyone had his ark and died with it. Maybe Benno had one on his back too, invisible, just as invisible as the one Pakulat was carrying. Maybe everyone carried an ark like that. Terrible, thought Pakulat, turning pages. And reading. Terrible? Why terrible, exactly? Maybe the world was beautiful only because it was so confusingly varied. Didn't people travel to foreign countries in order to see something exotic? Weren't they absolutely nuts about foreign travel? Pakulat didn't need to travel. Benno was foreign country enough for him. A person who hadn't experienced a war. Could there be anything more foreign to Pakulat than that kind of person? Funny, thought Pakulat, turning pages. And reading. And looking for clues that would suggest an ark. But he found none. Pakulat couldn't imagine how anyone could live without an ark. Naturally, he hoped for a world in which that would be possible. He had worked for it all his life. But he couldn't really imagine what it would be like: living without an ark. Because he really couldn't imagine what it would be like when you no longer had to protect yourself from floods. When you just lived and lived and lived. When there were no extreme situations anymore that forced you to extreme positions. Frenetic positions. Was Pakulat frenetic? For the time being anyhow, rest was unthinkable. Only Benno seemed to think about it. Yes, he seemed already to be living somehow in this unreal world, this green kid, this good-for-nothing. He seemed to attach no importance to discipline and great importance to imagination. The imagination of the individual. Ampère. Although he wrote *Venceremos*: we will — and he thought: we have. Weak in grammar, thought Pakulat. I must make him strong, thought Pakulat. Trembling with cold. Bleary-eyed. He squinted up at the sky, which the war had mutilated. And again he lived through minutes that he couldn't choose. Over and over he had to get through them, the minutes added up to hours, days, weeks, months, maybe to years. Still today Pakulat lost time on the war, irrecoverable time, maybe years. Not only his sky, even his days were mutilated. Although he had a strong power of imagination. One that produced collective farms in jail. No weather for flying, thought Pakulat. And watched the students get up and enter the university building, casually, and he thought, maybe they have no ark at all. Maybe they live without this weight. Maybe they didn't even know what it is, an ark. Because it was totally senseless to drag yourself around with such a thing nowadays, when the absolute flood threatened. Did Pakulat seriously believe he would survive it with a ridiculous ark? Ought to chop it up, thought Pakulat, you can do something about the flood by chopping it up. Everyone should chop up their arks, thought Pakulat, everyone, all of them.

And turned pages, reading. He read the last entry. *We're playing harmless dance music, twist and that sort of stuff. Then a few numbers for close dancing. By request. The studs from our class always request crap like English waltz and slow fox-trot. But I don't have Mitschurin blinders on my eyes. I've been watching the tall guy the whole time. He thinks when I take my horn and play, I'm gone, but I can still see every pimple on his nose. I can see his eyes fumbling around on Kat's sweater all evening. And as I'm playing one of those lousy, slow fox-trots to fulfill the clubhouse director's cultural plan, the tall guy rapes Kat with a bow and wants to drag her onto the dance floor. I'm there and knock him dead.*

Pakulat deciphers the last sentence again, reads, reads. But there it is. 'Dead,' it says. Dead, thinks Pakulat. It takes a while before the last word Benno wrote in the book penetrates his consciousness. When it does, it hits him like a blow with the brass knuckles. He tries to stand up but doesn't succeed. Something is pressing him against the bench. The big blue eye moves back and forth, nystagmus-like, but it can't make anything out. Dead. Lost. The end.

He sits there a while longer, then someone helps him up. And asks where he can escort him. But Pakulat doesn't want an escort. He wants to go this road alone. The last one. To the police.

The police don't know anything yet. Pakulat tells them what he knows. And leaves again. And carries on his back what he had just now recognized as ridiculous and anachronistic. He has nothing left but this weight. The chance to rest that it suggests to him is a lie. He knows it's a lie. But he doesn't want to know. He knows too much already.

The city is bearing the fog on its head. The skyscraper balances the amorphous hulk. It has curled itself up and rocks over the city like a many-headed cloud. Pakulat coughs and has to stop frequently, because he can't get enough air. He starts toward the construction site. But he has to turn around again. The heavy air forces him to turn around. The end, he thinks.

'The end,' he says as he unlocks the outside door. He shuffles through the hallway, drags himself from floor to floor, past apartment doors, some of which have rough plywood surfaces instead of carved wooden frames and glass panels, and checks to see that the hallway windows are bolted. When he reaches the door of his apartment, he stops. And unlocks the mailbox first. Newspapers well out of the mailbox; several newspapers fall at Pakulat's feet. And a note. The note says: *Dear Father, I'm sick of being blamed, am applying for jobs in Schwedt. Salud.*

BOOK ELEVEN

Chapter 1

OH, THOU JOYFUL . . .

The hunting report from Venice almost seemed to Laura proof of her suspicion that Beatrice had fallen into the hands of political blackmailers or some such villains. Apparently, they had psychically devastated the trobadora to such an extent that Beatrice now believed her own lies. In this case, letters would be of no use. Laura went to the nearest people's police station with the plea that a search for Beatrice de Dia be initiated. The police sergeant said there would be difficulties, since the GDR did not currently maintain diplomatic relations with Italy. The Writers' Union and the Ministry of Foreign Affairs also promised to do what they could. On Christmas Day Laura's parents arrived about three. The snow in the courtyard had square and rectangular outlines of carpet dust. Instead of spruce, bunches of green cabbage leaves in net bags hung at the kitchen windows. Wesselin had already played himself into a sweat. He hastily set the crash helmet that Olga Salman handed him onto his head, asking at once and numerous times throughout the afternoon if more company was coming. The living room smelled of resin. Later, of smoldering candlewicks. Wesselin didn't go to sleep until all the new toys had been packed into his bed. He put the freight-train locomotive from his grandfather under his tummy. Clinging to Laura's sweater were fibers from the Santa Claus beard that she had cut from a mask and fastened to her ears with rubber loops like gas-mask goggles. During her performance she watched Wesselin in disappointment. The effect seemed out of proportion to the effort. She had worked half a day sewing the outfit, stuttered out her first sentence, Wesselin strolled around the room. Laura made her voice even deeper. She spoke into the mask beard as if into a pot, sweating. When Wesselin started singing, she thought haste was called for. Soon she returned to the room, makeup removed, and explained her absence as going shopping. Her son asked for two slices of rye bread. He devoured them at great speed. Free of anxiety, Laura drank schnapps with her parents. Olga Salman rejoiced over her husband's retirement, which was coming up in October of the following year. Johann Salman cracked nuts and grumbled about the incense candles that his wife and daughter took turns putting into the belly of the wooden miner. Later Laura served *Neunerlei*, nine different dishes, in the blue air. With the TV on. If Jesus of Nazareth hadn't been born 1,971 years ago, Laura would have invented him that evening.

Chapter 2

EXCERPT FROM AN INTERVIEW GRANTED BY ALFREDO MAURER, PUBLISHER OF THE MELUSINIAN BOOKS, TO A *SPIEGEL* CORRESPONDENT; THE WEST GERMAN NEWSMAGAZINE PUBLISHED THE INTERVIEW WITH THE TITLE 'MATRIARCHAL NUDE OVER THE MATTRESS'

SPIEGEL: Herr Maurer, you were facing bankruptcy before you threw yourself into piracy. The Melusinian books have made you a millionaire. Do you owe your business success to the leftist vogue or to your director of advertising?

MAURER: Ach! Piracy is such an ugly word. I don't like ugly words when we are talking about ladies.

SPIEGEL: According to our information, the Beautiful Melusine is not a lady but a mystification.

MAURER: Very true, one can't pirate what nobody owns.

SPIEGEL: Did you pay the Beautiful Melusine no royalties because she is nobody?

MAURER: I paid her no royalties because she plagiarized the books.

SPIEGEL: There are famous authors nowadays whose fortune is founded on plagiarized books.

MAURER: Since stupidities are continually repeated, I, as a tolerant human being, can have nothing against the fact that truths are sometimes repeated too. I would characterize the Melusinian books as educational literature.

SPIEGEL: You are floating on the wave of religion. Not much more can be gotten out of Jesus, but the old Greek gods are still a fallow field for marketing. That is why the Persephone poster was such a knockout – I believe every daughter of women's lib who takes pride in keeping up with fashion has the matriarchal nude hanging over her mattress. Herr Maurer, you have a sixth sense for advertising, but for poetry?

MAURER: In this connection I would like to quote from the 64th Melusinian book, which the Beautiful Melusine copied from Peter Hacks. To wit: 'Christianity is not true in the sense that what it tells about took place or what it believes makes sense. The truth that it contains is only accessible to those who do not believe it is true. Whoever does not need to believe it can make use of it. This explains the fact that artists, when they met God in his wretchedness before the house of the Lord, after – admittedly – initial embarrassment, were eager to adopt the beautiful and transparent old man. Goethe was ahead of them here too; the exemplary nature and merit of the *Faust II* finale cannot be praised highly enough. Humankind learned from him that the religion of yesterday is the art of today. The deal is, as they say, to the advantage of both sides. Religion owes its postmortal resting place to aesthetic consciousness; only there does it have immortality. Aesthetic consciousness owes to religion, which understood itself during its lifetime as a world definition, a hefty heritage of poetically preprocessed reality. By no means does the author have in mind only the beauties of Christianity worth preserving. What he expressly intends to speak of are the insights worth preserving. Of course, the insights of mythical or mythically colored dialectics are of a prescientific kind; this does not mean that they have become superfluous. Science does not know everything. And at the place where it does know, it is still far from being useful for art. The graphic way of comprehending, which transforms not only the mind but also the attitudes of the comprehending person, very often achieves, in the case of practical judgments, the richer and truer result. Modern art is again making use of the great images . . . '

SPIEGEL: Elegant and brilliant, Herr Maurer, but hardly edifying for flipped-out types. Do you think that all the Persephone-poster buyers are also Melusine-book readers?

MAURER: Melusine-book buyers, that much is certain. Who says that products must deliver what their advertisements promise?

SPIEGEL: In any case, the matriarchal advertising poster is misleading; with it, you are intentionally or unintentionally doing the groundwork for certain leftist forces. And you cannot deny that the Beautiful Melusine is an occult object, Herr Maurer.

MAURER: Why?

Chapter 3

Benno Pakulat most personally

The winter was mild. Early February already springlike. Beatrice was still missing. On 11 February Laura dialed the telephone number 22 88 020 and requested Benno Pakulat awake. Request confirmed for the following day. Rendezvous at the Weißensee dairy bar. As Laura entered the establishment holding Wesselin on one arm at the agreed-upon morning hour, Benno whistled the scale up and down and looked Laura over, also up and down. As she went past his table, he said, 'Damn.' Then he discussed her shoes, which lacked high heels, with another man; they estimated her bust measurement as ninety-five centimeters, her age as thirty-five. They recommended hairspray to control her hairdo better and lauded the advantages of the full-figured type in general and in particular. Since Laura had sat down with Wesselin in a corner of the bar, Benno had to speak very loudly. He ordered a double vodka for himself and Laura and drank to her health while she tried to convince the server there had been a mistake. Later he went to her table, said excuse me, but they must know each other from somewhere, and sat down on the chair next to her. He insisted that Laura look over the wine list and asked her preference. Since she alleged that she had none, he pressed his knee against hers, ordered three rounds of slivovitz, and threatened revenge for the insult it would be if she didn't drink up. Although Laura was neither appreciative nor amusing but speechless, he paid for everything and escorted her out of the bar. In the doorway he slipped his hand as if by accident over one cheek of her behind, to check the tissue structure. Since he could find no shortcoming, he asked Laura if she had plans for the evening and invited her to the Cinema Internationale. An inner struggle that was becoming increasingly visible on her face now distorted it into a grimace but finally released her yawn and loosened her tongue, so that Laura spoke. 'Look here, you have ordinary manners!' — 'No, outrageous ones,' he replied. 'They just don't strike you that way, because you're not a man.'

Chapter 4

Benno Pakulat personally

Benno's reply exceeded all of Laura's expectations. So she held Wesselin out to him. Then her right hand and said, 'Laura Salman, if you like, we can be friends.' Benno took them mechanically and then stood baffled, Wesselin on his left arm, Laura on his right. If Wesselin hadn't bitten him on the ear, who knows how long he would have stood like that. As it was, he cried 'Ow,' and Laura explained to Wesselin that he mustn't bite Herr Pakulat. 'How do you know my name?' asked Benno. 'Well,' said Laura. And Benno also said, 'Well,' because her name was familiar to him too, somehow, 'but where from?' — 'Do you dream a lot?' asked Laura on the Weißensee's grassy shore, which was covered with breadcrumbs. 'Too often,' answered Benno. 'Why?' — 'Because,' said Laura. The benches and paths were visited by the nonworking population. A young man stood out in that crowd. His way of walking, you might describe it as swimming in air, accentuated the rarity of his type among retirees and women minding children, whose enjoyment of the flattering morning was impeded by physical or pedagogical tribulations. Laura was no less satisfied with Benno Pakulat's gait and stature than with his dreaming and waking intelligence. Wesselin was fascinated by Benno's pale mustache. He tousled the mustache, tasted it, and sang to it. Benno tolerated it with unseeing eyes. After Wesselin had yanked out a clump of his hair, Laura put her son back into his stroller. She tried to stem the ensuing roar of protest with a bunch of keys. But Wesselin threw the apartment keys out of the stroller. Benno quickly plucked them from the dust and said, if you please. Then he weighed the treasure in his hand before sucking in his stomach to stuff the keys into the pants pocket of his free leg. At a bench he asked would it be all right, addressing her as 'lady.' He sat down as awkwardly as he had bowed. And sat stiffly, as if bone-injured, legs and body in a straight line with the beginning and end of his back barely touching the bench: actually, he was lying down. Laura suspected that he was on sick leave. Benno asked if the child was a boy or a girl. The question pleased Laura. She pressed the handlebars of the stroller down to give Wesselin a good view of the ducks and geese strolling across the breadcrumbs. Benno asked Wesselin if Laura was his mother. Laura told Wesselin to say she was his grandmother. An old man was spearing paper with a nail-tipped stick. He dragged the sack he was collecting it in. At that, the dust lying loosely on the paths rose up in clouds. Here and there sparrows bathed in it. When the geese were quiet, the noise of the traffic from Klement-Gottwald-Allee could be heard. Benno tapped the toe of his left shoe against a front spring of the stroller and said, 'Bent.' Laura said the damage to the chassis was due to weakness of the material. Benno predicted a crack in the metal if she kept putting her weight on one side of the stroller. Laura said any broken springs would be Benno's fault, since Wesselin, for lack of keys and mustache, had to make do with spring fowl. There was more throwing of breadcrumbs. Planks that the boardwalks to the public baths were mounted on jutted out of the lake, visible two meters above the water. Most of the rental boats lay at the dock. 'I'd like to have that kind of grandmother too,' said Benno to Wesselin, without changing his position. His arms lay on the backrest of the bench. They occupied it. Laura sat curled up at the left, scraping the toes of her shoes in the sand. On the way home Benno said Laura had a peculiar way of pushing. Not the way women usually do, holding the handlebars with both hands, sometimes also leaning forward over them, bearing down on them, as if to demonstrate their right of ownership physically. At that, Laura also realized she was in the habit of pushing the stroller one-handed, not walking symmetrically behind it but half next to it. Like a man, said Benno and asked if Laura had quit her job. Out of curiosity she waited in front of a hardware store where he bought sewing machine oil. Of course, he used it to oil the stroller wheels in the hall beside the building door. The apartment key was returned to Wesselin as Laura expressed her intention of returning to trolley driving in a year and a half. When her son was old enough for nursery school. As soon as Wesselin was diapered and fed, Benno knocked on the door of Laura's fourth-floor apartment. She opened it. Benno pushed the stroller one-handed toward her as far as it would go, then toward himself, repeating this several times, probably quite a while, but the wheels hadn't squeaked before either. Then he shoved the stroller up to the pasteboard door behind which three electric meters were installed. His other hand hoisted a cleaning rag like a flag. The flag unexpectedly flew past Laura. Benno told Wesselin it was a handkerchief. Wesselin already had his thumb in his mouth: overture to sleep. The grownups stole out of the nursery into the kitchen, where Benno oiled all the doors of the stove and took a good look at Laura's toolbox. She expressed amusement at the show. He praised the assortment of tools, after establishing its relationship to her gender, and invited her to come and see his toolbox some time. Laura and Benno burst simultaneously into laughter. But Laura's mood deteriorated. Because she'd had more than enough of shows like that. Benno bent his knees until his face appeared in the mirror, tugging his stubbly chin and arranging strands of hair on his forehead and in front of his ears. Laura suspected the back of his head lacked roundness under the abundance of greasy hair. Since he remained in his apparently uncomfortable position similar to that of dancers leaning backward to go under a rope, she asked him if the beard stubbles had grown during the night shift. And she pointed out Lutz's shaver under the mirror. Benno said, chicks think unshaven men are masculine, and slowly straightened up again. He only moved slowly. Sometimes stiffly too, as if he had muscle cramps. But he didn't confirm Laura's suspicion. For a while they exchanged descriptions of housing construction sites and company accidents. And at one point, Laura sensed the odor of scorched iron right under her nose. Then Benno talked a lot about children again and wanting to have several of them. And Laura also talked a lot about it. But more specifically. Unwrinkled skin, unstained by tobacco, at such close range required her to be principled. She said that our children are not our possessions. They are sons and daughters of life's longing for itself. They come through us, not from us. We can give them our love but not our ideas. We can give their bodies a home but not their souls. For their souls live in the house of tomorrow, which we cannot visit, not even in our dreams. If we wish, we can try to be like them. But we cannot make them be like us. Because life does not go backwards and does not stop at yesterday. Benno listened in amazement. When she had finished, he said, 'My words, that's my speech, lady, word for word my specialty speech. I lifted it from someplace once, and I always fire it off when I need to get on somebody's good side. Guaranteed effective, it's the truth, and a fence is no better than a thief, lady, only I can't remember when I passed the hot goods on to you.' — 'But I do,' said Laura. 'Don't act so mysterious,' said Benno. 'I am mysterious,' said Laura. 'And I'd like to have you,' said Benno. Laura acted surprised and countered that he could be her son. 'Ach,' said Benno, 'but it doesn't bother you that my brother, who I've seen you with, could be your father. Talk about the high road, but take the path of least resistance.' Laura protested that Lutz didn't show his age and offered proof that Benno was mysterious too. 'The devil looks after his own,' said Benno hastily. 'Her own,' Laura corrected him. She countered the marriage proposal that followed with a question that Lutz had occasionally put to her. She said, 'Have you ever seen a dead person?' — 'No,' said Benno. 'But if you think it will make me older, I can do it now.' And that same evening Benno decided to take a leave from the staff of the State Enterprise Construction to seek a temporary position as a funeral orator with the municipal undertaker's office.

Chapter 5

THE STORY 'GALLOONS,' BY WHICH LAURA INTRODUCES HERSELF TO BENNO OVER AFTERNOON COFFEE AND CAKE

Galloons: Until 1943 my mother managed to avoid obligatory war-effort work altogether. Then she became a homeworker. The income was modest, neither was it interesting, in view of comprehensive rationing and regular air raids. When the alarm sounded, my mother left the embroidery frame in the apartment. It was about one meter long, half a meter wide, stood on a sawhorse, and belonged to the Vogelbein company, which had engaged exclusively in the production of military galloons since the beginning of the war. The business offices and drop-off for goods were located in the Vogelbein family's apartment. My scanty memories of the old part of the city stem from delivery days when the air-raid reports were favorable, so that I was allowed to go with my mother. We lived in the northeast suburb. A fifteen-minute streetcar ride gave me the impression of a great distance. Even before the war my parents seldom went into the city. The city: that meant the center. Houses, stores, stench were clustered there; to me it seemed that immense riches were assembled there, and old men whom I suspected of being the kind who used candy to lure little girls into tenement apartments with trapdoors. The Vogelbein company negotiated with its female employees in a tenement apartment. Herr Vogelbein exceeded my expectations inasmuch as he was not only wrinkled and bald-headed but also had a strawberry birthmark covering the entire right side of his face. Once he kissed his wife's hand right before my eyes. I'd never seen anything like that before and found my suspicions indirectly confirmed. My mother believed Herr Vogelbein was a well-traveled man because he often told his employees about safaris. The hallway of the tenement smelled of old fecal matter, the apartment of glue and dust. It was cluttered with ugly neo-baroque furniture and plush accessories on and under which fabric, felt, braid, piping, stripes, cardboard, various twines and yarns as well as gold and silver colored tin stars were piled in shoeboxes. The boxes were battered, the red plush shabby. My mother deposited the finished epaulettes and collar patches on the red plush cover of the oval center table, where a birdcage also had its place. A pair of parakeets scattered feed through the bars; the male could sing 'Lili Marlene.' Deer antlers on the walls. In my mother's presence, I wasn't afraid. She made a delivery every two weeks. Frau Vogelbein had trained her. Frau Vogelbein was younger than my mother and towered a head taller than her husband. My mother was soon embroidering the collar patches better than her boss, she quickly achieved precision in braiding the epaulettes as well, she was a trained tailor. The collar patches, destined for officers, were embroidered with silver thread. On green cloth with a cardboard template glued on it. The silver thread had to cover the template evenly on the diagonal. It oxidized easily, sweat blackened it, which is why my mother kept the heat low and washed her hands often. The epaulettes were made of felt-covered cardboard pieces onto which plaited or stitched-together braids had to be sewn. The pieces of felt were of glowing colors that indicated the weapon genres. My eyes caressed the fabric covetously. Herr Vogelbein cut the square pieces out himself and counted them himself too. He never miscounted. Only an occasional piece of piping, which was usually added to the trim of the felt-covered cardboard, or a piece of cord or stripe were left over. I would immediately sew it onto doll dresses. Braid seemed to me unsuitable for this purpose. It consisted of two wicks wrapped with gray stripes, rarely silver or silver gray. One wick had to be stretched a little with a tongs when the curve for the buttonhole was being shaped. When the air-raid warnings lasted longer than the time needed to get dressed, my mother would stretch wicks. I was allowed to help. For embroidering and plaiting, she needed peace and quiet. When my father was on leave from the front, she worked nights and listened to the London radio. The officers' epaulettes were plaited with four strands. My mother sewed the weave onto pieces of cardboard with the required shape stamped on them. While plaiting, my mother also used the tongs to make the curves come out flawless. She refused my request to plait an epaulette myself. Although piping was measured generously, she could not tolerate wasting material. I plaited my braids with four strands and tried to imagine what Herr Vogelbein would do if I sewed myself a traditional peasant girl's cap with appliqués made of some of the splendid felt, like those I had seen in a fashion magazine at the dentist's office. I had heard from an older girlfriend the fact that men sometimes killed little girls, and my mother had not denied it. Tormented by dread and curiosity, I brooded over motives for the deed. I was also interested in how the little girls died. I received scanty, incomprehensible information about this. Apart from uniformed soldiers on leave, whom I counted not as part of the masculine genus but of the military, in the fifth year of the war there were very few, indeed, increasingly fewer young men to be seen on the streets that were busy with women, so the world seemed more and more mysterious to me. I didn't fear the bombs, for I knew that God had his hand on me. When I dreamt about him, he wore plaited epaulettes with three golden stars. The center of the city burned, along with the Vogelbein family, on March 5, 1945, shortly after my mother had picked up material. She processed it by the stipulated deadline and in the following weeks made phone calls and visits to authorities trying to find out who had taken over the company. Her inquiries were unsuccessful. At the end of May, I asked my mother if I could cut the felt pieces off the epaulettes. I received permission to do so in July and started sewing appliqués on the cap right away. In August my mother and I went to sew, for free room and board, in the home of a farmer with a large family in the Erzgebirge; he had already taken all my outgrown clothes as well as half our bedding and cutlery in exchange for potatoes and linseed oil. I swapped the cap for a homemade liverwurst.

Chapter 6
Proclamation for Laura

Laura's story stirred Benno's pride in his father, who had passed away six years earlier. After that, Benno had given notice in Schwedt and returned to Leipzig. To the apartment in his parental home, which he had scorned until then. He lived in the apartment for two years. Because he couldn't make up his mind to sell the house. Only after the roof had been blown off by a storm and he couldn't come up with the money to repair it did he turn the house over to the communal housing administration. He moved to Berlin – a shortage of workers had helped him obtain authorization to move. His brother Lutz, who had lived there a long time, smilingly dismissed Benno's decision to keep their father's garden plot in Leipzig as sentimental. No sensible person would travel two hours by train to spend his weekend in a garden-plot community with chemical wastes flowing through it when he had the lakes of Berlin right under his nose. Benno didn't care if people thought he was a sensible person or not; he spent many weekends in the smelly community. Which was probably going to be torn down soon, the grounds were already scheduled for a new housing district. So he first took Laura and Wesselin to Leipzig to show them his father's cottage before presenting his room in Berlin to them. The greater part of the cottage was occupied by the toolshed. Here was collected everything that used to be directly and indirectly needed for a set of carpenter's tools: angle iron, mallet, pickax, cross ax, carpenter's ax, broadax, claw hammer, various bucksaws, handsaw, groove saw, backsaw, various chisels and drills, tongs, crowbar. Wesselin threw himself enthusiastically on the tools and started playing with them at once. Laura called the collection a museum. Benno suggested storing the treasures in the cellar when they had an apartment together. 'Won't they rust down there?' asked Laura. 'If the cellar is damp, we'll have to store the tools in the attic,' said Benno. 'An apartment without a suitable cellar or attic is really unlivable for us, indubitably.' — 'Indubitably,' said Laura too. Later, when Wesselin was already asleep and the moon was shining on the white blobs of foam floating past the cottage on the water, Laura talked about her time in Heidenau. When she had worked as an engine driver for the district construction company. Shoptalk in the damp air. Kisses. 'Old Wittig, who was a member of our team at the time, had a collection of tools like that too,' said Laura. 'Everybody knew Wittig, a real character, at festive company occasions he would sometimes enter the stage unnoticed and perform "The Little Frogs" and other comical songs with gusto. The event organizers feared him because he was unstoppable, he only read union newspapers, he rejected radio and TV. I think it's getting more and more difficult to assert oneself as a real character. The mass media level everything out. My grandfathers could build cottages as a matter of course. Without having been taught how. My father didn't try. If I hadn't helped raise buildings myself, I would feel dependent in my apartment. Not sovereign. I think my cellar would be dry enough.' — 'Lady,' cried Benno at that, scooped the clammy Laura into his arms, carried her into the living room of the cottage, and stoked the stove until it glowed.

Chapter 7

Wherein the Reader Finds a Story That Laura Tells Benno at the Midnight Hour on the Cottage Sofa

Shipment: One day, when a big shipment of rare animals for the zoo had arrived at the Schönefeld airport, the customs official discovered an extra crate during delivery. In the crate sat a king. The zoo director had not ordered him. He refused to accept the king. He justified his refusal as follows: a) on principle, if he were to accept everything that was brought or sent to him unsolicited, he'd soon have to use his employees for animal feed. Also, the whole concept would be destroyed; this was a zoo, not a barnyard. And b) he argued based on the interests of the visitors to whom a subsidized enterprise of a pedagogical nature had to be accountable. And c) he insisted on serious business. Contractual partners who violated the contractual agreements could expect neither hard currency nor exchange animals. On top of that, there was, to the best of his knowledge, no base of experience related to keeping kings in zoological captivity. He ordered the shipment to be sent back to Asia at the sender's expense. Forklift trucks maneuvered thirty-one shipping crates with fifty-seven animals onto trucks. Which transported the load carefully to the quarantine area. The most expensive animal was a girl giraffe. Her crate was two meters eighty in height. The costs of transporting the king were lower, yet considerable when compared with lions, hyenas, and vultures, because of his accessories, for a king without accessories is not a king, while an animal needs nothing in order to be an animal. Throne, crown, robe with a train, and other insignia took up half his crate. It was lined with velvet. His golden slippers rested on straw. The director looked it over after his initial anger had subsided. Shortly a keeper ventured to approach him and the crate, expressing political concerns. To the effect that the unrequested shipping of the king could have been prompted by political, possibly even progressive motives, perhaps the sender's country was in a state of civil war. The fact that a king was neither shot nor incarcerated but rather deported did not necessarily cast doubt on the sender's revolutionary position but might indicate a complex internal political situation. The keeper thought the novel manner of deportation, at first glance disconcerting, was a political gesture. The zoo director thought it was a provocation but declared himself ready to have the king transferred to the quarantine station until the facts of the case were clarified. The king was entrusted to the politically qualified keeper's care. He soon regretted his initiative. Because the king refused to take any nourishment, even refusing liquids if they were served to him in a standing position. While the keeper, forced to his knees in an extortionary manner, had to serve delicacies from the specialty shop on Unter den Linden, the zoo director made inquiries and carried out an extended exchange of letters. Without result, probably due to turbulent internal political conditions in the king's country of origin or because the new government was overwhelmed. The zoo director suspected that the return address was wrong. He reclaimed the letters he had signed.

When these efforts also came to naught, he ordered that the king be forcibly habituated to a normal diet of 1,900 calories with 70 grams of protein per day and quartered in the lion house. He can be viewed there from 9:00 A.M. to 6:00 P.M. weekdays as well as on Sundays and holidays in a glass display case decorated with climbing plants. Next to Ira, the Bengal tigress, and the silver lions. The keeper believes that having these neighbors challenged the king's vanity and induced him to break off his hunger strike so as not to lose his physical attractiveness. Since the king still refuses to speak – whether from general exclusivity or only because the available conversational partners do not seem to befit his station has not been determined – his name and nationality are still not known. The word 'King' is engraved on the brass plate. Visitors read it in astonishment and exchange historical knowledge and opinions about procedural issues. Many women write in the complaint book that the exhibit would be politically more convincing if king and robe were displayed separately, some doubt that the semiprecious stones on the crown and scimitar are genuine, a few demand that the king be disarmed for security reasons, most of the men are in favor of having him shot and stuffed. From these reactions and from communications by letter, the zoo director believes it can be concluded that the exhibit has a certain pedagogical usefulness. However, he has not yet presented it at the Friedrichsstadt Palace. Only on Saturdays, on the day of fasting, is the king permitted to leave the cage for a time. Usually he takes advantage of the opportunity for a walk in the park. Since the golden slippers, train, and other insignia would interfere with walking, the keeper lends the king leather shoes and a trench coat. The clothing makes him unprepossessing and inconspicuous in the stream of visitors, without his collar and leash nobody would know he was a king.

Chapter 8

Principled speech to Benno, delivered by Laura over a glass of red wine

Herta? That's Frau Kajunke to you. Tenants talk about a lot of things they don't understand. My neighbor gave me her trolley key when I had to retake a test. The one lying in the bookcase there, the copper one. Collector's item. One doesn't have to be a funeral orator in order to become more closely acquainted with death. Without Herta the S-Bahn would still be just a means of transportation for me, something you ride and that's the end of it. I don't deny that I changed my profession partly from curiosity or that I prefer traveling occupations. But the best can lose its shine when it's right in front of you every day. Herta made me curious, not about the S-Bahn but about her, first of all. I can call her Herta, she trained me. Challenges are educational. Personal ones in particular. The person can show herself in words or directly. The stronger the person, the stronger the effect. Teachers, for example, to the extent that this word designates the profession and not the activity, are magicians. A TV press conference that the newly elected President of Chile, Dr. Salvador Allende, held for West German journalists, was dominated by the sheen of pride that disqualified the interviewers. The good fortune of experiencing a proud personality is unsettling. Unsettling experiences of this kind challenge people. Without challenges they degenerate. Since Herta had a difficult start as one of the first women trolley drivers, she preferred to train women. From her I acquired the habit of standing while driving. Left hand on the switch button, right hand on the brake valve, ahead of me the ribbon of track that the train eats up, at sixty, at eighty kilometers per hour, bridges, steep railway embankments, brown from the rust of the brake dust, train stations, also rusty, houses, signal lights green, yellow, red, quays, silos, you feel the thump of the rails under your feet and the speed of the train and how full it is. The over-filled commuter trains ride heavily and gobble a lot of electricity. You can really feel a train only if you stand. Your decision to deliver funeral orations for two weeks was effective, perhaps a defiant reaction, also a compliment for me. Don't let anyone tell you that you look older when you're unshaven, Benno; after all, a woman doesn't make herself look older in order to conform to her older husband. Ach, Benno, I believe you have more worries than you realize. By the way, a carpenter with training as a crane operator is, of course, superior to me; I can only identify damage, you know? Lately regulation no. 2 keeps coming to me in a dream: *all clear ahead – be prepared to stop*. I pull the lever of the driver's brake valve slowly toward me, the power of the train rears up under my feet. I pull into the station to respectful applause. Always the Ostkreuz station. Never fear: all the traveling people in my family are sedentary. Herta drives umpty-thousand passengers every day and never arrives herself. Shift work makes it hard on her these days. Hard on her health. She too started as a car cleaner. Two years on the washing ramp, I was there only six weeks, and my hands were already ruined from the lye and pumice powder. Without pumice or whiting, you can't get the rust off the cars. Ever since I've been driving, I like the smell of brake dust. Incidentally, not all the tenants call Herta by her first name. A woman colleague who brought me a box of candy in the hospital when Wesselin was born was in a rage about an accident. 'Anyone who wants to kill himself should buy a noose or turn on the gas or something,' she said, 'just because of this suicide our money is down the drain,' she said. Obviously, with delays like that, your bonus is gone. People say *du* to Herta because they think she's a volunteer. People don't like to give up well-loved habits. Could be that they need something to feel contempt for. In order to enhance their uprightness. The married women still ask her why she doesn't want to get married. But she doesn't get in their face. She drives. It's understandable that they didn't want to hire you because of your age. It surprises me that they hired you at all. Lack of personnel same as everywhere else; nobody wants to work as a funeral orator any more. From the number of invitations to hold wakes, I gather that you find consoling words for widows. For the ones who have a corpse to show. Herta doesn't have one. She still likes to drive. But she doesn't like time off. She used to spend her day off sleeping or driving a special shift. Now she sits herself down in front of the TV and has examples held up to her. Or she listens to records. Or she reads a book. Sometimes a man still strikes up a conversation with me when I have the night shift, she says. Sometimes one rides along in the conductor's car until I've finished my route. For simplicity's sake the gentlemen turn to a waitress or a woman conductor or the likes of us, she says. At first that ploy was offensive to me, she says. My friendship with Herta created antagonism for me. In the company too. Not officially. After all, Herta has four or five activist's medals in her jewelry case. I don't expect that a forty-eight-year-old woman exists for you as a woman, I only expect that she should exist for you at all, as a human being. Herta says that many men of her generation are crippled as human beings, either through experiences in the war or through experiences after it. They have just as much difficulty coming to terms with this damned surplus of women any other way. She says that most of them are incapable of loving, they think they're doing a woman a favor by permitting her to love a rarity. Maybe that kind of offer was the reason why she once turned on the gas. He who doesn't love, lives separated from himself, says Herta. And defends herself. But she lives relatively free of lies. Herr Buschmann's wife preaches loudly in the corridor that married men were always taboo for her. As if she didn't know that of the few men of this generation who survived the war, even the biggest dimwit found a wife. For Herta there are only married men. You are wrong if you think this embarrassing problem has disappeared meanwhile, died out, praise God. Many people think love is a seasonal phenomenon that appears in life between seventeen and twenty-five, period. I tell you: anyone who recognizes only this season has no talent for love. Herta got married at nineteen, her husband was granted a three-day leave for the wedding, then he went back to the front, and she never heard from him again. Six years later they declared him dead and her a widow. Most women of this generation are widows without ever having been married. Herta knows this, of course. She has a talent for love. Talented men are highly regarded. Talented women are not — officially. The fact that most of these women struggle through life more quietly makes them neither less talented nor more normal. We owe all of them respect equally. You didn't experience the war in air-raid shelters as I did, you experience it this way. Leave your temporary job, Benno, ring the doorbell of my neighbor Frau Kajunke if you want to get acquainted with death a little bit.

Chapter 9

Laura calls 22 88 020, asking for the Beautiful Melusine in person in order to consult with her

Scene: *Laura's room.*

Time: *Night in late winter.*

Laura is shoveling ashes out of the tiled stove into a bucket. Leaves the room with the bucket. The stove door remains open. When Laura returns, she sits down, knitting in front of an electric heater. Noises similar to those made while cleaning the chimney. Cloud of soot from the open stove door, then Melusine.

LAURA (*indignant*): What a mess, yesterday I beat the carpet, couldn't you be a little careful?

MELUSINE (*brushing off her human upper body, which is covered by a blackened sweater*): The chimney is too narrow. I've got scratches all down the armor on my back. But if it doesn't suit you, I can fly away again.

LAURA: Stop! Of course, I would rather have had Beatrice. How come you can produce Benno and not Beatrice?

MELUSINE: Because every larger act of magic that I do is subject to approval. The approvals are arbitrarily granted or denied at the highest level; Persephone can only mediate. Marriage-initiation requests are usually processed benevolently by Mr. Lord God. I assume that you called me about the marriage-initiation situation.

LAURA: Yes. That is, no. More precisely: I'm not sure. She who must do without the support and advice of a woman friend in tricky situations is up the creek without a paddle. Could you stand in for Beatrice for a moment?

MELUSINE: I could if I can.

LAURA: Certainly. You know Benno inside and out. Is he really the way he talks and acts?

MELUSINE: Yes.

LAURA: Does he love Wesselin?

MELUSINE: Very much.

LAURA: Does he love me as a representative of my gender or personally?

MELUSINE: I believe personally as well. But if you don't love him . . .

LAURA: My marriage and all subsequent marriagelike situations were based on love. On my side, at any rate, that's certain. And love, which as you know effects a wonderful narrowing of consciousness, always cast the men in such a favorable light that I overlooked their egotism at first: I was building on sand. For me only the opposite route would be possible now, if any at all. I feel friendship for Benno. If, in addition to love, he also feels friendship toward me, actively, I mean, I would risk marrying again.

MELUSINE: Without love on your side?

LAURA: It will grow if there is peaceful accommodation.

MELUSINE: Do you think so?

LAURA: One must face great decisions as one does death. Of course, every human being knows he must die some day. But his body doesn't quite believe it. He lives as if he were an exception. And it's the only way he can live.

MELUSINE: A man from the generation of twenty-year-olds would have come closer to your ideas, of course. But you want to keep the age difference as small as possible. Why, actually? The situation with new moral customs is like that with new scientific theories, of which Max Planck once said that they gain acceptance not because the proponents of the old scientific theories became convinced of the new ones but because the proponents of the old theories die.

LAURA: Thank you. Actually, I have an appointment to meet Benno tomorrow morning at the registry office in order to post the banns. I think I'm going to go. Actually, I was there once already. To ask how the new marriage law regulates names. I had already lost my name once by marriage under the old law. That was at age twenty-one; at the time it only hurt my feelings. I got it back through divorce. Forever, I thought, in the Soviet Union women can keep their names if they want to, I was actually sure of my ground and only wanted confirmation. The woman at the office kindly explained to me that married couples must carry a common name, either the man's or the woman's, according to the new marriage law too. According to the wishes of large segments of the population, she said. Really, what large segments are those, I said, laughing scornfully. Generosity costs nothing when you have the traditions on your side. The woman switched to a decisive tone of voice, emphasizing that she was not the complaint department, anyway several young men had already been there who were prepared to give up their names. I yelled, I'm not some young man to whom the label under which he becomes a man is unimportant, I'm a finished woman. When you impose a different name on a forty-year-old person, you wound his integrity. My name is Salman and my son's name is Salman – and that's that. That's more or less what I babbled. Spitting into the wind, of course, shooting peas at the wall or rather the law. If I want to spare Benno, whom I also believe to be a finished person, from having his integrity wounded, of course I must give in. As a consolation prize for my capitulation, I am granted the right, because of my minstrel activity, to add my name to the family name: Laura Pakulat-Salman. Not the other way around: even the sequence is rigidly prescribed. It aggravates hell out of me. But I can't invite you to the wedding, unfortunately.

MELUSINE (*takes hold of her reptilian tail and passes it over the top of Laura's head three times*): You have my blessing. (*Off through the door of the stove.*)

Chapter 10

BEATRICE RETURNS

On 10 March 1972 Laura read in the newspaper *Neues Deutschland* that the law on the termination of pregnancy had been accepted by the People's Chamber of the German Democratic Republic by an absolute majority, with fourteen opposing votes. The news prompted Laura to take off her clothes and stand in front of the mirror for a while, taking stock of her no longer state-controlled assets. Seeing them as property to be taken for granted seemed a learnable task. On 13 March Benno gave his last funeral oration and returned to his construction job the next morning. On 17 March at about 8:00 A.M., Beatrice de Dia stood before the door of Laura's apartment. Weary but beautiful as ever. In the first moment of surprise, Laura could think of nothing better to do than call for Wesselin. Then she clasped her friend in her arms, welcomed her loudly, and immediately thanked her for Benno, who outshone Lutz. Wesselin wasn't yet used to his mother's being loud. He clung anxiously, already crying, to her skirt. Suddenly he stopped. Laura suspected it was due to nature's call and headed toward the potty. Then she spotted a small animal next to Beatrice's right pant leg. Which she would have recognized as a dog right away if there hadn't been a corkscrewlike horn towering from its head between the ears. Making bleating noises, Wesselin patted its pale coat with his little hands, stroking it, he kissed the animal on the nose, peered into its ears, pulled its tail. The animal tolerated everything. Silently. Not until Wesselin, tempted by the red color of the harness on its head, bit eagerly into the leather, did the animal make a sound. It barked. 'So it is a dog,' said Laura, even before making sure that the corkscrewlike horn was fastened to the harness. A leash led from the harness to Beatrice's elbow. 'Are you going to palm this mongrel off on me as a unicorn?' asked Laura exuberantly. 'Heaven forbid,' said Beatrice, handing her a little alabaster box, 'your City Council Assembly mandate was a hoax too.' — 'But your election to PEN wasn't,' said Laura and bombarded her friend with curiosity. At that, Beatrice declared she was sound as a bell in body and soul, fell into an armchair with satisfaction, and said, 'There really is no place like home.'

Chapter 11

Wherein the reader finds excerpts from that memorable speech by Dr. Ludwig Mecklinger, Minister of Health Services of the German Democratic Republic, in which he justified the law on termination of pregnancy to the People's Chamber on 9 March 1972

Mr. President!

Most honorable representatives!

The draft bill before the house was brought to the People's Chamber by the chairman of the Council of Ministers to implement a mutual decision by the Politbüro of the Central Committee of the Socialist Unity Party and the Council of Ministers.

Its point of departure is that equal rights for women in education and the professions, in marriage and the family in the German Democratic Republic shall also be linked to the woman's right to decide on her own responsibility whether to carry a pregnancy to term or to end it prematurely.

The draft bill provides that a decision to terminate a pregnancy, hitherto made by government commissions at the district or regional level, shall be granted *in trust and substantially expanded* to women by the socialist state, in keeping with their rights and their dignity in socialist society.

Women will be given the possibility, beyond that of contraception, to counteract the biological accident of a pregnancy and to freely decide to pursue wanted motherhood.

Again and again, we find that an unwanted, unplanned pregnancy creates extraordinarily complex problems for women in marriage — including those in which the desire for children is firmly established. Not infrequently, successfully begun or soon to be completed professional developments are called into question or marriage crises are triggered. The personal happiness of the wife and husband, the happiness and harmony of the marriage and family can be overshadowed and endangered by severe psychic stress, which sometimes seems hopeless to individual persons.

Naturally, our socialist social order can claim for itself — this has long since been proven — that no woman, no marriage, and no family need be left to its own devices to solve their problems on their own. The assistance, advice, and welfare services that are daily called upon by government offices, the employees of the Health Service, and other social forces for the solving of such problems are diverse and effective. But we would be mistaken about life if we believed that in every individual case the conflicts which often accompany an unwanted pregnancy could be eliminated in this way.

In the last few weeks since the publication of the mutual decision, I have had many confidential conversations with doctors, especially gynecologists. In these conversations doctors expressed the feeling of being liberated from a great psychic burden by the forthcoming new legal ruling, because in their office hours and in the clinic they were often confronted by the serious consequences of self-abortion and back-alley procedures.

Many doctors also pointed out that they are often the only ones in whom the woman confides the serious concerns triggered by an unwanted pregnancy, initiating them into their difficult situation without making it public. They called attention to the fact that hitherto the doctor could respond to great personal suffering and inner deprivation, including the psychically based threat to health, only with good advice and a helping ability to empathize. The legal ruling will, therefore, protect many women from severe damage to their health.

Most honored representatives! Making legal rulings of this kind, which enable women to determine the timing of pregnancy for themselves, was supported in particular by the revolutionary workers' movement. It regarded the meeting of this demand as an important step in the process of the social liberation of women and as an indispensable next logical step toward recognizing and granting an elementary right to women.

This problem has found eloquent expression in sociopolitical literature of past decades as well as in art and drama. The Communist Party faction of the German Reichstag forwarded a resolution in October 1931 to lift legal control of termination of pregnancy. In so doing, it denounced the double morality of the exploitative society that made expensive terminations of pregnancy possible for women of the ruling class while leaving working women on their own in desperate situations and with tormented consciences via hypocritical hollow phrases and cold legalese.

The property owners of the exploitative society have always found and still do find a way to eliminate a pregnancy that is inconvenient to them, while many working women, wives, and mothers are forced to take actions that bring them into conflict with the law and their personal ethical views. Under conditions of capitalism, the revolutionary workers' movement demands the decontrol of termination of pregnancy, assuming that the exploitative society is not in a position to solve social problems in general or those of women in particular.

Fulfilling this demand in socialism has a fundamentally different point of departure, as is shown also by the legal rulings in other socialist countries.

The decisive motive for giving women the right to decide on carrying a pregnancy to term is derived from equal rights for women, which can be realized in socialist society. In this logical step, a humanly understandable desire, respected by the workers' and farmers' state, is fulfilled for many women, marriage partners, and families simultaneously: the desire that women can prepare for motherhood with joy and anticipation and that the child will be surrounded at birth by a climate of being wanted and of responsibly prepared security. Wanted children mean happiness and fulfillment for the woman, the man, and the family. Wanted children are the goal and content of every harmonious marriage in socialist society.

Most honored representatives!

Marriage, family, and motherhood are under the special protection of the socialist state. This principle is anchored in article 38 of the Constitution of the GDR. The development of healthy, harmonious, and happy marriages; the founding of lasting families; the fostering of love for children; the heightening of the joy of giving birth are indispensable attributes and a principle concern of socialist politics. Let us remember that our republic set down a clear declaration of universal protection of women, mothers, and children as well as equal rights for women in the very first year of its existence, in September 1950, with the statute for the protection of mothers and children and for women's rights.

The GDR's family law book of 20 December 1965 sets itself the task of promoting the development of the family in socialist society. It is intended to help all citizens, especially younger people, to consciously shape their family life.

In our socialist state, the right to work, to education, and to equal pay, which is emblematic for women's equality, has been realized. Today it is already taken for granted in social praxis. Diverse measures to alleviate the lives and responsibilities of women in family and profession were put into action — and others will follow.

This consistent policy of the socialist state simultaneously created those favorable conditions for comprehensive health care for working women and mothers, whereby the GDR assumes a respected international position in important health policy decisions.

We are not content with these successes. The struggle to save and to sustain the lives of our youngest citizens will be continued with great intensity, as will the battle on behalf of the life and health of the mother.

The planned legal ruling — many citizens also point this out in their statements on the published common decision — agrees completely with the principles of our socialist state's family, social, and health policy. Indeed, beyond that: with its positive effects on wanted motherhood and conscious family development, it can and will promote love for children. It will help strengthen many marriages, support harmonious life in many families, and be an effective contribution to the social development of woman in her role as mother and worker.

The women of the GDR will make responsible use of the right granted to them. Hundreds of thousands of our women, along with their husbands, demonstrate this responsible awareness toward society and its development by giving birth to children in the interest of personal, family happiness and the requirements of society, introduce them to life with great love and care, and raise them to be dependable, strongly principled, knowledgeable, and forward-striving citizens of our socialist state. Such an attitude toward children and family will always have the strong and effective support of the socialist state.

The published mutual decision of the Politbüro of the Central Committee of the Socialist Unity Party and the GDR's Council of Ministers has found strong approval in the population of the GDR. The citizens value the decision as the logical next step of a societal development in the GDR by which equal rights for women were achieved.

In this connection the government believes it is desirable to inform the People's Chamber about questions that were raised in recent weeks by citizens in discussions with respect to the proposed legal ruling. Some citizens fear that the law on termination of pregnancy could encourage signs of immorality among young people and in particular that young people's desire to found a family could be displaced by an attitude of convenience. We do not share this opinion. Our young people have always justified the trust placed in them by the Party and the government. In recent years they have often proved their highly developed sense of responsibility in the decisive focal points of our social and economic development — and they continue to do so today.

Our responsible young citizens in young marriages do not want to give up the happy experience of family, of children. They know very well that the family has a firm place in socialist society, that the founding of a family is promoted by society, and that children experience the great love and care of the socialist state.

Fostering love for children, strengthening the family in socialist society, and heightening the joy of giving birth will always be a fundamental concern of socialist policy in the GDR.

Some citizens express the concern that women could suffer damage to their health by exercising their right to choose.

Of course, even a termination of pregnancy that is expertly performed by a doctor is, like every other surgical procedure, not entirely without danger. But it has been proven that the possible health risks associated with a termination of pregnancy performed by a specialist and based on current scientific knowledge are not at all in proportion to the serious injuries resulting from self-abortions and irresponsible quackery that our doctors had to treat in the past, injuries that not infrequently resulted in disability for the woman, in some tragic cases even in death.

Thanks to advances in medicine and the achievements of the Health Service, the women of the GDR have for some time had the possibility of avoiding unwanted pregnancy with safe means of contraception. These means of contraception, proven to be the best method of individual family planning, are being further researched and expanded.

In the future our women will make even greater use of these means of contraception in exercising their right to determine the timing of pregnancy themselves. In this, they will be supported by the doctors and other employees of the Health Service through comprehensible individual education and through intensified activity of the counseling centers for sex and marriage.

The Council of Ministers has also been informed that religiously devout women relate their reservations about the legal ruling to their religiously motivated moral concepts. In this respect, however, it must be clearly and unambiguously stated that the matter of concern in this law consists in granting a right to women commensurate with the achieved equality of rights in socialist society. Of course, it is left up to the woman's discretion to make use of this right or not.

In the draft of the law, restrictions on a legally permitted termination of pregnancy are determined in the interest of protecting the woman's health and life. Thus the pregnant woman has the right to terminate a pregnancy within twelve weeks of conception. In an implementation decree, the Minister of Health Services will, among other things, establish clear guidelines for how the woman can proceed with her request, that is, without a written application, to her family or company doctor, to a gynecologist in an outpatient medical institution, or to the appropriate pregnancy counseling center. The Minister of Health Services will define the doctor's responsibility to inform the pregnant woman of the nature of the surgical procedure and as part of this responsibility, to advise her on future use of contraceptives. These will be confidential discussions in which our women are interested and the content of which is obviously strictly subject to the physician's pledge of confidentiality.

The preparation for, performing of, and postoperative treatment of a termination of pregnancy permitted by this law are legally treated the same as an illness for purposes of work and insurance. This ruling is commensurate with the basic law that entitles all insured citizens of the GDR to take advantage of medical treatment free of charge.

The draft bill before the house also provides for distribution of contraceptives free of charge. Hereby the government wishes to particularly emphasize, in the interest of women, the desirable advantages of this method of preventing pregnancy as compared to termination of pregnancy.

Sex and marriage counseling, which is already used by many young citizens, is increasingly becoming a meeting place where the citizen turns in confidence with intimate questions of his marriage and its development to expert advisors, who respond to his trust with help and advice.

The Health Service will increase its efforts to clarify still unexplained causes of some cases of childlessness to help fulfill the unrealized desire for children in many marriages. The great contribution made by women and mothers to our societal development has always had the special appreciation of the party of the working class and the government of the GDR. The GDR will continue the path of comprehensive protection and promotion of working women, mothers, children, and the family by purposefully employing its social, scientific, economic, material, and cultural resources under the leadership of the party of the working class.

I ask you on behalf of the Council of Ministers to cast your vote for the bill before the house.

Chapter 12

Wherein They Finally Get Married

Even after Beatrice had slept three days and three nights, she preferred to spend her time in Laura's armchair. The dog on her feet. Her forehead smoothed by contentment. Her lips pursed by lethargy.

For the only words that crossed them were the few needed to assert that the GDR really is the promised land for women. But Laura, in her compulsory settledness, urgently awaited news of the great, wide world: travel substitute. Not a sentence about foreign lands and people, not a word of explanation or apology for the telegrams from Italy and the hunting report. Not even utopian speeches or hair-raising theories. Wasn't Beatrice ashamed of thus ignoring her friend's justifiable demands for housewife compensation? Was psychic cruelty the thanks Laura got for her stationary activity? Had the trobadora, protestations to the contrary notwithstanding, perhaps suffered physical and psychic damage? Laura's disappointment was alleviated by the fact that she constantly felt she was being watched. In contrast to before, Beatrice followed her friend's household activities with interest. Wordlessly at first. After a week she began asking Laura questions. How did you make a roux, Beatrice wanted to know, what detergents did you use for laundry that must be boiled, did paper diapers crumble, why did Laura hang her curtains wet in the windows. Laura was glad to answer the questions. The more so because Beatrice commented to Laura that in all her travels she had never seen a man as sweet as Benno. Benno commented to Laura that a poet as interested in housework as Beatrice seemed to him a little scary. But since he experienced love as indirect proof, of an aesthetic kind, that there is a God, one miracle more or less made no difference to him. After a beautiful orgasm, he had accepted Laura's story of the trobadora's previous life more readily than a newspaper report about Ireland. On the third day after her arrival, Beatrice asked Laura, 'Are you happy?' Laura answered, 'Without the abolition of paragraph 218, the pill was a solution for superwomen. That is, for people who never make a mistake, forget, miss a step. The medication alone could liberate women from fear only relatively, not principally. Only now does what belongs to us really belong to us. The effects are still unforeseeable. At any rate, my life would have turned out very differently if I'd had possession of my body from the time I was a girl. I wouldn't have planned my profession only with reservations, would have wasted less time with sublimated romances, would have chosen more intense lovers, wouldn't have married Uwe. Indeed, personalities living in fear develop very differently than others, if at all. They think differently, feel differently, produce different things with their hands and heads. Physical unfreedom is surely scarcely less crippling than political unfreedom. And no original achievements can be expected from cripples. Up to now, men have played destiny for women. That is past. But it will surely take a very long time before the female sex learns to use the productive force of sexuality in a sovereign manner. Together with all previous woman-friendly measures and laws, legal equality has been realized in our state with the new law. Only on this basis does moral equality have a chance to grow; it cannot be prescribed. I understand why you now feel really at home here.' Beatrice took charge of all the private organizational preparations for the wedding, which was celebrated in a socialist manner on 9 May in the clubhouse of the State Enterprise Construction at company expense. With all the members of Benno's brigade, their wives, Laura's parents, the singing club 'Salute,' representatives of the company, Party, and union leadership, and the registrar of births, marriages, and deaths. After the civil ceremony the team leader presented flowers and an electric grill as a collective gift; the representatives of the company, Party, and union leadership presented speeches, flowers, and books; the singing club sang FDJ songs and fight songs. The club kitchen rang up no less than 46 asparagus cream soups, 58 servings of rump steak with mushrooms and *pommes frites,* 57 bowls of ice cream, 31 bottles of white wine, 18 bottles of red wine, 110 bottles of beer, 21 bottles of seltzer water, 4 bottles of pop, 12 glasses of fruit wine, and 64 cups of coffee. Beatrice sang a wedding song that Paul Wiens had been commissioned to produce on short notice instead of the canso for Professor Wenzel Morolf, before the band, 'Green Gold,' got their instruments going. Laura's parents applauded enthusiastically. The song convinced them of its singer's existence. The bridal couple didn't miss a dance. Since the band played remarkably many English waltzes and similar indecent pieces for close dancing, Benno and Laura took turns leading, in order to save their energy for the real dances. During the wedding night the Beautiful Melusine watched over Wesselin's sleep.

Chapter 13

Wedding song, composed on commission by Paul Wiens, set to music and played by the singing club 'Salute,' performed by Beatrice de Dia, reproduced here in the lowercase spelling advocated by the poet

amidst the wedding party
  you're seated hand in hand.

thus sing i ONE to welcome
the future in and witness
your formally attested
  matrimonial intent.
my dear young people, marriage
  is not an easy state,
it means, and not just sometimes,
a harmony of voices,
  a slow-combustion flame.

TWO: as newly wedded partners
  you may well bill and coo,
a nest for your child feather,
live brotherly together,
  your hearts will take wing too,
desire much and much render,
  with one another rest,
with every limb and member
  each treat the other best.

THREE: yet at the height of love-play
  as you cling and entwine,
remember: we are many.
and feelings oft will vary
  throughout your love and life.
desire fuels ardor.
  time urges us on harder.
be with us as we rally!
  be a man, and be a wife!

FOUR: he who this song has written,
  by beatrice bewitched,
to lovers all sends wishes
that life be beer and skittles
  and bring a bag of tricks
to use when it seems fittin',
  fair slowly merry quick
and lifelong be committed
  through thin and so through thick.

Chapter 14
A KIND OF ULTIMATUM

The morning after the wedding, the minstrel informed her trobadora that she was leaving shortly on a trip. 'Where will your honeymoon take you?' asked Beatrice. 'I'm traveling alone,' said Laura. 'And Benno is keeping Wesselin?' asked Beatrice. 'Benno is going to soccer training camp,' said Laura. 'You're keeping Wesselin. Did you get your introduction to housework for nothing? I've been stuck at home long enough; now you're taking over the stationary post.' Beatrice could find no way to counter Laura's logic. Admired it, actually; the image that the trobadora had made of her friend during her travels had meanwhile become a role model. Which Beatrice resolved to emulate. The newspapers she had been reading since her return reinforced her efforts along these lines in principle. So she reluctantly asked what Laura's destination was. And Laura promptly replied, 'Almaciz or someplace like that.' At that, Beatrice thought that, for various reasons, it was high time to suppress her reluctance to tell stories, which was based on reluctance to remember. And before lunch she had described her experiences in the Rapallo area to the newly wedded couple. The narrative is found in abbreviated form in the next chapter.

Chapter 15
RAPALLO AND OTHER THINGS

We arrived in Rapallo on a Saturday afternoon. We, that means my recently hired traveling companion – whom I will call Simon; the gentleman's name and nationality are unimportant – and I. A brief, warm drizzle. Orange trees along the streets. All the large shops and the banks of course closed. And I had run out of lire. I only had dollars with me, in a money pouch worn next to my skin, just barely a quarter of the amount that the Beautiful Melusine had magically provided me. Since I feared that I would really be taken for a ride by taxi drivers and waiters if I paid with dollars, I called upon Simon to ask a confidence-inspiring young traffic cop where to find an open currency exchange. The policeman, very friendly and helpful, wrote down the address of a tobacconist and gave us detailed directions. The tobacconist was also very obliging. The next day we happened to pass a chart of the exchange rates and realized that we had been swindled out of 1,500 lire. After our arrival we stowed our luggage at the train station as always and studied brochures for reasonably priced lodgings. We finally chose the hotel The Palms. The shriveled daughter of the proprietress, whose dignified bulk sat enthroned in one of the lobby armchairs, discussed prices and showed us two rooms. The more expensive one had a balcony from which a patch of sea could be seen. I decided on the more expensive one. Simon accompanied me for free room and board. A man who knows his way around and how to live, of French extraction. After paying a deposit on the room, we had eyes for the city. Which looks small. Like a frame for a bay. Promenade with palm trees and restaurants, of course. Steep coast on both sides where the bay opens out, with villas clinging to it. Pines. Cypresses. Mist. Toward evening we fetched our luggage in a taxi. For reasons of economy, we never used porters at train stations or other anonymous places. Each of us carrying his own suitcase. Fair. But as soon as we approached a hotel where we wanted to get out of the cab and be treated like guests, I had to degenerate into a lady. That is, act arrogant and carry nothing. To swim as you please along the beach in Rapallo and the surrounding area is just as impossible as, for example, on the French Riviera. Either the shores are private property or built-up strips of swimming pools. The so-called free beach that you can enter without paying a fee was a small heap of stones where refuse was washed up by the sea, even in Rapallo. Local children squatted cheek by jowl on this heap. Children on vacation went with their mothers to the pool that corresponded to their degree of middle class. One rarely sees whole families traveling. The good provider with a livelihood sends wife and children on vacation in summer, continuing to work during the greater part of this time while also resting up from his family. Consequently, there is a surplus of men in the big cities in the summer, at the vacation spots a surplus of women. On Sunday, contrary to all good sense, we looked for footpaths to unsupervised pieces of coast and, of course, found only highways. On Monday we decided to visit the pool next to the girls' boarding school. Entrance fee the equivalent of five marks, a nail to hang your clothes on in the common changing cabin three marks per person, obligatory use of deck chairs. The deck chairs stand in dense rows like movie seats. On cement. In Cannes and Nice mattresses are spread out on sand in a like arrangement. They vary in quality, according to the price range of the pool, and are shaded by variably attractive umbrellas, which one must also rent. The beach of the Hotel Pallas in Nice has sifted sand that is free of footprints in the morning. Between the sheet-covered mattresses are partitions, the first row of mattresses corresponds to the first floor, behind the last row of mattresses is the snack bar. Since we didn't give the pool attendant a tip, he placed us in the second-to-last row of deck chairs. Since the southern sun cannot be endured for long when you aren't moving, we also rented an umbrella for the equivalent of six marks. And dozed for two hours, boxed in by women and odors of oil and sweat. The women here talk as little among themselves as the passengers in first class. Only now and then did we hear a commanding word to the children, who mostly stayed in the water. After dozing away two hours, I no longer felt like swimming. We left, although we had not nearly sat our money's worth. In the afternoon to Portofino by ship. Wonderful sail along the bays. Overcast sky above the picturesquely somber vegetation of the steep coast. Leaden sea. Hothouse air. Portofino's harbor lies hidden. Narrow, angled entrance flanked by overgrown rocks. Suddenly the former fishing village bares its idyllic buildings for the tourists. Half-way. Like streetwalkers in low-cut dresses baring their breasts. In the buildings are nothing but restaurants and shops. In front of the buildings, male and female street vendors hawking souvenirs and crafts on tables, chairs, and trays. A large selection of pillow lace. Variable prices. American women bargained for large lace tablecloths and admired ancient lace makers in traditional costumes, who could be viewed working on the pillows. I bought an alabaster box. Ascent to the castle, which was for sale. We often saw signs with the words *da vendere* on lots and villas. From the castle garden and other secret places to sit, we had a view of the somberly beautiful splendor of the landscape, which the German painter Feuerbach favored in his pictures. Here and there a blossom still hung on the magnolias. On the oleander bushes abundance in white, pink, and red. These armlike pine branches! Return by ship as far as St. Margarita. In the hope of somewhere discovering a path that would yet bring us to a walk along the beach. A one-hour march in airstreams and exhaust fumes on the shoulder of a highway. After supper a search for Simon's friend Gianino. Who lives on Via Santa Maria and many years ago had arranged a tour for Simon through Genoa's houses of pleasure. We walked and walked; the Via Santa Maria stretched out. Only now did I realize that the little face of Rapallo's coast is deceptive. Hidden behind it is a sober town stretching far into the country. Which is growing; the house numbers on Via Santa Maria had already been changed twice. Gianino's address was no longer correct. But we were able to ask our way to his home: as a member of Italy's Communist Party, he was well known. Gianino, a black-haired fifty-year-old, greeted us passionately, apologizing for his undershirt and his wife's apron. He said they had just come from their places of work. He from his second, where he worked from 4:00 to 9:00 P.M. as a pool attendant – from 6:00 A.M. to 3:00 P.M. he worked as a lathe operator. He also asked us to excuse him for sending his wife to earn money at the pool. 'But only until September,' said Gianino. 'Then the three-piece furniture suite will be paid for.' He showed it proudly and said he was sorry not to have known about our visit, which is why the vases were missing from the buffet in the hallway. Assurances on both sides of uninterrupted leftist loyalty. The wife poured schnapps for her husband and the guests – not for herself. A robust figure, flat-featured face; she arranged her arms leisurely under her breasts. During our visit she stood in the background when she wasn't waiting on us. She spoke only when asked a question. Briefly and shyly, like a child. She was Gianino's age. She treated the simple furnishings and her husband with care, as if they were treasures. A stone floor, scoured smooth. In a little side room, Gianino played us a record with his voice on it. He introduced himself as a member of a traditional singing group that performed Genoese songs every Saturday and Sunday – mainly at Party events, of course – and was booked solid until September. But of course the group would accept an invitation to the GDR any time. He called special attention to the soprano part, which was sung by a man. While the record was playing, his wife turned out the light in the hallway. When Simon happened to mention that I am a writer, Gianino's black eyes suddenly got big, and from then on he paid attention to me. Toward midnight he drove us back to the hotel in his tiny car. Gianino doesn't take the car to work. Because the round-trip highway toll would be two hundred lire, not including gas. The proud owner of that little car gets on his bicycle every morning and then changes to the train. 'Here everyone is Catholic,' he said, 'politically, you understand. So they can stay on top. That's our dictatorship.' As we parted, we raised our clenched fists in greeting. The next morning a side trip to Genoa. By bus. Anyone who wants to see something of this coast must resort to movable containers, ships, cars, or buses; a mere pedestrian doesn't stand a chance. I had studied old guidebooks and was curious about the imposing buildings of the old city. We wandered around a long time trying to find the old city, receiving contradictory information from local people; three of them shrugged their shoulders when asked where the old palaces were.

Finally we found what we were looking for, somewhere in between new office buildings. Hemmed in, obstructed, dilapidated. The inexorable pace of this harbor city permits no piety whatsoever. The monument fig leaf, which is usual in other cities, is recklessly disregarded here. The side streets between the trivial old buildings reminded you of crevices. That become narrower toward the top. At the bottom of these very tall black dungeons are junk shops, children, prostitutes, marijuana dealers. Again Simon revealed his romantic inclination for vulgarity. For him as an observer, it was a particular variety of the exotic. As an involved party — at one time in Paris directly involved — I flee these sites of degradation. For the sight of them makes me wild with rage. Blind. Vindictive. Devoid of utopian inspiration. Before long Simon advised spaghetti in order to shake off a man who had been following us from the bus station. We chose a tiled room where longshoremen were eating lunch. Cheap. The exhausted waitress wrote out an honest bill. After our arrival in Rapallo that evening, when we were eating ice cream in a restaurant on the promenade, the waiter claimed not to have change, disappeared with a thousand lire, and didn't come back. He ignored Simon's calling for a while. Finally he condescended but didn't even make an effort to pretend he'd forgotten our four hundred lire. I mention these bothersome details that one constantly encounters not to denigrate the Italians by any means. On the contrary, I think the little people's efforts to fleece the tourists are completely legitimate. Those who see themselves continually and increasingly dispossessed of the beauties of their country at least have a right to material revenge. Can an Italian sit on a dirty heap of stones that is called public beach without getting raving mad? How is an Italian woman who has to make her way through life alone with her children, because unemployment has forced her husband to sell his labor in West Germany, supposed to develop sympathy for affluent tourists? A railroad strike kept us in Rapallo longer than planned. The strike helped us get some undisturbed sleep. Before that, the express trains whizzed past behind the hotel; it sounded as if the tracks led right through the room. Above the bed a reproduction of a Madonna with lowered eyes. A greeting from a strange man on the street, literally 'good day' or 'good morning,' must be understood by a decent woman strictly in terms of its implied meaning. The implied meaning is defamatory. A silently rejecting, hostile reaction is expected. Otherwise the status of slut may be directly or indirectly assumed. In this Catholic country the seducer who uses dastardly language still has great chances. For example, with girls whose mothers doll them up for the evening to parade along the promenade. Strictly guarded. Italian morals allow for female human beings in the manifestations of girl or mother. Everywhere in the city, there were moving automats with seats in the shape of animals, cars, or rockets that, after insertion of a coin, rocked children for a few minutes or lifted them into the air. My longing for an unsupervised stone increased. Simon suggested taking a ship to San Fruttuoso, where he knew of an isolated monastery and nothing else. The ship passed rocky walls, towering steeply out of the water. A stiff wind urged the ship and water toward the rocks. The monastery was no longer isolated but surrounded by restaurants. Which had left no remnant of undeveloped ground in the little rocky niche. Rental beach where the stones were gray-and-white striped like the palaces and the gravestones of the Doria family; some had oil clinging to them. A lace maker showed us the gravestones for a fee. On the water old men in boats hung around, wanting to show you the Christ of the Abyss, for a fee. The cost of seeing the statue of Christ sunk into the sea was too high for me; I contented myself with the documents of its good deeds. The church was full of pictures of shipwrecks and photos of those who had been saved. At noon we treated ourselves to two deck chairs for 2,400 lire and four sandwiches for 1,000 lire. The actual experience of this excursion was the walk to Portofino. Local people whom we asked the way told us the ship departure times. What we were planning can only seem harebrained to a southerner. But my longing for a road without traffic had by now taken on fanatical proportions. This one was guaranteed to be free of traffic. A good hour's climb up stairs. Mostly shadowed by laurel trees and bushes that appear green and juicy but are hard and prickly. At unshaded stretches where the stones radiated like glowing ovens, the heat made you dizzy. After only a half hour, the strain suppressed all capacity for enjoyment. I staggered unseeing through blooming myrtle bushes. And would perhaps have collapsed if a building had not unexpectedly beckoned at the top. On the shabby house you could read *Osteria Turistica*. In front of it stood two dilapidated wooden tables. One had a white tablecloth. The farmer's wife brought rolls, salami, and Coca-Cola at normal city prices. Her grandson covered his eyes with his hands to make himself invisible to us. Above us, a roof of grape leaves and grapes. Descent through the silvery arches of an olive grove. Celestial penumbra. Which made you forget all the strain. Under our feet gray-white striped stones of the sort we were carrying in our pockets from San Fruttuoso: the path was paved with paperweights. Above our heads was peace. The olive branch is its symbol because it can suggest it.

Chapter 16

Beatrice de Dia at the factory sponsoring Aufbau-Verlag

When Aufbau-Verlag learned of Beatrice's return, they invited her to lunch. Over turtle soup the editor-in-chief revealed that the subjects described thus far would not carry the montage novel and suggested several supporting subjects. In this way Beatrice learned indirectly of the documents forged by her minstrel. But remained calm and promised to keep to the contractual deadline. Beatrice narrowed down the suggested supporting subjects to:

Petrochemical Combine, Schwedt (Sponsor of Aufbau-Verlag)
The Thomas Müntzer Agricultural Production Cooperative, Eichwalde
State Enterprise Elite Diamond, Karl-Marx-Stadt
The Forestry Company, Suhl
State Enterprise Electrocarbon, Berlin
GISAG Combine, Leipzig
State Enterprise Potash, Zielitz

Only a week later an Aufbau-Verlag bus loaded with writers and editors left for Schwedt. Beatrice was assigned to a group that was to visit the company's department of TEN, *Technische Energienorm*. Mornings at the workplace. Afternoons in the meeting room. Evenings in the clubhouse. The electrical engineer G. led the tour of the workplaces, which were located in a montage hall. There they observed skilled workers, generators, transformers, cranes, wall news sheets. There contacts were established by means of looks and handshakes. There the electrical engineer G. defined heavy current and strove to explain what the visitors should understand by high-voltage installations. Beatrice took notes. Key words noting the engineer's complaints about the shortage of workers, before being repaired the generators and so on had to be cleaned, but there were no cleaners, there were only skilled workers, the desire to qualify had become so strong among his workers that he had to restrict them. The trobadora needed four full-sized pages to record the description of a total energy loss in the petrochemical combine. The

TEN department had been in operation for thirty-six hours without a break when that happened. During such accidents, which, thank God, happened rarely, since the machinery and equipment were overhauled as scheduled, the department workers were literally pursued by the clock. Which gobbled thousand-mark bills like an elephant eating hay, so to speak. Spurred on by the horrible feeling of becoming poorer by the minute, they searched feverishly for the defect on such occasions. Engineer G. admitted that his wife claimed he was married not to her but to the company. One evening spent working for the Party, two for qualification, two for AWG, but he did regularly spend the weekend with his family outside the city. Because he came from the Erzgebirge and didn't tolerate low-lying areas well. After lunch, which the visitors took in the dining hall with the brigade, the poet Pomerenke read in the meeting room. Pomerenke asked them to excuse the fact that he wrote only poems. His editor participated avidly in the discussion, which had to do with the Vietnam War. Beatrice read excerpts from a communiqué from the Supreme Command of the Armed Liberation Forces of South Vietnam about the great victories of the offensive during the month of 30 March to 1 May 1972. From 8:00 P.M. until midnight dancing with the brigade members and their families.

Chapter 17

The excerpts read by Beatrice from the communiqué from the Armed Liberation Forces of South Vietnam about the great victories of the offensive during the month of 30 March to 1 May 1972

Our people's resistance battle to save our nation from the American imperialists has entered a new phase and is continuing at a very favorable moment. To launch the victorious position and realize the decisions of the central committee of the National Liberation Front and the Provisional Revolutionary Government of the Republic of South Vietnam, the army and the people of South Vietnam have revolted, attacking the enemy on all sides and on a large scale, destroying the enemy's political and military forces.

Our army and our people have revolted and attacked in all combat sectors from Tri Thien to the Mekong Delta. We have fought continuously and most courageously for a month, and our army and our people have achieved glorious victories and exceptionally great successes on all sides. Powerful blows were dealt to a large segment of the enemy's elite forces, great quantities of the enemy's war materials were destroyed, and many of the defense lines built up by the enemy in over ten years were broken. The control and oppression apparatus of the U.S.-Thieu clique was toppled from the local to the provincial level; in many villages the plan for 'peacekeeping' was foiled, and many large areas were liberated.

In almost all provinces, our countrymen have risen up powerfully to become master of their own country, and many large areas in the provinces of My Tho, Ben Tre, Kien Phong, Kien Tuong, Rach Gia, Ca Mau, Can Tho, Soc Trang, and Tra Vinh have been liberated.

The armed people's liberation forces have made continuous progress, carrying out large-scale operations in cooperation with various arms of the military service and dealing powerful blows to the enemy. In a short period of time, we have decimated many divisions, regiments, brigades, and tank units of the Saigon puppet army commanded by U.S. military advisors and extensively supported by the artillery of the American Air Force and Navy 7th Fleet as well as by several units of the American ground troops and the mercenary troops of Pak Tschong Hi.

By coordinating the actions on all sectors of the front, the army and the people of all of South Vietnam have strengthened the partisan war, launched powerful attacks on the American and the mercenary logistic bases, destroyed a great number of camps, airports, and harbors as well as hundreds of tons of enemy weapons, bombs, missiles, and other war material, broken through strategic enemy transportation lines, blocked off streets, made waterways unusable, stopped airlines, caused the enemy many difficulties with respect to the mobility of replacement troops and suppliers of ammunition, and impeded the delivery of foodstuffs and war materials, so that the enemy troops surrounded at all sectors of the front have gotten into a most complex situation.

Chapter 18

More and more, Beatrice settles down and in

When Beatrice had returned from Schwedt, she began putting the theoretical knowledge she had gained from Laura to practical use. She wallpapered Laura's apartment with help from Benno, helped him move out and in, and gave her services as nanny so that the young couple could go dancing. Sometimes Beatrice let words suffice, however. For example, she declared the concrete ceiling that fell down on Laura's head several times a week to be a baldachin. Beatrice banished the frustrated trolley driver's longing for people and train stations with statements like: 'The more a human being can do without, the greater he is.' If Laura complained that her husband didn't like to wash his hair, Beatrice would say, 'Eyes that see only what exists are blind' and that sort of thing. At any rate, the trobadora's various helpful acts subdued Laura's wanderlust. Olga Salman sent her daughter letters every week, in which she wrote about her husband's retirement as if it were the beginning of real life. Olga gave 8 October as the date of his last trip. 'Will your mother go with her husband on his last trip?' asked Beatrice. 'No, why?' answered Laura and looked uncomprehendingly at Beatrice. 'Has she ever gone with him?' asked Beatrice. Laura smiled at her friend's unworldliness. But was very well satisfied with her diligence in studying. Indeed, she felt a satisfaction similar to that experienced by parental authorities when their instructions are followed. However, Beatrice's messenger work seemed to her too much of a good thing. During her excursion to the Petrochemical Combine Schwedt, the trobadora had met an editor of the weekly newspaper *Sonntag*, who had recommended that she take an unpaid position. However, the offer had not seemed modest enough to Beatrice, which is why she had decided on the messenger job. She wanted to study the grassroots subjects recommended to her by Aufbau-Verlag while on vacation – unpaid vacation, if need be; she didn't grant herself any other special favors. Like her messenger colleagues, she spoke contemptuously about those desiring to travel as people who wanted to compensate for their inner emptiness by consuming experience. Chance and the editor brought Beatrice into contact with a simple woman's documents, which captivated her. Reminded of Uwe Pakulat's words in Paris, Beatrice produced a legend based on the documents, experiences in the GISAG Combine-Leipzig, and other Bitterfeld impressions.

Chapter 19

First Bitterfeld fruit: The Legend of Comrade Martha in Testimonials

I wanted to make an image of a human being because he didn't want one. I met him by chance, like love itself, in testimonials: her. A woman.

Martha Lehmann by name. She had the habit of writing messages on the monthly rent slips, that is, on the backs of postal payment receipts, which, according to the printed form, are not to be used for messages for the recipient.

M.L. 8 March 1945 Our Rudy no longer with us, six months now. Unbelievable. Helmut wounded on 5 February in house-to-house fighting, on 3 March 1945 released from infirmary in Landsberg (Warthe). Denmark. Waiting for address. Our Walter in Hungary (monastery). Papa retired and gardening. Mama letter carrier, Leipzig no. 21. Two big raids on 27 February and 7 March 1945. God was merciful to us.

B. One of this woman's sons, Walter Lehmann, submitted a sketch of her life to a literary competition of the newspaper *Sonntag*. To illustrate it, he had enclosed a selection of those rent slips pasted in like an album: self-testimony. Along with it, testimonial papers from people who knew Martha Lehmann personally. I would like to testify for this woman because I did not know her personally.

M.L. 11 May 1946 Peace trade fair. Glorious weather. And exhibits at the exhibition center. Papa retired. Mama railroad worker. Helmut school principal in Stahmeln. Rudy is buried in Russian soil, unbelievable. Walter at teacher-training institute. Now there is peace. Thank God.

B. Lucky circumstances had brought the extraordinarily everyday documents to my attention. They moved me as elevated subjects rarely do. And in a manner that made me want to talk with this woman and describe her. Martha Lehmann expressed her aversion to publication to an editor who transmitted my request. Only while drafting a letter meant to change Martha Lehmann's mind did I realize that her refusal was the most precious part of this paragon.

M.L. 22 July 1946 My Lehmann is no longer with us. Simply unbelievable. Helmut a school principal. Rudy is buried in Russia. Walter is taking teacher exams. I'm at the railroad. Now there is peace. But my two dearest men are missing. Why? My Lehmann, my Rudy.

B. I believe that Martha Lehmann's modesty was also perfectly honest. Women have not yet entered written history in substantial ways, they are just beginning. The tradition of their ways of working can be felt, not measured. Legendary.

M.L. 11 April 1947 Now peace is here! But we miss Papa and Rudy very much. Unbelievable. Helmut a school principal in Stahmeln. Walter a teacher in the south. Mama a gate attendant in Möckern, booth 121. Now the worst cold is over, and there were already several thunderstorms the first of April. Walter has already sowed various seeds and pruned the hedges, and I am turning over the earth, since I like to do that. Ach, my Lehmann, the first spring without you in the settlement. You hardworking man, thank you for everything and for the sugar beets.

B. In this old woman's beauty shines the tough, boundless power of love for the living. This humble pride. Untouchable. The communist movement is founded on such people. They are fulfilled in it. Extraordinary events will incite even empty-headed people. For Martha Lehmann everyday life was not ordinary; no life can achieve more.

M.L. 16 December 1948, Booth 121 Just now (9:45) a train full of homecomers passed through toward the Möckern barracks. Some of them waved joyfully to me, some gazed fixedly. How wonderful it would be if our Rudy were among them. Couldn't a miracle happen? Maybe it will . . . Mild weather.

B. Martha Lehmann was not in God's graces but in her own. She set an example because she didn't set one. The world can be rallied to an alliance without specific news from people like her. With such news I live more securely. For it unveils the glory of the way; goals can be dreamed of easily, even without assistance. I place the beauty of this old woman beside the reports of the Eighth Party Congress.

W.L. When the first heavy freight train roared past my mother's gate-attendant hut in 1949, she stood at the track with a little red flag and greeted the engine driver, Paul Heine. The red flag was thirty-one years old. She had made such flags for her sons for the 1918 November revolution, so that the boys could demonstrate with the revolutionary sailors of Wilhelmshaven.

M.L. 5 May 1950, Booth 399, Rackwitz My Lehmann has been gone from me almost four years now. And our Rudy five and a half. Simply unbelievable. On 1 May I joined the parade from Mockau to Leipzig. Was there in 1900 too. And 1919 with Papa in Wilhelmshaven. He gave me a bouquet of violets.

W.L. Mother is from a working-class family, born in Leipzig as the eldest daughter of a pattern maker. From childhood on, work was the elixir of her life. First, she took care of her numerous younger brothers and sisters, then worked as a nanny for other people, worked as a maid here and there, before and after school. When it got too crowded at home, she entered service as housekeeper at a Bavarian manor. There she met the baker's apprentice Eduard Lehmann and traveled through Germany with him looking for work. She gave birth to his first son in a mansard room in Leipzig East, the second in a servants' quarters near the Potsdam palaces, and finally me, the third and last son, in 1916 in Wilhelmshaven, where my father had finally found permanent work at the imperial navy yard.

M.L. 3 August 1950, Booth 399 Night shift three times in a row. My Lehmann is resting in Wahren, Rudy in the East. Oh, how I miss my two dear ones. Now there is more to eat and to smoke again, and I can't give you any. Unbelievable.

W.L. During the First World War, my mother worked as a letter carrier, later as a seamstress at the quartermaster's; she worked putting up posters and taking tickets in one of the newly opened suburban cinemas. During the inflation years, she took a handcart and milk cans on commission and delivered milk, 170,000,000 marks a liter for skim milk and 360,000,000 marks a liter for whole milk. My father tried running a small rye-bread stand at the weekly market, after that a confectionery booth with rich baked goods. Yet all these small businesses yielded no profit for my parents, despite their great diligence, because competition from the big market stands was overwhelming, and our good-hearted mother gave too many goods away to the hungry children who constantly camped around our stall.

M.L. 21 April 1951, Booth 45c, 8:30 A.M. Saturday My Lehmann has been gone from me for 58 months now. Still unbelievable. Why? My Rudy 79 months in foreign soil. Unbelievable. Why? Today fifth year of the Socialist Unity Party. Weather cool, calm. Planes circling in the sky. Hopefully, the peace treaty of 1951 will yet be realized. 9:00 A.M., sun coming through the clouds. Now the sowing and planting will begin. Hoeing, weeding, and watering.

W.L. Indeed no beggar, whether old or young, left us empty-handed. The poverty all around worried my mother. Again and again, she looked for a way out. A relative regularly sent her the *Leipziger Volkszeitung*. Gradually my mother became convinced that the working class is capable of turning the tide of poverty. My mother asked my father, who had been a union member since his apprentice days and then joined the SPD, the Social Democratic Party of Germany, to take her along to meetings. Father refused these requests because he thought politics unsuitable for women; Mother was supposed to take care of the boys.

M.L. 10 May 1951, Booth 401 Three Saints' Days, storm, on 9 May very hot, on 8 May two thunderstorms. Summer almost here now, again without my Lehmann and without our Rudy. I miss them both very much, the pain keeps getting bigger.

W.L. My mother made many trips to the various school offices, trying to get a better education for her sons. Her persistence won out; Helmut, Rudy, and I attended secondary school, where, to our parents' pride, we sat among officers' sons, the offspring of directors, and the children of rich businesspeople. During the economic crisis my father – formerly a baker in Leipzig – worked as a day laborer in civil engineering, my mother sewed tirelessly as a home-worker.

M.L. 2 December 1951, Post 399, Rackwitz Beautiful weather. Mild. Worked from 1:00 P.M. until 6:00 A.M. Almost missed the noon train in Neuwiederitzsch, but the conductress had a heart and held the train a minute longer.

W.L. My brother Rudolf joined the KPD, the German Communist Party, was put in charge of literature and provided our mother, who thirsted for knowledge, with books by Gorki, Tolstoy, Sinclair, and Andersen Nexö; told her about discussions at the evening political training sessions; patiently explained concepts from the foundations of Marxism to her, now and then also secretly taking her along to events where Ernst Thälmann spoke to the workers of Leipzig. Mother hid Rudy's Marxist literature in the house and made margarine sandwiches for him and his comrades, mostly impoverished Jewish students.

M.L. 5 January 1952, Railway Board, Mockau The undersigned pledges 3 percent of her wages to the reconstruction of Berlin.

W.L. In discussions with our father, Mother defended her progressively minded son. My father resolved the conflict in our family in his own way: He burned newspapers and letters from foreign comrades addressed to my brother, called the 'rabble-rouser' obscene names, and finally threw him out of the parental apartment.

M.L. 5 August 1952, Booth 45c After the 7623 from the main station has crossed, 2:54 P.M. Stubble on fire in three places from flying sparks. I did all I could with the shovel, but when an east wind suddenly came up, I called the main station to be on the safe side. The fire spread so fast because the stubbles were too tall. At first, I thought it was straw, but it was the stubbles that had been blown down and fed the fire. Soon the fire department arrived and put it out. After the P-503 from the main station crossed at 3:44 P.M., the fire department left again. Of course, I had let down the gates.

W.L. While my eldest brother pursued a teacher training course, my mother devoted all her love to me, the youngest, who up to then had watched the family political battles uncomprehendingly. So I provided my 'banished' brother with food, played messenger between Mother and emigrant, and was now systematically educated by my mother for my brother Rudolf's idea. That is, I received for study several volumes of the AIZ, the *Workers' Illustrated Newspaper,* with its stirring photo montages by John Heartfield, also simple books by Maxim Gorki. And Mother kept a strict check to be sure that I read a section of Gorki every day by the light of an oil lamp.

M.L. 8 October 1952, 11:00, Autobahn, Taucha Rain showers. Cold. Third anniversary of the GDR. 19th Party Congress of the Communist Party of the Soviet Union. On 7 October harvested some of the winter pears. Then it rained and I stopped. Today I picked some more. Ach, my Lehmann, my Rudy, it's no good without you, so alone.

W.L. When Ernst Thälmann spoke in an election meeting at the Volkmarsdorf market in Leipzig-Stünz, my mother took me with her to hear him. Had there been unity between the people of Leipzig and all German workers at that time, the Nazis could not have assumed their fateful, dark supremacy one year later. My brother Rudolf was arrested by the Gestapo at his workplace in a Leipzig secondhand bookstore and thrown into the infamous Elisenburg.

M.L. 30 June 1953 Papa dead seven years. Unbelievable. Many storms, rain, and much sun in June, the right weather for all the plants. Picked the last sweet cherries on 28 June, raspberry harvest will soon be over too. Many gooseberries. On 17 June a greater disaster prevented, thanks to our Soviet friends. The Rosenbergs were executed after all at 3:00 A.M. on 20 June.

W.L. My mother's pain was boundless. But the example of the mother from Gorki's novel that Rudolf had given her to read could inspire her. She worried intensively about her incarcerated son's family. She hid his abundant notes from his meetings in the depths of her kitchen cupboard. Marxist literature from here and abroad that is irreplaceable today was burned at night in the kitchen stove.

M.L. 8 May 1954 On the day of liberation 10 marks for aid to Korea.

Leipziger Volkszeitung, 1954 Mother Lehmann works as a gate attendant out on the Taucha track. She performs this responsible work, day in and day out. She is there in all kinds of weather. And there are many other things she is involved in.

At Christmas Mother Lehmann donated twenty marks to People's Solidarity for a West German freedom fighter. She writes letters to West German patriots. In one letter she demands of the West German federal court that the unlawful KPD trial be dismissed. 'There is still much that we must do for peace,' Mother Lehmann says over and over. In her field of work at the Taucha station too, she is constantly working to make our government's recommendations come true. Mother Lehmann is continuously busy. She wants to help convince people of our government's peace politics. She sells brochures and says simply, 'That is my part in the struggle for peace.'

W.L. In the inferno of the Second World War, my brother Rudolf was released from prison and drafted. He fell in action in the Ukraine in 1944.

M.L. 8 September 1954, Post 46, Taucha, 1:00–9:00 P.M. Ten years ago today my Rudy had to lose his life. Why my Rudy. I still can't understand it. My wonderful son, so friendly, willing, and hardworking. And how good my Rudy could have it now. All the fruit in Papa's garden would please our Rudy too.

W.L. The black-edged letter from the mayor of Leipzig with the laconic message that 'your son has died a hero's death for the *Führer*, the people, and the fatherland' was a severe shock to my parents. But strangely, my mother, who had wept so many tears during the months of my brother's imprisonment, who to my father's horror had shrieked loud curses for the insane brownshirt drummer in the cellar during the nights of bombing, was now unspeakably sad but could weep no more tears.

M.L. 13 August 1955 On the occasion of our *Landsonntag*, Sunday volunteer farm work, I would like to make my contribution too and donate 10 marks for our freedom fighters and 10 marks for aid to Korea.

17 December 1955 Dear Comrades, enclosed 10 marks for our freedom fighters.

7 June 1956 On the birthday of our president, Wilhelm Piek, I had pledged twenty hours of reconstruction work in the sport forum. Enclosed is documentation that the pledge was fulfilled.

W.L. At our father's side, Mother joined the SPD in 1945. In April 1946 they were both taken over into the SED, the Socialist Unity Party.

M.L. 16 April 1957 Dear Comrade Oehmichen, Unfortunately I must bother you again. But I didn't receive any Solidarity stamps. Förster said there are none yet. How is such a thing possible? The week for Algeria was from the seventh to the twelfth of April. Today is Thälmann's birthday, and I cannot stop thinking about it unless I do something for our Party. I have a snapshot of my deceased son, Rudolf, from the field. He was playing chess with three other friends, without his uniform, on the day of Thälmann's birthday on 16 April 1944. And in memory of my son, who truly fought honorably for our cause, I ask that you accept this small gift for Algeria.

W.L. While my father, an invalid and retired, took care of the household, my mother reported to the German State Railway in 1945, joining the *Trümmerfrauen,* the women who cleared away the rubble. Later she worked on the track and qualified as a signalwoman at age sixty.

M.L. 29 May 1958 In honor of the Fifth Party Congress of our Socialist Unity Party, 20 marks for the Communist Party in France.

W.L. Our mother was happy when she learned in 1959 that Mansfeld miners at a workers' congress and in a subsequent proclamation, which took place in Eisleben in front of the Lenin monument from Puschkino, had decided to create an Ernst Thälmann monument as a return gift to the locality of Puschkino near Leningrad. Mother immediately pledged eighty-five hours of wages, equaling one hundred marks, for this memorial. She said in her pledge, 'For the memory of the shining example of my son Rudolf.'

Leipziger Volkszeitung, 1960 We thank you sincerely for the ten marks sent to us, which we used for summit luggage.

M.L. In 1961 I will take on the following commitments:

1. Organizing the advertising for active visibility.
2. Production pledge of 16 hours for the Solidarity account.
3. Donation of 10 marks every month, as long as I am working.
4. 20 hours of NAW.
5. A subscription to the *Leipziger Volkszeitung* for the West, as long as I am working.

W.L. After the little signal workers' posts were eliminated, my mother went to work in the luggage processing department.

Fahrt frei, 7 August 1962 Despite her seventy-three years, Martha Lehmann of the ticketing and luggage processing department at the Leipzig Main Station does not yet wish to retire, because she knows how much our workers' and farmers' state needs every helping hand to build socialism. She not only does her work but also discusses current events politely and in an exemplary manner with her colleagues and the customers. At her workplace, she regularly organizes a visibility advertisement, which her son usually paints for her. Month after month, she donates ten marks and more for international solidarity. In her neighborhood everyone knows her as a tireless building representative and collaborator of the National Front.

M.L. 8 October 1963 (Agitation book) Today on the platform, a woman railroad employee asked me what kind of decoration that was (I was wearing the emblem for anniversary of the republic). When I had explained it to her, she said, I don't pay attention to political stuff. I told her she should read the newspaper more, then she would be up to date. She said, I don't have time for that. It is shocking how few women read the newspaper. Over and over again, I advise women to read the newspaper, men sometimes too, for then they can understand all the connections between the actions taken by our GDR.

Editor of the Leipziger Volkszeitung, *14 June 1963* We have gladly accommodated your request to add your name to the list of those who protested the unlawful incarceration of Dr. Grasnick in West Germany.

M.L. 7 October 1964 Fifteen years of the German Democratic Republic. I would like to say thank you to our government for the law that allows retirees to keep on working, if they wish to, according to their abilities. I still remember how a few young people said to me and my woman colleague in 1943, you should long since be in the ground; you're just eating everything that should be for us. My colleague and I were just coming from work. She was later killed by a phosphorus shell.

Leipziger Volkszeitung, 16 September 1968 Readers recommended Martha Lehmann this time for our LVZ present. We are glad to grant this request, for the eighty-year-old railway worker still works tirelessly day after day for the benefit of the women and men in the dark blue uniforms. On the top floor of the railroad administration building where the conductors spend the night or allow themselves a restful break after a strenuous shift, she keeps the rooms spotlessly clean with her bucket and broom. When someone is absent because of illness or vacation, Martha Lehmann takes over a full shift without thinking twice about it, although she was actually going to work only half days. This still young railroad woman regularly attends Party meetings at the main train station; she collects the contributions of a German State Railway DFD-group, the Democratic Women's Alliance of Germany. In 1963 she received the Medal for Outstanding Achievements for her work, and for three years she has worn the State Railway Service Medal Step II. Every month she donates twenty marks for Vietnam and other peoples fighting for their freedom.

B. Martha Lehmann was aware of the historical greatness of the program to which we have dedicated ourselves in community. Not often: always. That is why campaigns by no means had a routine character for her, that is why no task was too insignificant for her. Modestly, she lived a great life.

Kuntze, Senior Civil Servant of the State Railway, Stationmaster, Leipzig Main Station, 8 March 1969 International Women's Day 1969 takes place under the banner of the twentieth birthday of our socialist German Democratic Republic. In these twenty years of socialist progress, our women and girls have made outstanding achievements. Every day they help organize the complex tasks of the commerce and transportation service in all areas of our station. You, Martha Lehmann, have especially supported the continuing improvement of our work in the social and technical field. For this, I express thanks to you and recognition as well as a commendation according to the railway ordinance of 18 October 1956, along with a book prize.

B. Every kind of work was creative for Martha Lehmann: self-creating. Martha Lehmann told the editor who was to announce my visit that she knew she did not have long to live now that she had left the workplace.

Martha Lehmann died of old age the evening before the first of May. I received the news of her death as I was preoccupied with giving us a report of her life in documents.

W.L. In December 1971 my mother brought me a little picture of Thälmann from her last workplace. This photo of our Ernst, so dear to us workers, had followed my mother nearly twenty-five years to her various posts. It was always decorated with flowers, artificial ones or from her garden. It seemed to her, she often told me, that with this picture not only did the revered workers' leader speak to her, but also that Rudolf was watching her during her daily work. I hung the rather unprepossessing photo in its faded gold frame in my classroom, next to the pictures of Walter Ulbricht and Lenin.

B. One cannot make an image of Martha Lehmann, because she did not make one of herself. Her life was one: complete. It can rightly stand next to working-class leaders. Let us remember Comrade Martha in mourning and rejoicing.

Chapter 20

Melusine intervenes

On a morning errand, delivering galley proofs from the editor to the printer, Beatrice heard scraps of invective. Which fell from the sky.

Since the sky was overcast, she couldn't see the source. The fragments of speech made no sense to her. And so she went unchallenged to the State Enterprise Electrocarbon of Berlin after work to attend a union meeting of her sponsoring brigade. She was greeted as she passed through the gate of the factory. Rubble lay in front of hall 3. The factory train held Beatrice up. When the train was past, Melusine blocked her way. 'Are you trying to compromise me?' Beatrice whispered furiously. 'No, but listen,' said Melusine, 'you act as if women were the only people left in the world. You write about nothing else. You're discrediting the intentions of the Persephonic opposition, you're not meeting your obligations. We don't want to put ourselves in the place of Mr. Lord God. We merely want to take half of the celestial burden from him. In friendship. Mr. God is actually totally overworked. And no less lonesome than a certain Johann Salman. Or do you think it's fun to practice a profession for decades that interests his wife only monetarily? Do you think he would have chosen this provider role if he'd had a choice? Enough of this ahistorical moralizing, or we'll cut your thread of life.' Beatrice, who had expected praise, begged her offendedly to lower her voice. Melusine asked when her sister-in-law was finally intending to deliver the promised protest songs, for which her travel had been financed. After a whistle-alert, the Beautiful Melusine took off and flew away in a northerly direction. Unnoticed by the plant security. Beatrice arrived at her sponsoring brigade shortly after the start of the union meeting. Where the discussion was mainly about measures to reduce export debts.

Chapter 21

Wherein the Reader Finds Volker Braun's 'Song of Communism,' which Beatrice Delivers Instead of a Self-Authored Protest Song to the Impatiently Demanding Melusine

1

Someday, and it will be soon,
The rivers will flow uphill
And nobody will be cold anymore
And the sun will rise in the winter.
Then the table will almost set itself—
Brothers, a pleasure!

Our life is no longer a rivulet
But overflowing abundance.
   Communism can only be the work
   of many people.
   Brothers, do not leave us alone!
   Together we can do it –
   Comrades, when will your revolution come?

2
Someday we can succeed
We will all decide the plan
And no one will have to bow down
And no coward will toady his way to the top.
Thinking our own thoughts
Is a pleasure for us
Our life is no longer a rivulet
But overflowing abundance.
   Communism can only be the work
   of many people.
   Brothers, do not leave us alone!
   Together we can do it –
   Comrades, when will your revolution come?

3
Someday, if only it were soon!
There will no longer be yours or mine
The oceans will mark the borders
And the countries will all be one
Love will unite not only two –
A pleasure for all
Our life is no longer a rivulet
But overflowing abundance.
   Communism can only be the work
   of many people.
   Brothers, do not leave us alone!
   Together we can do it –
   Comrades, when will your revolution come?

Chapter 22
Second Bitterfeld fruit: Farewell to Pauline

1

There was a man who lived with locomotives for fifty-two years. When his last day of work was approaching, I wrote to the man, asking permission to accompany him. He wrote in reply that I shouldn't go to any trouble, especially since it was only a short run, he'd been off the long one for four years, at this time of year, it got cold toward morning too. Unauthorized persons, including even shunters, were prohibited from riding along anyway. I addressed a petition to the Ministry of Railroads, Department of Engine Operations.

2

For I gathered from his written reply that neither daughter nor wife could have gotten ahead of me. The daughter was none other than my minstrel Laura. I had been fascinated by Laura's parents at her wedding: Johann Salman had left the celebration before dinner. Under protest from his wife. Accompanied by her. He justified his early departure with the rheumatism of Whatzisname (his word). Which Whatzisname would that be? You know, Schuricht, no. 27, whom the railroaders' newspaper *Fahrt frei* had already mentioned twice, with praise, of course. Did Johann Salman look as if he would be friends with an s.o.b.? But the wedding guests, with the State Enterprise Construction representatives in the lead, not only grabbed uncomprehendingly for Salman's shoulders, on the other hand, their wineglasses – for there wasn't room for all the hands on his shoulders – they also asked if this railroader Schuricht used male hot-water bottles with ears at night. Damn fool blabbing (Salman's words), Schuricht needed milk, a half-liter of fresh milk from the dairy every morning, and *Quark*, German farmers' cheese, when they had it, that keeps a person going and cures lameness, what did they mean, railroader! Schuricht was an engine driver! Still was one. Although for a year he'd been chairman of the retirees' get-together, which of course only engine drivers attended, what was so funny about that? 'A tragedy,' said Salman, referring to the fact that the state railway was now forced to hire just anybody willy-nilly because of personnel shortages. 'Salman-Gustav would turn over in his grave,' Salman-Johann told the silenced wedding guests. 'In those days an engine driver was still somebody. My father wore a hat on his locomotive. Yessir, one of those hard ones, a bowler. Well, that was the style of hat in those days. But think what it was like even longer ago. Then the engine drivers actually wore top hats. Those were the days! Of course, at that time the drivers didn't do any grunt work — like nowadays, for example. The stoker had to do all that. Real slave labor, no thanks. I fired that boiler for eleven years, I know what it's like. Four years as stoker and seven years as reserve engine driver, because I wasn't promoted. Back in my day, when I had finished my training in the metalworking department and went to work as a stoker, my engine driver forbade me to climb onto the locomotive from the side where the driver's seat was. That's how it was in those days.' The company manager drank a toast to Salman and tried to bring him back to the men's table where war stories and prison-camp experiences were being exchanged. Wife Olga said nastily that his leave had been granted for the wedding, not for any old sniveling nitwits (her words) who didn't let doctors help them because they knew it all themselves. But Johann Salman refused to be deterred from his responsibility. Schuricht-Emil was in bed with an engine driver's injury, widowed for two years now and still no prospect of another wife — women nowadays were ruthless. And in Emil's building they also had jobs; Salman couldn't entrust the care of the engine driver Schuricht to such distracted people. Trust was good; control was better. Salman had to go back; the nonstop no. 40 was leaving at 6:02 P.M., let's go! Johann looked at the electric clock in the hall, pulled out his pocket watch, opened the spring lid, compared them, and established an inaccuracy. In the case of the hall clock, of course. With the snapping sound made by the closing watch lid, Salman put an end to all arguments. The party secretary paid tribute to Salman's proletarian solidarity with a toast.

3

I justified my petition as business, enclosing a letter from the German Writers' Union. It identified me as a French poet writing a work rooted in the State Railway of the GDR and requested support. One week before the deadline, I telephoned the Railroad Ministry, Department of Engine Operations. A male voice informed me of strict regulations that had been issued after a well-known accident and described possible endangerment of the transport by adverse behavior such as talking, interfering with work, failing to follow instructions, general and particular dangers of engine driving, and the complex legal situation in the event of an accident. I was persistent. The male voice summoned me to the office for an interview.

4

The voice reminded me of bridegroom Benno's brigade leader. Who was also seated at the men's table at the wedding celebration. Next to me. Johann Salman saw to the generic purity of the company around the table but didn't even act surprised when I rapped my knuckles on the tabletop. Didn't he count me as a woman? Was he ready to count me at all, since he bluntly disputed the existence of miracles? His demonstratively discreet behavior toward me during the party, in unobserved moments indicating chummy agreement, soon made it clear that Johann Salman took me for a spy. A spy on vacation or something like that – at home you didn't need to stick strictly to your legend, you could feel free to make up lies about Whatzhername and eight hundred years, everyone had to relax some time. Especially if they came from that crazy capitalism where cars choke off people's air supply. 'If I were chairman of the City Council, I'd ban all cars,' Salman announced to the tipsy group, 'all of them. The old Germans didn't have cars either.' Olga Salman announced at the women's table that the amoebas of the Ruhr River were immortal.

5

Dressed in my best, I made my way to the border where the office was. Solitary. A delicate red-brick façade with a baroque balcony on the second floor. The scrollwork damaged by bombs. A large, standardized side wing, rear building with barred windows, clubhouse in the courtyard, on the other side of the barricade. The engine operations department was housed in the rear building. A guide led me through the corridors, whose colorfully tiled floors reminded you of old butchers' shops. The outer office was occupied by two small, shabby desks of unequal height, their sides touching each other, where two women were seated. My presence was announced to the director via intercom. After a while he opened the door and handed me the requested confirmation: 78.75 square centimeters of white cardboard identified by the number 005088 and the label 'Authorization.' The black printed text authorized the holder, upon presentation of an ID, to a round-trip ride on a steam locomotive on the Karl-Marx-Stadt Main Station–Rochlitz route on 8 October 1972.

6

I notified Johann Salman that I had official approval. In a formal but not unfriendly letter, he wrote down the trains that were available for my trip there, advised wearing solid shoes, pants, and in general practical, old, even cast-off clothing, and offered to let me sleep on his parlor sofa. Johann Salman's second-to-last run was a night shift. His last one seemed to me a sort of intimate act that it would be improper to watch. At the wedding Olga Salman's face expressed embarrassed disapproval when Benno and Laura exchanged kisses. At first, I assumed it was jealousy. Then I recalled certain times after expired love affairs when the sight of erotic displays of affection was unpleasant to me too. At such times I longed for inner calm that allows desire to diminish. At 842 years of age, I experienced the loss of pressure to narrow one's consciousness by the convention of individual sexual love as a gain. In sovereignty. Could a sixty-year-old woman have a similar experience after thirty-seven years of marriage?

7

I boarded the nonstop train to Karl-Marx-Stadt in a state of cheerfulness that was new to me. Up to now, I had traveled less to collect knowledge about the route and more to keep my soul muscular: capable of great emotions. Now I sensed a comprehensive, expansive interest, a calm curiosity, not probing: roving. Superficial? My obsession to try to grasp the world from a single point, focused, possibly in one person, had left me. The actual surroundings, not manipulated by passions, came to the fore in multiple ways. Fellow passengers on the train, Mitropa waiters, door lock, compartment smell, dialects, types of luggage, whistle signals, brake noises, windows, platform construction, the shape of fields, and the nuances of foliage colors. Following Salman's instructions, I had practical, old, cast-off articles of clothing with me in a suitcase. In Karl-Marx-Stadt the morning mist still hung in the streets. I refrained from taking a detour over the Sonnenberg, where my poetry generator had stood, in order to combat my rampant obsession with remembering. In one of those narrow trolley cars described by Laura as Gothic, which constantly have to manage steep curves and switches on a narrow-gauge track, I was slowly jostled out of the valley basin. Up onto the northeast slope of the suburb, to the building that was my goal. Its slate-covered pointed roof bore chimneys and antennas, I looked in vain for the steam dome repeatedly mentioned by Laura. The oval attic skylight windows had metal crosses. Wire grates to block snow had been installed near the gutter. Below the gutter were gray drain troughs shaped like icicles, black rimmed. The longest ones reached to the aluminum sills of the attic windows. All the windowsills of this building were covered with aluminum, polished until it gleamed. The cellar windows had embossed grates. Of course, the building did not run on rails. It stood inconspicuously in line at the edge of the street. And its large size also turned out to be an exaggeration on Laura's part.

8

Olga Salman greeted me with friendly obsequiousness. Before taking me into the parlor to her husband, she announced my arrival in the manner of a servant. Yet not by name, but in code. She said, 'It's Whatzhername.' Johann greeted me with a homeowner's dignity. A long handshake as among statesmen. During which it did not escape me that he was checking out the firmness of the flesh of my hand. Nevertheless, he remained composed. Smiled representatively. Cleared his throat. His wife stayed at the door. When Johann Salman had found the start button for his prepared welcome speech, he thrust his right foot and right shoulder decidedly forward and spoke, 'So, welcome to the workers' and farmers' metropolis, and unfortunately we don't speak French, but the station master was discreetly informed of the situation by me. Also, the route is made for books in the fall, splendid foliage, if we're lucky we'll see deer, wild boars are not unusual, any amount of rabbits. For technical essays or novels, you'll have to ask me, of course, so you don't write anything incorrect. Three signal books are already waiting for you. By request my wife will bring you whatzitsname and other specialties of the Erzgebirge region, but don't spread any lies.' I promised Salman to love the truth. 'Don't promise too much,' he whispered conspiratorially. Olga watched me through the reading lenses of her bifocals.

9

After this thoroughgoing greeting, Salman led me to the buffet on which a small granite plate stood. Flanked by vases. The vases stood on lace doilies. The granite plate, black and polished, was mounted on a pedestal. In contrast to gravestones, the letters on the pedestal were engraved. They acknowledged appreciation of engine driver Johann Salman's loyal service. The plate bore a silver relief of a tender locomotive. 'It's lucky that this fiasco is finally over,' said Olga Salman as an aside.

10

Johann Salman inquired about the Renault workers' political awareness and disappeared back into the furniture. Whose proportions would have suited a ballroom. The little parlor was so full of them that only a small path remained. Carpet. Smell of floor wax. On the walls framed photos of Laura and Wesselin. I sat down under the rubber tree that was spreading out next to the television. Salman sat beside the tiled stove. Relaxed. Can an engine driver be relaxed when his last trip is imminent?

11

His hair was completely white, somewhat receding on his forehead, and contrasted starkly with his yellowish dark skin. A wide side part, grayed iris with light spots. On the backrest of the armchair were two embroidered pillows, presumably karate-chopped into shape so that four pointed corners stood up. Salman held his head stiffly as if the four-pointed crown were hard to bear. His hands were displayed on the edges of the armrests. Large flat-fingered hands, hairless, the veins hardly bulging under the skin on the back of the hand, in general strikingly smooth as if greased. His thighs touched the armchair sides. Legs positioned at right angles. Felt slippers. I recalled a French popular song whose refrain goes: 'A woman can only be a woman for a man. A man is the whole world for a woman.' The heralded whatzitsname that, according to Johann's instructions, would be served by Olga was not to be understood as Schuricht no. 27, as at the wedding, but rather as buttermilk coffeecake. The couple communicated by vague hints. Their code was based on such extreme economy that one must assume they were a unified organism. Does a healthy human being talk to himself? When Olga asked, for example, 'D'you want any?' Johann not only knew that 'any' meant a particular kind of tea. He also knew he need only answer 'the one out there' to make clear that he would prefer a bottle of beer, which was stored in the pantry. We drank it to German-French friendship. In consideration of Salman's kidneys, Olga had to warm the beer. Johann included his kidney damage among the typical disabilities of engine drivers that were traceable to train air heating up the front of the body and cooling off the back. When the buttermilk coffeecake, a pastry made of grated potatoes, had been consumed, Salman showed me a calendar. It was thumbtacked onto the inside of the right upper kitchen cupboard door. Starting in May his working days were numbered. In a continuing, descending row. The tenth of October was marked '1.'

12

At 1:00 P.M. Johann Salman checked to see if Radio GDR was broadcasting its time signal punctually. His comparison against his pocket watch, on whose silver spring lid the relief of a locomotive could be admired, yielded no cause for complaint. Satisfied, Salman stretched out on the kitchen sofa. As soon as Olga started rattling dishes in the washbasins, he fell asleep. I expressed surprise. Olga replied that a real engine driver couldn't exist without racket. The louder the racket, the better the sleep. 'I'd like to know what's so interesting about that noisy bunch. Or do you want to write something about me? In my day, a civil servant was considered a good match, an unemployed man couldn't support a family, that's why my father talked me into it too. But if I had it to do over?' Olga wrassled (her word) the pots more violently. Johann started snoring. I dried the dishes. Even before the last noisemaker had been stowed in the kitchen cupboard, Olga turned up the volume on the radio. Because she wanted to talk with me undisturbed. To this end, she led me into the parlor. There she dug the gown I had slept in for 808 years out of the massive, highly polished buffet. Then she looked at me again through the reading lenses of her bifocals, raising her chin. Wide lower jaw, thick black eyebrows above brown eyes, pert pointed nose, well shaped, like everything else about this woman. The decisive expression of this harmonious form had faded, to be sure, into a pinched look. I said that I had given the gown to Laura for safekeeping. Olga said, 'She doesn't need it anymore. Now that she has her Benno, she doesn't need it anymore.' The gown lay carefully folded and wrapped in mothproof paper in a plastic bag. Although the embroideries were damaged, Olga called the gown priceless. She said an antique shop had offered her 420 marks. That had made her suspicious. So she had gone home to try it on. And sure enough, she had slept wonderfully in it. Sixteen hours without interruption; she hadn't experienced anything that glorious for ages. Miracles were really invaluable. She whispered the latter sentence. Then she was silent, expectantly. I tried to spot the stratum of bitterness in her face. Curiosity came to light. Pride. And she was better preserved than her husband, in any case; this was not merely simulated by her dyed brown hair. Could another man have been 'the whole world' for Olga? Was such a thing even replaceable? 'The life span is not an irrefutable law of nature,' Olga Salman declaimed, tossing a well-thumbed magazine onto the table in front of me. Between advertisement photos, which were sharper and more colorful than objects can be, the text read: 'Most gerontologists believe that an average age of eight hundred to nine hundred years is achievable.' Not via sleep miracles, as I soon realized. Did Olga Salman long to extend her empty life tenfold? I identified the magazine as a West German product that was prohibited from import. Olga Salman read aloud, 'Since 1950 researchers have been pursuing a problem that in the past was the province of quacks. All other life forms develop from protozoa. Today they live either in water, as always, or they settle in foreign organisms as disease germs. The dreaded amoebas of the Ruhr are such unicellular organisms, for example. When the protozoa mature, they divide. New unicellular organisms arise from the old ones. But a corpse is never left behind. The protozoa are immortal. The human body is fundamentally nothing more than a collection of just such unicellular organisms. Its flesh and blood are composed of about a thousand billion unicellular cells, whose basic structure differs not at all from the basic structure of those unicellular organisms that float in a puddle of water beside the street. The unicellular organisms in the human body have specialized. Some of them form muscles, for example. Others provide them with nourishment, and so on. But there is no decisive difference from the protozoa. Except that the cells living in cooperation somehow carry the verdict of death in them. Forty to fifty divisions of human cells can be achieved in a test tube. Then it is suddenly over.' — 'I'll throw that paper in the stove yet,' said Johann Salman, who, awakened by the relative quiet, had entered the parlor unnoticed.

13

After supper I lay down, following Salman's instructions, on the kitchen sofa. He parried my protest that I couldn't sleep before ten o'clock with the statement: 'Engine drivers and cosmonauts must be able to sleep at any hour of the day or night, on command, yessir.' Since Salman's explanation did not put my nature to sleep, I used Olga Salman's magazine for that purpose. Thus I found out that the reason why body cells die is not to be sought in the genetic material of deoxyribonucleic acid (DNA) but in the cell protein. Every single one of the human body's thousand billion cells is practically a fully automatic protein factory. It works with complicated systems of production and monitoring. Nevertheless, it too sometimes has defective products, rejects, so to speak. That wouldn't be the end of the world as long as the dross remained the exception. But it could happen that a falsely formed piece comes forth not just accidentally, but that the molds become defective, continually producing rejects. Then the situation is more dangerous. It becomes really grave, however, when there is a breakdown of a mold that was intended to produce new molds. At that point, a catastrophe could no longer be stopped. The rejects would predominate, production would collapse, the cell would die. Aging is nothing other than that escalation of production errors and death nothing more than the great error catastrophe. Half asleep, I read the conclusion that means can and must be found to remove the faulty protein from the cell and replace it by new protein. I took with me into a short sleep the prediction that the 1970s could become the decade of rejuvenation, a life expectancy of 150 years would be a certainty by the year 2000 and an average age of 800–900 years was definitely achievable. I dreamed that gerontologists displayed the stuffed and mounted deposed goddesses Persephone and Demeter in the Berlin Museum of Natural History.

14

At ten minutes to one, Salman woke me for trip number 17, time to go. He already had his vest on over his shirt. The vest front was stitched with four pockets of different sizes, appropriate to the contents. The left breast pocket was a sheath for a glasses case; the other had quilted compartments from which pencils with metal point protectors protruded. The lower pockets were embossed. A silver watch chain stretched from a waist-level buttonhole to the waist pocket. While saying 'time to get up,' Salman took his watch on its chain from his pocket. Then he opened the spring lid, holding the watch between his thumb and middle finger; the thumb pressed against the hinge, the middle finger bending back the catch and pressing against the winder. 'Twelve fifty-eight,' said Salman, lifted one foot out of its slipper, stepped on the seat cushion of the sofa, and moved the hand of the big kitchen clock. The hand was rusted, the numbers too. While I got dressed, as instructed, in the practical, old, cast-off articles of clothing and solid shoes, Salman turned his back. He rubbed spots of rust from the brightly polished iron plates of the stove with steel wool, packed the steel wool back into his work satchel, also six pears, a beer bottle filled with tea, and an aluminum case in the shape of a semicircular slice of a long loaf of bread. Its two interlocking halves were held by a ring from a canning jar. Shortly we were eating whole-wheat bread from the health-food store, butter and homemade currant jelly, and drinking chicory coffee with milk that stood ready in a pot covered with a warmer. 'My wife always used to make fresh coffee for me every time I had to leave for work,' said Salman, 'my mother always got up when my father had the night shift, no two ways about it, yep.' Salman's curt 'yep' at the end of certain sentences could not have the common meaning of 'yes' but rather the opposite. This opposite was fired off ahead of time. Prophylactically, before a disagreement could come up. We left the house an hour before the shift began.

15

The night was mild. An almost summery breeze. Clear sky. Bright, the stars curiously enlarged to firmament machinery, the sounds of the still distant launching hill also clearly audible already. I trod the path laid with granite flagstones at Johann Salman's left side. Large flagstones, worn smooth, here and there slanted. Next to the gas lanterns, the flags hanging on poles from most of the windows looked red, otherwise black. I didn't assume that this decoration had been provided for the engine driver but said that I did. Salman gave me fundamental instruction in history, to create due respect for the anniversary of the republic's founding. He said that during the First World War he and the baker's sons had rung the bells in the church located to the right of the path on a hill shored up by walls. Sometimes the two boys' pants pockets would be bulging with raisins. The three of them could gobble them up safely under the bell cage. I interpreted this memory as a sign of melancholy, which up to now I had waited for in vain. I observed Johann Salman's surreptitiously swinging gait. Past the church the paved street went downhill. An unreinforced footpath, a fence to the right of it. Meadow beyond the fence. Old trees, then two half-timbered houses. Salman showed me a birdhouselike accessory with two spheres in it on the gable of the second house. The spheres were the size of tennis balls. They had been fired at the house from Napoleon's cannons in 1813, said Salman, assuring me he wasn't trying to make a stink. He thought I was a spy with high political qualifications. Steep curve to the left, also with remnants of a village that I wouldn't have expected from this industrial city. For I knew only the Sonnenberg quarter, the newly rebuilt center, and the VEB Elite Diamond. Between two old porphyry buildings, a cinder path branched off, leading left along the launching hill. Allotment garden plots at the right. Salman walked without hurrying, taking short steps that made grinding noises. Again and again, uniformed men came toward us. On foot. On motorcycles. Salman knew all of them. They greeted each other by calling out their first names. For my information, Salman said their surnames and numbers from the side of his mouth. For example: 'Richter 36, Georgie 8, Winkler 13, Müller 143.' Johann Salman's number was 2. Salman 1 had been his father, Gustav. The youngest of the men coming toward us were in their mid-fifties. The launching hill was lit by a floodlight. As we passed the second of the three boiler houses, Salman peered through a hole in the windowpane and said, 'She's in there, we're in luck, when she's in there, we'll get her, it could have been the case that she's out, shortage of engines, special trains, of course we don't like to see it when other people use our brigade's engine, not long ago we got her back totally filthy. I wouldn't care to hear what you would say if you had to lend someone your shoes and got them back all worn-out.'

16

Salman addressed the sleepy doorman as Richard and introduced me as 'Import from France.' He said that since no steam locomotives were used there anymore, the French railroad was selling its drivers abroad. Cheap, the GDR had paid with nylon socks from Oberlungwitz. Richard was wide awake in a moment, blurted out 'Johann,' and to demonstrate his professional qualities added that he knew all the company employees by name; his other qualities he expressed by exclaiming, 'I've seen the whole world.' While writing out a pass, he explained his boast. Which showed that his whole world consisted of Poland, France, Rumania, Greece, and the Ukraine, which he had attacked as an enlisted man in two world wars. Richard's son had been killed in action in Russia at age seventeen, Salman explained at the engine drivers' locker room. Which was located in a brick building. I had to wait there until Salman returned after changing clothes, the engine personnel were only masculine. No wonder then that I stood out as a rarity – like I would in a barracks. On the way to the engine command, we also waded through curiosity. Stares, shouted questions, and whistles. Salman waded solemnly. A line of people at the engine command counter. Salman introduced me as the director of the Paris Locomotive Museum, who had been delegated to production. The engine supervisor, a wizened man of sixty, was brooding over an open schedule book. His pencil traced columns of numbers and lines. Besieged by telephones. When two or three phones rang at once, he would curse to himself, 'money-grubbing shysters,' 'dumbbells,' 'busybodies,' which apparently meant something like 'Just a minute, wait your turn.' Salman and the engine supervisor were soon calling numbers to each other through the counter window. My permit was recognized as valid after it had been compared with written instructions from the station manager concerning my identity. The stoker had already picked up the engine key. 'According to the rules,' said Salman; rules were half of life, yep. Again, that curt 'yep' that presupposed disagreement, shorthand for the question: That doesn't quite suit you, hmm? In the next room, which was just as meagerly furnished, orders that had to be looked over before starting work were hung and spread out. Salman did his duty and checked it off in a book. Then he helped an engine driver named Karl to fill out his work sheet. His commentary on this at the oil pump: 'Ever since I've known Karl, he's asked questions. For at least twenty years he's been asking the same thing, godogod. Our headquarters is an old-folks' home. The last one far and wide; who else is still running on steam nowadays? And even here we're in the way. We couldn't get into the buildings all summer long. First, they were working on the turntable, then the channels were being paved. The entire steam-engine company running on one single channel — nothing but screw-ups and delays. And what we got back was one building, would you believe it — the competition is spreading out next door. And of the two chimneys that belong to the building, the office set aside one for its new steam-boiler installation. I wouldn't have believed I would outlive my profession.'

17

Through the two open gates of the engine shed, a harsh light fell on the smooth, worn pairs of rails that led to the turntable. Four engines stood under the flues. Pounding noise from the air pumps, hissing, metallic clattering, echoing cries. Salman escorted me to engine number 86 063; on its polished manufacturer's plate were the words 'Henschel & Co. 1932.' When I saw the stoker with a smoky oil lamp tinkering on the iron colossus, I stood still involuntarily. Expecting an explosion — since my reawakening I'd had to memorize orders that prohibited working with uncovered lights. The oil torches reminded me of home and Almaciz. Salman introduced the stoker as Ott-Willi and me as 'French union delegation,' asking, 'How's she doing?' I thought the question referred to me. Ott-Willi waved me off and moved three steps away. Then he answered at a volume that more than compensated for the distance. 'She's got dents on her wheels, Whatzisname was up there, you can't make a silk purse out of a sow's ear.' Salman placed his hands on the flattened spots on the wheels and said, 'Idiot.' Was he as intimate with Ott-Willi as with his wife, so that mere hints were enough here too? My hope that, despite the ban on talking to the workers, I would still learn all kinds of things from overhearing them disappeared. Ott-Willi raised that hope again. He asked me if I'd already been to the canteen and was promptly reminded of a story. 'Before I drove with Salman-Johann, I fired for Rucksack, actually, his name was Richter 87, but an engine driver who only comes to work with a rucksack naturally has his nickname ready. Rucksack is a coffee lover. If you look for him after work, you'll find him in the canteen. With a cup of coffee. So one fine day I'm looking for him, I go to the canteen and what do I see? Rucksack sitting there with two cups. "Whoopsadaisy," I say, because my Richter-Walter could never be too thrifty, "are you in a generous mood today?" I say and get ready to take a sip. Then Walter says, "wait a minnit," makes me bring the full cup up onto the engine, pours the coffee into the fire, and says, *"Weil de heide su schie gelaafen biest, kriegste a ne Dass."* — "Because you ran so well today, you get a cup too." ' I couldn't get used to the dialect as quickly as to the scratchy smell of smoke, iron, soot, and lubricating oil. Ott-Willi was about the same age as Salman but skinny. Emaciated, probably from the hard work — except for his cheeks. Amazingly, they were not sunken. Did he carry supplies of anecdotes in his hamster cheeks? I learned that at least two months would pass before the dents, ground in by insensitive braking, would be evened out. 'I won't be around to see it,' said Salman as he helped me up the ladder to the driver's cabin. 'Here on the right, the big wheel, that's the steering wheel. Turn it to the left: back up. Turn it to the right: go forward. And here's the most important thing: the controls. And if you want to take a look into the firebox — here. Well, there's only a reserve fire in there. Maybe that idiot thinks it's all right to mistreat it . . . ' The warmth radiating from the rear wall of the furnace fostered certain feelings in me too that are usually aroused only by living beings. The sixty-five-year-old Salman was, meanwhile, climbing around with monkeylike sureness on the steaming colossus, tinkering with wrenches, hammers, oilcans, steel wool. He always had some steel wool in his hand. Usually in the left one. Only when repairs required both hands to be bare did the crumpled knot disappear temporarily into a pocket of his protective suit. Water could stand in exalted drops on the back of the suit. Like in the drain under the engine. Salman held the lamp flame up to all the places to be oiled, in order to get me better acquainted with Pauline. Pauline was the name of engine 86 063. In spite of Salman's orders to pull in my noggin (his word), I bumped myself several times on Pauline's nether parts. If I lowered my head, oil or water dripped down my collar. Then trickled down my back. Preparation time. Two hours, that was the regulation, yep. The curt 'yep.' Did Salman assume that after reading the familiar magazine,

I shared Olga's opinion that, given a life expectancy of seventy years, our approach to life was out of proportion to the effect?

18

At 3:36 Pauline rolled onto the turntable. At 3:44 Ott-Willi announced her on the switch tower intercom. A croaking voice reported that the exit was clear and gave the order to drive at sight from switch tower to switch tower. We passed wait signs, forward signals, barricades. On the launching hill, which was still lit by a floodlight, the night retreated into the sky. Far above and beyond the upper electricity network. Then it sank again. Mild draft. Salman had assigned me to the right-hand door behind the engine driver's place – standing room only. Ott-Willi swept up with a twig broom after he had fired. At switch tower 6, Pauline was hitched between two engines, which also had to take over a train from the main station. Further orders through the loudspeaker. The first engine, a fifty-eighter, answered with an 'attention' whistle. I made a note of that. Salman demanded that I strike it, because commands really had to be repeated orally. Even across such distances, yep (curt): that would be fine bellowing (his word). The electricity network grew denser. Salman called it 'snarl.' He spoke only with contempt of the main station too. He called it 'the ones over there,' as if he were talking about the West. 'The ones over there don't get their hands dirty,' he said over the noise of the train, 'the whole bunch electrified or running on diesel, all the steam-engine drivers are shoved over on us, but we're still good enough for the grunt work over there.' Gruff words. Salman enjoyed them calmly. Like enjoying a liqueur. Olga Salman grumbled nastily.

19

At the entrance to the main station hall, Salman showed me the place between the tracks where he had survived the air raid on 5 March 1944. 'In a sugarloaf, that's what they called the concrete bunkers – the house that Ott-Willi built for his dog is bigger. That night, when the city burned along with over 3,668 people, I concocted more plans for the future than I ever did before or after. Homeland.' The passenger train was ready to go. Salman guided Pauline slowly up to the baggage car, which he called 'pack-meister,' doing it 'by instinct,' he said. And in fact, no impact could be felt. You couldn't even hear the bumper touch. 'Yep,' said Salman, as curtly as possible. Did he perhaps suspect that I was reluctant to admire his precision work with a colossus? Salman's simple dignity. His calmness, which could not be based on fatalism but rather on the ability to surrender to the course of life. Although it always ends badly: with death. Nothing more certain than that. The magazine professors, however, did not fix irrevocable death until about a thousand years: after the loss of brain cells, which, in contrast to the other cells, do not keep on dividing after the person's birth and thus are not in a position to replace the loss. It seemed clear to me that, under such conditions, death loses its bad reputation. The religions of the hereafter would become superfluous; suicide would probably become one of the most frequent ways to die. Youth worship would disappear, awareness of values would rise, the time of active maturity would increase. Women would no longer be forced either to wear themselves out with a double burden or to renounce an essential side of self-realization but would have ample time to devote themselves, in turn, to children and their professions. To several professions, according to developments in the sphere of production. Getting through life with a single profession as Salman had would become impossible. The stresses of education would no longer consume half the lives of researchers, which could immensely increase scientific productivity. Now people would have time to explore and colonize the planets and distant solar systems. It's questionable, however, whether life would not lose intensity by being stretched to such an extent that there would be no high points. It's questionable whether it doesn't need its ubiquitous negation in order to be experienced as precious, to be used and exhausted in the struggle to assert oneself. It's questionable whether gerontology even seems justifiable with goals such as those mentioned, considering that eighty thousand people starve to death every day on the earth. At the wedding Salman had asked me about a certain Canetti whom he assumed to be a colleague of mine, a professional colleague, not in an honorary capacity. He said he'd heard on the radio that this man refused to recognize death. Salman said that cursing the inevitable or calling it into question was pigheaded (his word). He lived in harmony with it. He also included morals in it. Did he live in an ideal world? Did he always say farewell in such a gruffly composed way because he sensed that postponement meant the loss of these illusions? The chalked writing on the heating board specified an atmospheric pressure of one. 'In winter you have to heat with an atmospheric pressure of four,' Salman explained, 'in freezing cold,' he said and grimaced as if a draft were blowing into his face, 'cold doesn't mean anything to an athlete like me; only in the last two years have I dreaded winter. This year I'll be retired at an atmospheric pressure of four. Behind the stove, there you can stand snowdrifts.'

20

The platform came to life. The first travelers boarded the workers' train, which consisted of old passenger cars with many doors. Brake test. Brief palaver with the shunter about brake blocks and me. 'Latest decision from the railroad administration,' Salman finally said seriously, acting surprised that the shunter hadn't been informed yet, 'starting in '73, steam locomotives can only be driven by female personnel, yep. The men have to retrain for diesel or electric.' Salman was standing in the light of a covered lamp that illuminated meters, water gauges, schedule holders, and the big, shiny lever of the steam regulator on the black rear wall of the boiler. Ott-Willi cast a glance at the water level and the boiler's air-pressure gauge, turned a little wheel to operate the supply pump, and shoveled coal into the fire, grinning. The sounds of doors closing multiplied. The station clock read 4:48. Salman took out his pocket watch, compared, nodded: The station clock was right. Were there more exact clocks than station clocks? 'Yep,' Salman said curtly, 'but it could be . . . who knows . . . somehow . . . but with the railroad it comes down to the minute and . . . anyway: my watch is accurate. Because it's an engine driver's watch, not a . . . how do I know what goofy kinds there are. Salman-Gustav kept on schedule with this watch, down to the minute. What am I saying? Down to the second! Yessir.' Salman snapped the relief-decorated lid shut. Attention. For the shunter that meant: end of palaver. For Ott-Willi it meant: Is steam up? 'Eyuh,' answered Ott-Willi promptly. Repeated door-slamming. Commands called out by the supervising attendant. A green signal light fell through the oval windowpane of the driver's cab. The attendant raised his signal. 'Clear,' said Ott-Willi at 4:50. 'Clear,' Salman confirmed, opening the whistle vent deliberately, then the regulator, 'time to go.' Passenger train 3271/72, Karl-Marx-Stadt/Rochlitz, departs the main station. Also deliberately. Salman seemed not to know haste. Was he so balanced because he was satisfied? With himself; could a man who had proven himself as a provider not be satisfied? At the time he got married, women got the problems of existence off their backs by marrying. A man couldn't get them off his back because of his gender; he had to stand up to them: be successful, strong. And if he failed, it was all over for him as a man and in general. Olga Salman had never had to bear such responsibility or work that hard. Her life was empty of existential fear; did she have a right to complain that it was empty in other ways too? No wonder that a man like Salman, who paid for the money he earned with great physical wear and tear, felt superior to his wife. She was probably more intelligent than he, certainly stronger of character, judging by her facial features, all her life she'd had to act small and weak, but Salman had had to overcome his gentle soul all his life, didn't that count for more? Dawn. Salman called my attention to the new high-rises, to cooling towers, the thermal power station, the hog farm. But the banner of sparks still reflected its glow on the moist roofs of the cars. First stop: Glösa. Two men got on. Salman knew them by name.

21

At the Heinersdorf stop, where no platform was to be seen, only grass and field all around, three persons were waiting in the dark. Ott-Willi identified one of them as Lang-Fritz, that snake. Rucksack had often gotten mad at that snake. Because he always had something to bitch about, either because there was too little heat or too much, because the train had gone too far or not far enough; there wasn't a day when that sock maker hadn't made a stink. To get revenge, Rucksack had driven through the Heinersdorf stop on his last run. Giggling. And he had called out to the snake, *'Heide mußte laafen.'* — 'Today you have to walk.'

22

The fog hung thick in the Chemnitz valley. The engine's regular, rocking movements heightened the effects of fatigue. I held my head out into the damp, cold draft to fight down my yawning or at least to hide it from the two old men. They showed no signs of tiredness. When I leaned out very far, I could clearly hear the knocking produced by the flat spots ground into the wheels. Salman called it 'racket.' Sunrise. The foliage colors heralded by Salman exceeded my expectations. And rabbits and deer were also to be seen. Any amount of unbarricaded rail crossings, which necessitated whistling and activating the signal bell. I was cold. Between the Wittgensdorf lower station and Wittgensdorf upper station, Salman cleared his throat at a volume suited to the train noise. 'Eeyuh,' answered Ott-Willi, reaching for the shovel again. One foot on the constantly moving support tank, one on the cabin floor, the stoker swung the coal shovel toward the open fire hole, balancing the shaking movements of the engine with legs spread wide. Heat shot out. Ott-Willi threw the coals precisely aimed into the two-meter-deep box, again and again, each shovelful thirty pounds. Then he reached for his coffeepot that stood keeping warm on the metal above the fire door. Salman's bottle stood next to it. Shortly before the entrance to Auerswalde-Köthensdorf, it fell down. Salman's curses added to the noise of the fall. On top of that, the rhythm of the sixfold rail impacts: tatatatatatum, tatatatatatum . . . Panting, the engine climbed the winding turns of the route, following the course of the scum-bearing Chemnitz River, crossing it over low bridges. The textile factory VEB Doppelmoppel came into view, VEB Graziella, Textile Works Clara Zetkin, all fully illuminated. Salman saw it with satisfaction. He would rather drive freight trains that served these plants than drive passenger trains, which he called grunt work. What? Were perhaps the closed cotton cars for the Schwarzathal-Dietensdorf spinning mill or the tank cars with chlorine and hydrochloric acid for the Fewa branch plant in Moosdorf more interesting to him than workers' commutes? I immediately shot back an argument in defense of caring about people. Salman replied calmly, 'Do you think it's fun for an actress when she has to leave the stage for the prompt box because of age? Sure, the work has to be done, trains that stop at every wide spot in the road have to run too, but when you've done big runs all your life . . .' — 'Is delivering to those plants a big run?' I asked in reply. 'Bullroar,' answered Salman, 'you can't get away from shunting. But shunting has to be learned. Some never learn it and ram every load to smash. It's the engine driver's calling card, so to speak. Like docking and casting off for a ship's captain. A person has his pride, after all . . . ' Said he and drove into Schwarzathal-Dietensdorf half a car-length farther than usual. I felt guilty for violating the rule against conversations with the personnel. A few travelers, who stood precisely at their usual platform positions expecting a particular door to stop in front of them, shook their heads. An old worker said indignantly, *'Muß mer a noch a wink laafen.'* — 'We still have to walk a ways.'

23

Ott-Willi and Salman used even short station-stops to clean, oil, and work on the engine. Only in the village of Stein, where the effluents of the rag-processing plant had given the river a color similar to that of steam-engine oil, did Ott-Willi pull another anecdote out of his hamster cheeks. Because Rucksack had also braked incorrectly once in a while. Oftener than Salman, he conceded quickly, when he saw his engine driver reaching for his pocket watch. So, as he'd said, Rucksack had braked incorrectly much more often than Salman-Johann; it was no exaggeration to say almost always, and once he had brought his train to a halt before the tunnel instead of after. 'So I think to myself, hey, I think, cautious as I am, for my friend Rucksack has a violent temper, and what do I hear? "She doesn't want to go in the tunnel," I hear. Then Rucksack gives the engine a slap on the back of her boiler and says, "Be not afraid, I am with you." ' — 'I don't understand what Laura sees in that electric rattletrap,' Salman fills in. 'It would give me the creeps to drive around in such a stupid contraption, where all you can do is identify damage, not repair it yourself. Nobody can talk to such a mess of wire.'

24

Pauline's speed was never more than fifty kilometers per hour, usually less. In keeping with the schedule. In Göritzhain we drove past the paper factory, which usually showed appreciation to Salman for good service with defective tissue paper. Olga used it for sewing patterns. Men or women in railroaders' uniforms stood at attention in front of the signalmen's huts along the route as we drove by. Salman greeted all of them by touching the visor of his cap and murmuring their names. Our route crossed the Chemnitz River twelve times, until it flowed into the hollow at Wechselburg. As we drove into Steudten, Salman said to Ott-Willi, 'Margitta has a new leather coat on today.' At 6:23 arrival in Rochlitz. 'Everyone out; this train ends here,' the station loudspeaker croaked. The passenger cars were unhooked. Pauline drove to the water crane. Break for breakfast — except, a shunter from Güterboden asked Salman if he could change a few cars, there was no shunting engine, try to stick your hand in a naked man's pocket. 'So,' said Salman calmly and let his watch lid snap shut. So, no break for breakfast. So, shunting. It wasn't part of the shift. 'Eeyuh,' said Ott-Willi. I made a note: 'Solidary behavior.'

25

Salman satisfied the curiosity of another shunter, who finally hitched seven empty cars for the sandpit to Pauline, by introducing me as 'lady electrification expert.' 'She wants to electrify our routes, down to the last one. She'd wire the whole sky if she could. And we steam-engine drivers sit in our engines like we're in a cage and can't get out. Won't that be a fine state of affairs, when my Pauline is plastered all over with warning signs for electricity and the stoker can't use the poker any more, because otherwise he'll roast? High time to end it.' The conductor brought the brake slip for the empty train no. 9504 (fourteen axles). In Steudten the empty cars were exchanged for fourteen sand cars. Four hundred forty-eight tons, which I wouldn't have guessed the little sand heaps on the open cars to weigh. And now of all times, it started to rain: filthy weather (Salman's words). Pauline skidded on the wet tracks. During ascents they constantly had to be sprinkled with sand. Pauline took longer ascents little by little, pulling jerkily like a horse. Ott-Willi hastily stuffed his hamster cheeks with bread now and then, chewing whenever he had a chance. Because he could hardly let the shovel out of his hand all the way to the Karl-Marx-Stadt main station. Now hunger also forced Salman to stoke samwiches (his word) in between times. In quick succession, sections of track where, Salman asserted with his mouth full, many drivers had gotten stuck with a sand train. Salman had put up a piece of metal above the engine driver's window. It kept the rain from running down his collar. A stretch with a single track. At the main station entrance, it goes across a path of ten change points. We crossed a Leipzig track and a Riesa track, two engine tracks from the main station headquarters, two Dresden tracks, one repair-shop track, and three freight-train tracks. 'Don't drive so slow,' roared a voice from the switch tower. 'Eeyuh,' said Ott-Willi. Salman enjoyed his last chance to completely block the electrified main station traffic at least briefly. Shift no. 17 tomorrow afternoon wouldn't offer that kind of opportunity. When the sand train had been transferred to Products 6 and unhitched, Salman drove Pauline home. Again, at sight from switch tower to switch tower. Arriving at headquarters, coal and sand and water were taken. In the boiler house the relief driver asked, 'How's she doing?' And this time I didn't assume the question referred to me. The way home led across black cinders that crunched under our shoe soles. The launching hill to the right and the garden plots to the left. Brake shoes squeaked. The cries of the shunters mixed with the metallic clanging of bumpers colliding against each other. But my ears were already so toughened from shift no. 17 that I could effortlessly ignore the shunting noise. Many older men came toward us, whom Salman greeted by name and was greeted by name in turn. One, to whom Salman called 'G'morning, Moritz,' yelled back, 'Hullo, Johann, are you done?' — 'Tomorrow,' Salman answered at the same volume. 'When it tastes best, it's time to stop.'

26

Back at home Salman found food on the table and his wife in bed. Lumbago. 'The old Germans didn't have lumbago either,' Salman grumbled into the bedroom. 'I can't remember a single time in the last three years that I was sick in bed,' Olga countered nastily. 'And who's going to pick up the milk tomorrow morning?' asked Salman after taking off his uniform. Later he told me about Bellman, a baker who closed his prosperous business at age sixty-four and took a job as factotum in a bar. 'For fifty years Bellman had to get up at 3:00 A.M.; now he goes to bed at 6:00 A.M.. Time to go, time to go.'

Chapter 23

THE FRIENDS BECOME APPRECIABLY CLOSER; THIS DISTANCES THEM

Beatrice read her second Bitterfeld fruit to the young couple and asked them for an evaluation and suggestions. The report moved Laura to tears. Benno praised the intent and said it was too bad that no one had portrayed his father, Oskar Pakulat, whose contributions truly overshadowed those of Johann Salman. At that, Beatrice brought Benno the thirty-fifth Melusinian book. And he read. And cursed. And criticized. Especially the description of the ruckus between him and his father; he said those were intraparty clashes, so to speak, that shouldn't be made public. And it was indecent to publish intimate details such as diaries, would old Pakulat have let these intimate details get into the hands of this writer Morgenstern or Mohrenfern or whatever her name was? Must he not have known this Mollenkern rather well, in fact? How else could she have described him in such detail? Was she maybe one of the ones he'd put on his short list, until his dying day old Pakulat had thoughts of marrying again, a nutty old guy, but fooling around with women writers? Benno honestly wouldn't have thought him capable of that, trumpet flourish! The trobadora calmed Benno with a minestrone soup, which she made without a cookbook. Benno gave the minestrone a rating of 47 Tender Loving Care units. He converted a tender, well-done steak to 38 TLCs, a full bath to 50, taking Wesselin for a ride was 20 to 60, getting up in the morning minus 80, washing windows minus 290. Since Beatrice went out of her way to emulate Laura even in small details, Wesselin soon accepted her as a mother-substitute. But didn't call her Mama. This word he used only for Laura or Benno. Then Beatrice withdrew the montage novel and promised the Aufbau-Verlag to fulfill her contractual obligations with a future-oriented novel instead. Its major figure would be a young construction worker. For the summer, Benno applied for a vacation trip to the Baltic Sea from the union leadership of his company. 'I'd rather go to Almaciz,' said Laura. At that, it seemed to Beatrice, for various reasons, that it was again high time to suppress her reluctance to tell stories, which was based on reluctance to remember. And so while working the pastry dough, she described her experiences in Rome to the happy couple. Wesselin, who couldn't stand it when grown-ups listened to each other instead of to him, interrupted the story several times by singing. The dog, Anaximander, interrupted it by barking. The story can be found in shortened form in the next chapter.

Chapter 24
Rome and other things

I pictured Rome – I have no idea why – as a pastel city, with sandstone-colored or white buildings of the kind found in southerly coastal villages. I expected the former capital of the Roman Empire to look charming! Sometimes our desires show rigorous disregard for our historical and art-historical knowledge. I wasn't even prepared for the sultry tropical weather that greeted me as I got off the train on Sunday afternoon. And so, unprepared with plans as well, we set out to look for a room. I naively. Simon grinning. And I even asked him why he was grinning, since you can get to know a city most quickly by getting your feet on it. I saw no reason not to follow that naive custom at this time. For once, Simon didn't contradict me, which should have made me suspicious. After only a few steps, sweat plastered our clothing to our skin. In the shade of buildings that could appropriately be called colossal and imposing, we dragged along for about an hour. Gasping for breath. And ever more slowly. In bad shape for hotel negotiations. From the top of the Spanish Steps, a first view of the city. The above-mentioned words suited the impression thus gained as well. Not a trace of pastels; the city's prevailing color is ochre. Youthful tourists in ragged underground look were roasting on the stairs. Romans were not to be found at this time of day, even in the shade. Unless extraordinary circumstances forced or tempted them. A soft-drink vendor had positioned his cart in heat position behind the uppermost balustrade of the Spanish Steps. I rushed up to him and ordered a drink without asking the price; he opened a tiny bottle, emptied it into a paper cup, and demanded four hundred lire. At the time that was approximately two marks thirty.

Refusing to accept it at this point would have led to a scene and an embittered verbal duel. Which would have ruined the mood. And it was also doubtful that we would have been able to settle the duel in our favor. So I only berated him with, 'Usury!' and the vendor berated me, in turn, with, 'Do you think they treat me with kid gloves?' Defeated, we wobbled down the steps. And absolutely could not properly honor or enjoy the quiet in the streets. Almost only parked cars during the Sunday siesta. Occasional streets where parking was prohibited could be viewed naked. We took quarters in the Cruce de Malta Hotel near the Spanish Steps. In the manner described earlier. Putting on my ladylike lazy act took the last of my energy. Indifferent even to hunger, I fell into bed and found neither strength nor desire to roll over from my back to the side. I started my Monday early, resolved to take health considerations into account. Modestly. Coolness on the streets. Noise. Stench. In the old city, which is innocent of sidewalks, pedestrians burrow their way through the car traffic as best they can. Not one of the famous plazas can be seen. Their paved surfaces, usually artistically patterned and reproduced for your admiration on postcard versions of older photographs, are buried under metal. Rome is one gigantic garage. Like Paris. At the time, the Roman Forum and the Coliseum were not yet closed due to danger of collapse and lack of means to restore them. So I viewed the Forum for two hundred lire. Walked around in the scraps of ruins left after centuries of use as a stone quarry with my city guidebook like all the other tourists. I experienced the ancient structures preserved here and elsewhere in the city as incarnations of undisguised authoritarianism in their style and proportions. I admired the intactness of this patriarchal style, its open declaration. The way you admire a beast of prey at the zoo. The image of being eaten by the beast is not one of my ideals. In front of the architectural monuments were street vendors hawking plastic reproductions of famous sculptures and sets of slides. Michelangelo's David was for sale on every street corner in various handy sizes, unbreakable. The supply of souvenir junk was overwhelming. In the vicinity of Vatican City, it took on gigantic proportions. Which in their own way correspond completely to those of St. Peter's Square and St. Peter's Church. This building instantly convinces everyone who enters it that they are, at most, a speck of dust. The reigning pope is the preferred motif of religious kitsch. You can buy photographic postcard sets of Paul VI, depicting him in six different prayer positions. His picture adorns wall plates, ashtrays, cups, beer glasses, neck scarves, and room thermometers. His portrait is worked into articles made of shells and plastic forget-me-nots. Washable. The most extensive assortment is offered by the vendors in St. Peter's Cathedral. For example, rosaries are hawked in innumerable designs and price ranges, hanging by the thousands on revolving necktie stands. Shamelessly flourishing sales of stamps and money. The male State of Vatican City has, however, employed women for the vile mammon work in this gold mine. They wear nuns' habits, understand many languages, and calculate exchange rates in their heads. At the entrance portal of St. Peter's Cathedral are liveried men, powerfully built, like bouncers in bars. Their work is similar to that of the tavern business, except their job is to put not drunken men out in the fresh air but mainly indecently clad women. A list of what is considered indecent in the State of Vatican City is posted on both sides of the portal in Italian, French, English, and German. I can't remember the details of the regulations; I only know for sure that women wearing sleeveless dresses, miniskirts, and hot pants are forbidden to enter the shrine. My dress satisfied the Vatican's requirements. Directly behind the entrance on the right is Michelangelo's splendid marble Pietà; a twenty-eight-year-old woman was the model for the Virgin Mary. She holds the thirty-three-year-old Christ on her arm like a bouquet of flowers. This risqué work of art, which boldly contradicts the posted moral guidelines, was mutilated shortly after my visit by a religious zealot. Understandably. One cannot simultaneously castigate the flesh and worship it. We strolled around for a while in St. Peter's Cathedral, whose size and riches are so overpowering that I couldn't summon any feeling for its beauty. From the cool of the church back into the heat. Which had meanwhile developed into noonday heat. We fled under the fourfold colonnade to the others who had also fled. Their buses were parked around the obelisks in the middle of the square. Caligula had long ago absconded from Heliopolis with the red monolith, Nero had installed it in the Circus Maximus. In order to obtain enough columns for St. Peter's, Sixtus V had completely gutted the Septiconium built under Septimus Severus. We asked some tourists and pilgrims camped in the colonnade where to get a hearty lunch nearby. The menu at the German sisters' pilgrims home was recommended as guaranteed to be close by and hearty. We followed the recommendation because we didn't think ourselves capable, in our climate-weakened condition, of paying attention any longer. Across a stairway, we trustingly entered the pilgrims home like we would a GDR restaurant. Relieved of responsibility. The cashier at the entrance wrote out a voucher in German script. Discipline was required in exchange for the relief and the modest price. You couldn't choose a seat; they were assigned, by young nuns wearing habits. First, the places at one table were filled with diners, then the next. Even two exhausted pilgrims, who had taken refuge with their cross-laden breasts in a drafty corner, were called to order by relentless friendliness. The food was brought to the table in large bowls from which everyone could take as much as he pleased. Noodle soup, schnitzel, boiled potatoes, carrots, pears: food for hunger, nothing elaborate. Only the wine was portioned out in one-quarter liter carafes. Praying was not a collective duty. I was seated between two American women. The younger one didn't talk, because she wrote postcards while eating. The older one, a kindly, spindly nun wearing a habit, asked whether I came from the States too. 'From Berlin,' I said. 'East or West,' she asked. 'Democratic,' said I. 'Are you traveling with American Express too,' she asked then. And I asked her to repeat the question because I thought I hadn't heard correctly. But the old woman was really incapable of imagining that anyone could travel without American Express. It and the pilgrims home seemed like shelters to her, which she went back and forth between in the incredibly worldly Rome. She recommended various nice churches that I absolutely should see; the most charming would be St. Paul's, where her sister had fallen. On the back of her head, unfortunately; while admiring the frescoes that depict scenes from the life of St. Paul, she had such an unlucky fall that she had to stay in bed and hadn't been able to attend the charming mass at St. Peter's grave today. The nun said that tomorrow she was hoping to see the Holy Father, who presently resided in the summer palace, Castel Gandolfo, and wasn't making official appearances. It seemed self-evident to this woman that she had to pay dearly to get a view of the pope. Back to the hotel along the dirty onyx-colored water of the Tiber. Under plane trees along the bank, through sawing sounds. Rome's cicadas are immune to noise. Again I paid for my attempt to ignore the siesta law with complete exhaustion. In the evening Simon took me to the Pincio to recover. Which he remembered romantically from a visit eleven years ago. The splendid park on the Pincio Hill, where we enjoyed the sunset, following the advice of the guidebook, was meanwhile crossed by streets in all directions. Near them, cars were parked in which young people made love, primarily in the form of petting. We spent Tuesday in Trastevere.

On the other side of the Tiber Island, the pressure of Rome's colossal size disappeared; I walked with a spring in my step. The main street was densely edged by vendors' tables offering immense assortments of junk, at first religious junk, later secular. On the main street a few tourists still stood out here and there; on the side streets the residents went about their lives un-gaped-at. Simple people, poor people, many children. The children lent dignity to the shabby streets. Probably Paris, where traffic had banned children from the streets almost entirely, had seemed to me strangely rigid, indeed foreign because it lacked this dignity. Flyers lay on many streets of Trastevere. With the intriguing inscription 'Sexuality.' The inscription was deceptive. The flyers preached marriage as a practical and healthy institution with great advantages. One advantage, for example, was that by leading a moderate life, a person can free himself from useless juices that cause epilepsy and other illnesses. Religious innovators were promised hell. Recently the clergy began wearing civilian clothes on the street. Only in Trastevere did we still meet a few who were recognizable by their black. One cowl-wearer was ripping Communist Party posters, announcements of an election meeting for the city council, off an old wall. The meeting date was five weeks earlier. —Wednesday: Vatican museums. Why should I pretend I approached Rome differently than any ordinary tourist? One can't get to know and hate this flourishing industrial branch if one doesn't work through it. I was interested in this barbaric phenomenon, which is as remote from relaxation as from adventure. Simon didn't escort me in museums and churches because you can't smoke there. It didn't bother me, because a woman can move about easily in these places, even without a male companion. You advance in a stream of humanity flooding toward the goal, you don't have to ask the way there. The streambed is heterogeneous. To the left the immense, heat-reflecting protective walls of the State of Vatican City, to the right the exposed wares of the ice-cream and soft-drink vendors. Arriving, I purchase a ticket for five hundred lire in the throng, enter a screw-shaped round structure, and fling myself through the marble. Blindly, bombarded by the gum-chewing English of American visitors; some of them run in groups, some alone. The ones who are alone hold radios to their ears; you can borrow them. The radio-equipped ones look inward more than outward, hasten from sculpture to sculpture, from bust to bust, they hasten through billions-worth like puppets on invisible wires. Sometimes the marble is arranged according to motifs. Halls full of marble animals are on display, army commanders, emperors, artists, alabaster tubs. One can wade for hours through pagan art. On which I didn't immediately notice the standard vine leaf; I thought at first that the Vatican had collected only male statues whose sex was covered. Not until the Laocoön group did I notice that the popes did not seize art in a doctrinaire fashion but only displayed it that way: with uniform plaster ready-to-wear over the sex organs. Tourists' crying children grew quiet in the halls where mummies were to be seen and they could cool their hands on polished granite statues. But the children were quickly yanked along and were soon covering their eyes with their hands again, to protect themselves from the onslaught of goblins and painted suites of rooms. Extracts of artistic life piled up like mountains of skulls. Now and then, I allowed myself a glance out of the opened windows into Vatican City. Splendid façades and gardens could be admired, with pines, cedars, fountains, colossal battlements, idyllic corners. And lawns of a perfection that had exorcised all lawnlike qualities. The green carpets and the no less perfect gravel paths were empty. No footprints anywhere. Only the cicadas enlivened the sacred off-limits area with their sawing. Black limousines parked before the façades. A long, narrow passage leads to the Sistine Chapel. I expected churchly coolness, quiet. Heat and noise greeted me. The heat came from the bodies closely crowded together. The noise reminded you of excited soccer audiences. I stood confused, then strangely bemused, indeed, soothed in this tumult. Suggestive harmony fell from the walls, at first glance brownish. Only gradually did colors appear from the tinting. Perhaps I too involuntarily contributed exclamations of wonderment and amazement to the palaver that hung at a constant volume in the room. Anyone who makes his way through Vatican magnificence and oversized objects to this space must experience it as simple, severe, small, humanly proud, and of an absolutely obstreperous sublimity. Sacrosanct for those who prescribed the institutionalized vine leaves. Not even God's representatives on earth dared to mutilate Michelangelo's art.

Lunch with a literary agent, arranged by Simon. I was told that if I wanted to obtain a hearing as a poet in capitalist countries, I had to acquire eccentric quirks and arrogance in order to call attention to myself personally. Literature obviously needed the same noise that must be adjusted in type and volume to the rapidly changing fashions prevailing at any one time. The literary agent thought my narrative fantasies were outdoor flowers from a society where human beings can live in innocence. The gentleman did not think that such plants could grow in the inexorable pace of capitalism, not even in a greenhouse there. As greenhouse plants, their cheerfulness would turn into cynicism. He gave my plants hardly any chance in his country, thought the future looked increasingly bleak for the marketability of literature, confessed to existential angst; he expected me to answer the question of whether I would like to live in his country with 'no.' Any other answer would have disappointed him. I had similar experiences during other encounters in such circles. Melancholy over expensive schnapps. Discussions of the most recent call-girl scandal, which all the newspapers were circulating. The call girls were daughters of the highest social circles, the customers were elderly stress-plagued men of the same class. The girls had to act out genuine feelings — desire, passion, bondage. Buying a woman didn't appeal to the rich businessmen, they wanted to buy love. A place of refuge where they could take a vacation from themselves. The girls needed money for luxuries appropriate to their class. I paid for my travels with the loss of wanderlust. Paid dearly. Nevertheless, I too threw a coin over my shoulder into the Trevi Fountain before leaving Rome. But until the Communists have taken power, I cannot repeat Goethe's exclamation at the top of my voice, 'Oh, how happy I was in Rome!' For a woman of character today can only be a socialist. And she must enter politics if she wants to achieve humane conditions for herself. In Italy, above all, and in other capitalist countries, she first has to enter politics; anything less is emancipatory faddishness. Moral relations can only be revolutionized after the revolutionizing of economic relations. One cannot take the second step before the first. In the GDR the first step has long since been taken. Now we are working on the second one, selah.

Chapter 25

Wherein the reader finds a provisional appraisal of the Vietnam War, prepared by a member of the Stockholm Institute for International Affairs (SIPRI), copied by the Beautiful Melusine into her 311th Melusinian book

In the Vietnam War the United States has extensively tested new military tactics and new technologies.

In the area of tactics are:

- the extensive deployment of Air Cavalry (infantry in helicopters);
- the use of herbicides to destroy crops and forests and of bulldozers to level small strips of land;
- so-called open fire zones for artillery and air force, whereby there is hardly any differentiation between 'civilian' and 'military' targets;
- the use of 'fatigue gases' on the battlefield, both to extend conventional firing power and to contaminate areas or close them off;
- meteorological warfare, the deliberate generation of rainfall;
- resettling of the population, sometimes with subsequent destruction of the settlements by fire, bulldozers, or artillery;
- the deployment of mercenaries from Thailand, (South) Korea, and the Philippines; subsidies for so-called ghost armies — often in ambiguous uniforms and under unknown command; deployment in Laos of a special air fleet, the CIA-supported Air American;
- finally, the selective murder of residents who maintain relations with the Communists.

In the technological area, the following innovations deserve attention:

- thirty carrier systems for CS gas, a powerful tear gas;
- flying 'fire ships' and flying 'cannon boats,' which light up the night sky and are equipped with miniartillery (repeating machine guns with extraordinarily high rate of fire);
- signal sondes that react to light or warmth, to mark persons at night;
- first-time testing of U.S. Terrier ground-air-rockets and of Shrike antiradar rockets;
- prolonged deployment of weapons that are aimed exclusively at persons: containers of bomb bundles that explode in the air, dart bombs, splinter bombs, bullet bombs, and so forth; bombs steered by laser beams or TV cameras;
- special machines for tactical aerial recognizance and electronic defense, especially over the South China Sea and North Vietnam; unmanned 'drone' aircraft for aerial photography and electronic defense; ground sensors that detect pedestrian and auto traffic behind the enemy lines (these sensors function in various ways: seismically, thermally, etc.) and then transmit their information

to circling aircraft or drones that in turn transmit it to computers on the ground, which then call air raids ('electronic battle field,' 'electronic war'). Sensors with which tunnel systems can be detected from the air were also developed.

The effect of these methods of warfare and new weapon systems over ten years is considerable. For comparison, in the First World War only 5 percent of all war casualties were civilians; in the Second World War this percentage rose to 48 and in Korea even to 84 percent. But in Indochina an estimated 90 percent or more of those killed are civilians. As the Pentagon made known this year, since 1 January 1961, 863,577 'Communists' were killed in Indochina. Most probably, a majority were civilians (wounded persons were not mentioned in this report). According to the latest estimates of the Kennedy Subcommittee for Civilian Losses, 400,000 persons were killed and 1,300,000 wounded in South Vietnam since 1975 alone. Thus presumably, more than a million civilians have perished.

In the Second World War the Americans dropped approximately two million tons of bombs over Africa, Europe, and in the Pacific; during the war in Korea, 1950–53, the total was just short of one million tons. Between 1965 and the end of September 1972 alone, approximately seven million tons of bombs were dropped over Indochina, more than half under Nixon's presidency.

An estimated twenty-six million bomb craters were produced during air raids in Indochina between 1965 and 1971. Twenty-one million are located in South Vietnam alone. The amount of earth removed represents ten times the amount excavated in building the Suez and the Panama Canals together. It would cover a connected area of 13,000 square kilometers – one-thirteenth the surface area of Vietnam.

Between 1965 and 1971, nearly seven million tons of artillery ammunition were fired, that is, even more than in the bombing.

Billions of flyers were dropped over Indochina in psychological warfare operations. Given a total population of 49 million, the distribution equals about one thousand flyers per person.

Of the ninety thousand tons of chemicals that were deployed as weapons by the Americans, seven thousand tons were CS gas; the remainder were defoliants. From 1962 to the end of 1970, the crops destroyed would have been sufficient to feed two million people for an entire year.

Based on statements from the Pentagon, it can be concluded that 20,000 square kilometers of forest were sprayed and, for the most part, have withered. A total area of 3,300 square kilometers of forest and bush has been leveled by bulldozers so far. There were also attempts to burn down already defoliated forests with firebombs and napalm. Thus in April 1968, 2,000 square kilometers of the U Minh forest were eliminated by over seventy fires. The fire raged for over a month.

Bomb warfare, artillery fire, and the destruction of crops and forests were the reasons why at least 85 percent of all refugees in Indochina left their settlements. Approximately one-third of the peoples of South Vietnam, Laos, and Cambodia fled — 6 of 17 million South Vietnamese, 800,000 to 1 million of 2.8 million Laotians, and 2 million of 6.7 million Cambodians.

According to official estimates, $126 billion were spent in full costs for the war in Vietnam between 1965 and the end of 1971. That amounts to around $3,000 per inhabitant of Vietnam or $500 per American. Based on experiences with the costs of earlier wars — the Civil War, the Spanish-American War, and the First World War — a cost calculation was presented to the U.S. Congress, according to which the expenses for veterans and survivors of the war yield a total amount that is 100 to 300 percent over the initial budget of the war. As a consequence of the public debt caused by the war, this sum will rise by an additional 10 to 45 percent. Based on the sample year 1971, the war in Vietnam could possibly cost the United States a full $300 billion.

In addition, the United States bears the complete costs of the Korean and South Philippine troop contingents in South Vietnam, for the Thai contingents in Laos and Cambodia, and also for all the regular and irregular forces of the Laotians and Cambodians.

Deployment of a fighter-bomber costs $12,300, a remote B52 bomber $45,000. It takes $500,000 to train a pilot. On 16 March 1971 the Defense Department announced that a total of 7,602 aircraft had been lost over Indochina, among them 4,318 helicopters. (At the end of last August, the number had already reached 8,362; of these, nearly 4,000 were lost over North Vietnam.) The numbers are considerably lower than those reported by the other side as shot down. Hanoi claims that 4,000 planes were shot down over North Vietnam by 1972; according to reports from the Vietcong, in South Vietnam between 1961 and 1967, 7,690 aircraft were shot down or destroyed on the ground (presumably including

South Vietnamese aircraft). Pathet Lao forces claim to have destroyed around 1,000 aircraft between May 1964 and April 1969.

Since 1965, 2.3 million Americans have served in the military in Vietnam. According to statistics from the end of November 1972, 45,914 American officers and soldiers have died in Vietnam. An additional 10,287 perished in incidents or accidents outside of battle action or through illness; 303,522 were wounded. At least 70,000, if not 100,000, Americans have fled to Canada to evade the draft.

The South Vietnamese government estimates the number of casualties of their regular armed forces at 164,642, but American military sources believe the true number is substantially higher.

Chapter 26

Third Bitterfeld fruit: The Tightrope

Professor Gurnemann, director of an academic institute that studied the atomic structure of matter, employed a woman physicist on his staff. Her name was Vera Hill and she lived in B.; the institute was located outside the city limits, inconvenient to public transportation. On a peninsula whose inhabitants preferred to get around on bicycles and stared at outsiders. When the accelerator, long since out of date and ripe for demolition, had been built, the institute had been the talk of the village. Ever since local women had been hired as lab techs and reported that the physicists worked with scissors and studied films, the physicists counted as insiders. Vera Hill brought the research center into disrepute again. Stragglers from a town meeting who found themselves in the local tavern one spring evening decided at a late hour to take a written complaint to the institute director. He resided in a little neo-Gothic brick building, a former chocolate factory. When the delegation to deliver the paper wanted to pass through the entrance, the doorman opened the window but didn't greet them; on such occasions he customarily said, 'Good morning, Frau Doktor,' to Vera Hill; the two male delegates were asked to show their identification. The doorman read the personal information of those seeking entry to the director's secretary over the phone. Later he wrote out two passes with carbon copies, handed over the documents with a suspicious look, and pressed a button that produced a buzzing sound and opened the gate ensconced before the entrance to the brick administration building. The delegates' feet trod on patterned tiles that covered the corridor and vestibule like those in old butcher shops. Professor Gurnemann's office had a wood floor. He received the delegation in traditional costume. Fashionably orthodox physicists at the time wore their white lab coats long, those at the other extreme wore short ones with slits up the sides. Gurnemann, in a shortened, unslit lab coat, strolled the three-steps-long passage between desk and bookcase. These furnishings and the armchairs, which the guests were immediately asked to sit down in for lack of space, had clawed feet. Brass. When the two men had described the scandalous events verbally and handed over the accusing paper, the professor said, 'In investigating the structure of matter, the high-energy interaction of elementary particles is of utmost importance. Here we are dealing with pure interactions that are least disturbed by secondary effects and thus permit the most profound insight into an elementary process that actually occurs in nature. Although we cannot yet achieve the high energy levels of cosmic radiation with artificial particle accelerators, the accelerated or artificially produced particles are preferable to those of cosmic radiation for such experiments, since their natural and initial energy are unambiguously defined.' Gurnemann stopped talking. His assumption, ever since the giant oaks next to the new building had been felled, that the institute was again suspected of producing atomic bombs proved to be incorrect. Regrettably, the ridiculousness of the new rumor seemed to surpass that of the old one many times over, which caused Gurnemann to assess the chances of refuting it as slim. In any case, the claim that a female employee of his institute was crossing over the top of the village twice each workday could only be refuted at a cost. Misuse of research workers' time for unscientific purposes infuriated the professor. He did not smoke, occasionally drank wine until midnight at most, then he withdrew from the event, no matter what, and in general was preoccupied with consistency. His institute conducted research from 7:35 A.M. to 4:45 P.M. five days a week. The delegates asked Gurnemann to pay particular attention to the section of the document describing the threat to public morality posed by the apparition. Gurnemann recalled the two-room apartment that Dr. Hill lived in with her son. The son was three years old; the apartment was furnished with two beds, a table, three chairs, armoire, carpet, and bookcases. Walls not covered with regular patterns of wallpaper but tangible stone. Whitewashed. Originally, but meanwhile gray beneath the dust that the wind from the nearby gas works still blew through the window cracks and that the heat from the stove raised to the ceiling. This seemed not to bother Vera Hill. Gurnemann knew a gifted Hungarian colleague who attended international conferences with a toothbrush and pajamas in a paper bag. But Gurnemann definitely believed walking on air was an idiotic slander. The ability to speak while reading, which he had acquired during his term of office, came in handy again. He had large eyes, noticeably far apart, behind bifocal glasses. He read through the lower lenses and spoke. 'Since the investigation of particle structure is essentially carried out via scattering experiments, it is also necessary to be thoroughly familiar with the nature of the bombarded particle. Thus the hydrogen bubble chamber, in which only protons are present as scattering particles, has the best qualities for detecting particles and particle tracks in scattering experiments. The disadvantage, that neutral particles leave no tracks and the transformation path of the gamma quanta in liquid hydrogen is very great, is more than compensated by the fact that extraordinarily precise measurements are possible in the hydrogen bubble chamber, and thus the existence of neutral particles can be inferred by disturbing the impulse and energy balance of all the charged particles. The most favorable initial energies of the incident particles are in the interval 3 to 15 giga-electron-volts because, first, here the measurements are still sufficiently precise, and second, it is possible to produce kinetically all recently discovered particles or resonances of interest.' The abundance of written material that was spread out before Gurnemann, charging among other things offense to public decency, harm to public health and worldview, power outages due to short circuits, endangerment of youth and unsafe traffic conditions, occupied the professor's attention to such an extent that, despite having gained time while speaking, he still had not thought of a convincing argument. This angered him and moderated his judgment of fellow administrators who employed no female scientists. Noticing that the delegates' faces were distorted by respect and distrust, he continued. 'Dr. Hill's department is studying filmed interactions of positive pi-mesons with 4 giga-electron-volt energy in hydrogen bubble chambers. At present she is working with two-armed events. First, the geometry is calculated on the computer. Then the events are studied for completeness with the help of a probability test, the so-called Fit program. In this way the elastic interactions can be unambiguously separated from the inelastic interactions. In the cases where only one neutral particle is present along with the charged particles in the final state, the nature and qualities of these particles can be determined. In this way the cross sections for the channels with two charged particles are determined. In addition, the individual reaction channels are studied in detail, especially with respect to the existence of mesons and nucleons in an excited state in the various channels.' Professor Gurnemann could no longer resist the thrills produced by these detailed statements and pursed his beautiful lips. He then whistled, not through his lips but through his teeth; however, he asked the secretary to bring coffee. Although the absurd report had already sent him into an excited state. Because it was conclusive in itself and thus not lacking a certain elegance. Most pleasing was the supernatural aspect of the alleged phenomenon. Involuntarily Gurnemann remembered Vera Hill's mouth, the wide, arched lips with threads of lipstick in their creases, the skin looked puckered. A married couple in the thrall of a sect had seen the Holy Mother in this woman and interpreted this as a sign that the village would be spared in the event of atomic destruction of the earth. But even those complainants who charged trespassing and invasion of privacy, accusing Vera Hill of possibly or actually looking into their windows and balconies, as well as the defenders of public morality, traffic safety, and dialectical materialism, all the undersigned testified unanimously that Vera Hill crossed the village twice each workday, specifically around 7:15 A.M. and 6:00 P.M., in a southwesterly or, conversely, a northeasterly direction, walking on air. Their statements as to how high and how fast differed; the owner of an orchard alleged, in her request for compensation of damages, that Vera Hill had knocked down yellow plums and cherry-tree branches with her briefcase. A short circuit at about 5:50 P.M. on the third day of Christmas, which had left the village without electricity for over two hours, was likewise blamed on Vera Hill. The tavern keeper thought that morally sensitive citizens and children could not be expected to tolerate the sight of lace-trimmed black nylon underwear and garters. Gurnemann recalled long, slender thighs, put the document into a file folder, served the guests coffee, rubbed his hands together and promised to investigate, sipped the foam of his coffee, and asked if he could keep the document. The delegates reminded him of the list of those to receive a copy that was appended to the document; it named the institute as one of seven institutions. At that, the professor sent the men away with a handshake. Acutely unnerved, for he feared that his request for hard currency to purchase an English computer would not be granted. Without it, the institute would not be competitive internationally. The computer building was in the planning stages, its financing was secured, the oaks had been felled. Gurnemann abandoned his coffee, threw his winter coat over his white lab coat, crossed the courtyard in long strides, and kicked open the door of the institute building. It smelled of scorched capacitors. Lab, workshop, library, and computer were housed on the first floor; on the second floor were the cells of the experimental physicists. Each cell had a blackboard with a tray for chalk and erasers, a desk with scissors, ruler, and protractor hanging on its right side, a chair, bookcase, coat hooks, a typewritten inventory of the furnishings in a plastic envelope, a square window with milk glass in its lower half, blue tile floor, two meters by four meters forty-six, and a door painted a different color than all the others, each one unique like the entrances to beehives. Frau Hill was assigned to a cell behind a lime green door. The door was locked. Gurnemann knocked with both palms, since he assumed that Vera Hill had earphones on and the tape player running, which she described as an instrument of cognition, since, as she said, true science and true music are rooted in the same thought process. Gurnemann did not deny that scientific thought had a poetic element but did not think Hill was more talented than he, because neither of them could get along without the assistance of sensory constructs, which is why he insisted on discipline and chalked his initial on the still locked door. The lab workers considered this form of reprimand an insult to their honor. On the third floor, where the theoreticians' offices were located, the corridor walls were covered with pictures of saints — Copernicus, Galileo, Giordano Bruno, Newton, Cavendish, Coulomb, Ampère, Galois, Gauß, Minkowski, Maxwell, Planck, and Einstein. In response to his question, the theoreticians Hinrich and Wander informed Gurnemann that Dr. Hill, after receiving a telephone message from the nursery school, had left the institute about a half hour ago, her son had apparently taken ill or something. Gurnemann, himself the father of small children, vacillated between principle and compassion, asking jokingly by which means the woman had left the institute. 'By air,' the theoreticians replied. At that, Gurnemann briefly doubted his sanity. Although he was hardened; the director of the mathematical engineering department was a fanatical hang glider; an electronics specialist had married his fiancée's mother, two of the theoreticians who worked on the third floor of the institute were sleepwalkers, he had not yet been faced with air walking. He still believed it was a figment of the imagination. Recently a malicious figment, which could, perhaps even was intended to, damage the reputation of science in general and his institute in particular. Obviously, mystical ideas had infiltrated the materialist worldview of his research team, without his having been informed of such scandalous events. Was he being excluded from institute gossip because of his position? Were staff scientists posing as sect members in order to topple him ideologically? Or they could be trying to deceive him. Intentionally or unintentionally, for the same reason. Weighed down by dark premonitions, Gurnemann withdrew to the villa, also located on the institute grounds, that was provided to him as an official residence. There he spent the rest of the day in front of the TV. During the night he got the idea that the rumor was a plot by Hill to get revenge and swore to refrain from all extramarital intimacies from now on. In the morning he woke up with a headache but in a mellower mood, because he had remembered with pleasure that Hill was one of those rare women who didn't want to get married. Also he valued her manic way of working and her habit of not forcing conclusions but letting them evolve. Filled with confidence that the confusion would resolve itself in a rational, natural way of its own accord, Gurnemann had a good breakfast and set out for Vera Hill's study a second time, where, to his delight, he actually found her. He said good morning. Holding her hand in his, he found his errand absurd, whereupon he felt embarrassed and asked about her son's health and the progress of her postdoctoral thesis. Her answers were encouraging. And tersely given; if Gurnemann hadn't been abruptly asked the real reason for his visit, he would have kept it to himself. He stated it in a subordinate clause. The main clause was a compliment. Vera Hill pushed aside her bangs by smoothing both index fingers over her brow from the center outwards. As usual, she seemed able to close her mouth only with an effort, although her bite was normal. Gurnemann suspected too that she always had something in her cheek, at least her tongue. To be on the safe side, he apologized for the absurdity of the suspicion, which of course neither he nor any other reasonable person believed even for a moment. 'Why?' asked Vera Hill. Gurnemann asked her to help him dispose of the matter pragmatically as quickly as possible. He said an institute like his was so vulnerable financially that even a delay in the flow of hard currency occasioned by absurdities could inestimably diminish scientific opportunities. 'The absurdities increase scientific opportunities,' said Vera Hill. 'Those of our rivals,' said Gurnemann. 'Do you see me as a rival?' asked Hill. The question annoyed Gurnemann. Vera Hill saw it in his face, which is why she explained that without the timesaving shortcut on the tightrope, she wouldn't be able to finish her postdoctoral thesis by the deadline, since, unlike him, she did not have access to the labor of a wife or maid. When she had done her shopping after work, picked up her son from nursery school, made supper, eaten, drawn pictures of cars and other objects requested by her son, bathed him, told him a story and put him to bed, also washed dishes or laundry or mended a hole or chopped wood and carried briquets up from the cellar, with the help of the rope trick she could be back at her desk by about 9:00 P.M. thinking about invariances; without the rope, an hour later. Also had to get up an hour earlier without the trick. After less than six hours of sleep, she couldn't come up with any useful ideas. Gurnemann spoke beseechingly and at length with her about the unreality of this means of transportation. The next day Vera Hill lost her balance on the way home. The lamplighter discovered her shattered body in the front yard of the public library.

Chapter 27

Laura takes preventive measures

Beatrice's third Bitterfeld fruit was a chance product. Which had been occasioned by an encounter in the Thomas Müntzer Agricultural Production Cooperative. The trobadora, who was there on a study visit, became acquainted with a cattle breeder. Who spoke to her affectionately about his hardworking wife. His wife worked as a lab tech in the nearby academic research institute. Her curiosity aroused, Beatrice visited the lab worker. From whom she learned that the institute was directed by Professor Gurnemann, a friend of the Professor Wenzel Morolf so admired by Beatrice. Thus the fruit grew. But then Beatrice was displeased with it, not only by the accidental way that it originated. However, she now went systematically to work on her new novel. Visited Benno often at the construction site, obtained permission from the company director to lend Benno, the nail driver, a helping hand after an appropriate period of instruction and training. She took the work upon herself, especially during cold and rainy weather. And studied technical manuals about the montage method of construction and socialist leadership. When the union chairman's secretary got sick, Beatrice wrote and copied the draft of the collective's contract. Laura got wind of pedagogical levers in Beatrice's travel reports. Which is why she gave them only limited credence. She was able to get Wesselin potty trained in time for Christmas. With Santa Claus as a pedagogical lever. This year Benno played the role of Santa. Laura had to lengthen the costume she had stitched together a year ago to fit him. 'And why was Santa Claus so tall?' was the first thing Wesselin asked the morning after the excitement. Holidays. During which strategic U.S. B52 bombers continuously bombarded densely settled regions of the Democratic Republic of Vietnam. Beatrice took over the kitchen work from Laura during the holidays. Also systematically. This made Laura uneasy. Indeed, she even started to resist. And it seemed to her high time to talk with Beatrice with preventive intentions about her grandmother's bad posture. She told the following story: 'The entire time that I knew my grandmother, her most favored position was stooped over. Standing, her calves, hollows of knees, and thighs in a straight line. To her last days she could maintain this position any length of time without feeling a rush of blood to her head or other ailments. In this position she washed the floors, waxed, weeded, planted, cut mushrooms, and gathered twigs. Her hands liked it better in the dirt than on floorboards and linoleum. In front her calf-length skirts were crumpled by her shoes, in back the skirts revealed her legs, clad in topstitched or hand-knitted stockings, above the elastic garters under the knee. She had acquired the ability to work in a stooped-over position in her younger days. As a servant girl. The entire time that I knew her, she hated birds.'

Chapter 28

Olga Salman's petition to our dear Frau Persephone, delivered by Beatrice de Dia, copied by the Beautiful Melusine into her 396th Melusinian book

Dear Frau Goddess Persephone,

From Frau Dia, who is a good friend of yours, I learned that you can occasionally do something for people like us. Well, I wouldn't say no. You see, the few Sundays and holidays when my husband didn't have to work you can count on your fingers. When other people went for walks or on outings, I sat home and waited. In the warm seasons when other people are traveling, the railroad had holiday bottlenecks, in bad weather less so. Toward the end of the year, the administration always tried to take care of the vacation backlog somehow, but naturally not at Christmas or New Year's, God forbid. My husband could practically retire two months earlier, that's how much vacation backlog he had collected – railroad, my life. I waited nearly forty years for the day for this fiasco to finally be over and Sunday to be Sunday and holidays holidays. Six months ago it was at that point, but if you're thinking we were now going on outings or traveling, you are mistaken. My husband says he was on the road long enough. And he sits. And stays put. All day he hangs around the apartment from early to late, asks what there is to eat morning, noon, and night, sticks his nose in the cooking pots, hangs his head out the window, wants to go out on the balcony the minute I sit down at the sewing machine, which is in front of the balcony door, sleeps in front of the TV, demands to be waited on when I've sat down, starts talking to me when I pick up a book, the rest of the time he's mute as a fish. I used to be able to read a few lines or do some tailoring when my husband was at work, now all I do is run to the kitchen, day in, day out. So if you could do for me something similar to what you did for your friend Beatrice, I would have no regrets.

Respectfully,
Olga Salman

Chapter 29

Laudatio for the poet Guntram Pomerenke on the occasion of his induction into PEN, delivered by Beatrice de Dia according to the model that was intended for the trobadora on the same occasion a year earlier

Anyone who has once seen Guntram Pomerenke will scarcely be able to forget him again. I sat across from him for over two hours during a solidarity rally for the release of Angela Davis. After that, my friends and certain colleagues declared me to be abnormal because I had not fallen in love with Pomerenke. To tell the truth, to this day I don't understand my abnormal behavior. For what poet of the German language can equal him? The length of his short fingers is in ideal contrast to the width of his shoulders. The high arch of his breast is brought out to perfection by fitted shirts. One guesses the gently defined leg musculature, comparable to that of young dancers, shoe size forty-one. A dark complexion. His skin spans his arms tightly – is it presumptuous to draw conclusions about the whole from those parts that I am familiar with? Moderately padded with fat, it hides the network of veins. Narrow skull similar to that of greyhounds, which, as we know, are wolf hunters. Voluptuous brown covering of hair. Under his nose, trimmed to a length of one to two centimeters, on the chin approximately five centimeters, the hair on his head reaches his shoulders. Gifted amber-colored eyes. Their gaze is no less penetrating than Pomerenke's verses.

Chapter 30
In which Laura finally makes a shocking discovery

'Our vacation in Warnemünde wasn't bad,' said Laura to Beatrice on 3 January 1973, 'and practically a gift. But for next summer could you have your sister-in-law, Melusine, conjure a visa for Almaciz for a change.' – 'I think Almaciz is a fable,' said Benno. 'Thinking is not enough; one must also believe,' said Laura. At that, it seemed to Beatrice high time to seek a compromise with Melusine, for various reasons. Negotiations along those lines took place on 11 January on the roof of Osterstraße 37. As is well known, the roof was surrounded by a balustrade-like wall that was meant to hide the chimneys and simulate steam heating. Since no proper fire could be started in the stoves connected to the hidden chimneys because they didn't draw, the chimneys had to be made taller after the fact. However, the secret negotiations helped lend the walls a function after all. Melusine gave Laura the prospect of being transported. No more could be achieved at the moment, since Persephone had already set aside her entire yearly allotment for Olga Salman. The negotiations took place in a sisterly atmosphere. At their conclusion Beatrice presented her sister-in-law with a draft of the first chapter of her future-oriented novel. On 28 January, when the cease-fire arranged as part of the Vietnam agreement had been in force for one day, Laura noticed that Beatrice had even begun to look like her. 'Why are you training yourself so hard?' she asked, shocked. 'Do you want to double me? Do you want to render yourself superfluous?'

Chapter 31
Olga Salman's wish is granted

The cheerful hope that her life would take a cheerful turn had already left Olga Salman as soon as the petition had left her hands. She had lost the strength to hold onto cheerful hopes. All she could hold onto were dark hopes. Not because her life had been especially hard. Its emptiness had embittered her. And marked her: the corners of her mouth had turned down. She had lost all curiosity. All that interested her on television was the weather report. A remnant of pleasure in shopping still remained, it stirred at the sight of fabrics. But the thought that Olga Salman wouldn't get out of the house anyway banished her pleasure in sewing, made purchasing fabrics seem useless. Olga Salman, the tailor, had uncut fabrics lying in cupboards! Even her daughter wouldn't have believed it before seeing it with her own eyes. But she had overlooked it. The way daughters do. Parents are closer to their children than children to their parents. External activity into which Olga Salman had retreated more and more was her purpose in life since Johann Salman's retirement. She swept or mopped the apartment every day now, fetched milk from the dairy every day, although she had a refrigerator, beat the rugs every day. On the carpet frame that was set up in the middle of the bleaching plain. On a foggy morning in early March, when she was busy beating rugs again, she heard a strange clattering and rustling. It came from above, out of the grayness. Visibility was about ten meters. With eyes turned skyward, Olga Salman headed through the garden gate to her vegetable patch where she was going to dig a leek for the bean soup; there the Sphinx landed beside her. On the roof of the cottage. Woman down to the navel, below that dragon, the apparition corresponded to the image of the Beautiful Melusine that Beatrice had described to Frau Salman. Thus Olga Salman was startled but composed. 'Are we starting?' she asked matter-of-factly, turning around to see if she was being watched. The building was invisible in the fog, their apartment, the bleaching plain. 'Do I have time to take off my kitchen clothes, shall I let my husband know?' — 'Your husband will find out from me, it's enough if you take off your apron, in three hundred years even your best dress will be out of style. I wasn't granted more than three hundred years, or would you rather sleep less than three hundred years?' — 'By no means less,' said Olga Salman, 'I'm thinking, a lot will help a lot, and one should take what is given to one, it's being given to me, isn't it?' — 'As an exception; Persephone thinks a pact with you would be unproductive. In your case she favors charity, that is, elixir; the cottage is stable enough to sleep in temporarily. In forty-three years we will own a Bulgarian cave monastery, then you'll be transferred there.' — 'We?' asked Olga suspiciously. 'I thought Frau Persephone was in charge of everything.' — 'In actual fact she is in charge of nothing, are you ready?' — 'Always ready,' said Olga Salman. And let the Beautiful Melusine escort her into the cottage. Salman's old kitchen sofa stood there, surrounded by bundles of firewood, sawhorse, chopping block, and tools. Johann Salman had rented the cottage to use as a shed, mainly for the stockpiling of firewood, which this man had practiced ceremonially for years. He couldn't live in peace without a head start of three or four winters. Olga needed the same head start for canned goods, which were stored in the cellar and filled it up. The house and garden were controlled by the communal housing administration in trust. The owner had moved to Swabia in 1945. Olga Salman brushed the dust from the sofa, took off her smock apron, lay down under the sofa blanket, put her folded apron under her head, and looked expectantly at Melusine. When the Beautiful Melusine had made sure that the window shutters were locked, she took a vial from under her left wing and handed Olga Salman the half-filled container. Olga drained it in seven swallows, shuddered, and compared the taste of the elixir to beech-tar cough syrup. Then the Beautiful Melusine took a spindle from under her right wing, pricked Olga Salman in the finger with it, and the magic began working immediately. Johann Salman, who was informed in writing the same day, ate his noon meal in the railroaders' club from then on. On weekdays he ordered a dish that cost seventy pfennig; on Sundays he laid down one mark twenty. Unshaken in his conviction that ruled out miracles. And he saw no reason to change his principles, which forbade discussions of things that do not exist. While sawing or chopping wood, he covered his wife's face with a clear plastic sheet to protect it from dust. On Women's Day he replaced the old kitchen sofa with the new one.

Chapter 32

Which the Beautiful Melusine copied from the GDR book *Intimacy between Men and Women* by Dr. Siegfried Schnabl into her 103d Melusinian book

It is clear that from the perspective of the continuity of the life process across generations, organisms with separate sexes are a life unit, which can only realize the automatic sexual reactions contained in their life paradigm by mutual effort. Since the realization of developmentally prescribed behavior patterns reconciles the entire life process, the successful experience of copulation is an important individual, harmonizing element of life . . .

In copulation the conditioned sexual reflexes undergo confirmation of success upon the experience of pleasure. This experience, called orgasm, is accordingly a necessary element, typical of every higher life form, harmonizing the total life process.

The most striking difference between the sexes today, confirmed clinically and by past and present surveys, is that the woman — on average in the total female population, not in every individual case — experiences orgasm much less often than the man; in fact (according to available scientific literature and roughly calculated according to our own investigations) at a ratio of one to ten. This result demands that the conditions observed today be changed.

Chapter 33

Laura is transported

On 11 February 1973 the Beautiful Melusine betook herself unobserved under the marital bed where Laura and Benno slumbered hand in hand and waited there until the subject had fallen soundly enough asleep. When Laura began to murmur while dreaming, Melusine thought she was ready for flight. So Melusine rolled out from under the bed as noiselessly as possible, lifted the down coverlet, separated the couple's clasped hands, conjured Laura into a fur-lined overall with a hood, and loaded the sleeping woman onto her armor-plated back. Then she opened the window and flew away with her passenger. Over Magdeburg, Cologne, Mannheim, Reims. It didn't start raining until just outside of Paris. Soaking the election campaign posters pasted everywhere on the walls. The Beautiful Melusine was satisfied with the proportion of left-wing campaigning. She shattered a window on the top floor of the Musée de Cluny with her tail, flew several rounds over the Latin Quarter until the rain stopped and the moon burst through the clouds, and finally, since the museum guards had not been awakened, neither by the noise nor by any alarm system, steered through the empty window directly to the staircase in front of the eleventh hall. Landing. Opening of the door with a skeleton key. Unloading of the payload. Melusine unbuttoned Laura's fur and sprinkled her with a somnambulizing elixir. It left brownish spots on Laura's face that reminded you of freckles. Melusine cursed. At Persephone, who had been in Hades for three months now as Pluto's wife; was her bad mood a reason to deliver inferior quality? Had Mr. Lord God not granted her anything better? Damn official channels! The nightgown seemed to Melusine too thin for a tour, the overall too heavy. So she took Laura's nightgown and overall off and led her naked into the eleventh hall. The hall was round. Moonlight illuminated the wall tapestries. They required the ideal perfection of the circle. Six tapestries into which a noble lady with a unicorn had been woven, also lions, wolves, leopards, monkeys, chamois, rabbits, all kinds of birds, trees, and blossoming plants; the male variety was absent. All the creatures seemed to be equal on the red background, leveled out. A suggestive peacefulness as under sunny olive trees. Laura strolled around the room for an hour. Without getting cold. She stayed longest in front of the sixth tapestry. It displayed a blue and gold tent held open by the lion and the unicorn. The fringed curtain hanging from the tent roof bears the saying, *A mon seul désir.* Return flight over Frankfurt (Main).

Chapter 34

Wherein the Reader Finds an Article from the Newspaper *Neues Deutschland* in 1973, Which the Beautiful Melusine Copied into Her 161st Melusinian Book

Rome (ND). An Italian woman from the remote area of Pescara gave birth to her baby in a cave and lived there with it for two years. The case only became public now after part of the cave collapsed and the mother, Lucia Colella, and the child were taken to a foster home. Lucia, who was twenty-two years old at the time, had been driven out of her parents' home in Caramanico because she was pregnant and refused to name the baby's father. Although the residents of Caramanico knew that the young woman was eking out a living with her child in a nearby cave, nothing had been done to help her during those two years.

Chapter 35

Wherein Laura Tells Benno Her Love, Disguised as a Story

Playtime: I take the pistol that was offered to me thirty-three years ago, I was six years old then, the boy's name was Ferdinand. For ten months I met him every day in ground-floor rooms of the old school. There a gaunt spinster named Fräulein Riedel had organized a preschool kindergarten. I brought my breakfast in a red shoulder bag made of cardboard. My mother went with me the first day. While we were getting ready for roll call and the assembled children were being lined up according to height, Ferdinand held a red pencil in his left fist. Chatter, warnings to the rhythm of hand clapping, commands amplified by the echo of the hallway arch played around his head, which was covered with dull black hair. I stood in the noise as if in the sounds of an organ. Up high, twenty-one steps led to the portal of the old school. Nine chestnut trees shaded the façade. They towered over the slate roof. The chestnut trees in the cemetery next door did not reach farther. As soon as the line had been formed, the assistant reported to Teacher Riedel. I stood at the front of the roll-call line, Ferdinand beyond the middle. He wore brown stockings attached to garters, the red pencil behind his ear. At the neckline of all her dresses, Teacher Riedel wore the brooch of a Nazi women's organization, which pushed and wrinkled the skin of her neck. After we had fallen out, the assistant rolled a pot with breakfast cocoa through the hall, like garbage collectors rolling trash cans. The rooms were large and so were the doors and windows, everything about the old school was high and large. The ceilings lay in twilight even on sunny days when no lamps were lit. Anyone who climbed those twenty-one steps ascended into evening in the summer. In winter, when the leaves lay on the forecourt, stoves filled the rooms with dark smoke. These stoves had cast-iron outer shells, similar in shape to a sugarloaf, with relief patterns. Friezes of naked men with helmets and swords were to be seen, rearing horses, contorted and fallen horses, letters of the alphabet and flowers. The janitor constantly had to stoke the fire to keep the convex stove doors red-hot. Ferdinand traced the stove horses onto paper with his red pencil. Sometimes I brought him some from a roll that had been given to my father by a worker in the paper factory. Ferdinand needed a lot of paper. When his right hand got tired, he switched the red pencil to his left hand. Teacher Riedel reprimanded him for this. Also for his unparted hair, all the other boys had their hair parted. The teacher had a tight bun at the back of her neck, with hairpins stuck into it. I liked women whose earlobes were stretched out by earrings. Cacti stood on the windowsills. Each window frame had a gear attached near the ceiling that could be moved by link chains. The sound reminded you of winding grandfather clocks. My aunt Jenny had a grandfather clock with a Westminster gong; the sound of the gong was so pleasing to my ears that I occasionally ventured forward to be allowed to open the ventilation flaps at the upper window. This task was only given to obedient older children. Ferdinand wouldn't have had a chance. He spoke very little when asked. I didn't know what to say when I sat next to him. Rarely, he would look up from his paper and stare. Mostly toward the window, probably down the steps to the street crisscrossed with tracks, down the slope that we sledded on in winter, down to the launching hill of the shunting yard. Inspired by pain, I wished myself after him, rode on various freight trains, on the roof of a locomotive from forty-four, exciting smells of soot and iron but not as nice as before. Ferdinand redefined locomotives to caterpillars and caterpillars to fog and fog to lizards. He didn't let anyone or anything distract him from his words, not even Teacher Riedel, whom he usually got to leave him alone by naming mushrooms. He called me Negus. I believe he despised reality. When no activities had been arranged, the boys played close combat and the girls played hospital. The bandaging unit was fenced in by chairs and cradles. Sometimes it wasn't big enough for all the wounded. I collected doll bedding and waited. When Ferdinand finally showed up, shot or dead, I put them on him as bandages. He tolerated it reluctantly. From other girls too; I hated everyone who touched him. Especially his mother and sister. She had shortsighted eyes like his and crippled legs. Without calves, supported up to the knees by chrome splints fastened with leather, which pulled on her high shoe tops. This pretty girl dragged the toes of her shoes over the ground, I liked watching it. The low tables were covered with green linoleum that smelled of floor wax. Some of the chair seats pulled threads out of stockings and skirts. The walls of the toilets were smeared with excrement. I suddenly held back, my interest in watching and inventing sexual games had diminished too. Giving way to new, unheard-of torments; when there was ground mist the old school stood in clouds. Swayed, trembled, I walked as in a dream. The plaster of the façade had burst and fallen off in many places. Then the square porphyry blocks stood naked. Their color reminded me of frostbitten hands or kohlrabi. Inside the school building, it was cool, even on hot days, like in the church next door. The porphyry came from nearby quarries that are now full of garbage. Twice Ferdinand went with me to the graveyard. He shot with the pistol, I threw sticks at chestnuts. He considered the nuts we collected to be his property, although he had only gone 'bang' with his mouth; he had no caps. I wasn't allowed to try it, I couldn't even touch it. Nobody was allowed to try it or touch it; it was a semiautomatic Mauser pistol. Ferdinand always had the gun with him. It even made a bulge in the short dark blue knit pants that he wore Sundays to children's worship hour. The fact that his mother could force him to such unmasculine actions intensified my aversion to this woman. I went because of the organ. Never to Sunday school, there they only had a harmonium; the pastor played it himself, often the wrong notes. He spit when he talked. Ferdinand sang off-key. I was ashamed. Also because of his stretched-out stockings. He was never allowed to wear kneesocks sooner than I was. He was forbidden to swim in the river; he didn't have a father, either. I was sorry for him. I threw stones at him when there was an opportunity. Best of all, I liked to go to the railway embankment by myself, climb up a dwarf oak tree, and imagine that I was touching his dull hair. Not until fourteen years later did I feel even approximately that misunderstood and like the center of the earth. On the last day Ferdinand offered me the Mauser. I didn't dare believe it, had waited ten months for a sign, this one was too momentous for me to take seriously or accept at all. I ran away and never saw Ferdinand again. Thirty-three years later I return, take the bad plaything, and say thank you.

Chapter 36
Death of the Trobadora Beatrice

Beatrice excitedly followed on television and radio the elections of the French National Assembly, which took place on 4 and 11 March 1973. Not as optimistically as Melusine, who had not left the site of these events since the beginning of March. During the night from 4 to 5 March, Beatrice, Benno, and Laura downed three bottles of wine. During the night from 11 to 12 March, they downed six bottles of wine. The election victory of the left-wing parties sent Beatrice into such a state of enthusiasm that around 3:00 A.M. she started singing the 'Marseillaise.' Laura made toasts to the Paris of the future, where people, animals, and plants would live on Red soil. Benno discovered freckles on Laura's face and announced that summer had arrived. On 12 March he came to work late, that was a Monday. Laura was nursing her hangover with coffee. Beatrice took a bucket and chamois and climbed onto the windowsill. 'I don't understand how a trobadora can fall all over herself to burn up her enthusiasm this way,' said Laura before going into the kitchen. When Beatrice had washed the frame of the living-room window and polished one pane to a shine, the Beautiful Melusine appeared in the sky. She circled Osterstraße 37 three times. Then she disappeared in an easterly direction. Beatrice waved to her with the chamois. And in so doing, apparently lost her balance. In any case, Laura found the window empty when she entered the living room again with Wesselin a short time later. The dog, Anaximander, sat howling next to the scrub bucket. Shrieks and calls for help resounded from the street. They came from the crowd of people that had formed around the victim. When Laura reached the street, the ambulance had already arrived. The doctor confirmed the trobadora's death. One day later Laura's tear-swollen eyes read the following in the newspaper *Neues Deutschland*:

'The upturn of the left-wing parties, which won an additional 87 seats in the National Assembly, and the decline of the right-wing coalition, which shrank by over 100, from 372 to 271 delegates, has seized the attention of the French people. Although the election law is not always directly addressed, many publications point to the flagrant contradiction between the proportion of votes and the distribution of the delegates' mandates.

'As a matter of fact, the left-wing parties received a total of 46.54 percent of the votes – but only 178 delegates, while the right-wing coalition, with only 40.88 percent of the votes, received over 270 seats – and thus controls more than a majority of the seats – in the new National Assembly.

'The élan that brought the left-wing parties together in working unity in recent months, leading to a dynamic election campaign founded on a mutual program of government, is described in the lead article in Monday's *Humanité*. It says: "The French left wing is emerging from the elections with new strength despite the rigorous campaign of the ruling parties and the other bourgeois factions.

' "Communists, socialists, and the leftist radicals have won dozens of new seats. Our party alone more than doubled the number of its delegates. The left-wing electorate remained united in the face of right-wing attack. The right-wing coalition's losses would have been much more serious if the election procedure were not so unfair, if it did not deny a large segment of the French people fair representation, indeed, any representation in the National Assembly, if this election procedure did not disadvantage the Communist Party in particular."

'The article states that it is now necessary to continue moving forward, in the opposition and by means of democratic action, to win over millions more French people for the powerful hope represented by the leftist unity. "Everything, everything proves that it is possible to create a large and stable coalition of a majority of the people, which can open up a new future for France. This was only the beginning; the struggle will continue."

'The bourgeois newspaper *Le Monde* confirms, in an analysis of the election results, that the unified Left was able to win more votes than the three previous ruling parties but nevertheless receives fewer seats in the National Assembly. The newspaper emphasizes that the First Secretary of the Socialist Party and the General Secretary of the French Communist Party were not entirely wrong in condemning the election procedure. "When the number of votes received by the entire left wing in the 490 voting precincts on 4 March is added to those received on 11 March in the 424 voting precincts, the result is a total of 11,090,427 voters, while the ruling parties and their supporting factions have a total of 9,009,432 votes. Thus a minority of allocations corresponds to a majority of seats."

'Statements by the trade unions CGT and CFDT emphasize that after this upturn of the leftist parties, they are in an extraordinarily favorable position for new campaigns to fulfill the justifiable demands of the workers.

'There are also voices on the side of the ruling majority that warn against ignoring the demands of the unions after this election.'

SEVENTH INTERMEZZO

Wherein the Reader Learns What the Beautiful Melusine Copied from Irmtraud Morgner's Novel *Rumba for an Autumn* into Her 42nd Melusinian Book in 1964

When Uwe realized that the marriage wasn't just a crackpot idea but had already been settled with Berta, he left immediately. To think about how he could prevent it. He had to prevent it. Valeska wasn't there; he had to do something so Berta wouldn't make herself miserable because she couldn't say no. She still called him Katschmann, not Edgar but Katschmann, but she couldn't say no. So Uwe had to say no, she couldn't make decisions. She always left decisions up to others. She was too good, she was good to the point of lacking character, to the point of self-sacrifice, a great conciliator before the Lord, always had been. Uwe had to do something. He went to see Kantus.

Naturally, Kantus was still awake. He shuffled toward him in huge felt slippers and said, 'Do you know a place that sells salami?'

'Now?'

'Of course, now. Eight hours from now you can buy it from any lousy butcher. Now . . . '

'In the middle of the night?'

'My appetite doesn't go by business hours,' said Kantus.

Uwe knew that appetite. He said, 'I've just left a drunk.'

'I don't booze,' said Kantus. 'I'm just hungry for salami.'

'With red wine,' said Uwe.

Kantus socked Uwe in the ribs with the back of his hand and pushed him into the smoke-filled room. Kantus had a two-room apartment, but he only lived in this room. He slept in it too. The one that Uwe had once stayed in stood empty. Kantus slept on a bed frame that stood on piles of books. The tabletop lay on a crate in which the literature of German Romanticism was stored. If he wanted to read E. T. A. Hoffmann, he had to take the table apart. Along the walls from right to left, the history of philosophy from antiquity to the present, books about gliding, economic history, German and foreign-language belles lettres in alphabetical order, art books, cookbooks, magazines; the balcony door was piled shut with Marxism. Other than that, the room was furnished with two hard chairs.

'Berta says you booze too.'

Kantus sat down on the mattress, under a blue cloud. He balanced it on a curving stalk of smoke that swayed to and fro at the end of his cigarette. He rolled the cigarette carefully in his lips to the left corner of his mouth. When it was wedged in the left corner of his mouth, he was in a mood for conversation.

'I've just come from Berta's,' said Uwe.

Kantus squinted his left eye to keep the smoke out.

'Berta has a lot to do,' said Uwe.

Kantus opened his mouth a crack but said nothing. He only gripped the cigarette between the two teeth he still had. And at that, Uwe didn't say anything either. One could easily get the last word with Kantus. But not the first one. The first one belonged to him. He chewed it for a while by moving the cigarette back and forth with his lips, then he spat it out like spitting out a tobacco quid, splat, but without taking the cigarette out of his mouth, and then you could talk. But not before. Uwe had given him several openings. To no avail. Kantus didn't want to. What was there to talk about anyway on such an occasion. Katschmann wanted to marry Berta. She had decided to marry him. Probably, Franz had become a stranger to her when he came back in 1955. And he had remained a stranger to her, presumably because he maintained silence about why he hadn't gotten in touch since 1937. At any rate, she hadn't objected at the time, when Katschmann gave Franz to understand that he didn't appreciate his visits. Later, when Franz was in and out at Valeska's, Berta learned his story. Since then, she visited her daughter more often. Probably Berta had asked Franz over to her place this afternoon, to let him know her decision. And Katschmann in his drunken condition had taken Uwe for Franz. But Franz had been there. Uwe had smelled it. Katschmann didn't smoke. Berta had surely let Franz know her decision, for in a sense, she was still engaged to him. Engaged for thirty years. But that was her business. Uwe wasn't going to get mixed up in it. He had no right to get mixed up in it. Valeska did, but he didn't. He had his own problems. He said, 'I have great material for an article.'

Kantus rolled his cigarette a little way out of the corner of his mouth.

'If I sell the story well, maybe the place will even be shut down. I have nothing against science, but we can't afford luxuries in this tense situation. Economy measures have been in force for months, we run ourselves ragged after relevant examples that have something to them journalistically. I don't see why I should close my eyes to what's going on in this case. Exploratory research is necessary, all right, they can explore all they please for all I care, even if they have no idea where it's leading, but when that luxury costs this much money, I'm opposed to it. I'll start with the topical political tag line, I'll relate it to the latest news about the situation in the Caribbean, and then I'll say right up front that I'm opposed to such costly research in this situation. We're a small country, the enemy is right in front of our nose, we can't afford to be extravagant. Right?'

'So you want to undermine them?'

'Yes.'

'And what kind of people are they?'

'A bunch of eggheads; the West Germans think I'm a spy, an English professor said that if the Americans start beating up on Cuba, Russia won't intervene militarily because it can't risk a nuclear war for six and a half million people. An Armenian, his name is Paremusian or Taremusian or Karemusian, I call him Prince Igor, claims that the Americans won't risk an invasion simply because then they'd be all washed up in Latin America, a guy from Hamburg is convinced that it's going to blow up this time, he got stinking drunk the day before yesterday, but the next morning he took part in the debate again as if nothing had happened. I don't believe any of these people are against Cuba, but most of the ones from the West are against the Soviet missiles on Cuba. Only they don't get fanatically worked up about it; probably they can only get worked up about their statistical material, I think they believe that they belong to a family of a chosen few, the only ones who are allowed to anticipate a societal situation. A Swabian told me they had one guy at the institute who rarely washed; supposedly he says that as a physicist, he doesn't need to. The ones attending the conference all wash; some of them are even rather elegantly turned out. The local director, I call him Monsignor, is a damned good-looking man, of course, there are also boring types; probably they all put their pants on one leg at a time too, even the eggheads, but they're a bunch of queer fish, I don't feel comfortable among these people.'

'And that's why you want to undermine them.'

'The article will appear in the series The Productive Force of Science, but what they're doing in this institute only costs money, so I have to say something about it.'

'Who's forcing you?'

'Katschmann also thinks I have to say something about it.'

'And what do you think?'

'I've been thinking it over, back and forth, for three days. I shouldn't have accepted the assignment.'

'And what does the editor think?'

'The boss thinks I should finally get something down on paper, something you can talk about. You can't cross the bridge until you come to it. But I can't write. I just can't get anything done. Not even with the material I've collected.'

'Maybe the material isn't any good?'

'The material is exactly right,' said Uwe. He laid it out to Kantus. Franz stuck his cigarette to his lower lip and read.

'Well?'

'The air is too dry for talking here. I say let's go to a bar.'

They went. They looked for a while. Uwe rejected the smelly corner bars that would be closing soon. Franz rejected the ventilated taverns with coat-check rooms. Finally they agreed on a cellar bar that was open all night. They entered through the hatch.

A little cabin, sparingly lighted and ventilated, music from the foredeck box; people are dancing on the floorboards. Uwe and Franz sit down astern and order vodka. A bottle. Franz always ordered a bottle. Berta was right; he boozed. Maybe that's why she didn't want him any more? But why did he booze? People don't booze for no reason. Did Kantus have a reason? For eighteen years he certainly had one; he didn't talk about it, but if you sit in jail as an innocent man for eighteen years, if you cut down trees for ten years instead of typesetting newspapers, your own newspapers at last, that was certainly a reason. Only he wasn't boozing when he came back. He only started that later. Maybe on account of Berta. Maybe on account of Katschmann. Maybe because sometimes being put monstrously to the test is easier to bear than everyday life. Why didn't he ever talk about those eighteen lost years? He'd been strong enough to survive them unbroken. Did he now lack the strength to remember them?

'So you want to undermine them,' said Kantus, 'but you aren't quite brave enough.'

'I'm brave enough.'

'But you need encouragement.'

'Advice,' said Uwe.

'You can only talk about such complicated things if you understand a whole lot about them or nothing at all.'

'A journalist must be able to talk about everything.'

'I'm no journalist,' said Kantus. 'I'm a typesetter.'

'But you can help me. You're the only one who can help me. If you hadn't helped me back then . . . '

'Good Lord in heaven, don't forever be clinging to people.'

'Sorry,' said Uwe.

'Stick to the matter at hand for a change. Even if that's harder, even if it demands more than antipathy or love.'

'I do, but for me the matter at hand has a face.'

'What kind?'

'Yours,' said Uwe.

'Windbag,' said Kantus and poured another vodka down his throat. He threw his head back as if he were swallowing a pill; a small head, a small face, totally wrinkled, mouse gray eyes. The biggest part of this man was his eyes. He always squinched them shut, to adapt them to his body, which was spindly. Uwe wondered how this spindly body had been able to withstand such hardships. Getting punched in the kisser by your enemies hurts, but when you get it from your friends. Uwe said, 'Plischka advised me to change jobs.'

'Every Communist has bruises,' said Kantus, 'if you don't have any, you aren't one.'

'The physicists don't have any,' said Uwe. 'Do you see the tall guy over there, standing on the right, next to the entrance, now he's going to the bar; yeah, the tall black-haired guy in the Superman sweatshirt, that's one of those people. Shall I invite him to our table?'

Kantus stuck his lips out like a snout, out beyond his nose. He could do that because he only had two teeth left in his upper jaw, two long thin incisors with just enough room for a cigarette between them. Uwe was happy to see the snout. He had actually expected something else. Kantus was starved for people, he always wanted to be introduced to all kinds of people, in order to question them. Recently he had interrogated a Cambodian prince on a tour of the print shop about card tricks. When you went out with Kantus, you had to be prepared for all kinds of things. Kantus seemed to have no inhibitions whatsoever. He had shown up at a reception in a baggy, stained suit and socked a minister in the ribs with the back of his hand. But today he seemed tired; he said, 'I'm really not in the mood to let any queer fish spoil my schnapps.'

'Me either,' said Uwe. Of course, he had to keep Kantus from getting the impression that Uwe didn't want to because he was feeling inhibited again. Or because he was afraid of this sweatshirt giant. So he went on to say, 'The dark-haired guy's girlfriend said he talks whole notebooks full when he's drunk. And that seems to be the case; he's wobbling pretty well, maybe we should listen to him for the fun of it. You probably think I'm exaggerating, but you'll see . . . '

Kantus rolled his eyes out so far that one could have grasped them with a buttonhook like people used years ago to unfasten brass buttons from the fabric when they wanted to polish them. He rolled his eyes to the right and the left as if he wanted to measure out his face, and that was ominous. Whenever his face got too small for him, he was up to something. Uwe tried to draw his attention to a woman, but Kantus said, 'Fine, invite the boy to our table.'

And then, if he didn't want to make a fool of himself, Uwe had to get up, emerge from the crowd, everyone stared at him, of course; there was nobody who didn't stare at him and see how he was sweating. He had to walk across the wobbly floorboards, which were unoccupied just then, that's all he needed, the bar heeled over, he took big strides, the upper leather of his left shoe was ripped near the little toe, he offered Dr. Wenzel Morolf a sweaty hand. Morolf didn't know what to do about it for a long, long time. Uwe explained it to him, also for a long time. Morolf leaned down toward him; it took forever until Morolf recognized him. It's hard to remember the faces of people who are not personalities. Later Morolf came astern with him, the way back took only a moment.

Morolf rapped his knuckles on the tabletop, laid a trumpet on it, and plopped down on the bench.

Then he reached for the vodka bottle, which by now was half empty, and quickly finished it. He set it back down in front of Kantus, with his eyes closed, he wiped the back of his hand across his lips and then his whole face; he said, 'I shouldn't have turned around.'

'You should have left some in the bottle,' said Kantus.

It seemed to take a while for the words to reach Morolf. When they did, he forced his eyes open. It was hard for him to keep them open, his face was contorted by the effort. But he wrenched himself out of his drunkenness, was everyone getting drunk today, he leaned back, crossed his left leg over the right, and jiggled his right foot.

'A quarter liter . . . '

Morolf's eyes, which were hidden under his steep forehead like under a roof, glittered.

'In our village a guy guzzled down a liter that way once.'

'Aha.' Several times. Inflammatory.

'Another guy as tall as you, Gustav was his name, people called him Gust, he could do the work of three people and drink as much as ten,' said Kantus, checking the drunken guest out with his mouse gray eyes, from top to toe, from right to left, embellishing his pal Gust with many contradictory qualities in order to gain time, he could talk while thinking about something quite different; then he spoke jerkily as he was doing now, his cigarette stuck between the two long thin teeth, what was Kantus thinking as he said, 'It was hot, we were working in the field, I was still a child at the time, the reapers made a bet, if Gust could finish a bottle of schnapps without falling down, the ones who were betting against it would stand a round of beer. They brought the bottle, Gust drank it down at one draught, threw it in the straw, fell down, and was dead.'

'Aha, you're one of those who'd like to bite my head off and so forth. But it floats, you can depend on it, it floats and if it doesn't have a trumpet, it sings scat until it runs aground in Lesbos. There I get patched back together.'

Uwe poked Kantus in the ribs with his elbow.

'You should drink a cup of coffee,' said Kantus.

'I have to work, everything else is unimportant,' said Morolf. He said it as if there could be no doubt as to what everything else was.

Kantus drummed his fingertips on the tabletop. He had remarkably flattened fingertips. His nails were cut straight across. When someone at the print shop brought him something he couldn't decipher, he would make a point of getting up from his machine, take the illegible text to a table, and drum his fingers until he had it figured out.

'You're wanting to work in this condition?'

'It's not important if an idea is true or false or even if it has a clearly recognizable meaning, but whether it produces fruitful work,' said Morolf. Slowly, with longish pauses during which his child's eyes, which didn't suit his face at all, grew still. Sometimes he paused in the middle of a word, but you could understand him easily; the noises of the city were not to be heard in this cabin.

'My son-in-law told me a lot about you.' Morolf laughed, he opened his narrow-lipped mouth a crack and forced air through his teeth, spasmodically, his hunched shoulders twitching.

'Unfortunately, we have to be going,' said Uwe.

'I don't,' said Kantus.

'I don't either,' said Morolf. 'I prefer to work nights.'

Kantus rolled his cigarette into the left corner of his mouth and said, 'I understand.'

'Why?'

'I have my best conversations at night,' said Kantus.

'Who with?'

'With myself,' said Kantus.

'Then we're on the same wavelength. Waiter, a vodka for the old man.'

'Stolichnaya,' said Kantus.

'Or Wyborowa?'

'Stolichnaya, I like to drink something from home.'

'Are you from there?'

'Well, yeah,' said Kantus.

'From what area?'

'Various,' said Kantus.

'I studied there, my last six semesters.'

'Where?'

'In Moscow.'

'Tell about it.'

'What?'

'Doesn't matter. I was last there seven years ago. Tell about it, go ahead.'

Morolf started talking. Now he paused only briefly. And his eyes, which were dark, had many lights, as if he were standing in front of a Christmas tree or an illuminated Ferris wheel. And in a short time Kantus was walking through Kitaigorod with Morolf, quickly; Morolf seemed to be in a hurry. And then they went to Red Square, past the Vasily Cathedral, where a kvass wagon stopped. Kvass, said Kantus, rolling his eyes. They went through the little door on the right next to the Kremlin gate, the theater on the left, and then the white bell tower with the gilded onion roof. Freshly gilded, says Morolf, freshly gilded, says Kantus, and the giant bell Tsar Kolokol and Archangel Cathedral and Maria Annunciation Cathedral and Uspensky Cathedral, yes, says Morolf, and in the booth in front of the great Kremlin Palace red *winogradny, winogradny*, says Kantus; he had already forgotten Uwe. He squinted up at Morolf. The wrinkles in his wizened face rippled. It looked as if a light wind were ruffling pleated needlework. Morolf was the source of the wind. Blowhard, thought Uwe.

Kantus swung both his arms out, putting on a show. He said, 'Now let's have a big bowl of *pelmeni*, huh?'

Morolf reached for his trumpet, playfully pressing the valves one after the other several times, pursed his narrow, ascetic lips, put the mouthpiece up to them, but laid the instrument back on the table and expelled the air he had pumped into himself out through his nose. 'I'm not hungry,' said Morolf.

'Or a keg of kvass?'

'Today I'm only drinking schnapps,' said Morolf.

'Why, *Bratjez*, why, little brother?'

'Because I've lost her.'

'Ach.'

'Yes,' said Morolf.

Kantus laid his hand on Morolf's hairy arm; he'd pushed his sweatshirt sleeves up so that everyone could admire his furry arms. Kantus left his hand there. He had forgotten that he'd lost Berta and that he wanted to help Uwe.

'That buck Aristaeus tried to rape her,' said Morolf, 'but she knocks him unconscious and runs away, because she wants to tell me the news piping hot. To make me jealous, she knows that I'm raving jealous, and she's looking forward to the effect and, of course, doesn't watch where she's going. And steps on a snake, just on the right one, some poisonous creature that bites her right away, of course, well then. If someone dies of cancer or a heart attack, okay, but something like that. So I take my horn and descend into Tartarus to bring her back; I take the passage that stands open at Aornon. And when I get down there, I take up my horn and play. I play the Basin Street Blues and the Potato Head Blues and the West End Blues, I play for all I'm worth. And I bring them all around, Charon, Cerberus, and the three judges of death. And for the damned, I play one more number, free of charge.'

Kantus kept edging closer. He aimed his mouse eyes at Morolf's sweatshirt as if he were trying to read through it. But he said nothing. He only drummed his fingertips on Morolf's lower arm.

'Of course, Pluto won't budge,' says Morolf, 'everyone swings; he doesn't move a muscle. But with the Wild Man Blues, I get to him too, and he allows the beautiful girl to return to the upper world. Of course, he stipulates conditions. He says I can't look back until she's safe in the light of the sun. So we take off, she and I. I'm ahead. In the passage it's pitch-dark. I play "How High the Moon," so she can find her way. When I reach the sunlight, I turn around to look at her, jackass that I am. I can't wait when I see the sun. Waiting drives me crazy. And with women I can't wait at all. So I lost her, forever, and that's why I'm only drinking schnapps today, understood?' He wiped his gruff face again, all over with both hands, which were very beautifully shaped, he groaned softly; his forehead was split by a vein.

'And I spoke with her just this morning,' said Uwe.

'With who?'

'You know, with her, the lab tech who was working at the gap meter this morning; that's who it is, right?'

Morolf opened his mouth a crack again and expelled bursts of air spasmodically through his teeth. He laughed so loud that the couple dancing on the floor got slightly out of step with the beat. They kept time to the beat with their hips. One foot pivoted back and forth on its sole four times such that the toes pointed inward twice and the heels twice. A movement similar to that usually applied when you squash an insect underfoot. Meanwhile, the free leg kicked twice into the air. The arms were used to maintain balance. When the man slowly went down on his knees without interrupting the movement and slowly straightened up again, his outstretched arms hung quietly in the air like balance poles. As soon as the man went to his knees, the woman did the same, eyes half shut too, the dance required full concentration. But Morolf's arrogant laughter had irritated even these transfixed dancers. Only Kantus didn't get irritated. He preached reason and reacted according to feelings. People he liked could get away with anything. Obviously, he had taken a liking to this Morolf right away. Boozers always took a liking to each other. And Morolf was soaking it up, without asking questions; Uwe had to watch him taking it in, soaking it up.

'What are you actually working on?' asked Kantus.

'I don't work,' said Morolf. 'I do research.'

'Is there a difference?'

'Yes.'

'What kind?'

'The same colossal difference that a bored married man feels when he sleeps with his girlfriend.'

'Oh, hell,' said Kantus.

He'd been caught off guard again. He fell for every rhetorical trick. And his ears were as red as if he were in a hot bath.

'Why does a married man get bored?' said Morolf. 'Because there's nothing about his wife that he thinks he doesn't already know. But people are curious. So he breaks the commandments, finds himself a girlfriend, and sins. I can be curious every day without breaking the commandments, and I even get paid for it.'

'Paid well?'

'Good ideas are expensive.'

'So.'

'But we sell them dirt cheap.'

'Why?'

'A little country isn't rich.'

'Why do you work in this little country?' asked Uwe.

'Because I'm for order. Scientists are for order. Human beings can't tolerate chaos. They fight it, either with religion or with science. I fight it with science. Here. Of course, I could do it in America too; at every international conference there are people who buy up physicists, best offer, optimal working conditions, money and so on, for me, order and clarity have a great aesthetic appeal. I think that here, in comparison to that buyer's country, order prevails, in principle, not absolutely. The endlessness and inaccessibility of absolute truth ensures that the best is preserved for us: enthusiasm and reverence.'

Kantus socked Morolf in the ribs with the back of his hand. A sign that he was extraordinarily pleased with him. Morolf hadn't said a word about the city, but Kantus was pleased. Kantus said, 'So you do research. Why, actually?'

Why, why. But naturally this Morolf thought it was great. They both thought the other was great. Uwe caught himself looking over at Morolf again. At this ugly man who absolutely couldn't compete with Monsignor. Uwe ordered a bottle for himself.

Morolf took a piece of blue chalk from his jacket pocket and started drawing abstract patterns on the scoured tabletop, sliding the tip of his tongue back and forth between his teeth. And then he delivered a long soliloquy. He said, 'Kepler writes in the dedication of the *Mysterium Cosmographium*: Indeed, we do not ask what benefit the bird hopes for when he sings, for we know that singing is a pleasure for him because he was created to sing. In the same way, we must not ask why the human intellect expends so much effort to investigate the secrets of the sky. Our Creator joined the intellect to the senses, not only so that human beings can make a living — many species of creatures can do that much better with their irrational souls — but also so that we can advance from the existence of things, which we observe with our eyes, to the reasons for their being and becoming, even if no further benefit is connected with this. And just as the other living creatures and the human body are maintained by food and drink, the human soul, which is different from the total human being, is kept alive by that nourishment found in knowledge, enriched and, to a certain extent, challenged in growth. Accordingly, whoever carries no longing for these things within him is more like a dead man than a living one. Just as Nature sees to it that the creatures never lack for food, we can say with good reason that the diversity of natural phenomena is so great, the treasures hidden in the firmament are so rich in order that the immortal spirit may never run out of fresh nourishment, that man may not feel satiated with the old nor find rest, but rather that in this world a workshop may always be open to him for the exercise of his intellect.'

The long soliloquy made an impression on Kantus, of course. He was drunk but much differently than Katschmann. Katschmann collapsed into himself, Kantus grew when he got drunk. And the ideas that he got into his head grew too; he seemed to be impressed by everything about this beanpole guy who claimed to suffer from a photographic memory. Probably he suffered from much more. Anyone who could speak in a polished style when someone had died on him was not normal. Presumably, all people were dead for him when he was pursuing his science.

Uwe said, 'Excuse me, but we are a little country. When we spend money, we have to ask what the benefit is.'

Morolf said, 'Research in the area of applied science leads to reforms. Research in the field of pure science leads to revolutions. You'd probably like to undermine us a little?'

So he'd noticed it. He was treating him so contemptuously because he had noticed. Probably he was even a little afraid of Uwe. And he was trying to cover it up by speaking about it as if incidentally. One always states the most serious things incidentally. His sweatshirt was smeared with blue chalk. Maybe he was also blue from bruises. Uwe always did everything wrong. With Valeska, with Kantus, with everyone. But just now, that had been right. That finally showed this Morolf that

Uwe wasn't just anyone who had to be glad if the doorman nodded to him. What this Morolf published was read by a few specialists, perhaps. What Uwe wrote was read by millions. When he thought about his newspaper's circulation, he felt either better or worse. This time he felt better. He poured Kantus a schnapps. Kantus drank it without saying thank you; he sat enthroned under the blue cloud that he constantly fed from his cigarette, blinking his eyes enthusiastically and asking question after question, as if he had to catch up on something. Now for example he asked, 'And what do you do research with?'

'With great technical extravagance and with ideas.'

'And how are ideas produced?'

'By reflecting with one's imagination. Actually, a premonition of a great connection is the driving force of research. The Pythagoreans' faith, their trust in a simple mathematical core of all law-governed connections in nature, including those we do not yet understand, is just as alive in the natural sciences even today.'

Kantus nodded. Uwe at least admitted it when he didn't understand something. Right at the start, when he came to the institute, he had told Morolf straight out that he had no clue about the stuff that this elegant science was about, but Kantus nodded.

'The internal connection of a new realm of experience appears understandable to us only when the laws that determine it are stated simply in mathematical terms. Planck says that as long as physical science has existed, its highest, most desirable goal has been to solve the problem of summing up all observed and still to be observed natural phenomena in a single, simple principle that allows the calculation of past and also, most particularly, of future events from present ones. It is in the nature of the task that this goal neither has been achieved today nor ever will be completely achieved. But it is surely possible to come ever closer to it. We all dream of a kind of world formula. Ignorantly, no doubt. Heisenberg drafted one once.'

'I've been told that at your institute they only measure and calculate.'

'That's true, coincidentally.'

Kantus poured himself and Morolf a drink from Uwe's bottle. Uwe's glass remained empty. Uwe thought, I'm a person who never gets to the issue.

'But what does imagination have to do with a dry science?' asked Kantus.

'New ideas don't arise from the rational intelligence, but from the artistically creative imagination,' said Morolf. 'We ask Nature questions. Formulating such questions requires the greatest expenditure of imagination. Physics is an extremely sensual science – every other true science is too, by the way – one constantly lives at the edge of mystery and is entirely surrounded by it. Some people say we are unworldly, because we are closest to the world. People with the ability to concentrate are usually called absentminded. However, one person alone can no longer accomplish anything nowadays, not even a genius. Within a given line of research too, the peculiar nature of our subject forces us to collective work. An individual researcher would remain stuck on the same special topic for many years if he closed himself off from collective work. He would eventually achieve results that would be hopelessly out of date or which had such insignificant value that it would be better to dispense with them. The scientific personality would atrophy from such a way of working. The mechanization of science and the abstractness of the subject by no means takes away the exciting moment from our work. The struggle with the unknown is always a sensual experience. For Dante, all the battles that he fought intellectually were battles with Pergalotta. In the *rime petrose*, Florence is the Pergalotta; he plunges into politics as into a love battle. In the *Divine Comedy* he himself is instructed – paradoxically by the immortalized Beatrice, whom he loved after her death in boyish ascetic excess for quite a long time, until the retaliation came – as follows: "Only through the senses can intelligence grasp / that which it will later elevate to rational thought." '

Big show. That was the thing for Kantus. Uwe poured his glass so full that the vodka spilled over its cracked edge.

They were saving on light too, except for the illuminated music box there were no lights on, three schmaltzy songs for a mark, at the next table some people were comparing their lecture notes, in that noise comparing lecture notes, in that heat. When Morolf held the flame of his lighter to Kantus's cigarette, jealousy tormented Uwe so sharply that he felt a desire to throw his glass at Morolf's head.

'Why did you become a physicist, of all things?' asked Kantus.

'In the eighteenth or nineteenth century, for example, all talented people became poets. Today all talented people become physicists.'

'And play the trumpet,' said Uwe.

'Yes,' said Morolf.

'In an orchestra?'

'Yes.'

'Which one?'

'In our institute's band,' said Morolf. 'Next Saturday we're performing in the conference hall.'

'What are you performing?'

'Cool. For local consumption we'll also play a little old-time, but other than that, mainly cool.'

'You probably just came from a rehearsal,' said Uwe, and he thought the way he said it wasn't bad.

'No, from the airport,' said Morolf.

'Is the conference over already?'

'No.'

'Oh, so just a few of the gentlemen have flown back.'

'A woman fell to her death,' said Morolf. 'The weather situation was not very favorable. When you have only weak upcurrent areas, it's hard to stay up. You have to watch out so you don't get nauseous. When I notice something like that, I sing loudly to release the tension. Maybe she felt sick and lost her nerve, that can happen. It happened to my flying instructor too. Someone who has fallen to their death like that is not a pretty sight. I didn't look at the girl at all.'

Sympathetic silence. Suddenly Kantus came out of his smoke. 'You're a flyer?'

'Actually, I have no time for flying,' said Morolf. 'I'm thirty-one, I've run out of time.'

'Glider pilot?'

'Yes,' said Morolf.

Kantus threw his schnapps-sluggish arms onto his shoulders. 'We must drink to brotherhood, brothers call each other *du*.'

And they drank to brotherhood under the blue cloud, and Uwe watched, and then Morolf had to tell Kantus what it's like, that which he knew only from books and which was his life dream: flying. And Morolf talked and talked; you could have filled several notebooks with his polished speeches. When Uwe's bottle was empty, Morolf said, 'Our present knowledge of the world of elementary particles is not sufficient to describe their physics mathematically without contradictions. Probably the experiments that will give the theory its decisive impulse are still to be done. Or we are thinking with false axioms.' Morolf spoke faster and faster. His black eyes stared toward the ceiling. But stared right on through it, toward some distant moving point, so it seemed. He spoke so rapidly, it seemed he wanted to catch up to that point. 'It is quite certain that we are facing a revolution in physics, comparable to the one that was set in motion by the discovery of Planck's energy quantum and led to the overturning of classical physics. Most people didn't notice it until forty-five years later, when the bomb fell on Hiroshima.'

'Yes,' said Kantus, 'I wanted to ask you about that all along. I just didn't dare, *du verstehst*, you understand. You don't have to answer me if you don't want to or can't or aren't allowed to, what do I know. My son-in-law claims that what you're doing still has no military significance, but you can feel free to speak openly with me, you don't need to explain to me why we have to build bombs.'

Morolf lifted his chalk-smeared hand to his head. When he took his hand away, there was a blue spot on his forehead. 'But you mustn't think that the question surprises me,' said Morolf. 'It would have surprised me if you hadn't asked. For forty-five years people didn't notice that a modern physics exists. Then came the bomb; then they understood it. Since then, physics means the bomb. Maybe forty-five more years will have to pass before this cliché is replaced by a new one. At the moment, at any rate, it's still considered chic to write about this cliché. Every journalist who takes pride in himself writes about it. Of course, the findings of science never before played such a powerful political role as that of nuclear physics, and some physicists have a screw loose because of it; they're always looking back over their shoulder. I look back over my shoulder sometimes too, today I made that mistake again, it's virtually modern for plays with physicists in them to be staged in madhouses. Möbius is the most brilliant physicist of all time, but he flees into a madhouse to protect the world from his discoveries, because it's not ready for them. As soon as he sees, he turns around and leaves the world to the lunatics. Anyone who constantly looks back over his shoulder will constantly be a loser. If we want to win, we must summon up the strength not to be blinded.'

'So it's true that you're working on problems that will maybe have practical significance in eighty years?'

'Yes,' said Morolf.

'And that's what the conference is about?'

'Yes.'

'Every day we print calamities in our paper and you . . . '

'Yes,' said Morolf.

Kantus got up and drained his empty glass, standing. Morolf stood up too. Uwe remained seated. Kantus told him he ought to write this. Kantus reached about as far as Morolf's fourth rib. Kantus was on such a roll that he even socked the waiter in the vest with the back of his hand and introduced him to Morolf. He ordered a round for all the guests.

BOOK TWELVE

The gospel of Valeska, which Laura reads as a revelation on the trobadora's burial day

Three days before her death, Beatrice had told her friend Laura about a strange encounter. Which Laura interpreted after the fact as a premonition of death. The trobadora claimed to have recognized, on the train to the potash mine in Zielitz, a man she had once met in Hades. While she was on her quest for Anaximander. But in Hades the man had still been a woman. Valeska Kantus by name. The incredible aspects of the report had not bothered Laura in the slightest. On the contrary, since Beatrice was hiring on in factories for study purposes, Laura interpreted her lies strictly as a symptom of excessive creative pressure. Beatrice had turned over to Laura a manuscript written by the man who, while still a woman, had allegedly been snatched from the jaws of clinical death following a traffic accident. Laura read it on the day of the trobadora's burial. As a revelation. It reads as follows:

The Gospel of Valeska in Seventy-Three Verses

Since no one has told my story up to now, I feel moved to write it down myself from the beginning. So that all may hear the simple teaching.

1

In the seventy-second year of the twentieth century, there lived in Prenzlauer Berg in Berlin a woman with a doctorate. She worked at a nutrition-science institute. Her husband, Rudolf, had the same profession and was employed there too. The woman's name was Valeska.

2

Since there was no prospect of getting an apartment together in the foreseeable future, due to an extreme housing shortage, Valeska had not resisted getting married on principle. Rather, as on other occasions, she trusted a sort of natural progression by which difficulties could sometimes take care of themselves, like mail piling up on her desk. Filled with such optimism, Valeska enjoyed two beautiful honeymoon years with Rudolf. And she was not at all afraid that these ideal conditions would end, for she counted on Rudolf's lack of interest in all nonscientific activities.

3

Rudolf pursued his research convinced that he was the greatest scientist in his field. All his friends overlooked this inspiring buffoonery in him. None of them would have overlooked it in Valeska. And delusions of grandeur were the farthest thing from this woman's mind. She thought of herself as a team member who could be replaced at any time, who was surprised herself every time she finished a project successfully. But after her victorious defense of a sensational hypothesis based on a series of experiments with Wistar rats, Valeska encountered something on the way home that she interpreted as a vision. Disconcertingly, it was her own face.

4

At home Rudolf greeted her with roses and the announcement that in two months they could move to an apartment together. He had been busy behind the scenes. And wanted to surprise Valeska. In this, he had succeeded. Differently than he had intended, to be sure. Tempestuous evening with ample lovemaking. Rudolf celebrated all happy events in the natural way. Valeska was skilled at adapting. Even screamed louder than usual. Since she was actually unable to enjoy the lovemaking.

5

That night, which Valeska spent sleeplessly, she drank three cups of coffee. In her student days a half-liter of this beverage had enabled her to memorize an anthropology textbook for an exam in one day, to flawlessly deliver rigorously organized speeches without an outline, and to smooth away every kind of lovesickness with diffuse feelings of elation. Considerately, Valeska resisted the almost uncontrollable urge to pace the apartment. Lay quietly at Rudolf's side instead. Listening.

6

Rudolf's apartment sounded like the sea. Mornings, evenings, best of all at night, when the traffic subsided. The addictive noise was produced by a fountain in front of the building. Four hummocks of water bubbling up from a blue green tiled basin. The tiles simulated Adriatic waters, cleanliness at the very least. In summer Valeska's son couldn't walk by without wading in it. Besides children, adolescents and older people waded there in hot weather. Middle-aged people, who could no longer blithely count on their charm nor yet on equanimity, refrained from this pleasurable activity. Valeska refrained from it.

7

Aware of the rocking of the mattress caused by her husband's involuntary rolling over, Valeska thought about Joan of Arc's enviably opportune encounter. Which had also included voices. Strange ones, of course. Male ones, obviously: the Christian God is male. By convention, Joan of Arc was a vessel. Can a woman whose body was governed by the state in Valeska's country until the enactment of the law on termination of pregnancy on 9 March 1972 suddenly be a vessel of herself?

8

Could Valeska's second marriage have been her explicit wish? After all, she was wonderfully relieved to be living alone with her son ever since her divorce had permitted her, officially as well, to bear all the burdens of existence alone. Indeed, Valeska suffered from an intense distaste for practical regulations and pieces of advice dished out by people who were for practical purposes idle. She strictly denied their competence. Preferably in silence. Which is why Rudolf perceived her hatred of patriarchal conditions as insignificant, that is, not to the detriment of her beauty. Rudolf had rented an apartment on the corner of Friedrichstraße, in the building known by the name Bonkburg. The disconcerting vision that had appeared, with voices, to Valeska on the way home had followed her there. And she couldn't shake it off, no matter how she tried. And it absolutely didn't fit into a shared apartment.

9

For Rudolf was used to housewives.

10

Shaken in her faith in natural progressions that sometimes take care of problems by themselves, Valeska concentrated strenuously on the light in Piran to bring this encounter into the Berlin apartment. Really irretrievable, impossible to repeat. On the market square, a statue of a poet shielded its eye with its hand. The other hand played a harp in the hollow where the sculptor had left out the heart. Valeska stood unshaded, blinded, marvelously redeemed as if by requited love. The lighting lay misty over the water, upon it in dove blue and pink patches that were rocked up and down and against each other, also mixed together by the waves. Such water on flat, limestone-covered earth; dazed by pastels, light on her feet, Valeska stepped onto the sea and made her way through the fishy boats.

11

Yes, miracles! Paths of least resistance. Walks over water instead of corpses. Quick relief. A different kind that takes generations could be of no interest to Valeska during this night. For she could not banish the belief, which had come to her on the way home, that she was a scientist who could not be replaced at any time. At that, she said involuntarily to herself, 'One ought to be a man.'

12

Softly. When Rudolf couldn't sleep at night, he listened to the radio. As the first light of dawn was breaking through the curtains, she got the idea, at the sight of the sleeping Rudolf, of recanting her sensational hypothesis.

13

Rudolf woke up around eight in a bad mood and indulged it in his usual way. Such that he couldn't wait for Valeska to get up and dressed but made a beeline for his coffee. He was in the habit of taking it in the hotel restaurant across the street. It was distinguished by excessive prices and slipshod service. Rudolf never got tired of complaining about the waiters; he was a regular customer. Valeska was serene in the face of quirks when she could explain them away as symptoms of fatigue. On this morning stubbornly happy. Though anticipating silly looks. When a woman steps out of this apartment house entrance alone in the early morning, legend assumes that she is coming from work. In Valeska's case unjustly so because of the civil ceremony; those kinds of romantic legends amused her intellectually, less so in a practical sense. Not for moral reasons but for the sake of comfort. Entering hotel lobbies and restaurants alone was also not exactly comfortable for her at the time. However, Rudolf was waiting for her; that made it easier. Valeska was inclined to let him wait a little. In general. And because these beds were much better than the ones in her apartment. And because she'd had more than enough of responsibilities and machinations. The minute her son was away visiting his grandparents, her housewifely debit awareness failed absolutely, which is why she unresistingly followed Rudolf's financial extravagances. It certainly would never have occurred to Valeska to leave her apartment for breakfast.

14

Valeska was strangely out of sorts. Not because of Rudolf; at forty a woman knows that men are in the habit of giving in to their moods, because they are poorly trained by a range of responsibilities. Moods decrease with increasing amounts of responsibility of an opposite kind.

A working woman with three children can no longer afford moods; this is described by clever people as a cheerful nature or a well-balanced personality. Since Valeska had only one child, she could occasionally spare a little time to marvel at her cheerful nature, which had found recognition at the institute too as a kind of gift from God. Valeska deliberately thought less often about Rudolf's changeable feelings, which were described by his friends as passionate. A woman cannot live without pragmatism.

15

The bedcover smelled of tobacco and fish. Familiar. Valeska drew her thighs up to her belly, making bulges in the white-covered wool blanket here and there, from side to side. Her right toe got caught and touched wool. Valeska assumed there was a hole in the duvet cover. Apropos of this, also that the damask was heavily soiled; she didn't let herself look. Rudolf never paid attention to these things. He had other interests. He was convinced that talent consisted of the ability to concentrate intently on one object for a long time. Undisturbed. Which is why his hand could easily fly out if Valeska's son made himself unwelcome at the wrong time. Valeska demanded fairness of herself. It is more blessed to give than to receive. It's easier to live by such maxims when you don't have to scrutinize daily the various standards by which they are usually measured. The shared apartment looming on the horizon obviously wouldn't be able to satisfy needs for those sorts of psychological tricks. Valeska cursed the grossly expensive crystal palace, where these traveling executives of various nationalities, skilled workers, and their fashionably dressed wives with artificial hair jostled each other at the smorgasbord. The news that the Interhotel Panorama in Oberhof was going to be turned over to vacationing FDGB members had done Valeska's heart good. Damn restaurants.

16

The next moment, Valeska found herself on landlady Grbic's balcony. Next to the Ploce gate. Sitting. Over the sea, as if on it. It had a harsh blue color from the low sun. It warmed up at noon when the bora died down, summery. The island of Lokrum stood out black against the flat sea. Palm fronds blocked the view of the Dubrovnik harbor. The fruits on the orange tree were turning yellow. Sweat lay in the crease of her belly. 'My daughter married and moved to Sweden,' said Frau Grbic loquaciously, 'Sweden, can you believe it, I was there once for three weeks visiting; terrible, that climate, an uninhabitable country, better to be a beggar here than a millionaire there.' As soon as Frau Grbic fulfilled her promise not to interrupt, Valeska started spitting olive pits through the balcony grating again. While diving into cottony white bread and milky coffee from a carton. It was the end of October when Valeska had sat thus, bare-skinned, on the sea, no, sat enthroned; those were breakfasts. One year later the prospect of drizzle and other unpleasant events prevented Valeska from satisfying that kind of hunger immediately, as was her habit.

17

Valeska felt fear.

18

A very ordinary fear; it did no good to indulge in silly stylized memories of business trips: expedient lies. In the end, the best advice for a local married man whose wife was not satisfied with local conditions affecting her gender was to take her to a foreign country like that one. Capitalist countries were too well suited for such purposes. Because they made you wild with rage. 'Uninhabitable for women,' Valeska had declared after her first business trip to Paris. Her friends, who had expected effusive descriptions, saw her verdict as camouflaged words of consolation for those who had stayed home. Or as a dogmatic streak. Provoked by this reaction, Valeska insisted that nowhere in the world did women live better than in the GDR, which triggered indulgent laughter. And the exclamation, 'Faith healer!' Now her trust in a natural progression that would work to her advantage had been shown to be blind. To be sure, even in this country no woman could tough it out without opportunism nowadays. But in this particular case, Valeska's well-intentioned reliance on this means, so damaging to character and health, must be described as reckless. Anyway she had already shared an apartment for seven years with one man, who was just as accustomed to housewives as Rudolf. So she knew only too well what was in store for her.

19

'One ought to be a man,' Valeska said involuntarily once again. Despite certain scientifically encumbered suspicions, which Rudolf possibly even found secretly pleasant, in an everyday sense he was versatile. Freud's model image of penis envy as characteristic of women, along with passivity, narcissism, and masochism, could not be inconvenient for Rudolf. Up to now, Valeska had been able to overlook his manners in general, which were domineering, because she knew his particular ones. And because she rarely saw him. His particular, loving behavior could apparently be sustained without the idea of having to subjugate women. There he needed no humiliations, violent acts, or other chauvinistic grotesqueries; in matters of love Rudolf was beautiful in the utopian sense. Valeska didn't want to let the preciousness of these truthful moments get buried by the detritus of long-established habits. Anyway, she was old enough to know that friendship could only exist among equals. And at best, erotic friendship would remain when the fires of love had subsided. Provided that Rudolf loved her as a person, not merely as a representative of her gender. Dilemma. Valeska pounded her fists on the pillow, beat the mattress with her heels, cursed: granted herself, since she was relieved of maternal duties and alone in the room, a leave from this gift of God. So that she finally pulled herself together and slammed the window shut, which locked out the addictive noise. Then she decided to breakfast on whatever leftovers were in the refrigerator and get the coffee machine going.

20

Inspired by injustice, she swung her feet onto the pillow, then flung them over the edge of the bed, and came abruptly to her feet before the mirror. A site she was in the habit of seeking out for dressing and undressing. In her own room an Empire mirror had been installed for such occasions, the most expensive piece of furniture in her apartment. Rudolf's rented mirror cast unflattering images. Valeska was used to it. Which is why she always looked only fleetingly. She was unwilling to go along with the custom that demands eternal youth of women without technical amenities, from which a certain accommodation can be expected. She bounded into the stuffy air of the kitchen nook, turned on the anodized-metal appliance. Steam rising, delicious smell, soon the stimulating drink was warming her tongue and throat. An expectation of diffuse euphoria. In front of the mirror, where Valeska was trying to reduce the puffiness of her tear-swollen eyelids with a wet washcloth, she involuntarily uttered the perverse wish for the third time in her own voice, which sounded strange to her.

21

Then fleeting glances at her waistline, belly sucked in, were followed by attentive ones. Then intense concentration. Not that Valeska's sense of beauty was shaped only to accommodate demand, which generally increases with increasing bust size, but Rudolf's mirror showed too little. More precisely: nothing. Except nipples with shrunken, pale areolas, wreathed by sparse curly hair. It prickled her palms pleasantly, like Rudolf's. This loss of flesh threw Valeska back onto the bed before she had really grasped it. That is when she discovered the growth. It lay tucked along her closed thighs, also suddenly sparsely haired. Valeska spread them at once, so as not to damage anything, examining in confusion the regular folds of the pouch along the seam, which was half-hidden. The member lay slanting toward the left curve of the groin, smooth skinned, uncircumcised, two freckles at the tip. Valeska quickly hoisted herself from the mattress with her hands and took a few careful steps through the room. Legs apart. An unfamiliar tension made itself felt, a local heaviness, pressure, similar to after a bruise, a physical event, comparable to falling ill or gravidity, arbitrariness – pleasant, though. Valeska took hold of it and found the freckles in the middle of an offshoot. Hurried back to the mirror. Not a caffeine hallucination. Up to now, she had usually found pleasure in the changeability of these growths. As objects. As part of her own body, the attachment struck her as a bad joke, which she unhesitatingly blamed on Rudolf's bad mood.

22

Valeska's son was convinced that Rudolf could do magic. Maybe not because of those cheap tricks whereby the new father made buttons and stuffed animals vanish and reappear again. Maybe Arno already saw through these bluffs and overlooked them because the idea of being friends with a magician was precious to him. But it also seemed possible that Arno's faith was not shaken by silly tricks because he trusted his instinct. It is well known that a child's instinct is absolutely superior to that of adults, which has been destroyed by thinking. So, following her son's physical wisdom, Valeska forgot her vision, her wish that had come true on her, as well as the invigorating drink from the coffee machine, and explained her transformation, which incidentally had also touched her head, as a magical act of revenge. Retaliation for a remark about Rudolf's domestic nature. Valeska had made the remark not long ago, very carefully, garnished with a joke so as not to hurt Rudolf's feelings; as usual, she disregarded her own hurt feelings. Short but not sweet: she had criticized Rudolf for never having anything to eat or drink in the apartment when she visited him. Duly noted. Incidentally, the refrigerator was empty on this appalling morning too. Rudolf replied that shopping could not interest a scientist. When he brought academic visitors to Valeska's apartment not long afterward, she explained the lack of supper by remarking that she was a scientist. Poisonous atmosphere and the declaration that he could not stand women with affectations. Valeska replied, 'If you'd prefer a man with affectations, I have no objection to being considered as such.' The appendage with various follow-up arrangements seemed to her an act of striking back.

23

Valeska burst into immoderate laughter. In view of the growth, on which legions of myths and power theories were based. Proof of having been chosen. Key to a privileged life, scepter of domination: a little flesh with wrinkly, at best blood-engorged skin. Valeska lacked the appropriate role training for a serious, self-admiring glance to her midsection: the prejudice.

24

On top of everything else, it turned out that the physical differences between men and women were modest compared with cultural ones. Valeska had guessed this. But she hadn't wanted to know it for sure. Sometimes one experiences truths as too true.

25

Since Valeska had to finish analyzing a second series of experiments on Wistar rats, she thought that she couldn't let incidental events hold her up for long. Not even miraculous ones. Of a kind that, like everyday events such as a sudden illness of her son, a missed period, broken water pipes, closing of the nursery school due to scarlet fever or mumps, the unavailability of children's tights in a certain size in the department store, and similar impediments to research, had the common characteristic of not being influenced by thinking about them. Valeska had laboriously trained herself not to think about objects that couldn't be influenced by thinking. For reasons of economy of behavior. Now she was not in a position to make use of her suddenly acquired privileges with the luxury of a clear conscience. If she had been able to choose a gender, she might, following her erotic curiosity, have chosen hermaphroditism. The one that had fallen to her she could at best consider to be a uniform of privilege. Which is why the continuation of the gospel is narrated without a change of name. Also without a change of grammatical gender.

26

Valeska especially appreciated the inconspicuousness of the uniform. Joan of Arc had chosen a too conspicuous disguise in order to make use of her military talent. Which is why she was granted only two years before the scaffold.

27

Valeska recalled certain exercises that Rudolf occasionally did in the morning when he had to refrain from love because of time or other reasons. So Valeska flexed her arm muscles, whereby the offshoot subsided to a size that could be tucked away. Incidentally, Valeska did not see any apparel problems in store for her, since she had always preferred pants, to escape the time-consuming tasks of adjusting skirt lengths and other dictates of fashion. Even her hairstyle, smooth and cropped at the nape of her neck, was compatible with her newly more severe face, because it was downright modern. The latest men's fashions gave machismo-weary men the opportunity to discard certain external attributes of power, a substitute for action perhaps, a game, in any case: known as 'partner look' in fashion jargon. Since Valeska had the advantage of having been trained to take great changes in one's own body in stride, she was able to accept her reflection in the mirror.

28

When the telephone rang, she mechanically lifted the receiver to her ear. Rudolf's voice. Flatteringly conciliatory, he asked if he could order artichoke hearts with crabmeat for her while waiting. She stammered something about an upset stomach, then a phone call from the director of the institute that obliged her to leave early for Moscow. 'Your voice sounds so funny,' said Rudolf, inquiring with tenderness in his voice about her health. Tones like these will put a crimp into even rigorous plans. Valeska had no rigorous plan, rather, none at all, could only lie through her teeth in this hardly usable, scratchy voice. It already seemed impossible that Rudolf was at fault for her conversion, his manner of speaking was thrilling; she loved him as much as ever.

29

She loved him as much as ever? This rush of passion finally brought Valeska to a degree of understanding of the far-reaching consequences of her altered situation. Seized again by fear, but of a quite different sort, she slammed the receiver down on the cradle. No doubt about it: Rudolf was lost to her if he discovered her condition. Why had the transformation not effected a change in her affection as well? Valeska felt much worse than she had last night. Helpless. Desperate. Knowing only that she had to hide from Rudolf somehow.

30

For lack of usable escape plans, Valeska resorted to her first white lie: Moscow. Surprisingly, her business visa for a consultation with professional colleagues from the Institute for Simple Organic Compounds of the Soviet Academy of Sciences, which was to take place in twelve days, had already reached Valeska, a hopeful sign in this confusion, it seemed to her. In difficult life situations, she always sought and found some auspicious signs or other and did not consider it disgraceful to believe in them. On the contrary, she had even developed a special theory about the health-promoting power of life deception. People who were unable to believe in their lucky star seemed weak to her. Phone call to the airport. Booking of a flight. Calling in sick to her institute in R. near Potsdam. Delayed takeoff due to fog. Landing in snow. Valeska had expected to see the birches of the Sheremetyevo Airport in leaf. Mid-October. She lived on a street where the seasonal conditions of the flora could only be discerned from newspapers.

31

Moscow was a distinct city. Berlin, by comparison, seemed a blurry place. Already upon arriving at the airport, Valeska noticed this strangely pleasant distinction: friendliness flourished much more clearly here than at home, its opposite as well. Formalities were dealt with either sincerely or indifferently. Taxi drivers talked like old acquaintances or not at all: no readiness to oblige. Entry via Volokolamsk Avenue. Smoky gray frost brightness that covers up colors, palpable. A pedestal hoisted the red brown tank barricade up from the plain. The taximeter ticked unusually slowly. In an exchange of words about her inadequate summer coat, the driver accustomed Valeska's tongue and ears to the harder, softer medium of communication. Stopped and waited matter-of-factly at a telephone booth in Kitaigorod, where Valeska announced her arrival to her surprised friend Shenya. The phone booth stood on a slant. And made a run-down impression from the inside also. Nine years ago when Valeska visited this city and country for the first time, those kinds of rough edges could upset her because of idealistic expectations. Today she was happy about her business trips because of this peculiar, uncompromising nature, softened by untidiness. Moscow was absolutely the only conceivable place for a person like Valeska to flee in Valeska's desperate situation. Because for her, as for the female sex in general, there was only one escape: flight to the fore. At this point

Valeska wouldn't have undertaken business trips to Paris, Rome, and other places from the past under any circumstances.

32

Shenya promised Valeska that a hotel room would be approved, of course she had time for Valeska, not the faintest suggestion of inconvenience, organizational complications, shortage of time. Many verbal kisses and hugs, which Valeska, as always, could not immediately return without an effort. First, she had to unlock that which they call 'soul' here. Get used to the fact that it is worn openly, without embarrassment, in this country. Refreshing area. High-pressure weather system. Dry air. Windless. Which meant that Valeska's summer coat was almost adequate. Trench coat. The feminine version was indicated only by the direction of the buttons. Which is why Valeska wore false eyelashes and abundant makeup. Actually, the disguise was only intended for the passport control, to verify her identity with her papers. In her telephone conversation with Shenya, however, she explained her altered voice range as bronchitis, contrary to her resolve. Because an erotic joke, which Valeska couldn't resist, was received in silence. At that, she lost the courage to confess her conversion to Shenya. Was immediately reminded of the moral strictness that was also customary in this country. One wore one's soul without embarrassment but above the waist nonetheless. Did not mention other things. Valeska remembered that she had never yet spoken with Shenya about unmentionable matters. She immediately detected conservative tones in Shenya's voice. This trip was a crackpot idea!

33

Date with Shenya that evening at the Peking Hotel, where a room was supposed to be available for Valeska and actually was. The women at the reception desk there offered their services to the guests but not their looks. Display was not considered part of service. They wore clothing-protective smocks, their age unconcealed. At the agreed-upon time Valeska waited in the hotel lobby, similar to a train station. Shenya teetered resolutely across the marble floor in high heels, embraced and kissed her, gave her flowers, asked solicitously about her health, the bad state of which she believed she could detect from her changed appearance. The makeup counterfeited severity of age. Witchlike.

34

The doorman at the restaurant refused to admit the two of them. Unescorted. Because the Peking was a respectable place.

35

What? And at that, friend Shenya did not knock over a table in rage? She didn't demand to speak with the manager? At that, she said, 'Come,' and drew Valeska away?

36

When Valeska had calmed down to the point of being able to gather her thoughts, she recognized the propitious moment. And was determined to use it. 'Just a minute,' said Valeska and washed off her mask in the nearest ladies' room. 'Pardon me,' she said to the indignant restroom attendant, who had not failed to notice the now visible beard stubble. With an effort she managed to delay being thrown out, in order to gain time for constructing her explanation. Valeska had resolved to take great care with the form of her explanation. But when she saw her friend waiting unsuspectingly beside the reception desk, luckily in an armchair, all the resolutions left Valeska's mind. And Shenya got the truth in three sentences.

37

Nevertheless, Shenya exceeded her wildest expectations.

38

Such that Valeska could escort her friend through the restaurant on her arm without interference. To a table with glaring place-settings. High above it, gaudily colored ceiling paintings. The columned hall was an expensive reproduction of Chinese temples. Shenya, a woman of the generation that had been widowed by the war and, married or unmarried, forcibly emancipated, hid her sovereignty, as always, behind boyish composure. She had her hair dyed brutally black, when she had time. When she didn't, she wore white roots with equal dignity. On that extraordinary evening, orange lips. But no attempt to cover up wrinkles with makeup. Or to repress her belly with a girdle. She had carried three children to term in it, one right after the other, raised them on her own while studying on the side; that left little time for sleep and other beauty treatments. Apparently, she saw no reason to be ashamed of the marks on her body. That had always impressed Valeska about her. Pleasurable smoking, during which Shenya occasionally rolled her imitation-amber cigarette holder from one corner of her mouth to the other with noisy clicking of teeth. Since her brown eyes were set very close together, her eyes could be piercing on extraordinary occasions.

39

Now, for example. Up to now Valeska had seen such lightning bolts deployed only in defense of brilliant hypotheses during the tribunal-like working meetings at their institutes. Which either directly supported or directly contradicted Shenya's conviction. Shenya was convinced that an economically supportable synthesis of foodstuffs would replace traditional means of production in the foreseeable future. Gigantic factories would then be able to produce all the food needed for the population. Agriculture would be a thing of the past, except perhaps for the cultivation of fruit and flowers. The industry that supplied agriculture with machinery, fuel, fertilizers, and pesticides would also become obsolete. Many professions would then change. It would be necessary to tackle projects that required collaborative work by chemists, biologists, physicians, and economists. Shenya was determined to combat in this way the fact that twenty-five million people starve to death every year. With rational fanaticism. Valeska said she had overlooked irrational fanaticism up to now. Shenya retorted coolly that phenomena which scientific wisdom had not dreamed of before now would seem normal to a true researcher, thoroughly desirable, meeting his highest expectations, absolutely auspicious. Because they were in contradiction to all previous theories: that is, challenging. Spurring one on. Inspiring. Valeska had to describe her transformation to Shenya down to the last detail.

40

Shenya listened with rapt attention.

41

After dessert Shenya took notes. She regretted that she wasn't a biophysicist. Nevertheless, she asked Valeska not to pass the material on for the time being. Intelligence is usually not enough to make a scientific discovery nowadays. You also need luck in getting access to material, which, as a consequence of highly technologized research that requires collective work, presupposes that you hold a certain position. Shenya was a simple staff member. She saw an opportunity. For she not only believed in the mysteries of this world, she knew about them without seeing. She called this unknown, unnamed quality 'radiance.' She despised people who thought themselves modern because they believed in science as in a religion. She proved, often and with relish, that presumptuous intellects of a conservative type found this religion substitute handy for trimming down the world to make it understandable. She, however, was never able to manage without explanations. She was silent for a while, looking for a provisional explanation. Didn't smoke, either. But noisily chewed the empty cigarette holder from one corner of her mouth to the other: Shenya's specific thinking noise.

After a while she took the mouthpiece abruptly, also specifically, from between her teeth, filled it, and declared, 'In order to enter history, you had to step out of history.' Valeska liked the effective statement. She kissed Shenya's hand with rapture. Her first official kiss on the hand. The masculine privilege of paying court is one of the very earliest pleasures of the human race. Later, love in the communal apartment.

42

Without thinking. After both of them had been pleasured, it occurred to Valeska that the apparatus, tried out for the first time, had functioned without feelings of dominance or visions of subjugation. Shenya was not spoiled, thus enthusiastic.

43

'But my son won't be enthused,' said Valeska after the sweaty exercise. 'Three fathers? Sometimes I actually think it's doubtful whether children need one, but not even patriarchal laws doubt that they need a mother. What the hell will I tell Arno?' 'The truth,' said Shenya, adding that the child would not be missing out on anything. On the contrary. There followed panegyrics that Shenya intoned in traditional Russian recitation style: with a disguised voice. Opera sound. After an unexpected descent into everyday style, she strove arduously not to forgive Valeska for having been ready to reject her own vision at the sight of the handsomely sleeping Rudolf. 'A scandal, to deny yourself when your own wish had already come true on you,' said Shenya, 'scandalous training, not wanting to admit that faith, which can move more than mountains, can move more than mountains, victim drill.' The last word drowned in rasping consonants. It was a sign of excitement in Shenya when her Slavic accent got the upper hand. She had started learning German during the war. In some military hospital where she worked as a nurse's assistant, taking care of prisoners. To cap it all off, she took a volume of Rousseau from the bookshelf above the bed and read aloud: 'The education of women should be aimed toward men. Pleasing them, being useful to them, endearing themselves to them, educating them when they are still boys, caring for them when they are adults, standing by them with advice, making life pleasant for them — all these are, at all times, the duties of women, and they should learn this from childhood on.' — 'You seem to have totally forgotten that I'm a man now,' Valeska objected, 'do you think it's pleasant listening to writings that generate such man-hating in this condition? Certainly no humane state of affairs can be achieved by acts of retaliation. This Rousseau must have been a provocateur.'

44

Shenya tapped the iron bedstead with her cigarette holder in various places. Sounds of a triangle in different pitches, depending on the thickness of the pipes. Valeska plunked in reply but not as melodically. Because she couldn't help thinking about the handsomely sleeping Rudolf. Even felt like talking about him. But she refrained from doing so for reasons that were not yet clear to her. Shenya was, without a doubt, the more beautiful sight. Not physically. Of course, to be fair, Valeska had to trace her friend's assets back to disharmonic realities. Perhaps Shenya was only proud and not at all inclined toward being an extraordinary character; maybe her generic affiliation had forced it, little by little? Because Shenya too had probably not escaped constantly doubting herself, reflecting about herself, testing herself, resurrecting herself; that fosters human virtues such as modesty, tolerance, patience. Nothing forced Rudolf to doubt himself. His generic affiliation allowed him to be convinced that he was the norm. 'Why did I actually love this Rudolf?' Valeska suddenly asked out loud. The past tense was incorporated as a trivializing tactic. But Shenya seemed not to notice. She dropped her jaw. The skin of her face promptly sagged in other places as well. Shadows burrowed into the creases, a kind of sadness, age in any case. Only in her voice was there still energy. 'I think that when one can say precisely why one loves somebody, one has stopped loving,' said this voice. It sounded as if it were reporting on a laboratory experiment. The sound and sight shocked Valeska. 'Would you like for me to remain a man?' she asked in confusion. 'Of course,' said Shenya, 'if you ask, you must also listen to the answer, but you can forget it again straight away. Short and sweet: the question "why" permits a motivation. Or two. Ten, for all I care. Fortunately, human beings are a universe. Incalculable. If they were not mysterious, love would be reduced to sex. Creative intoxication would not exist because there would be nothing to discover, wasteland far and wide; you have to get ready for great successes with women.' – 'Oh for crying out loud,' said Valeska.

45

In between conversations, activity in the communal kitchen. A wonderfully run-down vaulted room with four women in charge of its condition. The four-room apartment used to house four families, eighteen persons. The chickens were still not sufficiently thawed, for which reason they resisted Shenya's efforts to halve them for quite a while. Shenya cursed this unhandy form of nourishment, especially the bones.

Valeska told her she was using mother curses. And described a future luxury version of synthetic meat: cutlet with plastic bones inserted. She thought: shamelessness, to parade around such a mouth and such a nose uncovered! This Rudolf also looked just the way he was. Absolutely uncomfortable for everyday life, sometimes even insufferable. But for holidays! Rudolf was a man for holidays: travels, intoxication, religion. Since he thought he was the greatest, he couldn't doubt that he also deserved the greatest: everything, in other words. When he was on a train trip with Valeska or on a plane or in bed, he had shown her the world as if it were his property. Was well versed in everything, showing off his treasures with childish pride of possession. Eager, intent on amazed, admiring glances. At such moments of uninhibited curiosity, his bright-colored eyes usually had the ghost of a squint. Beautiful, confusing sights, blue notes between sensuality and fanaticism, 'anyone who can't summon up the strength to disregard historically developed moral distortions will not attain a lucid moment,' said Valeska. 'But do you, therefore, necessarily have to become homosexual?' asked her friend.

46

When the chickens had been dissected according to the instructions of a Georgian recipe, Shenya fried them on both sides, weighing down the halves with book-filled bowls. 'If you have other heavy objects in your household, of course, you can also use them to flatten the chicken,' said Shenya and talked a lot about Valeska's theory. The practical elaboration of which could open up possibilities for helping these one billion people in Latin America, Asia, and Africa who are undernourished due to an insufficient supply of protein, vitamins, and minerals. She said the present state of affairs led to high infant mortality, a low average life expectancy, and reduced capacity for physical and intellectual work among these people. Unexpectedly Valeska and Shenya found themselves crafting plans as in the old days. When their friendship was not yet threatened by erotic greediness. Valeska even missed the pressure against her ribs and might have gone looking for her bra if Shenya hadn't given her a new opportunity to wallow in jealousy. Shenya couldn't stop herself from casting Rudolf and his opinions in a bad light. The strivings of women's rights advocates seemed to him, in view of the fact that twenty-five million people starve to death every year, to be trivial, not seriously on the agenda, because societies only gave themselves problems they could solve. 'The legitimate, lawful realities of his country have already far exceeded conservative thought, and not only on the part of the male inhabitants,' replied Valeska in the manner of recitative, baritone. There followed arias suggesting which amino acids and which kinds of sugars must be mixed and heated in which proportions in order to simulate the delicious fried-chicken aroma that rose at the sides of the improvised constructions.

47

The following evening Valeska met the remaining residents of the communal apartment. Dinner from 6:00 to 11:00 P.M. The oilcloth was piled with appetizers, then with Ukrainian *pelmeni*, tarts, tea. Informal. None of the women aspired to prove housewifely perfection; rather, they openly scorned it. Shenya noted with satisfaction that the three male guests quickly isolated Valeska from the female guests. Soon the men were sitting together. Discussions of politics and technical subjects. Language of conversation: Russian. Valeska found the Georgian the most difficult to understand, not only linguistically. The German physicist's vocabulary was no less faulty than the Yugoslav's. When the Georgian meteorologist said 'we,' Valeska involuntarily edged her chair away slightly. Of course, she had to submit to the merciless Georgian drinking customs, like the other male guests. But unlike them, didn't dare complain about it. So as not to expose herself as feminine, that is, effeminate, that is, disreputable. Valeska heartily envied the women their freedom with respect to drinking. The vodka had quickly separated the women friends from the real men. The men embraced each other, showed off with dirty jokes and conquests; they were no longer capable of noticing Valeska's reserved behavior. The Slavophile physicist, who worked in Dubno, told the Dalmatian soccer trainer about adventures with Dalmatian women. The trainer replied that he would stab his wife in the ribs with a knife if he found out and retaliated by telling his Berlin adventures. 'And what if she found out?' asked the physicist. The trainer answered with the Serbian proverb: 'There is a difference whether I spit out the window onto the street or whether somebody on the street spits through the window into my apartment.' Laughter. Valeska disappeared once in a while to stick a finger down her throat. Thus she relieved herself of the alcohol but aggravated her situation. Because her unbenumbed ears could not help overhearing the women's vicious comments. Marina, Raja, and Polina concentrated their hostility on Valeska as the only man capable of defending himself. Shenya, meanwhile, was silent. Which is why Valeska suspected her of choosing the female members of the dinner party tendentiously. That the males had been invited for propaganda purposes seemed to Valeska as good as proven. 'And I thought it would be a fun evening,' said Valeska. 'I thought so too,' said Marina, a secretary, adding that she was fed up with the kind of equal rights that allowed women to work like men and like women as well. Raja, a twenty-four-year-old electrical engineer, said, 'Me, get married? Too expensive.' Polina said polemically that she actually wished to have the conditions of the previous century back, when men at least supported their mistresses. Shenya seemed to be waiting for something. Valeska was depressed by the prospect of possibly being condemned all her life to put her head and more on the chopping block for other people's mistakes if she didn't want to take off for Paris, Rome, or similar places that indisputably belonged to the past in this respect. Her mind strained to explain the hostility as disappointment over the halting progress of change initiated by the revolution. A consolation that couldn't seriously console. Thus her socialist worldview moved Valeska after midnight to counter the militant opinions of Raja, Marina, and Polina with the miracle.

48

At that point, the men were long since asleep in Polina's room. Shenya was in a victorious mood. Valeska described the miracle carefully. Celebration in Raja's room until noon the next day.

49

Raja described the miracle as an ultimatum. Marina said, 'Deus ex coffee machine.' But Polina, a teacher, asked, 'Where is the gospel written down?'

50

'Nowhere,' answered Valeska.

51

Fired by new insights, Shenya gave up her scientific plan and released the material. For Valeska.

52

'Why me?' asked Valeska. 'You can't count on evangelists,' said Shenya.

53

Valeska stayed eleven days in the communal apartment. Then she flew back to Berlin in order to avoid meeting Rudolf and the other colleagues from the institute who were expected at the working conference in Moscow. Of course, there was a low-pressure weather front. This adventure-thwarting grayness. Even under normal circumstances,

Valeska found it difficult to begin any activities that required hope before the winter solstice. Since Polina thought a sudden reverse transformation was not impossible, Valeska resolved not to spend time brooding but producing knowledge of the world. Optimally. That is, highly energetically. The greatest insights into unknown worlds are opened up to people by people who open up. So on with it.

54

Among certain acquaintances whom Valeska was easily able to seek out in a short time, since active measures were recognized as normal for her gender, two were positively essential: Lena and Wibke. The negatively essential ones remain unmentioned for reasons of propaganda.

55

Valeska met Lena in the House of German-Soviet Friendship at the Kastanienwäldchen, where she was reading poetry translations. Prepared on the basis of raw translations, Lena didn't speak any foreign language seriously. Supported herself and her daughter on freely rendered poetry translations, since these were generally paid several times more than original ones. Because she liked Valeska, she answered the question of whether she liked being a woman under present conditions in the affirmative. Valeska replied that she wasn't one of those men you had to lie to in order to prove you were a full-blooded woman and to counter all suspicion of being a bluestocking, which full-blooded men hate like the plague. Thus began their friendship. Which, however, could not really thrive, due to lack of time. Lena rushed through her days, up at six, take her child to nursery school, stoke the fire, tidy up, write poetry, shop, pick up the child and play a little, do laundry, cook, bathe the child and put her to bed, clean the apartment, possibly read a book or watch TV; such a hectic life is detrimental to love. One evening when Lena's life companion, who traveled around the world in the same profession, called from Cracow, Valeska said, 'Why don't you dump the entire household business and say I won't do that, I'm a poet. Why the devil don't you acquire a few affectations, which tradition has denied you because of your gender, why don't you just set your daughter on your life companion's desk sometime — beg pardon, what one doesn't know, one must learn — and take off for the airport. Naturally, people would think you're an unfit mother, irresponsible, they'll feel sorry for the poor man and so forth, who cares. On this treadmill you can only live far below your possibilities. Which is in no way merely a private matter.' With these and similar statements, Valeska nearly betrayed her origin.

56

Valeska wrote to Raja in Moscow that she had found a woman writer who would surely be able to describe the miracle. She described Lena as a gentle, modest woman.

57

Raja wrote back that Lena's good character traits, possibly also her talent, disqualified her. In order to enter history, women urgently needed not art but a genius. For example, a prophetess.

58

Wibke was not yet a woman when Valeska met her. Wanted to be one as fast as possible, however. A demonically painted girlish face. Speeches permeated with cigarette smoke and abundantly peppered with 'frustration' and similar jargon words, breasts swaying untrammeled under her sweater, sumptuously faded jeans. When she forgot to act determinedly cool so as to suggest a hard-boiled character and let her erudition in foreign affairs show, the beautiful draft of a human being was clearly visible. A high school student who was dissatisfied with herself: she thought that sixteen-year-old girls who could not yet speak from experience were sexual wimps. Which is why Valeska didn't want to shirk her duty. Although at first she didn't feel much desire: she shared the preference of young men for women in their thirties; indeed, she was a little afraid of the task. But certain solidary feelings remained with her from her former condition. Above all, the memory of her defloration, which had been done so unremarkably that Valeska could think about it only with bitterness to this day. Any woman who is introduced to love in such a way can lose the ability to love even before she has won it. Tradition blames such frigidity on nature, not on traditions. Wibke experienced the event lusting for sensations. Athletic seriousness. Three weeks later she introduced a boy from her high school class as her boyfriend. After that, the two visited Valeska regularly.

59

But Valeska still found Shenya the most beautiful of all her female intimates. Perhaps because the presentiment of the end that befalls human beings after their thirtieth year intensifies their capacity for experience. The fact that nothing in life is more certain than death enters seriously into consciousness at that age. Suddenly a feeling for time starts ticking. Wibke couldn't feel the preciousness of time, the irrecoverability of the moment. She wanted to traipse through dairy bars with Valeska, to be 'in' on as many occasions as possible. Her face was a hollow space: a charming draft. Shenya sought occasions that took her outside of herself. When loved, she could go wild. Her face was filled in. Filled out. With riches of life she had claimed and rubble. Tradition neutralized a woman marked by decline, while a man with gray temples was considered interesting. And, of course, a reasonable choice for a young woman. In the opposite situation, one spoke of 'desecration of mummies' and 'mounting your grandmother.' No wonder that in private, Shenya was absolutely enchanted by the miracle.

60

One day she flew in because she wanted to spend a night with Valeska. At that, Valeska had her friend's emotional fireworks on her conscience. For she was unable to respond in kind. Shenya was too familiar to her, despite the transformation a sort of 'I' form. Valeska was unable, even with supreme effort, to raise narcissism to the stage of passion. She mourned the loss of their old friendly relationship. For she had once read enviously of historical friendships between men that, without being homosexual, were of a beautiful intensity: a mutual undertaking reinforced them. At best, an idea. Elaborating and defending it created bonds. That sort of activity between men and women was mostly short-lived, because it was threatened by sexual tempests. But friendships among women were even rarer than solidarity. In part, because friendships need time. The hobby of most women was the second and third shifts: housework, children. But Valeska and Shenya, despite the daily journey from the diverse acts of stooping that are indigenous to housework to those heights where ideas are to be found, had still summoned the energy for a great friendship. 'I give up,' said Valeska that night. 'If I have to pay this dearly for my vision, I don't want it. Being a man isn't much use to me anyway, unless my past and my role socialization are magically removed too. One ought to be a woman with a man's past!' Shenya abruptly let go of her. Rigid with shock. Her eyes wide open with fear, staring at Valeska's body. As if a catastrophe were to be expected. But nothing happened. When saying good-by, Shenya urged Valeska fervently not to stray or let herself be diverted from her outrageous path but unwaveringly to appropriate nature, first of all her own: to tackle the making of humanity head-on.

61

But Lena, Wibke, and other friendly contacts also struggled in vain against Valeska's longing for the beautiful luxury, Rudolf. Her fear of being discovered by him remained.

62

Valeska shut herself up in her apartment. Relatively capable of working due to the news that Rudolf had fallen ill with scarlet fever in Moscow and was hospitalized. A pleasant awareness of being part of a discovery that could make the predatory characteristics of human beings obsolete lightened the burden of the November weather. This plunging downward toward winter, the increasing lack of light. Rudolf had always considered Valeska's pet ideas about the possible moral consequences of research to be sentimental and thought that butcher was a thoroughly human profession. Producing synthetic foodstuffs instead of the irrational detour via the production of animal flesh seemed to him, above all, laden with serious economic consequences. Valeska hoped that customs that could renounce violence would come from a future industrial exploitation of the institute's work, a humanizing of human beings. That is the manuscript with which she wished to enter history. While transferring statistics onto tables, she realized that the miracle could serve the same goals. In an extortionary manner.

63

Then she started recording the gospel.

64

And while writing forgot about eating, fear, and caution.

65

Such that the sound of the doorbell could distract her from her resolutions and get her to open the door.

66

Rudolf stood before her. Came in as usual. Kissed Valeska as usual. Took off his and her clothes as usual.

67

Later it occurred to Valeska that she should be afraid. Later it struck Rudolf that the naked Valeska was disguised.

68

At that, they realized that if necessary, they could do without the images that they had made of each other and that others had made for them.

69

Then they knew that they loved each other. Personally — miracle of all miracles.

70

And they gave up their apartments and moved in together. And they lived there in ideal marital relations.

71

With Arno. He was the least surprised about the miracle; to him the world seemed miraculous anyway. Without being asked, he tried to persuade three nursery-school teachers who were not in charge of his group to undergo transformation. Since Valeska's behavior toward her son had not changed, he called her Mama as he had always done. But was less jealous of Rudolf.

72

So as not to transgress prevailing concepts of morality, Valeska set aside her masculine body temporarily during lovemaking. By swallowing a tablespoonful of tincture of valerian and intensely imagining herself for a moment as produced from a man's rib. Rudolf loved the pungent fragrance for unerotic reasons. Each time he hoped that Valeska would retain her female state for a while afterwards. Because he wanted a break from the egalitarian division of household duties that was now taken for granted. Maybe he slept with Valeska so often because he longed for this respite so much. So far, Valeska did not grant his wish. She assumed her masculine body again with the help of coffee, the vision of her own face and words, as has been told.

73

Raja, Polina, and Lena proved to Valeska by their own experiments, which worked out for them easily after studying the gospel, that the words 'one ought to be a man' are not absolutely required for the transformation to be successful.

My teaching, which urges women to believe in themselves and in the transformation just described, is pragmatic. Shenya advised me to work miracles in order to spread word about the teaching. Since then I've learned a few, I can walk on my hair, make rain, multiply loaves of bread. Of course, that won't be enough. Because people believe great truths more readily in unlikely clothing. If I had the prospect of winning over a majority of women to a temporary transformation by having myself nailed to the cross, I might accept even this means. The danger of humanity's self-destruction through war causes me to see as right every means that can extort peace.

BOOK THIRTEEN

Chapter 1
Laura is summarily appointed to the Round Table

Between Caerleon on Usk and the future but a little closer to Caerleon, a building had moored at a height of about fifteen kilometers. Its anchors lay in the clouds. The castlelike building was made of the same material. In the sixth century the legendary King Arthur resided there with his wife, Guinevere. He assembled the twelve bravest and noblest knights at a round table. After Arthur's death in 542, the Queen of Sheba took possession of the castle. In a still unexplained manner. The means or connections she exploited to attain immortality are also still unknown. It is clear only that since 511 she corresponded with the imprisoned Persephone and her mother, Demeter. A very few extant letters, which today are preserved in Cardiff, the capital of Wales, are the primary source of insight into the divine plans. Whose principles have not changed up to the present day. The deposed goddesses not only demand their old rights but absolute dictatorship. The Queen of Sheba assured the goddesses in writing that she would support their plans. And probably actually did support them for several centuries. She turned over the left half of the castle and the hall to the strategic council, to which Persephone appointed proud, politically talented women for her purposes. The Round Table stands in the hall. During the sixth century there were at most twelve women assembled at the table. In the twelfth century, when the Beautiful Melusine pledged her collaboration through a pact, there were already forty-eight women who belonged to the Round Table. In return for prolonged life, all had been required to officially pledge that they would pursue reinstatement of the matriarchy. The secret opposition, which won a majority in 1871, succeeded in the ninth decade of the nineteenth century in winning over the first men for the Round Table. Since all participants at the Round Table wear masks, one must rely on guesses. But it seems certain today that prominent working-class leaders hide behind some of the guest masks. Incognito is required. The Beautiful Melusine can only enter castle Caerleon when she has exchanged her Sphinx shape for a normal human body. The lengthened life span of the participating men is achieved with elixirs, which the women were able to save by the strictest economizing. Concerns on the part of the mask wearers, male and female alike, who declared that divine magic tricks could not be expected of working-class leaders, were dispelled in an article by the Marxist theoretician Felix Durr. Since 1918 the Round Table has had equal representation of men and women. At yearly intervals. The rest of the time, the active members work at their assigned locations according to the resolutions passed by the Round Table. Only the standing secretariat remains in Caerleon. Party congresses of the workers' parties are transmitted via monitors to the secretariat. On 14 March 1973 Laura Pakulat-Salman was summarily appointed to replace the honorary member Beatrice de Dia, who had died an accidental death. During the night from 14 to 15 March, Laura was flown to Caerleon by the Beautiful Melusine so that she could accept the appointment document in person. The paper was presented to her by the Greek philosopher Aspasia, who had once brought Laura the hunting report from Venice. Penthesilea and Tamara Bunke were present as well. Since then, the document hangs above the Pakulat-Salman marital bed.

Last chapter

Wherein the reader finds the first of Benno's thousand and one stories, which he tells the sorrowing Laura at night, in Beatrice's style, to console her

Beatrice de Dia, a beautiful and noble lady, was the wife of Sir Guilhem de Poitiers. She fell in love with Sir Raimbaut d'Aurenga and composed many fine and beautiful songs for him, which can be found in anthologies of old Provençal troubadour poetry. Next to the distinctive verses of Raimbaut d'Aurenga. He loved the game of playing with difficult rhymes and the ambiguity of words. The metric structure of his works reflects great refinement. Convinced of their exclusivity, the chronically indebted count constantly tried to find complicated words ending in -enga to rhyme with Aurenga and showed disdain for all unaristocratic verse artists. For this reason Beatrice felt compelled to mention her noble status in her 'Canso of Love Betrayed,' as well as her intellect, beauty, loyalty, and passion. Superfluously. In practice, the gentleman didn't think a bird in the hand was worth two in the bush, as would seem logical. To him, a bird in the hand was worth two in the hand. This experience with the cult of the Virgin Mary occasioned the contessa's departure from the medieval world of men. By unnatural means. The sorceress demanded seven talents for each year of sleep. The trobadora's fortune was enough for 810 years of sleep. When she had handed over the money to the sorceress and pricked herself in the finger with a spindle, the magic began to work. Only for her; husband and servants died in the usual way, per the agreement. A hedge of roses grew up around the château. While it was still visible, robber barons tried repeatedly to break through the hedge of thorns. Later people took it for an impassable hill and went around it. In the spring of 1968, an engineer who had been hired to build a highway in the area decided to blast the obstacle out of the way. As he and the explosives specialist approached the red-blossomed mountain of roses to discuss where to place the charge, cursing the fragrance for lowering the construction workers' productivity, the hedge suddenly gave way and opened like a gate. The engineer was dumbstruck. Until he saw the château; then he cursed even louder. For he was anticipating endless negotiations with the Office for Protection of Historic Monuments. The curses awakened Beatrice. After rubbing the sleep out of her eyes, she fell instantly in love with the engineer as a consequence of extreme abstinence and wrote many fine and beautiful songs for him. At first, he refused to hear them sung out loud because he was married, later because he wanted to get divorced and marry Beatrice. At that, the lady thought she had gone from the frying pan into the fire and turned toward the East. She traveled through a land in which women were paid less when they did the same work as men, and one in which they received equal pay for equal work. There she settled down and took a job with the State Enterprise Construction in Berlin. No campaign without the company's own trobadora, no meeting, no festival. Inspired by the songs of Beatrice de Dia, the State Enterprise Construction fulfilled and exceeded its production plans. The housing shortage in the GDR capital, Berlin, disappeared. On Saturdays the tenants would sometimes act like men and women, pulling weeds and collecting trash from the squares in front of their doors. On Sundays Interflug planes sprayed the trobadora's golden words on the pedestrians. Then the proletarian solidarity of the city's residents, internationally established, even overcame the barrier of the family. For, of course, this country was a land of miracles.

STRUCTURAL PLAN OF THE NOVEL

Resolutions

Book One

Book Two

GLOSSARY

ABF. Arbeiter-und-Bauern-Fakultät (Workers' and Farmers' Faculty). A special division established at universities in the GDR to provide the necessary preparatory work for university study for students, especially workers and farmers, who had not had the advantage of attending a college-preparatory high school. The Workers' and Farmers' Faculties existed in the GDR from 1946 to 1962, when they were gradually phased out because they were no longer necessary to achieve the desired goal. (interm. 3)

Abi, Abitur. School-leaving exam, prerequisite for university study. (interm. 2, 6)

ABV. Abschnittsbevollmächtigter der Volkspolizei (Section Authority of the People's Police). A member of the People's Police who is responsible for a specific area or neighborhood. (bk. 10, ch. 14)

AIZ. *Arbeiter Illustrierte Zeitung* (Workers' Illustrated Newspaper). Communist weekly newspaper during the Weimar Republic. (bk. 11, ch. 19)

Aufbau-Verlag. The GDR's largest publisher of belles lettres, publisher of Morgner's *Life and Adventures*. (bk. 4, ch. 3; bk. 8, chs. 6, 8)

Battle of Fehrbellin. Decisive battle between Sweden and Brandenburg in 1675; the victory for Brandenburg was an important step toward the Prussian monarchy. (interm. 6)

BdJM. Bund deutscher Jungmädel (League of German Girls). One of the Hitler Youth organizations, for girls between ten and fourteen years of age; there was another organization, the Bund deutscher Mädel (BdM), for girls aged fourteen to eighteen. (bk. 8, ch. 28)

Beate-Uhse shops. Stores that sell items to enhance sexual fantasies, named after their founder, West German businesswoman Beate Uhse. (bk. 10, ch. 19, 8).

Bitterfeld Way (Bitterfelder Weg). Refers to cultural policies developed at the 1959 and 1964 conferences held in the industrial city of Bitterfeld, GDR. The aim was to integrate the world of production into the creative arts and thus to increase the workers' level of cultural literacy, influence, and participation. The emphasis on production was seen as a decisive break with intellectualized Marxism. Authors were expected to experience the lives of workers by working in a factory or other enterprise before writing about them. *See also* production line research. (Bitterfeld Fruit, bk. 11, chs. 19, 22, 26)

Braun, Volker. 1939–. Dramaturge at the renowned Berliner Ensemble, playwright, and poet, Braun was one of the oppositional voices among the GDR's prominent authors and intellectuals; like Christa Wolf, Christoph Hein, Stefan Heym, and others, he remained in the GDR to the end. (bk. 11, ch. 21)

Brigade. Term used in the GDR to designate a work team in a factory, on a collective farm, or in other state enterprises. The term was taken over from the Russian; its military origin reinforces the concept of class struggle (*Klassenkampf*). Brigades were usually named after Communist heroes and heroines, important dates in history, and so on.

Budjonny, Semjon Michailowitsch. 1883–1973. Soviet leader of the Red Cavalry in the civil war. Katerbaum (interm. 6) earned this nickname by his bravery in uncovering corruption.

Bunke, Tamara. 1937–67. 'Guerilla Tanja,' born in Argentina to German emigrant parents, returned with them to Berlin after the war, served as Che Guevara's interpreter when he visited the GDR; later accompanied Che to Bolivia, where she died. For many years the GDR did not recognize her. (bk. 8, chs. 22, 23)

Castro, Fidel. 1926–. Premier of Cuba since 1959, he was a symbol of socialist revolution throughout the world. It is his picture that Oskar Pakulat recognizes above his son Benno's bed. (interms. 5, 6)

CFDT. Confédération Française Démocratique des Travailleurs (French Democratic Confederation of Christian Workers). French trade union. (bk. 1)

CGC. Confédération Générale des Cadres. French trade union of white-collar workers. (bk. 1)

CGT. Confédération Générale du Travail (General Confederation of Labor). Communist trade union; the largest French union. (bk. 1)

Cuba Crisis. References in the intermezzos to Soviet missiles in Cuba make clear that the autumn of *Rumba for an Autumn* is the time of the missile crisis of 1962. In book 6, Laura remembers her experiences 'during the Cuba Crisis of 1961,' but mention of the blockade indicates that 1962 is meant, rather than the Bay of Pigs invasion of 1961. The incorrect date may simply be a mistake, or perhaps the author intentionally has Laura confuse the two events.

DEWAG. Deutsche Werbe- und Anzeigengesellschaft. The GDR's advertising agency. (bk. 4, ch. 7)

DFD. Demokratischer Frauenbund Deutschlands (Democratic Women's Alliance of Germany). The GDR's official Communist women's organization, which sought to attract women into political life by means of educational events, continuing education courses, counseling centers, and so on. (bk. 11, ch. 19)

Dietzgen, Joseph. 1828–88. Early Marxist philosopher. (bk. 8, ch. 3)

Dolle-Minna Movement. Dutch feminist group of the early 1970s; the women called attention to sexist behavior by in-your-face role-reversal actions, such as whistling at men on the street. (bk. 10, ch. 19, pt. 6)

Fahrt frei. The GDR railroaders' newspaper; the title means 'the way is clear.' (bk. 11)

FDGB. Freier deutscher Gewerkschaftsbund (Federation of Free German Trade Unions). The only officially permitted union organization of the GDR. Founded in 1946, the FDGB sought to encompass the GDR's entire working population in instilling acceptance of the state's social and economic policies. (bk. 12, 446)

FDJ. *See* Free German Youth.

FEN. French trade union. (bk. 1)

Force Ouvrière. French social democratic trade union. (bk. 1)

Free German Youth (FDJ; Freie Deutsche Jugend). The only officially permitted organization for adolescents in the GDR, the FDJ played a major role in political indoctrination, in leadership training, and so on. Membership in this organization was more or less obligatory after age fourteen. (bk. 1, ch. 11) The organization's slogan is 'Storm the Fortress of Science' (Erstürmung der Festung Wissenschaft). (bk. 10, ch. 12)

Good scholar medal (*Abzeichen für gutes Wissen*). An award given by the Free German Youth for demonstrating good knowledge in the area of politics and ideology, conferred on the basis of a test. Three levels, gold, silver, bronze. (silver: bk. 1, ch. 27; bronze: interm. 4)

Gori. Birthplace of Stalin in the Georgian Caucasus. (interm. 4)

Grundlagenstudium. The foundation course in Marxism-Leninism (Studium der Grundlagen des Marxismus-Leninismus), part of the core curriculum required of all students at GDR universities and colleges, to be completed during their first six semesters. (interm. 4)

Guevara, Che. 1928–67. Prominent figure in the Cuban revolution, a hero of twentieth-century revolutionary movements. After leaving Cuba, he trained and led guerrillas in Bolivia, where he was captured and executed in 1967. (bk. 8, ch. 23)

Humanité, Humanité Dimanche. The central newspapers (daily and Sunday, respectively) of the French Communist Party. (bk. 2, ch. 2)

Interbrigade. International brigade of volunteer fighters. The term originated during the Spanish Civil War (1936–39), when such brigades from other countries joined the fight against Franco. (interm. 6)

Interhotel. Luxury hotel for international visitors to the GDR and for the privileged. Interhotels were located in the capitals of the GDR's administrative districts (*Bezirke*) and in popular vacation spots. (bks. 9, 12)

Intershop. Shop where imported (usually from the West) foods, alcohol, and other goods could be purchased, with hard currency. The prices were comparable to prices in Western shops, that is, much higher than in ordinary GDR stores.

Jean Paul. 1763–1825. Real name: Johann Friedrich Richter. German author of popular novels, known for his whimsical style, sentiment, ingenuity, and attention to details of everyday life. (bk. 1, ch. 11)

June 17, 1953. The date of mass strikes and demonstrations by workers in many cities throughout the GDR, sparked by a raising of work norms. The uprising was suppressed in Berlin by Soviet tanks; not surprisingly, only local strikes took place after that. The uprising was portrayed in the West as a spontaneous act of outrage by the workers; the official GDR view was that it had been provoked by Western agents provocateurs. (bk. 8, ch. 22)

Kirsch, Sarah. 1935–. Best known for her poetry, for which she has received several prestigious literary prizes, Kirsch also published stories, reportages, and translations of works by other poets. She left the GDR for West Berlin in 1977, in the wake of the GDR's expatriation of dissident singer/songwriter Wolf Biermann in 1976. She has lived in West Germany since 1983. (bk. 8, ch. 27)

Kollontai, Aleksandra M. 1872–1952. Revolutionary who advocated radical changes in traditional Russian customs and institutions, including the practice of free love, removal of the stigma attached to single mothers and illegitimate children, and improvements in the status of women. As a Soviet diplomat, she became the first woman to serve as a minister of foreign affairs, with assignments in several countries. (bk. 2, ch. 8)

KPD. Kommunistische Partei Deutschlands (Communist Party of Germany).

Krupskaya, Nadezhda K. 1869–1939. Lenin's wife, secretary, and collaborator, author of *Memories of Lenin*. (bk. 10, ch. 13)

Leuna. A large chemical company near Halle/Merseburg, it produced nitrogen for explosives during World War I. Leuna II was built nearby during the early years of the GDR. (bk. 5)

Magazine (*Magazin*). A monthly magazine for literature and in-depth reportages, the only magazine in the GDR that published pictures of nudes (one picture per issue!). (interm. 5)

Magazine for Women (*Frauenmagazin*). The official publication of the DFD. (bk. 4, chs. 20, 21). *See also* DFD.

Mitschurin, Ivan Vladimirowitsch. 1855–1935. Russian biologist and plant breeder. In the 1960s, associated with the idea of superior agricultural products through agricultural technology in the GDR; the name evoked a 'one-track mind.' (interm. 6)

National Committee (Nationalkomitee Freies Deutschland). A pro-Communist organization for the reeducation of German Nazi officers in Soviet prisoner of war camps. (interm. 4)

NAW. Nationales Aufbauwerk (National Reconstruction Works) A GDR organization for 'voluntary' participation in postwar reconstruction work; later a synonym for unpaid work. (bk. 7, ch. 15)

Neues Deutschland. The official newspaper of the GDR's Socialist Unity Party (SED: Sozialisitsche Einheitspartei Deutschlands). (bk. 11, ch. 34)

Objektlohn. The policy of paying workers after completion of a specific 'object,' such as the wall of a building or other part of a project, rather than by the hour. (bk. 6)

October 7. Date of the founding of the GDR in 1949, a state holiday *('Tag der Republik')* (interm. 3)

Paragraph 218. The section of the German penal code forbidding abortion in all cases except when there was a 'medical indication,' that is, a health problem that, in the opinion of a physician, would endanger the woman's life if the pregnancy were carried to term. A long campaign by West German feminists to abolish Paragraph 218 was unsuccessful. In 1972 the GDR legalized abortion on demand during the first three trimesters. (bk. 11, ch. 11)

PEN Club. International writers' association; the letters stand for Poets, Essayists, Novelists. Founded in 1921 in London, it had centers in all member countries. (bk. 10, ch. 5; bk. 11, ch. 29)

People-creating art (*menschenbildnerisches Volksschaffen*). An allusion to the policies of the Bitterfeld Way, which aimed to promote artistic creativity for and by working people (*künstlerisches Volksschaffen*). (bk. 8, ch. 15) *See also* Bitterfeld Way.

People's Chamber (Volkskammer). The GDR legislature. (bk. 11, ch. 11)

PGH. Produktionsgenossenschaft des Handwerks. Production trade cooperative, an enterprise in which the members (workers, craftsmen, or farmers) managed their cooperatively held property according to state regulations. (bk. 4, ch. 21)

Pieds noirs (literally, 'black feet'). The name given to French settlers returning to France from Algeria after Algerian independence in 1962. (bk. 1, ch. 19)

Prenzlauer Berg. A section of Berlin (East), a former working-class district that became the center of the 'alternative culture' scene in the 1970s and 1980s. (bk. 4, ch. 4; bk. 12)

Production day (*Produktionstag*). Time when students were scheduled to work in production, which was considered a necessary supplement to their academic study. (interm. 6)

Production line research (*Produktionsstudieneinsätze*). According to the policy known as the Bitterfelder Weg, authors were expected to spend time working and observing in factories or other enterprises in order to learn the reality of the workers' lives before writing about them. ('Resolutions') *See also* Bitterfeld Way.

SA. Sturmabteilung. Hitler's Storm Troopers (brownshirts). (interms. 1, 6)

S-Bahn (abbr. for *Stadtbahn*). Berlin inner-city commuter train.

Schwedt. Town on the Oder River at the Polish border, location of a large petrochemical combine, end point of the pipeline from the Soviet Union; because of higher wages and 'frontier' conditions, an attractive place for people who wanted to begin a new life. (interm. 6)

Self-criticism. Members of the Socialist Unity Party were expected to analyze their errors and failings according to the principles of Marxism-Leninism. (bk. 4, ch. 14) *See also* Socialist Unity Party.

Serpukhov. Nuclear institute south of Moscow. (bk. 8, ch. 26)

Shawm. A double-reed wind instrument, favored by Communist marching bands such as the one recalled by Oskar Pakulat from his activist days during the Weimar Republic. (interms. 5, 6)

Shawm Twist. Benno Pakulat's adaptation of his father's favorite marching song in the style of popular music of the early 1960s. Because the Twist (a dance) originated in the United States, the insult to Oskar Pakulat's Communist past is all the more profound. (interms. 5, 6)

Sinn und Form. One of the major journals for literature and culture in the GDR, founded in 1949. It published literary works, criticism, and theoretical pieces. (bk. 9, ch. 1)

Skat. German card game for three players. (bk. 7, ch. 15; interm. 6)

Skobeltsyn, Dimitri. 1892–1990. Soviet physicist known for research in the field of cosmic radiation; received the Stalin prize for research in 1951. (bk 8. ch. 26)

Socialist Unity Party (SED: Sozialistische Einheitspartei Deutschlands). The GDR's Communist Party, the result of the merging of the KPD and the SPD in 1946.

SPD. Sozialdemoktratische Partei Deutschlands. Social Democratic Party of Germany.

Stoph, Willi. 1914–. Held several important posts in the GDR government prior to becoming prime minister in 1964, a post he held until 1973 and again after 1976. In 1970 he and then West German chancellor Willy Brandt began negotiations on the normalizing of relations between the two Germanies. (bk. 9, 6)

Störtebeker, Klaus. Legendary pirate of the Middle Ages who, like Robin Hood, took from the rich and gave to the poor. Beheaded in Hamburg in 1401. (interm. 4)

Subbotnik. Designation for obligatory 'volunteer' work on reconstruction projects in the early years of the GDR; derived from the Russian word for Saturday. (interm. 3)

Summit luggage (*Gipfelgepäck*). A reference to the unsuccessful summit meeting between then U.S. President Dwight D. Eisenhower and then Soviet Premier Nikolai Khrushchev in Paris in 1960. (bk. 11, ch. 19)

Thälmann, Ernst. 1886–1944. Communist leader who was chiefly responsible for molding the KPD (Communist Party of Germany) into a Stalinist organization. His working-class origins and ability to speak the language of the masses made him a cult hero. Along with many other Party functionaries, he was arrested in March 1933 and eventually executed in Buchenwald. (bk. 11, ch. 19)

Ulan. Cavalry soldier in an elite regiment. (interm. 6)

Ulbricht, Walter. 1893–1973. Communist leader and Stalinist hard-liner, a key figure in the Party during the short-lived Weimar Republic, he fled abroad after Hitler's accession to power in 1933. One of the founders of the National Committee. Returning from Moscow to Germany in 1945, he was given the charge of organizing an administration in the Soviet-occupied zone. At the founding of the GDR in 1949, he became deputy prime minister; later he became head of the council of state and also served as secretary general of the Socialist Unity Party (SED) from 1950 to 1971. (bk. 9, ch. 6) *See also* National Committee.

Ustaše. Croatian fascist organization. (bk. 8, ch. 22)

VEB. *Volkseigener Betrieb*, literally 'people-owned company.' The designation for the GDR's state-owned enterprises. (bk. 4, chs. 3, 4, and often)

Volkssturm. Nazi territorial army; recruited boys and old men to form a militia of untrained fighters from September 1944 until the war's end, under the command of Heinrich Himmler. (bk. 9, 'Petrification')

Wartburg. One of the two automobiles manufactured in the GDR, more expensive than the Trabant (Trabi), driven by workers; named after the famous historical fortress in Eisenach.

Wiens, Paul. 1922–81. GDR poet who also published reportages, essays, and translations of the works of other poets; married to Irmtraud Morgner for some years. He was among the more conservative writers, supportive of official policies and until his death an IM (*Inoffizieller Mitarbeiter*), that is, an informant for the Stasi, the GDR's state security police. (bk. 1, ch. 9)

Workers' consumer co-op (*Konsumgenossenschaft*). Generally referred to simply as '*Konsum*,' these co-ops sold food and most goods needed for everyday life. Nearly 90 percent of goods were purchased at the *Konsum*.

Writers' Union (Schriftstellerverband der DDR). Founded in the early years of the GDR by writers returning from exile, such as Anna Seghers, Bertolt Brecht, and Johannes R. Becher, the Writers' Union eventually had nearly one thousand members. Only writers who had already published could apply for membership. The Writers' Union facilitated the obtaining of visas for foreign travel and provided grants to members; it also attempted to influence cultural policy. (bk. 6)

Young Pioneers (Junge Pioniere). Members of the GDR Pionierorganisation Ernst Thälmann, the socialist mass organization for younger children (first through seventh grades). (bk. 4, ch. 10) It was led by the Free German Youth and aimed to develop the children into 'all-round socialist personalities.' Its slogan was 'always ready!' ('Immer bereit!') (bk. 4, ch. 5; bk. 11, ch. 31). *See also* Free German Youth.

Youth pal (*Jugendfreund*). Members of the Free German Youth addressed each other as *Jugendfreund*. (interm. 3) *See also* Free German Youth.

In the European Women Writers series

Artemisia
By Anna Banti
Translated by Shirley D'Ardia Caracciolo

Bitter Healing
German Women Writers, 1700–1830
An Anthology
Edited by Jeannine Blackwell and Susanne Zantop

The Maravillas District
By Rosa Chacel
Translated by d. a. démers

Memoirs of Leticia Valle
By Rosa Chacel
Translated by Carol Maier

There Are No Letters Like Yours: The Correspondence of Isabelle de Charrière and Constant d'Hermenches
By Isabelle de Charrière
Translated and with an introduction and annotations by Janet Whatley and Malcolm Whatley

The Book of Promethea
By Hélène Cixous
Translated by Betsy Wing

The Terrible but Unfinished Story of Norodom Sihanouk, King of Cambodia
By Hélène Cixous
Translated by Juliet Flower MacCannell, Judith Pike, and Lollie Groth

The Governor's Daughter
By Paule Constant
Translated by Betsy Wing

Maria Zef
By Paola Drigo
Translated by Blossom Steinberg Kirschenbaum

Woman to Woman
By Marguerite Duras and Xavière Gauthier
Translated by Katharine A. Jensen

Hitchhiking
Twelve German Tales
By Gabriele Eckart
Translated by Wayne Kvam

The South and Bene
By Adelaida García Morales
Translated and with a preface by Thomas G. Deveny

The Tongue Snatchers
By Claudine Herrmann
Translated by Nancy Kline

The Panther Woman
Five Tales from the Cassette Recorder
By Sarah Kirsch
Translated by Marion Faber

Concert
By Else Lasker-Schüler
Translated by Jean M. Snook

Slander
By Linda Lê
Translated by Esther Allen

Daughters of Eve
Women's Writing from the German Democratic Republic
Translated and edited by Nancy Lukens and Dorothy Rosenberg

Animal Triste
By Monika Maron
Translated by Brigitte Goldstein

Celebration in the Northwest
By Ana María Matute
Translated by Phoebe Ann Porter

On Our Own Behalf
Women's Tales from Catalonia
Edited by Kathleen McNerney

Dangerous Virtues
By Ana María Moix
Translated and with an afterword by Margaret E. W. Jones

The Forbidden Woman
By Malika Mokeddem
Translated by K. Melissa Marcus

Absent Love
A Chronicle
By Rosa Montero
Translated by Cristina de la Torre and Diana Glad

The Delta Function
By Rosa Montero
Translated and with an afterword by Kari Easton and Yolanda Molina Gavilán

The Life and Adventures of Trobadora Beatrice as Chronicled by Her Minstrel Laura
A Novel in Thirteen Books and Seven Intermezzos
By Irmtraud Morgner
Translated by Jeanette Clausen
With an introduction by Jeanette Clausen and Silke von der Emde

Nadirs
By Herta Müller
Translated and with an introduction by Sieglinde Lug

Music from a Blue Well
By Torborg Nedreaas
Translated by Bibbi Lee

Nothing Grows by Moonlight
By Torborg Nedreaas
Translated by Bibbi Lee

Bordeaux
By Soledad Puértolas
Translated by Francisca González-Arias

Candy Story
By Marie Redonnet
Translated by Alexandra Quinn

Forever Valley
By Marie Redonnet
Translated by Jordan Stump

Hôtel Splendid
By Marie Redonnet
Translated by Jordan Stump

Nevermore
By Marie Redonnet
Translated by Jordan Stump

Rose Mellie Rose
By Marie Redonnet
Translated by Jordan Stump

The Man in the Pulpit
Questions for a Father
By Ruth Rehmann
Translated by Christoph Lohmann and Pamela Lohmann

Abelard's Love
By Luise Rinser
Translated by Jean M. Snook

Why Is There Salt in the Sea?
By Brigitte Schwaiger
Translated by Sieglinde Lug

The Same Sea As Every Summer
By Esther Tusquets
Translated and with an afterword
by Margaret E. W. Jones

Never to Return
By Esther Tusquets
Translated and with an afterword
by Barbara F. Ichiishi

The Life of High Countess Gritta von Ratsinourhouse
By Bettine von Arnim and Gisela von Arnim Grimm
Translated and with an introduction by Lisa Ohm